THRESHOLD

THRESHOLD

CHRIS JOHNSON

Threshold

Copyright © 2014 by Chris Johnson

First Edition

The prologue contained in this work was previously published as *Prequel*.

Thanks to Patrick Saikas and Chip Smith for their contributions to this work.

ISBN-13: 978-1496133113

ISBN-10: 1496133110

This work is dedicated to Duane Garrett and William Gibson.

***

How is it

That this lives in thy mind? What seest thou else

In the dark backward and abysm of time?

If thou remember'st aught ere thou camest here,

How thou camest here thou mayst.

Prospero, "The Tempest"

***

PROLOGUE

The diesel fuel glittered, amorphous prisms swirling in the morning sun, radiating out from the generators and pick-up trucks sitting idle and mostly submerged in the K-Mart shopping center parking lot, the home of the traveling two-bit fair. Shallow waves rippled across the floor of the Tilt-A-Whirl, but only the bottom bucket of the Ferris Wheel was underwater. The few other rides and attractions were in various stages of submersion. Hundreds of yellow hard plastic ducks from one of the midway games floated along with trash, fallen limbs and leaves across the expanse of the sixteen-acre lot, turned temporarily into a suburban pond.

"Well ain't this some shit." Sheriff Lucas Garnto had not run for sheriff because he wanted to deal with this kind of nonsense. After retiring as a senior foreman from the big J.P. Stevens woolen mill, he just didn't have a lot to do, and his wife Susie—accustomed to spending her days watching *The Young and the Restless*, getting her shopping and hair done, gossiping with the girls—did not appreciate his gloomy presence around the house. She had encouraged him to run for office, "to make a difference." It was not that she did not love him, or enjoy his company. She both loved him and enjoyed his company. They could still share a good laugh together every night. He even enjoyed helping her out in the kitchen, and she enjoyed having him there. But in their thirty years of marriage she had created a routine for herself of which he was not an everyday part, and his everyday presence had pushed her to push him.

While not especially well-known in the close-knit community of Laurens County, Georgia, he was widely-known, so had nonetheless run for office against a popular incumbent who died shortly before the election, and against a black man who had no chance of winning in a town where the Moose Club, the Elks Lodge, and the Country Club (it just had *Country Club* on its sign) had yet to admit a person of color for any purpose other than cleaning or cooking. He spent most days quietly shepherding drunks home, investigating the occasional domestic dispute, and keeping bootleggers from getting overly ambitious. It was a dry county, but Sheriff Garnto looked the other way whenever he could—he believed in everything in moderation. The site before him was anything but moderate. It was an unbelievable mess. But, the rest of Dublin, the county seat of Laurens County, looked pretty much the same. In the distance he could hear the sound of chain saws clearing roads—they had been at it since Saturday.

"At least it didn't get the Piggly Wiggly." Spence Johnson, the chief of the Dublin Fire Department, looked on with some satisfaction at the wall of sandbags he and some other members of the United Methodist Church had barricaded around the entry of the grocery store, and, just to be neighborly, around the Tog Shop Shoe Outlet next door—a store which none of them really gave a rat's ass about. But, it would have seemed spiteful not to save it, too. The water had risen only four inches up the 18-inch sandbag wall, but it held tight. Last week's bread and last year's sandals were safe and dry.

The Piggly Wiggly was where most of the members of the Hilltop United Methodist Church and First Baptist Church shopped, and where their children worked part-time jobs to pay for gasoline for the Camaros and Mustangs their parents bought them for their sixteenth birthdays. The Winn-Dixie across town was where most of the members of First Presbyterian and Wesley Monumental shopped, and where their children worked to save up to buy their cars. The A&P was where the Church of God people shopped, along with people who used food stamps, and the people who worked there just worked there, often buying their groceries on credit for work they hadn't done yet. The produce truck came through on Thursdays, and stopped at the Piggly Wiggly first, then the Winn-Dixie, then the A&P. Most of the colored folk did their grocery shopping on Tuesdays, because for years, before all the agitation, that had been the only day they were allowed to shop. There were no signs on the doors, not anymore, but everyone knew their place. That was just the way it was.

"Damn kids." This was not the first time teenagers had covered over the single, center stormwater runoff drain of the parking lot to amuse themselves by creating a temporary swimming pool and at the same time creating a public nuisance to annoy grownups. There was not, after all, a lot to do in Dublin. But it was the first time they had done it prior to an unrelenting and record-setting rainfall, with a travelling fair in the lot.

The relatively steep slope of the lot was never a great asset. The handful of young people in Dublin who had taken to skateboards found the slope ideal for practicing their jumps and spins and whatnot. However innocent the kids may have been—the sheriff privately thought that kids getting fresh air and exercise should be encouraged—they scared the blue-haired ladies, so at least a couple of times a week he would be called to come clear the kids out. Long, heavy car doors on the downhill side of the slope were difficult or impossible for children and the elderly to close. Abandoned shopping carts would meander down from the Piggly Wiggly and K-Mart, and congregate in small clusters around the big drain until a bagboy from the grocery store, or one of the managers from the K-Mart who needed a cigarette break, would journey down to the center of the lot to corral the carts into single-file order and return them to their proper homes.

The managers of the K-Mart, the sheriff thought, were going to be lucky if they had jobs this time next week. When the electricity had gone out on Friday, they just locked the doors and hoped for the best, which turned out not to be very good. The four inches of standing water that did not make it into the Piggly Wiggly did make it into the K-Mart, from what little they could see. Somebody was gonna have hell to pay.

***

The rain began the previous week around noon on Wednesday without much fanfare or notice. It started as a warm, gentle spray that rinsed early spring pollen off tool sheds and magnolia leaves. Schoolchildren on their way home that afternoon walked unchaperoned and without umbrellas or raincoats, running and skipping in shallow barely-there puddles. By midnight Wednesday, it was a real rain, and the planners of that Saturday's St. Patrick's Day Parade were in early panic mode.

The St. Patrick's Day Festival was in fact a month-long event of which the parade was only a part, with a Leprechaun Marathon two weeks prior, a Miss St. Patricks's Day Pageant at the Veteran's Administration Hospital auditorium, and a pancake breakfast at the junior high school, with local leaders of industry and unpopular teachers serving as chefs and servers. The festival was the community event that defined the community. The impossibly small number of people who might actually be able to claim any Irish ancestry in the community was simply overlooked by the people of Dublin, who cheerfully and dutifully wore their green and gold Dublin High School Fighting Irish team regalia year-round. But the parade was the anchor of the festival, and the floats, which had been stored in barns and warehouses throughout Laurens County, were already being spruced up for their annual trip down Bellevue Avenue.

By Thursday morning, it was raining in earnest, a relentless, gusting rain, with wind swirling the chilled water in blasts under school catwalks and porticos. Children were dressed in their wet weather best, which for the city school children meant rain boots and slickers, and for the poor county children mostly meant wet feet all day and a plastic trash bag with holes cut out for their heads and arms. Streams sprung into creeks, and ditches filled and spilled into lawns and rose into fields. Streets and sidewalks were no longer visible, and parents had been called to pick their children up from school. Not all did—not all had phones. Many did not have cars.

Late Thursday afternoon, a school bus turning off of Highway 441, the main state artery twisting through the county, turned uphill onto a slick red clay road and skidded into an overflowing ditch. There were only six children left on the bus, and they were not seriously injured, but the driver dislocated his elbow, and the operator of the county's only tow truck that could handle the bus said it would have to sit there in the ditch until the rain stopped—the wet clay was just too slick to get any traction. And, the bus had three feet of water running through it, gushing out the emergency door at the back of the bus, which wouldn't help the process.

As a member of the Parade Committee, Sheriff Garnto had voted for just calling the whole thing off. The emergency meeting of the committee had been called by the mayor at the sheriff's request for 10pm Thursday evening, even though the mayor had suggested he knew what the outcome of any such vote might be—"You might as well try to cancel Christmas, Sheriff," he had said with resignation. But he called the meeting anyway.

That afternoon the weather forecasters in Atlanta had said to expect rain through at least Monday, and the sheriff did not have the budget to call in even more overtime deputies from the surrounding counties to help with the inevitable traffic accidents and lost children and who knew what else the rain would cause. But the rest of the committee was unmoved. Representatives of the Rotary Club, the Pilot Club, the Civitans, the Christian Women's League and all the rest were united in their opposition to cancelling or even postponing the parade. After an hour and a half of debate, the vote had been taken, and Mrs. Dottie Cotton, silver-haired matriarch of the town and president of the Junior League, a woman whose every deliberate movement suggested her fingernails were still wet with lacquer, called out gaily down the table with what the sheriff considered senseless enthusiasm, "A little rain never stopped us before, Sheriff Garnto! Who knows, maybe we'll even get a little luck of the Irish and that rain will just pass us on by. Now let's all get home and get some rest. Tomorrow's going to be a big day!"

Tomorrow *was* a big day. Between Wednesday at noon and Friday at 6:00am it rained 19 inches—a record by most any measure. The soil was completely saturated. The school board had contemplated cancelling classes, but with what seemed like half the town's parents preparing in some way for the parade, cancellation wasn't really an option. Plenty of children hadn't shown up—busses weren't able to navigate many of the washed-out dirt roads that still crisscrossed the town's less-travelled neighborhoods. Some children were home alone, some with relatives, some were seen wandering in packs playing in the rain. No one thought much about it—Dublin was one of the safest communities in the state, after all—until 11:09am. That was when it happened.

Reports of exactly what *it* was varied widely, but from points as far away as Lake Lanier north of Atlanta, to Albany in southwest Georgia, but stopping short of Savannah to the south, the sky fell. Hard and thick and loud and above all heavy, like the crystal streets of Heaven had just fallen through eternity to crash on the flat fields, loblolly pines, trailer parks and mill towns of middle Georgia.

Later estimated to be up to five inches thick where it fell in Dublin and throughout Laurens County, its thickness diminished in an irregular pattern radiating out from the town. At its far edges, the sheet was really no more than a smattering of hail and raindrops almost a quarter inch big. Still, it was enough.

Since most every rain gauge in the state had been full for at least a day, estimates of the thickness of the sheet were eventually determined largely by the census of dead livestock and birds, overturned trees and downed telephone poles and power lines. In the months and years to come, Dublin was determined to be the epicenter of a meteorological event. A weather anomaly. An unprecedented act of God. Providence. Revelation.

"Bullshit." Sheriff Garnto was not looking into the future at 11:10am. He was standing in his suddenly dark second-story office, looking through the window, down through the pouring rain at his deputy sheriff Eric White struggling to get up from the pavement. Just a minute before, the sheriff had been sitting at his desk with an oversized city map attached to a cork board, flagging with blue pins where his officers would be for the parade the next day. State patrolmen were marked with red pins, and officers borrowed from other towns marked with green. Volunteer traffic guards were marked with yellow. And then a shock of blue-white light had blazed through the window behind him like a million flash bulbs going off at once, filling his office. The entire building shook. It wasn't a rumble, like with the thunder that had been fairly consistently barking across the sky for the past two days, but an honest shaking that might have caused cracks in the foundation, or pipes to bust. Or fire. Or worse. Outside he heard cracking, breaking, crunching, tinkling, hissing, honking, barking, screaming, crying and other sounds he didn't know what they were.

At first, he thought it was an explosion, or maybe several of them. From the screams he heard from other parts of the courthouse, some others must have thought the same thing.

The electricity in his office had immediately died, and when he stood up to see if the power was off all over town, or just at the courthouse, he saw with some amazement that every tree surrounding the courthouse had been stripped of branches, or uprooted from the earth, or both. A monumental magnolia, older and taller than the courthouse itself, with roots that had snaked over the soil, and a trunk as big around as the desk where he had just been sitting, was now just a pile of splintered branches, leaves and young blossoms. A cluster of roots was standing upright twelve feet high, like some immense spider web, the dirt being rinsed from the mass by the now once-again just-pounding rain.

And then he saw Eric, sprawled face down on the ground like a linebacker who had just been sacked. Eric had, in fact, been a linebacker for the Fighting Irish in high school until he graduated fourteen years ago, and he still had the build to prove it. Yet he lay there like some kind of cripple struggling to stand up. The sheriff's second-in-command would not be helping with the parade, or anything else, for some time.

"Bullshit, bullshit, bullshit," he muttered to himself, without any thought of what he was saying. Then aloud in his deep, calm, carrying tone, "Eleanor, are you out there?"

Eleanor was the sheriff's secretary, a woman in her sixties—he didn't know how old, exactly—who kept the order part of law and order together in Laurens County. She had been a fixture in the office for nearly thirty years, through six sheriffs. She wore a smart two-piece skirt-suit every day, with sensible black patent heels that matched her sensible black patent purse, and kept her hair in a loose silver perm. She was a childless widow, and wore only clear fingernail polish. She knew every penny spent on a paper clip or hour of overtime for the past ten years off the top of her head, and whether to call the mayor's wife or girlfriend when she needed to find him. The sheriff figured her to be the most grossly underpaid public servant in Georgia, but he never told her that. At 11:10 she was usually on her way to go pick up their lunches in styrofoam boxes from Ma Hawkins Diner down the street—Friday was fried chicken day.

"I'm here, sheriff. What on Earth was that?" She came hastening into his office, opening the office door without knocking for the first time in her life, and stood beside him at the window. She let out a soft scream, almost a whisper, then stopped herself, clipped it short and swallowed it. She could not scream in front of the sheriff. This was her town, and she could see instantly there were things that had to be done. "I'll see what can be done sheriff, you go see about Eric."

"Yes, ma'am. I'll be right back."

***

He was not right back, as she had suspected would be the case. Once she had found someone to get the emergency generator going, she relocated to the communications office with her Rolodex card file full of contacts. She locked her purse in her desk drawer, but brought along her Visine, a pack of Juicy Fruit gum, a yellow tin of Bayer aspirin, a stack of steno pads and three sharpened pencils. She knew it was going to be a long day, and an even longer night.

It took a while for her to get something like a handle on what had happened, or at least what the immediate results were. But she had the results of it in her textbook-perfect shorthand, filling the pages of two steno pads. After an hour it became clear that help would have to come from Atlanta, and quickly. She stopped compiling her inventory of downed trees, missing children, and stranded motorists and focused her attention on making certain the sheriff's voice was heard in Atlanta. It would be her voice, but everyone in the capital knew that her voice was the sheriff's voice—regardless of who the sheriff was. Laurens County was the third-largest county in the state, and was well-known and well-despised throughout it as a moneygrubbing speed trap, so calls from the capital to the sheriff's office were a common occurrence.

After an hour she was able to get a radio call into the Eatonton Police Department, which was the nearest town that still had telephone service to the capital. She had anticipated chaos, but the complete lack of organization at the state level took her breath away. She should have known better after thirty years, but there appeared not to be a single person in the capital who had both mental competence and the ability to pick up a phone. That she was having to communicate through a radio dispatcher in another town who had his own crisis to deal with didn't help, but she had somehow managed to effectively communicate that however bad things were in Eatonton, things were a lot worse in Dublin. She didn't know how bad things were in Eatonton, really, but when she asked the operator "Do you have a busload full of children dressed as leprechauns missing from your elementary school, and a deputy sheriff with a concussion laying on the sofa in the magistrate's chambers because there's no way to get him to the hospital, and dead people strewn across your county? Because we do," it became apparent that no, things were not as bad in Eatonton.

When pressed to find someone with a lick of sense who might not be fielding calls from desperate civil servants like herself, she finally lighted on Stick Strickland, a Dublin native who had stayed in Atlanta after graduating from Emory's law school. At 30, still single, and working as a clerk in the capital, many of the people of Dublin feared the worst, but right now he might be their best hope. *Walter Strickland*, she reminded herself before asking for him. She couldn't remember offhand why they had called him Stick to begin with. *Baseball? Was he skinny?* She just couldn't recall.

She couldn't speak to him directly in any event, but was able to relay through the Eatonton dispatcher with relative efficiency the catastrophic hit Dublin had taken in the storm, and the need for emergency relief as soon as possible. He would get ahold of the people necessary and contact her back within the hour. But if she could, "would she send someone to check on his mother, and tell her Stick loved her and was doing all he could?" She wanted to ask if it could wait until after they had found the missing children and retrieved the corpses, but she held her tongue.

When she got the radio call back, it was at 2:00pm, and directly from Colonel Ed Barfield, the commissioner of the Georgia Department of Public Safety. She was simultaneously comforted and alarmed to be hearing from him directly.

"Is the sheriff available, Ms. Allen?" She hated this *Ms.* business.

"No, sir," she replied, "I'm speaking for the sheriff. He's got his hands full right now. The whole county is a crime scene."

"Who's the criminal?" he shot back, in something like jocular fashion. The lilt in his voice suggested there was still patience for humor in Atlanta.

"Well, I don't know sir, but whenever we have to use colored push pins on a map to tell between the injured, the critically injured, the missing children, and the dead that are still sitting out in the rain, I figure if a crime hasn't been committed yet, one will be soon. And we're running out of pins."

He paused and said with a new, quick, but not forced sincerity, "I see." *That wiped the smile off his face*, she thought with some satisfaction. She didn't know what he looked like, but she had a pretty good idea. Career law enforcement officials in Georgia had a fairly consistent profile it didn't take an FBI agent to put together:

Old, white, bald, with jowls like hound dogs; fleshy, greasy fingers; and shit-eating grins that belied the fact they couldn't believe their good fortune. Typically, Eleanor couldn't either. The state was run by men who lived on fried chicken, moonshine, and faith in their own good sense. Hopefully this one would know better.

"Well, Ms. Allen, we have a situation here that might make things a little worse before they get better."

"Let's have it before we lose the connection."

"The unprecedented rain of the past few days has created a situation at Lake Sinclair that was getting unmanageable before this morning. After the event at 11:09 this morning, it is beyond unmanageable. We are opening the flood gates at 3:00pm. You all have one hour to evacuate all the people you can. There is too much at stake here."

Silence.

Lake Sinclair was a man-made lake in Baldwin County, northwest and upstream of Laurens County. It was 15,000 acres of muddy pond carved out of the red clay of middle Georgia, damming up the Oconee River to generate hydroelectric power. *Money*, Eleanor thought with a touch of uncustomary bitterness. *There is too much money at stake here. Power is money. Money is power. And the people who live in the river basin of the Oconee River have neither.*

She started tapping one fingernail on the red *Talk* button of the desk microphone in front of her, the plastic making a hollow staccato. It was a nervous habit she had mastered years ago, and was not aware she was doing it. She was thinking.

The Oconee River passed through Laurens County, less than a quarter mile down a gently descending bluff from where she was sitting. It was already cresting over the banks—the 21 foot flood stage was passed Thursday night when the good people of the Parade Committee were pressing on with their genteel indifference to the storm battering the town around them. Eleanor had been sitting quietly at the table taking dictation. The notes were in her desk drawer waiting to be typed.

When they opened the gates in Milledgeville, death would follow as certain as night follows day.

"Are you still there Ms. Allen?"

"Yes, Colonel. An hour will not help us any more than two minutes. We have no way of getting to those people. We have no way of getting anywhere fast. It looks like a warzone hit by a hurricane here. We need help before we can get to those people. And we need time."

"Help is coming, I assure you, ma'am. But unfortunately, time is one thing we do not have. The engineers at the dam wanted to open the gates two hours ago. If the dam goes, not only will we lose one of our primary sources of power for the state, no one knows what the consequences for the whole power grid in the entire southeast might be. Every hospital and nursing home from Miami to Charlotte or even D.C. might be without power if we don't open those gates. The decision has been made. Please notify the sheriff immediately and confirm back that he has been notified. My assistant will stay on the line. The National Guard has been deployed and men are being airlifted to your Armory, but they will not be there before the overflow reaches you. We'll be in touch."

"Wait." She had raised her voice. She sat back in her chair, holding her breath at her audaciousness, "Please," she added with the proper deferential pleading layered onto her natural tone of authority.

"Ma'am? We have a lot going on here. You aren't the only folks in trouble." He ignored her impertinence. He just wanted to move on. "There's a lot to do."

"Yes sir, I know. But what was it? What was that thing that happened this morning? And how much water is coming?"

"We don't know. And, we don't know. Goodbye. Please keep someone on the line."

And he was gone.

She didn't believe that business about the grid, which she did not exactly understand, but she believed everything else. As bad as everything was, it was about to get worse. She radioed the sheriff and communicated the news in the same brisk, emotionless tone, almost word for word, as she had received it. While she believed him not to be an emotional person, the destruction he had seen today, and radioed in to her, could not help but have some impact on him. Men were not naturally capable of experiencing trauma in the way women were—she had always believed that. The proof was in the eyes of those shellshocked Vietnam veterans who left the V.A. hospital and wandered around town whispering to themselves, with their pints of liquor wrapped in brown paper bags.

She waited.

"Bullshit. Bullshit. Bullshit." The words came out in rapid fire, like three quick shots from his Colt 45, but still managed to change in tone and expression—the first came out as rage, the second as confusion, the last something like a sob, with a crack in his voice. The grieving process reduced to an instant. There was silence, and then the sheriff came back more in his customary tone, with something like hurt and bewilderment in it, "How could they make this decision without involving us?"

Eleanor's reply was ready and succinct. "We would never have agreed to it. You know it, I know it, they know it. And since they have decided to do it, they have to do it before we can object, or get protesters and TV cameras or whatever else they imagine in place to stop them. As far as the rest of the world will be concerned, this will all be one big wet tragedy. It's coming, and we have fifty minutes before they open the gates, and what, another twenty or thirty before the water gets here?"

"I don't know. Eric would know. He knows about that sort of thing. Is he up yet?"

"No sir. That was quite a knock he took."

"Right. Get back on the line with Public Safety and tell them I've been informed."

"Yes sir."

"Fifty minutes," he repeated numbly, as to himself.

"Yes, sir. Fifty minutes," she repeated back, and got back on the radio where the young man was waiting for her.

"Thankya'ma'am," he said, all in one breath, "Ya'll take care now." And he was gone.

***

They did not have fifty minutes. By Eleanor's calculations, the floodgates at the Sinclair Dam must have been opened as soon as she said she would notify the sheriff, because by 2:37pm she could hear it coming. Above the rain, above the babble of voices on the radios in the communications room, above the box fans whirring, they could all hear it. They had been warned. Apparently, that was enough.

She had seen firsthand a tornado in Columbus, Georgia, when she was ten. And she and her husband had been honeymooning on St. Simon's Island when there was a hurricane in south Florida, and the waves had been monstrous, incessant, arrhythmic, unnatural. Both had been loud, incredibly loud, and she had been scared, and her parents had held her when she was ten, and her husband had held her as they stood on the beach.

She was not scared now—she was too old and experienced in death for that. But she could feel the terror of those dirty children in their clapboard shanties down by the river not knowing what was about to hit them, but hearing it, feeling it come in through the soles of their bare feet and work up through goose pimples on their arms up to the backs of their necks. The physical reality of fear. And it would, it would hit them, it would hit hard, it had that sound, a thousand thousand trains moving straight for them, just them, because that's how it feels when something is coming straight at you, whether it's a fist or a baseball or a car or a train or a thousand thousand trains, they're coming straight at you, just you, and no one else.

How many would be swept away? She did the closest thing she ever did to pray, which was to clear her mind for just one moment, which was also the longest she could block out the sound.

She walked across the hallway with Lieutenant J.T. Carls, the emergency dispatcher she had been sharing the communications room with, over to the window in the sheriff's office, where they stood and watched the rain to the east in the direction of the river, listening to its churning. Even from the second story, they could not see the river itself, but they could see the bridge, the four lanes that connected Dublin to East Dublin, or more properly, connected East Dublin to Dublin. No one in Dublin liked to think of themselves as being connected to East Dublin. The other side of the river was the other side of the tracks—nothing pleasant, nothing good, nothing *Dublin* happened in East Dublin. The woolen mill was there, with its vats of dyes and chemicals and stink, and the hundreds of workers who poured out at the end of each shift, tired and filthy, to go home to their shacks in East Dublin or maybe across the bridge to the Dairy Queen or A&P. The workers for the 3-11 shift who lived on the Dublin side of the bridge were headed in now. The two lanes headed east were full of tail lights and brake lights as they crept through the rain, but the lanes headed west into Dublin were mostly empty, just a few sets of headlights. The far end of the bridge, some 600 yards across the river, was veiled in rain.

More people from the courthouse, including the Superior Court Judge, Carl Breshears, came in to see the prospect from the same window, though it was not evident there would be anything to see—just rain. The window was starting to fog up with their breathing. They were really watching the sound of it, mighty galumphs of waves of water galloping through the scrub and majestic oaks, young pines, and thickets of weeds that spread out from the riverbed, now suddenly becoming river. They stood in silence.

"You all heard about the dam?" Eleanor asked. She looked in the reflection of the window at the people standing behind her. Silent nods and a single murmur of assent were the only reply. She considered if news could travel faster anywhere than a courthouse in a small southern town.

A 1973 Corvette in Fighting Irish yellow pulled slowly by the courthouse, with its radio blaring, and Eleanor could hear through the rain the lyrics "put your camels to bed… got shadows painting our faces…" as the car went by. *Midnight at the Oasis by Maria Muldaur*, she thought. She liked to keep up with music.

And then from farther away she heard a sharp crack like a cannon, then another deep crunch, and a final mighty groan, and the bridge was gone. It was just gone. All the cars, and the truck, or was it two trucks? Gone. Like some child's sand castle swept back into the sea, nothing from nothing into nothing.

"J.T., get the sheriff." She turned and looked back at who was there. "Judge, we've got to get flares and barricades up on both sides of the bridge, now. Right now. Bo, can you go down to the storage room and get some barricades and flares and put them in the back of the judge's car and go help him get them set up? I'll try to get someone on the East Dublin side of the bridge moving."

"Yessum," Bo replied, not knowing how he felt about putting rusty metal barricades in the judge's immaculate Cadillac, but what Eleanor said do, Bo did. He had been working as a handyman in the courthouse since before even her time, so he knew when not to question her. He paused before asking, "Would it be alright if I left peanut here with you?"

Eleanor looked around in the near-darkness, then realization dawned and she looked down and saw for the first time that Bo's 10-year-old grandson Michael was standing among them, as still and quiet and black as a shadow, except for his eyes, which were wide open in confusion. He had not seen out the window. She didn't think the courthouse was the right place for him to be at the moment, but didn't want to waste time trying to determine why he was there or where he might possibly go. She knew he would get more in the way at the river than with her, so she quickly replied, "Of course, Michael is one of the best helpers I could have right now. Come along, Michael."

She headed to the door, but paused as the judge's voice suggested somewhat weakly from the window, "Eleanor, perhaps we should pray first?"

She stopped and turned and looked back at the window, where she saw the judge's reflection looking back at her through the rain-streaked glass. She believed, as did many in town, that he had a mistress in the capital, which was why he did not take his wife to the legal and political gatherings there. She replied as she turned back around and walked out the door "Why don't you get going and I'll pray enough for us both." She did not look back.

J.T. followed her back into the communications room, Michael in tow. She sat the boy down in a straight-backed wooden chair on the wall behind her, handed him a legal pad and a pencil, and said "We're going to be very busy in here Michael. Can you sit here and be very quiet for me?"

"Yes, ma'am," he answered.

"I heard your Papa Bo bragging that you can draw a map of the United States with all fifty states and their names. That's a thing I for one would like to see. Would you care to show me?"

He smiled a bashful smile but replied back with an unmistakable touch of pride, "Yes, ma'am." He started drawing immediately. Before she turned back to the wall of microphones and speakers and blinking lights, she tore a piece of still-wrapped Juicy Fruit gum in half and offered it wordlessly to the boy. "I'm not allowed, ma'am," he said in an almost-whisper.

"Just this once. I won't tell." He took it with a conspiratorial grin, carefully unwrapped it from the paper and foil, and put the evidence in the trash can. Then they both set to work.

The judge and Bo borrowed some black slickers with *SHERIFF* in big yellow letters across the back from the supply room along with the barricades, loaded the light green car as quickly as two men in their sixties in the pouring rain could, and set out. *Sumatra Green* was the actual name of the car's color, but it was somehow indecent-sounding to the judge, so he never told that to anyone. Bo had never been in a car with white leather interior, or with a judge. His anxiety was somewhat lessened when they heard Mike Carlson announce on the WMLT radio station that "the bridge to East Dublin has been washed out. Please avoid that area. Rescue workers are on their way and need access to the river."

The judge wondered silently what rescue workers Mike was talking about, since every uniformed officer and able-bodied man in the county was already on some task Eleanor had set them to. He switched the channel over to the other local station, WKKZ, where he heard nothing but static. Their tower must be down. Hopefully the good people of Dublin had battery-powered radios and were listening to Mike.

The good people of Dublin *were* listening to Mike. Unbeknownst to the judge, Mike was Eleanor's first point of contact at 10:30am that morning when the generator had finally been cajoled into operation. After that, she began providing the radio station with updates, which Mike delivered each half hour so that people could conserve their batteries by turning on their radios only for what he was calling "official updates from city hall," but which were really no such thing.

At 6:00pm Friday, the elementary school leprechauns were found safely tucked away on a Mennonite dairy farm, and their names read out on the radio so their parents would know they were safe. By 10:00pm that night, Eleanor had a legal pad with the names of the missing on one sheet, the dead on another, and the injured needing care on a third.

***

The Georgia National Guard arrived in a Bell 205A-1 helicopter around 11:00pm Friday night at the Armory, home of the 148th Support Battalion in the 48th Infantry Brigade. The Armory was a cavernous brick, metal and glass building on Highway 441 where it cut through town, surrounded by an assortment of camouflaged military vehicles and cannons behind high metal fences topped with barbed wire. It sat across the highway from the Burger Chef restaurant, and next door to the Oxford Shirt Company. It had seen more than its fair share of activity during the Vietnam mess, but by noon the next day would be the bustling headquarters of the recovery and cleanup effort.

The sheriff met them there at midnight to review the situation *on the ground*, as the uniformed men kept saying, and was annoyed to find that this was only the advance team of six men he was meeting—the commander of the unit was still in Atlanta resting and would be down first thing the next morning. The commander would read the report being prepared by the advance team on his way down in the Chinook transport helicopter that would be loaded up overnight with the materiel determined necessary by Sergeant Robert Samuels, the 32-year-old leader of the advance team. Mike Blankenship, who looked barely old enough to be out of high school, was introduced as a captain, though it was unclear who or what he might be captain of.

Forty-five minutes and four radio calls into Eleanor later, Sgt. Samuels knew as much as anybody in the county, except the sheriff and Eleanor themselves, what the conditions in Laurens County were. They were miserable. The generators at the hospital would continue working until sometime late Saturday, and while the doctors were busy, things weren't unmanageable, as they had been preparing for a St. Patrick's Day influx and were overstaffed.

The morgue was another story—it was full, and they would need to come up with a proper makeshift by morning. First Baptist Church had already opened its fellowship hall to people whose homes had been taken out by trees, but there would be more of those come morning. The V.A. hospital had gone on lockdown immediately when the power went out. It surprised the sheriff to learn the V.A. could go a week without any outside assistance—the lockdown was more to keep civilians from coming in for meals and water than to keep patients from leaving. People in town would in fact begin running out of water and food Sunday morning if not sooner—a situation anticipated by the Guard, who were coordinating in Atlanta with the Red Cross to get everything necessary where it was needed in the state. Without power, the city could not supply fresh water, and the power company had yet to provide even a suggestion of when power might return. "We have every man and every truck out there working on it" was the only answer the power company would give, and that was not a real answer. Samuels had told the sheriff, "It means they don't know shit."

Sgt. Samuels' presence was, after all, a calming influence on Sheriff Garnto. Like Eleanor, Samuels could organize and prioritize information in his mind, identify gaps, ask smart questions, visualize possible outcomes, all without sitting down. That had never been Sheriff Garnto's way—he needed time to sit, ponder, write out lists, and carefully reconsider, before making what was still usually the right decision. But even then, he wasn't necessarily good at seeing the thing that was not there. If he knew the thing that was missing, he could find it, but he was limited. He knew that, had always known that, and admired folks who had what he called imagination, which was just not something he had a good deal of. But this Samuels had it. The colonel had sent the right man.

So when Sgt. Samuels suggested the sheriff get some sleep before the colonel arrived, he agreed. They found a stash of cots in one of the seemingly endless Armory supply rooms, and before he settled down for a few minutes shut-eye, he went out to the CB in his patrol car to call into Susie. He hadn't spoken to her in a few hours. He imagined she had been listening to the Regency ACT-4 police scanner he kept on his nightstand, until he remembered she had no electricity—when he had shown up at the Armory, the power was on from a generator, and he had forgotten while he was there that the rest of the town was still dark. When he had stopped in earlier, he brought her fresh batteries for their portable CB, and told her to keep it on. He called her on CB channel 37, the one they had agreed on years ago in the case of an emergency. She apologized sleepily that she had dozed off while listening to the radio. She said things sounded so awful, were they really that bad? He told her he thought they were that bad, maybe even a little worse, but to go back to sleep.

"I will, sweetheart. You get some sleep too. Happy Saint Patrick's Day." She had said it automatically, still almost asleep, without a trace of irony. This was the day the good people of Dublin—and *she is one of them, one of the good ones*, he thought—looked forward to all year. To not say it would be to not say *Merry Christmas* or *Happy Birthday*.

"Happy Saint Patrick's Day," he replied. "Goodnight."

He radioed in to Eleanor that he was going to get a few minutes sleep and suggested she do the same, without much belief that she actually would. He left his radio with Sgt. Samuels and said to come get him if there was a new crisis. He lay down on the taut green canvas stretched across a creaking aluminum frame, the sound of rain and distant radio clicks, static and voices echoing softly through the barren Armory hall. He looked at the 12:17 digital display of the gold Timex watch he had been given when he retired from the woolen mill, and mentally went down the list of the workers who were missing. Not missing. Dead. In the river.

He had known them all. Not well, but he had known them. He tried not to remember the sight of the jagged slabs of concrete pancaking their cars down into the riverbed. Even if he had the equipment, a rescue effort would not have been possible. The volume and velocity of water coming down the Oconee was beyond the capacity of any men or equipment he knew. It was like the river was alive, expanding, angry, hungry, just devouring everything it touched. As the officers had stood considering how they might try to get to the one potential survivor in a car still miraculously upright and only half in the churning water—it was a silver 1970 Nissan Skyline he knew to belong to the 2nd shift inspection line manager—a massive live oak twenty yards up the steep red clay embankment fell on the car, nearly flattening it, and as the tree was washed down the embankment, it pushed the car into the river, and within seconds both were simply gone, swallowed up in the churning, foaming mass of muddy red water. He turned back to his patrol car with its rooftop lightbar flashing red and blue in his eyes, sat down inside, punched the vinyl dashboard, and sobbed for a full four minutes. It was the first time he had cried in his adult life. He navigated a path home to put on some dry socks and have a cup of coffee with Susie. Without electricity he had to settle for a warm Coca-Cola, but that had been just fine.

When he called into Eleanor to find out where he was needed next, she directed him to the Dublin Junior High School. They were starting to set up a temporary morgue in the gymnasium, and a crowd was gathering. And on it went. Each time his radio crackled through the afternoon, it foretold with cruel accuracy yet another communique of some new misery—they never radioed with good news, even when there was any.

It had been a long day.

***

It had taken Eleanor a good while to coordinate names with the woolen mill—who had shown up, who hadn't shown up, and then who hadn't bothered trying to make it to work—but with the assistance of CB radios it was finally completed around 4:00am Saturday morning, and there were only 18 people who should have shown up for work that were unaccounted for.

When parents, spouses, siblings, friends and neighbors figured out they could use the radio station as a lifeline, many began setting out either on foot or in their cars to make their way to the courthouse building or the radio station. Seeing the growing danger in this situation—it was still raining, and there were trees and power lines down everywhere—Mike suggested and Eleanor agreed that they establish a dedicated CB channel—18—for people to call in on to the courthouse if someone was missing, or if they could provide the location of someone who was thought to be missing. The lists grew through Friday night and into Saturday morning. For every one person that was located and scratched off a list, two more would be added. It was a sorry business.

The dead were never mentioned on the radio. A group of pastors, deacons, and their wives were contacted with the names of those who had been found dead, and they were working their way through the community the best they could, notifying the next of kin in person.

A network of CB and ham radios formed and began coordinating information on separate channels and providing it to Eleanor directly to cut down on some of the confusion on channel 18. People in radio communication were asked to go door-to-door to see if their neighbors were home, and safe. This prompted many more ambulance calls throughout the afternoon. The mayor's wife was located at the Country Club, where she had been with a number of other ladies and a florist finalizing plans for a *Leprechaun VIP* breakfast early Saturday morning. The mayor had not been found.

When the judge and Bo had finally shown back up at the courthouse with the food around 8:00pm the night before, they found most every light off except for desk lamps where people were looking at maps or printouts from the 1970 census. Bo was taking the food up to the jury deliberation room while the judge was rounding up the remaining workers at the courthouse to join them there. The judge found Eleanor looking as she always did, fresh and ready to teach Sunday school, and J.T. looking like he'd spent all day chasing two greased pigs around a roller rink.

"Well, look at that," the judge said as he walked into the communications room and looked down at Michael's legal pad. "Eleanor, you better watch it. Looks like Michael's after your job."

"What's that?" Eleanor replied, turning round. She had not paid Michael any real attention throughout the day, except to ask how he was doing and if he needed some water, when she had excused herself twice to the ladies' room. She had forgotten to ask to see his map of the United States, which she regretted now, seeing it sitting on the chair beside him. She was actually very genuinely interested in seeing it—she had simply forgotten. And unlike most of the children she interacted with, which wasn't many, she had been waiting for him to interrupt her and demand her attention, and that had never happened. "I'm not much of a mapmaker, your Honor. I hope they don't add that to my job responsibilities," she added.

"No, Eleanor, he's been busy over here copying your shorthand." Michael looked instantly, almost comically guilty in the way only children who haven't learned to lie properly can look. His bottom lip dropped as if to speak, then closed tightly back up over his top lip as if to stop himself from speaking. Eleanor stepped in to save him from the awkward moment, saying "I told you all he would make a great helper, your Honor, and you see now I was right. You did make it back with some food, I hope? And the mayor?"

"The food we have, the mayor we do not. Bo is taking the food up to the conference table in the deliberation room. Why don't ya'll come get something to eat?"

J.T. looked back hopefully from the communications panel in front of him, one ear still covered with the black-vinyl-covered pad of the headphones connected by a fabric-covered cord to the switchboard. He looked as if he could use a sandwich. *And possibly a jigger or two of bourbon, and a good night's sleep*, the judge thought.

Eleanor told J.T. to go first and she would keep the airwaves calm. "Go on, Michael, and get yourself something to eat," she urged him.

When they were all gone, she unplugged J.T.'s headset and turned the broadcast speaker at his station on to a low volume. There was an indistinct babble of voices echoing around the room, from the two broadcast speakers, and the bank of CB radios, but none of it was directed at the courthouse for the moment. She walked over to look at what Michael had been doing, and looked at the map, which was drawn with more exactness than the children's placemats at Ma Hawkins Restaurant, and with the capitals all neatly lettered, spelled correctly and located accurately—as far as she knew—with small stars. Then she looked at what the judge said Michael had been copying, but he hadn't been copying anything. He was writing.

He had apparently been watching her take shorthand notes throughout the afternoon, and at some point during that time, taught himself, and began taking dictation from his own thoughts, and written a letter to his father. *Is that even possible?*, she asked herself. It seemed more likely than that a colored boy, or any 10-year-old child, would just happen to know Pitman shorthand. Gregg shorthand was still taught in both the city and county schools as far as she knew—it was what all the girls knew, and what most every woman taught in Laurens County used in the secretarial jobs most of them had. She learned Gregg in Dublin High School herself in her junior year from 1936-1937. She had mastered it before the Christmas break, unlike most of her classmates, many of whom never quite understood that they weren't learning a new language, they were just learning a way to quickly record the one they already spoke, or any language.

When she graduated high school in 1938, Miss Eleanor Thompson enrolled in the South Georgia Teachers College south of Dublin in Statesboro, where she learned Pitman shorthand, a style much more suited to her. The variety of strokes lent itself much more easily to her natural style of writing, which was fluid and elegant, with long, tall, slender strokes. When she completed her four-year degree there, she did not go into teaching—there was a war on. She wanted to be a part of the war effort, and so had gone to the Carnegie Public Library in Dublin each day to look at the job notices in the *Atlanta Journal*, the *Atlanta Constitution*, and the *The Washington Post*. In 1941 she responded to an advertisement in the *Post*, and was called for an interview to Knoxville, Tennessee, to be prepared to work immediately. She soon found herself the subject of a series of background and personality tests, and after being granted *Top Secret* security status, began work in a small pool of secretaries for the architectural firm of Skidmore, Owings and Merrill, which was selected by the federal government to design what would become the city of Oak Ridge, Tennessee, home of the Manhattan project.

It was through the endless meetings of architects, engineers, designers, contractors, scientists, military personnel, and government officials that she learned firsthand how government works and doesn't work. The meetings really *were* endless—the work preparing for, building, maintaining and expanding the Oak Ridge site went on twenty-four hours a day from the time she started until well into 1945. Even with the end of the war in sight, in the summer of 1945, it was not over until it was over. Then, on September 2, 1945, it was over. For her, at least. It was time to go home.

She had met and married a civil engineer from Columbus, Georgia in 1943, and they decided to head back to Dublin, where she could finally tell her family where she had been and what she had been doing for the past four years, and her parents could meet her husband. As far as her family had known, she had been working as an administrative assistant at a pants factory. They knew pants were important to the war effort, but never fully understood her commitment to her job until after it was over and they could read about it in the paper. She had been home only once during that time, and that was for the funeral of her only sibling, a sister, Alice, who died of complications from pneumonia in December 1942.

She wasn't sure what she would be doing after the war, but she knew it wouldn't be teaching. In Oak Ridge, she had been hired away from the architecture firm by the Army Corps of Engineers, and gained respect among the men she worked with. They never asked for her opinion on war matters, but as the war went on she found herself transcribing her own words more than she would ever have imagined. *What do you think, Eleanor?* always preceded those entries in her notes. She never took it upon herself to interject, even when there was a name, or a common sense answer, or even a reasoned response to a complex question she could provide. She knew her place.

And when she returned to Dublin, she found another place. The tiny old lady who had been answering the phone for the sheriff since sometime before the Depression finally retired from her post, and after a brief interview with then-sheriff Pete Sumpter, Eleanor just sat right down and took over. Dublin was booming, as always, and there was plenty for her and her husband Ellis to do. Preparations for the new Veterans Administration Hospital that would open in 1948 were underway, and over the next few decades, she saw plenty.

But she had never seen this. She wasn't even sure what *this* was. A rainstorm disrupting the flow of life, of life itself, was uncommon but not unheard of. The sheet of water that had broken the city down was unusual, certainly, but probably not unprecedented, either, she suspected. Yet a child, able to pick up in hours, maybe minutes—who knew—a probably entirely-foreign system of writing. Without any guidance. Without a single question. It unnerved her. She hadn't paid proper attention to what she was reading as she looked at it. She re-read the letter, focusing on the content, and not the impossibility of the writing itself. It read:

> *Dear Dad, I hope you are somewhere safe and dry and not alone. I am at the*
> *court house with Papa Bo and Mrs. Eleanor. I like Mrs. Eleanor. She treats*

me nice. I don't know if you know the big bridge went down, but it did. There are so many people dead and people who nobody knows where they are. Papa Bo said we could not go see you at the V.A. and ride the Ferris Wheel across the street because you left the hospital Wednesday morning and didn't come back before the sky fell this morning. You are on the missing list there because you left A.M.A., but I do not know what that means. I do not think it is the same thing as A.W.O.L. because you never went A.W.O.L. and I know you would not desert us. One of the officers out helping people today radioed in to say that a black man in his late twenties or early thirties had been seen walking in the rain and talking to himself, saying "He can never tell," over and over again, and that he was scaring people. I think that was you, and I promised you I would never tell and I never will. I know you were not talking to yourself. I understand. One day mom will understand too. I think you scared her too, but she will come back. I hope your dreams have stopped, and that you can get some sleep. Papa Bo said the medicine they give you at the V.A. helps, but I do not think it does. I think only the liquor you get from across the street from the V.A. helps, but I do not tell Papa Bo that. He does not like that you drink. I do not like it, but I know it makes everything better for you. I do not know how to get a letter to you but I wanted to write something in Mrs. Eleanor's writing, so I wrote this. I love you, your son Michael, Peanut

She sat down with the legal pad in her lap and looked back at the map, trying to make a connection between the letter and the weather and the boy, and she couldn't. She did not know if she was more frightened or saddened by what she had read, but she was shaken by the utter strangeness of it all. She could not make sense of it. The letter explained a great deal, but left her with questions that she could not reasonably ask the boy or Bo or anyone. It just then occurred to her that it had not been her business to read the letter in the first place.

Was it some sort of child abuse the boy was referring to? Did Bo bring Michael to the courthouse to protect him from his father? She thought it unlikely.

She had not even known Bo's son had returned from Vietnam, and as far as she knew, Michael's mother had died years ago. Shellshock, flashbacks and hallucinations seemed the most immediate and obvious answer for many of the questions she was asking herself, which multiplied as she looked back at the letter. There were so many gaps. So much strangeness. So much disorder. The boy was just 10.

"Is anyone there? Eleanor? J.T.? 418 calling dispatch." The voice was calling from across the room. It was the broadcast speaker. An officer. 418. Jimmy. Eleanor did not know how long she had been lost in thought. She took Michael's legal pad and sat down at the communications desk, slipping the letter under her own paperwork while pressing the red button on the microphone. "Sorry Jimmy, I'm back."

"We found the Sirmons family down an embankment off Turkey Creek. That's going to be a 10-79."

Eleanor looked down and saw she had the list for the missing. She began crossing through their names as she reached for the list of the dead.

"Light a flare and leave it on the embankment to the nearest access point to the car. We'll get somebody out there. Head on over to New Bethel Church. Reverend Shoals is unaccounted for, and the flock is nervous."

"10-4. If it's like every other church in town, the steeple's knocked off. We got steeples everywhere. And the Shrimp Boat is just gone. En route. Over."

The Shrimp Boat was a restaurant in a building the size and shape of a large shrimp boat. It served cheap frozen battered seafood on greasy paper plates, and Eleanor considered its destruction no great loss. Its presence had in fact always mildly distressed her—a ship just sitting there in the middle of town, next to a car wash, hours from the nearest ocean. There was just something impertinently incongruous, unseemly about it to her.

She turned back to her lists, calling out on the radio to officers, establishing times and locations and destinations, coordinating with the hospital and fire department with a dexterity and efficiency that J.T. lacked despite his years of experience. The most critically injured had made it to the hospital hours earlier, but more kept straggling in. As roads were slowly cleared by volunteers with chain saws, people continued trickling into the emergency room, some in cars or the back of pick-up trucks.

The judge, Bo and Michael returned from eating after a relatively short time. J.T went to get an update on Eric, who was being looked after by Jackie, the court stenograph machine operator. After conferring with the doctors at the hospital earlier in the day, it was decided that as long as Eric was breathing, he was safest where he was.

When Eleanor reported the news of the Sirmons family to the judge, she discovered they had attended First Baptist Church along with him, so it would be likely that he would know whoever the children in the car were. After some brief discussion about the suitability of the judge and Bo going on such a mission—down a steep embankment, in the rain, at night, when there was no hope of actually saving anyone—Eleanor acquiesced to the judge's fallacious reasoning so she could return to the work at hand. She then noticed Michael, who was looking distractedly at the chair where he had left his letter on the legal pad.

"Why don't you leave Michael here with me, Bo? I believe I can put him to some good use," she asked.

"Yes ma'am. That creek ain't no place for a boy this time a'night. You mind Mrs. Eleanor now, Peanut."

"All right then, ya'll take care now," the judge said, and the two men turned and left.

"Yes sir, I will," Peanut said as he watched the shadows of the two men fade into the black corridor. He said it with the calm conviction of a child who always behaves, without being reminded—but there was an uncomfortable sadness about his features that made Eleanor uneasy.

She looked at the boy, her face expressionless, and asked, "Michael, are your block letters as neat as your shorthand?" She knew the answer to this question—she had seen his block letters on the map, but this seemed a plausible introduction to the other questions she had for him.

"My what, ma'am?" He was looking at her in genuine confusion.

"Shorthand. That's what we call the kind of writing I do that you wrote your letter to your father in. I didn't read the whole thing, don't worry," she lied without thinking or pausing, "I was just so impressed, I had to see. You've never done that before? "

"No ma'am," he replied looking down at the marble-patterned asbestos tile floor.

"Did you figure out how to do that just by watching me?" She was now actively ignoring a radio call coming in from one of the officers.

"No ma'am, I didn't watch you write. I used the way they used to figure out the higher-o-glyphs." He looked up from the floor at her with an unabashed curiosity—*Would she understand?*

She did, almost instantly. Everything Egyptian had been all the rage since the Tutankhamun exhibition had opened at the British Museum a couple of years before. On the cover of *National Geographic*, *Parade*, and *Science* magazines, among others, if the boy hadn't picked it up from one of those, the story of the decoding of the hieroglyphs had probably made it into the school curriculum. She could see how it might make an excellent teaching tool. Here was the proof. But still. The boy was 10 years old.

"I see," she said, and then, "Well, how about it? Are your block letters as neat as your shorthand?"

His shorthand *was* neat, she thought, and then she considered with some momentary pride that while neat, his shorthand did not have the grace or fluidity of her own. She checked herself—Was she jealous of a ten year old who had just discovered and mastered the basic concepts of shorthand on his own? That was petty, and Eleanor was not a petty person.

"Yes ma'am, I print just fine." His reply was cautious, curious, and yet confident. He had abilities, and he knew.

"Well then why don't you sit here by me and translate my lists so that someone besides the two of us can read them? Come tomorrow morning, we're going to need them, I'm sure."

They set to work, legal pads spread on the narrow laminate worksurface beneath the wall of blinking lights and speakers and dials. J.T. returned a few minutes later, and looked curiously at the pair, but Eleanor silently motioned him to sit down and get to it. They worked into and through the night. Around 4:00am Michael had finally begun to tire, and Eleanor suggested he put his head down, and he did, sleeping almost instantly. J.T. had no family to go home to, but still looked at Michael with some envy, until Eleanor suggested he go find a sofa to rest on for a bit.

They had not heard back from the judge or Bo, but this was no great surprise. They were still without a radio or CB in the car, and had probably found a hundred other things to take care of on their way out and way back. Eleanor hoped so—there was much to do.

When the sheriff woke the next morning it was to the smell of bacon frying in the Armory kitchen, and the sound of rain still pelting the building. It was past eight o'clock, and he soon found, much more to his relief than he was willing or ready to admit, that he was no longer the man in charge. The echoing, cavernous hall had been filled to overflowing with a vast amount of equipment and what seemed to him an inordinate number of people. How he had managed to sleep—on an army cot—through the arrival and unloading of so many crates and boxes was beyond his understanding.

"Morning, sleepy head," called Blanks, walking in with a styrofoam cup of coffee in one hand and a clipboard in the other before the sheriff had even managed to stand up. The young captain was smiling, clean-shaven, and apparently well-rested. "The command is in from Atlanta, but I guess you can see that. The Lieutenant Colonel, Gerald McAfee, arrived with the last load in. He'd like to start getting things moving."

Things were already moving—the colonel just wanted to get the sheriff involved and made to feel a participant. But his participation would be that of an advisor, and a go-between for the community. It was a limited role, but an important one.

On their way to the folding tables and chairs where breakfast was being served on sea foam green melamine cafeteria-style plates, he glimpsed some of the diverse array of equipment coming in—telex machines, pallets full of gas-powered generators, welding equipment, several backhoes, a pontoon boat, scuba equipment, chain saws, gasoline cans, sledgehammers… it seemed endless. Four very well-behaved bloodhounds sat on the cement floor by an open door, looking out into the rain.

He couldn't help asking "Scuba gear?"

Blanks kept walking along with him, answering "Retrieving bodies from cars in moving water is something of a specialty, sheriff. We have a team flying in from

Baltimore to assist."

The burst of hope and energy he had felt upon wakening was gone instantly—his stomach sank, and his hunger with it. A part of him just wanted to go back and crawl on the cot, or better yet, to his own bed, and his wife, and coffee.

"Good," he replied without emotion, then "How's the power situation?"

"More crews arrived overnight. Some from Alabama made it already, more are coming in later from Mississippi. The South Carolina and Florida crews will be covering everything from Savannah up through Metter, and the Tennessee, Arkansas and North Carolina crews will be covering everything from Macon north."

"What about the Georgia crews?"

"The Georgia crews will primarily do the local line work. The out-of-state crews will mostly be working on the major transmission lines. It's going to be a slow go getting everything back running."

It was a slow go, but the people at it, at least those in the Armory, were moving very quickly—walking, talking, writing, even eating with a hive-like efficiency. The morning was spent with more introductions than the sheriff could keep up with, multiple radio calls into Eleanor, and finally the very welcome news that he could go home to have lunch with his wife—and take a warm meal to her.

He spent the afternoon at the courthouse mostly assisting Eleanor, who had struck up an immediate kinship with the colonel over at the Armory—their no-nonsense approach to every possible situation had bonded them in their first conversations that morning. Well before the sheriff woke up, they were comrades in arms against a common foe—chaos. They both seemed to abhor it, and their shared emergency management style seemed to consist of two steps: One, make an inventory; Two, take action. The only consensus they seemed interested in making was with one another. When he had arrived at the courthouse after lunch, Eleanor had called him into the communications room to ask whether or not he thought they should ask for more gasoline to be trucked in from Atlanta, he told her he thought she had a pretty good handle on things, and she hadn't asked for his opinion since. He was sometimes included in making inventories (*How many restaurants in town have working gas stoves?*) and taking actions (*Why don't you process the release paperwork and let all the non-violent offenders out of lockup so we can put those officers to some useful purpose?*), but his role now was largely perfunctory. He could see that.

The judge and Bo made it back just in time for a late lunch of leftovers from the day before. They sat in the communications room regaling J.T. and Michael with stories of their recent adventures. Some were so gruesome they agreed without speaking should not be shared with a boy Michael's age, or possibly anyone if it could be helped. At a pig farm right outside of town, a farmer who had apparently been braining in sows crippled by the storm had been found half-eaten and trampled in filth, with a bloody mallet clamped in what was left of his fingers. His skull had been entirely flattened. A woman had been found naked on the floor of the U.S.A. Carpet Outlet on 441 South—and her clothes were nowhere to be found. It looked like she had been brought there naked, possibly already dead, and used in the most uncharitable way. But not all the stories were so gruesome. Half of a chicken farm had collapsed outside the small town of Rentz, and the judge and Bo had spent an hour helping gather up thousands of chickens in the rain, and the story the two of them told had Michael laughing out loud, and even Eleanor cracked a smile, though she pretended not to be listening as she sat at the communications switchboard, soldiering on with the day's work.

***

By midafternoon Saturday, and multiple check-ins with the radio station, the CB users, and ham radio operators, Eleanor was able to narrow the list of missing from 18 to three, not including those assumed in the river. The mayor was still missing, as were two young boys. She sent Jackie Sirmons, the court stenographer, to ride by each of the boy's homes to independently verify that the boys were not there, and that the parents did not know where they were. When Jackie returned two hours later, she reported that the boys were not at their homes, but also that none of the boys' parents were especially concerned—Josh Landrum, eight years old, and Jonny Vinson, ten, went to church, school, and Boy Scouts together. They had known each other since preschool, and both boys were in fact boys, and this was, after all, Dublin, and there were only so many places they could be. They would turn up sooner or later. For boys their age to not appear at home on a Friday night was not an unusual thing—*I thought I told you I was spending the night at their house* was an entirely common phrase in the lives of Dublin parents, particularly on Saturday mornings. Chances were they were at a friend's house where there was no radio, or, even more likely, at one of several forts they had helped build and/or maintain in a stand of woods across Woodlawn Drive from Moore Street Elementary and behind the back yards of the houses on the north side of Roberson Street. They would show up.

Made of discarded bits of wood, metal siding, old signs, and busted up doors and windows, the little shacks—which might have been called *clubhouses* in some other neighborhoods, or *homes* down by the river—were called *forts* by the children around Moore Street because they were used as forts in an ongoing game of War, or Cowboys and Indians if girls were playing, that had been fought without significant interruption since the beginning of time, or at least since the beginning of the neighborhood—there were men in their forties who could recall the names of the forts that had been around when they were adolescents living in the neighborhood's then-new ranch-style homes. The tradition of naming the forts had faded in popularity over time, but not the forts themselves.

At any given time over the years there had been as many as eight, and as few as two forts. The weekend of the storm there were four. The neighborhood parents knew more or less about the forts, but not exactly where they were. They did not know that one of the forts—the main fort—had actual twin beds, one of which had dog-eared copies of *Playboy* under it (a copy of *Penthouse* had disappeared the previous fall, and the culprit had never been found out). The parents had suspicions, but for the most part let the forts exist in the world of childhood—their kids were good kids, and they would be in the real world soon enough.

Teens that had outgrown playing make-believe would nonetheless use the forts for making out, smoking cigarettes, or playing hooky—until they got cars. College students returning home for Thanksgiving or Christmas break, in need of some nostalgia or marijuana, would volunteer to go find a younger brother or sister to bring them home for supper. The problem for college students was that with one exception, the forts moved. As a fort would begin to rot or fall apart, or particularly bored or industrious kids would decide to build *the best fort ever*, they would scavenge the best parts of one of the old forts, but leave it somewhat intact as a sort of decoy. Lots of people, including most of the children who attended Moore Street Elementary, and the teachers and principal, knew that the forts existed. But without one of the neighborhood children to act as a guide, finding an active fort could be difficult. And unless someone from outside the neighborhood was spending the night over, it was against the rules of War to show where the forts were. And no one from the outside was ever allowed to know where the main fort was, ever. It was the best fort of them all, because it was real. It was referred to as *The Treehouse*, and it had proper walls, a floor, a ceiling, and a door. According to legend, it was built in 1968 by a guy named Stevie Mitchell in the last month before he left for Vietnam, as a present to his younger brothers Vince and Coty, because he was convinced he was never going to come back alive from Vietnam. He was right—he died May 2, 1970 from Viet Cong shrapnel during Operation Toan Thang. His parents, who had been fighting about the war since before America entered it, finally got a divorce, and the mother moved with Vince and Coty to live with her sister in Chattanooga. After that, his father moved back to Helen, Georgia where his family was. Most of the kids who used the main fort now were too young to remember any of the Mitchell boys, or a time before *The Treehouse*. At some point in the fall of 1973 a POW/MIA flag appeared on the back wall of the main fort, and just sort of stayed there, without anyone knowing where it came from, or exactly what it meant.

Most things that showed up at the main fort stayed there. It was close to 600 square feet, built between two giant live oak trees in a grove of them spreading out from the steep, deep ravine of Cedar Creek. Normally dry during the summer, the creek sprang to life at the first sign of a summer rain, the result of overdevelopment upstream, but it typically disappeared just as quickly. In the spring, though, it was usual for there to be two-to-three inches of water bubbling along beneath the entry to the fort, hidden away under the spreading branches of the oaks, invisible to everyone but God. One of the reasons no one was ever able to find it—including parents, principals, and even the police—was that it was not in the stretch of woods behind the houses on Roberson Street, where the rest of the forts were. It was across the street from those woods, across Brookhaven Drive, past the *No Tresspassing, Keep Out, Violators Will Be Prosecuted* signs posted every ten or fifteen feet. The owner of the property, Dyson Caruthers, was as old and mean and spiteful as Noah's own Billy Goat, a man who always looked ready to kick in the teeth of the nearest child. A retired, part-time locksmith, he regularly wrote scathing editorials about the immorality of the people and politicians of Dublin for the *Courier-Herald*, which they printed mostly for entertainment value, and he would go to the library to confirm they were printed—he would never subscribe to such an awful paper, which was another frequent topic of his editorials. Whenever he saw young girls in halter tops in public, he would point and curse "Jezebel! Jezebel!" in a dramatic stage whisper that would have been funny if the harlots in question weren't first and second grade children. Choosing the easy way out, most parents told their young children he was one of the veterans from the hospital who was very sick, and that everyone should pray for him. What they really wanted to do was punch him—he wasn't sick, he just enjoyed being a mean old man, and was a deliberate thorn in the side of everyone he came in contact with. It was as though he started playing a caricature of a hateful geezer at some point in the early 1950s, and had just been unable to stop. Instead, he had refined his persona until it bordered just this side of evil—some said he crossed it, but it really wasn't so.

Caruthers stayed up late on every Halloween night, sitting in a folding aluminum chair on his immaculate lawn, daring trick-or-treaters to step on his property, his face so set in its livid expression it looked like a mask. He held a notepad and pencil to record details of the automobiles that would visit his lonely corner of the world, where Garfield and Grant Streets met. To try to prevent any risk of identity, dozens of cars would coordinate to ride by his house in both directions at the same time, pelting his house and car with eggs they had let ripen for days in anticipation of the annual skirmish. They avoided hitting him directly—that somehow seemed out of bounds—but he learned not to stand up or move, because the boys were aiming for near him, and Dublin boys have good aim. When his house had last been rolled, in March 1972, it appeared to have been subjected to some sort of mummification ritual—no brick, no window, no door could be distinguished beneath the horizontal and diagonal lines of toilet paper engulfing the house, and most of the roof was covered as well. Hundreds of rolls of toilet paper had been used. An editorial in the next day's paper suggested that Christian Charity should lead some of Dublin's youth to help the old man in his cleanup effort, and two of the Methodist Youth Fellowship groups joined together to remove the toilet paper. Caruthers sat in his lawn chair, facing his house, cursing them and their whole generation while they worked to return his home to its usual pristine state.

So the brazenness of the main fort, built squarely in the middle of enemy territory, on the property of the man most likely to attempt to have even a casual or accidental trespasser arrested, was what made it so perfect. The man himself appeared too old and feeble to to ever venture anywhere near the center of the property where the main fort was nestled by the creek. He patrolled the perimeter of the property regularly, particularly right after school ended each day, cruising up and down the street in his black 1963 Dodge 440 sedan, stopping to pick up any litter he might see, and waiting for a car to ride by so he could raise his fist and yell at it. But he never saw the children as they darted in around his warning signs. Their secret system of crossing the street, the 150-wide-open-yards from woods to woods, had never failed, but they held their breath, each and every time, eyes wide at their own audacity, their hearts racing in time with their feet.

Eleanor knew nothing about the main fort, or any of the forts, though she knew Dyson Caruthers as well as anyone in the county. She somehow even knew the jump-rope-rhyme about him: *Dyson Caruthers, Didn't Have a Mother, Sold His Sister for a Dime, Got a Nickel for his Brother, He's so Damn Old, He Thinks Hell is Cold, So I Asked My Mama to Knit Him a Sweater.* He had stopped speaking to Eleanor directly in 1962, at the insistence of the then-sheriff, when she had finally threatened to quit if they couldn't get the man to stop calling and wasting her time. He didn't stop calling, but if he ever got her on the line, he would just hang up. She was never sure what the sheriff had said to him, but two sheriffs later, it still had its effect.

When Jackie explained to her what the parents had told her about the forts— Jackie graduated from East Laurens schools, and had no idea about anything at Moore Street, including the forts—Eleanor radioed out to Darryl Burke, the driver of one of the paramedic vans, "419, this is dispatch."

"Go ahead, dispatch."

"Darryl, it's Eleanor. You grew up on Woodrow Avenue didn't you?"

"Yes ma'am. Something you need over that way?"

"If you're in that neighborhood, could you do us a favor and check and see if two boys, Josh Landrum and Jonny Vinson, might be hiding out in some kind of fort you boys keep over there?" An unexpectedly long pause followed.

"Yes ma'am. We're not far from there now. We'll work our way over."

"Thank you boys. Over."

"Wait, Mrs. Eleanor, one quick question. Has anyone seen or heard from Dyson Caruthers?"

"Not that I'm aware. What does Caruthers have to do with anything?" She then realized she had gone several blessed days without thinking of, hearing, or reading the man's name.

"I may have to go into his woods. I don't want to get shot." Darryl wasn't entirely joking.

"If you see him, tell him Mrs. Eleanor sent you there on official police business." Eleanor wasn't joking at all.

"Not the sheriff?" Darryl asked in mild surprise and amusement.

"Not if you're talking to Caruthers." Eleanor said it with finality and authority.

Darryl laughed and said "I wish I'd known that when I was eight years old. We're en route. This might take us a while. Over."

The woods on both sides of Brookhaven Drive had been almost but not entirely destroyed. The trees weren't shredded to pulp like most of the woods in the county, but they were broken and twisted, heaped in haphazard piles, like a game of Pick-Up-Stix writ large, wet and deadly. There were some isolated pine trees still standing out in the open field, and, where Cedar Creek cut through the Caruthers property, a small but dense cluster of cedar, scrub oak, and ancient live oak trees stood with their branches locked into each other, holding each other in place in the wet soil, shimmering in the sun-streaked rain like a mirage.

Darryl began working the ambulance over to Moore Street Elementary before Eleanor was off the line. He parked in the back parking lot of the school, which was being set up as a Red Cross Distribution Center in the front, in the cafeteria. When he got out of the van and said to his partner, Doug Austin, "This should only take me a few minutes," he was not entirely surprised when Doug responded "You don't really believe I'm going to miss this chance to see the fort, do you?" He was laughing, but serious and excited as he got out and followed Darryl across Woodlawn Drive.

Doug had attended Central Elementary across town, and grown up on Williams Street. His little league and bantam league baseball and football teams had played at the small Hillburn Park recreation complex, adjacent to Moore Street Elementary, so he had heard rumors of the main fort for probably 20 years, but like most children not from the neighborhood, he didn't really even know if it existed. Lots of kids who had spent the night with neighborhood kids over the years had played War, and so had seen the scrawny little forts behind the Roberson Street houses, but they had never found the legendary main fort, *The Treehouse*, because they were always looking in the wrong woods, and they were looking up.

The two men stood in the rain, in their Laurens County Ambulance Service rain slickers, trying to determine where to cross the ditch. It was overflowing with water, and was easily five feet across at the narrowest point they could see. They walked half a block to the stop sign at the corner of Woodlawn and Brookhaven, where they found a spot closer to four feet across, and each goose-stepped over the ditch without disaster. Darryl started walking quickly towards the oak and cedar cluster in the middle of the destruction, trampling the remnants of the *No Trespassing* signs as he went.

"Really? Here? You kids had fucking balls!" Doug was laughing, and a little out of breath. "Right here in Caruthers' own woods? That is some shit, my friend. If he had found out, his head would probably have like, exploded or some shit. You kids had fucking balls!"

"Nope, not us." Darryl called back behind him. They were both shouting to be heard in the rain. "Just Stevie. Stevie was the one with the balls. And the brains."

"Who's Stevie?"

Their legs were quickly tiring from the strain of the mud, and their progress had slowed as they backtracked around unsteady-looking piles of pine trees.

"Stevie Mitchell," Darryl answered. "We were best friends growing up. You probably didn't know him. Sorta quiet guy. Anyway, when he got drafted he decided he wanted to do something for his little brothers. He came up with the tree house idea, I don't remember where from. But it was actually his dad who came up with the idea of building it out here. His dad fought in Korea, read all these fucked up books on military strategy, like Caesar, and the Nazis, just every fucking thing."

They were standing in the thicket of trees, and Doug was looking at Darryl expectantly, looking up into the canopy, waiting for something to appear.

"Well, what do you think?" Darryl asked. The look on his face was of a familiar amusement—like showing a tired old card trick to a child seeing it for the first time. *Now you see it...*

"Where is—" Doug faltered in disbelief. "What the fuck? What *is* this?"

He had followed Darryl's gaze to look at what appeared to be the remains of an old, dead live oak tree fallen between two others. But the initiate could see and hear the rain bouncing off the oak tree. It wasn't dead, because it wasn't real.

"You, you *made* this? How do you get in it?"

"I didn't make it, Stevie made it. And his dad, but it was mostly Stevie, I think, anyways. His dad was a camouflage specialist for the military, covert something something ops. He says you can make anything disappear if you want to bad enough. The problem most people have is that when they think about something disappearing, they think about something like a magician with a bunny—they think the thing isn't there anymore. They aren't looking for it so they don't see it, but the bunny is still there. So the trick is to get people to not look for what is there, so they won't see it. It's about appearance, not about disappearance, not about physical reality. I can give you his dad's number if you want. He will talk to you about it for hours. Hours. I mostly helped bring stuff in and put it together."

Darryl was walking around the oak tree cluster to the side of the trees overlooking the steep drop to the racing creek. The other side of the ravine was only 10 feet or so away. The trees on the far side of the creek had weathered the storm in the same pattern, with pines trees mostly down, oaks and cedars mostly standing.

"Be careful coming down. The handholds are going to be slick. The trick is to try not to use your feet for leverage, just use your hands." And then, like a five-year-old on a strange, partially-buried set of monkey bars, Darryl quickly but carefully dropped over the side of the ravine and descended to a narrow ledge of wet, red clay about twelve feet down and projecting out about 18".

Doug eased himself down to the wet ground, and reached down for a handhold he was sure would not be there, but it was. And it wasn't a rope, or a root, it was a bent piece of metal, a proper handle projecting out from what looked like a muddy red clay embankment, but was actually some kind of painted or stained concrete surface. He grasped the handle and swung himself down, reached down and found another, and then another, and another, and felt his feet touch the slippery shelf of mud. It was real wet clay, but visually indistinguishable from the fake wall it was next to. He kept hold of the last handle as he steadied himself and looked around. It was like being in a diorama at the Museum of Natural History that shows animals in their natural habitat, but dropped into the actual habitat it was a copy of. And they were virtually identical—it was only where tiny bits of the concrete surface had begun to wear away over the years that one could see, up close, that there was a difference at all.

The exposed roots of the oak trees sprung out from the wall of red earth and hung down over the side of the ravine in knobby tendrils. He looked around for Darryl, didn't see him, and called out for him.

"In here," Darryl responded, laughing, from behind the curtain of roots. Doug parted the roots and passed through them, and through a metal-framed doorway hidden in shadows behind them, to enter the strangest place he had ever seen. Part bomb shelter, part kids' room, part juke joint, part clubhouse, part hobbit hole—there didn't seem to be any order to the place whatsoever, other than paradise for a ten-year-old. It was remarkably, almost incredibly dry, even though the entire structure was underground. It didn't smell any more like mildew than any teenage boy's room might. There was a Pink Floyd poster on one wall, but on the floor beside one of the sofas—there were two sofas—sat two Barbies and a G.I. Joe doll obviously abandoned mid-play. There was an overhead fluorescent light on—the fort had power.

The ceilings were eight feet tall, and the room was paneled with eight-by-four foot panels of plywood. Where one of the panels had been removed, pink fiberglass insulation was visible.

"Oh my God," Doug began. "This is fucking unbelievable. But I don't under-stand—" he began, before Darryl cut him off.

"I will bring you back so you can marvel at the amazing amazingness of it another time, and I'll tell you everything I know. But our mission here is complete—those boys aren't here. We need to get back to the truck."

"Oh, come on, gimme five minutes," Doug started, but Darryl cut him off.

"No. Our truck is probably already drawing attention, and who knows who's been trying to get hold of us." The ambulance radio was mounted under the dash, and they had no portable radios.

"Do we go back out the same way?" Doug asked as he followed Darryl to the door.

"You were never very good at war, were you?" Darryl responded with a laugh as he turned out the light and shut the door, which closed with a deep metallic thud.

Going out the other secret way necessitated them sloshing through the creek—it was ice cold and came up above their knees—but Darryl insisted it was necessary. When they reemerged at the school, it was from the opposite direction they had entered Caruthers' property.

Darryl mentioned casually, almost in passing, as an afterthought, "Doug, you know if you ever tell anybody about that place, someone will kill you, right?"

Doug laughed, and turned to laugh with Darryl, who wasn't smiling. "You're not serious? Who? Who would kill me? You?"

"Just don't tell anybody."

"It's almost in plain sight now. Somebody's bound to see it."

"No one ever has, and no one ever will. Just don't tell anybody."

"Alright, alright, I won't tell. Damn it's cold." His quick change of subject marked his unease with the topic—he knew, somehow, that Darryl was telling him the truth.

They had fresh uniforms in the ambulance, and went into the school to change into them. Colleen Colquitt, the school principal, was standing smoking under the front portico, a Mid-Century modern slab of concrete in the shape of a boomerang, held up by five conical columns. "You boys go swimming?" she asked as they ran in from the rain. The paramedics knew all of the principals and vice-principals in the county on a first-name basis.

"I thought I saw my daddy's German Shepherd out in Caruthers' field, thought I'd try to get it before Caruthers makes a jacket out of him," Darryl answered. "But if it was him, he got away."

"We haven't seen the old man," Mrs. Colquitt responded, in a tone that suggested she hadn't given it a second thought. "I guess he'll be down here soon enough to get his signs back up."

After the men changed clothes they grabbed some apples and oranges from the Red Cross folks in the cafeteria and headed back out into the rain.

"Eleanor, you there?"

"10-4, Darryl. What'd you find?"

"No boys, and no recent trace of them. That's not to say they weren't in the woods, but if they were there it's gonna take a dog to find 'em out. It's a mess. Trees all over the place, same as everywhere."

"I'll let the Guard know to take the dogs when they can. Did your fort survive?"

"Eleanor, I'm a grown man, what would I have to do with a fort?"

"10-4. Thanks Darryl. If you could head on out to Colonial Mobile Estates? Somebody's stuck under a tractor trailer. They're not out yet, but they're going to need a lift to the hospital directly."

"10-4"

Eleanor turned from the control panel of the communication room and looked at Michael and asked if he had ever built a fort.

"No ma'am," he answered, looking up. "Should I have?"

"I don't know. I never did, either. I never even heard of such a thing until today. Sounds like a lot of running around getting into mischief and not a lot of doing homework to me."

"It sounds like it might be nice though. Maybe not the war part. Do you think they really fight?"

Eleanor laughed, "No, not these children. I imagine they have wooden rifles, maybe the ones that shoot rubber bands at people. Maybe those noisy cap pistols. Not a lot more."

She turned to go back through Friday's list of who had knocked on doors in the different neighborhoods, found Caruthers, and put a call out on C.B. channel 18 for Sly Deloach. He answered, "10-4 Mrs. Eleanor, I'm here."

"Was Caruthers home yesterday?" Eleanor asked.

"His car was home, still is. He didn't answer the door, but that ain't nothing from him."

"Can you try again? If he doesn't answer I'll send a car by."

"10-4, Mrs. Eleanor"

He reported back in 20 minutes that he got no answer, but went to the back door to knock—it was a sliding glass patio door—and he saw Caruthers spread out on the den floor as dead as yesterday. The house seemed to be in fine condition—not even a leak. But there he was face down on the floor, with a housecat kneading the flesh at the base of his neck. Deloach tapped on the window to shoo the cat away, but it just looked up at him defiantly. He didn't mention the cat to Eleanor.

"10-4, Sly. We'll see to it."

She added Caruthers to the list of the dead, and wondered if there was anyone, anywhere, who would be sad the man was dead.

And a thought, not fully formed, rose almost to the point of consciousness, of who, where, would be sad if she died, but before it became a complete thought she whisked it away, without deliberate awareness, and she radioed the Armory for someone to transport Caruthers. Immersing herself in the work before her, she immediately forgot what she almost thought.

***

It was mid-afternoon when the call came in from Jack Dominy, a patrolman out helping direct traffic at the intersection of Moore Street and Jefferson Street, saying that the mayor's car had been found. In fact, the patrolman himself had spotted it, when he had gone to relieve himself back behind the Candlelight Motel, which sat at the intersection. The motel itself was a marker of bygone era of travelers to and from the coast, a place where decent people could pay a reasonable price for a clean bed and a warm bath on the long drive from Atlanta or Nashville to the Atlantic Ocean. It had become derelict over the years, home to travelling salesmen and other shady characters. It was one of Dublin's few hot-sheet hotels, as the locals called them, where trysting couples could have their way under the guise of having lunch at Dublin's only Chinese restaurant, which had taken over the once-popular Vegas-themed Candlelight Lounge. As incongruous as it was authentic, the Lucky Shamrock Chinese Diner was operated by second-generation immigrants who appeared to speak just enough English to take orders and make change. Order sweet-and-sour-chicken, and it would arrive. But ask for directions to a barber, or what time it was, or where they were from, and any and all of the family would point, smiling and nodding, out the restaurant's front door to the front desk of the hotel. They were all completely fluent in English, both verbal and written, yet found that playing hapless Chinese immigrants saved a great deal of time.

But the restaurant still had no power, and the motel had no public restroom, so the patrolman had just gone around the corner to take a piss in the motel parking lot. That was when he recognized the mayor's car peeking out from under an uprooted live oak tree, which looked massive beyond reasoning, reclining in almost taunting ease across the windshield, hood, and body of four cars, and the better part of a fifth.

After he made the call into J.T. at the courthouse, Jack went to the front desk of the motel and talked to Patty, the manager, who explained that the car had been there since all hell broke loose Friday morning. When he asked if the mayor was at the motel, Patty looked up from behind the cheap paneling and pealing Formica of the reception desk and answered with a question of her own—"Who's asking?"

"What do you mean who's asking? I'm asking."

Patty crushed her Camel filter into a black melamine ashtray overflowing with cigarette butts and pulled her long black hair behind her head and shoved it through a fat rubber band. Her features were vaguely American Indian, probably Cherokee, with something dark and European thrown in, that gave her a seductive but distinctively don't-fuck-with-me appearance. She focused it on the patrolman.

"Look, Jack, I don't need no trouble. I got enough with all these goddam carny folk runnin' all over the place." The manager of the fair had negotiated a week's stay with her for ten of the rooms, and it seemed like a good bargain until the storm hit, and now it looked like they might never leave, or never pay if they did leave.

"Is he here or not?" Jack had been down this road before with Patty in the middle of domestic disputes that had turned ugly. But this was not the time.

"Well, he ain't no registered guest. But he might be in room 36. That's where the girl from the fair who was taking gentlemen callers was the last time I seen her."

Jack half-laughed as he asked her "You running a whorehouse now, Patty?"

"Get your sorry ass outta here before I call your wife and tell her you're down here lookin' for company."

His wife Carol and Patty had sewn shirts together at the Oxford Shirt Company straight out of high school. They weren't good friends, but knew each other well enough to speak when they met.

"How do you know I'm not?" he laughed as he was walking out the door, and added, "You ain't got no damn phone, no way."

"Out!" she screamed at him, laughing. Then she lit another cigarette and went back to work on a macramé owl she was making for her mother-in-law's birthday. Smoking while doing macramé work was a delicate art—but she had mastered it.

When J.T. said he would send someone over, Jack never expected to see the judge, much less Bo. The two seemed the least likely pair in all of Dublin to send to such a scene. Yet there they were, standing in the rain in their *SHERIFF* slickers, looking at the scene with the deliberation of a couple of seasoned detectives from a 1940s matinee thriller.

"Well, he ain't with the girl," Jack told them shortly after they arrived. The girl had not been in room 36—she hadn't been in there since Thursday, she said, she had been with her man in his room. When pressed, she acknowledged she may have had a cigarette with the judge in room 36 late on Thursday night, and he might have stayed over. But he had got up and left sometime Friday morning. When exactly she couldn't say, but it was before the big fallout.

As far as the patrolman, the judge, and Bo could collectively reason, the mayor was either in the car, or had walked somewhere else and got caught by the storm. It was conceivable he had stopped off at the Lucky Shamrock for a cup of coffee—they opened early in the morning for whatever motel business they could get—but it seemed unlikely. The three agreed that the best course of action would be to see if he was in the car, but with the rain still coming down it was impossible to tell. After briefly considering trying to move the tree, they decided it would be easier to try moving the car.

They went from room to room, and got the six strongest-looking men they could find to help move it. With no electricity, most of the guests had the doors to their rooms open, anyway, and without any way to get anywhere, they had nothing to do. Moving a car from under a tree in the rain wouldn't normally qualify as entertainment, but in the current situation, it would seem to do. The possibility of seeing a dead mayor provided some additional interest to the work. Patty left her macramé work in the office and locked the door when she saw the judge and Bo arrive in the Cadillac, and joined them by the Coca-Cola machine out back.

All but one of the men worked with the fair. The other was a machinist who had been in town to repair a weaving loom at the woolen mill. When they were all assembled, and each had spent a few minutes trying to see what they could make of the cars and the tree, they made their plan under the dry overhang of the building, looking out onto the sodden lot, its uneven pavement pocked with potholes not distinguishable under the expanse of water covering everything in sight.

It was decided—mostly by the judge, who was more in the habit of deciding things than the others—that the men would push the back of the car in a slow rolling motion just to move it enough to be able to tell if the mayor was in the car or not. Not one of them had voiced a suggestion that the driver of that or any of the cars under the tree might be alive.

The judge and Bo stayed with Patty under the overhang, her cigarette smoke filling the outdoor passage. As the men walked out into the rain, Patty called after them "Ya'll ain't never gonna move that car." She had already expressed the same opinion several times, but a final taunt seemed in order. All of the motel guests had come out to watch the goings-on, and they served as her audience, and she hoped would bear witness to her wisdom, should she prove right.

The biggest problem at first for the men was just getting some traction—their feet were in the remains of a cluster of azalea shrubs that was nothing but mud and clay and sticks. Their feet sank in up to two inches when they first stepped onto it, and when they hunkered down against the front of the car and began to push in earnest, they went in to their ankles. One man went in almost to his knee, and he lost his bearing on the wet hood and hit his head on the car's fender.

A lot of swearing and grunting and mumbling was taking place, and the car wasn't moving, so the judge told Bo to "Come on and let's show these boys how it's done."

Bo followed the judge out into the rain, and was stationed in front of the car to provide information about the movement, if any, of the car, while the judge made himself foreman of the six-man crew, and bellowed out "On the count of three now fellas. One, two, three, Heave!"

No movement, and Bo called out, "Nothing, Judge."

"One, two, three, Heave!"

Then there was a slight shimmer of something like movement, or it might have been lightning—Bo wasn't sure—so he called out, "That looked like we might'a got something."

"Alright, one more time, now. One, two, three, Heave!"

A creak in the lowest octave of nature followed, and at once the car skidded forward, then back, and the oak, so mighty and immovable, rolled with a wet and metallic crash from the hoods of the cars onto the ground, and into and onto Bo, and sent the car skittering back into the men who had just been pushing it. And just like that, Bo was dead. A man who had lived through… what? How much had he lived through? The judge wasn't even sure. Bo was already a grown man, or what seemed like a grown man, when the judge was still a child. He was at least 75 years old, and likely much older. He was probably the son, certainly the grandson of a slave. He had lived such a long life, seen the world through so many evolutions and revolutions, and this, *this* was his end. Here, in this place, surrounded by carny folk and whores.

The judge looked on in horror at what he had done—and he knew he had done it. He had used his authority to strong-arm these men into injury and death for what, his amusement? So he could feel important? So he could feel worthwhile? The shame of it washed over him, and with every drop of rain came another doubt, and soon every decision he had ever made came into question, the reverberations of years of justice weighed with his careless human hands. He stood there motionless in the rain, weak with guilt, with shame, with remorse. He did not hear the screams coming from all sides, didn't hear anything at all until the distant sound of Jack calling into J.T. awakened something deep inside him, and connected the horror in front of him with the communications room. He turned and yelled, "Jack, NO." It was his battlefield voice, and it resounded through the rain and bounced off the walls of the motel like a cannon.

Jack silenced his radio at once. The judge walked to him under the overhang, wiping the rain from his face, and said "His boy, the boy, his grandson, Michael, is probably in the communication room right now, listening to every word. God help me, I will tell him myself, but not like this. Just tell J.T. who to send, don't say who for." He turned back and walked into the rain, and knelt at the body of a man he had known all his life, but hadn't really known at all until the past day. He had learned about Bo's struggles with his son, the joy of raising his grandson, who was such a wonder and a mystery to him. He had learned that Bo was a World

War I Veteran. How had he not known? But he hadn't. And now the man was gone, and it was his fault. He wanted to go home, to his wife, to his bed, to be dry again. He could hear sirens in the far distance, and a part of him wished they were coming for him. For all the men he had sent to prison, he knew very little about it—he had never set foot in one. But he thought he would rather go there than to the courthouse, to face that young boy Bo was so proud of. That Bo had just left so alone in the world.

The courthouse was only a few blocks away, and he turned and started walking to it, leaving the carnage behind him. Someone else would clean it up, he knew. The town was suddenly bustling with teams of men to deal with just this sort of thing.

"Judge," Jake yelled after him, "Where you headed? Don't you think you need to stay here?"

The judge stopped and turned around, "No, sir, I don't. I think I've done enough here, wouldn't you agree?"

"Well at least take your car. There's no reason to walk in the rain." Jake looked at him quizzically, both concerned for the man, and wanting some assistance in cleaning up the mess. It was the judge's mess, after all.

"There's no reason not to walk in the rain, Jake. No reason at all." With that he turned and left, and didn't look back.

Patty lit another cigarette and looked over at Jake, her face alive with both shock and excitement. "What the hell just happened here?"

"I'll be damned if I know, Patty."

She cocked her head at him sideways and asked "And who the hell is gonna pay for it?" She stretched *hell* out into three long, luxurious sing-song syllables: *hey-ey-yull*.

"God only knows, Patty." He walked into the rain to meet the arriving ambulances. The other men weren't dead, but at least two had what appeared to be concussions, one had a broken leg, and all of them had bruised and broken ribs. Patty leaned back against the brick wall, exhaled a long, particularly satisfying breath of smoke, and whispered half to herself, "Amen, brother."

Michael woke up at 4:00am Sunday morning and could not go back to sleep. He had woken up several times during the night, and been scared each time. It took him just a few seconds to remember that he was at Mrs. Eleanor's house, and that he was in her guest bedroom, and that Papa Bo was dead. But they were scary, those seconds—they wandered out into the house, the quiet, the night, the rain, the darkness, and took some time to come back. Each time it took him a while to go back to sleep. The strangeness of the house itself made him feel like he was in some foreign land, even though he was only a few miles from his own bed. The sheets were hard, and scratchy, and smelled like a whole box of detergent. The pillows were bought from a store—his pillows at home were good homemade pillows, blue and white striped cotton ticking plush with chicken down feathers, pillows that his mother and grandmother had made, when they were both alive, back before he was even born. He knew those pillows, that place, those smells, those people. Here, he didn't know anything. He felt a million miles from anyone or anything he knew, there alone in the darkness.

The 4:00am awakening was different. He was still scared when he woke up, but as the realizations of time and place arose in him, his senses were aware something had changed. For the first time, he could hear Eleanor snoring softly through the walls and doors. And he had not heard it before because of the rain. The rain had stopped. "Is it over?" the boy whispered aloud in a soft, silent, rasping croak.

He tip-toed to the window and opened the drapery panels there. Unfiltered moonlight, strong and bright and bold, cut into the darkness like a movie projector, casting the boy's shadow behind him onto the floor and the bed. Motes and flecks of dust invisible in the darkness seemed as real and substantial as the boy himself in the fullness of light. The moon's low position in the sky—he was looking straight ahead, and almost directly at it—told him it was almost morning.

He left the bedroom door open and used the moonlight to find Eleanor's kitchen, where he found two craft-paper grocery sacks from the Winn-Dixie sitting on a diner-style breakfast table beside an arrangement of blue plastic daisies and silk ivy sitting in a woven basket. One sack was filled with food, the other with clothes and things for him. When they had come in the night before, after stopping by Bo's house to pick those things up for him, they had both been very tired, and Eleanor suggested they brush their teeth and go straight to bed, using the illumination from a battery-powered camping lantern set on the kitchen table to find their way. The lantern was still there, and he turned it on the lowest setting, which was still enough to fill the room with a soft, white, artificial glow. The night before, Eleanor had the lamp on full power so the light would reach through the house, and the sharp angular shadows it had cast made the house seem stranger and scarier than it did in the paleness of his pre-morning solitude. A window above the sink let in some moonlight as well, but it was facing away from the moon, and the light was muddy and gray.

On the top of the food sack, he found the thing he had been looking for—an old Cool Whip tub filled with homemade peanut brittle. Ida Mae Edmonds, a neighbor and family friend who had helped Bo care for the boy, had brought the tub over to Bo's house while Michael was gathering his things. The portable lantern's cool fluorescent light was spilling out from the screen door where Eleanor stood outside looking in, casting her shadow out into the Quarters, when Ida Mae walked up and asked, "That you, Mrs. Eleanor?"

Jefferson Terrace was the official name of the neighborhood, but not even many of the people who lived there knew it. The Quarters, short for *Colored Quarters*, was the hardscrabble neighborhood situated convenient to nothing where every colored person in the city of Dublin was still unofficially required to live. No real estate agent in town would even show a property outside of the Quarters to a colored person, or he would find himself the subject of a variety of intimidation tactics, from the cold shoulder at church on Sunday, to threatening letters, or mutilated animals on his front porch or car hood. A colored Veterans

Administration executive transferred to Dublin found himself unable to buy a home or rent an apartment for his family that would not be considered *ghetto* back home in Baltimore, so the transfer never happened. The people of Dublin did not consider themselves racist—for the most part, they just wanted things to stay the way they always had been.

Things in the Quarters were not much different than any slum anywhere in the world. The people who lived there, though mostly subjugated to abject poverty, still found ways to make life bearable, orderly, even joyful, for those who chose it. The flat, hardpan, rocky dirt in the Quarters wouldn't grow so much as a turnip in most places, much less the luxurious turf of the gracious lawns on Bellevue Avenue, but the porches of the beaten-down shacks were lined with containers of shade plants, and old wash pots and buckets filled with tomato plants and zinnias speckled the barren landscape in summer, and wild petunias grew up in profusion from wherever one of the tiny seeds could get a foothold in some crack in the chalky clay earth, and their warm acidic smell filled the streets. In winter, when the porch plants were all moved indoors, and the rocking chairs on the front porches sat empty, the Quarters were as bare and desolate and grey as any prison on Earth.

The police were never called into the Quarters, because the police found it somehow impossible to drive out of the Quarters, past the single monumental oak that marked its entrance, without at least one colored man in the back of a car, regardless of whether or not he or anybody else was guilty of a crime. As far as most of the police were concerned, living in the Quarters—that is, being colored—made you guilty, by default, by nature, by God, of something. So the people there took care of their own, whenever they could. If a chicken or a bicycle or a watch went missing from the Quarters, one of the preachers of the four prominent colored churches would be contacted, and he would call the other three (the preachers all had phones), and each would call his deacons (most of whom had phones), and they would get it taken care of. The chicken, bicycle, or watch would almost always reappear. More serious matters were likewise "kept in the Quarters," as they liked to say.

Whenever a chicken or a bicycle or a watch went missing from Dublin—the real Dublin, where the white people lived—a police car would show up, pulling slowly and silently onto one of the ten north-south streets or twelve east-west streets that defined the neighborhood. If the crime was something particularly noteworthy, like the missing purse of a preacher's wife taken from her car during church, several cars would appear at once moving in from different directions like a skulk of foxes moving in on unsuspecting prey. It didn't matter if there was a witness who could clearly identify the white features, or even the name of the white man who had actually taken the purse—someone from the Quarters would be taken in. At the first sighting of a police cruiser, a whistle would cry out, a sharp Whip-Poor-Will, until one or two more had taken it and it was carried through the Quarters. *Run*, it said, *hide. They're here.* Everyone who heard it would disappear quick.

The officers would dutifully ask the first few black men unlucky enough to be on the street, or on a porch, or just riding up on a bicycle, who had not heard the warning, or been unable to move in time, "Boy, where you been?"

If that boy, regardless of whether he was ten or sixty, didn't have the right answer, off to the courthouse he went, knowing he might never return, knowing that behind him, people had stopped peeping out of windows and walked back onto their porches, were gathering in groups in the streets, deciding who would be best to go let his mother, or his wife, or his children know.

Eleanor's 1971 blue Pontiac Bonneville had first drawn attention well before it pulled onto the two submerged white cement strips that made up the Isaacs' short driveway. Word had made it to the neighborhood earlier in the day that Bo Isaacs was dead, and the whereabouts of his grandson was a question no one could answer. They couldn't answer the question of where his son was, either, but they all knew that he could be anywhere—they had heard about him wondering around town, about him leaving the V.A. hospital. They knew there wasn't much that could be done for him, even if they could find him. They all knew that. He had come back from the war changed, a stranger to them.

But Michael, he was another story. He was one of them. He was book-smart in a way most of them weren't, but he was still one of them. His papa had seen to that. "This boy here gonna have a place at the table, yes he is," Bo had been saying since the boy first learned to read.

People had been moving from porch to porch all afternoon and into the evening, dodging the rain and carrying what scraps of news they had, but none really knew anything other than Bo had carried Michael to work with him on Friday, then Bo had been seen riding around in the judge's Cadillac, and down at the bridge. Nobody remembered seeing Michael at the bridge, but nobody remembered not seeing him, either. Always thoughtful, and almost always silent, he disappeared easily in most situations.

The community was coming together in grief, but it was in some confusion as to how much and exactly what kind of grief to be in—had the tree rolled onto the boy, too? If not, where was he? The answer came with the Bonneville, when the headlights turned into the yard of the Isaacs home, and the old white lady got out with the boy. "He was with that white lady, praise the Lord" became answer enough, and much of the grief turned into prayers of thanks.

Still, they weren't sure how to approach the lady. Did the boy even know his papa was dead? When they first saw the Bonneville, someone ran over to the Edmonds' house to get Ida Mae—the Edmonds family knew more white people than anybody in town, and knew better than anyone how to talk to the ones they didn't know. Ida Mae, like her mother before her, worked as a domestic for Judge Breshear's family, and his parents before that, keeping house, preparing meals, and generally making life manageable for people whose lives seemed otherwise unmanageable, despite the wealth and privilege of their distinguished lineage.

Ida Mae had slipped a rain bonnet over her hair, got an umbrella, and filled a Cool Whip container with peanut brittle her mother had made the week before. It wasn't much, but it was something, and it wasn't the real reason she was going, anyway.

Eleanor had been happy to hear her name called, and even happier to see it was Ida Mae calling it. The two had known each other, at least in passing, for over twenty years, with Ida Mae running into the courthouse on occasion to drop off lunch or a forgotten paper while the judge's wife sat in the car, and Eleanor sometimes running for the sheriff to the judge's house to get him to sign a warrant or a restraining order on a day off. While it was only a passing acquaintance, it passed for true friendship to Eleanor when she had turned and seen Ida Mae's inquisitive expression turning into a smile of recognition.

Eleanor wasn't racist, not at all. But she didn't have any colored friends, either. It was not by way of exclusion, it was just the result of the pattern of her life and the times and places she was raised in. The real truth was that she didn't really have many friends at all. She knew people whom she liked, and admired, and a few she even trusted to some degree, but nothing any poet would ever call a friendship. Her husband, before he died, had always said, "Let's see them cards, Ellie!" It was an old joke, from when they had first been dating, that she played her cards too close to her chest. He wanted not only to see her cards, but also to see her chest, and the expression reminded her long after he was gone about his desire for her to be more open with people. He was a naturally outgoing, warm person that everyone wanted to be around, and he believed her unwillingness to let people know her the way he knew her—warm, caring, generous, and funny—prevented her from having the sorts of friendships he enjoyed so much. But she never had changed. In fact, after he died, what had been a quiet reserve sharpened over time and habit into a stiff guardedness. People knew she was smart, and strong, and that was enough for her. Most of what she called friendships were simply the tired remainders of relationships her husband had formed. So for her to hear her name called, in a kind way, by a woman she knew, in this dark and quiet neighborhood that she had been to only a handful of times in her life, was more than a relief, it was a real pleasure. "Ida Mae, thank goodness," she exhaled.

It was to her own surprise that as Ida Mae walked up the steps, Eleanor opened her arms out to the woman, and Ida Mae walked right into them, giving her a warm and familiar hug, a gesture as natural to Ida Mae on that porch as walking up the steps themselves—she had known and loved the Isaacs family all her life, and they had been in this house all her life.

"You all heard?" Eleanor asked in a low whisper as the two women separated, and they stepped back instinctively to a dark corner of the porch, where they could just make out each other's faces. Ida Mae removed her hair bonnet, shook it dry, and folded it neatly into a pocket.

"Yes ma'am. It's awful. Just awful. Seems like there's no end to the sorrow around here." It wasn't a complaint, just an assessment, and an accurate one from what little Eleanor had seen of the Quarters, and most all of what she had heard. "I just don't, know, Mrs. Eleanor. I just don't know." She paused, seeming to realize how long she had been talking, which wasn't really that long, but was for her. "I'm sorry to go on like this, Mrs. Eleanor, ma'am," she continued, "We just been so worried about Michael. Nobody knew what happened to him. We heard about Brother Bo this afternoon, and didn't know nothing else. But this is a blessing, him here, him alive. Praise the Lord. Praise the Lord. How's he doing? Does he know about his papa yet?"

They were both still speaking in whispers, the rain on the tin roof of the porch preventing any suggestion of their conversation carrying from where they stood on the porch.

"Please just call me Eleanor, Ida Mae." She didn't feel like being Mrs. Eleanor at the moment. "Yes, he knows. The judge and I told him this afternoon. It was hard on the judge. Me too, to be honest. I don't know many children, but I suspect there aren't many like him. He asked for his daddy, but nobody seems to know where William got off to after he left the V.A. on Wednesday. Michael seemed to think he may be wandering around town," she felt no need to mention the letter, "but nobody in town has seen him today that we could find. Has anyone around here seen him?"

"No ma'am. I pray for that boy. I kept him when he was littler than Michael. Known him all his life. But not since he came back from Vietnam. It's like he don't know me, or anybody, except Michael. I know Brother Bo was worried, but he don't say much about family, except to dote on Michael. He kept pretty close."

Eleanor smiled grimly, but before she could say anything more, Michael was standing there with the screen door open looking at the two women. His eyes adjusted from the glare of the lantern, and as Ida Mae's face emerged from the darkness, his face opened into a smile that filled his whole face—even his hair looked happy to see her. As much as Eleanor had been happy to see a familiar face, the boy was that much more thrilled, comforted, and relieved.

After some small talk on the porch, the three walked inside, and sat at the comfortable kitchen table, with salt, pepper and Tabasco huddled together beside a napkin holder. Eleanor realized while she was sitting down that she had never been in the home of a colored family before, and looked around to find that there wasn't that much visibly different from her own. And the house was actually much nicer on the inside than the outside let on. Sitting at the table, she would never have guessed there was a tin roof on the front porch. She could have been in her own neighborhood, except for the many framed photos of colored people on one prominent wall, and the house was immaculate except for some wet foot-prints they had just brought in. The walls and trim were freshly painted drywall, the living room furnishings comfortable and up-to-date, with a console television nicer than her own.

"So, Michael, where you headed off to?" Ida Mae asked almost as soon as they were seated, looking pointedly at the grocery sacks.

"Judge Breshears said I was to stay with Mrs. Eleanor 'til daddy comes home," Michael answered without any hint of his feelings about it.

"How does Mrs. Eleanor feel about that?" Ida Mae looked up to Eleanor with genuine curiosity and some concern—*Why is this white woman taking this child of ours?*

"I like having Michael around," Eleanor answered, and it was true. She did not want to express her own misgivings in front of him. "As soon as we can find William and let him know how much we need him back here, we're sure everything will work out fine." They weren't sure of any such thing—far from it, and Ida Mae knew it.

Eleanor continued, "Michael wasn't able to tell us about any other family we might be able to track down. Do you know of anyone, Ida Mae?"

Ida Mae looked with concern at the boy, caught herself, rearranged her face into a smile and said "Well, he has us. And we're close enough to family, ain't we Michael? You know you're welcome to come stay over with us. Ola Mae might not even notice you ain't one of her own grandbabies."

He just smiled, at once understanding and not understanding what was happening.

Eleanor hesitated, feeling the delicacy of the situation. "Michael, how about this. How about we talk to Judge Breshears tomorrow? He said for me to take you home with me and let you stay at my house tonight, and I'm not one to disobey the judge." This wasn't entirely true, but she thought it would have an effect on Ida Mae, and it did.

"That's the truth, Michael. You don't never want to get on the judge's bad side, Lord knows. Maybe I'll even have a word or two with him myself tomorrow. Mrs. Eleanor gonna have her hands full at that courthouse,"

Here Michael spoke up for the first time, interrupting her to say "I like it at the courthouse. Me and Mrs. Eleanor, we get by just fine."

It was such an old man way of speaking, so like Bo, that Eleanor and Ida Mae looked up at each other and smiled.

"Alright, we don't have to decide anything tonight Michael. You got some clothes and your toothbrush?" Eleanor asked.

"Yes, ma'am. And I got us some food, too." He had been listening to the radio reports carefully.

"I don't think we'll be running out of food, Michael, but bring what you need.

And we'll see about tomorrow tomorrow. Now why don't you run on back out to the car? I have some other business I need to discuss with Ida Mae."

"Yes, ma'am." He went to pick up the two paper sacks from the kitchen counter, but Ida Mae called him back, saying "Michael, come take this peanut brittle. Ma made it and was saving some for Brother Bo. It was his favorite."

She held out the white container to him, and he took it almost reverently, and placed it in one of the bags. Then as he was struggling to get both bags off the counter, Eleanor called out that he should just take one, and that she would bring the other with her.

When he was down the porch and the women heard the car door close, Eleanor asked Ida Mae quickly, in an unnecessary whisper, "Is there *anybody* else in the family? On his mother's side maybe?"

"Not that nobody knows. It was so strange—none of her folk even came to her funeral. And there ain't nobody else 'cept Willie. Whatever's gonna come of that boy?"

"You mean Willie?" Eleanor asked, confused.

"No, Michael," she began, then paused, and continued, "Both, I reckon."

Eleanor let out a sigh, and responded, "Well, the judge feels mighty responsible, personally, for Michael not having his grandfather. The judge aims to see that the boy is taken care of, and from what I know of the judge, he will."

"Yessum," Ida Mae replied, off in thought.

"But can you please look around the house, see what you can find—anything—that might help us find some family who might be willing to help? I don't know that Willie will ever be fit to take care of him from what I've heard. What do you think?"

Ida Mae considered, then responded, "Well, I don't know about *ever*, but not now. No ma'am. I don't know if Willie's fit to take care of himself right now. But things change, you know."

"Yes," Eleanor replied, "That they do." She stood up, preparing to leave.

"Would you mind looking around, seeing if you can find anything?"

"No ma'am. I'll look tonight. I'll send word to the courthouse if we find anything."

The two women walked out the door, pulling it to, but not locking it behind them—this was still Dublin, after all. Eleanor had a grocery sack in one hand, the lantern in the other, and Ida Mae walked her to the car with her umbrella. Michael saw, and he slid over the wide front seat and opened her door for her. Ida Mae walked around the car and after he rolled down his window a crack, she said loud, over the rain drumming on the taut umbrella fabric, "We sho' do love you, little Michael. You get word to us if you need anything. We be praying for you."

"Yes, ma'am, Miss Ida Mae." He and Eleanor drove away into the night, away from the Quarters, away from everything he knew as home.

* * *

So he took the Cool Whip tub with him into Eleanor's den, where two recliners sat facing a television-stereo console on one wall of windows, and on another wall was the biggest collection of books he had ever seen outside of a library. From floor to ceiling, from wall to wall, were almost nothing but books. There were some framed pictures, and a few binders that were labeled with dates on the spines, but the rest of the shelves were all filled with books of every shape, size and color. He put the peanut brittle down on the television, and turned the light on the lantern up just enough so most of the shadows went away. He spent the next hour peering through the books, looking for something to take to the courthouse with him that day. None of the books were for children, he was pleased to see. He was less pleased that many of them were cookbooks and engineering textbooks and the like, but he was stopped short when he ran across something called *The Book of Common Prayer*.

He sat down with the book, and began reading by the light of the lantern. He realized almost immediately that while the prayers might be common, he didn't know them. But he liked them, at least what he understood of them. It wasn't long before he got back up to find a dictionary, and by that time, there was the faintest blue-pink glow on the horizon, visible through the translucent shears. He opened them wide, and sat in the recliner as the sun rose, reading the Prayer for a Sick Person, the Prayers for a Sick Child, for Strength and Confidence, for the Sanctification of Illness, for Health of Body and Soul, for Doctors and Nurses, for Pain, for Sleep, for Mourning. On and on the prayers went, orderly and rational, but layered and lyrical. They were so different from the prayers at his church, at Papa Bo's church. The prayers there were rich and loud and vocal, the people cried out earnestly for God to hear them, and he knew that they were honest prayers, but something about them made him uneasy. He had long secretly believed that Papa Bo was the same way—whenever the church got too exuberant, with the screaming and the crying, they both felt uneasy, out of place, even though Papa Bo was a deacon. He had been a quiet deacon, tending to the physical needs of the church, donating money, helping out the sick. Whenever there was a big vote or some controversy, Bo would usually *keep praying on it* until the others had made a decision. He was just quiet that way, and always had been. That's why Michael thought he would have liked the prayer book—it just laid everything right out there, simple and neat.

He hadn't intended for the peanut brittle to be a sacrament, but that is what it became. Ida Mae said the candy had been for Papa Bo, and so that is what he made it. He opened the Cool Whip container, took out a cluster of the candy, ate it, and read out loud, but in a whisper, "Almighty God, we thank you that in your great love you have fed us with the spiritual food and drink of the Body and Blood of your Son Jesus Christ, and have given us a foretaste of your heavenly banquet. Grant that this Sacrament may be to us a comfort in affliction, and a pledge of our inheritance in that kingdom where there is no death, neither sorrow nor crying, but the fullness of joy with all your saints; through Jesus Christ our Savior. Amen."

He lay back in the recliner and looked up at the ceiling, and that is where Eleanor found him, asleep, an hour later. She turned off the lantern and looked out at the steady rain, which had returned, and thought to herself, *No common prayer is likely to help us now.* She went to the kitchen and decided to put away the boy's things. She was impressed at his food selection—canned tuna and sardines, a jar of pickles, saltine crackers, bouillon cubes. To her way of thinking about children, he should have brought a bag filled with bubble gum and baseball cards. She realized, again, how very little she knew about children in general, and this child in particular. There was some hard cheese in her refrigerator that was still good, and she cut off some squares for them to eat with the crackers for breakfast. She became aware at some point that though it was raining, there was real sunlight for the first time in days.

She left the cheese and crackers sitting out on the kitchen table for Michael and went to her bedroom to dress. She would not be wearing another skirt-suit. She chose a pair of khaki-colored pants and a lilac sweater, and white canvas lounge shoes she usually wore just for puttering around the house. She knew they would get dirty in the swamp outside, but she could bleach them, and she had no intention of destroying another good pair of her patent pumps.

The rest of Sunday was almost relaxed compared to the previous two days. Eleanor was due at the courthouse to relieve J.T. of his duty at 10am, when she would continue working to determine who, exactly, was still missing. With the rain beginning to diminish, and expected to end before Monday morning, there were new problems.

Overall, Eleanor was not displeased with the progress being made. All of the known dead had been successfully retrieved, except those in the Oconee, where the water still churned downriver with an audible, almost tangible rage. But this success led to its own problem, as the temporary morgue set up in the Dublin Junior High School gymnasium was growing increasingly grotesque with each passing hour. The county coroner, Doc Parry, was doing all he could to get everyone identified and everything sorted out properly and by the book, but he was only one man, and the hospital morgue and every funeral home in the county were full. Georgia Power had promised to begin restoring power on Sunday afternoon, but that also presented its own set of problems—stoves and machinery left on when the power went down would be on when the power was restored, and fires and injuries were an almost inevitable result, regardless of good planning. People who had been scared to leave their homes Friday or Saturday were anxious to get out and see the damage first-hand, to see their businesses, schools and churches.

It was late afternoon when the parents of Josh Landrum and Jonny Vinson showed up at the courthouse looking for Eleanor. Their sanguine comfort in the safety of their children began disappearing over the night Saturday night and vanished entirely Sunday morning. After the boys failed to appear at First Baptist or Hilltop United Methodist, and no one at either of those churches reported hearing anything about the boys' whereabouts, the parents traveled from possible household to possible household, each more unlikely than the last, then through the remnants of the woods behind Roberson Street looking for the boys in the forts and remains of forts. "Jonny," "Josh," they called out in the rain, "Josh," "Jonny," bogging through the wet muddy earth. When they arrived distraught at the door to the communications room, Eleanor took them to the sheriff's office where she spent an hour with the four of them. Her news of the previous day's efforts, and that the National Guard's bloodhounds had already been through the woods looking for the boys Sunday morning, provided the parents with a certain sense of shame—the idea that a secretary in the sheriff's office had been more actively concerned for their children than they had been was distressing to them. It robbed them of the ability to demand *Why aren't you doing anything to find our children?* It made them accountable for their own inaction, it made them the target of their own unarticulated rage at their overwhelming inadequacy in the situation. No plausible single action, no reasonable coordinated effort they could conceive of had not already been attempted. When Eleanor finally suggested that the best place for them to be was their homes, which is where anyone with news of the boys, or the boys themselves, would be sure to go first, they listened to her. On their way down a dimly lit corridor, towards a rectangle of rain-filtered sunlight framed in aluminum by the massive glass front doors, Jonathon's father paused and asked the others, "Should we ask to speak to the sheriff?"

The three stopped and turned to look at him, and his wife answered, "I think we just did, Chuck." Her voice contained no trace of sarcasm or resentment, or even a hint of wonder. It was a tone of inevitable, dispassionate truth. It was the voice of a mother whose single concern was her missing child. No one in that building could find her child—there was no need to go back in there. Before they stepped down the wet granite steps, she perched on the edge of the shallow covered portico, her eyes focusing rapidly on each pile of debris, on each store entryway—the F.W. Woolworth, the Diana Wig Shop, Howard's Record Store, Ma Hawkins restaurant. Their awnings were all ripped to tatters, and hung limply on their frames, like banners for a wartime parade abruptly and permanently cancelled. She did not see her child, so they moved on.

It had been forty-five minutes since the sheriff arrived at the K-Mart parking lot, and no progress had been made on clearing out the water. No one knew exactly what to do. The National Guardsmen kept sentry at each of the four main entrances to the lot, two on each of the entrances on Highway 80, and one at each point where Westgate Street terminated into the shopping center at the rear of the lot. Two more were stationed at the entries to the Piggly Wiggly and the K-Mart. They were unnecessarily menacing, in the sheriff's view—rifles did not seem necessary, though he was more aware than usual of his own firearm strapped to his waist.

Small clusters of firemen and deputies and townspeople lined the top of the hill along the side of the highway, looking down into the water, listening to the whining creak of the light, lingering wind buffeting the metal skeletons of the amusement park rides rising up out of the water. The sheriff noticed over time that the plastic ducks were making a slow but steady journey to the center of the pond, a logarithmic spiral interrupted only when the wind blew one of the little ducks off course. This meant to him that however small it must be, there was a flow of water down the drain. Sooner or later, with or without their interference, the lot would be dry again, but they needed it sooner. The rain had stopped earlier on Monday morning, as predicted, and most people seemed surprised—the inability of forecasters to predict the storm had robbed the meteorologists of any faith the people who had suffered through the storm might ever have had in them.

The carny folk had shown up just as the rain stopped, but were keeping a safe distance back from the others. They were looking suspiciously at the uniformed men and the townspeople, as though they might somehow sneak off with the Ferris Wheel or Tilt-A-Whirl.

The problem of how to remove the plywood, or whatever the kids had covered up the drain with, while not insurmountable, was still a problem. The shop owners and store managers had begun to arrive, eager to get in and assess the damage. The

Dublin Twin Cinema was connected to the K-Mart, but to the east and slightly uphill from it, and had suffered no visible damage. The Dublin Mini-Mall, which was really just a corridor of small shops stretching back perpendicular to the K-Mart façade, had presumably suffered no damage, though no one had yet gone to check. The Sears storefront, next to the Mini-Mall entrance, was at the opposite end of that stretch of the shopping center from the K-Mart, and had suffered no damage.

The sheriff's goal was to get the Piggly Wiggly open. The roof of the A&P had almost entirely collapsed sometime during the storm, and even the labels on the canned goods deep in the shelves were soggy or missing altogether. The Guard had decided that opening up just the Winn-Dixie, which had made it through unharmed and now had power, would be a mistake—even in Dublin, they considered there might be a run on the place if word got out it was the only place in town to get food. The Red Cross people, while nice enough, and providing sustenance, were not handing out fresh chickens or pork roasts. The reality that there were no fresh chickens or pork roasts in the stores, which had been without power for days, really made no difference—the grocery store was an anchor in the lives of the people who lived in small towns, and Dublin was no exception. It was not just a place to buy food—though without gardens or any way of feeding themselves, it was that, primarily—it was a also part of the culture. Women dressed well, put on makeup, checked their hair before going grocery shopping. On Saturdays men would go to the store with their wives, but linger in small packs in front of the store, sharing that week's news, while their wives were inside gossiping up and down the aisles. The information they shared was the same, only the means and method of delivery changed.

Sgt. Samuels had been at the site at 6:00am that morning, and saw the lights come on in the Piggly Wiggly. He made a visual assessment from the front windows of the store, and saw that the store appeared to be intact. But they had to have the parking lot drained so people could get to it. Walt Starling, the manager of the store, had shown up with a cleaning crew around 8:00am, eager to get in and see what was what, but he had not been allowed in until the sheriff showed up. And even then, he wasn't allowed to take his crew in with him, just one of the National Guardsmen, to make sure the store was safe to let in anyone else.

After some discussion about the water situation, Sgt. Samuels put in a call to Cpt. Blankenship at the Armory to bring the scuba gear and a diver to go down and attach some chains to the obstruction. The Oconee River was still moving too fast for anyone to go in the water for the bodies there, so the thinking was the scuba gear might as well be put to good use. Now that the rain had stopped, the stormwater drains were able to begin dumping water in the Oconee River in earnest, and the streets were beginning to clear. The parking lot obstruction would only need to be moved a couple of feet in any direction to get the drain working properly, and the lot would be clear of water in a matter of minutes. Then they would just need to remove any debris, and life could get back closer to normal.

As word of the plan was spreading around the edges of the parking lot, there was some commotion at the entry to the Piggly Wiggly. The sheriff looked over and saw Walt Starling yelling in his direction, his hands cupped like a megaphone around his mouth, and then waving frantically in a beckoning gesture. When the sheriff started walking in that direction, Starling and the National Guardsman who was with him disappeared back inside. The sheriff quickened his pace as he felt the eyes around the parking lot following him.

When the automatic doors opened into the store he yelled out "Walt?" and heard a muffled cry from somewhere in the back of the store, "Back here, sheriff."

There was something vaguely unsettling about the store, but the feeling was indistinct. The smell of rotting meat and vegetables was sweet and cloying, but not overwhelming. He walked down the center aisle with pet food on one side and bottled soda on the other, not entirely sure of his destination. The empty store, and the hard, echoing squish of his wet cowboy boots on the terrazzo floor made him uneasy, and he wanted to draw his pistol, but he settled for resting his hand on its butt.

"Sheriff?" he heard from behind the butcher counter at the back of the store. He walked around the counter toward the voice, turned a corner, and saw the two men standing in front of a refrigerated storage room, the door open before them, chill spilling out. The looks on their faces were confused, alarmed. The sheriff looked inside and on the left he saw giant slabs of pork and beef hanging from hooks connected to a chain conveyor belt in the ceiling, stretching back to the end of the long refrigerator. To the right he saw a row of pallets stacked with boxes of Jimmy Dean sausage patties and Hormel hot dogs. Four bare 40-wall bulbs illuminated the meat locker. He looked at the men and said with some impatience, "Well, what is it?"

"Look-a-there," Walt responded, pointing down on the floor between the first two pallets. It was a pair of very bony, filthy feet, apparently belonging to a girl, as the men could see the hand-sewn hem of a daisy-patterned dress partially stretched down over scabby knees.

The sheriff walked around the corner and saw, to his amazement and relief, a red-headed girl he had never seen before holding a boy that had been missing for almost three days. Both their eyes were closed, but her arms—almost sticks, they were so thin—were wrapped around the boy like a mother's would be. She couldn't be more than 10? 12? But the boy—black hair, freckles, eight or maybe ten years old, this had to be Josh Landrum. *Is he dead?*

He was not dead. He was breathing, but slowly. The air was not just cold, it was thick somehow. *How long have they been in here?*

"Boy. *Boy!*" the sheriff called, to no effect. He reached out and gently tugged on one of the boy's wet canvas tennis shoes, muddy white with green laces. "Josh, wake up son."

"Huh?" The boy murmured, waking as if from a deep sleep, "Whut?" As his eyes opened and he saw where he was, and the two men looking down at him, he jerked back away from them, withdrew his feet from the sheriff's touch, then turned and saw the face of the girl who was holding him, and let out a short yelp.

She bolted upright, eyes flashing bright, wide awake with panic, and the boy spilled from her embrace onto the cold unfinished concrete floor of the freezer. He began to scramble to his feet, as if to run away, but the sheriff pulled him up and into his arms, and said, "Whoa, whoa, now partner," as at the same time the girl darted like a sparrow around them, ducking beneath the boy's kicking legs. She was stopped by the two men still standing in the door, whose clutches on her grew tighter as she twisted and squirmed to get away from them. The Guardsman was trying to hold her with her back to his chest, his arms wrapped around her waist, but she was fighting like an animal, utterly instinctive. Walt was trying to grab her arms and legs as they jerked out in his direction, but the force of her blows was terrific, inhuman. Walt tried circling around the pair for a better angle, but the violence of her movements was causing the Guardsman to buckle and shuffle and duck. It was chaos, out of nowhere, and whatever the sheriff had been expecting, it wasn't this.

"Wait just a minute now," the sheriff began, but he was cut off by the boy who began yelling at the top of his lungs "Help! Help! Help!" Then catching his breath, then again "Help! Help! Help!" Then catching his breath, and beginning again. His shrill cries, which seemed immense relative to his size, like a dog whistle, distracted the men holding the girl. She kicked the Guardsman hard in the groin, and took off running before she even hit the hard green-speckled floor. She was halfway past the dog food before the overweight grocery clerk even turned around good.

"Stop her!" The sheriff yelled to no one in particular, over and in between the boy's howls for help. He had Josh's arms pinned down beside him in a sort of bear hug, but was unsure what to do about the boy's legs, which continued their piston action, hammering whatever they touched.

When the girl got to the front of the aisle she saw a crowd of men running towards the store, through the water, jumping the sandbags. She turned to run back to the back of the store, but the Guardsman had made his way up from the floor, cursing in pain, and was almost on her with a nylon leash he snatched from a Hartz Mountain pet supplies display. She saw him with the rope and started screaming, as though she were being sliced open. He yelled to the grocer behind him, "Come help me get this girl before she kills somebody."

Walt Starling was no hero. He was in fact a coward. He had lived his whole life in fear of one thing or another. And as a coward, he had a much better understanding of fear than the trained recruit barking orders at him. "Put down the rope," he said.

Pudgy, bald, middle-aged, wearing his white grocer's apron, he held no real authority in the world, and probably wouldn't have dared speak to a man in uniform in that way in any other setting. But this was his store, and he was used to giving orders and being listened to in this place, so his voice had an authority in the grocery store it had nowhere else.

The Guardsman turned and looked at him in outrage, saying "You think I'm going to—"

"Yes, you're going to put down the rope," the grocer interrupted, as he walked around the man holding the braided nylon. He could see the girl was honestly terrified. It wasn't of them, he knew. But somehow he did not think she knew that.

Her shrill screaming filled the empty aisles as he moved slowly toward her, and still from the boy in the back, "Help! Help! Help!" Breath. "Help! Help! Help!" His voice was starting to scratch and squeak from the effort.

Walt began in a voice that was loud enough to carry, but not yelling. "Miss, please stop screaming. We're just here to help you. My name is Walt Starling. The kids call me *Mr. Wiggly*. I'm the manager of this store. I'm just trying to make sure you're alright. Are you alright?"

The kids did in fact call him *Mr. Wiggly*, and they called his wife *Mrs. Piggly*. He couldn't blame them—he thought she had grown into a pure-T bitch and a lardass to boot since they married, and he was willing to live with the ignominy of being Mr. Wiggly for the secret pleasure of knowing every schoolchild in Dublin knew his wife as *Mrs. Piggly*. He thought giving the girl this little weapon, this little piece of information, might calm her.

He was mistaken. He wasn't even certain she had heard him. She looked behind her and saw the end of the aisle was now blocked by what looked like a literal army—several men in camouflage with weapons drawn were blocking her path to the exit. She looked back at Walt, stopped screaming, swallowed hard, and said in a loud, high, carrying voice, "Where am I? I didn't take nothing, I ain't got nothing. Let me go."

The cries of *Help! Help! Help!* continued from back behind the meat counter.

"You're at the Piggly Wiggly. You're safe here. This is my store. And we will, we will let you go, of course we will, of course you didn't steal anything," he said, wondering whether in fact she had stolen anything. She was the perfect picture of East Dublin white trash, except even they knew to wear shoes in a grocery store. But it was more than that—she was wet as a drowned rat, and her flesh had been cold as Christmas, more than just skin-deep, when he had held her briefly as she struggled to get out of the freezer. She was visibly shaking. Was it fear, or was she sick? There was fear in her eyes, but there was something else. Her lips were cracked, and there was a rasping in her voice. Dehydration? How long had they been in that freezer?

The cries of *Help!* suddenly and abruptly stopped from the back of the store, without any diminution in volume or terror, and the silence was jarring.

"What'chall done to that boy? Who is he? What'chall done to us? Why're we here?" The girl snapped her head in quick sharp pivots, turning from face to face to face with such a fierce mechanical movement that Mr. Starling expected to hear a click from the base of her neck.

When no one answered her, she looked back at Walt, who had stopped just a few feet from her, and said "Look here Mr. Wiggly, I ain't done nothing, and I got to get home." Her face was making strange contortions. She looked at once as if she wanted to cry, to sleep, to bite someone. He realized in an instant that she was in fact wild—desperate with fear in a way that even he had never been.

"We will get you home. We want to get you home and make sure you're safe.

Now what's your name?" The tension and adrenaline coming from the crowd of men was making Mr. Starling nervous and a bit scared himself. He had never seen a gun drawn in his store before. He was having to hold his sphincter tight in fear the chill coursing through his bowels might cause him to mess himself. He could not imagine what must be going through the girl's mind.

"Where's my daddy at? Why ain't he come looking for me?" She was still looking from face to face, like a trapped animal, making sure no one was coming closer. *Ready to bolt*, Mr. Starling thought, but where, over the top of his soda display? Through the wall of armed men? He thought she looked ready to try.

In the distance he heard a siren wailing. He knew it was an ambulance, or maybe even two, less than a minute away from the sound of it, but he knew also that the siren was not going to lower the level of anxiety in the room. The girl heard it too. She cocked her head like a wolf pup.

"What's that?" She asked, eyes still turning from face to face, but now even looking up over the shelves of dog food and soda as though she expected to see people coming from over the racks of groceries.

"That's just an ambulance. The paramedics are going to want to make sure you're alright. They won't hurt you. No one is going to hurt you."

"We can't afford no doctors." She began shaking her head from side to side, and finally, she did begin to cry. The siren was now a few hundred yards away, and she seemed angrier than ever. Her face, translucent, pale and freckled when he had first seen her, was now almost the same shade of angry red as her hair, her freckles now barely distinct under her tears.

The siren stopped. Several of the men broke from the crowd at the end of the aisle and walked outside to meet the paramedics.

"It won't cost you a thing. I'll take care of it myself. That's my promise, I give it to you right here in front of God and everybody. Now why don't you tell us your name and where you live so we can go get your ma and pa and get them to come take care of you? I bet they're worried sick."

The girl looked only at him now. She thought he looked just like Mr. Whipple from the toilet paper commercial she had seen on television, and that gave her some comfort. "Vicky Dewberry is my name. My pa is Carl Dewberry and my momma done run off. I got a new ma. We don't live nowhere."

Good Lord, Mr. Starling thought to himself, but aloud he asked, "Well, does your daddy work anywhere? Maybe we can find him there."

"He's the 'lectrician for that fair out yonder." She pointed behind her in the general direction of the parking lot.

That explains everything, Starling thought, but he said aloud, and with a smile, as if this was good news, "Well that's just fine then!"

Two paramedics had worked their way through the crowd and were standing at the end of the aisle behind the girl's back, looking nervous with a collapsible canvas stretcher standing between them. One, holding what looked like a giant tackle box, nodded a single nod to the grocer and pointed down to the floor with one finger.

"Alright, Vicky, the paramedics just need to give you a quick look over to make sure you're alright. Let's just sit down right here where we are." He squatted in the middle of the floor crossing his legs to the best of his ability, now eye level with the 20 pound bags of Alpo on the bottom shelf to his right and wooden crates of bottled Coca-Cola on his left. He gestured for her to sit as well.

She turned around to look at the paramedics in their pristine white uniforms, and glared at them suspiciously until the one with the tackle box tugged the stretcher from the other man's hand and leaned it against the metal shelving. "We ain't taking you nowhere. We just want to make sure you're alright. Can I come listen to your heart? My name's Darryl."

The girl half-shrugged, half-nodded as she eased to the floor in a single fluid movement that left her sitting cross-legged and upright. The paramedics approached slowly and smiling. As the first knelt down he said, "Alright now, just breathe normally, this won't hurt a bit, and we'll be done in no time. You look just fine," and as she began breathing, the other paramedic walked around behind her.

She turned to see what he was doing, but it was too late. The needle was already in her arm, and she was unconscious before she could resist or utter a word.

The boy had fallen silent not by any effort of the sheriff, but through sheer exhaustion. He had kicked and screamed and flailed until he was out of momentum—a wind-up toy quickly unwound. The sheriff's arms were still encircling the boy, but holding him instead of restraining him. The boy had not fainted, nor was he asleep, but his limbs were limp, dangling, as the sheriff hefted him onto his hip and carried him down the coffee and peanut butter aisle to the front of the store. His head lolled on the sheriff's neck, looking away from the man and down at the floor, at the flecks of green granite and glass sparkling in the polished floor.

"Your parents sure are going to be glad to hear you're alright, Josh," he said as he started walking down the aisle. He wanted to keep talking so the boy would listen to him and not the grocer talking to the girl on the next aisle—it did not sound like things were going well. The boy did not respond.

"How long you all been in that freezer?" he asked. No response.

"How did you get in there, anyway?" Again, no reply.

"Who's that girl you were with?" The boy turned his head so that his lips were almost touching the sheriff's neck, and he answered softly, "I don't know."

"You don't know what son?" The sheriff asked. They were at the end of the aisle. The boy's icy wet clothing had soaked through the sheriff's clean dry shirt—he was sure the boy would have pneumonia, if not something worse from all that raw meat.

"Any of it, Sheriff Garnto," the boy almost whispered. "I don't know any of it."

He thought it was a good sign the boy remembered he was sheriff, at least.

Some of the men clustered around the entrance to the store watching the standoff with the girl backed away as the sheriff came through, and outside he gently lowered the boy to a gurney that was waiting for them on the other side of the sandbags, at the edge of the giant pond.

Another set of paramedics were there waiting, and gently strapped the boy down.

"We'll take it from here, sheriff," one said as he prepared an IV drip of fluids and sedatives for the boy.

"Josh, have you seen Jonny, Jonathan Vinson?" the sheriff asked as the needle entered the boys arm. He wasn't expecting the boy to know, and wasn't even sure why he was asking.

"He's gone, sheriff." The boys eyes closed, and the paramedics rolled the gurney to the silent ambulance, collapsed its folding legs, slid the apparatus into the doors, and disappeared into the morning, lights flashing, but the siren silent.

***

It was after 1:00pm when the diver finally resurfaced. He had been underwater for close to 20 minutes, which was about 18 minutes longer than the sheriff had been told he would be down. His only mission was to go down and see what was blocking the drain and determine what would be best to remove it with. All manner of chains and hooking gear, as well as a Bucky's Towing tow truck, were in place, waiting. The sheriff was sitting in his car at the top of the lot, coaxing salted peanuts from a bottle of Coca-Cola, when he got a call to go meet with the diver, *Pronto*.

He walked across the lot, down to the water's edge, where the diver was talking in hushed tones to Sgt. Samuels. The diver's face was ashen white, but the sheriff knew nothing about either the diver or diving, so he didn't know if that meant anything or not, until Samuels said "Sheriff, we have to get these people out of here."

"What? Why?"

"We have a situation."

"We have about a hundred situations." He was already exhausted, and it was barely lunchtime.

"We have another one. That Jonny Vinson you've been looking for? Does he wear leg braces?"

The sheriff's heart and stomach sank. "Yes."

"Well, he's down there. And sheriff, he's tied to a four-by-eight piece of plywood covering the drain. And he. He's been." Samuels stammered. "There's something wrong."

The diver spoke for the first time, in a controlled but anxious monotone, saying "His lips are sewn shut. Sewn shut. And his eyes are wide open."

"What the hell are you talking about?" the sheriff asked, hearing but not comprehending. "He's tied to the board? How? Are you sure?"

"Some sort of half-inch rope, looks like jute, but hard to tell underwater. His hands and feet aren't tied, it's his whole body, the rope is criss-crossed over him like a spiderweb, with him bound under it. But his eyes," and here the diver vomited a little, then swallowed it back down. There were dozens of people watching the three of them closely. The tow truck driver was probably close enough to hear them, the sheriff realized too late.

"Okay," the sheriff stopped the diver before he could say anything else. "It sounds like a prank got out of hand, but we can handle this." The sheriff wasn't sure if the words he was saying meant anything, he was just saying something to fill the silence so the diver wouldn't say anything more. He took the two men by the elbows and turned them so that all their backs were to Bucky and the crowd at the highway, and began speaking with a quiet urgency, "Can we get a tarp secured over the boy underwater and get him and the board up without dislodging him from it?"

"I don't think I can do it alone, but yes, it can be done," the diver replied after a moment's hesitation.

"Can we get some assistance on this? I don't think Bucky is up for the job. At least, he's not who we need here." He gestured with his thumb behind his back to the man who was working very hard to appear not to be listening for any word that might drift his way. The sheriff privately thought that none of them were up for the job. *What the fucking hell?*

"Sure," Sgt. Samuels answered, "Why don't we talk in your car? Duncan, why don't you come sit with us in the back seat, so you don't have to answer any questions from the locals." It appeared the diver's name was Duncan. On the way to his squad car, the sheriff told Bucky they weren't going to need the tow truck after all.

"You shore sheriff? I don't mind hanging around if they's a chance y'all might need me." He was looking at the sheriff and the two men walking towards the squad car with deep suspicion.

"No, I imagine Mrs. Eleanor has plenty lined up for you this afternoon, if not the triple-A. We'll get things taken care of here. Just go on and take care of business."

"So what was it down there?" Bucky asked, gesturing with his chin to the mass of water.

"A mess too big for me or you to clean up," the sheriff answered in a noncommittal yet final tone as he walked away.

Bucky's truck pulled off a few minutes later, but as the three men were sitting in the sheriff's car, they saw the driver reappear at the top of the hill on foot, and talking with a group of men there. *He heard*, the sheriff thought.

"He heard," Sgt. Samuels said aloud. The other two men repeated his words in confirmation.

On their radios, they arranged with the colonel at the Armory for the boy to be transported by helicopter to the forensics lab in Atlanta after he was recovered from the water, and after he had been identified by his parents. Everyone agreed the identification should be done on the helicopter, and Eleanor dispatched the sheriff to the Vinson's home to transport them to the Armory, and try to prepare them for what they would see there. He wondered how he would prepare himself.

As he pulled away, he noticed that the crowd of people at the top of the hill was growing, quickly. He didn't understand how word was spreading so fast until he remembered that of course the tow truck had a CB in it. *Half the county will be here in half an hour.*

But there was nothing for it. He headed for the Vinson home, which he knew, because he had been there to play penny ante poker with Chuck Vinson, and their wives were friends as well.

He found Chuck in the yard, picking up fallen pine limbs. When the man looked up and saw the sheriff, the color drained from his face and he dropped the sticks he was holding where he stood. The front door was standing open, and he called out for his wife, his voice cracking, "Cheryl, get out here."

Almost instantly she was there, walking down the three short steps of the almost-new ranch home.

"What?" she began as the sheriff opened his door to get out. "Well, what? What is it? Where's Jonny?"

Chuck was reading the sheriff's face more accurately than Cheryl was—she was looking for and finding hope, he was looking for and finding truth. He held his wife from behind, his arms clutching her arms to him.

"I'm sorry to have to tell you this," the sheriff began, and watched the hope drain from Cheryl's face in an instant when she heard the word *sorry*. By the time he began "We found him a little while ago," her face was emotionless. Not frantic, not sad, just devoid of any human emotion or warmth, as though a switch had been flipped into the *off* position.

Chuck began sobbing behind her, his grief bending his body in mild convulsive gasps, but her body did not bend. She was rigid in her grief. Chuck's tears fell onto her shoulders, but she did not cry.

"Where is he? Where's my Jonny?" she asked, her voice without any inflection—she might have been asking the whereabouts of a baking dish she needed. The sheriff for the first time smelled an overwhelming scent of artificial lemon and saw that Cheryl was holding yellow latex gloves. The flesh on her fingers was almost raw—white, pink and fleshy. He wondered how long she had been scrubbing.

"He's being transported to the Guard now," the sheriff answered.

"Why?" she snapped back at him. "What happened to him?" She was pulling away from her husband's clumsy, wet embrace. All business, for now, none of the foolishness of grief.

"We don't know, exactly," the sheriff wished he had planned out with a little more precision what he was going to tell them and how, "but the circumstances are a little odd. It may be some prank that went bad wrong. We don't know. We're going to send him up to the forensics lab in Atlanta so they'll be able to tell us. But we need you to come identify him."

By now the husband's sobs had subsided. "Prank?" he asked. "What kind of prank? Who would pull a prank on Jonny?"

It was a fair enough question. Jonny was an extraordinarily popular child, particularly for a boy with muscular dystrophy, unable to participate in most of the activities of boys his age. Diagnosed with Duchenne Muscular Dystrophy at the age of two, he experienced imbalance and trouble walking from infancy, and was wearing leg braces by the age of four. He was never able to run, and by the age of seven had exaggerated trouble even walking. His slow, awkward, crablike movement made strangers uncomfortable, but the people of Dublin, particularly those children with whom he had grown up, knew him to be an entirely approachable, otherwise perfectly normal child. He loved comic books and Boy Scouts, and sat in the score booth at little league games. He laughed easily, loudly, and often, and worked hard to make the morbid condition of his body less discomforting to others. He outwardly regarded his handicap with a self-deprecating, jocular humor that left him for the most part immune to the taunts, stares and laughter that, while infrequent, still punctuated his life. His classmates protected him jealously, and at school he was perfectly safe from any sort of unkindness not consistent with the general uproar of children. But the farther away from his own school he ventured, the more unkind the world became. When he was six his parents had taken him to the Georgia State Fair in Macon, and the open staring, pointing and laughter made him feel like more of an exhibit than a visitor to the fair. *Mama, what's wrong with that boy?*, he heard over and over again, with laughter both nervous and hateful. When he would look their way and their eyes would dart off, but just a little too late. After a miserable two hours, his mother had finally had enough and said

"My head just can't take any more of this noise. Let's go home." And they had all been glad to go. Actively ignoring the cruelty of the world had taken just about all of their energy.

But this, whatever *this* was, was beyond the general cruelty of people, even of children, the sheriff thought, and he knew that he was not doing a good job of preparing the Vinsons for what they were to shortly see. What he would be seeing for himself for the first time.

"I don't know who would want to hurt Jonny," he answered her question after a moment lost in thought, "but we will find out. Why don't you put on a coat and come on with me. I'll bring you back here when we're done." *When will we be done with this?* he thought to himself.

The couple took several minutes to get themselves together and close up the house. She returned first and sat in the front seat of the squad car without asking, leaving her husband to sit alone in back as the three of them rode in silence. The sheriff considered giving them more detail as they rode along, but realized how little the particulars of their only child's death would mean to them in the end. Jonny was dead, and however strange or cruel the manner of his death might be, the only question that mattered was the eternal one, which was as unanswerable as it was insistent. He held his silence.

***

The Chinook helicopter with another diver, mechanics, and the necessary supplies showed up as the sheriff was pulling away from the parking lot on his way to the Vinsons. It landed 80 yards from the water and parallel to the road at the top of the hill beside which the majority of the onlookers stood, and at close to 100 feet long, the aircraft blocked the view of the water to most of them.

As soon as both divers were underwater with their supplies to secure the tarp to the plywood, the crowd of people at the top of the hill began slowly shuffling forward, and dividing as if to see around the helicopter. There were over a hundred of them, young and old, men and women, boys and girls, white, and colored. And, their movement seemed less premeditated than pack-like and instinctive—they all wanted to see. They had heard what Bucky heard or thought he had heard, or some version of it made even stranger in the multiple retellings.

When Sgt. Samuels saw what was happening, he shouted at the crowd to "Y'all stay back, now. We need you all to stay back up at the top of the hill." It was a crime scene, but he couldn't say that aloud, not yet. He was gesturing with his hands in a shooing motion.

The people paused and looked at one another. The Guardsmen and local deputies with their weapons were looking at the sergeant for guidance. After a moment, Bucky the tow truck driver stepped forward in front of the rest of the crowd and said, his voice at once nervous and strong with fear and anger, "I heard what ya'll said about that boy being tied up and drowned down there and him all butchered up. We got a right to know what's goin' on 'round here."

The *butchered up* part took Samuels by surprise, but he had no way of knowing what the man thought he had heard. He saw for the first time that there were people with cameras—several of them, including one with a professional-looking Nikon with a telephoto lens on it, probably a local reporter. He thought it would not end well—the expressions on the faces of the onlookers were determined. But it was his job to keep them back, so he replied with more authority and force of conviction than he felt, "I don't know what you think you heard, but that ain't it. You'll know what's happening when we know what's happening, but until then, you need to stay back. There." He pointed to the top of the hill.

To his surprise, after some muttering, the people did slowly back up the hill. Samuels got in the car and radioed to the men around the perimeter of the lot not to fire under any circumstances, but to try to hold the crowd back if they moved forward again. He called into the Armory to get more men, and described the people with cameras to them. It was decided they would wait until the several roads into and away from the area had been barricaded before they would actually use the hydraulic winch and electronic lift in the aircraft's cargo bay to remove the boy from the water and load him onto the aircraft. Once the helicopter was gone, the remaining officers would deal with the crowd, and no one would leave until all the cameras were confiscated. The twin rotors of the Chinook were started up, both to prepare the aircraft for departure and to deter anyone from coming close. With each set of the twin rotary blades measuring in at 60 feet in diameter, they made for a large, loud, visible, and deadly deterrent when in motion. The wind generated from the rotors set the nearby Ferris Wheel to creaking in earnest, from what had been gentle, like a porch swing, into a metallic, insistent, hee-hawing. The Highland Swing seats that were not underwater began to move erratically, as though filled with sullen children.

Meanwhile, even more people had gathered. There was nowhere left to park on either side of the road at the top of the hill, and even some employees and patients of the Veteran's Administration Hospital across the road had walked over to see what the crowd was gathering for. Many appeared to have joined with the carnival people, still watchful over their mostly-submerged possessions, where they had a closer view of the retrieval effort than from the road.

When the divers emerged from the water, even though only six minutes had passed, it was to an entirely different scene, one full of a tangible tension in a growing crowd. Each diver led a length of chain trailing behind him into the water. Samuels went to meet them and explain the situation, and two other Guardsmen from the helicopter, both mechanics, retrieved the chains from them and connected them to the chain from the hydraulic hoist. The divers got in the aircraft, and a few minutes later, when Samuels received word that the necessary roads were blocked and the men required to secure the perimeter were in place, he and one of the mechanics stood by the water's edge, ready to lift the board and carry the boy to the aircraft, while the other mechanic prepared to operate the hoist once the board was out of the water.

Things went well at first. The hoist, which was typically used to lift loaded cargo containers and tanks into the helicopter, was able to retrieve the board with incredible ease, even considering the pressure of the water. In fact, the mechanic kept the motor at much less than full power to prevent the board bouncing up the pavement once it was free from the water. At the first sight of the surface rippling, the movement of the chain was slowed to the lowest setting, and the tarp-covered board slid out of the water. Any noise from the chain and plywood scraping the pavement was masked by the thumping of the helicopters' blades.

Then, as Samuels and a mechanic walked down to lift the board and carry it to the helicopter, a series of shots rang out—several rounds of shots, from different directions. What sounded like two small-caliber handguns and a long-range rifle were popping off rounds. People started screaming and running for cover, which was nowhere to be found in the wide-open expanse of the parking lot. They knocked each other down as some made for the amusement park rides, which were closest, while others ran for the Piggly Wiggly, and some for the corridor of shops over by the Sears. But since few had any idea where the shots were coming from, most just ran to the first thing they saw, but all away from the water. Samuels and the mechanic dropped to the ground at the first sound of gunfire and began crawling on the pavement toward the helicopter. As they neared the craft, they were startled to see the other mechanic jump out of the craft and run with a gun drawn past them towards the boy. They turned and looked and saw their mistake.

Sgt. Samuels knew at once the bullets had been fired as a diversion, because there, around the plywood, which had been pulled free from the chain, stood three men, including the tow truck driver, who had cut the tarp loose and were standing looking down at the boy in awe.

In a heartbeat, swarms of officers and National Guardsmen flowed into the parking lot from every direction, herding the people back into the parking lot. A group of three men in suits emerged from a sedan that had just appeared at the top of the hill. The three walked rapidly, in unison, weapons drawn from concealed shoulder holsters, directly to where Bucky and his two companions were gaping at the boy. Bucky saw the three strangers approaching and started to bolt until he saw the barrel of a sleek, small pistol aimed directly at him. He faltered, and the man gestured with his weapon for him to get down on the ground. He did, and the other two followed.

Bucky began blathering in a voice several pitches higher than his usual drawl, in something like a childlike whine, "We didn't do nothin'. This ain't right. This here ain't right. You can't—"

"Sir," one of three cut him off, "you're in more trouble right now than you can possibly imagine. In a minute or so, cars are going to be here to take the three of you off somewhere that I don't have to look at you any more today. If you would like to stay conscious during that time, be my guest. If you would like to be unconscious, just say one more fucking word."

The people who had run into the corridor of shops extending back beside the Sears had come running back out again almost as soon—they had discovered a colored man sleeping there, who, upon awakening, jumped up and took off running in the only direction possible—towards them. Once clear of the Mini-Mall, they all scattered again. The colored man took one look at the helicopter and bolted back around the Sears into a stand of woods behind the shopping center. The deputies discussed on their radios whether or not to go for him, but the order came through from the Guard commander that the first priority was to secure the shopping center parking lot, and get those cameras. In any event, the man was long gone, and there was only so far, and so many places he could go—this was Dublin.

Considering the number of guns, the amount of running and screaming, the level of anxiety, and the presence of moving helicopter blades, the lack of any deaths or serious injuries seemed as improbable as the boy lying dead at the center of it, his eyes open, fixed without moving on the sky above him. He was blocked from view by a wall of men—once Bucky and his accomplices were taken away, no more chances were being taken. With the tarp now unusable, a parachute was located within the helicopter, and it was wrapped around the boy and the board, and they walked him, surrounded him, as in a procession. Sandbags were taken from the entrance to the Piggly Wiggly and used to weigh down the flimsy parachute material in the gusts blasting from the rotors. The cargo bays slammed shut, and the helicopter lifted straight up into the air, sending debris flying across the lot.

In the midst of all the commotion, few besides the fair workers had noticed that the great shimmering pool of water that had been at the center of chaos a half hour before, had quickly, quietly, almost stealthily vanished into the drain at the center of the lot. Hundreds of hard plastic yellow ducks, Coors Light cans and Coca-Cola bottles littered the lot, now glimmering in the sun, the black tarmac iridescent with the remains of diesel fuel.

Accustomed to being blamed for whatever went wrong wherever they went, the carny folk began executing their departure with a startling, efficient determination almost at once—it was what they had been waiting for. Not even waiting to see if the rides were still operational, they began the process of disassembling the Tilt-A-Whirl, the Highland Swing, and other rides, games and concessions with a speed and agility that suggested this was not the first time they had made haste. Even after one of the sheriff's deputies told them they shouldn't plan to go anywhere anytime soon, they continued their fevered pitch of activity so that when word came, they could be gone. They did not yet know that the rope used to tie the boy down had been identified as likely being theirs, or that a young girl belonging to them was lying sedated at the hospital, as bewildered doctors observed, measured and monitored her. The carnies were in the thick of it, they felt sure, but they had no idea how deep.

Over the course of the next few hours, everyone was interviewed—there were several dozens of detailed interviews—and names, addresses, phone numbers were taken down from even the most casual of bystanders. During that time, a shift in the consensus of the crowd seemed to take place. Not all of the uniformed men could keep the onlookers from swapping stories before or after they were interviewed, and as word spread of the colored man who had been sleeping in the corridor of the Mini-Mall, and this was put together with the story from a few days back of a colored man who had been roaming town repeating the phrase *He can never tell*, along with the information that the crippled boy's lips had been sewn shut, and that the colored man had run off into the woods, a concern formed that grew quickly into a mild panic with episodic expressions of rage and frustration at not being allowed to leave until everyone was questioned. By the time the interviewers got to the last of the onlookers, they found themselves being increasingly questioned, instead of questioning.

When a man in his forties, sandy-blonde hair peeking out of a train engineer's blue-and-white-striped bill hat, was called up by name and asked by an officer with a clipboard what he had seen, he responded through clenched teeth, "Why're ya'll still here questionin' us when you should be out lookin' for that nigger what done this to that boy?"

The interviewer, realizing the futility of further questioning, let the man go, and went to report to his superiors what the man had asked. They decided to let the crowd go, but not without first gathering them together in the center of the lot, where the deputy sheriff, Eric White, back at work for the first time since he was knocked to the ground Friday morning, spoke to the crowd. He did not use the megaphone that was standing by, but his own natural, loud, bass voice. "Folks," he called out, "it's been a long day, and we appreciate ya'll being so cooperative. We got a lot to sort through. We don't know anything yet. And we don't need anybody jumping to any conclusions based on what somebody might or might not have heard about something they might or might not know anything about. Everybody just get on back home now. Let us take care of this."

It was an unsatisfactory speech, and he knew it, and he also knew for certain that if they didn't find that colored man before that crowd did, he was as good as dead. He tried unsuccessfully to get the sheriff on the radio, and settled for J.T. at the courthouse, who said he would pass the news on as soon as the sheriff was back in radio contact. Eleanor was on the radio with the colonel at the Armory almost as soon as J.T. could say "over."

She did not look over her shoulder to see Michael's reaction to the news that was travelling through the communications room. She knew that to do so would only confirm him in the fears he had written in his letter. She decided he would only hear her doing everything possible to help the man that he thought was his father.

He did look up when he first heard the words *colored man* from the deputy sheriff on the other end of the radio, and he had seen Eleanor's spine shift and back straighten. That was all he needed. She knew, and he knew she knew, and he wanted to cry, but he didn't. He looked back down into the *Book of Common Prayer*, and kept reading.

***

It took Parrish Stevens, the county coroner, a good while to get to the Armory. He had no radio or CB in the temporary morgue—there was no obvious need for one. The ambulances and National Guard trucks had been dropping bodies off, but with less regularity now. He was alone except for a guard at the door to keep out families and gawkers. The cataloging of death was, as usual, a low-key and lonely business.

The state crime lab would do the autopsy and determine the cause of the boy's death, but Doc Parry, as everyone knew him, would need to officially declare the boy dead and sign the papers saying so before Atlanta could accept him. Doc had never been so busy since being elected coroner. He was a retired surgeon, and had what everyone in Dublin considered plenty of money, but he still needed something to do besides play golf on the raggedy greens at the Country Club, and being coroner gave him purpose without giving him a whole lot of work to do. Up until the past few days, that was.

He knew precious little about the very poor—he had never been poor, and he found such people distasteful. He simply did not care about the trifling needs of people he did not know half a world away. Nor did he care about the trifling needs of people he did not know half a mile away. In fact, he cared little for anything or anyone, besides money and what he could do with it to entertain himself and refine his life. The pervasive, casual racism characteristic of the south was at once more generalized and intense in him—he despised anyone who did not share his perspective of the world, regardless of color. So when he had been a surgeon he had required poor white people to make payment arrangements in advance before he would operate on them, just the same as he would any colored person. He did not consider himself a racist, or even unkind—just a very practical Christian. The superiority of his understanding was evident to him in his success, so he did not tithe, because he believed the church to be a poor steward of his hard-earned money. He told himself that if they were more prudent with money, not always giving it to the poor, he would be more willing to give his money to them. And he was just unaware enough of himself to believe it.

So Sunday afternoon, when the diminishing rain allowed the National Guard to begin retrieving bodies of the shanty-dwellers from the banks and basin of the Oconee River, he was more than appalled, he was very literally sickened. He had to deal with the *river rats*, as he thought of them, on occasion, as part of his regular duty as coroner, but before the storm he had always been able to schedule the task of dealing with them for the end of the day. That way, he could limit the time between touching the bodies of the poor and the time his wife Connie would be waiting for him with his drink of choice—Bombay gin shaken over ice with just a splash of vermouth. She typically had the gin poured and waiting in a shaker by 5:00pm every weekday, and would have the ice in the shaker before his car made it from the street to the carport, and poured into his martini glass before he made it to the front door. But some days she had errands to run, and he had to fix his own. He made certain whenever he was going to be working on a river rat that she would be home when he was done, and his drink would be ready for him. The liquor wiped away all of the lingering discomfort he felt after touching the poor, working as a spiritual disinfectant, cleansing his mind in the same way the surgical hand scrub cleansed his fingers, palms, and forearms. It was a deep, thorough, and satisfying experience for him, a purification ritual necessary for his wellbeing.

It was an experience made all-the-more necessary by its absence, as he worked his way through body after body in the makeshift morgue of the Dublin Junior High School gymnasium. The thought of gin crept around the margins of his mind as he called out autopsy notes to the tape recorder perched on a lectern beside him, his voice echoing back to him from the empty bleachers and basketball goals. First on Saturday afternoon, then all day Sunday, and again on Monday, he had begun to feel like some third-world has-been. He became more and more sickened not only with each corpse—each more grotesque than the last—but also by the lack of cleansing salvation his gin should have been providing. In short, by noon on Monday he needed a drink. So when the light-skinned colored man in camouflage clothing appeared on the other side of the cafeteria table on which a dead, muddy, urchin was stretched out for him to officiate into death, he was not in the mood.

"What is it?" he asked sharply, his beady narrow eyes glaring at the man, before the man could even speak.

"Dr. Stevens, sorry to interrupt, but the colonel needs you over at the Armory. We'll have you back here in no time."

That was an offer and a promise the doctor could live without. He noticed the stripes on the sleeves of the man's garment and ignored them—the army had given too many uppity young men rank, as far as he was concerned. It was a false rank—based on nothing more or less than a man's willingness to kill another man, or lead other men to kill other men. They were animals, all of them, colored and white trash alike.

"Look around you, boy." The doctor gestured with his own dirty, gloved hands at the lifeless, wet piles of bodies and muddy clothing littering the gymnasium floor like autumn leaves after a hard rain. "I've got my hands full here. You can tell your superiors if they need my services, they can come here and ask me like a gentleman. I do not serve at the pleasure of the military."

The last bit was not entirely true—he had been more or less following orders from the military for the past two days, but enough was enough. To leave would only postpone the time when he could finally be done with the miserable gymnasium once and for all, and he had no intention of leaving, particularly not at the request of some low-ranking colored man. He looked back down at the young body on the table, and was pleased to see and hear the man turn and walk away. He was less pleased to first hear, and then to see, the young man return with another young man, this one white, also in uniform, some few minutes later.

"Sir." It was the white man.

The doctor looked up. "Can't you people see I've got my hands full here?" His hands were in fact full—he held what looked like a stainless steel dental instrument in one hand and a wooden tongue depressor in the other. He gestured to the room around him. The two men looked only at him, ignoring his suggestion to take a look around.

The white man spoke again, his voice as neutral and calm as a telephone operator. "My name is Sgt. Alan Cone. I won't take up much of your time sir. But for our report, I just need to verify that you are Dr. Parrish Stevens, coroner of Laurens County, and that you are denying an official request from the commander of the Georgia National Guard, along with the Georgia Bureau of Investigation, and the Federal Bureau of Investigation, to assist in the investigation of a child's murder, by performing your duty as an elected official. Is that correct, sir?"

"God," he threw the instruments he was holding across the gymnasium floor. "Damn it." He glared at the young men, who looked back at him without expression.

"Just a *yes* or *no*, please sir, and we'll be on our way."

"Fuck you people." The doctor was red in the face, his gloved hands grasping the table, palms down, fingers curling under the edge. He could feel hard, dry lumps there, which he knew, even through the gloves, were wads of old chewing gum. He wanted to flip the table over, let the dead child get the two pristine young men with their high-and-tight crew cuts as dirty as he was. He was seething with rage. He was seething with confusion. The powerlessness he felt in the situation was so foreign to him he didn't recognize it for what it was. Wealthy white surgeons weren't answerable to the riff-raff standing in front of him. Couldn't they see he was wearing a bow tie? Didn't they know what that meant?

"Sir, is that a *yes* or a *no*? We have our hands full as well."

"Are they full of dead people? Because this gym is." He moderated his tone, even and low, to keep from screaming at them.

"No sir, we just have the one. And he needs your attention. Now. Are you coming or not?"

He breathed in an out for a full minute, before finally answering with the only rational response he could muster.

"Yes, I'm coming," he spat out, as though the words scalded his tongue. He paused and looked at the two men with a kind of burning hatred. "But I'm driving my own goddam car." He started walking, removing his rubber apron and gloves as they walked. He threw them down beside the door as they exited.

The gurgling call of a lone Purple Martin, separated by the storm from his mate in their northern migration, was the only sound in the gymnasium, besides the rain, after the door slammed. The tape recorder just kept running, recording the emptiness, which wasn't really that different than what it had recorded before.

No one said anything as they got into their separate vehicles, the men in their jeeps, the doctor in his 1973 Mercedes 280 four-door sedan, painted Caledonia Green, purchased to take place of pride in the parade, with the mayor, or Miss Saint Patrick's Day, perched on the hood. But not this year.

On their way to the Armory, he retrieved an unopened fifth of Bombay gin from under the driver's seat he had secreted there that morning. He slowed down just enough so the man in the jeep directly ahead of him wouldn't be able to see him tilt the bottle up into his mouth. Just three quick shots, and he was better. The warmth traveled through him even before the liquor touched his tongue—just holding the bottle had been almost enough. But not enough. By the time the third swallow went down his throat, he was himself again. He couldn't smell the river rats on him. He wasn't livid with rage at the men who had interrupted his day. He was Dr. Parrish Stevens again, and when he got to the Armory, he was going to let the superior of that uppity yella fella get an earful. How dare they send some illiterate, ill-mannered subordinate to fetch him like he was the hired help? He had had just about enough of it. Yes he had. He had indeed.

He never got the chance.

The gate to the chain-link fence enclosing the Armory's front parking lot was pulled closed behind the doctor as he pulled onto the gravel behind the other men. Two nights before there had been a scramble for some WD-40 to get the gates moving at all. The rubber on the wheels to the gate had long since rotted off, and the two men stationed at the entry had to pick-and-lift the gate away for vehicles to get into the lot.

Once they were parked, the doctor got out of his car and headed for the front door of the Armory building, before Sgt. Cone called out "This way, Dr. Stevens," and motioned him to a small gate near the front of the building, set in the tall chain-link fence surrounding the yard. The opening was just tall enough and wide enough for a man to get through, and another guard was there and already in the process of opening the gate for them.

The doctor was through the yard, which was filled with cannons, jeeps, and stacks of barrels and crates everywhere, all in drab military green, with some camouflage here and there. When they turned a corner around to the back of the building, he saw a Chinook helicopter, its cargo bay doors wide open, and dozens of men in various military uniforms, both combat and dress, with and without weapons, standing around both inside and around the helicopter.

They all looked up or over or around as he entered the yard, and he became intensely aware of being out of his element. They had all been awaiting his arrival, he could tell. They knew he had caused trouble. They were looking to see if there would be more. He noted with some dissatisfaction the number of colored men in the group and decided he would wait for his indignant response. A letter to Senator

Hutchins suddenly seemed a more fitting method of expressing his outrage. The men before him looked ill-suited to receive it.

A silver-haired man in full dress uniform, resplendent with bars of ribbons, stripes, and stars, walked forward and stretched out his hand with a welcoming smile, saying "Dr. Stevens, thanks so much for coming. I'm Colonel Barfield, with the Georgia National Guard. We know you're busy, and we appreciate all the work you're doing, and we apologize, but we have a little situation here, and you're the only man who can help us."

The men standing around were pretending not to listen, standing in small clusters, finding busy work, looking absently at clipboards with lists and manifests.

"I'm happy to do what I can, Colonel" was the doctor's only response.

"That's just great!" The colonel's smile and voice were wide and welcoming, like a game-show host. He wasn't the gravelly-voiced army commander from a movie, but the reassuring captain of a cruise ship. He continued, "Well, this young man here, it's unfortunate really, what's happened to him, but because of the nature of his injuries, the sheriff wants him taken up to the crime lab in Atlanta before there's any, um, deterioration. You understand, I'm sure." He gestured vaguely inside the helicopter. "We have the death certificate already prepared for you, it just needs your signature and the date."

One of the men darted forward and handed a clipboard to the colonel, who handed it to the doctor without looking at it. The doctor saw in some amazement that it was an official State of Georgia Certificate of Death, with all of the information typed neatly and accurately. Behind it was Dublin's official form for a preliminary autopsy, the page almost filled with notes—more than the doctor himself would typically have made. Behind that was the carbonless triplicate form requesting the autopsy from Atlanta. The white original and the canary yellow copy would travel with the body, while the green copy would remain in a file in the courthouse. Normally the doctor's own mostly illegible scrawl—he couldn't read it himself, really, but he could remember what he had written—would have been where he saw rows of neatly typed information.

"But who—" he began, before the colonel interrupted him with "That Mrs. Eleanor of yours, of course. She's something else, isn't she?"

"Yes," the doctor responded, "she is." Of course it would have been Eleanor, the doctor realized—she had been the one who had made the forms in the first place. But the details on the form seemed beyond her, and he couldn't help saying so. "But how could she know? *Algor mortis*? *Livor mortis*? Eleanor couldn't possibly—"

Again the colonel interrupted, smiling. "No, no, of course not. Eleanor simply completed the form. One of our own men completed the preliminary examination almost as soon as the boy was retrieved from the water. He said the decomposition would begin to increase significantly once the body came into contact with warm air after being in the cool water. He wanted to make sure the report was as accurate as possible."

"Yes, of course." The doctor agreed, but was seeing that much of the report—his report, he realized—was not only not accurate, it was as vague and incomplete a report as he had ever seen or submitted. For each entry, there was both a place to include information, and a box beside the word *unknown* to indicate uncertainty. Time and date of death, *unknown*. Place of death, *unknown*. Industry, home, or public place, unknown. Principal cause of death, unknown. Other contributory causes, unknown. Accident, suicide, or homicide, unknown. Unknown, unknown, unknown, checked down the page.

He realized the colonel was holding a pen out for him to take. "May I see the body?" he asked, as he looked up and took the pen.

"Oh, yes, of course. You realize the circumstances are a bit unusual, which is why we're assisting the sheriff in this. Want to nip any speculation in the bud, you understand. Tensions are high enough around here, as I see it." The colonel was leading the doctor to the helicopter, where what appeared to be a parachute was weighted down with sandbags around what could have been a pile of anything, but which the doctor realized as soon as two men started removing the sandbags, must have been the boy.

It was a boy he knew. It was a boy whose parents he knew. They had come to him early in Jonathan's life to see if there might be a surgical procedure to improve the boy's condition. They had already met with a specialist in muscular dystrophy at the state hospital in Augusta shortly after the boy was born, who had assured them there was no surgical or other cure, but it hadn't stopped them from asking, from setting up a pointless appointment. He had only confirmed what the doctor in Augusta had told them, but he understood the needs of parents to do all that they could, what they thought was right.

Doc's own children were grown, living off in Atlanta and Macon. He had raised them the same way he had been raised—firm but kind. Like his parents did for him, he had cut his children off without a dime when they had gone off to college. They hadn't thanked him for it—not yet—but he was sure one day they would. In the meantime, they called to speak to their mother regularly, at times when they knew he would not be at home, and they would return home for Thanksgiving or Christmas each year, in rotation with their own inlaws. His children only visited together, and with their whole families, so as not to risk the chance of being alone with him, which was always awkward, and marked by long silences. They were attractive children, and smart, and hard-working, and successful in their own right, but not as successful as he was. Not yet, in any event. So he knew what it was to care for, or at least about a child, if not how to be close to one. Not close the way the Vinsons were. He saw the family frequently over the years, the three of them, at the Piggly Wiggly and the like, mother and father both doting, coddling some would say, the cripple boy, who was nonetheless always smiling if not laughing, making his way the best he could on his shriveled, twisted legs. The boy had always called out to him, "Hello, Doc!" which always embarrassed him, because he could never remember the boy's name, so he responded with what he called all boys whose names he couldn't remember, "Hello, little fella!"

And here he was, this boy, this little fella, this Jonathan, laid out before him like a, like a, *what?* He did not know. The crisscross of the rope suggested something like a spider's web, but with a mockery of natural symmetry, without any grace or balance or delicacy. It was not from nature, this web—the clumsiness of the construction, the rough brutality of the jute, the uneven texture of the plywood all spoke to the inefficient workings and doings of man. He moved forward to the edge of the board and looked down into the boy's face, at the eyes, still open, still looking up, and then he saw the mouth, saw the lips that weren't there, sewn shut, with what he immediately recognized was surgical—beyond surgical—precision. It was as though a well-calibrated machine had done it, as exact and elegant and mechanical as a Jacquard loom. The thread was not like any thread the doctor had seen—shiny and translucent, gossamer-thin, disappearing where no light struck it. And then he saw the perforations themselves—there was no blood, or hint of a trace of blood, as though each tiny hole had been cauterized before the thread, if it was thread, had been used to... *what?* His line of inquiry faltered. He could not think beyond the physical presence of what was before him, to try to explain the how or why of it.

"What is this?" he asked without turning his head, his eyes fixed upon the features of the boy. "What did this? How?" A part of him wanted to ask if the boy was really even dead—his still-open eyes looked so alive, so urgent, so desperately in need to speak.

The colonel continued in his calm, assuring voice, with well-practiced authority, "Well, now, we don't know exactly, do we? That's what the autopsy is for. That's why those boxes for *unknown* are there for us to check off, right? Sometimes all the answers aren't right there before us. But we'll get the answers, rest assured."

The doctor turned and looked at him, his features deranged into an expression unused to expressing ignorance, or amazement, or bewilderment, and attempting to show all three at once. "How?" he blurted out, believing at the same time the colonel would have no real answer to the question. He looked around him and asked himself for the first time, *Who are all these people? What are they doing here? For this one boy?*

"These sorts of things are more common than you think. With all the hallucinatory drugs floating around these days, and, well, you watch the news. These are troubled times. But we'll get to the bottom of it. And the quicker we get this young man to Atlanta, the sooner we'll be able to put this to rest. If you would just sign there," he pointed to the clipboard, "We can get moving. The boy's parents are on their way in, and they'll want some privacy."

The doctor realized at once that whatever was going on, whatever was going to happen, he did not want to witness any parent seeing this, whatever it was. He held the clipboard to his waist, clumsily inked his signature and dated it on each of the forms, and turned without another word to leave the yard.

The colonel caught him by the arm and said, "Dr. Stevens, you understand that as this is an ongoing investigation, you shouldn't speak about the boy's condition to anyone, correct?"

"Yes, of course," the doctor replied, pulling himself away, and stumbling as he went, weak with disbelief at what he had seen, at the lies the colonel had told him so effortlessly, at the realization of how very, very small and insignificant he was, of how very little he knew.

As he approached the fence, the guard there was already in the process of opening the gate, but not for him—the Vinsons and the sheriff were walking towards him, Cheryl two steps ahead of the two men. He felt an impulse to duck behind a stack of 50-gallon drums, a reaction unknown to him in adult life, and rarely in childhood—he was not a man to hide from anything—but this woman he felt he could not face, would not if he could. But she was there, marching, almost running towards him, and then she was through the gate and clutching him—"What, what is it?" she demanded, her teeth clenched, her eyes wild and frantic. He just pointed his arm back behind him, around the corner of the building he had just rounded. She ran. Her husband followed. The sheriff stayed behind.

"Everything alright there, Doc?" the sheriff asked, more concerned about the cause of the doctor's discomfort than the doctor himself. He knew Doc Parry to be a self-righteous, arrogant, bigot, and he had no use for him.

"See for yourself," the doctor replied, and began walking again, slowly, as if in a stupor, as liberated walking back through the chain-link gate as any prisoner of any prison, on being set free.

He sat in his car in the Armory parking lot, slugging shot after shot of the gin, until there was nothing left. He did not even look to see if anyone was watching—he did not care. Twice, he almost wretched. He was a daily, but not usually a very heavy drinker, and he hadn't eaten so much as a sandwich since leaving his house that morning. By the time he put the key in the ignition, his vision was doubled, and his thinking almost entirely disordered. He was driving to a place he knew in East Dublin where he could buy another bottle for three times its retail price from a man who could also set him up with a woman, and had on occasion over the years. He loved his wife, in an abstract way, the same way he loved his children—they completed his ideal of what a successful doctor should be—but there were some things she could not do for him. Things he would never ask her to do. He didn't need those things tonight, but he needed someone who would keep him warm, and his wife was never warm. At least, she was never warm to him.

As he rounded the courthouse and headed towards the bridge to East Dublin at full speed, he noticed strange yellow lights blinking in the distance. There were indistinct, unfamiliar shapes shifting in his drunken haze, each in multiples, some appeared to be moving, some almost steady. He was having a hard time holding his head upright, and keeping his eyes open. He had forgotten where he was going, or why, and even where he had been. He knew he was trying to get away fast for some reason, but he could not remember why. Still, he did not slow down.

He never saw the orange and white barriers as his car crashed through them, and he flew at full speed into the void where the bridge had been. The weightlessness of flight awakened something in him, and he held his head upright, with his eyes barely open, just in time to see the jagged concrete slab rising up out of the moving water, putting his long day to an end.

The two colored men who had been picking up limbs out of the road jumped out of the way when they first heard and then saw the doctor round the courthouse and speed down the road toward them. They tried waving him away, but he had paid them no mind.

"That was Doc Parry! Why you reckon he in such a hurry?" the younger of the two asked.

"He must'a found out one of them folks down at the bottom of the river owed him some money."

The younger man went to marvel at the car in the river, the older man walked to the courthouse to let Mrs. Eleanor know there was another one dead.

***

"What do you mean, *she's gone?*" The sheriff was looking at Nurse Howard with something like hatred—in that moment, he despised her as the living presence of everything that had gone wrong in the past week. She was standing behind the laminate counter of the nurse's station, beside the receptionist sitting at the giant telephone switchboard, looking past him at every one of the faces in the waiting room turned round to look at his raised voice. His back was to the room full of people, who were crammed into every chair, sunlight piercing the thick haze of cigarette smoke to land on dusty plastic plants and old copies of *Highlights for Children* and *National Geographic*.

"She's not here, *sheriff*." She said *sheriff* with some contempt and even more sarcasm. She had managed even less sleep than he had since the storm broke, and she was not in the mood. They had known each other since high school, and each knew the measure of the other. She pulled herself upright—at 6'1", she was taller than she sheriff and could easily take him out, with wits or a swift kick. "She left. Her daddy came in, picked her up like a sack o' potatoes, threw her over his shoulder, and marched out the same way you just marched in. Like he owns the place."

She crossed her arms over her massive bosom, made to seem even more enormous by the tightly-cinched belt beneath it, separating her upper and lower halves into a tall, forbidding hourglass. Her pristine white uniform annoyed him—he was still wet from the morning.

His face turned red as his lips. "And you just let him take her?"

She responded speaking down to him in slow, crisp, clipped schoolmarm diction. "This is a hospital, not a jail. And no one told us she was a prisoner, in any event. If you wanted her kept here, you should have sent someone to see to it."

"Well can you at least tell me his name?"

"Whose name?

"The man who took her."

"No, I cannot tell you his name, because I don't know it."

"Godammit Edna, you mean to tell me—" and here he was cut off.

"Luke, why don't you come to my office where we can talk about this in private." It wasn't a question. She turned and walked away from him through a swinging door that led through a series of supply and filing rooms to a public hallway where he caught up with her. The pale green linoleum floor glared with the reflection of overhead fluorescent lights, and the clunk of his boots echoed through the corridor. Her shoes were silent. Her office, as he knew, was just down the hall on the left, where it had been since she was promoted to Assistant Director of Nursing more than 10 years earlier. The director had apparently been visiting relatives in Mississippi when the storm broke the week before, and decided to stay put. At 57 years old, the director spent most of her time at the hospital in meetings made unproductive by her presence, and in her office reading *Reader's Digest Condensed Books*. She mostly got in the way when there was real work that needed to be done, and all the hospital staff had been quietly thankful that she was gone, leaving Edna in charge during the storm and its fallout.

She walked around and sat in the swivel-based slat-back oak chair behind the ancient oak desk. The chair had a multicolored crocheted seat cushion her sister-in-law had made for her, but it didn't make the chair any more comfortable. She reached into her desk drawer and pulled out a pack of Virginia Slims and lit one of the slender cigarettes with a desk lighter that was a four-inch cube of white marble. Disposable lighters disappeared like hope in the hospital.

"Well?" she asked, looking at the sheriff through her exhaled puff of smoke. Her hair was still naturally jet black, but set in a permanent wave that framed her face in unnatural curls. She wore only lipstick in an almost-indiscriminate looking shade of red that suggested she was wearing it as a matter of function, not interest. As he looked at her closely for the first time, he could see she was exhausted. There were lines on her face he had not seen before. He had cooled his jets during the walk to her office, which he realized was probably her intention. A row of vertical filing cabinets with neatly typed labels lined one wall, there was a furniture store picture of a mountain in springtime on the other, and two windows on the wall behind her, looking onto the employee parking lot, which was full of cars. She had a black rotary-dial phone, a Month-at-a-Glance desk pad, and a cheap crystal jar filled with sugared orange slices on her desk, along with the lighter and ashtray, but nothing more. She wasn't giving anything away. She hadn't in a very long time.

"Edna, I'm sorry. But we need to find that girl. Did anyone here recognize her? Or her father?"

"Nope. Nobody. Why does it matter? What did she do?"

"Maybe nothing. I don't know. Can we talk off the record? Patient-confiden-tiality kind of?"

Edna did not care for this turn of the conversation. She had been content in her dislike of Lucas Garnto since ninth grade, when she had an unreciprocated crush on him, though she had stood almost a foot taller than him at that point, and was among the first girls in their grade to develop full, proper breasts. He had rejected her publicly, cruelly, in the way that schoolboys will, and she had never forgotten it. She suspected he hadn't, either. She hadn't voted for him, and she didn't want to be in his confidence now. But she also wanted this conversation over with so she could get on with her day, which would be another full one.

So she responded "Yes, off the record. One public servant to another. Go ahead."

"You heard about Jonny Vinson?"

"I did." Everyone in town had heard about Jonny Vinson by now, probably even in the Quarters.

"Well, about half an hour before we found him, we found that girl and Josh Landrum huddled together in the Piggly Wiggly's meat cooler."

"Yes, I know about all that."

"Well, maybe not all. Before Josh's sedatives kicked in, I asked if he knew where Jonny Vinson was, and he told me Jonny was gone, but that's all he said. That girl was scared half out of her mind. I don't know if they did something or saw something or maybe a little bit o' both. But something happened. She told Walt Starling her father was the electrician for that fair in the lot. The fair people say they don't know anything about any such man or girl. I'm sure they're lying, but they're just carny trash who want to get out of town quick as can get. And, well, I don't blame them for that. But if Josh knows something, that girl probably does, too. We need to find her. Do you know her name?"

"The whole hospital knows her name. Part of it, anyway. Her father came busting through the doors like Yosemite Sam, just spinning round and yelling and spitting *Where's my Vicky at? Who's got my Vicky? I know she's here. Somebody best tell me where she's at.* He scared the staff half to death before I could get to him and make some sense of what he was saying." She paused to take a drag from her cigarette, and exhaled before continuing. "But she was telling the truth, or I think she was, about the fair. It makes sense now, anyway, the father said something about having to get back on the road soon, he didn't want them leaving him, something along those lines. Even when he wasn't yelling, he was crazy. I would have thought he was drunk, but he didn't have any smell on him at all. Still, he was talking in fragments... disconnected thoughts coming out together. It was like somebody was flipping a channel switch in his head."

The sheriff couldn't stop himself saying "And you just let him take her?"

She could have been affronted by the question, but saw the justness of it. "There wasn't a lot we could do to stop him. I told him he needed to fill out the forms before he could take her, and he said he *didn't fill out no forms to bring her in here, and he wasn't filling out no forms to take her, and he didn't have no insurance and we weren't gonna squeeze him for every penny he done made.* And there was some sense in that, to be honest." She took another long drag from her cigarette. "And we didn't know she was part of, or maybe part of, any crime scene, or what have you. But Lord. That girl was sick, burning up with fever. We don't know what with. Josh is, too. It's not pneumonia, at least it's not in their lungs. We're just going to have to wait and see how they, or at least he, will respond to the antibiotics. How's Chuck and Cheryl doing?"

He didn't want to talk about Chuck and Cheryl. "Better than can be expected, I suppose. I better get back to them. I was hoping to have something to tell them." He stood to leave, and continued "I'm sorry about earlier. We could all use some rest. Could you please give Eleanor a shout when Josh wakes up? I would leave a man here with him, but I can't spare one."

"Do you really think he's really going to be able to explain, well, whatever it is that happened?"

"We're gonna have a lot of sleepless nights around here til somebody does. Thanks, Edna." He turned to leave, his boots clunking.

"When did you start wearing cowboy boots, anyway?" she called as he passed through the door. He turned and looked at her.

"When I was running for sheriff. They told me if I wanted to be sheriff, I had to wear 'em."

"You look like a jackass, you know." She smiled at him, with a look that was at once sarcastic and almost forgiving. He returned it.

"Yes, I know. Thanks, Edna." And he was gone.

***

The meeting late Monday night between the National Guard higher-ups and the Laurens County higher-ups was scheduled for 9:30pm, and in name was the *Region 6 Emergency Relief Task Force Committee* meeting, but in reality was a meeting to figure out what the hell to do next, and the sheriff was looking forward to finding out just what that was, because he didn't have a clue.

When he left the hospital that afternoon, he did not go to the Vinson's house, where he knew neighbors and church folk would be bringing platters of food, but back to the K-Mart parking lot, and found the people from the fair all but ready to leave town. He knew that they'd already settled up with Patty at the Candlelight, and he could see they were ready to make tracks as soon as the Ferris Wheel was dismantled and packed away. He found the manager of the thing, and asked to speak to the electrician.

"Ain't got none," the manager said without hesitation. He was covered with grease and sweat. He was wearing an old Colonial Bread uniform shirt with an embroidered name patch that said *Henry*.

"Carl Dewberry, then."

"He done gone. We ain't seen him since Sat'day."

It was a lie, but the man looked him straight in the face when he said it.

"Where was he headed?"

"We picked 'im up in Alabamy. Maybe back that-a-way."

"Alright, I get it. You don't know nothin' you ain't seen nothin'. But can you at least tell me what he was driving?" The sheriff considered taking the whole lot of them down to the courthouse and interrogating them for a few hours, but from previous experience, knew that the results would be more of the same, except he would have a courthouse full of carny folk, and there wouldn't be a pen or a stapler left in the place by morning.

"Red Ford pickup, 62, 63, beat up."

"Right. Thanks. Where you folks headed from here?"

"Alabamy. Folks 'round here don't need no fair."

"Right."

He hadn't even called in the truck. By his own rough estimate, with Alabama's population of about three million people, there were probably half a million red Ford pickup trucks in the state. If Alabama was even where he was from. If he was even driving a red Ford truck. If he was even driving, and not stashed somewhere with the girl in one of the concession trucks until the fair was safely out of the county. He wasn't sure a crime had even been committed or witnessed by the girl, much less the father. Their disappearance gave every impression of something being wrong, but they were carny folk, and used to being among the least and lowest wherever they went. And with a dead boy not a hundred yards from where they had set up camp, tied up with what looked like their rope, they were probably right to pack up quick. So, he had let them go. He could find them again if he needed them.

He sat at the conference table looking over reports and lists Eleanor had compiled, waiting with Deputy Sheriff White, who looked like he'd rather be just about anywhere else, and the Recently-Deputy-But-Suddenly-Acting Mayor Nelson Harding, still in shock from the death of his friend and boss, and Eleanor, who was there to take notes, and fill in any gaps the sheriff might need filling. He was, after all, seeing some of the reports and lists he was looking at for the first time, though his name was at the top of each of them. Spence Johnson, the fire department chief, was at the far end of the table talking about the day's events in whispered tones with the deputy sheriff, trying to make sense of what they had seen and heard, but not getting very far.

At 9:31pm, they heard a stairwell door at the far end of the building open, and the patter of wet leather and rubber soles making their way down the dimly lit corridor. As the sounds neared the open conference room door, and the group stood to meet them, they looked at one another with puzzled expressions—how many shoes were they hearing? The sheriff and Eleanor, the only two to speak with the colonel, had been under the impression it was going to be a small group, the four from Laurens County and maybe another four or five from the National Guard. But it was obvious from the sounds of shoes both very near and very far away, that there were at least ten or more of them arriving. Before anyone could speak, the colonel was walking in the door.

"Our apologies for being late. It took longer to navigate some of these roads that we anticipated. Thank you for taking time to meet with us this evening." Following in behind him were fifteen more men, which seemed like a lot.

He first introduced himself to Eleanor, whom he had not met in person, then introduced the other men to one another. Among the men were Commissioner Barfield from the Georgia Department of Public Safety, his assistant, the Southeast Regional Commander of the Army Corps of Engineers, a Response Coordinator for the Red Cross, Samuels, Blankenship, and the other men the colonel described as "here with me," and introduced by first name only.

"We will be meeting in turn with the leaders of your neighboring counties tomorrow, and from there developing long-term strategic goals for getting life back to normal. But it seems as though Dublin has some different—and some more pressing problems than your neighbors. Before we get to that, let's look at where we are right now." One of the four here-with-me men got up wordlessly and pinned a magnified aerial photograph of the county to the wall. It had been taken that morning and developed and printed in Atlanta that afternoon.

The colonel spent the next half hour discussing the assessments that had been made that day, referencing the map throughout. Most of this planning had been made with Eleanor, and there were unlikely to be any changes based on what the sheriff or acting mayor thought, but it was necessary to walk them through the rationale for the decisions. After all, there would be some roads fixed the next day, and some not repaired for weeks or possibly months, and everyone needed to be on the same page. The sheriff and mayor made no objections.

"Eleanor, could you put down your pen?" the colonel asked, and she did. "The rest of our conversation is going to be a little more delicate. We don't want to embarrass or cause any more grief for any individuals or families in town, but we do need to have some frank talk here. The physical recovery is going well, better than expected. But the social recovery is wavering. With the electricity coming back on, people will be urgent to get back into homes, to work, to school. Before that can happen, we will need to get the displaced people now in the schools into some sort of temporary housing. Where are we, Ron?"

Ron Thompson, the Red Cross Response Coordinator, provided an update on the housing situation—68 families totaling 207 people were still in shelters across the city, and would need permanent relocation. Priority was going to families with small children and elderly in the households. There seemed to be enough empty housing in Dublin to make it work. In the end, they may need to bring in some trailers, but that would be the worst-case scenario. Everyone would be housed by Friday at the latest. Everything had gone exceptionally smoothly in the shelters until word reached them that afternoon about Jonny Vinson. Parents had grown anxious about being out in the open in strange places with their children when there was a monster roaming the streets.

"Right," the colonel interrupted. "About this monster. The folks around here seem to have decided the monster has a name—Corporal William Isaacs, a veteran who had the misfortune of sleeping in a public hallway near where the boy was found, or at least that's the chatter we've been picking up. Is that consistent with what you've been hearing?"

The sheriff nodded slowly. The acting mayor spoke up for the first time, saying "Folks been showing up at my house all afternoon. Janie—that's my wife—she says she's scared. I don't rightly blame her. They want that Isaacs boy's head on a stick. And they want to make sure we all know it."

The colonel looked at him questioningly and asked "Why would they go to your home and talk to your wife instead of coming down to the courthouse and talking to you?"

"Well, because this is Dublin," the mayor answered.

The colonel looked at Eleanor and the other Dubliners, and they nodded in agreement.

"Will they hurt him if they find him? We know they are out looking for him. We would like to put a curfew in place tomorrow until we can get this all settled."

No one answered at first, then Eleanor spoke. "Scared people everywhere make poor decisions. Tired people everywhere have bad judgment. Dublin is no different. There may be places racism doesn't exist—I'm sure I don't know—but not for a hundred, or even 500, maybe even a thousand or more miles from where we are, would a colored man be safe in the circumstances Willie was found in this afternoon. I don't mean to be impertinent Colonel, but you're not from around here, are you?"

"No, I'm not. But that doesn't mean I can't—" he began, before Eleanor cut him off, saying "Understanding human nature only takes you so far in understanding the nature of a particular people, in a certain time and place. Put a curfew in place, by all means. Nothing good happens past eleven o'clock in this town, anyway. But our best chance of saving Willie Isaacs is to find him before anyone else does."

The colonel considered, and responded, "We need Corporal Isaacs alive. Word has come down, not from the top, but from close enough, that Willie Isaacs remains an asset of, or rather to, an asset *to* the U.S. military. What you all may be willing to tolerate around here to keep the peace is, well, your business. But when it involves the U.S. military, and it does in this situation, you need to understand the rules aren't quite the same. So, how do we find him?"

They spent some time working out a deployment strategy for the next morning to find Corporal Isaacs. It was decided that they would not let it be known they were looking for him—if the townsfolk heard there was a *manhunt* on, no one liked to think what might happen. They would say they were on a *final sweep* for victims and survivors, which wasn't a bad idea in itself.

By the time they wrapped up the meeting, it was after midnight. They had discussed Doc Parry's replacement—they were bringing in four coroners from the

Atlanta area to finish his work at the junior high in one day. The local newspaper was supposed to be up-and-running by Thursday, and someone would need to sit down with the reporters to discuss the events and progress being made on them. It was decided that since the new mayor knew the least, he would be the best person to send over—the *Dublin Courier-Herald* had its offices across the street from the courthouse. Schools would reopen on Monday. The National Guard would be bringing in a delivery of 47 caskets from a warehouse in Nashville. If the weather stayed clear for the rest of the week, it was possible the dead would be buried and life could somehow begin to return to normal.

The sheriff and Cpt. Blankenship were dispatched to Colored Quarters first thing Tuesday morning to see if Corporal Isaacs had returned to his father's home there, or was otherwise roaming the streets, or sleeping under a porch—everyone was told to keep their eyes wide open, as he could be most anywhere.

As they approached Fairlawn Drive, the morning sun piercing white into their eyes, they found him. At first they could not be certain it was him—it was just a silhouette of a man—but they knew. Dangling from the giant live oak, like just another branch broken and mangled in the storm, with a cluster of three mangy dogs sniffing at his feet and the ground beneath him, the corporal hung from a thick knotted rope.

As they neared him, and the blackness of the silhouette diminished, and the blackness of his features was revealed, they could see his feet were bound, and his hands tied behind his back. He was stripped naked, and his penis and scrotum removed in a series of rough, jagged cuts, as with a dull bread knife. The strip of white fabric gagging his mouth pulled the flesh of his cheeks deep back into his skull, and his tongue stuck out, swollen and blue-black like an overripe plum about to burst, caught between the fabric and his bottom teeth. The tear tracks from his bulging, almost-closed eyes were still wet.

As the two men got out of the camouflaged jeep, the dogs scattered from the puddle of blood and feces unable to soak into the saturated soil. The men walked as close to the body as the smell allowed them.

The sheriff looked away, into the stillness of Colored Quarters, and could feel the eyes on him from behind every curtain, every just-cracked door.

"WHO DONE THIS?" he yelled, with a ferocity that strained his vocal cords, an echo from back beyond the far corners of the Quarters. The silence rang back at him.

His face was red, the veins in his neck visible, pulsing, alive with rage, a molten, kinetic despair racing through him. "SOMEBODY COME TELL ME WHO DONE THIS. I KNOW SOMEBODY SEEN."

Minutes passed. Somewhere in the distance, a rooster crowed. A wooden screen door slammed shut. And then nothing.

Nobody would tell. He knew that as sure as he knew his own name. He knew that as surely as he knew the death of this man would be declared a suicide. It had taken him a minute to come to that realization, but when he knew, he knew.

"Bullshit, bullshit, bullshit," he finally muttered under his breath, and then he took a deep breath, and then another deep breath, and then aloud, resolutely but quietly, "Blanks, pull this truck up where I can get up there and cut him down." He reached into his pocket and pulled out a short pocketknife he always carried but typically only used to pick his teeth.

"Sheriff, this is a crime scene, shouldn't we wait for forensics to get here before we cut him down?" Blanks was tentative, looking at the anger still simmering on the sheriff's face.

"Blanks, this ain't a crime scene. You're in Dublin now."

"With all due respect sheriff, it doesn't matter where we are—I'm looking at the murdered, mutilated body of a U.S. Army officer."

The sheriff inhaled, and exhaled, and turned to look at the young man. The young man who had no idea where he was.

"Blanks, this is Dublin, and all you're looking at is a dead, crazy nigger that the good folks of Dublin have put out of his misery. If you want to stir up some shit, we can come back here next week and find another, or maybe two, hanging in this same tree, or maybe all of Colored Quarters burned down." His voice was calm now, the color draining from his face, leaving a pale, sad exhaustion in its place.

"I just heard you yelling that—" Blanks began, but was interrupted by the sheriff, who said "You heard me yelling for justice, but you won't find it here. Not here. Not now. This is not Montgomery, Alabama, and there are no bridges left for anyone to march across. I care about these people more than I do your justice. I want them to live. The best way for them to live is for this to end. Now. And they know it. That's why they're not here, now. They want peace more than they want justice. They want their children safe."

They looked at each other, then Blanks looked off into the Quarters, sighed, got into the jeep and eased it up until the front fender was almost touching the dead man's body. The sheriff climbed onto the hood of the jeep, looked up, grasped the rope above the corporal's head with one hand, and began slowly sawing through the rope with the other. He kept his eyes on the rope, watching as each fiber split, holding his mouth shut tight. His knuckles were white with the effort of holding the rope steady. Flies and gnats began swarming around him, into his eyes, first, then his nose and ears, their sound amplified, deafening in the silence, but he did not swat them. He wanted it over.

Behind him he heard Blanks begin vomiting, and the smell of that morning's bacon filled him, and he held his own vomit down as the corporal's body crashed to the ground in the puddle of filth, his head smashing on the fender with a wet cracking sound, like a hard summer melon bursting, before it fell with finality to the muck beneath.

He looked down and out into the rising sun, and screamed an ancient, guttural yawp unlike any sound he had ever made or heard before—an old man's misery, a birthing woman's wailing, a starving infant in search of a breast, a dog thrown down a well. It was all of them, it was all of him, it was everything, and he had nothing else. He clung to the rope with one hand, standing unsteadily on the hood. For several minutes neither of them spoke or moved. Then he listened as Blanks called in to make the report, and became aware that he *could* hear him—the buzzing of the insects was gone. He looked down and saw the gnats and flies had followed the corporal to the ground, where they danced around him, a swarming, glistening shadow growing in the morning light.

***

"Mrs. Allen?" There was a tap on the frame of the open door to the sheriff's office, where Eleanor was sitting at his desk, a half-cup of coffee sitting in a saucer with a teaspoon resting on it. "May we have a word with you?"

She looked up from the desk without expression and saw two men in camouflage standing in the opening. They were two of the first-name-only men from last night.

"Why yes, of course," she replied after a moment. One of the two oxblood-leather guest armchairs was occupied by Michael, still reading the prayer book. He looked up, and the two men noticed him for the first time, and both looked startled.

She turned from the men to look at the boy. "Michael, why don't you go sit and read in the deliberation room while I meet with these gentlemen? I'll come get you in a bit. It's almost lunchtime."

"Yes, ma'am," he said, but he said it to the men, who could not seem to take their eyes away from him, and he in turn kept looking at them. They made him visibly uneasy. He walked slowly towards the door, and after they closed the door behind him, they could hear his sneakers making slow, deliberate steps down the hall.

"How can I help you gentlemen?" They had turned back and been looking at her, but had forgotten her in apparent contemplation of the boy who had just left.

"May we sit?" asked the taller of the two. He had the name *Hardwick* stitched to his jacket, the shorter one had the name *Coles* stitched to his. Apart from the difference in their height, they were essentially the same person, with generic European features softened through generations of the American melting-pot. *They could disappear into a crowd as easily as a whisper*, she thought.

She had been appraising them since she first looked up, and something was not right about them. She hadn't paid them much attention the night before, but now she could see something was off. They were in standard-issue camouflage, but they did not wear it well. It wasn't new, but it was as though the men were in costume. They were uncomfortable. The shorter one had reached up nervously several times to brush away hair from his eyes that was not there. The military haircuts were new—brand new—possibly only a day old. The taller one, Hardwick, was carrying a slender aluminum Halliburton briefcase with a combination lock—something she had not seen in person in thirty years. As she motioned them to sit down, she wondered if the names stitched to their uniforms belonged to them. She thought not.

"The sheriff is out just now, as I guess you know?" She had been waiting to hear from him all morning, but hadn't, other than J.T. had let her know the search for survivors ended almost as soon as it started, which she understood to mean that Willie Isaacs was dead. The other information she received in whispers in the courthouse, and she suspected to be mostly gossip—yet she feared the truth behind it.

"Yes ma'am," said the Hardwick man as he sat down in the chair vacated by Michael. The men sat in the two chairs, facing her. "It's you we're here to see." He paused and cleared his throat. "Before we go on, we need to let you know that this conversation is entirely confidential. Your security clearance has been reinstated. You may not repeat anything you are about to hear under penalty of federal law."

"My what? I haven't...I don't..." She was caught off guard, even with her suspicions of them. She wasn't sure what she had expected, but it wasn't that. She pursed her lips down and tapped a nail on the desk. From some far corner of her mind recollections of thousands of pages, tens of thousands of pages of letters, telegrams, blueprints, stamped *Top Secret* in red ink came flooding back to her. That was a lifetime ago. That was before Hardwick and Coles had even been born. But they were sitting across from her, and they knew, and there was nothing for it but to get to it. She looked at each of the young men in turn, her shock turned into resolution, and replied "Yes of course, I understand. Shouldn't there be something for me to sign?"

She could not be in control of the situation, she knew, but there seemed to be a protocol not being followed that made her uneasy.

"No ma'am. There is no paper to sign. We are not here. This meeting is not taking place," replied Coles.

Her spine tightened, and her shoulders reflexively bristled. "I see" was all she said. She was not in control, would not be in control. This was their meeting. She waited, looking instinctively at Hardwick, who seemed somehow or other to be the superior of the two.

He spoke. "How well do you know Michael?"

"Michael? Michael who?" she responded, in genuine and profound confusion.

"Michael William Isaacs, the young man who just left the room." It was Coles speaking.

She was too dumbfounded to respond with anything but the truth. "I barely know him. Before the past few days I don't know that I would have recognized him on the street without his grandfather with him."

The two men looked at each other briefly, knowingly.

Coles began. "His father was killed late last night, before we could get control of the situation." He paused to let the surprise of the man's murder sink in, and it did—instantly, but she only responded with, "What *we* are you talking about, sir?"

"Does his murder not come as a shock to you?" asked Coles.

"My ability to be shocked has been somewhat diminished by the events of the past few days, gentlemen. Please speak plainly. Who are you? And, what is it you want?"

Hardwick spoke. "We are here on behalf of the federal government. We will not bother telling you what agency we are with. It would be a lie, and I suspect you would know it. We cannot tell you the whole truth. But we can tell you why we are here. We are here to make certain that Michael is quickly removed from this town, and taken somewhere safe."

Eleanor started in her seat. "Gentlemen, I have no idea who you are, or what your interest is in Michael. For all I know, you murdered Willie—Corporal Isaacs, if he is dead—murdered him yourselves to get hold of the boy. Heaven knows why. I have no intention of letting you take him anywhere."

The murder at least explained where the sheriff was, but did not satisfactorily explain why he had not contacted her. If there was a murder in Laurens County, she was usually among the first to know. But now, what?

Hardwick responded first. "Mrs. Allen, you're wrong—he is not safe here with you. After the atrocious brutality inflicted on his father last night, that boy will never be safe in this town, if any colored person can be said to be safe in this town. If anyone at all can be said to be safe. Have you seen, have you heard, what they did to that poor boy's father? What kind of monsters live in this town, anyway?" This last bit was unplanned, and immediately regretted as he saw Eleanor's response.

She bristled with indignation. "*Human* monsters. We're called *people*. And no, I have not seen, nor have I heard in any detail. I understand it was gruesome. But no more or less atrocious than what we've been doing in Vietnam for the past fifteen years, or what scared and angry people have been doing to each other since the Bible and probably before. And you may or may not have heard, but the sky fell last week, and a young boy was found mutilated yesterday. It has been a very long week, sir." She picked up her coffee cup and sat it back down without drinking from it. Her hands did not tremble.

"Are you justifying the actions of a lynch mob who tortured and murdered an innocent man?" Coles was genuinely interested, but it seemed an almost academic interest in understanding her viewpoint. He had no personal connection to the boy or his father. She could see that.

"Certainly not. He asked what kind of monster I am and I answered him." She nodded at Hardwick and continued, "Which was kinder, to my mind, than calling a perfect stranger a name such as *monster*."

"I did not call you a monster, ma'am." Hardwick suddenly looked 12 years old.

"How not?" she asked, prickly cold. "Am I not a person in this town? How am I not a monster if that's what we are here?"

"I apologize if I misspoke." He was almost mumbling.

"Thank you. And yes, you did, you did misspeak. We are not monsters, sir. We have our faults like everyone else. Crises like these bring out the best and the worst in everyone, as I'm sure you know. How should we be different?"

"You're right ma'am." Coles was stepping in to cover for Hardwick. "Emotions are high. We understand. But our primary concern right now is Michael."

"About that," she interrupted him, "How is it you seem to know so much about him? About his father? That his father was innocent?"

"We know," was his only reply.

"I see," she said simply. She understood.

"And we also know the safest place for Michael is away from here." Coles added softly.

"He has no family left. I began checking on Saturday when his grandfather died. You know about that, I assume?"

The two men nodded.

"What are you planning to do with him?" she asked. She had known for several minutes that whatever plan they had they would carry out with or without her assistance. That was why Hardwick's response to her question was all the more amazing to her.

"Well, that is somewhat up to you, ma'am," he said, with a tone that was almost, but not quite, imploring.

"Beg pardon?" She could not imagine how her very peripheral connection to this boy might entitle her to voice any real opinion about his wellbeing, despite her earlier protest at the suggestion of his removal.

Coles spoke quickly, in a measured way that indicated his words were prepared beforehand, if not rehearsed. "We are here to ask for your assistance. You once uprooted yourself and dedicated years of your life to support and protect your country. We're asking you to do that again. We want you to take Michael away from here, from what for him will only be a place of death, where his mental and physical well-being will be at constant risk. We need you to keep him secure, safe. Raise him as you would have raised your own child. Teach him. Mentor him. Guide him."

Hardwick jumped in before she could speak, picking up where Coles had left off. "We understand how sudden this all may seem to you, but our request has nothing to do with the events of the past few days other than the untimely deaths of the only family he knows. He needs protection, guidance, nurturing, not just from someone he knows, but from someone who loves and believes in this country, as his father and grandfather did. We believe you're that person."

"But this, this is just, just absurd." She looked at the two men, whose names she still did not know. "This is my home. Dublin needs me," she paused briefly, looking at the two men with undisguised incredulity, and continued, "I've never raised a child, much less someone else's child, and a colored child at that. I am a white woman. An *old* white woman. My qualifications for raising this child are what? That I took shorthand for some architects forty years ago?"

Coles smiled. "Since Bo Isaacs died, we have been running extensive background checks on everyone connected to the boy. Every teacher, every neighbor, every distant relation that even you can't track down. Anyone who has had contact with the boy. Anyone who might want to have contact with the boy. You're the one." He paused and looked at her with some curiosity sketched on his brow, and began, "Mrs. Allen, may I ask you a question?"

"It seems to me you should be asking lots of questions, but go right ahead."

"Why haven't you asked why we are interested in Michael?"

She answered without hesitation. "If you cannot or will not even tell me who you are, I can't imagine you will tell me why you're interested in Michael. Or if you even know yourselves. Or if you know *all* of it, whatever *it* is. But I'm fairly certain you aren't interested in Michael. He either *has* something, or *is* something, that someone somewhere needs. Michael is just a poor colored orphan boy from Dublin, Georgia. There are probably a few dozen just like him, maybe even one or two named *Michael*. He's nothing to the world, and certainly nothing to you. So there's something else. But I don't waste time solving puzzles I don't have all the pieces to. I don't believe you *have* all the pieces. Do you?"

"No. No we don't." Coles was still talking, and looking at Eleanor with a new interest. "But that's not all, is it Mrs. Allen? You've seen something, haven't you?" he asked her, with an almost-reverent curiosity. "What is it you've seen?"

"I've seen a very bright young boy deal courageously, or somehow completely avoid dealing with, the upheaval of his life, his town, his family—what he knows of it, at least." Her tone was casual, dismissive, disdainful—a brave attempt at a lie.

"How is he bright?" Coles replied immediately. He and Hardwick both were alert now, looking at her with frank anticipation, greedy for what she would say next.

She considered quickly and carefully and replied, "Bright like other children his age. I suppose he has more interest in reading than most children these days, and is better spoken. With better manners, too, you could say." She looked each of them directly in turn as she spoke.

"No," Coles said, shaking his head in a tight side-to-side, excited gesture. "That's not right. You have no idea about other children his age. There are no children in your life. You see them on the street, at church, and in the grocery store. That's all. Tell us what you've seen. Please. We already know he's special. That's why we're here."

She just looked at him, her expression unchanged. She did not like being outwitted. Had she been? She still wasn't entirely sure what the objective of this conversation was—the outcome the two men were looking for. Without an outright lie to men she believed to be federal officers of some sort, there was no way around it. She became aware that a legal pad holding Michael's letter to his father—his dead father, now—was on the desk between them.

"We're all special in some way, Mr. Coles," she said with a carelessness that hid her growing discomfort. "Michael seems to have a gift with language. Nothing extraordinary for a child so in love with books." She reached across the desk and removed the folded piece of paper from the back of the pad. "Here, see for yourself." She held it out between them.

Coles reached forward and took the letter. He looked at it without recognition, and handed it to Hardwick, who looked up at her from the paper and asked "This is his? He wrote this? What does it say?"

Shorthand—the secret language of women. She smiled, "He did write it. You can read it for yourselves."

The two men looked at each other with blank expressions. "We seem to be short on shorthand skills, Mrs. Allen. Would you be so kind?"

"It is a letter he wrote to his father. There's nothing of significance in it. The significance, if there is any, is that he wrote it. He taught himself shorthand in the course of an afternoon. I was impressed. But surely a talented child, even a prodigy, if he is one—I don't see how that could have come to the attention of federal agents in Washington before it was even in the local newspaper. What is your interest in this child?"

"We want to keep him safe," answered Hardwick, in a soothing tone.

"That's not an answer. Mr. Coles, do you have anything better to offer by way of an explanation for this extraordinary visit? This request?"

Coles hesitated before answering "Why would you not believe we are interested in Michael's welfare?"

"Oh, I do," she said, just a shade of bitterness entering her voice. "The same interest a farmer has in keeping his turkeys alive 'til November." She hesitated. "Have you seen pictures of the children who survived the attacks on Hiroshima and Nagasaki, gentlemen? Because I have. And as I assume you know, I played my very own small part in helping to cripple and burn and orphan them." The two men looked at each other uncertainly, and Coles began to speak, but she cut him off.

"Don't misunderstand me. I'm not a pacifist. I don't regret my part in what we did to Japan, or that we did it. The world can be a hard place, and we make hard choices in it. I love this country. But if you think after seeing what I've seen—up to and including this past week—after seeing all this, I'm to believe that the federal government of the United States has some paternal interest in the life of this or any child, you have greatly underestimated my ability to do simple math. Now speak plainly. Why are you here?"

Coles sighed, and began. "Michael Isaacs has for some time been of interest to the United States federal government for reasons we cannot disclose. As a result of the recent deaths in his family, we no longer believe he is safe here. Dublin—well, really no part of middle Georgia, or Alabama, or Missippippi, or the whole south for that matter—was ever really safe for Michael, or any black child. But with his grandfather alive, there was at least a loving home for him. That is gone. And now, he must go. We have a safe house in Atlanta where we want you to take him and stay with him while the arrangements are made for you to legally adopt and raise him. We have a property in the northeast where we would like to establish your home with him. Financial responsibility for the child and his education will be assumed by the federal government, provided to you through a monthly pension. As an orphan of a veteran, he will be entitled to military benefits until he is 18. Your needs, and his, will be met in any event. You will have parental discretion in how you raise the child, of course. Our goal is to keep him alive and healthy. Nothing more. We need your help. Will you help us?"

The question hung in the air. The question was so unreal and yet the answer seemed so definite and final to her.

"Atlanta?" was her first response. "But my life is here. Dublin needs me. Especially right now."

"With all due respect, Mrs. Allen, what Dublin needs right now is a wrecking ball." It was Hardwick, who seemed determined to offend the woman whose help he was there to ask for.

Before she could respond, Coles jumped in, adding "What he means to say, Mrs. Allen, is that Dublin, this whole area, is a mess. Emergency management specialists will be here for months—years probably—assisting in the rebuilding. There are plenty of people who can help the sheriff, the town. But, as you said before, emotions are high. We can't risk the anger shown to his father being extended to Michael. We have the authority to take him right here." He gestured to the aluminum case at his feet. "He will be leaving with us, today. You are the only person here qualified to leave with him. And, quite frankly, you're right, at least in part, about the federal government not being qualified to raise children—that's why we're asking you. We could put him into foster care, and monitor him there. We want something better for him. We want you."

She swiveled the desk chair around to avoid the intensity of their gazes. She stood and looked out the window, the morning sun providing crisp illumination to the scene outside. Piles of magnolia branches taller than a man still littered the bit of lawn in the courthouse circle, blocking a sidewalk that no one ever used. A truck loaded with creosote poles grumbled and chocked its way around the courthouse in fits and starts. Down the street, she saw two Southern Bell telephone trucks with their aqua and gold bell logos parked in front of the bus station. At the end of the street, where the bridge should have been, the barriers the judge and Bo had put in place just a few nights ago had been replaced by more substantial, permanent concrete barriers.

Her thoughts as she stood looking out the window were not about the boy, or the government, or Atlanta, but about herself. Over the years, she had made herself a fixture of Dublin. She had encouraged others to rely on her through her resourcefulness, her intuition. She had made a place for herself, but she could not trick herself into really believing the place actually needed her, even if the people of Dublin believed it. If she had died in the storm, everything taking place before her would still have happened—she had made no real difference, in the end. She had no family. She had no real friends. The church choir had more than enough altos. And that was the thought that stopped her—*If the composition of the Christ Episcopal Church choir is a consideration in helping the life of a young boy, you're a fool*, she thought. And the corners of her mouth twisted up into a resigned smile as she realized, *We were never really even that good.*

She turned round and asked, "What do we tell the sheriff?"

Both men exhaled. Coles answered, "The judge will speak to him and tell him he granted you emergency custody of the boy this morning, and ordered you to get him out of town."

"The judge?" she questioned back. "What judge?"

"Judge Breshears. We spoke to him this morning. We determined the sheriff should be kept as much in the dark as possible about our involvement. The judge understands, sees the wisdom in removing the child, and signed the temporary custody agreement this morning. It just needs your signature." He opened the aluminum case on his lap, removed a two-page stapled document from one of several dozen multicolored file folders, and placed it on the desk before her. She sat down, glanced at the front page, recognized it as a form she had seen a hundred times, turned to the second page and signed it. Once her mind was fixed, her resolution never faltered.

"What next?" she asked.

"Michael," both men replied at the same time.

"Yes," she answered slowly, in deep deliberation, "Michael. I suppose I must tell him. Tell him his father is dead. Tell him he is leaving. With me. Today." Was she prepared for this? Could she ever be if she wasn't already?

"Yes," answered Hardwick. "And today is important, because we believe Michael has an unusually good ability to distinguish emotional truth. You should always be emotionally honest with him. You can tell him whatever stories you need to cover yourself practically, especially during this transitional period, but in matters of any significance, tell him the truth. He will know if you're lying."

She just looked at the two men, choosing not to respond at all—she wasn't sure how to.

"After you've informed him about the move—we think it best if you ask him, but we have no doubt he will say *yes*, again, your discretion—we think it best for him to retrieve whatever clothing, small possessions, mementoes, etc, he wants to take with him now. Whatever is left we will pack and move into long-term secure storage in an Atlanta facility. It will be inventoried and a list sent to you. Should he ever want or need anything from it, you will have a number you can call, and we will get it to you." Here he retrieved from the briefcase a piece of paper with two columns with the headings *Resource*, and *Telephone Number*. There were *Medical, Psychiatric, Financial, Legal, Education, Logistics* and *Social* entries, with phone numbers adjacent to them. At the bottom of the otherwise plain page was a number: *Ref:#1021*.

"Anytime you need any type of assistance, you can just call the relevant number, provide the reference number, and you'll get the help you need. You won't need any of these numbers while you're with us in Atlanta, obviously, but we're giving them to you now so you know you're not alone in this."

"But there are no names here. I will not know *who* it is with me, will I?" she asked.

"No ma'am. But you *will* get the help you need," Hardwick concluded.

Coles picked up, "Sergeant Samuels, who has been working with the sheriff for the past few days, is going to continue here, taking over for you until a suitable replacement can be found. He's excellent, and the sheriff seems to like him, and he won't be on the county payroll. He will be here at noon. He has no security clearance—he is unaware of our visit. Tell him only what you would tell any civilian covering for you."

She nodded, and looked at her watch. It was 10:07am.

Coles continued, "By 2:00pm you should be at your home to gather your own things. Take just what you will need for two weeks. Anything else you need when you get up north can be sent up after you. Pictures, books, clothes, whatever you need. We will see that your house is maintained and secure, but if you decide you want to rent it out or whatever for extra income later, that is up to you, but it won't be necessary. You should be at the Isaacs' home by 3:30. The judge is going to arrange for Ida Mae Edmonds to stop by just after you arrive. She will already have been told as much as anyone in Dublin will know about your plans—just that you are going to Atlanta to take Michael to relatives. She will not ask any questions. She will tell the people in the neighborhood—the Quarters, I think you call it—just what the judge tells her. From there, you'll drive to the Armory, and we will transport you to Atlanta."

"Transport?" she asked.

"You'll be flying up, in a helicopter. It's all been arranged."

The next half hour was spent discussing more details of the arrangements that had already been made, plans that needed to be made, general expectations. Eleanor found her senses transported back to another time and place. An anxious energy of being a part of something clandestine, something important, that she hadn't realized for years that she missed, came flooding back to her. The details were exhilarating, the furtiveness intoxicating. It was not until the conversation was coming to an apparent close—the men's ability or willingness to answer additional questions was becoming increasingly limited—that she realized there were two funerals the boy would need to attend. In the working out of the details, she had briefly forgotten the reason for them: Michael.

"The funerals," she began, "he will need to," she began, and looked at the two men.

"His father will be transported to Arlington and buried there," Coles interrupted her. "It will be a proper military service. His grandfather will be buried here. Judge Brashears was fairly insistent on that. When you decide the time is right, you will be able to bring the boy back here, or take him to Arlington. He is a thoughtful young man, but not overly nostalgic, we don't believe, anyway."

"Is that what funerals are? Nostalgia?"

"You understand what we mean, I think." There was a pleading in his voice that Eleanor not become difficult again, and she acquiesced.

"Yes, I do. Still this is all as sad as it is strange, nostalgia or not." In her mind, she had begun packing.

Coles stood up, followed by Hardwick. He handed Eleanor a manila folder and said, "Your work for us will remain unofficial. This is your pay in advance for the first six months. But again, it is unlikely you'll need it. Thank you for this service. Your sacrifice is appreciated more than you can know." They turned to leave.

"One last question," she asked as they walked out the door. They paused and looked back at her. "Who are Coles and Hardwick?"

Coles looked back at her with a smile at once conspiratorial and warm, full of gratitude. "Nobody. They don't exist. They were never here. But they wish you the best, all the same. We will meet you at the Armory, then."

***

When they had flown past all that he could recognize in the growing darkness, from the unfamiliar perspective, Michael turned from the helicopter window and asked, "Is this what it's like? Is this what life is like? So much... hurt?" In the dim light of the control panel signals from the cockpit she could just make out tears welling in his eyes for the first time. She faltered, and before she could speak, he went on, his voice quiet, even.

"In books, life isn't like this. The Hardy Boys, they always come home to parents who love them, and roast beef and potatoes, and a mowed lawn, and a convertible, and everything is always nice, and there's always an answer for everything. No one ever dies and no one gets drunk and there isn't any war and there isn't any hate and all the questions get answered, but that's just not real is it?" His question contained his answer, as well as a lingering hope that it was wrong.

Always be emotionally honest, she remembered. She thought back upon her own life, weighed his question against her experience, and replied, "Michael, I think for most people life is somewhere in between. I'm sure those Hardy Boys had their bad days, too—they just didn't write about them, I'm guessing. My parents are dead, too, you know. When they died, those were difficult days for me. Very difficult. Very sad. I was much older than you when they died, and I guess I was lucky that way. In other ways, I wasn't so lucky. I loved my husband very much, but when he died, he left me alone, with no children, no family. Maybe that's why the judge thought it would be good for me to help you get a fresh start in a new place. Maybe I need a fresh start as much as you do." She realized the truth of what she was saying as she said it, and it both saddened and surprised her, on a day when she thought nothing else could surprise her. She was the perfect choice because she had no one, she had nothing—the rest was all convenience. She did not feel self-pity, or resentment. Through the course of the day she had grown to see the goodness as well as the practicality of their efforts, and now hers, in removing the boy, regardless of their reasons for it. Now she saw how neatly it all fit together, and it was at once comforting and a bit frightening to see how well-considered their actions had been. She began to think she might be the least perceptive person in the helicopter.

She reached out for Michael's hand in the darkness, and found it, so small, clinging to the nylon belt he was strapped in with. She pulled his hand to her, and held it clasped for a long while. She was looking out the window, a thousand miles from wherever they were, when she heard Michael ask, "We're never going back there, are we?"

She was pulled from her reverie, a jumbled collage of memories distinct and vague, loved ones and nameless faces, images both still-life and moving—songs, sounds, and feelings, asynchronous and nonlinear but somehow soothing. "I don't know, Michael. I really don't. But maybe we'll never want to."

A few minutes later Michael fell asleep, his head drooping down onto his chest, rocking with the vibration of the engine, swaying with the gentle turns of the aircraft. She looked at the reflection of the control panel lights twinkling in the narrow band of gold on her left hand, and knew that she would remove it when they landed in Atlanta. Ms. Eleanor Thompson had once been a woman of the world, so modern she helped build a nuclear arsenal, in her own small way. And, with a call into Logistics or Legal the following day, she thought she might be that woman once again—a new name for a new day. Suddenly, she was no longer a widow, she was a single mother, with a son to raise. Not her own son, but still—a son to raise. Someone to love.

She leaned forward and looked through the windshield of the cockpit, the sky full of stars, steady and bright, casting the landscape rushing beneath them into a ghostly impressionistic blur, and thought to herself *No, we'll never want to go back.*

Deep in sleep, despite the movement and the noise, Michael watched in his dream as the earth moving beneath them was quickly, quietly flooded. It wasn't water, but neither was it air. It was a layer of in-between, translucent and dry, and dense, but leaving everything it touched unchanged. It stopped just above the treetops. In it he could see phosphorescent forms spreading out into the distance, with some nearby, swimming along in the helicopter's wake, like spilled neon light bobbing along behind. Others seemed miles, hundreds of miles away, mere dots disappearing around the curve of the earth. In his lucid dream state, he dove from the helicopter and flew down, arms spread wide, to see the lights more closely. He wondered at first if they were jellyfish, and how they traveled so quickly from the ocean, which was so far away. He flew along with the aircraft, as if tethered, and the lights continued bobbing along behind, but the closer he got to them, the more indistinct they became, as if they were trying to hide. Then, he knew.

"I know," he said aloud in his dream, laughing, and flew back up into the moving craft, arms at his side, like Superman, and sat back down beside Eleanor. She only heard him mumble in his sleep. She looked at him, and saw him smiling, and she was glad.

Riber run and darkness comin'.
Sinner row to save your soul.
Michael row de boat ashore, Hallelujah!
Michael boat a gospel boat, Hallelujah!

"Michael Row Your Boat Ashore," traditional.

CHAPTER 1. CALLIE

"How'd ya do it?" they asked in unison.

Callie looked at the room full of people, and answered back in her head *How should I know?*

But that was not what they wanted to hear. They wanted to hear something inspiring, funny, touching. Something poignant, personal, moving. Something to make them laugh, or cry, or both. But above all, they wanted to hear something brief. She looked down at her watch, a Patek Phillipe men's Calatrava, a classic round white face with slender black Roman numerals, a circle of white gold banded to her wrist with a black alligator strap. A gift to herself. Time. So much time had passed.

Her life flashed before her in an instant, a PowerPoint presentation of still life portraits... asynchronous and overlapping, with layers of audio making words indistinct, feelings unclear... her Pat Benatar phase... her Nancy from Sid & Nancy phase.... her yoga phase... her office worker phase... her foster daughter... the time she was arrested... the time she was strapped down and couldn't breathe... the time she overdosed... the time she... the time she.... The time.

The meeting had already run over fifteen minutes, and there were dinner plans, movie dates, and actual dates to get to. She looked out at the circles of faces radiating out in rows of folding chairs from where she was standing, and saw some faces she had known for almost twenty years, some for a few days, and some she had never seen before, a few of whom were clearly high or nodding out. She honestly did not know how she had stayed sober for so long. It was eighteen years, to the day, since she had walked into her first A.A. meeting, filthy, high, bruised, bleeding, and shaking. She had been wearing cut-off denim short-shorts, a yellow My Little Pony t-shirt that was much too young and small for her, and white Keds that were more brown and grey than white. She hadn't had a penny to her name. And now she was standing in front of them with her straight auburn hair slicked back into a rectangle of tortoiseshell, and falling just to the top of her Armani grey wool sleeveless mock-turtleneck sweater. She wore tapered khaki Dolce & Gabbana trousers and flat Bottega Venetta strap sandals. There were no labels visible, but she knew them, and she loved them. They helped her define an identity that she was still sculpting, all these years later. They helped smooth off the rough spots of her character, the way she used elocution to distance her from her past. They weren't lies exactly, in her mind, just minor revisions of, or amendments to, the truth.

Many of the people in the room knew a lot about her—certainly more, she thought, than any other group of people in any other room would ever know— but none of them knew everything. Some knew that she had suffered sexual abuse as a child, but none knew that her father had raped her dozens, maybe hundreds of times. Some knew that she had worked as a prostitute, but none knew that it began when her father started renting her out at the age of ten, and that he always watched. Some knew that she had run away from home as a teenager, but none knew that it was at the age of 13 with a man with a Super 8 camera who had been filming as seven men took turns with her on the lowered tailgate of a pickup truck. When the last man refused to pay her father the full five dollars, and threw two crumpled dollar bills in the truck beside her, and walked away, laughing, her father went into a rage, not at the man, but at his daughter. He scrambled drunkenly into the truck, reached down between her legs, and began slapping her face with the wetness the men left there. When she didn't react, he started screaming at her, "Dirty whore, dirty fucking whore," over and over again, and began choking her and banging her head against the truck bed. The men, scared he might actually kill her, pulled him off her, and left him unconscious in the process.

When she came to, the photographer was the only man left besides her father, who was still knocked out in the bed of the truck. The man's camera was gone, and he had wrapped a blanket around her and put her in the back seat of a car she didn't know. He was standing beside the open car door, smoking an unfiltered Camel, nervous, looking at her. He asked, "Do you want me to take you away from all this? I can make sure nothing like that ever happens to you again. I will

142

take care of you."

It wasn't quite true, and it wasn't entirely a lie, either, but she had no way of knowing that at the time. She didn't know who the man was, or exactly where she was—just another small town in southern Alabama. What she did know, what she understood fully for the first time, was that if she stayed with her father, he would end up killing her one day, or getting her pregnant, or both, so she said simply, and quietly, "Get me as far away from here as you can get me."

And that is just what he did. He closed her door, got in the front seat, and took off west into the warm Alabama night. He said, "My name's Ed. What's yours?" She took several minutes to reply, looking up at the lights and shadows crisscrossing the pale blue roof of the car's interior. Her head was aching and sore, and she felt a little nauseous. *I don't want him to find me. Ever,* she thought. She responded by asking "What's the most beautiful name in the world?"

"That's easy," he said. "Callie." It was his mother's name.

"Then that's my name." She said it quietly, but with certainty, and finality.

"What's your last name going to be then?" He was straining to see her in his rearview mirror, but could not.

"I don't know just yet." She sat up, hoping it would make her less sick. Instead, she felt a long sharp blade twisting in the back of her skull, and she let out a soft aching moan.

"Everything all right back there?" Ed asked, a little nervously. He thought she might have a concussion, and wasn't sure what he would do then. "You probably shouldn't be sitting up."

"I think I'm gonna be sick." Her voice was thick and slow with nausea.

"Here, take some aspirin and have some Co-Cola." He fumbled around in the front seat with one hand on the steering wheel for a few minutes and produced first a white tablet and then a Styrofoam cup half-filled with soda, melted ice, and rum. She took the pill and drank the soda without question, and lay back down, with her head turned to the side to avoid the tenderness at the back of her skull. Her sleep was almost instant, and dreamless, uninterrupted by the stops for gasoline and coffee, or when he had stopped at a Goodwill store in Houston and bought a shapeless dress and sandals for her.

When she awoke, they were in San Antonio, Texas, and the sun was shining full in her face. She had rolled over in her sleep and her hair was stuck to the vinyl seat with dried blood. He had checked into a room at the Traveler's Oasis motel on Interstate 90. He got a room with two double beds, and was waking her up to go inside and lay down. When she got to the room, he gave her another of the white tablets, and again she was asleep in an instant. While she slept he found a pharmacy and bought peroxide and ointment to treat her head, as well as a small bottle of Chanel No. 5 eau de toilette, some lilac-scented glycerin soap, and a really very beautiful Kent hairbrush, made by hand from cherry wood, with soft white bristles. He also purchased a small cosmetics case with a nail-care kit for her to put the other things in.

All of this was laid out for her beside the enormous television on the dresser facing the beds. She was alone when she awoke, and had no idea where she was. It took her several minutes to recall the events from two nights before. At first the note beside the bath products didn't make sense to her—*For Callie*, it read—until she remembered her new name. Before she opened any of the products she went to the door of the motel room and stuck out her head, looking from side to side and peering over the cars into the lot, but saw no one. Then she opened each of the packages in turn, almost guiltily, and the smell of the soap and the Chanel overwhelmed her—they weren't like things she had ever smelled before. Her life had been spent in places that smelled of fried food, machine oil, dirt, and sweat. This, this pleasantness, this sweetness, was entirely foreign to her.

She took the brush out of the box, and tried to brush her hair, but it snagged on a mat of dried blood, and pulled at her scalp, which still felt tender. So she took the peroxide and the soap, and spent a long time showering, removing the blood, and letting the heat of the water wash down and through her, the scent of lilacs infusing the steam that filled every crevice of the small bathroom. She toweled off with a harsh, over-bleached bath towel and put on the dress and shoes he had laid out for her. She put a small dab of the ointment on the sore place at the back of her head, but found that she didn't need much—it was almost healed. She then spent a long while brushing her hair, marveling at the softness of the bristles. She was in the process of trying to figure out how the tools in the nail-care kit worked when he returned, and after a brief re-introduction, he showed her. He used the nail trimmer, nail file, buffer, and cuticle scissors in turn, patiently demonstrating each, and talking to her all the while.

When he finished, they left and he took her to a Denny's restaurant. As they sat waiting for their breakfast, he discovered she had never had real orange juice before. He reached into the pocket of the blazer he was wearing—red and blue houndstooth in an oversized pattern, with large lapels—and handed her an over-stuffed envelope.

"This is for you," he said, "but don't open it in here. Just put it in your purse." She had brought her cosmetics case with her, so she put it in there, asking as she did, "Whut's in there?"

He lowered his voice and looked around to be certain no one could hear them. "While I was waiting for you to wake up the other night, I went through his truck, and found it in the bottom of a tool box."

Her eyes grew wide in terror. She whispered, almost breathless, "That's his whole life savin's. He ain't got nothin' else. He'll find us. He'll kill us." The envelope contained $4,800 in cash.

"No, he won't. I threw his keys and wallet into the Mississippi River yesterday morning. The little notebook he kept with all the names and phone numbers of everyone he ever knew, I threw in there with them. He'll be scared to call the police, or should be anyway, because those other men who were there were from around there, and they'll see to it he stays quiet. They don't know who I am or where to find me. You're safe. I promise you."

"But, but, it was his money. It ain't right for me to take it like that."

"How much of it was his money, and how much of it was your money, I don't know. But he didn't treat you right. He didn't deserve any of it. You know that, don't you?"

"I reckon," she answered softly, her face twisted in confusion. She did not know.

"After we finish breakfast, we're going to go downtown to the Frost Brothers department store, and we're going to buy you some proper clothes. I want you to grow up to be an independent lady, but until then, I'm going to treat you like a princess."

And he did treat her like a princess. Not an actual princess, but to a young girl whose life had been had been as brutal as hers, characterized by rape, abuse, poverty and neglect, her new life over the next few months and years was an improvement. As an underage, underground porn star with high-rolling clients around the world eager and able to pay for her body, her quality of life improved. Bruises and scars were not acceptable, and she saw a dentist for the first time in her life—after she had flown in to meet him at the Newark Airport Hilton, the married father of two agreed to provide dental services in exchange for her company. Ed travelled with her everywhere she went. He was, according to the state of California, her father. Among his circle of like-minded friends—something the outside world would call a pedophile ring—was a State of California Health and Human Services administrator who, in the age of paper records, was ready, willing and able to create an identity for Callie Pennington, for the small price of monthly visits with her, and a private film, made just for him, of the two of them together.

Neighbors in the large apartment complex in West Hollywood where Ed and Callie lived together did not question the story of the two of them relocating from North Carolina because her daddy wanted her to be a TV and movie star—there were dozens of parent-child stardom hopefuls living in the same complex. Their different last names, and her lack of school attendance, were similarly dismissed—

most of the star-struck children had adopted names that sounded more cinematic than their real ones, and none could regularly attend school and still go on screening calls. And, Callie did have cinematic, if unorthodox, beauty. Neighbors suggested she might be a star one day—not knowing she already was one.

As an adult, she was not bitter about her past, nor saddened by it. To the contrary, she was grateful to have made it out alive and relatively whole. She had entered her adult life as a prostitute and drug addict, but in the early years of her recovery, when she had not only sponsored many young women like herself, but also volunteered at a number of women's shelters, she had seen much worse. Women who were brutally physically scarred, who were in constant pain from severe burns, who had lost the use of limbs, or could not reproduce, or recoiled at any human touch. Women who feared for their lives, for the lives of their children. Women who had so much less than she did. Women who had nothing but the possibility of hope. Yes, her life had been hard, but she had escaped. She was lucky, and she had spent long enough in fear and poverty to realize how fortunate she was. She had forgiven her father, and she had forgiven Ed, and the other men, but she had not forgotten.

It was well into her adulthood, several years into her recovery from drug addiction, before she could really even acknowledge she had been exploited. The men who had paid to use her were certainly pedophiles, and probably mentally unwell in other ways, and spiritually maligned, but they had provided her a way out of the life she had been living when no one else had bothered. No social worker, no Concerned Citizens Brigade, no Salvation Army had rushed in to save her. In her experience, the Christian Charity of the Deep South was limited to looks of pity and disapproval for the poor, the dirty, the hungry, the unpolished. It was not that she believed their particular shade of hypocrisy to be more or less self-interested than that of other religious people in other places, it was only that it was these particular people whose disinterest had failed her. Whatever they may have believed, or believed they believed, their actions belied the simple truth that they just did not care.

The men, though, they had cared for her. They may not have cared about her, but as a prize among pedophiles—a young girl truly grateful for their attention, eager for their affection—they made sure she received it.

Because of her slender build, she was able to last longer as a pedophile princess than most. But by the time she turned 15, Ed's sexual interest in her began to wane. She was not his primary source of income—he was an independent dealer of luxury cars—so her emerging adulthood created a problem he had not foreseen, though logic might have told him before he even drove her away from her father. He did not regret his rash decision that night in Alabama, but after two years, he began to feel it was time for her to move on.

So when he received a call that a Hollywood executive was looking for a red-headed girl who was young, but presentable—not *that* young—he remade the 16-year-old Callie, taking down the ponytails that had been part of her standard appearance, brushing out her hair in big curls. He covered over her freckles with a light layer of base, adding blocks of rouge, and rings of kohl around her eyes. She could have passed for the 19 year-old-daughter of Catherine Deneuve. He sent her headshot over to the studio. The next day, Callie went on an interview, to the executive's office, and she never spent another night in Ed's apartment.

Zach Duncan was an accountant who worked as an independent auditor for film production companies. It was an unglamorous job that still provided him with a glamorous lifestyle, particularly for a pudgy, balding, forty-something accounting bore. He had a huge home in Pacific Palisades, with mountain and ocean views, but it was lonely. The women he met at the movie premieres and parties were happy to take his compliments and his drugs, but he was not someone who could help their careers, so except for an occasional one night stand, usually with an older woman, usually a Hollywood hanger-on like himself, he drove home alone in his Mercedes coup, and masturbated to pornography with women half, or much less than half, his age. In Callie, he saw an opportunity to change all that. He had only been calling out for a young whore, but what he saw was the answer to his prayers. A beautiful girl he could shape into the woman of his dreams. He soon secretly paid Ed $50,000 cash for what remained of Callie's films, including the negatives, and locked them in a home safe—she belonged to Zach now, but she did not know to what degree.

Within weeks, he hired private tutors for the girl he called a distant relation. She came to him just barely knowing how to read, but within six months she was perfectly literate, and became a voracious reader. He hired a diction coach to remove her accent—he had learned, quite by accident, that some of his more observant neighbors had been referring to Callie as his Beverly Hillbilly Whore. She only really knew how to talk, act, and look like an illiterate child from southern Alabama, so during her first few months with him, she rarely left the house. Her new education included learning how to sit properly, eat properly, drink properly, walk, talk, and dance properly. She learned yoga, how to swim, and to drive. She began to learn French. She learned how to apply makeup, but not just how to put on a specific mask—she was taught the techniques, how to achieve effects. She was taught how to dress, how to shop, how to accessorize. Zach was startled to learn in their first interview—though it was one of the things that attracted him most to her—she had seen exactly three movies on a big screen in her life: *Jaws*, *Star Wars*, and *Freaky Friday*. He grew up in Hollywood, and loved everything about the movie industry. So, whenever he could, he would take an afternoon off from work and take her to movies, focusing on the classics that were shown in small specialty cinemas around town. That task he kept for himself—he wanted her to see the industry through his eyes. Through his job, he knew the best of the best people in Hollywood, and he got them for her. Each day while he was at work, she was working, too—becoming the young woman he wanted her to be. He told her he loved her, and she believed him. And she told him she loved him in return. And in many ways, both things were true.

She never considered leaving him any more than she had considered leaving

Ed, or her father. By every standard of life she knew how to measure, her life was getting better each day. As her manners and appearance improved, Zach began gradually to take her out in public, first just for quick lunches in Santa Monica restaurants, then dinners there, eventually taking her to upscale but unpopular restaurants in Brentwood and Beverly Hills at off hours, places and times he was unlikely to run into important clients. He knew more than half of Hollywood, so the chances of them eventually running into someone he knew were high, but he knew that if he was ever going to bring her out socially, he had to help her overcome her anxiety of not being good enough, of not fitting in. At the same time, he did not want her to be overly aware of just how beautiful, or smart, or talented, she really was. So when her vocal coach suggested that she might take a public speaking course at a community college, he deliberated before deciding that was too far. That much self-confidence in someone over whom he wanted to maintain authority and control, whose dependence he was nurturing, was just going too far.

It was during this time that Callie discovered how quickly she reverted back to the Southerner who lived buried inside her after just one glass of wine. Words she had painstakingly worked to pronounce like a good Midwesterner slipped back out with a deep Southern accent. But it was not a patrician Southern accent—it was hillbilly, it was comic, even to her own ears. So she did not drink in public, and only drank at home at Zach's suggestion. On certain nights, he liked her to be a little tipsy, but her tolerance was so low that the distinction between tipsy and drunk was marked by just a few sips of wine.

In early December 1979, she asked if they were putting up a Christmas tree. It was not something her father had ever done for her, but she could remember in the most indistinct way her mother putting up one, or possibly two trees, in places she could not remember, in the years before her mother left them. The question caught him off guard. As the child of a Jewish father and vaguely-Christian mother, they had never celebrated any religious holidays in his childhood, and he had never had a reason for decorating himself—he threw no lavish parties. But he instantly said *Yes*, and hired a florist to put a tree and festoon the front of the French Provincial façade.

Underneath the tree on Christmas morning were three large boxes, one small box, and a small envelope, all for Callie. The boxes were wrapped in silver foil with large aquamarine velvet bows, and she opened them first, finding three evening gowns: Halston, Kenzo, and Sonya Rykiel. The small box contained a key to a car—a red Alfa Romeo Spider convertible parked behind the pool cabana. The envelope contained an engraved card, in French, which took her a while to decipher: *Présentez cette carte pour votre robe de couture pour les Prix de l'Académie 1980.* It was signed *Valentino* in ink, in an almost illegible script. She was able to translate the rest of the card, and determined that it entitled her to a free dress from Valentino, but stumbled on the word *couture*, because she didn't know what it meant in English, either.

But she knew what the presents meant: She was finally coming out to Hollywood society. She learned that the gowns were for the parties leading up to the Academy Awards ceremony, and the card was for a Valentino couture gown, to wear to the ceremony itself. The awards were in April, which meant she would be flying to Rome with Zach in January to select the gown and be measured for it, and there would be a final fitting at the Valentino boutique in New York in March.

She still lacked confidence in her appearance—she knew what she liked, but was unable to distinguish between trendy and truly stylish. She had an idea of who she wanted to be, but was unsure how to get there, so she asked for and received permission to use the stylist who had been working with her, to help get ready for her coming out. His name was Antoine (it was actually Anthony, but he would only answer to Antoine), and he was the only homosexual she had ever known. He fascinated her, and made her laugh. He wore ascots, and French cuffs with ludicrously fake jewels in ostentatious settings. He called everyone, including Zach, *Darling, darling*, never just one *Darling*, always the pair. In restaurants, every waiter, every busboy, every anyone whose attention he wanted, he would just call out, "Darling, darling," and someone would respond. Every salesperson in town knew him, and loved him, even when they brought out something they loved, and he said "That's simply dreadful, darling, darling," they would laugh, agree with him, disappear and return with something else, again and again, until he said "Perfect, darling, darling. Who were you saving it for?"

She had travelled internationally before many times, frequently staying at the finest hotels in Europe, the Middle East, and Asia. But she had never been to any-place like the Valentino boutique, or experienced anything like it. She felt really and truly like Cinderella. She couldn't understand any of the rapid-fire Italian spoken around her in the atelier, but she didn't need to. There were assistants who spoke English, and Valentino himself, when he briefly appeared, spoke English with a beautiful but clipped Italian accent. More than that though, his eyes read her, and spoke back to her. He didn't know who she was, but he knew what she was, and he would still make her beautiful. After brief introductions, he asked her to stand, and pronounced with finality, "Not that one, the red. With the cape."

Zach had selected the black gown that was being pinned when the couturier arrived. An assistant interjected nervously, "The gentleman selected the black. He thought it most fitting."

Valentino glanced at Zach, and dismissed the notion with a firm wave. "Most fitting for her grandmother, yes? Look at this." He gestured to her hair, glowing cinnamon and pumpkin in the sunlight filling the studio. "Red. Only red. With the cape, I think. Yes." He turned round to face the girl. "Callie, a perfect name for such a beautiful young woman. I look forward to seeing you in New York." He made a bowing gesture, and was gone.

As soon as he was out the door, there was a flurry of activity to unpin the black gown and retrieve the red. There was no question—she would have the red dress with the cape, or nothing at all.

The whirlwind of activity in January become a maelstrom by the middle of March. Antoine had more or less moved into the mansion, helping Callie prepare not just her appearance, but also smoothing out the rough edges of conversation, filling her in on the Hollywood gossip on the people she would be meeting, and most importantly, building her back story. He knew how important a good back story was—he had been thrown out of his parents' house in the suburbs of Dayton, Ohio when he was 16, and had hitchhiked and whored his way to San Francisco, where he was able to work out a backstory of his own before landing in Hollywood two years later. By then, it was a tightly woven but compact and dramatic tale at the end of which he was a poor orphan from a plantation outside of Nashville, the last of a long, great family line.

Callie questioned, "Why Nashville? Wouldn't it be easier just to say you were from a farm outside of Dayton?" and he answered without a pause, "Nobody wants to meet anybody from Dayton, darling, darling. The point of your story isn't that it is about you, or who you want to be, it's about who they want you to be. This is Hollywood, darling darling, it's all about storytelling, its lies crafted into a truth more interesting than reality. Reality is so…. Real. So boring. The colors are just never quite right. There's always some dreadful relation chewing up the scenery, muddling up the narrative. You can see that, can't you darling darling?"

"Well, I'm from Alabama," she began, before he cut her off, "No, darling darling, you are not from Alabama. There is no banjo on your knee. There are no banjos in Hollywood. No one in Hollywood is from Alabama, and no one ever will be. No, that just won't do. Never let me hear you say that again. Don't say another word. This silly little lie you and Zach dreamed up—it's pitiful. The truth is probably more interesting, but that will never do, either. We have to create you—from the time you were born until the day you showed up here…no, darling, darling, no, until today. All this training, all these lessons—they have to stop. No one speaks any more French than you do. No one cares. You're as refined and elegant as any of the private day-school girls in town, probably more so—they're so crass, so incredibly nouveau riche, their labels hanging out all over the place, their second-generation cash, but nothing worth having, really. You have something worth having, we just need to shape it up a bit. You need a story. Let's go for a walk."

It was a perfect California day—bright golden sunshine, warm but not hot, just enough humidity to feel the lushness of the place without being oppressed by it, with a gentle cleansing breeze. They took the short drive over to Will Rogers State Park in her convertible, and while walking around the stables, the lie began to develop. "Kentucky. You're from Kentucky, darling darling."

Callie laughed, "I don't know anything about Kentucky. I've never even been there."

He ignored her, continuing on down a path with great swarms of shocking pink bougainvillea reaching up to the sunshine and darting out into their path, "The Penningtons helped start the Kentucky derby. Your Louisville family goes back for generations. You're horse people."

She laughed again, "I've never even been on a horse. I know nothing about them."

He looked off into the distance at the low-rising mountain peaks, "You were thrown from a horse when you were 13, and hurt your back. You haven't been on a horse since. You can't even discuss them. It breaks your heart. They shot the horse. His name was… Euclid."

"Why Euclid?" she stopped laughing, and looked at him, genuinely interested.

"The details, darling darling, they bring the lie to life. If you're vague, they question you. If you give them details, however irrelevant, it takes them down a path. You provide the contours, the shape, and they fill in the rest, like a coloring book. But they have to have enough detail to know how to color you in."

She looked at him curiously, but said nothing.

"Even if you told them the truth, the absolute truth, you couldn't tell them everything, and they would still fill in the gaps to make you whole. They would project their idea of you onto you, and once they do that, it's impossible to erase. It's over."

They were past the bougainvillea, into a glade of eucalyptus, the smell warm and rich and filling their lungs. "Zach went to the Kentucky Derby last year with friends from New York. You met at the Founder's Cotillion."

"Zach will never go along with this. Has he ever been to Kentucky? Is there a Founder's Cotillion?"

"Zach will go along. And there's always a cotillion."

"What is a cotillion, anyway?"

"I think it's just a party where southern belles put on hoop skirts and get drunk. But no one will ask. No one cares. They will picture some scene from *Gone With the Wind* with you in the middle, and that will be the end of it, darling darling."

The distant hum of bees filled the air in his pause, longer than before.

He began again, as though he had not been interrupted, "He was unlike any man you had ever met. I don't think there are any Jews in Louisville. There can't be that many, anyway, and certainly not in your family's clubs. He swept you off your feet. You never really fit in in Louisville, you were always different. This is where you connect with everyone—the Hollywood dream. Hollywood is filled with America's rejects. Your family has cut you off without a dime, but you love Zach, so when he asked you to come live with him, you said *yes*, instantly, and here you are, and fuck your family, fuck Louisville, fuck all. You found your ticket to the Hollywood dream—his name is Zach. And you love him for that, if nothing else."

"Do I have to love him? Do I have to say that?" She was a little frightened by the thought. She had said it before, but had meant nothing more than *I love being able to eat*, and *I love the things you do for me*. What Antoine was suggesting was quite different, she knew. Her relationship with Zach was fun and friendly, but besides the sex, which was actually quite infrequent, relative to her recent past, she had never thought of him romantically. Indeed, she had not really thought about him at all—she appreciated what he had done for her, but he was just one of a series of men who had been in control of her life in one way or another. She had never been asked to say she loved one before—at least, not for real.

"Oh yes, darling darling. You have to say it. And you have to believe it. You have to do it. You have to love him. That's the detail, the truth, that makes the lie complete. Everyone will probably know, or at least suspect, the rest is lies, but if you can get them to believe that part, they will be willing to believe the rest. Or at least pretend to, and that's all that matters." He stopped, and took her by the arm. "Tell me."

She screwed up her face into a serious, loving, innocent look, and whispered, "I love you," then burst out giggling.

"Not me, darling darling. Say you love him. Say it, and mean it." He was laughing, but trying not to. They each made a concerted, modestly successful effort to be serious.

"I love Zach. We have a perfect life together here." She was able to say it without laughing. It felt strange.

"Not bad, darling darling, but keep at it. Practice in the mirror when you're putting on your makeup in the morning, when you're taking it off at night, when you go take a piss. Watch your mouth. Watch your eyes—they'll give you away every time."

They walked on a bit, the path taking a sharp turn uphill, into giant cedars with long, low branches spreading out under a dense canopy of mottled green bristles. "That's enough, I think."

"Really?" she asked back, in some surprise.

"Oh, yes. We'll keep working on it, but really, the trick is to be more interested in them than they are in you—which isn't hard, because most of them aren't really interested in you at all. Ask about anything—their clothes, their shoes, their hair, their work—they would all rather talk about themselves than about you."

"Speaking of which, how was your date with that stunt double last night? I noticed you didn't make it back home til this morning."

He laughed. "That's my girl. You are a quick learner. He was amazing, darling darling…." Antoine launched into a story about his adventures the night before as they walked a low, rambling path through the park. After a few minutes, he paused in the story to ask her, "What was he wearing?"

"Who?" she asked.

"My date last night, Eric. What was he wearing?"

"Jeans and a denim jacket? Cowboy boots?" It was a guess. She couldn't remember exactly what he said the man was wearing.

"He was wearing ass-less leather chaps and a jockstrap. I never said what he was wearing—just that we were at a gay bar called *Cowboys*. You filled in the part I left out. That's how it works. Memory—it's tricky."

She laughed. "Okay. Do you think Zach would wear ass-less leather chaps?"

"We should find out," Antoine responded, with a smile, "but not tonight. Tonight we need to introduce Zach to *The Callie Pennington Story*. I think he'll like it, darling darling."

He did like it. As they sat having coffee and desert after dinner that evening, he also agreed that the intensive lessons could end, at which point Antoine exclaimed with his arms thrown wide above his head, "Eliza Doolittle, you're a duchess now, darling darling!"

Zach laughed, but Callie questioned back, "What? Who?"

Antoine's arms fell down with a dramatic sigh. Zach stopped laughing, stuck his fork into a serving of crème caramel with raspberries, and said with bemused exasperation as he raised the fork to his mouth, "*My Fair Lady*, 1964, nominated for 12, won eight Academy Awards, one of the most expensive musicals ever. Over the top, fabulous, we'll see it next week. You may even feel some special connection to one of the characters."

***

Without her tutor to guide her reading, her supply of books dwindled quickly. Zach had a small home office, which he called a study, because he never used it as an office—the massive ledger books were too cumbersome and heavy to carry back and forth to the office. If he needed to do actual accounting, which was rare—he mostly made the deals, and oversaw a small army of C.P.A.s who did the rigorous daily bookkeeping—he went to the office in Brentwood like everyone else. But his accounting textbooks from college were there on a generally neglected bookshelf, and one day, out of sheer boredom, she took one down. At first it made no sense to her at all, but then she realized it was an advanced text, and she looked for and found an introductory level book. Over the course of the next few weeks, in between yoga and movie matinees, she taught herself not only how accounting works, but why. She read deeply, going back into accounting theory, with works by James H. Rand Jr., J. Brooks Heckert, Keith Powlison, Warren G. Bailey and Howard Greer, some of which were only referenced in Zach's textbooks, and which she had to go to the library to find. Many of them were out of print, or were only articles in journals and business magazines going back to the turn of the century.

She peppered Zach with questions as soon as he walked in the door each day, and he was both amused and bewildered. That this young woman—child, really—could or would express any interest in accounting, much less sustain it over a period of weeks, boggled his mind, until one evening when he stretched his memory back to his own life at her age, and recalled his brief experimentation with bisexuality while he was a student at UCLA. He hadn't touched a man since, and the remembrance of it sent chills down his spine, but when he was 17 and drunk it seemed like a perfectly right and natural thing to do. He hadn't thought of it in years. He hoped she would never regret her pursuit of accounting as much as he regretted his sole, drunken, collegiate interest in sex with men.

He was pleased, at least, that he could answer most of her questions. Not all, but nearly all. Some of the obscure topics she asked questions about he had never studied at all, or at best parenthetically, as historical asides to contemporary practices. But he reasoned that there were few, if any, accountants in town not lecturing at university who would be able to spontaneously respond to her questions with any accuracy. And he knew for a fact that none at his firm could—they were mostly men with calculators where their brains should have been. They could determine with precision the effect of the most miniscule variances in rates of return and expenditures off the tops of their heads, but ask them for directions to La Jolla, and you might end up in Portland, or Nashville.

He was also pleased that it gave the two of them something to discuss, besides movies, which she seemed to have no real interest in. The famous people he knew and fabulous parties he had attended likewise held little interest for her—they were so abstract, so unlike anything she had experienced herself, that they were no more real to her than the movies he loved so much. She had travelled the world—more than he had, in fact—but as a whore, and he didn't like hearing about those days, and didn't want her in the habit of discussing her prior life. She didn't like talking about life before Ed took her away from Alabama, so the scope of her life available for easy discussion was really limited to her time with him—which he knew about. He had lived his entire life in or near Los Angeles, and had never been married or had any sort of real relationship with a woman. They had little to learn about one another, that the other wanted to know, and accounting provided a diversion.

It was during this time that Callie first began to think about herself as a person, to understand what an identity was, and what hers was. Having been robbed of the opportunity to have any sort of a traditional childhood, with very little interaction with other children, and having watched no one grow from childhood to adolescence, or adolescence into adulthood, it was in films and books that she first began to understand that children weren't always children, and adults weren't always, or at least hadn't always been, adults. No one had ever asked her what she wanted to be when she grew up, and it wasn't a concept she had ever considered. Even now, Zach was training her to be someone he wanted her to be—she understood that, with some guidance from Antoine. Distanced from the very real physical dangers of her past, and introduced to the idea that she would one day be something, she began to consider what it would be. And like teenagers everywhere, when she came up with answers, they were usually unsatisfactory, or implausible. She had never developed a secret fantasy life—never projected herself onto stage or screen or college graduation or the altar, or into a book or song, and she did not begin now.

Accounting, Antoine and the Academy Awards were enough to keep her busy.

Life for Callie seemed almost perfect in the weeks leading up to the Awards ceremony, full of seamless, careless days of yoga, salons, shopping, and sitting by the slate pool under an umbrella while Antoine lay baking in the sun, covered in baby oil. The first event Zach took her to was a political luncheon where businessmen and their wives, and a scattering of women executives and minor celebrities, ate cashew chicken, drank white wine, and vowed to end homelessness in Los Angeles. Callie was flawless—she never went off script, primarily by not saying much at all, and following Antoine's advice to ask questions. She wore a white silk Norma Kamali jumpsuit with the collar turned up, belted with multicolored silk cords. She wore flat white strap sandals, and just enough makeup to make her look old enough to be there. She kept in constant physical contact with Zach—just a hand, an arm, nothing too over the top, as Antoine suggested—so there would be no awkward questions: Everyone knew that she was Zach's—and not his daughter.

The first evening event she attended was a celebration of Oscar nominations at the home of one of the film's producers. It was a relatively subdued, mostly business affair. She wore the Sonia Rykiel—a black knit minidress with long sleeves. She accessorized with an old red silk handkerchief of Zach's knotted at her throat, and plum-colored suede knee-high boots. Her makeup was more adventurous than before—not quite on the cutting edge of fashion, but bold. She was the perfect picture of young Hollywood.

But young Hollywood had no idea who she was, and they buzzed and swarmed like locusts when she walked in the door with Zach. The other young women in attendance—and there were several her age, or even younger—recognized her as competition immediately, and for about half the evening made subtle inquiries around the room as to who she was, where she was from, how long she had been with Zach. Their collective wisdom, shared over coffee after the light outdoor supper of roasted salmon, revealed to them that she was nothing, that no one anyone knew anything about, and they conspired to get the truth.

Leslie, a young woman of about 20 whose father owned the house and was throwing the party, was the most entitled to encroach upon and separate Callie from Zach. When she found them, Zach was talking numbers with a group of other men, with Callie listening on in real interest, but Leslie was able to take Callie hostage by insisting that she must be bored, and that any girl in her right mind would prefer a tour of the home, which Leslie knew she could not have ever seen. The father of the house, unaware of the plot, and seeing in his daughter an unusual desire to be hospitable to his guests, encouraged their departure with a drunken gesture, and a "Go, go, by all means, take her and make her feel welcome."

Callie's grasp on Zach's arm tightened, and for about half a minute she stood firm in opposition to going, but when he gently detached her arm from his, and said "Go, have a good time," she knew she must submit. She was uneasy, but with no prior knowledge of girls—particularly this intelligent, cunning, world-weary-at-a-tender-age sort, raised in wealth, privilege, ease, and dissipation, with no real regard for anyone other than themselves—she was wholly unprepared for the trap laid for her. It was not the sort of thing that would have ever entered her mind, as even a vague possibility. Used to, and trained to, keep to herself, and mind her own business, the idea that people would ever try to maliciously interest themselves in her life never seemed real to her—despite Antoine's assurances that, despite the human race's general self-interest, it would happen sooner or later.

She expressed admiration when called upon to do so as they passed through the dining room, the screening room, the library, and on through the public down-stairs rooms. It was larger and she supposed more impressive than where she lived with Zach, but in her travels with Ed, she had seen larger and more opulent—she had literally spent the night in castles before, in the beds of royalty. So the display of wealth Leslie meant to impress upon her made less of an impression than anticipated. Still, it was only a prelude of the tour upstairs, which ended in Leslie's room, where they discovered to Callie's surprise, but not Leslie's, a group of Leslie's friends passing around a pipe emitting the sharp acrid scent of marijuana and a haze of smoke that was beginning to fill the room.

"Ladies!" Leslie voiced mock astonishment and admonition. "Are you trying to get me grounded? At least open a window. I have a trip to Monaco in two weeks. Goddamit."

"We tried, it wouldn't budge," slurred a girl with giant brunette curls, sitting on the floor with her back against the bed, a stuffed penguin wedged between her and a nightstand, which, like the rest of the furniture, was an oversized Rococo reproduction painted white with an abundance of gilding and ormolu flourishes. The rest of the room was awash in powder pink—the carpet, the walls, the ceiling, the bedspread, the upholstery on the armchairs, and the pleated draperies, which Leslie parted to throw open the French doors to the narrow balcony overlooking the front drive. The bed was covered with dozens of dolls and stuffed animals of various sizes, arranged neatly in rows, and sitting upright—the obvious work of a housekeeper. Callie wanted nothing more than to crawl into the penguin's vacant spot near the headboard and disappear.

Two other girls were sitting on the bed, and a fourth sat on a pink tufted pouffe at a low vanity table, scrutinizing her appearance in each of the three mirrors, and adjusting the two side mirrors so she could see both herself and the girls behind her.

"Girls, this is Callie, Zach Duncan's new girlfriend." She introduced each of the girls, and Callie, in fear of not remembering them, immediately forgot all their names. It felt like the first time she had gone through international customs with Ed—she hoped, that like then, all of the preparation would be for nothing. But she was wrong.

After Callie declined a hit from the pipe, Leslie motioned to one of the pink tufted Fauteuil chairs and said, "Sit, it will be at least half an hour before that horrible jazz combo shuts up and the DJ gets the dance floor going." Callie sat, and she couldn't help shaking.

One of the girls from the bed opened the bottom drawer of the nightstand and pulled out a bottle of champagne—"Callie, you have to have a drink. You can't

162

be the only one not drinking. Leslie, do you have any glasses up here?"

"I really shouldn't. Zach hates it when I drink," Callie protested. She tried to sound firm, but her habit of submission was obvious.

Leslie laughed and said "He told you to have fun. If he hadn't meant for you to drink, he wouldn't have brought you. That's what these parties are for."

"But it makes me kind of sick," Callie answered with the vague idea of inspiring some sort of sympathy in the girls.

"Me, too," slurred the girl on the floor, and pulled a small beaded bag from under the bedskirt, which she fumbled around in before pulling out a blue tablet. "Here, take one of these." Callie ignored her outstretched hand, and it slumped to the floor.

Leslie disappeared into a bathroom and returned with a ceramic cup, and filled it with champagne. She took the blue tablet from the girl's lifeless hand and held it out for Callie. "Welcome to the party, Callie," she said with a smile that was all perfectly aligned, perfectly white teeth. Everything about the girl made Callie nervous, but she felt trapped.

"What is it?" Callie asked, knowing that she wouldn't know what it meant when they told her. Zach took probably 40 pills a day, all sizes, shapes, and colors, and she had never bothered to ask what each of them did. She knew she would have to take it—she was just buying time.

"It's valium. It's like, for nerves, and it totally helps keep the champagne down."

"Totally," echoed the girls on the bed in unison. The girl on the floor appeared to move her lips, but no sound emerged.

Unable to endure the smiling girl standing before her with the pill and the cup full of champagne, Callie took the pill and swallowed about half the champagne. Leslie exchanged a smile with the girls on the bed as she sat in the other chair.

"The champagne tastes funny," Callie remarked, and Leslie laughed, "Oh, sorry, probably some toothpaste in the bottom." It was a crushed valium in the bottom, in case Callie refused the pill. "I'm going to have to talk to daddy about Anna Maria.

She has got to be, like, the worst housekeeper in Beverly Hills. Whenever I ask her to do something, she's all like, *No se,* like she doesn't speak fucking English. Fucking Mexican bitch. But enough about her. Tell us, Callie," and the questioning began. At first it was questions she had rehearsed a hundred times with Antoine—*Where are you from? Where did you go to school? How old are you? How did you meet Zach?*

But as the valium began to have its softening effect, the questioning became more pointed. *What airline did you and Zach fly in on? When did you graduate high school? What does your father do? With what firm? Where did he go to school? Where is your mother from? What was her name? What neighborhood in Louisville? Did you ride English? Who was your trainer? Do you know…..*

The increasingly intensive questioning did not end until Callie appeared to pass out. After a repeated chorus of "Fuck," "Fuck," "Fuck, fuck, fuck," from the girls, the two on the bed got on each side of her and attempted to rouse her from the chair while Leslie got water from the bathroom. Callie jerked awake once she was upright, and sprayed an almost cinematic volume of vomit over the bedspread and army of dolls and animals facing her, then she collapsed to the floor, her knit dress almost to her waist. The girls could not rouse her. Half an hour later, the smell of sushi and vomit overwhelming her, Leslie finally went to find Zach to let him know Callie wasn't feeling well. The other girls had found their way downstairs, where the DJ had finally begun playing Blondie, and the dance floor was full.

Getting her out of the house without causing a major scene had been much less problematic than he could have imagined. Zach carried her down a back stairway, out through the kitchen where caterers scurried out of his way, and into the car, where the valet stood waiting with the passenger door open for him. Zach had to stop twice on the way home, when Callie momentarily gained consciousness and looked as though she might be sick, but both times were false alarms.

He wasn't as angry as he was embarrassed—not so much by her behavior, as by his own expectations. He should never have let her out of his sight, he realized in retrospect, and he did not like making mistakes—especially one as easily foreseeable as this. He was more concerned about what she might have said to the girls before she passed out. When they got to his house, he fixed her a carafe of water and left her, in her ruined dress and boots, in a lawn chair by the pool—he didn't want her messing up the house if she got sick again during the night. And after all, he reasoned, it was a gorgeous night out. He went back to the party.

When Antoine arrived at 4:00am, he put a blanket over her, pulled a lawn chair up next to hers, drank some of her water, and whispered "Darling, darling, what is ever going to become of you?" before looking up into the star-filled sky for just an instant before he passed out himself.

***

"You two look like hell." Zach didn't bother pretending he spent the night at home. He was still wearing what he wore to the party, with the addition of sunglasses. It was 7:30am.

"Is there some reason we're sleeping out here? What did we do last night?" Antoine asked as he slowly stirred, with no recollection at all of the night before. "Where's my car, darling darling?" And then, seeing Zach was still in his clothes from the night before, he added, "And where have you been?"

"We weren't with you last night. Last night was the big party you've been helping Callie get ready for, remember? Apparently you forgot the part about not taking candy from strangers."

"Oh my." Antoine sat up fully and looked at Callie. There were faint crusty tracks on her face from the night before. "Well, darling darling, at least we know she'll make a lovely corpse." He looked away from the girl with a sigh. "Is there grapefruit juice? I need a refresh."

When Callie woke several hours later, Antoine was stretched out beside her, glistening in oil and a tiny Pierre Cardin racing swimsuit, maroon with white and blue vertical stripes. Air Supply was playing on the radio.

It took her several minutes to rouse into consciousness. She tried not to move, and did not want to open her eyes until she could remember where she was, how she got there. After several nonproductive minutes searching her memory, she gave up, opened her eyes and saw Antoine. "No more parties for me, I'm guessing?" she asked tentatively, her throat raw, her voice scratchy.

"I don't think you're getting off the hook that easy, darling darling. Have some water."

The next few days were spent recovering, repairing, reviewing, revising, and rehearsing. The backstory had not been good enough, the preparation not strong enough, but most of all, the actress had been overestimated in her role. Zach and Antoine both felt it, but without retrenching entirely, there was little choice but to move forward. Either she would be the amazing new Callie Pennington from Kentucky, or she would not. Zach was not content to have a beautiful bookworm sitting home waiting for him—he wanted a beautiful, young, smart, talented trophy wife. It's what he had paid for—so, the show must go on, however uncertain.

The next big event was the week before the awards, a huge affair sponsored by the International Press Foundation, a literal who's who of Hollywood, held at the Los Angeles County Museum of Art. They briefly attempted getting Antoine invited so he could chaperone Callie in Zach's absence—it wasn't entirely unheard of for a girl her age to be inseparable from her gay boyfriend—but in the end, it couldn't be managed. Zach just wasn't that important, Callie was nobody, and Antoine was just some trade technician.

It was almost a certainty that the girls from Leslie's bedroom would all be there, and what sort of mischief they might get up to was a complete unknown. But that they could, and would, was also considered almost certain. The girls' own bad behavior would make them that much more willing to have done with Callie once and for all—her downfall would vindicate their cruelty. If they could make her disappear, then she had never belonged. Everyone felt it, except Callie, who had no practice in the sort of domestic warfare she appeared to be engaged in.

The Halston was a long, flowing, black jersey evening gown, entirely backless, with a plunging neckline barely supported by Callie's modest breasts. It ensured that if nothing else, Callie would sit and stand up straight all night. Dancing was out of the question. Antoine convinced Zach that Callie must wear heels, regardless of how much she would tower over him. If he wanted a statuesque beauty, he had to let her be statuesque. And she was.

The evening began perfectly. Callie was young, beautiful, and radiant, and Hollywood loves anything young, beautiful, and radiant. Zach had vowed not to leave her side, so she felt a confidence going into the evening that she could not have imagined the morning after the previous disaster. Even when she saw Leslie approaching, she felt only momentary terror. Leslie though, was perfectly charming. She asked with apparent sincerity if Callie was feeling better, waved her mumbled apologies away, and introduced her date, the son of another industry executive. Everyone told each other how wonderful they looked, and that they hoped they would run into them later in the evening, then smiles and goodbyes all around. Everyone was loving being beautiful and rich, and being with everyone who was beautiful and rich. The masterpieces of art hanging on the walls were mere background scenery—no one was looking at it, no one cared. The night was about the people, and the only art that received even momentary consideration was that framed in glass, which gave the viewers the most cherished view of all—their reflections.

As the evening passed, Zach's pride and confidence in Callie grew. The important introductions he had been considering waiting to make at a later date he went ahead and made—titans of industry were delighted to meet this beautiful young girl, of whom they knew nothing, and asked nothing. She was gracious and demure, self-effacing without self-deprecation, the playful innocence of a schoolgirl in the body and trappings of a woman. Within an hour or arriving, she had even laughed at a joke. The energy of the evening—the sound and flash of the paparazzi filtered in through the open doors—was contagious, even to her. She felt for the first time that she was part of something special. She felt alive. She relaxed, and became the girl she was when she was alone with Antoine. Flirty, almost coquettish, with an entirely natural charm, Zach watched her becoming the girl he had pictured when she showed up in his office over a year before. This might actually work, he thought, for the first time in a long time.

When they were invited to the home of a popular producer for an after-party, he knew it to be largely because of Callie. He would never have been invited on his own. But he accepted graciously, almost eagerly. The invitations he received in Hollywood were because of what he was, not who he was, and those invitations were limited, almost a formality of doing business, the protocol and etiquette of the film industry, which went only so far. The doors of the after-hours crowd had been largely closed to him. He could see now how Callie might change all that.

Callie, though, was growing tired. She was wearing the highest heels she had ever worn for the longest she had ever worn heels, and on the unforgiving stone and cement floors of the museum. She had smiled the most she had ever smiled, and while having fun, had also been on high alert all evening, waiting for whatever was going to go wrong to go wrong, though nothing had. Zach was happier than she had ever seen him, glowing more than she was, by far. He could see all that, as well as her desire to go home, take off her heels, and snuggle up with a book. And he knew how to fix it.

When the rented limousine pulled around to pick them up, he gave the driver instructions not to the address of the party they had been given, but to Cowboys.

"Cowboys? The gay bar?" Callie was confused on every level she knew to be confused on.

"Yes, the gay bar. I need to talk to Antoine."

"Why? Is he coming with us?"

"No, of course not. You'll see. Besides, we can't just show up now. The host may not even be there yet. We can't be the first ones there." He turned to look at her. "Have you ever been to a gay bar?"

She lowered her voice in playful confidence, so the driver couldn't hear, "I've never even been to a bar, silly. You do remember how old I am, right?" He laughed at her whispering.

"Driver, do we exist?"

"I am in this car alone," called a voice from the front of the car, speaking for the first time that evening, and a window slid up electronically between them and the driver.

The bar was only a half-mile away the museum, though on a much less well-lit and well-travelled street. The front of the bar was nondescript, with no window, and no sign—just the street number under an inexpensive Colonial-style exterior porch light, not unlike one from a Sears catalog. The only thing that distinguished the building at all from the rest of the buildings on the shabby block was the number of cowboys in various states of dress and undress lingering out front, wandering to and fro around the corner to the dark lane behind the building. It was a busy night.

Zach hesitated before getting out, saying "Why don't you wait here. I may be a few minutes."

Callie laughed out loud, "Are you kidding? I've never seen ass-less chaps before. This may be my only chance."

"You're probably going to be the only girl in there. I don't even know if they'll let you in."

"If they'll let you in, they'll let me in." She followed him out of the car, and she was right—they were both let in, but only after they told the doorman they were looking for their friend Antoine.

The interior was made to look like the inside of a barn—probably more like a barn than most barns, from what Callie could remember of the few she had seen—and none of those had the Village People playing at a volume that made even thinking difficult. There were wagon wheels and saddles and coils of rope everywhere, and bales of hay, and hay strewn on the floor. The only light in the entire place came from scattered antique lanterns with dimmed chandelier bulbs in them. The street outside had been dark, but compared to the interior, it could have been broad daylight. It took several minutes for their eyes to adjust and find

Antoine, which they were only able to do because he was sitting at the bar, which had just enough light for the bartender to be able to function.

Callie snuck up behind him and covered his eyes before asking "Guess whoooo?"

"With all that Chanel No. 5, it must be Roger." He spun the barstool round, rolling his eyes as he did, "Darling darling, what are you doing here? I can't believe they let you in—there's a strict no-fragrance policy. Maybe they have an exception for actual women."

One of the men he had been in conversation with at the bar had spun round and was goggling at her animatedly, and broke in "This must be she. Is it she? It is she. But you're all wrong, love, it's not Rita Hayworth, it's Maureen O'Hara. That's the look. That's who she is. Hayworth had that giant nose. This specimen is just divine. I could eat you alive. Antoine's been going on about you for months. So lovely to meet you. I'm Rutherford."

Rutherford extended his hand, completely nonplussed by the fact that he was wearing only a leather harness, a leather jockstrap, and boots. Callie laughed, introduced herself, and stood aside to introduce Zach, who, in his tuxedo, was getting his own share of attention.

"Rutherford, could you keep Callie company while I have a few words with Antoine? But whatever you do, do not let her have anything to drink. And no candy."

"Of course love, she's in good hands. I'm a hand model, you know." He held up his hands, which were, Callie could see, remarkably beautiful, even in the near darkness.

"Is that a full-time job?" Callie asked as she sat down, and the other two men walked away. Callie spent the next half-hour learning about the many various films and television commercials Rutherford's hands had appeared in.

Forty-five minutes after they left, Zach and Antoine returned, and ushered Callie and Rutherford to a dingy bathroom meant for one, which all four crammed into. Callie kept her gown hiked up with one hand because she was scared of what might be on the floor, which she couldn't see at all.

"What are we doing in here?" she giggled as they closed the door behind them.

"Blow darling darling, we're doing blow," Antoine answered. "But not a lot. Not for you, anyway."

"Is that why we came here? To get blow? Did we get it?" Callie wasn't upset, she was just confused, and a little curious. She had no way of recognizing the tell-tale signs of a drug deal going down—the private conversation, the pay phone call, the stranger showing up 20 minutes later and having a brief, close conversation with the two men before disappearing out the door again. Everyone else in the bar paying any attention at all knew, but not her. She had never had any cocaine, in any event. Whenever she had been drugged, which she had been with Ed many times—many more than she could know or even guess—it had always been with depressants to make her more pliable, more patient in the hours the men would sometimes take with her.

"There are other places we could have gone, but this seemed to make the most sense. Thank you, Antoine," Zach answered as he unscrewed a black plastic lid from a slender brown glass vial almost the size of Callie's small finger. He fished his keys out of his coat pocket, and used one of them to gently scoop out a small mound of white pounder. "OK, Callie, watch Antoine."

Callie watched as Antoine closed his left nostril with the index finger of his left hand and Zach gingerly raised the key to his right nostril. With one quick snort, the small mound disappeared. Antoine threw his head back and flexed his shoulders. "Thank you, darling darling. Oh, this is fantastic. Bulk buyers always get the best stuff. Carlos would never sell this to me."

"Rutherford, you next," Zach said as he repeated the gesture with the key. Callie watched as a shiver seemed to travel through Rutherford's whole body—most of which she could see, and which Zach was making significant and unsuccessful efforts not to see.

"Now you, Callie."

Callie was less nervous about the effect the drugs would have on her as she was that she would embarrass herself in front of the men. She hadn't sneezed all evening, but as her eyes crossed to keep focus on the small mound of white powder approaching her face, and she increased the pressure on her left nostril, she felt an incredible desire to sneeze, or at least exhale.

She needn't have worried. The delicate white powder flew up her nose without a trace, and she closed her eyes.

The effect was instantaneous, and marvelous. A crystalline clarity spread through her face and head, travelled down her body, through her shoulders, into her pelvis, and down into her toes. She felt like she was waking up for the first time in her life. The sensation of being at the absolute center of the universe overwhelmed her. She gently moved each part of her body, beginning with her head and working down, feeling the electricity move through the contours of her body. Parts of her were coming alive that she had never felt before. She wanted to linger on each sensation.

"Callie, everything all right in there?" Zach asked.

"You have to breathe, darling darling." Antoine suggested.

She opened her eyes and looked at the three men, exhaling as she did so, a little breathless.

"Yeah, everything's allright." Callie answered. "It's perfect." The dim lights in the bathroom seemed brighter, the men's faces brought into sharper focus, their eyes sparkled, their lips so close to hers in the cramped small room.

Zach helped himself to a heaping mound of the powder, in each nostril. "Again?" he asked Antoine, and then Rutherford, without much fear of opposition. There was none.

When he came to Callie, she nodded, and he asked, "Are you sure?"

"Of course I'm sure. This is amazing." She had no hesitation.

"Okay then," he answered. "Other side. But this is it for a while."

172

The experience repeated and amplified the previous one, expanding to her limits of physical sensation. She let go of her gown, and it dropped to the floor. She grasped Rutherford's bare upper arm with her hand, and felt the warmth pounding through him. She looked at his chest, and it was glistening in the dim light. She wanted to touch it, to rub her hands against his chest, feel the coarse hair there, but she looked away instead. Where before she had seen nothing in the darkness, she could clearly see the corners of the bathroom, where black walls met black ceiling and black floor in near darkness. She watched Zach take his two hits from the key, and she wanted to wrap herself around him, to press her warm flesh against his, to melt into him. They all stood in silence for a minute, maybe two, letting the almost-pure cocaine serge through their bodies. They might have stayed there for hours, or all night, if not for a pounding on the bathroom door. They gathered themselves together, and left the bathroom. Donna Summer's *On the Radio* filled them as they worked their way back to the bar.

A look from the bartender told them it was time to go.

As they parted on the sidewalk, Zach and Callie headed to the limousine, Antoine and Rutherford to the well-worn path behind the bar, Antoine said "Careful, you two. Especially you, Callie. Take it slow tonight. You're gonna be running with the big dogs, darling darling."

"We will," Zach and Callie said in unison, and both smiled. As the two men turned and walked around the corner of the building, Zach and Callie looked at each other, reading something dangerous but uncertain in each other's eyes. Callie wanted to follow the two men—to see what they did, to be part of it, to abandon herself completely to whatever she could. Zach wanted to take her back behind the building, shove her up against the wall, lift up her skirt, and have her right there, with all the men watching, the men wanting it to be them he was pounding into the rough brick. They were both within a breath of saying something, but the moment passed, they got into the waiting open door, and the driver shut it behind them without saying a word.

Zach gave the driver the address—it was a 20 minute drive. "Could we get a little privacy back here?" he called in a jocular but serious tone, and the window went up again. Some indeterminate light jazz music began playing a little too loudly. And almost without warning, Callie's hand was on him, reaching down for him, grabbing him, in a way that told him everything before with her had been a lie, a fake, a show. She had never wanted him before, but she did now. She buried her face in his neck, licked him from the tip of his collar to his ear lobe. He gently pushed her back—he didn't want to deny her anything, especially this, this thing that he wanted more than almost anything, but not anything. He wanted Hollywood. He wanted to be at that party. But at the same time he wanted to be home with her. She took the hand that had pushed her away and put it beneath the halter of her dress, on her bare breast, cupped her hand over his hand, bent to him. He knew that if he wanted to, he could take her, right there, right then, in the car, any way he wanted. She wouldn't say no. She couldn't say no—he could feel it through her skin, see it in her eyes. *Yes, yes, yes.* Her vocabulary in that instant was reduced to the single, emphatic, infinite affirmative. For her there was no future, no past, no party, no Hollywood, just that primal urge to be, to really truly be.

"You're going to mess up your makeup, sweetheart," he said, pulling his hand from her blouse.

His voice in that moment was so disconnected from the moment itself, it put her immediately in mind of one of the foreign films they sometimes watched where the dialogue was dubbed poorly, running out of sequence with the images on the screen. She was disoriented, lost—she forgot for a moment where she was, who she was with, what day and time it was. It was as though the synchronicity they had shared for a minute, maybe two, had been purposefully, savagely, severed, leaving her alone again in the world. She could feel him softening in her grasp, the light summer-weight wool of his tuxedo pants disclosing without the possibility of contradiction that the moment had passed.

She sat back in the tufted vinyl seat, exhaled, and asked for a cigarette.

"I don't smoke, Callie. You know that. Neither do you."

"I need something." She needed to do something bad, something dangerous. Of all the things that went through her mind, a cigarette, somehow, seemed the most reasonable. "Would you rather me ask the driver to come back here and fuck me?"

The question caught Zach off guard. Her tone was absolutely neutral. He turned to look at her. He couldn't tell if she was joking. He wasn't sure whether or not she knew if she was joking. He reached forward and tapped on the glass, which went down halfway. "Could you spare a smoke for the young lady?" Zach asked.

"Anything she needs" was the driver's reply, and he handed back a cigarette and a book of matches.

This sounds like some goddam porno, Zach thought as he handed Callie the cigarette and lit it for her. *This has got to stop.*

"That'll be all," he said in the direction of the driver, and the window slid back up.

"Callie, look," he said, watching as she began inhaling the cigarette, remarkably without choking or even coughing, "I'm glad you're having fun, but let's turn it down a notch or two. These parties can get a little rowdy. Remember—you're with me. Let's stick together, just like we did at the museum. We're perfect together. We're a hit. Let's keep it that way. Remember what happened the last time I let you slip away."

The last time you sent me away, she thought, but she only said, "Okay." She wished she could remember what the driver looked like, but she had no idea. *Maybe he will be the one*, she thought, and just as quickly, *Which one?* The idea of a knight in shining armor was not a fantasy she had ever indulged in. The idea of being rescued from her life—any of her lives—had just never occurred to her. But here it was. She couldn't decide if it was Ed or Zach who had started the idea in her, but it had never been a conscious thought until just that moment, that she should be on the lookout for some him. Some him who would save her from….. what? She had

175

everything, or at least something worth having, which hadn't always been true. She didn't know what she was missing, but she knew what she wanted. She wanted more.

They rode in silence until they arrived at the towering stucco fence surrounding the estate where the party was being held.

"Your name's not on the list, Mr. Duncan," the driver called back apologetically to them from the barely-parted window.

In an impulse she regretted almost as soon as it was over, she called back "Ask for Callie," before Zach could speak. In less than a minute, the massive iron gates rolled back, and the car passed through.

She thought he would be angry, but he only laughed. "So I'm here with Callie, tonight. And I'm glad."

She smiled back at him. "Should we do some more, before we go in?"

It took him a minute to register she was asking for more cocaine. "Are you sure? It hasn't even been that long."

"I'm a big girl. I can handle it." She smiled, teasing. It was so uncustomary a gesture it took him by surprise. This naughty seductress, whoever she was, he had never met.

"Okay, but this is it for a while," he said for the second time in less than an hour. He gave her two small bumps, and gave himself four larger ones, as the car rolled to a stop and the driver opened the door for them. The sounds of Olivia Newton John's *Xanadu* were pouring from the open windows of the old-Mexico-style adobe mansion with terraces leading off of terraces filled with potted plants, spilling into the lush grounds with stylized gardens and fountains, all twinkling with party lights. People were everywhere, laughing, shouting to be heard over the music.

The party was more than raucous. It was pandemonium, planned to exceed excessive, a long list of superlatives to be remembered throughout the coming weeks and months—biggest, best, wildest, chicest, most expensive, and on and on. The theme, which only the host seemed to have prior knowledge of, was Arabian Nights. Giant striped tents filled with pillows and hookahs were scattered on the

176

lawn. Waiters and waitresses wearing gauzy, transparent high-wasted sarouel pants in the style of Aladdin, and little or nothing more, moved through the rooms and grounds carrying trays of champagne, vodka, and some strange spicy Middle Eastern drink no one seemed to be drinking.

The host, whose name Callie had to be reminded was Nick, had changed from his tuxedo into his own sarouel pants, but black velvet, with a matching jacket, unbuttoned, and nothing else. A collection of gold chains and medallions were nested in the tufts of black hair poking from under the jacket. He greeted them at the door and welcomed them extravagantly, with a bow and a rolling flourish of his arms. He was attended by two women dressed in their best *I Dream of Jeannie* harem ensembles, one of them holding a cordless phone, the other a notebook that apparently held the guest list.

As he rose from his bow, he stepped up to Callie and said with a grin, "I think you have a little something on your nose," and before she could react, he licked some white powder from the tip of her nose. "Delicious. All better now," he laughed, "Come in, have a drink, show yourselves around," and he disappeared into the dining room, where giant platters and pyramids of food stood untouched by the dozens of people clustered in the room. They followed him there, where Zach recognized some people, who were waving him over. He and Callie began the after-party much as they had the museum party, with meaningless and forgotten introductions, happy-all-around great-to-meet-you's. Callie was having a little trouble speaking, the little she did speak, but so were most of the people there, so it was neither especially noticeable nor remarkable when it was noticed. The carefree exchange of drugs—pills, powder, and joints—was open and unapologetic. A man she had never met asked for permission to run his finger down her bare spine—he was Los Angeles' most successful orthopedic surgeon—and he pronounced it perfect, and beautiful, and allowed his hand to rest in the small of her back for just a little too long, as Zach looked on approvingly. While they were in the study with a group of models admiring a recently acquired Chagall circus painting, an extremely blonde and extremely tan woman Callie had never seen walked up to Zach, pressed her lamé-covered bosom into his chest, whispered something in his ear, and grabbed his crotch, rubbing her thumb up and down without so much as a blush. Zach whispered something back to her, she turned and looked at Callie with a frankly appraising, and finally approving stare, smiled, and said goodnight, with a final squeeze of him as she turned to walk away.

And as they moved through the house, Callie realized that what passed for decadence in the front rooms was dull, sober chastity compared with the rest of the house. Couples, and trios, and groups of boys, and girls, and boys and girls, in various states of dress, danced, groped, and more-than-groped throughout the house. Every room, every corner of every room, was filled with them. But it was still Hollywood, so the orgiastic feel of the evening had a very cinematic sheen. It wasn't just hedonism, it was exhibitionism, staged by the world masters of stage-craft. There were no unsightly blemishes, no glaring lights, no awkward holds or rejections—the script called for a picture-perfect Hollywood party, and everyone was sticking to the script.

Some instinct told Zach to keep Callie at the front of the house, and in the gardens, which he did with some success for most of the evening. By 2:00am, he knew it was time for them to go home. Most of the people planning to keep their clothes on had long-since departed. The people they had been chatting with since midnight were those taking breaks from dancing, or having sex, or both. When the revelers had enough fresh air and respite, they would inevitably tell Zach and Callie "You should really come inside." As the evening progressed, and there were fewer revelers taking advantage of the cool ocean breeze, they found themselves increasingly alone, bored, and cold, whether in the garden or by the wilting mounds of food in the front rooms, where the windows still stood open to the night. The occasional shriek, or burst of laughter, or ecstatic moan, punctuated their isolation. Conversation was being kept up almost entirely by Zach, who was providing Callie with a rambling, frequently repetitive description of the people she had met that evening—who they were, what they were worth, who they slept with. But Callie's interest in these people did not increase upon meeting them. Zach may have felt some great fortune in knowing them, but they struck Callie as any other people she had known—perhaps cleaner, and prettier, and better-dressed, but still just people. Her chemical high from earlier in the evening had lost its edge, and Zach's droning acted as an extraordinarily effective buzzkill for her. He thought he was engaging her, but with each statistic or bit of gossip he provided her, she drifted further away.

During one particularly dull stretch of more than ten minutes without seeing another living soul, in which Callie commented they hadn't seen the host in hours, the two seemed to agree, without speaking, that it was time to go, and were walking towards the front door to leave, when Zach realized a gold Mont Blanc ink pen he had written a number with earlier in the evening was missing from his coat pocket. After a quick recap of the evening, they decided it must have fallen out when they were lounging on the pillows in one of the tents, and went to look for it.

The tent was lit only by candles, and was relatively dark, and most of the pillows, of which there were hundreds, had metallic gold trim, or were made of sari-like fabric with metallic fibers in the weave that glittered like the pen would. It was a slow process—they had moved around while they were in the tent earlier, and the pen could be anywhere—they needed to look through the whole tent. Callie removed her high heels and knotted her gown above the knees so she could crawl around better on the Turkish carpets covering the ground. It was several minutes before Callie discovered a girl with her eyes closed, buried—but breathing—beneath a mound of pillows. It took a moment before she recognized her as the girl from the floor of Leslie's bedroom, and even then she couldn't remember her name. She was considering whether or not to put the pillows back over the girl's face when she opened her eyes and looked straight up into Callie's face and said "You're, like, that new girl, aren't you?"

Callie was amazed the girl remembered her. "Um, yeah, I guess so. Are you alright?"

"Totally. I'm waiting for my, like, fucking mom. She's such a fucking whore. I've been out here for like, hours. You wouldn't believe the shit people have been like, saying in here. Some chick gave a guy a blowjob right there." She pointed to just past where Callie had just been looking for the pen under some pillows. "At first I thought it was my mom, and I thought I was gonna be like, sick."

They both seemed to recall the scene in Leslie's bedroom at the same time, and Callie wondered if the girl was making fun of her. But before she could say anything, the girl said "That was so like, major, what you did to Leslie's room. You're like, my new hero."

Callie fell back on a pillow and looked at the girl curiously, expecting a trick, or a trap. "Aren't you two friends?"

"Leslie doesn't have friends. She has like, allies and enemies and shit. She's like some renegade Gestapo commando thing running loose in Beverly Hills High. Everybody hates her. But, it's like, it's Beverly Hills, and, she's Leslie." She said it with a tone of resignation and finality, as though that was supposed to explain everything.

"You haven't seen a gold pen, have you?" Callie thought to ask.

"No, but some people found it earlier. I heard them give it to a waiter. Isn't it weird seeing all those waiters' things just bouncing around in those pants? It's like, creepy."

Callie had just called Zach over to tell him the news about the pen, when the very blonde, very tan woman from earlier appeared out of nowhere, breathless with laughter, red in the face. "What the hell are you two doing out here?" she demanded, looking around for, and finding, something to drink, in the form of an abandoned half-drank flute of champagne.

"It's not nice to bring candy to a party and not share, Zach," she said with a lecherous twist of her mouth that showed her age to be approaching closer to 40 than to the 30 her getup aspired to, as she half-stumbled, half-slunk her way over to where they were.

"Of course, sweetheart," he said distractedly, pulling the brown vial from his coat pocket.

She purred back in an oddly unsexy way, "I was talking about the girl, but I'll take some of that, too."

"Mom, you are like, so fucking gross."

The woman started—she had not recognized her daughter buried in the mound of pillows. "Goddammit Miranda, you're such a creepy little bitch. Get out of those fucking pillows. I've been looking for you for hours."

"No you haven't, you liar."

"Zach, Callie, meet my charming daughter, Miranda." She rolled her eyes with disgust.

Callie held her hand out to the woman, "It's nice to meet you. Miranda and I have met before."

"Lucky you. I'm Kate, her mother. Lucky me."

"Do you have to be such a total bitch, mom?"

"Yes, Miranda, I do. It's what I do best."

Callie interrupted the two to tell Zach the news about the pen. "Great, I'll go track it down. Callie, why don't you stay here with Miranda and Kate?"

"Fuck that. If you're leaving, I'm leaving," Kate answered before Callie could.

"I'm just going to find this waiter."

"Sounds like my kind of party. Let's go."

"Callie, do you think you'll be fine for ten minutes?"

"I'll be fine." She wanted to hear more about Leslie, about high school, what it was like. What she knew about high school she learned from movies and Antoine, and she was sure neither of them told the truth.

Kate wrapped herself around Zach with the desperation of a woman twice her age, and they made their way out of the tent, disappearing up the terraces and into the sounds of Kool and the Gang. The speakers around the lawn had been turned off since midnight, but the music from the house still drifted down into the tents.

"Do you have a cigarette?" Callie asked, not because she really wanted one, but more to have something to do. She sat on a pile of pillows, facing Miranda.

"No, but I have some valium. If you did like, just a half, you'd probably be like, ok."

"I better not risk it. We did some coke earlier. That was ok."

"Not for me. Mom goes crazy if I do any kind of powder. She's ok with pills though. They're all like, prescribed and shit."

"Cool."

"Sorry about the other night. Most people just get like a little loopy. It's just valium. That's a thing Leslie like, does. You're like, lucky it wasn't mushrooms or mescaline or some shit. If she would have like, had some, she would totally have done it. She's so like, fucked up. You can't even imagine."

"So the other night when you weren't talking, when you were on the floor, were you just pretending?"

"Fuck no. Whenever I'm around Leslie I get like blasted out of my fucking mind, totally like a retard in a coma. It's the best way to like, deal with her. Otherwise you end up stealing people's jewelry and prescriptions and shit. She stole some lady's Emmy award. It's what she does. You know, for kicks."

Miranda still had not moved from her nest of pillows. She hadn't even turned her head. The only parts of her plainly visible were her face and her feet, which were in hot pink leather ankle boots. They sat in silence for a few minutes.

"Is this fun? I mean, for you? Do you like these things?" Callie asked.

"It's better than TV. And high school boys. But no, it's not really fun. It's just what we do."

"Okay."

Another silence was starting to blossom out between them when they heard steps coming their way, a man's voice, singing out loud along with *Cars* by Gary Numan, playing in the distance. In no time, their host was there, his chill bumps glistening in the night air, sitting on the pillow beside Callie, with a casual, "Here you are, darling."

Callie turned to look at Miranda, whom she assumed he must know, but he was speaking to her. "No, you Callie. I've been sent to tell you Zach may be a few minutes more than he thought. He found his beloved pen, but he's been, um, detained. He said if you're cold you should come inside."

"Oh, okay," Callie answered, not sure how to respond. "Nick, do you know Miranda?" she asked, to buy some time, and also because she was so surprised she remembered both their names.

"I've known Miranda since before she was born. I'm her father. Well, in a manner of speaking. I was briefly her stepfather, but her mother's such a godawful bitch, I had to let them go. It was sad, but, baby with the bitchwater, you know how it goes. And she hasn't had a father since. Probably better that way." He leaned up and peered into the mound of pillows where Miranda still had not moved and asked, "Do you want a car home, babe? Or you can crash upstairs. If you stay out here, you're likely to wake up with someone on top of you. Or in San Diego, or some other godawful place. It's freezing."

It was true. Even with the tent to buffer the breeze, it was unseasonably cold for L.A.

"Okay, I'll stay. Do you have anything to eat that isn't disgusting?"

"Like what?"

"Like Pop Tarts?"

"I spent sixty grand on catering, and you want a Pop Tart like some valley trash?"

"Like, a Pop Tart on a silver tray served to me by a man whose penis I can see through his pants?"

"That's my girl." He stood and extended both hands to her, and she took them and rose as from a coffin.

"Wow, it is cold. Aren't you guys freezing?" she asked.

"Yes," Nick answered, "We're all going inside." He extended his hands to Callie, who stood, unknotted her dress and let it fall to the ground. She left her shoes where they were. She didn't want to leave where Zach told her to stay, but at least half an hour had passed, and she didn't want to be left alone, either. So she went.

As they approached the upper terrace leading to the front steps and around to the back of the house, he said "Miranda, why don't you head up to the blue guestroom. I'll send someone up with Pop Tarts. Callie, you come with me."

Miranda said goodnight and thanks and told Callie to have fun, before heading towards the front door. As they watched her head off, he turned to Callie and asked, "So, somewhere quiet or somewhere loud?"

"What?" Callie asked. She heard the question, but she wanted time to think.

"Do you want to head up to the dance floor, or do you want to be somewhere quiet while you're waiting on Zach? I have a screening room downstairs if you'd like to watch a movie."

"What kind of movie?" She was instantly on the alert.

"Whatever you want. I have hundreds." Nick's tone expressed disinterest and a little impatience.

"Okay, yeah. Downstairs."

"Sure, let's go this way." Rather than walking around to the front or back of the house, he went straight to the side of the house facing them. Behind a tall mound of shrubbery was a single flight of stairs leading down to a lower level of the house Callie did not know about—when he said downstairs, she thought he meant the main floor of the house they had been on throughout the evening. The quiet darkness of this lower place, which she could sense more than see through the glass door at the bottom of the stairs, made her uneasy. She stopped at the head of the stairs.

When he got to the door and began searching the unfamiliar pockets of his costume for his keys, he realized she wasn't beside him. He looked up and asked "Change your mind?"

"No," she began. It was a lie, and it sounded like a lie, she knew. "I just want to make sure Zach knows where I am. Will he be able to find me? Does he know you have a downstairs?"

"I will get you set up, and then I will let Zach know where you are, and get Miranda's Pop Tarts, and probably a hundred other things that have popped up in the past five minutes. I do have a party to attend to, you know."

This admonition, while mild, had the desired disarming effect—Callie was not accustomed to people being kind to her for no reason. In being less kind, he made himself less suspicious.

Callie hiked up her gown and walked nimbly down the steps, which were cold on her bare feet.

Nick did not turn on any lights as she passed him into a dark hallway. She had been in enough basement dungeons to know roughly the location of where Nick's would be if he had one—and it was near where she was walking into darkness. As though he sensed her heightened insecurity, he said in an offhand tone, "This is where my home office and screening rooms are. I keep a separate door for the tax man." Callie clung to this bit of truth as she stood there in the dark, waiting as he locked the door behind them—she had heard Zach counseling clients on the vagaries of deducting home offices spaces, and was hoping more than believing that she was just being led to a screening room.

Her eyes adjusted quickly to the almost total darkness—the moonlight had to slip around the shrubbery, down a flight of underground stairs, and around a corner through a mullioned door before it gasped almost sickly into the hallway. Still, she could begin to make out doors, shapes, down a hallway. Nick walked past her, took her hand, and led her down the hall. His hand was warm, almost hot, as it grasped hers, which was still cold from the night air. "You really are freezing. I'll turn some heat on for you."

He turned into a doorway, and when the door was shut behind them, he finally turned on the light. She was amazed to find that the thing she had considered least likely in the world appeared to be true: It was a screening room. Four rows of eight theatre seats sloped down gently to large white screen taking up almost the whole wall at the far end of the room. A large overhead projector mounted behind the seats declared that whatever else might happen there, it was a screening room. Lining the wall adjoining the hallway they had just entered through was a bank of floor-to-ceiling bookcases holding nothing but black VHS cassette tape boxes with neatly typed labels. On the opposite wall was a row of theater spotlights with different colored gels arranged in just such a way that the entire room was filled with a soft pink light. After the movement of a few sliding switches, the theater lights dimmed and a row of recessed canister lights in front of the bookcases came on to wash the wall in light, making the titles legible.

"Pick one," he said.

"Thanks," she said, and paused, and her silence gave have her ignorance away.

"It doesn't matter, just pick something. They're all good. I have a Pop-Tart to attend to."

She grabbed a box at random, from a top shelf, with the title *Amarcord*.

"Are you sure you want this? It's foreign."

She grabbed another, on the next bookcase, but with a more English-sounding title—*Tommy*. Nick seemed satisfied. "Ann Margaret was good, anyway. Take a seat, I'll get it going." He gestured to the theater seats with a sweeping gesture—the sole attendant of the world's smallest theater. She sat in the front row. As the credits began, he lowered the spotlights even more, but before he turned off the other lights, he sat down in the seat next to hers, dug around in his pocket and pulled out a brown vial almost identical to Zach's. From the mass of gold chains and medallions around his neck he pulled loose a slender, stylized crucifix, with the Jesus torturously thin, his hair and beard blocked off square like a beat poet. Zach turned it over and she realized with a laugh that she couldn't suppress, that it was a spoon, with a long deep gash running the length of it. He dug deep in the bottle and gave himself what would be considered more of a line than a bump, then repeated the gesture with the other nostril. "Want some?" he asked indifferently.

"Zach may be a while."

She knew as soon as she saw the bottle that she would be offered some, and knew as soon and even more deeply that she must refuse. But she did not. Nor did she tell him that the amount he did was too much for her—more than she had taken all night, combined. She just said with the same casual tone he had used, "Sure." But her body gave her away. She had begun shaking, and goose pimples peppered her arms, as soon as she saw how much he was doing. She wanted that much, too. She wanted it all. It seemed strange to her that in just those few hours, she had forgotten how much she had loved it, the way it made her feel. Seeing it before her again so close brought her back to life, awoke parts inside of her with a desire that was still foreign to her.

In a feeling that she could not have described until it had been satisfied with more cocaine, she realized watching the man raise the spoon to his nose that her own nose had been hungry, searching. Like a bloodhound that has lost a scent, but can remember the scent, can feel it in its nostrils, can sense it in the air, all around, everywhere, except where it should be, and then it is there, and life is perfect again. The one sensation they were born for, that they live for, that they would kill and cheat and bleed for—it was there, on the spoon, and she had to hold her chest tight as the shiver of completion ran across her face, to the edges of her ears, raced through her body again to the tips of her toes. And then again. And she closed her eyes, and held onto the arms of the theater seat, and lolled her head, feeling the blood race through this vein then that, carrying the electricity through her, filling her.

"You ok?" he asked.

"Yeah. I'll be right here when Zach—" but she just stopped there and sat back in the seat, her words gone, and stretched out her legs in front of her, one under and then over the other. She turned and looked at him, and with what seemed to be all the effort in the world, found the words "I'll be right here."

And that was the end. When she looked back on her life more than twenty years later, everything in her life before that point led up to it, everything after that point led away from it. It wasn't the moment she became an addict—it was the moment she found God, synthetic and pure, liberating, electric, and forgiving. It wasn't the moment she became a bloodhound—it was the moment she found the fox.

The rest of the tale was tragic, and sad, pure Hollywood in many ways. Zach of course had no idea where Callie had gone, had had no conversation with Nick, and was livid that she had left him there—and left her shoes. In the weeks and months to come, that would be the detail he remembered most about the evening, walking into the tent and finding only her shoes. He also remembered, with regret, not being able to ever locate the waiter with his Mont Blanc pen, for the simple reason that Miranda had it in her purse for hours before he began looking for it.

The next six days for Callie were like immeasurable time spent on a roller coaster without an end, that makes itself up as it goes along, the highs getting higher, the lows getting lower, the spins more complex, the spirals down more vertiginous—but never a straight path, never a pause for air, just constant movement and exultation, beyond the point where joy has meaning. The sex was almost endless from the moment Nick left the room—with herself, with him, with other men, with other women, in groups, in clubs, in a van, in a dressing room trailer, in the back room of a liquor store, on a pool table, twice, in two different houses. She had been having sex all of her life, but she had never wanted it. And now she did. When she saw a needle on the third day, she was no longer even with Nick— he had left her with his dealer. He was done with her, and needed to get back to work. But the dealer, he was just beginning. It scared her at first, but as soon as it slid in, and she looked in the eyes of the man who was looking at her like he was ready to eat her face, she wanted to eat his back. She wanted to claw, to tear, to bite. He was ready for her.

At some point someone suggested she needed something to eat, and she ate a half cup of yogurt. People more experienced than her kept suggesting she drink water, but the taste of it was foul to her—and it cooled her body down, when she loved the feel of burning from inside. It was a warmth concentrated in her center—her fingers and toes would get cold if she stopped moving for long, the blood racing to her center—the center. The whole world felt like it began and ended with her, in her.

On the fifth day, the paranoia set in quickly and permanently, and it was more distressing to her because she had never felt it before, didn't know what it was, didn't know there was a chance what she was sensing might not be real. She had been hearing voices in the background since she took her first bump with Zach in the bathroom of Cowboys, but there had been voices, or at least plausible explanations for voices, until the fifth day. It was just her then, alone with the dealer, with his guns, in his bunkered-down condo with curtained, shuttered blinds and video monitors showing the exterior of the building and the parking lot. It was the first time she became aware that there were no people who belonged to the voices she heard—she could see there was no one. But there were shadows now that she could see, that belonged to the voices. And they were moving, all around her, but just out of sight, always. She would see one sneak into a closet, and go looking for it, and find no one. Under the beds, behind the curtains, whenever he left her alone for more than five minutes, the shadows would return. When he told her to stay in the bedroom and be quiet while he met with an important client in the living room, he returned to find her crying, the sheets pulled up over her head like a child.

He was able to coax her down into manageability that night, and through a combination of cocaine, valium, and Xanax, he was able to make her play the way he liked to play. But by the morning of the sixth day, she was manic. While he was on the phone making an important deal, she interrupted him one too many times with her babbling, and he slapped her across the room. She was hysterical after that—she wanted to go home. She didn't know the day, or month, or where she was, or even the name of the man who had just slapped her. She had no idea where her Halston gown was—she hadn't seen it in days—so he gave her some gym shorts and a stained white undershirt, drove her to Zach's, and pushed her out of the car. "Fuck you, you crazy bitch. Don't ever let me see your face again."

She no longer had sunglasses—picked up and discarded in the blur of the past few days—and the sun bore into her eyes as she sat on the pavement. But the voices didn't stop. And the shadows, they were in the bushes, they had followed her. She looked around her, felt the neighbors looking through their binoculars at her from down the street. She made her way to the front door, and found it unlocked. She crept in silently, hoping to disappear back into the life she knew before the Cowboys bathroom.

But that life was over. Two men whose names she did not know were sitting in the living room, playing some very involved-looking game of cards that looked to have been going on for some time. The men looked up and smiled as she walked in. She recognized them, though she had never met them. They had been to the house a few times to pick up things from Zach. He called them his fixers. They were the men he called when he needed something—someone—fixed.

"Welcome, home, Callie. Zach's been worried sick about you," one of the men said.

"We were looking for you all over town. You're a hard girl to track down. We were beginning to wonder if you were ever gonna show back up. But here you are."

"W-w-where's Zach?" she stuttered, beginning to see the men clearly for the first time. Beginning to feel she was about to be fixed, but not certain what that meant. She wondered briefly if it was their voices she had been hearing.

"Zach's at work, sweetie. Somebody's gotta pay the bills around here, right?" he smiled.

"Why don't you come have a sandwich? You look like you could use one, babe."

"W-w-w-where's Antoine?" the stutter was getting worse, and she was starting to shake. She could just make out the gleam of a pistol, or a pen, but she thought it was a pistol, under one of the men's jackets. She was still close enough to the door that she could make it out, but she had nowhere to run to, no money, no shoes. Antoine was her only hope.

They looked at each other. "He's up in his room," one of the men answered. She could not distinguish them from one another even as she looked at them—she couldn't remember who had said which words even as he said them. "You want us to go get him for you?"

"N-n-no, I'll go," she said. But it was a mistake. As soon as she was away from the front door, they were up, and on her. One held her arms behind her back, the other began to repeatedly punch her directly in the solar plexus with force that could punch through walls. Before she could scream, he ability to breathe was almost gone. They let her drop to the floor, and she began throwing up gobs of mucus and bile, and she was trying to cry, but there wasn't enough oxygen. She tried to see, but couldn't. She felt the duct tape going around her head, over her mouth, over her eyes. She felt her hands being tied behind her back, then her feet, then her knees. Then one of them sat on her chest to keep her from convulsing while the other slid a needle into her arm. She didn't feel anything again until two days later, when she woke up in a dirty hotel room near the airport.

"Dirty little cunt, ain't ya?"

"Are we the last two men in L.A. to fuck you?"

"I've had tighter pussy in a nursing home for whores."

"Thank God you got an asshole back there."

"Even that wasn't great."

She had no idea where she was, who the men were, or what they were talking about. She opened her eyes—the light was blinding. But the voices had stopped. The two men kept talking, but the other voices, and the shadows, which had invaded even her sleep—they were gone.

"Where am I?" Every inch of her body ached. Some ached more than others, but nothing felt good.

"The very tippy top of shit creek, little lady."

"The City of Fucked Town, population—you."

"You have earned yourself a star on the Hollywood Walk of Fame of Stupid

Whores."

"But don't worry, you haven't wasted any time. While you've been knocked out the construction crew working on the new terminal at LAX have been coming in to visit you. Look, some of them even left you some tips." She didn't look, but there were crumpled dollar bills on the nightstand between her bed and the next.

"One of them asked if you were part of a donkey show."

"Another one asked if you dated the Harlem Globetrotters—all at once."

Here the men laughed. But the laughter was forced, more the recollection of laughter than real laughter. She guessed—rightly—that the men had been working on their comedy routine, such as it was, while she was sleeping. As she tried to sit up, she realized there was a length of rope knotted to each of her arms, disappearing off the sides of the bed.

"Seriously though, it's time for this to be over with. We're being paid by the hour, but we got other jobs we need to take care of, so this is how it is." The men were suddenly all business. "You're going to go away now. We're taking you to the airport, we're buying you a one-way plane ticket to wherever you want, but not this side of the Mississippi. Anywhere in the fucking world you wanna go. But you gotta go."

"What? I don't have anywhere to go." Her throat felt like someone had shoved hot embers down it while she slept, and it hurt to speak. The men had been moving around while they spoke, but one was now sitting at a table by a window with closed draperies, the other on the bed on her other side.

The man on the bed said, "Listen, girlie, you got it all wrong. You got nowhere to be here. You should consider yourself lucky to be alive at all. Very lucky. Yes, very lucky indeed. Our employer isn't very happy with you."

"No, not at all, he really is not happy. Happy is a thing he is not."

"The reason he did not see you, did not want to see you, was that he thought he would kill you with his bare hands if he saw you."

"Have you ever seen that happen? It ain't pretty. Bare-hands deaths just go on forever. On and on and on with the hacking and the wheezing and the snot. Just stupid."

"Total waste of energy. Bad kharma, too, I think. But we got a better way." Here the man at the table patted a revolver in a shoulder holster, plainly visible as he wore no jacket. Callie had to strain to see it from where she was tied down to the bed. Her vision was limited to everything from about three above the floor up to the ceiling, which was stained with brown spots.

She was too confused and in too much physical pain to be as truly frightened as she should have been, but the men understood that, too.

"Look," said the man on the bed, "There's already a dead nigger two doors down from here. We're gonna be setting that bed on fire before we're done here— nothing to do with you, but you know, economies of scale, why start two fires, right?—so it's easier for us just to shoot you and throw you in there with the nigger than it is to deal with any bullshit from you."

"But that isn't what our boss wants. That faggot that lived upstairs convinced the boss that he should let you live. Used good logic, played on the emotions, the whole bit, real class job—all bullshit of course—nobody cares whether you live or die."

"Most especially us. But he paid us to get you on a plane alive. So we're making the offer here."

"We're being generous, as it were."

"But if you don't want to cooperate, like we said, we got 20 gallons of gasoline and a 20-minute-wick, and Zach will never know the difference. For all he will ever know, you're in Nashville, or Amsterdam, or some goddam place—we just gotta show him a receipt for reimbursement—that'll be enough for him. He'll never know that you are, or might be, or might have been, whatever, a pile of ashes in this whorebag hotel. He did his part."

"Now we're doing ours. So what is it? Curtain number one, grizzly death, or curtain number two, free plane ride to your new life?"

"Can I talk to him, please?"

"Any more questions like that, and we're just gonna assume the answer is curtain number one. He don't wanna talk to you, ever. If you ever come on this side of the Mississippi again, we have his permission—his paid in advance permission—to kill you on sight. Even Antoine agreed—he said if you're stupid enough to come back here, you deserve it. Or something to that effect. But he didn't think you'd come back, anyway."

The man at the table stood up. "Enough of this shit. Are you going to shower, dress, go the airport, get on a plane, and never come back, never call, never so much as mention the boss's name again in your life, like a good little cunt, or do I just shoot you now?" While he was talking, he pulled the gun from the holster and walked over to the bed, and held the cold muzzle against the side of her neck. "Well?"

Six hours later she was on a plane to Atlanta. The man at the table went to buy the ticket—the airport was only four miles away—while she showered and put on some of the clothes Antoine had packed for her in a small nylon duffle bag he used to carry to the gym. There wasn't much, and nothing Antoine would call *perfect*, but she guessed in a vague sort of way that was how Zach wanted it. He wouldn't let Antoine let her have anything nice—that was over. It was all over.

She was in the shower for a long time. She hurt walking to the shower, and the water hurt her in different places all over her body. She drank for a long time, straight from the shower head. The water made her lightheaded, dizzy. She wondered when she had last had anything to drink, or eat, but could not remember.

When she looked in the mirror, she almost screamed. She didn't recognize the person there at all. She was covered in scratches and bruises, and appeared to have lost 15 or 20 pounds. Her eyes were sunken into her face, like death. Even at the height of her father's abuse, he had never allowed her to look, to be, so near death. And this, she reasoned, she had done to herself.

The man from the bed took her to the airport, and stayed with her until she boarded the plane. He was mostly quiet, but much more kind. Without his partner, his brutal persona seemed to weaken, and he grew less and less like a thug and more and more like the uncle he was pretending to be—not that anyone asked.

He handed her an envelope right before she got in line to get on the plane. It was a plain white envelope with her name, written in Antoine's incredibly stylized, loopy, swirly script. "For when you get on the plane. Not before." He looked at her uncomfortably, then went to the desk of the boarding gate, borrowed a pen and paper from the clerk there, and copied down a name and number from a small spiral notebook he carried. He handed her the paper and said, "If things aren't working out for you in Atlanta, give this guy a call. He ain't a nice guy, but he's fair. You ain't used to nice, noways, from what I seen. He can put you to work, if you ain't got nothin'."

She tucked the piece of paper in her pocket without a thought of ever calling the number, and thanked the man. As she headed through the boarding gate, he called out her name, and she turned around to look back. He snapped a photo with a camera he had pulled from nowhere—evidence, she supposed, that she got on the plane.

When the pilot announced they were crossing over the Rocky Mountains, she took out the letter from Antoine. It read:

Darling, darling,

I am so sorry. This is all just so awful. I blame myself more than I blame Zach, and somehow, I don't think you're to blame at all, but you're the one who's going to suffer. Or maybe not. I don't know. You have more pluck than you think. Here's a little something to get you going. Make it last. Zach says you will never call or write or see me or any of us again, and maybe that's for the best. But know that you will always have a place in my heart.

Much Love, Your friend, Anthony Romulus Edwards

She realized immediately that the purpose of the letter was to give her his full name, which she had never known. Like Cher, his idol, he only went by one name. But to be able to find him in a phone book, or find him at all, ever, she would need more than Antoine, and now she had it. There were four hundred dollars folded into the letter. She wondered how much more he had to bribe the fixers to give her the letter at all. And when he had done it, and how, and how brave he was. She began openly sobbing on the plane. The people around her, who had been looking at her with curiosity since before boarding began, shifted uncomfortably in their seats. After a few minutes, a flight attendant came to see if everything was alright.

"It's my nerves. Flying terrifies me. Can I have a drink please?" Callie asked. The woman brought her a Bloody Mary, and she stopped crying, and then another, and she stopped thinking, and another, and she finally fell asleep for the rest of the flight.

When she got off the plane in Atlanta, she had no idea where to go, or what to do. She had never been there—she chose Atlanta only because she had a vague recollection her mother was from there, or had family there. But she didn't know if her mother was even alive. She had a duffle bag with a few street clothes in it, $400, no formal education of any kind, and a skill set limited to the sex trade. She had never had a resume, much less been on an interview that wasn't for sex work. She knew how to drive, but had no idea where to drive to. She was exhausted. She took a taxi to the nearest, cheapest hotel the cab driver knew. She bought a newspaper there, and looked through the classified ads, and realized how little of the world she knew—she had no idea what a good salary was for a person who did not live in Hollywood. What can a person live on? How much does it cost to live? And, how does one do that? She did not think apartments came with electricity and water paid, but she did not know. There were many apartments for less than $400 a month, but she didn't know any of the neighborhoods. For most of the jobs and apartments, references were required, and she had no one. She ate dinner that night from the vending machines at the motel. The man at the front desk had given her some grief about not being 18—the legal age to register a hotel room in Georgia—but she protested, and when he took a good look at her face, and she told him she was paying cash, he let her have the room. She bought a pack of Virginia Slims, and the man gave her a pack of matches. When she woke up the next morning, she was down to $364. She knew she couldn't go on indefinitely without a plan.

The number in her jeans was for a man named Darryl. She didn't know the name of the man who had given her the number, but she didn't think it mattered. She called and identified herself to the man who answered the phone, who started laughing, saying "Callie, so soon! George just called yesterday and said I might be hearing from you in the next few weeks. So soon? Better if my regulars haven't seen you walking the streets. We can upmarket you. George says you know how to eat and dress and all that shit, a regular high class act."

She wondered if it was true—if George really had said those things. And why. And what else he might have said.

"Where you staying? I'll send someone to come get you so we can have a look."

She told him, and within an hour a white 1978 Thunderbird was sitting in the front parking lot waiting on her as she checked out. The man driving the car took her, without much conversation, to the condo tower on Peachtree where Darryl lived.

She walked into something like a disco den, with Flokati rugs, leather and chrome sofas and chairs, thick glass coffee and side tables, Ficus trees, and a generic sort of disco music with lots of violins playing not too loudly, but loud enough. Scantily clad women, and men in leisure and dress suits were smoking and having cocktails. Drugs and their various implements were scattered almost casually around the room. A disco ball spun slowly in the center of ceiling, trying with its small rectangles of reflected light to outshine the morning sun, which was fighting back with vigor through the window sheers. It was 9:30am. She was greeted at the door by a young man wearing skin-tight Jordache jeans, a white satin shirt unbuttoned almost to the waist, and bleached hair feathered back with a lacquered sheen of hairspray making it into something more like a hat than hair. He introduced himself as Billy, and asked as he closed the door behind her, "You alright, gurl?" She was still getting re-accustomed to southern accents. Antoine would have hated this boy, and she felt a pang of remorse at not having him with her so they could make fun of this Billy boy later.

"I'm fine. It's been a long week."

"Well I can see that. Come on in. Can I get you a drink? A Bloody Mary maybe?" His voice sounded genuinely concerned—but then she remembered she was back in the south.

"Sure. It's becoming my signature drink, I think." She wasn't sure why she was talking like such a grown-up anymore—the act was over. She was 17—she didn't need a signature drink.

"Darryl's in his room, waiting for you. Do you need to get ready?"

"What do you mean?"

"Freshen up. Little girl's room? Darryl's a back-door man, if you know what I mean."

She did know what he meant, but she declined, settling for the drink. It was strong, and spicy. She liked it, and she said so.

"Everybody loves my Marys," he responded, and then, "Well, you might as well come on back."

The door opened onto a man sprawled out in a black silk robe on a king-sized bed with red silk sheets, talking in exaggerated tones on the phone—not dramatic, or threatening, but expressive. There were dozens of pillows spread out behind him. He continued his conversation, waving the boy out, and gesturing to Callie to sit in one of two upholstered armchairs by the window. She sat with her duffle bag at her feet, not knowing exactly what to do or where to look. She sipped her drink nervously, but without making any noise. The man before her did not look exactly threatening, but as George had suggested, he didn't look especially nice, either. He looked like the successful owner of a used car dealership caught lounging at home. White fleshy skin with dark curly hair in sharp relief poked out of the robe at his legs and above the waist, where it was belted. Based upon the décor of the room, which was less like a discotheque and more that of a matador's secret bordello, with large, dark, heavy furniture and velvet upholstery, she was surprised not to find the man completely naked and engaged in some sex act.

He finished his call, looked at her with frank, appraising eyes, and asked "What the hell happened to you?"

"It's a long story."

"It always is. Alright though, we can fix all that up. Now, show me what you can do."

"I - I don't understand. I'm sorry." She was biting her lip. She knew she was interviewing to be a whore, but she had never managed herself as a whore—she had always been told what to do. She didn't understand the mechanics of the business. "I've never done this, exactly. I've done a lot, but… Just tell me what to do. I'll do it."

"But George said… alright, how 'bout this. You pretend you just walked in through a hotel room door. You found me laying here. You make me happy, I give you 500 bucks. Make me happy."

After a moment, she began an awkward sort of striptease, made more difficult by her jeans and peasant blouse.

The man started laughing, and said "Alright, we're gonna have to fix that too. Why don't you come sit next to me."

She sat on the bed next to him. She felt awkward, like she was playing a part she didn't know the lines for. "I'm not always this awkward," she began, feeling like she was blowing her opportunity not to live on the street.

"Would you like something to make you less awkward?"

"Not valium," she answered quickly, then smiled somewhat shyly and said "I think I may be allergic to it."

"Name your poison then."

She hesitated. "Maybe a little blow?" Without her makeup, with her hair hanging loosely down around her face, she looked more like 15 than the 17 she was, and her eyes could have been a hundred. But when she said blow, her eyes lit up like the child she had never been.

And so it began again, but with the drama slowed down, and under careful supervision. She was Darryl's private consort for the first four months, rarely leaving the apartment for anything. A nearly constant supply of cocaine was available to her, but Darryl kept a very close eye on her, monitoring her consumption. He had seen the type before, and unlike Zach, he knew how to manage her. At the very least, he knew that she needed managing. The first time she would look in a closet, or peek behind a closed curtain, he would begin cutting the cocaine with Xanax or valium or any number of other things, to bring her down without her being aware that he was bringing her down. Sometimes there would be no cocaine at all, when he could see the look of fear in her eyes that meant she was not going to be fun to play with anymore. When he began being bored of her, he started renting her out periodically, and as she began to come back more and more paranoid and delusional, he tired of her entirely, and moved her into a nearby apartment he kept for his regular girls. It was a matter of months before he grew tired of their complaints, and his customers' complaints, about her erratic behavior. He had cleaned her up and fed her while she lived with him, but since moving out she had just become a tiresome, paranoid junkie, barely skin and bones, not at all suitable for the high-dollar jobs he planned for her. He let her go.

She went from escort agency to escort agency. Word about how difficult she was had spread on the street—it was a very small network of businesses, even for a town the size of Atlanta. She could not stop using drugs, and she couldn't even figure out how to cook a chicken, much less how to run a household of her own. For the most part, she lived without power, without food, without clean clothing, or even a toothbrush.

Within two years of arriving in Atlanta, she was chained to a bed in the Bowen

Homes public housing project, where she could be had by any man willing to part with five dollars. It was two days after her 19th birthday when the Fulton County Police vice squad raided the orange duplex, and took her, sobbing and incoherent, down to the station. It was, remarkably, the first time she had been arrested. With her photo ID long gone (she could not say when or where it disappeared), it took three days for her fingerprints to be cleared by the F.B.I., and another day before a fax of her California driver's license picture arrived and positively identified her.

She ultimately was not charged with any crime—the vice squad wanted her cooperation to secure a conviction of the pimps and drug dealers who had chained her to the bed. When she repeatedly refused to cooperate, and appeared to be having auditory hallucinations, as well as syntax and speaking problems consistent with schizophrenia, they discharged her to Grady Memorial Hospital for a 72-hour involuntary observation, which led, within 18 hours, to her involuntary commitment to inpatient psychiatric treatment at a run-down state facility. She was discharged within a week—after the voices in her head stopped—and was back out on Cheshire Bridge Road within hours, already high, trying to find a customer or old friend who might hook her up with a place to stay, when an unmarked police car swerved off the road and into the parking lot of the Pink Palace strip club where she was lurking. She turned to run, but a voice, strong and deep, and dark, but clearly feminine, called out, "Don't you even think about it, bitch."

Callie turned to see a black woman in khaki pants, a white shirt, black nylon jacket, black boots, and thick black braided belt walking towards her—fast. The woman continued, "What the fuck are you doing back out here?"

Callie thought she recognized her, but had no idea where from. She didn't know anyone who looked like this—the woman had perfectly lovely hair, big shiny black rolls of Farrah Fawcett curls cascading down from a center part in her hair, and big firm hips not hidden by the black jacket.

"Answer me, bitch." The woman was standing in front of her, rage in her eyes, her voice, and the veins Callie could sense but not see were pulsing under the woman's dark skin.

Then Callie recognized her voice—she had been the neighbor in the duplex in the projects who used to come over to buy weed. Every once in a while she would poke her head into Callie's room, look at her lying naked and chained to the bed, and say something like, "When ya'll gon'let that white bitch go? She look wore out to me." Callie had always been too high to respond, but she recognized the woman's voice now.

"It's you," Callie said.

"Yes it's me, bitch." She was in Callie's face now, her voice raised and threatening to yell. "You refused to give evidence against them sorry niggers, now they might walk free. We cut that operation early so we could get your ass outta there and get you some help, and now you back out here? Oh, hell no. This ain't happening. I lived in the projects eatin that nasty-ass food for four goddam months, for nothin', a waste o'time cause o'you, and you think you just gonna walk up and down in front of this titty bar and shake your skinny white ass and get yourself chained to another bed, or worse? Hell no. Get in that goddam car. Right this goddam minute."

During this exchange, the officer's white male partner, who was driving, had been looking on in some amusement. His partner had been bitching all day about this girl, and then, out of nowhere, there she was. Out of all the hookers on all the streets in Atlanta, there she was. He opened the back door of the car, and Callie quietly got in, looking to him with terror in her eyes, but only getting a smirk back.

"Um, Delores," he said in a low voice, as he got in the front seat, "Where is it we're going?"

"Dutch Valley Road."

"Why?"

"Just drive, fool."

"Lights?"

"No goddam lights."

202

He was still smiling at her irritation as they wound through the hilly streets to the short length of Dutch Valley Road. It took a lot to get Delores worked up, and in the three years they had been on the vice squad together, he had never seen her like this. Unless she was undercover, she rarely raised her voice or even cursed at all. He wished he had a tape recorder to tease her with later.

"Ok, where to?" he asked as they turned onto the dead-end stretch of Dutch Valley. Delores pointed to a dilapidated two-story cinderblock building nestled in a cluster of scraggly oaks.

He parked the car in the small lot in front of the building, and Delores got out, saying "Wait here," to him as she opened Callie's door. "Come with me," she said to the girl.

They walked in through double metal doors at the front of the building, and the officer opened the doors to two empty rooms before she found a small group of people behind the third door, and they were sitting in a circle, clearly having a meeting of some kind. Delores walked in, pulling Callie in by her upper arm. "Who's in charge here?" Delores demanded of the group.

"Ma'am, we're in the middle of a meeting here," answered a voice from the circle, where all the faces had turned round to look at the two women.

"I know what you're doing here. I asked, who's in charge?" she replied.

"No one's in charge. We don't have leaders. I'm the chairperson of this group. And I'm going to have to ask you to either have a seat and join us, or leave, before I call the police."

"Honey, I am the police," she said, as she pulled back her nylon jacket to reveal a badge affixed to her belt. "Now, when I say who's in charge, what I mean is, if there was some mean-ass police woman about to call every building official, fire marshal, health inspector, and who the fuck knows all else, cause some bitches wouldn't answer a simple question, who in this room would you say you would want her to talk to before she did that, and got this whole goddam place shut down?"

A nervous minute or so followed, in which all of the heads in the circle eventually turned to one man, ancient and thin, with white hair flowing to his shoulders, a light touch of makeup, a blousy sort of white linen poncho, Wrangler jeans, and white flip-flops. Both of his arms were covered in dozens of bracelets, charms, beads, and he wore rings on most of his fingers. "Why're you all looking at me? I don't even have a key," he said in exaggerated mock horror, his fingertips closing over his lips as a look of comical innocence played across his face.

"Just go talk to her, Mama Ben, so we can get on with the meeting," the chairperson said in a voice that couldn't hide nervousness under pretend authority.

"Fine," the man apparently named Mama Ben replied, but pulled a Virginia Slims 100 from a white vinyl cigarette case, and lit it, replacing the lighter in the holder attached to the case, before he got up from his seat. As he started walking towards the door, Delores pulled Callie out of the room, and he whispered back to the room full of men as he walked out, "What fresh hell is this, girls?"

When the three of them were all out in the hall together, Delores said "Why don't we have a seat," and sat on a ragged sofa that looked like it had been snatched from a dumpster, pulling Callie down with her.

"OK, so Mama Ben, that's your name?" Delores asked, and the man nodded assent as he sat opposite them, his mouth just then full of cigarette smoke he didn't want to let go of, "Well, this is Callie. And I want you to fix this mess."

Mama Ben exhaled with a choke and a cough, saying "Beg pardon?"

"This mess right here, this wreck of a human being sitting on this sofa here with me, you can see her can't you? Take a good look. She's little, not much of nothing, but she's here."

"Yes, I can see. She doesn't look that bad, to be honest with you." In his time, and it had been a long time, Mama Ben had seen much worse.

"She aint had time to get good and truly fucked up again yet. She can still walk and talk, and for her, that's saying something. I watched and listened for over two months while this girl got raped, while she was chained to a bed in the duplex next to me in the projects. I was undercover, see, and this girl here, she fucked it all up. Nobody wanted a dead white girl found in the projects, when there was a police officer undercover, next door. Right?"

"Okay," the man answered, seeing the beginning not quite the end of the conversation.

"So we shut the operation down, moved in, got the low level hustlers, but not the ones we were after, cause Miss Callista here can't say no to the powder. Or to the men, even when she ain't tied down, from what we've heard on the street. She may be had more men than all you gays in there put together." Delores nodded to the closed door of the meeting room.

"Don't bet on that," the man responded.

Delores ignored him, and continued, "So, she hasn't been out of Georgia Regional for more than half a day before I find her walking Cheshire Bridge. So I brought her here, and now, I want you to fix her."

"That's not how it works," Mama Ben began, before Delores cut him off.

"I know how it works. My husband is in the program, eight years sober, thank God. I'm in Al-Anon, when I can go. I have a sponsor. I've worked the steps, I know. And I know how some of those men in those A.A. meetings are, too—they'll eat this girl alive, she'll be back out on the streets in no time. She doesn't want to be sober, I know that, but that's because she doesn't even know what it means. To want it, you got to have something to start from, and this girl here, she's got nothing. Nothing. No-thing. No one. No friends, no family. The people on her birth certificate in California, they don't exist—it's like she just appeared from nowhere in the middle of Los Angeles one day. Never been to a school, never had an immunization. We even checked with the Justice Department in case somebody got lost from witness protection, but they never heard of her, or the people on her birth certificate, either. You can help her. Will you?"

Callie looked up for the first time in the conversation—this was the first she had heard of any of this, and it scared her. What does it mean when the police know your whole life is a lie? Did they know? Her head went spinning away from the conversation, still a little high and not entirely sure if she was hearing everything right.

"What do you want us to do with her?" Mama Ben asked, a little interested, a little sarcastic, a little despairing.

"Save her." Delores' tone was flat, matter-of-fact.

"Can she be saved?" Mama Ben was looking at the girl with frank curiosity, and she looked away, at a bulletin board covered with community notices, at the floor, at the ceiling.

"Everyone can be saved," Delores answered matter-of-factly, standing up. "Callie, or Callista, or whatever your name is, I'm leaving. I don't know this Mama Ben, but he's probably your best chance of not ending up in pieces somewhere. I'm going to check back in here every so often to see that you're here. When there's a meeting here, I want to see you here. I don't want to hear about any boyfriends, any jobs, any relapses, any anything. Do what Mama Ben here tells you, and you'll be alright. Alright?"

"How do you know? You don't even know him." It was the first time Callie had spoken since she got into the sedan, and her voice was strangely defiant. It caught even her off-guard.

"I know enough. I know he's here on a Saturday night. I know that when I asked for who was in charge, they turned to him. I know he doesn't he want to have sex with you. I know he doesn't have any drugs. That's a start. If he's willing to help you, you have hope, and that's more than you had an hour ago. Just do right, girl. You'll be ok."

Delores walked out the door, and Mama Ben jumped up to follow her out. "Miss," he called after her, "Miss?" as the door shut behind him.

Callie stayed glued to the sofa, not entirely sure if what was happening was even happening.

Delores turned back to the man, who asked "May I have your card? Can I call you, if, well, something comes up?"

"Yes, here, of course" she pulled out a card, and smiled, for the first time in days, saying "My name is Delores. And you are?"

"The name on my driver's license is Benjamin Carson Withers, but I've been Mama Ben since before any of these little chickens were hatched," he said with a nod back towards the building behind him. "May I ask you a question before you leave?"

"Sure, unless it's for money."

"Why? Why do you care about this girl?"

Her smile faded, and her eyes lost focus as she considered. "You know, my husband asked me the same thing last night. It's hard to explain, really. At first I just thought she was some dumb-ass white girl, maybe with some real bad luck, fell on hard times. But we were doing audio surveillance—eavesdropping, I guess you'd call it—on everything going on in that duplex. The things I heard these men do to her—literally hundreds of them over the course of the past few months—slap her, punch her, rape her, go to the bathroom on her, in her. Sick mess. You know how many of them wanted to see her cry? That's what a lot of them wanted—most of them were high, but not all. It takes a lot though, to get that girl crying. Pay day was the worst. Every Friday, just like at the liquor store, with men all lined up outside wanting a turn. She never said stop, unless that's what they wanted her to say. She never tried to run away. She just lay there, took it. Those scabs on her wrists are from where they had her chained to the bed. I don't think they even needed the chains though, really—not as long as they had cocaine and a bed for her."

She paused for a moment, lost in reflection, then continued, in a softer tone, "But when she slept—every once in a while, they'd let her sleep, or make her sleep, when she got too crazy—she sounded just like a five year old girl. Just like my five year old girl. She'd talk in her sleep, see, and say the strangest things, in the sweetest little voice. Sometimes she'd laugh, sometimes she'd scream, sometimes she would talk about a secret fort in the woods, and playing cowboys and Indians, and she would cry out, cry for, her friends. That's what would make me sad—that this girl, who the way I figure it had more to cry about for herself than most anybody I know—was crying for someone else in her sleep. There's a girl somewhere in there that hasn't been destroyed yet. I can't help her—I know that. But I think you can."

"Well, we can give it a try. I've seen worse come out the other side." Mama Ben tucked the business card into his pants pocket, and turned to go back inside. "I'll be in touch."

"Thanks," Delores called out, "I'll be seeing you," as she watched the door close behind Mama Ben, who walked past Callie, going back into the meeting, and stopped, saying, "Well, come on, let's get started." The girl stood and followed him inside nervously. As they neared the circle, he guided her by the elbow, and pulled a chair into the circle, which expanded for her. "You don't have to say anything, just listen," he whispered into her ear. The meeting was over within ten minutes, and Callie's recovery had begun.

Eighteen years later, standing at the podium, holding the poker chip Mama Ben had just handed to her, in the room where they had first met, she was overwhelmed, as she had been each year at this moment. She let the emotion recede, with the wave of memory that had just washed over her, and finally answered the question, "How'd you do it," with a hug to Mama Ben, and sat back down.

CHAPTER 2. ATLANTA

The hugs seemed like they would never end. Standing outside the front of the Galano Club, the physical center of gay recovery in Atlanta, Callie felt as at home as anywhere in the world, and had felt that way almost since being dropped off there 18 years earlier. Still, she was ready to go get some decent coffee. She had stopped drinking the Maxwell House, or worse, swill served at the clubhouse years ago. The birthday party speaker that night—the one who shared his experience, strength and hope, in A.A. speak, but who actually gave a dramatic recitation of his life story, in the Galano tradition—was a black drag queen named Sam, whose personality was always in drag even when he was dressed like the Centers for Disease Control laboratory assistant he actually was during the day. He was just a few years younger than Callie, and she was his first sponsor when he came into the program, but 16 years later they were more like brother and sister than anything else.

When he stumbled down Dutch Valley Road into the Galano Club, wearing a spaghetti-strapped red-sequined mini-dress, clutching a matching evening purse, but noticeably missing breasts, shoes, and a wig, Mama Ben had looked over to Callie and said with a laugh, "Why don't you take this one, sister." When Callie realized Sam was high on crack, she was patient with him, for hours that stretched into weeks that stretched into months, like Mama Ben had been with her. Slowly, over time, she needed less patience. He came around, eventually, and worked with her through what they referred to obliquely as The Dark Time.

At the height of the parallel and overlapping crack cocaine and AIDS epidemics in Atlanta, the Galano Club was always an emotionally charged place to be. Someone was always dying, or dead, or wanting to die—for the pain to be over. Faith in a higher power was hard to maintain for many, sitting in a room where the faces of the young men were literally peeling away, some walking in with catheters plainly visible, some not able to walk at all, being rolled in in wheelchairs, their gaunt faces gasping for air through cracked lips, at 20, or 30, or 40 years old. It was painful, for those with and without faith, to watch their suffering. Belief in a hereafter did not lessen the pain of the here and now, for the sick or the well. "Pain," Mama Ben said one day as he helped Callie clean the chair of a man who had shat his chair during a meeting, "is always pain. Suffering is always suffering. We just see an end. We have hope. That's all that separates us from the people out there."

Callie and Sam, with Mama Ben aging gracefully at their side, made it through The Dark Time. They lost many along the way, but they gained more, in time. The circle of chairs that Callie joined her first night at Galano kept expanding. She arrived there in what was its first year—she got to see it grow and change, while she grew and changed within its walls, and outside. Her first months sober were hard—terribly hard—on her, on Mama Ben, on everyone who came into contact with her. The sense of self she had once tried to make into something real was not what she saw when she looked in the mirror. She did not see a beautiful young girl, or even a human—she saw the remains of something that might have been. As her mind began to clear, the sense of shame, of loss, of sadness, threatened to overwhelm her at times. Finding faith in a higher power—a creator, a god, a spirit of the universe—eluded her entirely for a very long time, and she struggled mightily with the concept that *the* God, or any god, cared about her personally. Her understanding of the Christian God, who was by far the most popular god in Atlanta, was gained mostly through the movies and television she had seen—she had never been to a church or any place of worship, not even for a funeral or wedding. Her understanding of Christmas was not unlike what a pygmy or aboriginal watching cable television might perceive—Santa, shopping, and family dinners. She began to feel, over time, very slowly, that there *might* be something out there. She developed a genuine interest in understanding every belief system she was introduced to, learning through both study and practice how each of the major, and many of the minor, belief systems of the world worked. She spent days at the library, and attended every variety of church, temple and mosque Atlanta had to offer. She picked up a belief here, a practice there, until she had something that she could recognize as religion in her own life—it was not a religion she shared with anyone, but it was sufficient.

It was during this same early time in her recovery, when she was living with Mama Ben, that she began exploring career opportunities. While comfortable, Mama Ben was by no means rich, or even well-off, and as much as he enjoyed having Callie around, both in his home and in his small flower shop, where he designed dramatic flower arrangements for the society ladies of Buckhead, he could not afford to feed and clothe her indefinitely. He told her as much when she was around two months sober, when both her thoughts and her appearance began to clear up a little—she was by no means clear-headed, but she was getting there. Yet she had no more idea at two months sober what she might be able to do for work than she had when she first landed in Atlanta two years earlier. Mama Ben made his first call to Officer Delores, who arranged for some vocational testing with the Georgia Department of Labor. It came back inconclusive. Callie had traveled the world, but her knowledge of it, her experience in it, was more limited than even the state prison parolees who regularly went through the vocational testing office. She did not know if she would like working with animals—she had never had a pet. She did not know if she would like working with children—she had never spent any real time with them, even as a child. She had never regularly cooked or cleaned or sewn or done friends' hair. She didn't know how to type or take shorthand. To virtually every question she was asked, her answer was either *No*, or *I don't know*. It was demoralizing to her not just that she had no skills, but also that she did not have even enough knowledge of herself to determine which skills she should try to learn. She rode the bus back to Mama Ben's tiny, cramped flower shop from the career assessment with the certain knowledge that she would never amount to anything.

Mama Ben dismissed her conclusion as nonsense, tied her hair back in a wide white satin ribbon he cut from a large spool, and asked her to mind the store while he delivered a rush order, as the delivery van was out for the afternoon, and there was no way to get in contact with the driver. Callie knew nothing about flowers, but she also knew from previous experience that the likelihood of anyone stopping in or even phoning was very slim. Mama Ben had many regular clients, including large midtown business firms for whom he provided weekly arrangements, but foot traffic was almost non-existent. She sat idly at the counter flipping through wholesale floral supply catalogs, and was surprised to see how inexpensive balloons were, and what the wholesalers suggested the return on investment might be. She got out the yellow-paged business directory, found a helium supplier, and determined that even with helium delivered, the cost per balloon would be nominal. She pulled the shop ledger from under the counter, and as she suspected, there was no efficiency in the flower operation—they were expensive, had short shelf lives, required refrigeration, and had to be kept on hand. There were seasonal fluctuations that could be anticipated, but there was always waste. Balloons, on the other hand, had virtually no expense, no maintenance costs, and could last virtually forever, compared to carnations. She attacked Mama Ben with the numbers as soon as he came back into the store.

He was not at all impressed with the idea of balloons—"Sweetheart, the only way my clients are going to buy balloons is if they're Gucci or Chanel—and maybe not even then," was his initial response—but he was impressed with the math she had worked out. From a pure accounting basis, her suggestion made complete sense, and she was fairly unrelenting. "But sweetheart," he said, "people can buy balloons in the grocery store. I've worked hard to build a reputation as a class act. I'm a great artist, you know," he said with mock affectation. "I can't be seen going downmarket."

"Even rich people go to the fair, and all kids like balloons. It's a fact." She wasn't sure it was a fact, but she knew she had a better idea than he did. "We're four blocks from the hospital, but nobody ever just stops in to buy anything. If you just tied some balloons to the parking meter out front, I bet you would get at least one customer a day."

He wasn't that interested in having a shop full of new customers wandering in off the street, but the shop was hard to find, even for people he wanted to find it. Nestled in a row of connected 1950s storefronts that stretched an entire block down Peachtree, each shop was virtually indistinguishable from the others, except for one with a giant slice of pizza painted over the entire front window. In the end, he gave in, and agreed to the balloons, on a trial basis. It was the first thing he had seen Callie get genuinely excited about since he met her.

He, on the other hand, was more excited about her math skills. The next day he called his contact at one of his clients, Arthur Andersen, one of the largest accounting firms in Atlanta at the time, and asked about getting Callie hired on in some capacity, even just answering phones. He was given the name of the temp firm they used, and the name of the contact there, and two days later, Callie began training to type and learning to use a calculator. Both skills came very quickly to her, and within weeks, she was answering the phone and preparing the correspondence of the Vice President of International Tax Accounting. It was a small department within a large office, so she received more personal notice from her coworkers than she might have in a larger secretarial pool. They noticed her very limited wardrobe, timidity, and general awkwardness in the place, as well as her incredible attention to detail, and an almost humorless devotion to following rules. If she was at work, she was working—no personal phone calls, no reading the horoscopes, no Avon catalogues, no engaging in harmless Monday morning gossip, even if prodded. Charletta, another temp from the same agency working in Payroll Accounting on the same floor of the office tower, suggested that "Anybody trying to be that good must have something baaaaad to hide."

Her boss, though, didn't see it. He just saw an intuitively smart girl that he wished his own children—spoiled, loud, demanding, lazy—were more like. She had a genuine interest in her work, and in his work, which no one in his family did. One week several months into her assignment, when he would be meeting with a client out-of-town for three days at the end of the work week, he decided to keep her for that time rather than have her temp somewhere else, even though there was not much work for her to do. Good temps were hard to find, and the possibility of her being poached by another firm, or someone else within his own firm, were significant. He gave her a busywork assignment that seemed real enough: Read and summarize the articles in the *Wall Street Journal* for the days he would be gone, as well as that month's *Journal of Accountancy*.

He returned on Monday morning to find on his desk each relevant article from both publications photocopied with Callie's summary of the highlights of each article attached to it with a paperclip. He was impressed with the clarity of her succinct writing style, and more than impressed, something like amazed, at her insight. She described how contemporary accounting methods were in contrast to, or enlarged upon, basic accounting principles—she recognized gimmicks and tricks, but she also recognized potential and value. He was so amazed, he did not at first believe it was her work. He thought it must be a practical joke being played on him by his office mates, so he called her into his office to question her.

He needn't have bothered. At that point in time, Callie did not yet have what might be called a sense of humor. The seriousness of her recovery from drug addiction had been so deeply impressed upon her that the idea of playing a practical joke on the man who was paying her, who was financing her new life of independence, would have been unthinkable. She could no more have played a joke on him than she could have flown to the moon.

She sat and answered his questions nervously—she was scared she might have gotten something very wrong, or that he was in some way displeased with her. The more questions he asked, the more pointed they became, and the more frightened she became, until he reached the outer limits of what she understood, and she could answer no more. He finally asked, "Callie, how is it you seem to know so much about accounting?"

She blushed—itself a remarkable effect for a young woman whose past would have suggested an incapacity for embarrassment. "I spent a whole summer a couple of years ago reading a bunch of old accounting books. I like it," was her response, which she sputtered out.

"Well, it was a summer well-spent, is all I can say. Have you thought about going to college? To get a degree? With an understanding like yours, you could go far."

She blushed even deeper. "No, sir," she replied. "That isn't really an option for me."

He regretted the intrusion into her private life, seeing how uncomfortable it made her. He let it pass for the moment. "I understand," is all he said, though in truth he didn't understand at all—he had grown up in an upper-middle-class family where the pursuit of the American dream was considered as obviously desirable as it was inherently attainable. Having never experienced real misfortune himself, his ability to consider its consequences was limited. He handed her his notes from his meetings, which needed to be typed up into a memo and distributed through interoffice mail and international fax—"Back to work, then."

While he let it pass for the moment, he did not let it pass entirely. The almost total lack of ambition he saw in the young woman was distressing to him. He recognized talent when he saw it, and he acknowledged to himself that anyone who had come into extended contact with her must have seen it as well. He determined that there must be some other source of her discomfort, or lack of self-confidence, or whatever it was. He likewise reasoned that the only explanation must be some mental or social anxiety problem. He also knew the office tower where they worked was full of people with similar problems—for every one person like himself who brought in and interacted with clients, there might be 15 or 20 people who sat looking at spreadsheets and memorandums all day, never interacting with the public at all. Accounting was still in large part a man's world—there were few women CPAs, and even fewer female executives at his level. Whatever Callie's problem was, they would just work around it. If he played his cards right, he thought he might have the most clever assistant in the entire firm, for about a quarter of what she might be worth.

Before he hired her on full-time, and she became an Arthur Andersen employee, he decided to test her in a more aggressive way. With the extensive company library at her disposal, she had a full week to identify an accounting irregularity in the corporate tax return previously filed for a new Andersen client by a rival accounting firm. He already knew the irregularity was, as did the IRS, but it wasn't public information—and no one under his management level knew what the problem was, only that Andersen was getting the client. He brought in another temp to cover for her, while she was doing what he called a special project. He gave her the assignment on Monday morning at 9:00am. She reported back to him on Thursday right after lunch. She didn't bring in a typed, formal report—she just knocked on his office door, with a sort of shrug of her shoulders, and said "I think I got it."

It turned out that she got it, what he was looking for her to find, on Monday afternoon, but had continued searching the massive document because she didn't believe she could find that easily something he had given her a week to find. So, she kept searching, and kept finding more and more irregularities, and explanations for them that had various degrees of sophistication and accuracy. What she found, and what the IRS missed, at least initially, were discrepancies in exchange rates and foreign valuations. Individually, the mistakes were minor errors, but collectively, they were substantial, and she reasoned, intentional. If the mistakes were systematic, they would have been consistent—which they were not. But by selectively applying inaccurate currency exchange rates, the other firm had significantly devalued the taxable income of the company. Bob was blown away.

Friday morning, Callie was presented with a job offer--$26,000 a year to be his executive assistant. From the $3.35 an hour she had been making, the new salary made her feel like a millionaire. It also made her nervous. It felt too good to be true. It would be enough money to move out of Mama Ben's place and get her own apartment, to be a real adult, to be, to do,…. What, she did not know. But she remembered the night of the party at the museum in Los Angeles, when she felt on top of the world. She had that feeling again now, and it scared her.

Over the course of the next year, her knowledge and understanding of accounting grew deeper and expanded in breadth, under Bob's direction. She did not become an accountant, and was not working towards becoming one. But her ability to knowledgeably discuss and utilize theories of accounting, especially when applied to international accounting, was significant. Many of the firm's best accountants could easily lose sight of what was before them when presented with two or even multiple currencies in the reports they were reviewing, but not Callie. She did not think of the funds she was looking at as currency at all, but as beans—Deutschemarks were German beans, Francs were French beans, and so on. It was simplistic, but simplicity was what was needed. By eliminating the exotic, inherently foreign nature of the reports, she was able to apply basic standards to them with ease that properly trained accountants, accustomed primarily to working in American dollars, took great labors to achieve.

By the end of her first year as full-time Andersen employee, she was regarded with suspicion by most, whose jealousy of her beauty, youth or talent had given way to contempt at her apparent disinterest in themselves. They had given up asking her out for drinks after work long ago. They understood that she couldn't drink, but that didn't mean she had to be antisocial, which is how they perceived her. The trained and educated accountants saw her as something of a freak, if an attractive one, and distrusted her as much as many of them wanted to have sex with her. She, in turn, rejected and distrusted everyone, not entirely excepting her boss, whose objective in keeping and training her she did not understand. He, sensing some of the burgeoning animosity in the office, encouraged her to develop friends there, but she replied that she didn't have time. And, it was true enough. Officer Delores still regularly, if less frequently, stopped by Galano and sat in the parking lot until meetings ended to see if she was there. And if she wasn't, and Mama Ben wasn't there to explain, there was hell to pay. Twice, Officer Delores showed up at work to interrogate her, and even though the officer didn't make it past the security desk in the main lobby, and was not in uniform, whispers of the visits made it all the way through the building. Whispers of *What do you think she did?* travelled up and down the stairwells.

One day early in March, the first real gorgeous, dry, warm, sunny spring day, Callie took her sack lunch out to a small park near the office tower, and sat on a bench for a little longer than her usual lunch hour. It was a few weeks after she identified a problem with reports coming from a branch office in the southeast, in which a number of executives in the office tower were embarrassed. She was surprised to be called into Bob's office, where he was sitting with the director of human resources, the director of security for the firm, whom she knew only by sight, and, somewhat incongruously, Officer Delores. It felt as though a cold hand had reached up from the grave and grasped her intestines. She wanted to run, to cry, to pee. The other shoe was dropping now, and she could see it in their eyes.

She stopped in the doorway and forced herself not to stutter when she spoke, which was difficult, but not impossible. "What's wrong?" she asked.

They saw the fear in her face, and looked to each other for guidance. It was the officer who spoke first, saying with something like a smile, "You didn't do anything wrong child, come on in, we just need to talk to you."

In that moment, she did look like a child, wide-eyed, small, and weak. But she walked in and sat in the armchair they had waiting for her. The others sat in a small circle, which reminded her of the Galano Club, and she truly wished for the first time in her life that she was at an A.A. meeting. She walked in and sat, and the security officer stood to close the door.

Bob began, "Callie, you're not in any trouble. None at all. You've done nothing wrong. Before we say anything else, I just need you to understand that, ok?" He wanted her to stop trembling. He wanted, for the first time, to hold her, but not like a woman, like one of his own children. He knew he could not, and the frustration of it forced him to continue speaking. "You've done nothing wrong." His repeating it didn't make it feel any more real to her.

218

The human resource director, Pam Spivey, an aging woman with silver rings of hair piled high on her head, cut to the business at hand, which she knew would be the quickest means of calming the girl. "Callie," she began, "yesterday afternoon I received this videocassette through interoffice mail." She held up a black VCR tape in her hand. Callie could see the word *whore* scratched into its top surface with deep, sharp, jagged cuts. "Several others in the office received copies as well, with other words carved into them. The tape depicts a young woman, many years younger than you, but who looks a great deal like you, engaged in sexual acts with a number of grown men. While we don't believe it is you," it was a lie, and it made everyone uncomfortable as they tried to look as though this statement was true, "we think someone believes it is you, or wants us to think it is you. But we're more concerned that the tapes were sent from within the office. We learned from Bob that he has given you some assignments that may have made you a target of internal animosity, and based on what we're looking at here," she gestured to the tape in her lap as she spoke, but did not hold it up again, "we are quite frankly concerned for your safety. Officer Cannon agrees with us." Here, she nodded to Delores, and continued, "but she disagrees with us as to how to proceed. We would like to identify and prosecute the person who did this. We do not want this person working at Arthur Andersen. Or even walking the streets for that matter."

Here Delores cut in, "But I'm more concerned about you. Your safety. We don't even know for sure how many of these tapes were sent out, or if more than one person may be involved, and likely never will."

Bob cut the officer off, "But we will try if you want us to. We can open a full investigation into this."

"But we will never be able to fully contain it," the human resource director cut in again. "The word about this tape has already spread through the office. You know how it is." Callie wasn't sure if she meant just the office tower, or Georgia, or the south, or offices, or just people in general, but she nodded her head in agreement anyway.

The firm's security officer spoke for the first time. "Callie, I'm Steve Whitfield, the head of security here. Not just for the building, for the firm's southeast operations. The tape here shows a girl no more than 13 or 14 years old, and likely younger. As a result of a Supreme Court ruling last year, just the possession of these tapes is a felony. As soon as I became aware they were on company property, I put a call into Fulton County, and received a call from the vice squad shortly after that. When I explained the situation, they put me in contact with Officer Cannon, who agreed to come down. We met just briefly before you joined us."

"And we agree," continued Bob, "that the level of protection you need you cannot receive here in the office. Your work has been more valuable to me than you know—which is why I think it's you, and not me, on the receiving end of this, whatever it is."

"And regardless of whether or not you want to look into pressing charges—it's unclear what charges you could directly go after, since you weren't the direct, intended recipient of the tapes—Arthur Andersen is prepared to keep you on at an increased current salary, with benefits, allowing you to work from home on the assignments you have been working on. As long as you aren't doing work for anyone else in competition with us, we see no reason to lose you," Pam said. She added with a smile, genuine and maternal, "Bob says you're a valuable asset. And if any company can recognize the need to retain valuable assets, it's this one."

Callie looked to Delores. She was still trying to process all of the information presented to her, and was still shaken from the first impression that she was going to be fired. She still wasn't sure what it all meant, but she would do whatever Delores told her.

Delores smiled and said, "Callie, I think it is a good offer, and a good solution. If we did try to prosecute this, even if we could identify the person or people responsible, you would almost certainly be called to the witness stand. A trial of this sort, involving a firm this prominent, would draw media attention from well outside Atlanta. I think a quiet solution will serve you best."

"Ok. What do I need to do?" was her quiet reply. For the many things she was grateful for in that moment, the greatest was that they not asked her if it was her in the films. She had been prepared to answer *Yes* just to avoid being asked to watch any part of any one of them.

There was a general easing of tension, a sort of collective sigh of relief that went through the room with her words—she was going to cooperate.

"Not a thing. We're going to install a dedicated phone line at your home for business purposes, for which you'll receive a stipend each month. Your paychecks will be deposited by wire transfer every two weeks. Your assignments and all correspondence will be delivered to Midtown Florist by messenger, no name. When you're done, you'll call Bob, and he'll send a messenger back over. Just to be on the safe side, the only people in the office who will know about the arrangement are the people sitting in this room. As far as everyone in the firm will be concerned, they will see you leave here today with the officer and never return. They may think you've been arrested—and we think it's ok if they do," Pam said. "When you don't return, they will assume you've been fired or quit. If word gets out about the payments to you, which may happen, people will assume its hush money of some sort. But, I don't discuss personnel matters with anyone in any event, so no one will ask me. Bob will tell them you decided not to come back, and that is what you can tell anyone you may run into on the street, if you ever do."

"Whoever is behind this will be much less likely to come looking for you if he thinks you're in jail, which is why we're going to let you leave with Officer Cannon, and," Bob began, then paused as if he were going to continue, finally adding in a tone that was more paternal than she had ever heard from him, "Callie, the increase in your salary is going to be sufficient enough for you to move into a secure apartment building somewhere. Please use it for that."

Callie wasn't sure how to respond, and before she could think of something, Delores said, "I can walk Ms. Pennington through the motions from here." It was the first time the officer had ever used her last name. It sounded funny coming from her. "Are we about done here? I need to get back to the assignment I was on when you called. And I'd like to give Ms. Pennington a ride home."

They said their awkward goodbyes, and Bob told her she would receive her first assignment in the next couple of weeks. Callie emptied the few personal things she had from her desk, and walked to the elevator bank, aware, as she walked, that every person on the floor, and some from other floors, seemed to be huddled in groups where they could see her leaving with Delores, in plainclothes, but still plainly a police officer of some sort. She had the feeling of being watched through the downstairs lobby, out into the street, to the officer's waiting car.

As they walked to the car, Delores spoke for the first time since leaving the meeting. "It may not feel like a break, but this is a break, girl."

"I think it feels like a break. It's just, you know, weird."

"That's 'cause you're not used to anything good happening to you. You just got a raise, and you get to work from home, 'cause some nut job buying kiddie porn recognized you." It wasn't a question—she knew. "Oh, and we still gonna find the pervert that did this. Not my department, but they're already on it. It just won't be connected to Andersen, or you, at all."

When they arrived at the flower shop, Mama Ben wasn't surprised at all to see them. Callie could see on his face that he knew everything. And for the first time in her life, Callie believed that there were people looking out for her, people caring about her, people working to keep her safe, make her happy and well. It was her first real glimpse of hope. The tenuous hold she had on life before that moment had been more suspicious, something like the possibility of hope, the belief in the possibility of something other than what she had known before. But it was in that moment, in the concern and love on Mama Ben's face, that she truly felt hope for the first time.

And it was in the next few days that she found the desire, and the courage, to find Antoine. She had discussed it with Mama Ben before, made lists and weighed the pros and cons, but had never quite felt right about calling him. She had never felt well enough to disguise the uncertainty in her voice—not from Antoine. But now she felt she could find him, could tell him she was safe, and with people who loved her. She could call him and not be ashamed of letting him down. She could let him know she finally had a good backstory, and it was real this time.

She began with Neiman Marcus, Giorgio of Beverly Hills, Fred Segal, and the chic little shops where Antoine loved to spend his days. She did not leave her name anywhere—she just said she was an old client looking to track him down. She sat with a copy of the Beverly Hills and Los Angeles yellow pages, copying out phone numbers, at the recently-opened Central Library of Atlanta, a building designed by the architect Marcel Breuer. She found the monumental brutalism and lack of symmetry somehow comforting, and she more or less set up office there—she sat at the same table each day whether she was working on accounting or looking for Antoine. The librarians liked her and knew her by name. Delores' suggestion that she would work from home turned out not to be very real—Callie needed a place to get up, and out, and to, each day, and it was the library.

What had seemed to Callie to be permanence in the Beverly Hills shops turned out to be a fabrication in her mind—not only were none of the salespeople she remembered still employed, none of the ones who were there remembered anyone named Antoine. In reality, the turnover of salespeople at those stores was extraordinary, as was the stores' own popularity among stylists. She decided, in time, that he had likely moved on to other shops now considered more chic. He may have even chosen a new name. All she knew for certain was that after six weeks, she had called more than 200 stores in Los Angeles, and only six had any idea who she was talking about, and none of those had seen him in a while.

The most direct way to find him would be to just go to Los Angeles herself, but she and Mama Ben both believed that there was still real danger for her there. So she decided, out of desperation, to hire a private investigator, and, in an abundance of caution, not to look for Antoine, but for his friend Rutherford. They reasoned that however lucrative hand-modeling might be, it could only employ so many people, and most likely only one man named Rutherford. And as an extra precaution, it was not Callie, but Mama Ben who actually made the calls and all the arrangements with the investigator. Two weeks and $250 later, Callie had Rutherford's phone number. She left a message on his answering machine: "You may not remember me, but you met me at Cowboys a while back. You were with a friend of mine. I'm trying to get in touch with him. If you know where he is or how to get in touch with him, I would love to hear from you." She left the number for Mama Ben's shop, and ended the message.

Two days later, Mama Ben called to let Callie know she could phone Rutherford, but suggested she make the call from the shop, which was consistent with the precaution they had taken all along. But the look on Mama Ben's face when Callie arrived the next morning was not consistent with his usual aura of maternal serenity.

"What's wrong?" Callie asked as soon as she entered the store and had a good look at him.

"I am an open book, aren't I?" Mama Ben replied, with an exaggerated expression of disgust, putting down a bunch of forsythia stems on the work counter between him and Callie. "I wanted Rutherford to tell you, and he wanted to tell you, but, well, sweetheart, Antoine died last year."

The remorse, regret, and sadness washed over Callie like a December rain. Ever since she heard the first mumblings about AIDS, each time she had watched some new friend or stranger wasting away, she had wondered *What about Antoine?* She did not immediately ask Mama Ben how he died—in her heart, she knew, knew she had known for some time, and realized that what she had dismissed as morbid reflection was actually intuition. She just wanted to know when.

"Last summer, I think. Here, sit down, call Rutherford. He will have the answers. I'll get you some tea." With that, Mama Ben turned the phone around so the rotary dial faced Callie, put the piece of paper with the number on it beside the phone, and disappeared around the corner of a partition wall that separated the front of the shop from the back. Callie picked up the phone and dialed, and was answered on the first ring.

"Hello. Hello?" His voice sounded eager.

She was afraid to speak. "Hi," she began, "It's Calli—", but she was cut off.

"Sweetheart, darling, oh my God, we were beginning to think we would never hear from you. Even when I spoke to your friend Ben yesterday, I still didn't actually believe I would be talking to you today. We've been looking for you."

"Mama Ben," was all Callie could think of to say.

"What did you say darling?" Rutherford asked.

"Mama Ben. His name is Mama Ben. My friend that you talked to."

Rutherford laughed. "He was serious then? I thought, well, I don't know what I thought, but what kind of name is Mama Ben? I had no idea he was serious. Well, good for him, I suppose. Anyway, he filled me in a little bit on what's been going on with you. It sounds like you're okay now. Are you okay, sweetheart?"

"Yes, I'm okay. He just told me about Antoine. A few minutes ago."

A deep sigh came from the Los Angeles end of the line. "I'm so sorry darling. It really is just awful. Antoine cared for you very much, you know. He wanted you to know that. Do you know that?"

For what felt like the first time in her life, she was crying, not from grief, or sadness, or pain, but from love. "Yes, I know," she almost whispered into the phone.

"He tried to find you. Even before you were on the plane, he tried to find you. He tried finding those goons again, but they disappeared without a trace, to Cincinnati or someplace. He even tried bribing Zach, but Zach just laughed at him."

Callie looked up from the leaves strewn on the counter, at Mama Ben, returning with chamomile tea in a ceramic mug. Her grief was interrupted by confusion. "How could Antoine bribe Zach? Antoine didn't have any money."

"Ooooh. About that. Yes, you're right. Antoine did not have any money. Antoine was nobody. But Anthony Edwards—a name, by the way, I didn't know existed until Antoine was hospitalized the first time—he was rich. Filthy rich. Not Rockefeller rich, but still, rich enough. Part of a family trust—used car lots, recycling plants, smelting operations—all sorts of ghastly things Antoine would never have discussed. A family dynasty, centered in Dayton but scattered around the Midwest. His family did disown him though—that part of Antoine's story was true. Not in the way Antoine described it, but true enough. But they couldn't disinherit him. The way the trust was set up, they couldn't keep it away from him once he turned 21. But he just had whatever dividends or payments or whatever were to come to him put into savings. He was scared the family might finally find a way to get him cut out of the trust, and he wanted something set aside, to retire on, back when we used to think about retiring. Now we just think about dying it seems. Anyway, he mostly lived off what he made, like the rest of us, but with the knowledge he could fly off to Paris like Nina Simone and live comfortably for the rest of his life without raising a finger."

"That's insane." Callie was more surprised by his life than by his death. Her tears were checked by her astonishment. "All that time? He had all that money?"

"Yes, darling. He couldn't get to it quickly enough to keep you in L.A., but he tried. And, well, now you have all that money."

"What?"

"He left everything to you. That's why I'm so happy to hear from you. The family tried in court last year to have the will annulled, saying he wasn't in his right mind, you know, all the usual crap. But the judge said no, that it was all perfectly legal. You are the legal inheritor of a one-twelfth share of the R.F. Edwards Family Trust. I hired the best attorneys in L.A. for you, but they were worth it."

The flow of information was overwhelming her, and she was grasping for words. She had to pull herself out of her thoughts to find what to say next. "Well, um, that was awfully nice of you, Rutherford. You've gone to an awful lot of trouble. You don't even know me. Thank you. But I still don't understand, really."

"Well, it wasn't just for you. It was for him, too. And for me. He made me his executor. I get six percent annually, and that's something, sweetheart. I introduce myself as Executrix Rutherford now. It pays better than hand-modeling, I can assure you. I only had two years to find you, then the money was to go to the Humane Society, I think just to piss off his family—he didn't even like animals, that I know of."

Callie was absently doing math in her head, and asked "Just the six percent of the revenue on my one-twelfth share is more than you make modeling?"

"Yes, darling. It's big money."

"I see."

"But the money was really just his way of saying he loved you. And he did. He regretted so much everything that happened the night of that party, especially his part in it. He felt so bad. So did I. That Zach was just a piece of fucking work."

"What do you mean *was*?"

"Oooooh. You don't still have feelings for Zach, do you?" Rutherford sounded uncertain as to whether or not to recite this part of his story—it was feeling like a story he had told before, or at least been rehearsing.

Callie had never considered the question, but decided to go with the obvious answer, and replied "No, of course not."

"Good, that makes this part easier. Six weeks after Antoine died, Zach got murdered. At home. Butchered to hell and back. It was all over the papers. Apparently he had been doing some laundering for some of his shady connections, something went wrong, you know, the usual. Everyone always wondered how he could afford to live so well. I mean, he was successful and all that, but still—how many accountants do you know who live like that? I mean, even in Hollywood?"

She realized the answer was *None*.

"If Antoine could have held out just a little longer, things would have been so different. But, well. Never mind. But you can come back now, sweetheart. You can come back to L.A. You don't have to stay there anymore."

"How did it happen? Antoine. How did he die?"

There was a pause, and then he asked, all the bravado and timing of the recitation draining from his voice, "Are you sure you want the details? Does it matter?"

"It matters."

"Well, then. It was quick, and painless. At least, as deaths go these days. After he saw the first lesion, he said *No more*, that he wasn't going out that way. He got ahold of pure pharmaceutical morphine from somewhere, and injected himself with 500 milligrams. From what I understand, about a tenth of that would probably have done it, but he wasn't taking any chances."

"Oh my God. Was he alone?"

"Well, sweetie, I think he was with you. In his heart, at least. But yes, he was alone, in a grove of eucalyptus in the Will Rogers park. He used to go there sometimes, after you left, to walk and get fresh air. Then his vision started coming and going and he had to stop driving. I took him there a few times. He left a note for me saying where he was—he had been more or less saying his goodbyes for a few weeks, making his arrangements—death has become so common now, it's like an everyday thing. He wasn't the first, and won't be the last. You know, I went the first 40 years of my life seeing a total of maybe six dead bodies, including at funerals. Now in the past year I've seen over thirty, and not all in funeral homes, which is where they should be, if you ask me. Anyway, that grove is where he died, and where he wants his ashes scattered. And, well, he wanted you to do it. To scatter his ashes. I have them here. We used to talk about you there, at the park, try to think where you might have gone, where they might have taken you. Zach wouldn't tell him anything, just that he would never see you again. He finally got tired of Antoine bothering him, started threatening him, and, but, well, that's all over. You're alive, and you're well. You can't imagine how happy this would make him, to know. And I'm kind of happy myself, to be honest. And not just for the business with the money. Antoine was so in love with you, he made everyone love you."

"In love with me?"

"Of course, darling. You couldn't see that? Just because he didn't want to have sex with you doesn't mean he wasn't in love with you. He absolutely adored you. Really, it's the purest kind of love, if you ask me, when friends fall in love with each other without even the possibility of sex. You could search all of Hollywood and not find a straight man more devoted to his wife than Antoine was to you. Ever. But you may find another one, one day. Not another Antoine—that's not possible. But another somebody who loves you just the way you are, just for who you are. And, well, if you don't, you can cry yourself to sleep on a mattress full of money, attended by an army of naked manservants. That's my plan."

Callie tried not to smile, but couldn't stop herself. She even laughed a little. But she didn't believe him, not about finding another friend like Antoine.

They were ending the conversation with plans for future conversations, the trip to California for her to sign papers, set up accounts, and scatter Antoine's ashes, and the conversation was winding to its apparent close, when Rutherford exclaimed, "Wait, wait, wait! I forgot the best part!"

Callie grimaced as she tried not to imagine her life with Antoine as a cocktail party story with good parts, or a best part, but realized it was too good a story for someone like Rutherford to pass up at any opportunity. "What's that?" she asked politely, but without any real warmth.

"The dress! The Valentino!"

"But I never went to New Yo—" she began and he interrupted, "I know, darling, I know. But just in case you tried to, Zach called up the Valentino boutique in New York and said for them to ship the dress to him here, and they said no, you had to come in for a fitting, and Zach said you were gone, and he was going to give the dress to someone else, and they said no, the dress belonged to you. It was a huge scandal, with lawyers and threats and the whole shebang, but as it turns out, the sales ticket was in your name, not Zach's. The dress belongs to you. It's waiting for you, in New York."

"How did you find all this out?"

"One of the girls from Neiman-Marcus here moved to New York to work at Valentino. So when the dress came in, and all the hoo-ha started, she recognized your name, and gave Antoine a call, knowing he knew you, and it sort of went on and on from there. Anyway, after they died—Antoine and Zach—I contacted Valentino, let them know I was looking for you, to hold on to the dress. It's in long-term storage, but it's waiting for you. Even if you don't want to wear it, you could have them finish it and donate it to a museum. It's couture, darling. You shouldn't just leave it lying in a box. And, Antoine really wanted you to have it, and he wanted to see you in it. Those snapshots of you pinned in it were so unsatisfactory—we both agreed on that. This may sound creepy, but I think he thought if you turned up dead, he would bury you in it. He never said it in just that way... I don't think he ever believed you were dead, not for a minute. Maybe it was just the idea that if you were dead, you deserved to be buried in couture. The whole point is, he never stopped thinking about you."

"I understand," she said, and she did. They said their goodbyes, and the call ended. She looked to Mama Ben, whose face had returned to its placid state of maternal imperturbability, and asked "What am I supposed to do?"

The first thing she had to do was tell Mama Ben everything Rutherford had said on the phone—he had been very cautious on the phone the day before, and Mama Ben was unable to pick up from what he overheard on Callie's end of the line what all Rutherford was saying. When he had the full story, he began by asking "Valentino? Couture? Really?" He gave Callie a visual assessment that made her uncomfortable—he had never looked at her body in that critical way before.

"Hmph. Well, yes, I suppose so," he said slowly. He looked back at her face, saying "I wish I could have been a fly on the wall. Valentino! But why didn't you ever mention that before?"

"It's just a dress. I didn't think it was that interesting."

He looked at her with sympathy both genuine and affected. "Bless your heart. If those drag queens at Galano ever find out about this, you're done for."

The attempted makeovers of Callie had begun almost as soon as she entered the clubhouse door, but try as they might, the men of Galano could not convince her to dress the way they would dress if they were her—either as hookers, or

Joan Collins, or Joan Collins as a hooker. On one memorable occasion just a few months earlier, when she was doing after-Christmas sale shopping with Mama Ben and a newly-sober drag queen, the man, who was wearing hot-pink leather pants, a lavender tank top, and what he imagined to be subtle daytime makeup, held up a confection of multi-colored sequins and tulle and asked Callie "Why don't you try this on?"

"Because I'm not joining the circus, I'm going to a sober New Year's Eve party," was her reply. Callie was tired, and bored of hearing the word *fabulous* from the young man's mouth. She wondered if he even knew what the word meant.

He looked back at her, in her worn Sebago dockside shoes, khaki pants, and drooping navy blue sweatshirt and said, "You know, just because you are an accountant doesn't mean you have to look like one."

"I'm not an accountant."

"Then you should change your costume, 'cause Halloween is over, honey."

"Bitch," she replied in her best drag queen demeanor, which was not very good.

"Bitch, please," he replied back instantly and on cue, with a waspish, dramatic hand gesture that was something between a snap and a wave.

She ignored him and turned to her friend, asking, "Mama Ben, do I look like an accountant?"

Every part of Mama Ben's face answered *Yes*, except for his mouth, which replied, "You don't look like a young woman obsessed with her appearance, but I wouldn't say you look like an accountant."

"What would you say I look like?" she asked, surprised, and surprisingly hurt for a young woman who actively concealed her figure, wore no makeup, and pulled her hair straight back into a rubber band.

"A lesbian mechanic on holiday to her family's lakeside trailer?" the drag queen interjected helpfully, as Mama Ben looked for the right words.

Callie and Mama Ben both ignored him.

"A color-blind drill sergeant just back from the Congo? A veterinarian's assistant on her way to hose out the kennels?"

Callie and Mama Ben both turned to stare him down, and stopped him before he could go on, which his tone suggested he had every intention of doing.

"Well, darling, you've never expressed any real interest in, you know, being chic or anything. I didn't know it mattered to you," Mama Ben finally answered. The drag queen had wondered off to a nearby sales rack, so they could speak earnestly without fear of becoming part of his vaudeville act, which seemed to have no end. "If it's something that matters to you, we can work on it. But why don't we go get some coffee? I'm exhausted."

They left the mall, and the subject had never come up again. But it seemed to have resurfaced in both their minds as Mama Ben had looked at her—in the same deck shoes, khakis, and sweatshirt—standing at the work counter, trying to imagine her in a Valentino dress.

"It might be time," he suggested, "to spruce you up a bit." She looked at him, a little hurt. "Oh, and me too, darling," he added, consolingly. "We can't go strolling into Valentino looking like people with jobs."

"You're coming with me? I mean, we're going? You think I should go? To New York?"

"If you don't go, I'm stealing your driver's license and going for you. I may not look like a twenty-year old girl," he said, pulling his long white hair into a chignon and looking in the reflective glass of a nearby flower case, "but for couture, I'm willing to pretend."

She laughed with him, and they began planning her makeover, and the trips— not just to New York, but to California—all the while aware that beneath the sheen of excitement lay the inevitable sadness of Antoine's death. They seemed to have come to an unspoken agreement that they would deal with it, in time.

And they did. On a warm blustery Sunday that June, teetering in heels down a path she thought she would never see again, Callie gathered with what was left of Antoine's friends to finally scatter his ashes in the eucalyptus grove. Rutherford and Mama Ben had both insisted on heels. Other visitors to the park that afternoon thought some sort of avant-garde photo shoot must be happening, seeing the young movie star whose name they did not know in the long red dress and cape, being escorted, at times held up by a group of men, some in jeans, some in leather, and an older man with white hair in a caftan and beads. But being Los Angeles, no one thought much of it, though some did linger, apparently trying to guess the starlet's identity.

The ceremony was short, and simple—Antoine's family had been invited, as a matter of course, but neither attended nor replied to the invitation. No one had any idea what religion Antoine might have been, so they settled on the only Episcopal priest they could find available that Saturday afternoon. The priest was Spanish, and spoke with an exaggerated accent, as well as a lisp, and no one understood much of what he said, but no one was really listening. They were thinking about themselves, reflecting on their own mortality, not unlike any other group of mourners on a gorgeous sunlit day.

Callie's cape kept whipping up, snapping the air, lashing out playfully at the men around her, until Mama Ben gently put his arm around her waist, and held the cape down for her. When the time came for her to sprinkle Antoine's ashes, Rutherford presented her a small, amethyst-colored glass Lalique urn with a motif of leaves and berries, capped with a silver lid. Before she took off the lid, she was scared the wind might blow the ashes into her face, or the faces of the men standing round her, but neither happened. The breeze calmed for just a moment, and she quickly took off the lid and tipped the ashes out. Before they hit the ground, a surge of warm air came rushing from the ocean, over the hills and down into the valley, lifting the ashes straight up into the sky, dispersing them, fleck by fleck, into the atmosphere, whisked away, and just like that, Antoine was gone. The elasticity of forever, which she had never contemplated before, entered Callie's head. Feeling dizzy, she handed the urn back to Rutherford, and turned to look at Mama Ben, who held her steady.

"He's gone, forever?" she asked quietly.

"Forever, for now," he replied.

They skipped the gathering at Cowboys, where mimosas were being served on the house, in Antoine's honor. Rutherford dutifully, if somewhat regretfully, toured Mama Ben around Los Angeles, showing him the landmarks of both the city and Callie's time in the city. Callie had changed into a Norma Kamali ensemble of a loose tunic with dolman sleeves and batik-print Capri pants. On their way to the airport that night, they passed by the motel where both Callie and Rutherford knew she had spent her last days in Los Angeles, but neither spoke of it. She wondered who was in those rooms now, where their lives would take them. Would they even get out alive? *Who decides?* she wondered, not for the first time, but for the first time directly connected with a specific place—*Who decides who gets out alive?* and *Who saved me?* and *Why?*

***

She found her answer to the last of these, or what sufficed for an answer, around two weeks later, when Sam stumbled down Dutch Valley Road and into Galano. He was still a grad student at Emory University, but just barely holding on. He was a popular performer at the Armory, a gay leather bar in midtown, and his cocaine-fueled drag shows there on Sunday nights had been cutting into his Mondays, and frequently his Tuesdays. His absence in the laboratory, and the decline in the quality of his research, had begun to be noticed by his research and thesis advisors, and their rebukes were one of the major motivating factors behind his decision to make that long walk to Galano. It was imperative to him that he stay in the research program, and it became imperative to Callie that he stay sober. She couldn't do anything for Antoine, but she could do something for Sam, and she latched onto him like a mother hen. When they weren't in A.A. meetings together, Callie would go sit with him in the Emory library, and they would work together— she on her accounting, he on his research. During this time, they discovered the most extraordinary kinship, and developed an ability to sit together for hours without speaking, then casually drift back into conversation, and out again. Theirs was a continuous dialogue that lasted for years as they grew up together in sobriety.

And now she was waiting for him, somewhat impatiently, to continue that dialogue. The bronze-colored medallion with the *18 Years* emblazoned on one side and *To thine on self be true* on the other was sitting on the table before her, for no particular reason. It was just doing what it was supposed to do—be a physical reminder of her past. She was waiting for him outside the Starbucks in Ansley Square Mall, chatting with some of the regular hang-out-after-the-meeting crew, catching up on gossip she missed during the week. The patio was a covered area where they could smoke and drink coffee and play cards for hours without interruption. A changing cast of characters played out as the evenings, and as the years passed. Tonight there was Eric, an aging, brash antiques dealer with a bad coke habit; Carlson, a wisp of man in a snug Armani Exchange t-shirt, barely 20, with six months clean from meth, but unable to put down his cell phone; Josh, an orthopedic surgeon who kept mostly to himself, but whose all-American looks, solid body, and apparent celibacy made him among the most sought-after of the Galano men; and Luc, better known as Luc-with-a-C, as he always introduced himself, a well-groomed, articulate shoe salesman at Saks Fifth Avenue, a person with a perfectly sublime knowledge of shoes and sex, but no apparent knowledge of or interest in anything else.

There were two other tables of post-meeting gatherers nearby, and Callie knew that as soon as Sam arrived, all the tables would join together, the real meeting-after-the-meeting would begin, and after a respectable amount of time to allow Sam to bask in the glow of his successful, if somewhat shaky, performance, she would be able to take off alone with him for chicken and waffles at an all-night diner that was a favorite hangout of theirs. But an hour had already passed. She was on her second triple grande soy latte with whip, and the conversation at her table was at a near standstill. Sam wasn't answering her texts, which was very unlike him—his work at the CDC required him to be on-call 24/7. When he told people he was a lab assistant at the CDC, most envisioned him as some sort of helper or cleaning person, which wasn't the case at all. He was a highly-regarded, very well-paid researcher, specializing in mind-numbingly boring investigations of amino acids in protein chains. But he was happy to let people think he mopped the floors. He had discovered over time that even when he told people the truth, especially those who had seen his luxurious pied-a-terre on Lenox Road, they still didn't necessarily believe him. He could see in their faces that they thought he must be a drug dealer, the child of an athlete or celebrity, or a criminal of some sort. The idea that a young black man could honestly, legally make enough money to live like a rich white person was viewed with suspicion equally among white and black people. His Driving-While-Black-Arrest-Averse Toyota Supra was in the parking lot, and Callie had parked near him. He was there in the shopping center somewhere, or at least had been.

Finally, at 10:20pm, more than an hour after the meeting ended, she got a text saying "B right there." Seconds later she saw him walking not from the parking lot, but down the sidewalk from the 24-hour Kroger grocery store at the other end of the shopping center. *What the hell?* He had no bags, and he was walking strangely, as though he wanted to run, but was trying to look casual. It was odd, because he almost always walked like he was on a catwalk, ready to take a turn and shrug off some clothing at any moment. The hesitancy in his demeanor was completely unlike him. The closer he got to them, the more she realized something was wrong.

"Hello, ladies!" he called out to the group, as was customary, and the men sitting at the tables began to stand to hug and congratulate him, most for the second time. But with the dramatic affectation of a 1930s silent movie star, Sam held out his arms and tossed back his head to keep them at bay. "Thank you, thank you," he said, "but I'm afraid I must delay your adoration. I've been called into duty, and someone has to pay for all this fabulousness," he continued as he gestured sweepingly up and down his body with fluid movement of his long, thin, toned arms. There were murmurs of displeasure and signs of disappointment—Friday coffee was where Sam usually held court, and without him it was typically a lackluster affair.

"Next week, darlings, I'll be back, promise," he said with his hand placed gingerly over his heart in the sign of a pledge.

Throughout this, Callie could feel a tension underlying his performance—and it *was* a performance, more than usual. He was trying to act like himself, and doing a very good job, but she knew him too well not to hear the faint jitter in his voice, to not see his usually carefree mannerisms suddenly characterized with a mechanical awkwardness. He was trying and failing to do something, but she had no idea what.

And then, out of nowhere, he asked "Could I borrow you for a few minutes, Callie? Oh, and you too, Josh." Callie looked first at Sam, then at Josh. Josh looked at Sam, then at Callie. Sam turned as if to leave, saying, "Come on darlings, bring your things, we may be just a moment."

Callie shrugged, but gathered her few things together, and called after him, "Do you want your drink? I got you a cinnamon dolce latte. It's cold. I can get you a new one."

"I'll take that one, darling, no time for a new one, chop chop," and he began walking back down the same way he'd come from, towards the supermarket. "Well, come on, you two."

Josh was in utter confusion. Except for a few times when they had first met two years back, Sam had never given him the time of day, unless they ended up next to each other at dinner or coffee somewhere. As he stood, he tried to get some information from Callie, but she had no more idea what was going on than he did. They started to follow Sam, who slowed down so they could catch up.

"Sam, what's going on? What's wrong?" Callie asked as soon as she was within distance to talk to him without raising her voice, passing him his drink as she did so.

"I wish I knew," he said. "This has been the strangest day of my life, and I've had my fair share of strange days. I look forward to telling you all about it, but we don't have time right now. Just follow me. I'm going to do some shopping, and I need you to just stay within earshot of me. You too, loverboy," he said over his other shoulder to Josh, still in forward motion without understanding why. The *loverboy* comment struck both Callie and Josh as odd, but for different reasons—neither had ever heard him use it, and while Callie could find no reasonable explanation for it, Josh could find no reasonable explanation for it to be coming from Sam. Josh had a past—but he could think of no reason for Sam to know about it.

"Are you alright, Sam?" Callie was growing more concerned with each word that came out of his mouth.

"Yes, darling, we just need to get moving," he said as they crossed through the automatic doors and into the entry of the store, where he pulled a grocery cart from one of the many standing waiting—there were few shoppers at that hour on a Friday.

"It's getting kind of late, Sam," Josh began, until Sam turned and cut him off with a look of determination, and said with less drama than dull earnestness, "Just follow me, Joshua Landrum. You'll regret it if you don't. I promise you." He turned and started walking until he found an aisle with no one on it. When he confirmed that they were both within hearing distance, he began, speaking quickly.

"Last night I received a call from my aunt Ida Mae. She tells me a cousin of mine I've never met is in Atlanta and needs to meet with me for breakfast this morning. I tried to put her off, but she won't take *no* for an answer. I agree, she gives me the man's name and number, I call, we meet this morning for breakfast. And he spent most of the day telling me the most extraordinary story, and in the most extraordinary way possible. The reason we're having this conversation in the grocery store is because the two of you are under surveillance. You have been for years. I've seen and heard some of the tapes myself, today."

"Sam, what the fuck," Callie began, but Sam cut her off, "Callie, do you trust me?"

"Of course I trust you, but—" she began, but he interrupted her. "There are no buts. You have to trust me. And you have to let me finish."

"I don't know you or trust you," Josh began with some heat, but his voice faltered as Sam turned on him with an expression that could stop a feral hog in its tracks.

"Romeo, you just shut your mouth. You're hardly one to be talking about trust. Callie, every word we've ever heard from this man has been a lie. Well, most of them, anyway. He's no more gay than my grandpappy. He's fucked more women than I knew a man could. Sometimes two or three at a time. They have video of that, too, loverboy."

Callie, astonished, looked at Josh, and saw it was true. They both wanted to stop walking, but Sam kept going. "We don't have a lot of time, people, keep moving."

"Why would anyone be interested in me? You're just not making any sense," Josh replied, but kept walking.

"And why both of us? We barely know each other," Callie added.

"You know each other better than you think. Or at least longer." Sam stopped in front of the granola bars, and started loading boxes of them into the cart. "St. Patrick's Day 1974, in Dublin, Georgia. Josh, you were discovered in a grocery store freezer with a young girl who disappeared from the hospital that same day, correct?"

Josh's mind turned sideways. He almost fainted in that instant—he felt himself slip back in time, into the sheriff's arms, then back forward into the grocery store where time seemed suddenly frozen. His eyes searched Callie's face as if she was a ghost. She looked to Sam, but he was already turning to move.

"Keep walking. We need to keep walking," Sam said, and pushed the cart forward.

"Yes," Josh said simply. He was trying to look at Callie as they walked haltingly, almost stumbling, to keep up with Sam, who stopped again abruptly to look at applesauce.

"Well, here she is." Sam appeared genuinely interested in the applesauce. When he found the right one, organic, with no cinnamon, he put all they had in his cart.

Could it be true? Josh dared not believe it—he had been dreaming of this girl for years, since he was a child. A girl whose face he could only remember in dreams, a girl whose existence he had been assured of, but had never entirely believed in. He had read about her in the paper, and the clippings were pressed in a copy of *Frog and Toad are Friends* he had kept from childhood. There had been cash rewards for information leading to the whereabouts of a girl, but not a woman, not a grown woman. In his dreams, the girl had never grown—she had been frozen in time, in 1974, as had he.

"Are you Vicky Dewberry?" he asked without caution, without embarrassment, without knowing what the answer might or might not mean. He just wanted to know.

Callie had not heard that name in over thirty years. She had been Callista Pennington for so long, that she sometimes forgot Vicky Dewberry had ever even existed. However surprised Josh may have been in that moment, Callie was overwhelmed. Her past had risen up like a loose floor plank in a cartoon, and hit her in the face, without warning, without any way of bracing for or avoiding it. She grabbed hold of a grocery shelf with her right hand, expecting to faint, or simply fall. She did neither.

Sam answered the question for her. "Yes, she is, but I didn't know that before today. And we have to keep moving. Josh, bring her."

Sam began inching the cart forward, looking back over his shoulder to confirm that the two of them were following him. He saw Josh take Callie by her left arm, and urge her forward, with the most gentle effort. She looked in his face, searching, and let go of the shelf. They began walking, and Sam put the cart in motion.

He continued talking as they walked, turning his head from side to side and throwing his voice behind him. "Callie, I'm sorry this is happening this way, or at all, but it has to be." He sounded genuinely sad, but also, still scared.

"Why, Sam, what's happening?" she asked him.

"I can't explain it. I don't understand it all, to be perfectly honest." His voice was uncertain, but determined. He was walking again. "But can the two of you accept that there are people who have been monitoring your lives, either for a very long time, or at least very extensively?"

"Yes," Callie said instantly, at the same moment Josh said "No."

Callie had two reasons for believing him—first, her past was buried so deeply that someone must have been doing at least one of those two things, and second, she knew Sam better, and loved and trusted him as much as she had ever loved anyone—he hadn't replaced Antoine, but had grown into some new place in her heart. Neither of those things was true for Josh, who neither loved nor trusted Sam, nor knew him well; and, he believed that the things Sam was presenting were things that could have easily been learned through an exhaustive internet search. He saw nothing profound, or even noteworthy—his chief suspect was gossip.

Surprisingly, Sam smiled, as he paused, took out his cell phone, made a few swiping motions, and handed the small device to Josh, saying, "They really do know what they're talking about. They said you would need convincing, but that Callie wouldn't. Press play."

As Sam began looking through canisters of dried nuts, the voice of a young man, possibly in his late teens or early twenties, soft, Southern, but not quite effeminate, began speaking: "Josh, you're never going to love me the way I love you, are you?" and a voice that was clearly Josh, but much younger, replied, "No, Will, but you're my best friend, and always will be." There was a brief pause, and then a woman's voice, slurred with drunkenness, began saying, "Fuck you Josh, just fuck you. Get the fuck out of here. Get out and don't ever come back, ever." By the end, her voice was screaming. There was a brief pause, and then the sound of an older man, with a deep middle-Georgia accent saying "Josh, you need to get back down here to Dublin. It's your mama. When I woke up this morning she—" Josh looked for and pressed the button to stop the recording. He saw that he had played only 22 seconds of a sound file that was over four hours long. He wordlessly handed the phone back to Sam, who put two value-sized cans of unsalted cashews into his cart.

"I don't understand—" Josh began, but Sam cut him off, saying "I don't need you to understand. I already told you, I don't understand. I just need you to believe. Do you believe me now?" Josh had just listened to recordings of three of the most intimate and sad moments of his life, stretching over 20 years. If his choices were to believe, or listen to the rest of the recording, he would choose to believe. "I believe you. But why? And who? And what are we doing here?" He gestured to the grocery store around them, but Sam wasn't looking at him.

"The who and why of that is on a need-to-know basis, and I don't need to know, so I can't tell you. Honestly, I don't think I want to know. But you will. The reason you're here is because the audio surveillance that is being done by satellite apparently has a difficult time with fluorescent lights." He gestured to the ceiling, which was an almost-solid bank of fluorescent tubes, whose gentle humming could be heard even over the store's music system, which was playing Whitney Houston's *I Wanna Dance with Somebody* at a volume that seemed unnecessarily loud in the nearly-empty store.

He continued, "Not only do they give off a slight hum, each tube gives off a slightly different hum. It's very subtle, apparently. But enough to throw off the aerial surveillance equipment, which follows you wherever you go, and automatically adjusts to filter out wavelengths that interfere with the reception of your voices. But so many different sound signals confuse it. In any event, you aren't their primary concern right now. Your monitoring has been mostly passive for the past several years, but apparently that is about to change, and before it does, you need to be under the radar. And it appears that going under the radar will put you on it. If you can see what I mean."

"I could see what you mean if you were talking about someone else, but Sam, I have nothing. I know nothing that could warrant the sort of thing you're talking about," Callie said, still somewhat astonished. "My life has been more interesting than most people, sure, but for the past 20 years I've basically been a surrogate mom to a bunch of gay men in recovery. Who gives a shit? I mean, are you sure the government—I'm guessing it's the government?—doesn't track everyone this way?"

"I'm not sure of anything. Except I can't believe how many calories these fig newton bars have." He put the bars back in their place and looked at her. "From what I understand, it isn't everyone, no. And at this point, it's less about what you have, than it is about what they have. I need some soup." He pushed the cart forward with a jerk and made a sharp 180-degree turn before stopping in front of a display of canned soup that stretched to the front of the store.

It occurred to Callie for the first time to ask, "Sam, what are you doing with all this food?"

"Well, love, when they realize you two have gone off the radar, they will go back to the surveillance tapes, realize where they lost you, hack into Kroger's digital surveillance files, see me be the last person known to be seen with you, and come looking for me. I've been trying to keep my head moving while I talk so they will be less likely to be able to read my lips from the surveillance, but it's harder than you think, really. To answer your question, once you two are safely on the road, I'm going into lockdown in the lab at the CDC. I'm taking enough food to be there for a week, but it's likely they will get in before that. The important thing is, by then you'll be long gone. We think you'll have about an eight hour head start, depending."

"Depending on what—" Callie started to ask, at the same time Josh began "I'm not going anywhere."

Sam looked at Callie with a smirk and answered, "Depending on how long that takes." He gestured with his head to Josh—both his own hands were full of reduced-sodium vegetable soup.

"This isn't going to take any time at all," Josh replied with anger for the first time, "because I'm out of here. I don't know what sort of X-Files reality show bullshit you have going on, but you can count me out." He turned and was walking away when Sam called out after him, "Your daughter needs you, Josh."

Josh stopped dead in his tracks, but did not turn around. He stood for a full minute without saying anything, looking into the middle distance at the end of the aisle where two-for-the-price-of-one cinnamon rolls were heaped onto a folding table with patriotic bunting.

Put out by this lack of response, Sam continued, "Did you think that of the literally hundreds of women you've had sex with, that not one would have a child? You did go to medical school, right? I know you're an orthopedic surgeon, but you still understand how human reproduction works? Well? Don't you?" Josh's continued silence was provoking him into anger. Sam's own father had abandoned his mother, and a successive string of violent and abusive men had taken his father's place. Any mention of abuse, or neglect, or abandonment, always filled him with disgust, and he could not keep it from his voice. "Your daughter is literally being tortured right now. You hide from your addiction in a room full of gay men, you hide from your past by never making proper amends to the people you've harmed, and when given the chance to help your child, you just stand there? With your back to me? When you should be begging me for the opportunity to help? Fuck you, you pussy." Sam was surprised by his anger, at the sound of his own voice rising, at the unmistakable tone of resentment that sharpened each word he had just spoken. So was Callie. She knew his childhood had been as unpleasant as hers in its own way, but she had rarely seen this side of him, or this part of him, so alive, so raw. She wondered why she wasn't angry. She knew Sam had information she did not have, but she reasoned that information was not what was informing his emotions. Yes, there was resentment—she heard that plainly enough. But fear, she decided, was the real culprit. Somehow, she was not scared. The things Sam was saying and doing were confusing, and his intentions were unclear, but she was entirely unafraid.

"Sam," she said quietly, "Whatever Josh is or isn't, we aren't going to change it on the soup aisle, here, tonight. Whatever it is that needs to happen, if we could do it with him, we can do it without him. We are invincible. We are woman. Hear us roar." She smiled, and was hoping for, and received, the smallest smile from him in return. She could see the anger washing away from his face in waves like a slow autumn tide. He was back in control, and she was glad. "What else do you need? And what else do I need to know? I feel like I'm still missing some parts."

She had taken the grocery cart from Sam and was turning it around in the aisle so they could go back the way they came, avoiding Josh, who was still standing motionless, looking lost, even from behind. She felt pity for him, but a second glance was all she felt she could spare—Sam was her friend, the only person on that aisle she loved. If it meant something to Sam that she help save Josh's daughter from being tortured, if that was really happening, she would do it. At least, she would call some of her attorney friends and decide what the best way to approach it might be. Even if someone was monitoring her phone, she reasoned that no one was above the law, and calling an attorney for help was a perfectly reasonable thing to do.

Except. Except. Except she did know someone above the law, or at least between the law, someone who had slipped between the cracks. She, herself, did not exist, not in any legal sense. She was a fictional piece of paper in one place, and a missing person in another—at least, she thought she might be a missing person. She did not know if her father, or anyone, had ever reported her missing. Since her first and only brush with the law 18 years earlier, she had never questioned how relatively easy her life as a fugitive—Was she a fugitive? She didn't think she was a fugitive. But, was it really this easy to assume an identity? Somehow, thinking about it for really the first time in years, which in retrospect seemed extraordinarily foolish, she thought it probably wasn't. Had someone, some group of someones, had a hand in helping her maintain her assumed identity? That would make it easier for someone to make her disappear, certainly, but why would they? The overlapping complexities raced through her mind with sickening speed, but with no outcome—she didn't have enough information to formulate a conclusion. She hadn't seen Delores in several months, but suddenly she wanted to call her. She had a thousand questions about law enforcement, and her brush with it, that had never even crossed her mind. The grocery cart had not yet completed its turn when she began to pull out her phone.

Sam saw the gesture and nodded in apparent agreement, "Yes, you should go ahead and take the battery out."

Before she could respond and correct him, they heard Josh call out from behind, his voice directed towards them, "You're wrong."

They turned to look at him, waiting for him to say something else, but he didn't. He just walked towards them, his arms awkward at his side as he moved slowly but with deliberation down the aisle. When he reached them, he looked Sam in the face and said again, "You're wrong. And you're not very nice, either. Where is my daughter? And what is her name?"

Sam looked at him appraisingly before he responded, with a degree of self-satisfaction that bordered on contempt, "There's nothing kinder than the truth, Josh."

"I don't know what all you've heard, but even if you'd heard everything I've ever said, know everything I've ever done, you still don't know the truth. Not my truth. The kindest truth you could tell me right now, is where my daughter is."

"We're the sum of the actions we take, Josh, not the decisions we make, not the feelings we have. We are what we do, nothing more."

Callie could feel the two of them preparing for some philosophical showdown, and wasn't interested in hearing it. "Boys, this isn't really the time, or place, is it?" She didn't wait for an answer, but continued, "Sam, you wanted him to come, now he's coming. What else were you going to tell us? If you could get to the part where this somehow involves me, I would appreciate it. I have no memory of 1974. At all." But even as she said it, she knew it wasn't true—there were memories, but she always thought they were memories of dreams, of her father carrying her down a hospital corridor where paper shamrocks were taped to the patients' doors, of walking through a creek, of a boy with metal legs.

After a moment's hesitation, Sam began moving the grocery cart forward again, and began to speak, "Josh, in 1994 you were at Augusta National for the Master's golf tournament. You were on the 12th hole, or green, or whatever they call it, when you met the daughter of a former instructor of yours from the Medical College of Georgia. Later in the evening, when the two of you were good and properly drunk, you had sex in the woods, I don't remember which ones. Anyway, eight months later she gave birth to a daughter. Fourteen years later, that girl, Jacqueline Lucille Etheridge, was placed into foster care and into the home of—" Here, he was cut off.

"Lucy? My Lucy? Josh is her father?" Callie was still trying to wrap her head around the idea that the man she had known as a gay man for the past two years was some sort of heterosexual Lothario, when this fresh news that her first and only foster child, taken in at the urging of officer Delores, was his child. It happened the year before she met Josh—or thought she met Josh, or could remember meeting Josh. "How can that be?"

Was it planned? Was Delores part of some sinister plot involving her and—*No.* She decided instantly that whatever was happening, why whatever was happing was happening, Delores had no more awareness of it than she did. Again, she retrieved her phone.

Sam stopped her with a word. "No, Delores can't help you. I made the same connection, but no, she is not part of this, whatever it is. She will be one of the first people they contact, if they contact anyone. A phone call to her now would only put her in jeopardy."

"They who?"

"I don't know, exactly," Sam answered. He was looking at cat food. "Which food do your cats eat, Josh? I can't remember. They all sound the same."

"Are my cats coming with us?"

"No, Mama Ben will look after them, but I need to pick up some food and drop it off. You're out of food, right?"

"Almost, yes, but how do you know that? Mama Ben knows about all this?"

"You put a reminder on your phone to pick up cat food. They, I mean we, hell, I don't know, I guess everybody has access to your phone, your computer, your bank accounts. Everybody watches everything. And, no, Mama Ben knows nothing, but he has a key to your place, doesn't he?"

"Yes, but," Josh began, but Sam cut him off, saying, "Well, there you go."

"I'm sorry, but who cares about my cats?"

"We're just dotting the T's and crossing the I's, as they say," Sam responded.

"Who says that?" Josh asked.

"Just shut up and get the goddam cat food," was the impatient reply.

"How much?"

"However much they have. Just get it."

Josh put the only four bags of the specialty cat food his cats ate into the cart, and Sam moved it forward almost instantly.

Callie realized as they were standing in front of the bags of cat food that other than what she had personally observed of and about Josh, she knew nothing. It wasn't only that she had been misled about his sexuality, if she had been—she didn't even know he had cats. She did a quick mental accounting of the time they had spent in each other's company over the past two years, and came up with a number around 96 hours. In coffee shops, restaurants, and just sitting around outside Galano with the smokers, she had spent almost four full waking days with this man, and she had begun the evening without even basic knowledge of him. Now, she began to see that their lives were somehow parallel yet asymmetric, like two cars that start a trip across the country on the same road at the same time without knowing it, perhaps passing each other on occasion, maybe eating at the same places, staying at the same motels, spending more or less time in different places, one then the other taking the lead. Now their lives were being laid bare before them, and the trip they had been on was being explained, but only partially, and in hindsight. But for what purpose she still could not see.

For his part, Josh was simply lost. As much as Callie wanted to call Delores, he wanted to call Mama Ben. It was a long time since he last felt as alone and alien as he did standing there with Sam and Callie. His path forward seemed clear, even if the destination remained unknown. His anger stemmed from the loss he felt, not the uncertainty ahead of him. As Sam had suggested with an almost cruel indifference, Josh was a sex addict. When he first sought counseling, the therapist had suggested that Josh begin attending 12-step meetings with other sex addicts, which Josh did, and he found himself surrounded with people whose problems he considered almost mundane, even trivial, compared to his own. This feeling was compounded in him by the inability to fully explain himself to any of them. After a year of trying the few 12 step meetings Atlanta had for sex addicts, with no success, and straight A.A. meetings, where Josh met newly sober and desperate women who leapt on and clung to him, Josh's therapist suggested he try out the Galano Club. The therapist had many gay clients, and he felt that Josh had little to lose by giving it a try. Josh had no sexual attraction towards men at all, but one of the few really intimate relationships he had ever had was in his late teens and early twenties with a gay man. At the very least, the therapist had reasoned, there wouldn't be the risk of him meeting even more women—which had been Josh's experience at A.A., N.A., C.M.A., S.C.A., and pretty much every other kind of twelve step meeting all over the metropolitan Atlanta area. Josh met Mama Ben—himself a recovering sex addict, among other things—for lunch at the IHOP on Peachtree one afternoon, and after a four-hour conversation, Mama Ben took Josh to his first meeting at Galano. And almost immediately, he felt at home. With the exception of Callie, who he purposefully avoided, there were no heterosexual women who regularly attended meetings there, and few lesbians. The attraction of the gay men to him was flattering, but posed no threat to his addiction. He made several friends over the course of his first few months of attending meetings there with Mama Ben, but the lies of omission, such as his heterosexuality, and lies of distortion, such as that he was an alcoholic, prevented him from developing true intimacy with any of the men there, except Mama Ben, who became his sponsor in his recovery.

Mama Ben was the only person, since he was six, he ever told about the voices. He realized, even at that young age, within hours of telling the startled young therapist, that it had been a mistake. The look on his parents' faces after their private meeting with the young lady told him so. He then pretended throughout his childhood that the voices weren't there, and his parents pretended to believe him. He found some small ways to manage the voices—listening to music or television with his father's headphones clamped over his ears worked, for a time, as did reading, and getting lost in a story. But these were very temporary fixes. He discovered over time that there was something like a pattern or a rhythm to the presence, volume, and number of voices he heard, but he could not understand it enough to meaningfully use the information to avoid them. With his parents' help, he might have been able to figure it out, he sometimes thought, but that was not and would never be an option for him.

Despite his advanced reading skills, he still did not perform well at school throughout his early childhood—his lack of attention and focus, not just a result of the voices themselves, but also the fear of them returning at any time—resulted in poor performance on achievement and placement tests. His performance at sports and even playtime activities such as model-building was considered weak by his parents and teachers, who believed him to be very bright. But the evidence to support their belief in him did not materialize up to and through the sixth grade.

And then, when he was 12, and he began exploring his body the way 12-year-old boys do, he discovered that the voices would go away whenever he touched himself. It was a discovery that changed his life, by removing the oppressive and daily fear that he was, or was going, insane. By that age, he knew from cartoons, televisions, and movies, that people who heard voices were not normal, not right, and should be wrapped in straightjackets and put away. Despite the fact that the voices he heard were indistinct, and had never actually said anything to him in words he could distinguish, he had secretly believed himself to be a danger to his family, friends and schoolmates. And now, this fear was lifted, providing not only relief from his aural anguish, but also significantly improved grades at school, agility in sports, and the ability to focus on the Boy Scouts projects whose badges had been beyond his grasp. But this presented a new set of problems, not beyond the ingenuity of a 12-year-old, but also not beyond the observance of parents who, though perfectly willing to overlook the fact that their son continuously had one hand in his pants pockets at all times, found it distressing to be called into Moore Street Elementary to meet with the principal, counselor and teachers who were less willing to overlook his newfound activity.

After a mortifying conversation with the school counselor and Josh's seventh grade teacher in which the words *compulsive, obsessive* and *deviant* were used a lot, his father's conversation with Josh seemed only mildly embarrassing. "Son, you can play with that thing as much as you want—just don't ever let anybody catch you at it," he said with something close to equanimity.

Josh, confused and ashamed, agreed immediately, and kept to his word. Unfortunately, the recent upturn of his report cards, which only he one could date back to his self-discovery of self-pleasure, began a reversal. His grades plummeted as he fidgeted in class, with distant voices murmuring in his ear, and he restrained his hand from reaching reflexively down in his pocket to make the voices stop.

After another visit to the school to discuss his declining grades, his parents sent him to the family doctor, who quickly prescribed a high dose of Ritalin, and Josh, within 72 hours, had to be sedated and hospitalized. The drug caused the distant murmurs to grow closer and more distinct almost at once. On the first day, he began to hear his name, and could make out infrequent nouns and verbs which he attempted to string together into meaningful communication, but he could not. On the second day he began to see shadows everywhere, in dark corners and open daylight, gesturing to and hiding from him. The third day, the police, an ambulance, and his parents were called to school where he had locked himself in a supply closet and was talking incoherently. He could not be coaxed out. When they finally broke down the door, he came running at the officers like a small rabid animal, with an open pair of scissors, and it was only the dullness of the blades that saved Sheriff Eric White's life. After Josh was taken to the hospital, the doctor who prescribed his drugs—the family doctor who had delivered him at birth, and seen him his whole life—explained to the officers that Josh had experienced a very rare, very violent reaction to the drug, but that he was fine.

But he was not fine. In the weeks that followed, his best recourse was to find times and places to be alone without drawing attention to his absence. At school this meant extended trips to the bathroom between classes—never during, no drawing attention. At home it simply meant staying in his room all the time, which his parents were secretly, guiltily, happy about—they did not know what to do with this strange young man their beautiful little boy was becoming. In sports, the occasional gropes and tugs that other boys used to emulate their grown counterparts provided him sufficient cover until he could get home and go to his room and shut the door and get under his bed covers. Church, though, proved at first to be a problem, because he spent so much time there. Between Sunday School class, the Sunday morning service, afternoon choir practice and the Methodist Youth Fellowship before the evening Sunday service, he usually spent between 8 and 10 hours at the church each Sunday—far too long to go without going to the bathroom, which is how he thought of it. It wasn't pleasure for pleasure's sake—in fact, he found no pleasure in it. It was a chore for him, like the diabetic kids with their insulin, but one that only he could know about.

The church was massive, and of relatively newly construction, but in the classical southern style, with a monumental sanctuary supporting a slender but aggressively aspirational steeple taller than the sanctuary itself. Built on the top of a gently sloping hill, the church was three proper stories tall, not including the soaring ceilings in the sanctuary at the top of the hill, or the steeple. On the lowest level, and partly submerged in the earth, was the recreation room, or *Rec Room*, as it appeared in church bulletins. A nod to the Methodist sensibility of engaging youth, it contained a pool table, ping pong table, foosball table, and a collection of matched sofas and chairs that could be easily rearranged on the linoleum floor for movie screenings, board games, informal Bible studies, or birthday parties.

Accessible either by four steps down from the rear parking lot at the bottom of the hill, or through the interior by descending an echoing cinderblock fire stair, the Rec Room provided the perfect solution for Josh because the same broadcast system that piped the church service to the children's nursery was channeled in through a speaker in the ceiling, allowing him to soothe himself while listening to the sermon. And he was listening, with intent and purpose, and not just to be able his parents' questions about the service. He wanted to learn about God. He wanted to believe, because he thought faith might provide an explanation, or remedy, for what no one else could or would.

But he did not have faith, and until he found it, his respite would be where he could find it. And he found it in the Rec Room. His first Sunday service there was entirely an accident—he was looking for a bathroom with privacy, and the toilets in the Rec Room were the only single-occupant bathrooms in the church. The Rec Room door was typically locked, especially during church services, but as frequently was left open, as it required a key to lock it. It was relatively easy to find a parent willing to unlock a door for events at 8:00pm on a Friday or Saturday night, but no parent wanted a call at 11:00pm or midnight to lock the interior door of a room with nothing of any real value to steal, in a building whose exterior doors were secure.

On a whim, he bolted down the stairs just as the Sunday service was starting, and he found the Rec Room door open, went inside, into the Men's Room, pulled the bathroom door closed behind him and locked it. He sat somewhat nervously on the toilet for the entire service, his pants around his ankles, his hand between his legs with only his thumb softly stroking himself, listening intently to the preacher's voice, which was muffled by the bathroom door and intermittent hum of air conditioning units nestled in the shrubs just past the Rec Room windows. When he returned the following Sunday, the Rec Room door was locked, and he retreated to an upstairs Sunday School classroom supply closet he found unlocked, and he spent the service in the company of hand puppets with the faces of donkeys, kings, and wise men, as he strained to hear the sermon from a hallway speaker through two closed doors. That Saturday morning he took his mother's keys from her purse before she awoke, bicycled to the Ace hardware downtown where no one knew him, and had a duplicate made of her master key to the church.

In the weeks that followed he repeated his first Rec Room experience, with the exterior and stairwell doors locked from the inside, and the wide metal window blinds closed. At first he stayed in the bathroom, sitting on the toilet, as a sort of precaution, but he left the bathroom door open so he could hear more clearly. His absence in the sanctuary wasn't noticed because all of the older children and teenagers sat together at the back of the church, and they snuck in and out of the service all the time, so his parents would never take note of his absence even if they were aware of it. However, they never noticed. His classmates knew that he was up to something—all of them had been together since preschool both at church and in Mrs. Choate's preschool, Mrs. Marshall's kindergarten, and up through the early grades at Moore Street Elementary. They knew Josh was a little odd, but he was more normal than odd, and he was a better-than-good athlete at every sport, so they let it pass. It was two of these schoolmates, both older, but who were nevertheless part of the group he hung out with, who helped him learn how to make the voices stop for hours at a time.

Easter Sunday was always a blow-out at the church, with part-time Christians arriving in their springtime best for their annual pageant walk down the nave in search for seats, to join their full-time Christian friends who kept the church going the rest of the year. When all the pews were full, folding chairs would be crammed into the center and side aisles until the only room left was to stand in the back of the church. Just before the service began, when he knew his parents were seated, Josh walked through the nave and out a door to the right of the pulpit, as if going to the bathroom down the hall, which he did. He then returned through the sanctuary, spotted and waved to his parents, and kept walking to the back of the church, as if to sit there, which he did not do, but kept going, out through a side entry door in the foyer in the front of the church, across the lawn to a carport, and through a meandering path within the church that ended at the stair down to the Rec Room. Once safely down the stairs and inside the room, he secured the doors, shut the blinds, and sat on a sofa upholstered in a synthetic pastel plaid. His back was to the windows, but he could see their reflection, and the horizontal bars of light spilling through them, in an oversized framed poster on the opposite wall that said *Keep on Truckin' With God!* in an orange early-seventies typeface two feet tall on a brown background—a remnant of an earlier decorating scheme that was never replaced. This was what his eyes rested on as he began the first part of a ritual developed over the past few weeks, which began with him touching himself through his pants as he listened to the church announcements—he listened to them carefully in case there were some mentioned in the service that were not in the printed church bulletin. The ritual would end an hour later, with him stretched across the pool table, the heels of both feet anchored in two corner pockets, and his pants and briefs pulled down just enough to free himself. The broadcast speaker was directly above the pool table, just a few feet from his face, and it was there he kept his eyes focused. He would lay there, softly caressing himself throughout the service, and at the end would be able to give his parents an articulate summary of the sermon—better, in fact, than they could have given themselves.

It was near the beginning of that Easter sermon, during the traditional scripture reading from the Book of John, that Josh heard the faintest metallic click from the stairwell, an echo from above, and then softly, but with the distinct shuffling and hesitation of people not wanting to be heard, the gentle footfall of two people descending the stairs.

He was as agile as he was alert, and before the unknown people even made it to the first stair landing, he was off the pool table and opening the bathroom door, which in that instant he realized provided a poor alibi. Better to hide entirely, he thought, and quickly surveyed the room. On the wall adjacent to the restrooms were two supply closets, one for sporting equipment and another for craft supplies and board games. He made his decision as the intruders turned down the second landing. He realized suddenly, and with some horror, that any of his classmates could do what he had done—most of their parents had keys. He unlocked the equipment door and pulled it closed behind him, and the color drained from his face as he heard a key turn in the stairwell lock. His pants were up, and he was clear of being caught, but the fear of what might have been gripped him in the almost-darkness. Light penetrated the closet door through a louvered grill right above his face. He stood on his tip-toes and watched through the grill with some amazement as two people he knew, but knew to dislike each other, pressed themselves against the door they had just closed and began to make out, aggressively thrusting and grabbing with tongues and fingers. The partial erection he had just a few minutes before, scared away by the intrusion, returned quickly and without encouragement.

Shut tight in the closet, the scents of leather, rubber, and vinyl from baseball gloves, basketballs, dodgeballs, footballs, baseballs, Frisbees, and all the rest, were close in upon him, filling his nostrils, seeming to seep in through his pores. He dared not move his legs at all—wedged between two green canvas rifle bags filled with wood and aluminum baseball bats, the smallest movement could set off a dissonant chorus of tinny clinks and clunks. He could only rise up on his toes, and reach down with his hand.

He watched as the girl, Jennifer Adams, a 16-year-old who the older boys said would swallow, take his friend Casey Lewis to a sofa, push him down in his seersucker suit, kick off her white sandals, hike up her eyelet sundress, and straddle him, grinding her crotch into his, through his suit pants, letting him run his hands all over her, pulling up her dress so high Josh could see her pale pink cotton panties, and Casey's hand reaching down into them. Josh unzipped his fly, and as if on cue, Jennifer rolled off of Casey and onto the sofa beside him, her hand finding and unzipping his trousers with the same practiced efficiency she might have used to unfasten her own bra, had she been wearing one.

Josh was marveling at Casey's good fortune much more than his own. Casey was a pudgy, pimply sapling stump of a man with flesh the color, texture and somehow even the smell of warm vanilla pudding. Fifteen years old, he could rattle off innumerable sports statistics and had a bedroom decorated completely with a sports motif, including a lamp with a ceramic football base, an alarm clock shaped like a baseball, and an intercollegiate wallpaper unifying the other diverse sporting elements; but, he threw like a girl, ran like a pig, and spent 90 percent of game time on the bench, and the other 10 in positions where he was least likely to lose a game for the team. That 10 percent was due to the generous support of Casey's ancient Dublin family to every noteworthy local cause, including generous support for the ballfields where he played so poorly. To not play Casey in a game was not a smart political, social, or career move—the influence of the Lewis family was as toxic as it was it was pervasive. He had just been given a brand new Pontiac Firebird with T-tops, tinted windows, and leather bucket seats a year before he could legally drive it by himself, but in Dublin there was no chance of him being pulled over by the police, or given a summons if he was. He was a Lewis.

Jennifer may have been thinking of the possibility of becoming a Lewis herself, or at least of cruising through downtown in that new car, as she began stroking Casey's penis with an expression of true longing on her face. Josh, at least, saw nothing to desire. He had very little knowledge, and no direct personal knowledge, of any penis other than his own. It took a moment, as he was waiting for Casey's penis to become erect, to realize that it *was* erect. What appeared to Josh to be a sad, shriveled, sorry thing the butcher might toss in with scraps, was actually Casey's fully erect penis. No more than three inches long, and diminishing in girth along its short length, it made Josh smile to realize that he was larger when completely soft than a mighty Lewis when a girl was stroking him.

That thought quickly passed. When Jennifer bent her head down over Casey's lap, and he pulled up her skirt and spread her legs apart, and pulled her panties to one side, and Josh could see Casey's sausage-stub fingers begin to fumble around and in her, Josh felt something strange begin happening to him that he couldn't understand or control. He had been aggressively stroking himself, fully erect, truly masturbating for the first time in his life, when a tremor began in the back of his legs, and his scrotum shriveled up like jumping in a cold pool, and his butt clenched tight together right before he felt a burning rip through his penis. He immediately let go of it, in fear that he had fractured or torn something in his manic stroking. He was alive with the terror of making noise, either from the sports equipment surrounding him or from himself—there was a noise that was trying to escape his clenched teeth with the same force that something was shooting from his penis, which was moving in spasmodic jerks of its own accord, as though searching for his hands. He realized as soon as he could think that he had just ejaculated for the first time. And as he stood in the dark with his eyes closed, he came to the realization that he had heard a noise, a metal clink—the baseball bats had shifted. It wasn't the cacophony he had dreaded, but a single, sharp, clipped, high-pitched clink. It was enough to scare them all.

The young couple had stopped. In the moment of his ejaculation, Josh didn't know or care what happened—his vision had gone away with his thinking and hearing—but looking again through the grate he could see the couple scrambling to arrange themselves, and, thankfully, looking through the blinds towards the parking lot for the source of the noise. After quick whispering Josh could not hear, the couple separated and departed, she up the interior stairs, he out into the parking lot. Josh waited over 45 minutes, until the beginning of the final hymn, to go to the restroom to check his appearance in the mirror there. As he guessed, his pants, shirt, and even his tie were ruined. But he was only partially distressed—the voices he had heard for as far back as he could remember were entirely, completely, absolutely gone. There was not even a trace of murmur. He raced to his parent's car to wait for them in the back seat, a nervous smile, something like happiness, stretched across his face. "How did you like the service?" his father asked. "It was awesome!" Josh replied, and in that moment he was as radiant as a young bride on her wedding day, in the honeymoon getaway car, off to begin a new life.

Monday was completely uninterrupted by any voices at all, though he remained on high alert for them. When he woke up Tuesday morning, he could hear the distant murmur of voices again, but he wasn't scared, or even very concerned. He took extra time in his shower that morning, to achieve the result of the church closet, and the voices were gone again, entirely, through the next morning. Over the next several months, the frequency with which he needed to quiet the voices increased until he discovered somewhat by accident, in the J.C. Penney dressing room, that by altering the situation, introducing novelty or an element of danger, he could come close to repeating the initial euphoria he experienced his first time. It wasn't many months before he had visited most every clothing store in town.

That fall he started 9th grade, and moved to Dublin High School, where he learned through the open locker room that he was what most of the boys bragged about being—really, very extraordinarily-well endowed. None of them knew how large he was because the incidental erections of adolescence weren't really possible for him. It took a fair amount of physical effort for him to achieve a real and proper hard-on.

He was still a virgin in the spring of his freshman year, when, due to a busy schedule and a lack of proper personal maintenance, the voices started returning around lunchtime the day before a big algebra test. He skipped his fifth period history class and went to the boy's locker room, as he knew there were no physical education classes immediately after lunch. He took his time soaping up in the shower, and had his head back under the water and both hands at work when the locker room door opened, so he did not hear the baseball coach and assistant coaches come into the locker room, back early from a trip to a regional athletics conference. He became aware of their presence only when one of them shouted "Jesus Christ!" and then another, "Put that thing away before you hurt somebody with it!" The men were not surprised at his being there, or his activity, as the sight of a boy being erect or masturbating in the locker room shower was almost as common as a boy showering at all. They were laughing at the comical proportions of his penis to the rest of him—when fully erect, it could not stand upright or stick out on its own. The weight of it forced it down between his legs, and its beer-can girth made walking awkward—his too-tight tighty-whities worked as a restraining device on most days, but not in the shower. As he started to recover from the shock of the men there laughing at him, he went to reach for his towel, and slipped in the water, almost falling. One of the coaches laughed, "He's tripping over the goddam thing." "I better not let my wife see that—she'd leave me in a New York minute." The men were red in the face with laughter, but had turned and were already walking away, still muttering in amazement, when one of them called back to Josh as he turned off the jet of water, "Don't miss sixth period, Donkey Kong."

By the next morning, the name was permanent. He had never thought of men, especially coaches, as being gossips, but he learned they were people just like everyone else when he walked into homeroom and the jocular raillery began that would last well into adulthood, up to and including his 25th high school reunion, where the guys wanted to know if Viagra worked on that thing of his. But on that day, they only wanted to know if it was true. "Hey, Donkey Kong, is it true?" "Coach said you got the biggest thang in Laurens County." "You've been holding out on us, Holmes," and on and on it went until after the bell rang and Mrs. Dorsey, the homeroom teacher walked in. Josh thought at first that she gave him a funny look when she walked into the room, but then decided he must be wrong, that there couldn't be a circumstance in which coaches would discuss such a subject in front of women. But his first instinct was right—he had been the primary topic of conversation that morning in the teacher's lounge. Josh wasn't yet experienced enough to know that really good gossip extends the bounds of decent conversation to every dark or potentially entertaining corner of human experience.

But another thing happened during this time that had not happened before— Josh became a person, a real, interesting person, whose name everyone in the high school knew. Dublin High School was a sprawling brick mass of 1960s architecture resembling nothing so much as the Pentagon on a much smaller scale, with a projecting corridor for each of the grades nine through 12, and a fifth for the entryway and administration offices. It was built to accommodate the students from more than a dozen widely-scattered elementary and secondary schools around town, and except for a few star athletes and pageant queen cheerleaders, there were few freshmen known by everyone at the school, but Josh very quickly became one of those few. Even the seniors who couldn't be bothered to learn the names of sophomores learned quickly who the Kong was. The first few weeks were uncomfortable for him, as people pointed, laughed, and made exaggerated gestures. There were girls who couldn't look at him without blushing, and other girls who looked at him with expressions of frank curiosity. But all that most people really knew about him at first was about his penis. In the weeks that followed, they also learned that Josh Landrum, the quiet athletic kid who (everyone who didn't know before, now learned) once attacked police officers at Moore Street, and that he was the kid who had been kidnapped in the Piggly Wiggly during the big storm when they were all little. He had become someone, someone with a history. He found himself actually playing in varsity baseball games. While he was very good, neither he nor anyone else anticipated that as a freshman he would be on the field during varsity games, but there he was, and playing at least as well as most of the seniors. He found himself invited to parties thrown by juniors and seniors, and people there became interested in talking to him about things other than his penis, which, while large, provided little ground for actual conversation. He remained quiet to the point of shyness, but his looks, which were never considered remarkable before, became nice, then good, then hot, to the young women who grew to know him, though except for a bit more confidence, and a greater likelihood that he would be smiling at any given time, his looks had changed very little.

That spring, Cindy Duncan, a senior, and the captain of the varsity cheer-leading squad, decided that the infidelity of her boyfriend and homecoming king Stewart Stevens was too much to bear, in part because she had never really cared about him, but mostly because she was bored. When she told him in the parking lot of the Hardee's adjacent to the high school that she was breaking up with him, he didn't ask why, only "What about prom?" The junior-senior prom was two weeks away; or, at least, the white prom was. The black prom was a week later.

"I'm going to take someone who knows how to satisfy a woman," she said in an overly-rehearsed, dramatic response, as she scrunched her face into something like sarcastic triumph that made her look more shrewish than is typically possible in a varsity cheerleader. She had not yet asked Josh, or anyone, to go to the prom with her, and she had no idea if he knew how to satisfy a woman. But she planned to ask him, reasoned that he must accept, and whether or not he would satisfy her was irrelevant—she planned to embarrass Stewart with reports of Josh's extraordinary talent even if she didn't have sex with him. She knew Josh would never deny having sex with her—no man in his right mind, much less a freshman, would call her a liar on such a score. She was beautiful, she was homecoming queen, she was Miss Saint Patrick's Day, she was the captain of the varsity cheerleaders, she was a Duncan, and she had been successfully manipulating men since before she understood what manipulation was. This was revenge, this was victory, this was *Fuck You* to the small town and simple-minded boyfriend she never wanted to see again. She was going to Duke University in August, would be pledging Delta Zeta, dating a Sigma Chi, and had no intentions of ever coming back. A weekend here or there, and Christmas, would be unavoidable, but she hated the town and everyone in it. She planned to fuck this freshman in a place, and in a way, where everyone would know it. Except, hopefully, her parents, and her future adoring audience —her plan was to be a television news anchor in Atlanta or New York.

It was the next day on the back patio of a keg party in the upscale Shamrock Estates neighborhood that she told Josh he was going to the prom with her, with instructions not to tell anyone that he was even going. When he told his parents of the secret plan the next morning, his mother still didn't understand why he had to rent his tuxedo from a store an hour away, but she agreed to it—she and his father were both delighted that their awkward, quiet, and frankly odd son was becoming so popular at school, and were eager to promote his happiness, now that they could finally understand how. They had no inkling as to the origin of his popularity, and the blind partiality of parenthood did not lead them to question it.

Cindy arranged with her parents for a limousine to drive down from Macon, 45 minutes away, to chauffer the couple around on the big night, to avoid the spectacle of her picking up and driving her own prom date, who had neither a car nor a license to drive one with. From a lifetime habit of providing Cindy with almost anything she asked for whenever she asked for it, this request was not extraordinary—they saw her recovering from the heartbreak of a recent breakup, providing a delightful surprise to her classmates when she arrived with Josh, and helping that promising young athlete become a rising star. They were in on the secret, but they dared not cross their daughter, who, when crossed, could linger in the sulks for weeks and even months on end.

The most popular prom attire that season was the massive Scarlett O'Hara-style ball gown complete with hoop skirt, but as it made even going through doors difficult, Cindy opted for the mature Scarlett look, in a red sequined mini-dress with towering heels, both bought in Atlanta. Also in contrast to the other girls at the prom, with their hair in giant cascading ringlets, Cindy pulled her hair up tight into a tousled pile on her head. When the two of them arrived at prom, two hours late, as planned, she looked not only ready for, but just from, having sex with Josh. He looked less gangly and uncomfortable than most of the young men that night, but he had never worn even a bow tie, much less a tuxedo, and the combination of overly-starched shirt, scratchy synthetic suit, too-tight pants, and merciless shoes made him question whether prom or football was more painful. Since none of his classmates knew he was attending prom, and he was unaware of Cindy's intentions for the night, he had been largely immune to the buildup of nerves in the days leading up to the event. But when he was getting dressed that night, after he awkwardly fastened his elastic cummerbund around his waist, and it flattened his shirtfront and trousers, he became very aware of how much could go very wrong over the course of the evening. To the bewilderment of his parents, 20 minutes before the rented limo was to arrive to pick him up, Josh went to the bathroom, took off all his formal attire, and took a quick five minute shower, just an hour after he'd taken his last one.

The prom was held at the National Guard Armory, one of the few places in Dublin large enough to hold hundreds of people, but that was not part of the school system itself. To avoid charges of racial segregation and discrimination, both proms had to be held off school property, and not officially associated with the school in any way. Both were private functions organized and paid for by the students themselves, at least ostensibly. In reality, adults guided, shaped, planned and financed the proms as much as, if not more than, adults did in towns where proms were held at schools. Though most of the students attending the prom that night with Cindy and Josh had no memory of it, the first year the segregated proms were held at the Armory was in the physical and racial aftermath of the big storm in 1974. Dublin's proms had been held there every year since, with the white prom and black prom alternating which dance was held first each year, just to be fair.

The first year the prom was held there, the Armory was not only the head-quarters for the regional storm recovery effort, it was also the headquarters for the National Guard, who were still actively helping fight the ongoing war in Vietnam. That year and the next two, proms were held on Friday night for the white students, and Saturday night for the black students. Military supplies and equipment were locked away in storage rooms inside and freight containers in the yard outside. A mirrored disco ball and paper streamers were strung up, a few potted plants were placed in front of a florist's portable lattice arch for couples to pose with, and music was played on a record player broadcast over the Armory's own intercom system. The location itself wasn't particularly menacing to the students—even in the early years, the tanks and helicopters of the Armory were a constant presence throughout the town—but the presence of the military men, looking on, and leering on, in many cases, as security, were discomforting to many. The antics of pre-storm prom diminished until after the war ended and the military materiel was decommissioned and moved away, and the Armory could be rented out without its personnel present.

Over the years since, the white prom had developed into a more and more extravagant affair, with a new theme each year, bands and disc jockeys blaring music over rented sound systems, and banquet tables filled with foods. The theme for the prom of 1985 was *Xanadu*, chosen solely by Cindy the previous fall, and dictated to the Prom Committee, of which she was not a part, as it took up too much time. She had envisioned entering the prom on roller skates, but gave up on the idea of the skates over the Christmas holidays, when she set up a mirror in her parents' garage and began practicing dancing in a dress while wearing skates. While it was possible to do, it wasn't possible to do well, and still be desirable, so she just let it pass. Being an object of desire was what Cindy had spent her life perfecting, and she wasn't going to blow it all at her senior prom. She lost her virginity at the age of 13, as a perfectly willing and even eager participant, with a popular 16 year old football player. Since sometime shortly after that chilly September Saturday night, she would pause before leaving her bedroom door each morning and look in the mirror and ask herself *Would I want to fuck me?* If the answer was ever *No*, she fixed her appearance before she left. She didn't just want to be attractive, she wanted men to want her, to very specifically want to fuck her, and she wanted them to know they wanted to fuck her. Passive desire wasn't sufficient for her. Even with much older men—her uncles, her father's friends and business partners, and occasionally even her father—she would hug just a little too long, press just a little too firmly, rest her hand on a forearm or back or even a thigh, until she got the reaction she wanted—a slight change in voice, a resistance, a nervous tensing of the body as it reacted or tried not to react to the beautiful young girl who touched them in the way they dreamed of being touched by young girls—almost. It was the unfulfilled act she wanted them to think about. And prom night, she wanted every boy and man at the Armory to be thinking about her, to think about how Josh would be tearing her apart, ruining her, for them, forever. She doubted he was actually as big as everyone said, but she planned to confirm the rumor as fact.

The arrival of the stretch Cadillac in the parking lot full of Camaros, Mustangs, and Toyotas, caused a stir. The smokers, drinkers, and dancers who need a rest were scattered around the parking lot when the limo arrived. Before the couple was entirely out of the car, someone had dashed inside to spread the news: *Cindy is here! With Donkey Kong!*

By the time the two of them passed into the main hall, through a curtain of thin silver Mylar streamers, nearly everyone had heard and was waiting for their entrance. The dance floor had emptied, and the wallflowers and the nobodies, geeks and freaks and nerds, the band and the chorus, jocks and stoners and dudes, all took their places beside and behind the beautiful young country club couples in the loose circle more or less surrounding the dance floor. Every eye was fixed on Josh and Cindy. The disc jockey, who was from a radio station in Atlanta, did not know who any of the high school students were, and was also incredibly stoned, looked up from a private reverie, mistook the stillness of scene before him, panicked, and quickly replaced the extended remix of *Funkytown* by Lipps, Inc., that had already been playing for eight minutes, with that evening's love theme, *Magic*, by Olivia Newton John, announcing as he did so, "Ladies and Gentlemen, please welcome to the floor, your prom king and queen in their special dance."

Voting had taken place as couples entered the dance hours earlier, and only a handful of people knew that Josh and Cindy were in fact not homecoming king and queen, or that as a freshman, Josh wasn't even allowed to be prom king—but it was too late to stop it without causing a scene and embarrassing Cindy, which no one, including any of the chaperones, was willing to risk. To a quickly deafening uproar of cheers, yells, catcalls and whistles, Cindy led Josh out to the middle of the dance floor without hesitation, wrapped herself in his arms, and began swaying, leading him with her body, just inches from his. This was her fourth prom, and she was accustomed to dancing with boys who had never danced with a girl.

Josh, never having been to even a dance, much less a prom, had his only personal knowledge of them from the movie *Carrie*, which he knew could not be an accurate indicator of how proms were supposed to go. He sensed something wasn't quite right, but attributed it to Cindy's careful planning, which he assumed he only knew in part. Cindy, accustomed to having things go her way, also attributed this fresh victory to her maneuvering. She had not planned specifically to be prom queen—it wasn't something she had given more than two minutes thought to, as she was queen the year before, as a junior, and that achievement could stand on its own, allowing her to appear gracious in allowing some lesser beauty to be crowned in her senior year. But believing in the saying that *God takes care of those who take care of themselves*, she accepted the ill-gotten rewards as more fruit for her labor. It confirmed for her that she was right—the breakup, the secrecy, the limousine, her date, and even her dress were just right, as was the rest of her plan; and so, almost as soon as they were on the dance floor moving, she began to put the remainder of her plan in motion.

"So is it true?" she asked, looking him directly in the eyes, for what to him felt like the first time ever. He had been asked the question dozens, perhaps hundreds of times, but never by anyone who appeared to have a direct personal interest in knowing the answer to the question—and since the day of his discovery in the locker room shower, it was always the same question. But the look in her eyes, on her face, and in the way her body seemed to be leading less and submitting more, suggested the reality of her interest.

It was the first question or statement of any import either had made since the car picked him up. Their talk had been mostly self-congratulatory discussion of how well their plan—her plan—was going. Its success so far was largely due to their having barely spoken or even acknowledged one another since she had first told him the plan, in keeping with the norms of how a freshman of subordinate social status might interact with a beautiful, popular, powerful cheerleading captain. Her ability to look past and through him in hallways, in the lunchroom, and in the parking lot, led him to question at times during weeks prior if he was really even going, or if he had rented his tux in vain, or for some trick, or joke. He could see in her face now, there was no joke.

First one spotlight and then another from the distant, opposite corners of the room latched onto them, and the warmth of the lights masked the rush of heat to his face, but not the color—it was nearly crimson in the hot white lights. The glare blinded them both in darkness and light as they turned slowly round, and the rest of the Armory became invisible to them, except where shards of light cut past them into the dark beyond, and lit a knee, a folding chair, or a face for just an instant before they spun away out of view, taking the light with them.

"It's true," he answered her, looking back at her directly, confidently, and then immediately doubting himself, wondering if or how what was happening could be real or true. She answered by closing the space between them, pressing herself into him, urging the tops of her breasts up past the sequin bodice holding them back from him. When he looked down and saw her gazing up at him with longing in her face, and he heard the renewed catcalls and whistles, he could feel himself, against his will, beginning to grow with an urgency never anticipated or experienced before. He needed no coaxing, no tugging or pulling or holding or teasing—he was, almost in an instant, full and completely hard, his erection threatening to escape the confines of his tight briefs. He knew, instinctively, that the flimsy rented pants would provide him no cover. Everyone would see. Everyone would know. But if he was with her, he didn't care—suddenly he wanted them to see. And somehow, he got even harder. She gasped with a smile as she felt him expand between them, and her face came alive with desire and wonder. Without missing a step, she spun in his arms, and pushed herself back against him as they danced, and looked out at the faces she could not see cast in their shadows. "Look out there," she whispered to him from the side of her mouth, talking back to him, and he bent down to listen. "Right now, every person out there wants to be us. Every. Single. One of them." And, for the most part, she was right. They were the perfect picture of teenage sexuality at its apex, in a room nearly full of teenagers.

She spun back around and looked up at him, the song nearing its end, and said "Kiss me. Now." He had never kissed a girl. And now he was being commanded, on the spot, to kiss one for the first time in front of half his school. He bent his head down uncertainly, and just barely had his lips parted when hers came up to meet him. She opened his mouth wide with hers, pulling him down into her, and the wetness of her mouth made him stumble. They stopped dancing entirely, and stood there making out, their bodies still moving to the slow pulse of the music, as the assembled prom-goers broke out in stomping, cheering, clapping. A chant began to emerge from the darkness, first from just one corner, and then it spread through the entire crowd: "Kong! Kong! Kong! Kong!"

Over the sound system, the DJ, who was still somewhat confused, and now more than a little aroused, said "Let's give it up for our king and queen!" The two finally separated, turned to face the spotlight, then Josh clasped Cindy by the shoulder with one hand, and with the other grabbed himself through his trousers and shook the bulge at the howling crowd. His face was an animalistic impression of sexual aggression, his emotions in that moment so primitive he wanted to bark, to howl with the crowd, to throw Cindy on the floor and take her right there in front of everyone. He was smiling, but his face was contorting in spasms. Cindy was laughing at how perfect her own victory was playing out. "Come on, let's get out of here," she said, and she took his hand to lead him back through the entrance to the parking lot—her work at the prom was done, and much quicker than anticipated. With his free hand, he was high-fiving hands whose owners he could not see, his adrenaline racing faster than it ever had before, and seeming to emanate from somewhere just below his scrotum. His eyes were stretched open, and he could only unclench his teeth to yell "Yeah! Yeah! Yeah!" He felt wholly out of control of his own body, and he loved it. It was a high he would spend the next twenty years chasing.

He lost his virginity shortly after they left the prom. It was not in the pool house at a crowded party as Cindy had planned—that was no longer necessary. She gave the driver directions to the now-entirely-derelict but still-convenient Candlelight Motel, with instructions to wait at an all-night diner down the block, where Josh would go for him when they were done.

The sex was frantic, almost dangerous—just putting himself inside her was nearly an act of violence in itself. Her vision turned white with stars, and she sucked air through her gritted teeth with an expression of pure anguish on her face. Frightened, he was preparing to pull himself out when she pulled him down on top of her, fully into her, and bit his shoulder to keep herself from screaming. He pulled up from her, and saw his blood on her teeth, saw through her layers of makeup, and for just an instant he saw a child there, like himself, uncertain of anything except just that moment—an unspeakable tenderness between them. And then she slapped him, and he pulled out and slammed back into her without mercy or hesitation, relentless, again and again, ignoring the guttural cries coming from somewhere below her neck.

It was over quickly, but not before she began sobbing, though he was not aware of it until he finished. He was resting inside her, breathless, his head spinning, his torso and shoulders covered with sweat and scratches and bites, when he looked up at her face and saw her tears.

"Should I—" he began to ask, but she cut him off with an angry but quiet "Get out." He quickly pulled himself out of her, but he was still completely erect, and this final pain, pain on top of pain, a knife through an open wound, when she thought the pain was over, was what sent her into hysterics, escalating in volume and pitch until she was out of words and was just screaming.

"Get out. Get out! Get out of this goddam room, you fucking freak. What the fuck?" She was up and hitting him, her muscular cheerleader's limbs slapping and jabbing and kicking at him. "Get out. Out. Rrrrruh. Rrruh. Gaaaah." And then she saw the blood on him, and then down between her legs, and her words came back. "I'm bleeding. I'm bleeding! Look what you've done to me." And she ran to attack him. He tried to take her in his arms, to hold her, but she beat her way free and ran to the bathroom and closed the door. He heard the toilet lid go down. He stood wondering what he should do. He looked down and saw to his surprise, that he was still almost completely erect.

For some time there was nothing but silence, then he heard soft whimpering noises, a sort of cry, like from a scared child, or small animal, and then a short muffled scream, but he didn't know what to make of any of it. It didn't seem normal, but he had no way of knowing what normal was in the situation. He wiped himself off, put on his underwear, tucked himself into it with some difficulty, and then just stood looking at the bathroom door.

"Are you okay in there?" he asked.

For a minute there was no response. And then, "I want you to get the fuck out of here."

"Really?"

"Yes, fucking really."

"How am I supposed to get home?"

"Do you think I fucking care?" There was another soft cry, the vocal opposite of the tone in her speaking voice, like there were two different girls in the bathroom, but he knew there was just her.

"Can I take the car? And, um, send him back?"

"Yes, just leave. Please. Just. Fucking. Leave." Her voice was calm, almost measured.

"Okay. If you're sure you're alright."

"Get OOOOOwwwwwOOUUwwwwUUUUUt."

Her sudden, howling scream scared him more than anything else had. He quickly put his clothes on, but carried his shoes and socks with him out the door. He walked behind the buildings between the motel and the diner, found the driver, and headed home. The driver tried to engage him in conversation, hinting, not very discreetly, at the good time he must have had, as well as how quickly it had ended.

Josh did not take the bait, and wanting nothing more than to get home and get in his bed, gave the driver directions to his home, along with the information that he had a headache. And his head did ache—within the course of less than three hours his life had been turned upside down, and he could no more understand all that had happened than he could predict its outcomes, but his mind was working determinedly to do both. His penis, which was finally deflating, actually hurt, and the confines of his briefs were not helping the developing soreness. He glanced at his watch and saw, with some incredulity, that it was still before midnight. His parents would still be up to watch Carson on *The Tonight Show*, and possibly even later, to wait up for him. As a fourteen-year-old, his parents did not consent to him being out past 12:30, even for prom, though his father had told him, as he was walking out the door earlier that evening, "If you're having fun, just stay out. I'll take care of your mom."

He put on his shoes and socks, and asked the driver to drop him off two blocks from home. There were no cars or people out, so he snuck behind a neighbor's house to wait a decent amount of time before heading home. He very quietly climbed the metal frame of the trampoline, its rusted springs creaking softly in the silent moonlight. He stretched himself out, looking up at the stars, almost perfectly visible, just one corner of the sky smudged out by a nearby streetlight. It took a moment for the silence to register with him—the perfect clarity of the silence. The removal of the voices during his previous endeavors seemed amateurish as he luxuriated in this new and complete silence. It seemed now that not only might the voices never come back, but as though they had never been there. He realized now that his hearing before had been left with something like streaks of residual sound, a filmy, grimy remembrance, and somehow an expectation, a fear, of the return of the voices—an absence, but not complete. Like a coffee cup waiting to be filled, the chill coffee remains an anticipation of the new. And now, there was none. No residue. No lingering fear. Just perfect, shiny clarity. He heard a dog bark in the distance, and the pristine canvas against which the sound was painted for him took him off into deep, silver sleep. His life as a sex addict had begun, a journey which would take him through hundreds of women in high school, college, various jobs, sex clubs, prostitutes, and finally the internet, a thing that didn't even exist back on that prom night, which was a peaceful oblivion of perfect, dreamless sleep. The next morning, the neighbors the trampoline belonged to were surprised, but not alarmed, to find him there—they knew it was prom night. They jostled him awake by drumming lightly on the taut nylon canvas, and the movement, as well as the sound of the springs, and the gentle calling of his name, woke him to a new and brilliant morning. That the perfect abandon of the night before might be anything other than a gift from God, he never even questioned, until it was too late.

***

"Josh. Josh." The voice was insistent, demanding. It was Callie. They had moved on without him, and now Sam was turning the corner into another aisle as Callie beckoned for Josh to move.

He joined her, and they found Sam on the candy aisle, but he no longer appeared to be in a great hurry. He had located butterscotch, and put six bags into the cart, and was casually looking over the chewing gum.

"Aren't we in some sort of hurry?" Callie asked when they reached him.

"We're actually about seven minutes ahead of time," he responded, looking at his watch. "Me losing my temper wasn't part of the plan, but, well, that seems to have put us ahead of schedule," he said with something like regret on his face as he looked at Josh, then added, "Your ride isn't ready yet."

"What ride?" "Who is it we're leaving with?" "Where are we going?" "Why aren't you coming?" The questions were stacked on top of one another, but it didn't matter—Sam had no answers for them. "I don't know. I'm just to have you at the loading dock of this store in six minutes. But we can't be ahead of schedule. I don't know why."

Callie finally expressed her underlying concern, and real response—she couldn't pacify Sam any longer, if it meant she was about to be transported by strangers to some mystery location Sam knew nothing about. "We can't do this, Sam. I can't just leave. You know that. You must know that. Lucy needs help—fine, we'll get her help. We'll get her the best lawyers money can buy. We have money. We know lawyers. Lots of them, good ones. But just disappearing, with strangers, to some place…. " Her voice trailed off as he turned to look at her. He was holding a ten-pack of grape Hubba Bubba bubble gum, but putting it back on its hook. His face was so very sad. He looked older in that instant than she had ever seen him, or imagined him looking.

"It's not just her, Callie. It's you. And him," he said, nodding to Josh. "You're not safe. You've never been safe, I don't think." He looked away from her with something like embarrassment, then with what appeared to be resolve, turned to look her directly in the eye. "Do you remember the night you met Ed? And he began the drive to California?"

Callie's face tightened, and her eyes widened almost imperceptibly. She was attempting not to show emotion. She had not said Ed's name out loud to anyone in almost 20 years, and never to Sam.

"They were there," Sam continued. "They were there all along the way, observing, measuring, monitoring, taking notes. They lived in your apartment complex in San Diego, flew on every plane you ever flew on. They were at Valentino, in the eucalyptus grove, in the projects in Atlanta. Every step along the way, your way, they were there. Preparing for, well, I don't know exactly what. But there is a list, and your names are on it. And they're coming for you. Not yet, but soon. That's why you have to go. Lucy is important, yes, but not to me. Not really. You are, though. I've seen some of what they watched happen to you, and what is happening to Lucy, too. Whoever they are, they have no limits, no mercy. You have to see that. I would rather you disappear a million miles away from here than have you experience any more of what you've been through."

Callie's attempts to restrain her emotions were preventing her from putting together the words to ask the questions she desperately wanted answered. All of her tools for keeping herself composed, for maintaining serenity in any situation, seemed to be just beyond her grasp. Her head was spinning, again. And again, she began to reach for a nearby shelf to steady herself, but stopped, and just wrapped herself in her arms. Still, she could not speak. But Josh, who had a few minutes more than she had to collect himself, asked the most obvious question: "How do we know that your cousin, or whoever these people are, aren't the ones? That he isn't some dupe in a larger plan, or conspiracy, or whatever this is?"

"It's confusing. I know. The people who've been tracking you could have killed you a thousand times over. Your death would have required a little cleaning up," he said to Josh, "But Callie, they could have killed you a thousand times, and no one would have ever known. But something has changed, and leaving, leaving now, is the only real chance you have. I believe that. I believe him—it's what he told me. Yours are not the only videos I've seen. They've done worse. Much worse. You'll see." He was looking into her eyes as he spoke, and the expression on his face said *And then you'll be as scared as I am.* He looked away, at his watch. "Four minutes. We need to move to the back of the store. Follow me." He left the shopping cart by the chewing gum, and walked to the back of the store, the other two following behind. Callie felt fear for the first time that evening, and for the first time, really, in years. The fear that she would never see Sam, or Mama Ben, or any of the people she loved ever again cut as quick and deep as a dagger. It did not pierce into her, but rather down through the center of her, the chill of it radiating out from her center to the tips of her fingers and toes.

When they reached the back of the store, Sam led them down a wide corridor with *Restrooms* in big block letters above its entry, at the end of which was a door labeled *Employees Only.* He led them in through it, into a poorly lit, cavernous space, and behind a stack of pallets laden with paper goods. He said in a low voice "In three minutes a truck is going to back up to that loading dock. Within two minutes, the assistant manager of the store will come back to sign for the delivery. He will open the loading dock door. The driver will open the back door of the truck. It will be a refrigerated cooler. The manager guy will freak out, because it is supposed to be a dry goods delivery. They will take the shipping manifest to the front office. When they are going out the door we just came through, the driver will say, *Well I'll be John Brown.* That's your cue. You walk through those strips of heavy plastic and into the truck, through to the back of the refrigerated compartment, and into the freezer compartment. You'll meet my cousin there. His name is Michael. I'll go back inside, check out and be on my way to Mama Ben's to drop off the cat food. And tell him."

"Tell him what?"

Suddenly distracted, Sam looked at the time on his phone, and switched the phone to silent. "One minute. Turn your phones off." He looked into her eyes. "Tell him that you're as special as he's always said, and so much more." His voice faltered. "I love you so much, Callie. You're my superhero." He hugged her, and the hug told her something she hadn't heard in his voice.

She pulled back from him. "You don't think you're ever going to see me again, do you?" She was suddenly terrified. She realized now the reason his performance had been off earlier, why even his walk down the sidewalk was all wrong. He was scared for her life. She had never seen him this scared before, not since he was sober. And now, he took too long to answer her before saying "I don't know, Callie." The tears welling in his eyes told a different truth—his words weren't a lie, but they were the product of his reasoning, not what he felt in the pit of his stomach.

"You're wrong. Whatever this insanity is, it will end, and you will see me again." She pulled her 18-year medallion from her pocket and handed it to him. "Hold on to this for me."

It seemed so much like a dream to each of them, with familiar faces in an unfamiliar setting and situation, that they looked to one another for confirmation that was happening was real, and found only fear and misgivings in each other's faces.

Josh looked on at their exchange with sadness, envy, and his own very different fear. He had no one to mourn his departure, or even notice it until he did not arrive at work on Monday. He was suddenly scared that he would never have that person in his life, with the love for him he saw in Sam' and Callie's faces. Even this daughter, Lucy, he felt somehow was at the end of a riddle he wouldn't be able to solve, or probably even understand. He wasn't a superhero. Maybe Callie was, but not him. He felt entirely alone in the midst of their sadness, and impotent in the face of whatever lay before them.

The rumbling of a truck could be heard approaching, the air being released from the brakes as it began to maneuver in the lane behind the store. "We have to stay quiet now. Stay out of sight until you hear *John Brown,*" Sam whispered. Callie held Sam's hand. The high-pitched chirp of the truck backing up to the loading dock put all of their nerves on even higher edge than they had been before, without anyone knowing with any certainty what it was they had to be scared of. Being caught hiding in a grocery store's loading bay was all they were technically guilty of. And yet, they felt frightened, and guilty well beyond any reasonable measure. Callie's own relatively constant guiding life principle of the past decade, to live in the moment, seemed suddenly as inadequate as it did naïve—while she had been living in the moment, someone else had been watching her, recording her, learning, preparing... for what? Her imagination came upon a wall. She had never been a fan of science fiction or government conspiracy movies or books. They were unavoidable in modern life, but they seemed so shallow to her, and counter-productive to what she sought in her own life. Participating in a media culture which seemed to encourage fear, while she was actively trying to eliminate fear from her life, just did not seem useful. She found herself wishing she had watched more X-Files, for some possible pointers. But it was too late for that.

The assistant manager of the store had arrived, and the blustering between the two men had begun. Over the sound of the store's own equipment and the engine of the truck just outside, they could just make out snippets of dialogue. "I just drive the truck, I don't load the cargo," and "I have buy-one-get-one on peanut butter and saltines tomorrow morning at 9:00am, and they gotta be here, I don't care what it takes. The rest can wait 'til Monday, but not the BOGO." They heard the voices becoming more indistinct, and for just a moment, Callie prayed, earnestly prayed that the words *John Brown* would not be said, or would not be heard, that it would all just go away, and be for nothing.

It was an unusual prayer for her, what the A.A. people called a *foxhole prayer*. Usually, Callie prayed for, and in, colors. She had given up on specific wants and needs long ago, then abandoned feelings and aspirations, finally giving up on words altogether. A dusty violet with just a whisper of red, a dot from a Seurat painting magnified to fill the universe—that was her perfect picture of peace, and all she had prayed for, or more precisely, prayed towards, for years. But standing in that strange place, staring into a crate filled with Bounty paper towels, that abstraction was insufficient. She very specifically wanted it to be over, to be a dream, to be a joke. In the midst of her prayer, it occurred to her that Sam might be part of an elaborate surprise for her 18th sober anniversary, but as quickly remembered the tapes they had heard, the information Sam had shared, and the fear in his embrace. There was no party. Before she could readjust her prayer back properly to ask that she not hear the words she was dreading, that would make it all real, she heard them, loud and clear above all the machinery. "I'll be John Brown."

She turned and looked at Sam, and threw her arms around him, her embrace suggesting she was no longer certain she would see him again. He returned her embrace, but only briefly, pulling her from him as he said, "It's time. You have to go."

"I'll call you."

"Michael will explain it all."

Now that the moment had arrived, it was Josh who was suddenly anxious to get moving. "If we're going, let's go." He moved past the two of them, to the void in the wall where the thick plastic sheeting hung down in strips, reminding him of the Mylar streamers at prom. He let the thought go, as held the strips back for Callie, who stepped in first, mindful of the small gap between the truck's floor and that of the loading dock. The surfaces were not level with one another, and the different textures required some calibration.

Over her shoulder, she whispered back, "Watch that step."

CHAPTER 3. THE TROLLEY

And just like that, the world of everything they knew disappeared behind a curtain of nearly-opaque plastic refrigeration strips. Light from the loading dock struggled to penetrate into the chill darkness of the refrigerated compartment they found themselves alone in. After the tension of the loading dock, the nothing-happening of the refrigerator left them awkward, looking for something to do, or feel, or think.

"What do we do now?" Callie asked, wrapping her arms around herself, her sleeveless sweater inadequate to the chill of the truck. Josh was formulating a response, and their eyes were adjusting to the shapes of the pallets of trays around them, when a door just a few feet away swung open, and light poured into the refrigerator. The silhouette of a man emerged and opened the door for them, backing into the refrigerator as he did so, urging them past him. "Come in, come in," he said quietly, with the conversational tone and warmth of an old friend welcoming them into his home study for a cup of coffee. They walked into a dimly lit and compact freezer compartment, filled with plastic trays of mostly-indistinguishable frozen foods, though Callie did recognize several quarts of her favorite ice cream bars—Haagen Dazs Pralines & Cream. Michael closed the door behind them, walked past them, and put his hand on the metal wall at the far end of the freezer from where they had entered. The metal panel slid back into the wall, and soft light poured from a room just beyond. "Come on in," he said as he gestured them forward. The door slid back into place after Josh followed Callie through it.

It took their eyes a moment to adjust, and their minds a minute more to accept their surroundings. They were not in a freezer, but in what looked to be the small, well-appointed futuristic living room of a very narrow New York brownstone, or a Space Station module with a Prada makeover. It was photo-shoot immaculate, with tonal greys and beiges, gleaming chrome and stainless steel, matte black enamel and warm veneers. But it was all just tucked in a freezer, in the back of a semi, somehow.

There were two small sofas, two armchairs, two small tables, built into or attached to the walls. The ceiling was vaulted to a center pitch running the length of the small room, and there were halogen lights on cables suspended from it. The effect was disorienting. Most disconcerting were what appeared to be windows encircling the entire space, including in the door they had just walked through. Standing in the middle of it was a handsome, thin, but athletic black man, about their age, in a grey knit jersey shirt, khaki trousers, and what Callie recognized to be Cole-Haan driving shoes. The man only had eyes for them, and he was beaming.

"Where are we?" Callie asked. "Who are you?" Josh asked, at just the same time.

"My name is Michael. Michael Isaacs." He had a big, toothy, boyish smile, the expression on his face taut with restrained anticipation, as though he were meeting a beloved rock star or author. "And, you're, I guess, in what I guess you would call my, my home. The closest thing I've had to one for a while, anyway. Here, sit," he gestured to one of the two upholstered grey wool sofas.

Josh and Callie looked at each other, but did not move. "Really, sit," Michael said, maintaining his focus on their faces as he sat himself, encouraging them with a gesture to follow him. "The driver will be back in a minute. Once we start moving, it will be a little awkward for you to stand. You get used to it after a while, but it's sort of like living in a really nice subway car."

"How can that be a window?" Callie asked, not moving, pointing back to the door she had just walked through.

"It isn't. It's a liquid crystal display, showing a panoramic view generated from cameras running the length of the truck. After my first week in here, I started getting really claustrophobic, which I'm not, usually, but you know, a week in the back of a truck, even with nice furniture. So one of the guys came up with this. It's not like a window, really, but it's good for keeping my circadian rhythm in check. I come in here at sunrise, sunset. Right before I go to sleep, I check in with what's going on outside.

"You, you don't leave this truck?" Josh asked.

"Not for more than six minutes at a time. Not for four years."

"Good God," Callie exclaimed, looking away from the truck and at Michael really for the first time. "Are you a prisoner here?" The tone implied the question *Are we prisoners here?*, but she somehow felt it would be both rude and pointless to ask—the door she had just walked through had no handle she could see. In fact, it couldn't properly be described as a door from where she was standing. Had she not just walked through it, she would have been hard pressed to identify a door anywhere in the room, if it was a room. It seemed like a room, but knowing it was in the back of a truck made it somehow *not* a room to her.

"No, of course not," Michael laughed, and then more seriously, "and neither are you, Callie." Then when Josh looked at him sharply, he added quickly, "or you, Josh."

"Can you tell us why we are here?"

"Yes, I can, and I will. But I really would like for you to sit down. Please. Standing isn't safe, really, until you get used to it. And sometimes not even then—the drivers know the cargo is fragile, which makes me scared to think what the driving would be like if they thought the cargo was not fragile."

"Doesn't the driver know we're back here?"

"Dear God, no," Michael exclaimed, again with a bit of laughter. "We have people of most every talent in the community, but no one willing to drive a truck around in circles full-time for years at a time."

"The community?"

"That's our name for us. Well, my name for us. We don't really have a name. We just sort of... are. Like an informal neighborhood block association. No membership, no signs, no get-togethers. Just a loose association, a community. Of sorts."

Without warning, the truck lurched forward, and Josh and Callie tumbled into one another. What was left of Callie's triple grande soy latté with whip went flying across the truck's interior, onto the ceiling, the floor, one of the tables, and one of the digital screens, which just then was giving them a view of the delivery lane behind the grocery store. It wasn't much of a scene, but the clarity of the image was startlingly realistic. Callie felt as though she could reach out, open a window, and touch the things she was seeing beyond—if she hadn't ruined it all with her latté.

"Don't worry, everything in here can pretty much be hosed down. Most of it can be hosed down with acid and still be fine—it's comfy enough, but it's all pretty industrial stuff. But do please sit down."

As they could feel a turn around the rear corner of the grocery store beginning at the front of the truck, the two took Michael's suggestion, and sat facing him from the opposite sofa.

"Before we get started, and I promise, I'm going to tell you everything, beginning to end, that I know, that I think is relevant, maybe even what's not relevant if we have time, I need to know something. Josh, how is your hearing?"

Josh looked at the man, startled, once again. The question about his hearing was his and Mama Ben's private code for *Are you hearing voices?* It was a topic he had discussed with exactly two people in his life, and he realized that this man Michael, for whatever reason, was choosing to protect his privacy, at least with Callie, at least for the moment. Michael paused to listen carefully for the voices, but heard nothing. "It's fine" was his only reply.

"Great. We were concerned that the information you received from Sam might have caused some emotional dysregulation, which we agree with your Mama Ben is the primary causal factor in your hearing problems."

Callie listened to this discourse without the least idea what they were talking about, but, given her own desire not to be questioned by Josh on information she believed Michael likely to have about her, should the occasion arise, she asked nothing.

"Okay," was Josh's seemingly indifferent response. In truth, he was much more than curious about how the knowledge of the voices he heard had been accepted, even understood, by this stranger, or these strangers. But he said nothing more.

By this time they had turned from the shopping center parking lot onto

Monroe Drive, and were heading northeast. "We should be good for a minute," Michael said, and jumped up with practiced grace in the moving truck, retrieved a towel from a cabinet that had appeared to be mahogany paneling, and wiped up the latté mess, disposing of the towel in a trash bin or laundry basket—it was hard to tell which—that had also been disguised as paneling. As Callie looked at all the flat surfaces, and Michael working his way around them, she realized she was in something much more like a ship's cabin than a motor home. "Is everything in here something else?" she asked.

"For the most part," Michael answered with a smile as he sat back down. And then he added, "So, what do you want to know first?"

He had not prepared a speech or presentation for them. He knew that everything he had to tell them would come out in time, but he wanted to give them some sense of control in the situation. He reasoned that their powerlessness, as well as the strangeness of the situation, would be frightening—it had been for him when he had been introduced to his new life environment, in much the same way. Answering the questions they wanted answered first, however irrelevant they may be to their ultimate goal, would provide them some comfort, and he wanted to make them comfortable. They did not know it yet, but he cared for and about them, and had for some time. He was being manipulative, but not mercenary—it was generosity, not guile, guiding him through his efforts.

Josh and Callie looked at one another, each giving the other permission to ask first. Midtown Atlanta was passing by them in slow but steady retreat into the night as the shopping center lights faded and the dense canopy of trees of residential lawns grew thick around them. Michael interrupted their politeness, suggesting "Callie, why don't you go first?"

"Alright, why don't we start with the basics. Who, what, when, where, why?"

Michael smiled. Callie's efficient mind, even when she was being kidnapped—for all she really knew at that point—was amazing to him, and had been for some time.

"Who. Well, I guess there are a few who's you will want to know about. The first one is me, I suppose. My name is Michael Isaacs. I attended Moore Street Elementary with you, Josh, until the big storm in 1974. My father was lynched right after the storm. He was accused of murdering a boy who was your friend. I was taken off, into protective custody, you might say, but loving custody, by a county clerk, Eleanor Thompson. You probably knew her as Eleanor Allen if you knew her at all." He looked to Josh for a reply, and received a shake of the head that included an urging for him to continue.

"We relocated to Brattleboro, Vermont, at the request of the U.S. government, though of course I didn't know it at the time. I was ten years old. The pieces started to fall into place more quickly than anyone anticipated, or at least anyone I know of. I was inquisitive by nature, I still am, really, and by the age of fourteen, I had pieced together that someone, somewhere, was taking care of me besides Ms. Eleanor. I just assumed it was family, some distant relation, and that she would tell me who in good time." He paused, as if considering how to proceed, and then continued.

"But that never happened. I graduated high school, and was accepted to the Massachusetts Institute of Technology—a school, by the way, which I never applied to. But it was relatively near Ms. Eleanor, and it was one of the few places on the east coast at the time to properly learn computer programming. I had been play- ing around with computers for years, with Ms. Eleanor's encouragement. I had a gift not just for language, but for programming language. It was such an abstract sort of thing at the time, no one really knew what I was talking about, or doing. I had a computer for years before anyone else in the town, or before even the town itself had one. I didn't think anything about it at the time—you know, how much computers cost, or how this retiree from middle Georgia could afford one. I just went with it, the way you do when you're a kid. But when I got to M.I.T., I started to realize something wasn't quite right. Even with my dad's life insurance and military benefits and state orphan funds—my mom died when I was three—it still didn't add up. We danced around it a few times, but I never directly pressed her—I was, and am, too grateful for everything she did for me, to make her uncomfortable. And that's what questioning her did—she wanted to tell me the truth, and I could see that, and that's why I let it pass. With me off at school, we had very little time together, I didn't want to ruin what time we did have."

Here he paused, and looked past them at the road beyond, the truck in a wide turn as they merged onto I-20 East, headed towards Augusta. "Do you guys want anything to drink? We have everything you like. Except lattés. We're still trying to work that out. But I can make you an espresso."

"No thanks, but I really could use the bathroom?" Callie was looking around the room hopefully for signs of a door, but saw none.

"Of course, sure, here follow me. Actually, why don't we go ahead and get you programmed in." Callie looked at him waiting for more explanation, but he was standing up, so she stood and followed him the few steps to the opposite end of the room from where they came in. He held his hands up to the image of the light traffic moving in front of them on the interstate, and started typing. The image of a keyboard appeared where his fingers were moving, and a rectangle about the size of an average desktop monitor screen appeared level with his face. He made a few poking and swiping motions in it, apparently opening and activating software, and typed a few more keystrokes. He then asked Callie to put her hands palm down with fingers splayed on the monitor-shaped cutout in the night sky. She did so, and felt the relative coolness of the screen, which surprised her. Within a few seconds, there was a beep from some indistinct place, and Michael told her she could put down her hands. As she did so, a picture of her appeared in the monitor box, digitally imprinted on the front of an image of a manila folder—this was her file, and, she guessed, her life. She recognized what she was wearing in the photo—it was a Donna Karan sweater she bought years ago, but had recently rediscovered, and worn twice in the past month. She could see from the image that it was taken at her eye doctor's office as she sat in the exam chair two weeks earlier. It gave her chills. "Can I read what's in that file?"

"Sure, but why don't you use the bathroom first? You can open the door yourself now. Just put your right hand on the wall, anywhere you see the exterior right now." She did so, and a small-door-sized panel slid back into the wall, taking the night sky with it, which was a little jarring—it was easy to forget it wasn't a window, even that close, even when she had just seen someone typing on it.

"Do the same thing to the next wall to get through to the bathroom. This is the sleeping compartment," he said gesturing to the room just before them. "The toilet is the door on the right," Michael called after her. "You come back through the same way. Just use your hand." The door closed behind her.

An overhead row of recessed lights like in an aircraft, dim but evenly distributed, illuminated two sets of three vertically-stacked sleeping compartments, both on the left-hand side of a narrow passage, and what appeared to be closets at the far end, where a door—this one clearly visible—sat nestled in the wall. She started to walk through, lightly bracing herself with her hand as she began moving through the corridor.

The sleeping compartment door closed behind her as she stood in front of the toilet door. He hadn't said how to open it, so she tentatively put her hand on the wall, and the door slid back. The toilet compartment was small—not airplane small, but small enough. The walls and ceiling were a beige synthetic surface, which looked easy to clean. The floor appeared to be sheet vinyl. There was an overhead light, and an exhaust fan. The toilet appeared to be one of those one-gallon low-flush toilets that were rarely efficient, but this one was. In all, nothing extraordinary, except for the reality that it existed at all. As she washed her hands, she wondered vaguely about the mechanics of the truck, but it was only a passing thought. On her way back she poked her head into what she guessed, rightly, was a shower compartment, and realized that it, too, was scaled on the old-town Prague hostel model—tiny, and not suitable at all for shaving her legs. She hoped she wouldn't be on the truck that long, but from what Sam had said, and the apparent length of the story Michael was beginning, she thought she might be.

As she approached the door, she paused to see if she could hear them talking, but could hear nothing—absolute silence, which she realized at that moment was incredible, as she was, to the best of her knowledge, in the back of a giant, rumbling truck—which was so loud it had made her own thoughts hard to hear in the loading bay at the grocery store. As the door slid back into the wall, she found the two men, as she suspected she would, in conversation, which abruptly ended when she appeared. *We all have our little secrets*, she thought to herself.

"What size are those beds?" was her question for Michael as she sat down, joining the two.

Michael smiled. "Funny you should ask. They're the biggest headache on the trolley. That's what I call this thing—the trolley. The guys who designed it wanted to make the beds as big as possible, and had custom mattresses made without much thought as to where the sheets would come from. Everything else on here we pretty much dispose of as we go through it—we don't wash pillowcases or towels. New ones show up when we refit, and the old ones go to Goodwill or whatever. But the sheets are a problem. We have multiple pairs of them, but even we don't have an endless supply of custom sheets. Those get laundered in South Carolina somewhere, I think—at least, that's where we get them. We have a refit tonight. It's not time for one, but just to be on the safe side."

"What's a refit?" Josh asked, wondering vaguely where one would even get custom sheets made.

"Right now the exterior of the truck shows that this is a U.S. Foods truck with Virginia tags. After the refit, we will be a different truck from a different place. We could be a FedEx truck from New Mexico, or a Wal-Mart truck from Georgia. We never know. It's all done with vinyl."

"Who does this, exactly?" Josh seemed genuinely interested.

"Some of the shadiest people in South of the Border, South Carolina. They think we're drug runners."

"South of the Border? You mean that truck stop with the giant sombrero?

It's a town?" Callie questioned.

"Of sorts, yes. That's the one. They have a big mechanic's shop where these trucks can be repaired. Our driver will pull into a service bay, and leave the keys in the ignition—his shift is over. Two hours later, another driver will arrive and find a completely different truck waiting to be driven off into the night. The whole process of changing the truck only takes 30 minutes, but there's always been a two hour window for precaution."

Callie looked at him thoughtfully for a moment, and cut off Josh, who had every appearance of asking another question, to say "I think we've ventured into how. Can we get back to who?"

"Right, of course. So, through my work at M.I.T. I meet all the big movers and shakers, east coast, west coast, D.C.—it was a relatively small group of people when you consider what the internet became. We had no idea back then, not really. Well, a few people did. But most of us were just busy working towards the next thing. I was writing code all over the place. I would get pulled off of one project and onto another. Technically, I was getting my undergraduate degree in Linguistics. What I was actually doing was a lot of work for the government barely disguised as independent study courses. I had an English course here, a public speaking there, but mostly it was late nights working on ARPANET, MILNET, NIPRNET, SIPRNET, all government and military computer networks that were being branched away from the public, university network that became what you know as the internet today. Mostly classified stuff, but my professors had the clearances, not me—it was technically them doing the work. At least, they were the ones getting paid for it. Anyway, one day, out of nowhere, my academic advisor, Dr. Trevor Singh, pulls me into his office to tell me I'm going to begin working for the new M.I.T. Media Lab. It's sort of a promotion, but one that doesn't really make sense—I was very good at what I was doing. One of the best. It wasn't especially pioneering work, no really great thinking going on, but it was some of the necessary mechanical work that was making the great thinking practical. Sort of like when they laid the first telegraph cable across the Atlantic—it was an easy enough idea, but it took lots of people on boats and docks actually handling the cable to make it happen. For all practical purposes, I'm an expert cable layer being pulled to work in the accounting office—so I ask him why, and he can't answer me. He just sort of looks at me and says 'You know, these things, they came from somewhere up the hierarchy.' It seemed plausible enough."

Michael paused and looked at the passing landscape. With each mile away from Atlanta, the buildings grew less dense. The interstate was almost empty. An occasional glare of headlights from an oncoming vehicle would illuminate the small interior, but not in the same way actual headlights would do. It was like how headlights on a movie screen illuminate a theater—just a white glow, without the intrusive intensity of actual beams of directed light. He took a sip of water. He could see from their expressions the two were growing tired of his narrative, so he sped it along.

"I spend the next few years working on the beginnings of software applications that became the basis for a lot of what we use today, or in more cases, the negative of it. For every one scrap of code that might be useful for guiding a robotic arm or camera lens, there might be 10,000 or 100,000 tossed aside. Anyway, a few years later I end up in southern California, doing research at U.S.C., but also working as technical advisor all over the place—there were lots of committees, working groups, subgroups, you know. Anyway, I'm at a conference in Sacramento where we're working on http markup protocol, working on standards, when I run into Dr. Singh. This is in 1996, and everything we've been working on for years is really heating up. Most of the internet is still porn, even more in the early days than now, but between AOL and all the list-serves, everyday people are beginning for the first time to actually use the internet on a daily basis. I even have Ms. Eleanor chatting with me through instant message. It's a really exciting time."

He sees a look of consternation on Callie's face, and realizes he has drifted off topic. "So anyway, Dr. Singh and I chat for a few minutes, what are you working on, how is your funding, are you publishing, you know, and we go back to our respective meetings, I don't think anything more about it. Later that afternoon, I'm getting ready to sit on a panel presentation. After I set up, I go to the bathroom, and when I walk out, I pass Dr. Singh. He slips me a piece of paper, without a word, and keeps walking. I assume it is going to be some sort of job opportunity—for all the online openness we were discussing, people were beginning to see the web as the next place to be the next Microsoft, to really make some serious cash. You remember Netscape, and CompuServe and all that stuff, all the next big things, right?"

The two nodded.

"So I'm walking down the hall, returning to my panel discussion, I look down at the piece of paper, it's folded into a sort of flat origami box—like those sort of paper footballs we used to play with at school." He holds up his fingers in the sign of a goal post, and Josh nods, as Cassie looks on blankly. "I open the first fold, and it says *open tonight*. I fold it back, slip it back in my pocket, and don't think about it again until that night when I'm getting undressed for bed—it falls out of my pants pocket. I open the first fold again, then the second, and it says *keep this paper moving*, and then the third, which says *as you read it*. I do what it says, thinking there may be some optical illusion I'm supposed to be looking for. I open the fourth fold, and it says *double helix 412,943*, and the fifth, which is a string of numbers I recognize as an I.P. address, and the sixth fold says *it's your life*, and the seventh, final fold says *eat or burn now, do not flush*.

"I committed the numbers to memory and immediately burned the paper. There were still ashtrays in hotel rooms in those days. I had no real idea what any of it meant, but Dr. Singh was not a man given to humor or practical jokes—I had never, and have never, heard him laugh. But I recognized the I.P. address as not being a location I knew. Cassie, do you understand how I.P. addresses work?"

Cassie shrugged while shaking her head no—she knew what they were, but had never had any real interest in understanding the internet any more than she had interest in understanding her toaster. Still, she asked, "Why aren't you asking Josh?"

"Josh has been actively blocking his I.P. address for years, as soon as he could figure out how." Josh blushed, as he realized that if Michael knew he had been blocking his I.P. address, he almost certainly knew what sites he had been visiting. It was at that point he gave up any pretense of having had a single truly private moment in his life.

Michael continued "Internet Protocol addresses are basically like zip codes for the internet. The numbers have meanings that can help people find people. 10022 is a fine Manhattan zip code, but most people would rather live in 10021, which is just north of it. People in New York know roughly where one lives if they have those zip codes. Beverly Hills 90210 isn't just a television show, it is a physically specific place. So if all I can tell you about a piece of mail is that it was headed to a zip code starting 9021, you can know the rough location in Los Angeles, but if all I tell you is that is has a zip code starting with 9, it could be anywhere in Washington or Oregon. 970 is Portland. 980 is Seattle. And on and on. And the internet is charted in mostly the same way, but I.P. addresses aren't necessarily constant, or tied to a physical place. Your phone, for instance, has an I.P. address. And in the same way people who work with mail a lot can recognize places by zip codes, people who work with the internet a lot can recognize I.P. addresses. And I recognized this one—to a point. The primary I.P. address for the Pentagon is 141.116.168.135. The address I was given began 141.116, but then branched away. So I could be relatively certain the address was a Department of Defense address, and was likely, but not certainly, physically housed on a server at the Pentagon. *Double helix* was a primitive type of encryption we used in the early days of the internet, and 412,943 told me that at one point in time the password was those two digits. *Double helix* meant that with the three digit sequence, one counting up, one counting down, all I needed was to know the correct sequence on any one day to determine the password on any day."

Cassie looked at him without the least bit of understanding or interest on her face and asked, and said with what she hoped was kindness, "Does any of this matter? I mean, really, I don't care. I'm sure it's very interesting and all, but can we just skip to the part where you figured out what the password was, and tell us what's there, and why it matters?"

Michael laughed, and blushed as much as it is possible for a man with skin as deeply black as his to blush—it was more like a shadow passing over his face. He laughed, and apologized, saying "Of course, you're right, none of this matters—I was just letting you know how cloak-and-daggery it was for me in the beginning. Yes, I figured out the password, and I didn't get caught—I never get caught. I get to the server and find files, text files, thousands of them, arranged by year, month, day. I open one, just a random one. Its named 7_1984_18.txt, and I open it not really knowing what to expect, and it's a transcript of my day. From the moment I wake up and yawn, until I go to sleep. It has snoring in brackets, like it's a screenplay I followed without knowing it. But it's my life. I don't remember any of it, of course—who remembers everything that was said on a random day from more than two decades ago, just some day in eighth grade? But it looked real enough. So I go back out to the year directory, open the 1996 folder, and open the most recent file, from two weeks earlier. That day I do remember. And that text file is a perfect transcript of everything I said, and everything that was said to me that day. This file, though, is more complex. There are references to files on other servers—apparently audio and video files. Also references to every commercial I heard, every song I heard, just on and on. There are a few places where the word *inaudible* is included in brackets—when I was on the subway, and when I stopped off at the Gap to buy some khakis. So, to make a very long story just a little shorter, from about two weeks after my mother died, when I was three years old, until the moment I stepped onto this bus four years ago, every movement of my life, every word I uttered, every cartoon I watched, every lecture I heard, was, whenever and wherever possible, recorded by the United States Department of Defense."

Callie and Josh both looked at him. It wasn't an entirely new concept—really more of an elaboration, a different version of what they'd heard in the grocery store about their own lives. "Is that what's in my file?" Callie asked.

"That's what's in your file." Michael answered, adding, "and yours, Josh."

"Okay, so, Department of Defense," Callie said matter-of-factly, not bothering to question the veracity of anything Michael had just shared with them. "If they are the enemy—I'm guessing they're the enemy?—who does this van belong to? Who is the community?"

"I don't know that they're the enemy, but yes, they are the ones who have been collecting all the data. As far as the community goes—" Here he was cut off by Josh, who interjected "Data? That's what we're going to call this intrusion into our lives? Data collection?" He looked appalled. He wasn't angry—not exactly, not yet—but he appeared headed that way.

"Well, that's what it is. To them, anyway," Michael replied in a soothing but matter-of-fact tone. "To them, it isn't about you, it's about the data you can provide. To them it isn't personal. You take it personally, of course. So did I. It's the natural, human response to being the subject of an investigation—but you're just a subject, you're not Josh. I'm not Michael. Callie isn't Callie."

Looking at him, Callie thought for the first time she could remember ever thinking it, *I'm not Callie.* "Who is the community?" she asked, clipping the thought for the moment—it was not the time for personal reflection, she felt sure—though she wasn't sure what it was time for, either.

Michael looked to Josh for his assent in moving the conversation forward, and received a small shrug of the shoulders.

"A loose collection of scientists, mostly researchers, programmers, and developers, and ex-military, and other specialists in various fields, who, over the years, have worked on your files—either the collection or analysis parts of them—or have been made aware of the D.O.D.'s efforts by others who have. Some are purely interested in the moral side of it—they don't like seeing the technology they've helped to create used in the way it is being used. Some are purely interested in the project itself—they could, for all practical purposes, be working for the D.O.D. But most lie somewhere in between. I would put myself in the latter category, as well as being one of the subjects. And I'm the only subject who has also joined the community."

"Have we joined the community?" Callie asked, but Josh, having had a moment to consider interjected, "Let's go back to this data thing. What kind of data? Why?"

Michael was beginning to regret not having structured their introduction more carefully. He had been looking forward to it, planning for it, within weeks of learning about Josh and Callie, but he had never actually worked out what would be the best way to move forward. He could see now, that was a mistake. "Okay," he said, "We have a lot to cover, but we have some time. I guess it's time for you to meet Trevor. He can explain better than I can."

"Your teacher? From the conference?" Josh asked. "He's here?"

"Yes," Michael answered, and lifted his head up in the general direction of the ceiling and spoke in a clear, authoritative voice, "Trevor." A moment later a voice replied back, "Yes, Michael?" and Michael responded "Do you have time to come join us?"

There were no speakers visible, but Trevor's voice sounded as clear as though he was sitting with them when he answered, "Sure, gimme a sec."

Michael lowered his head back down and began, "While we're waiting on Trevor, let me fill you in on a little more of my part in this. After I found the directory of my subdirectories, and I began digging around, it occurred to me there might be others. So I kept searching, and eventually I found my dad, and the two of you, and some other people from Dublin, and the more I searched, the more I found. Everywhere. All over the world. Of course the only people they can monitor exhaustively are those of us here in the U.S. The others they keep an eye on as best they can, but nothing like what they have on us here. In the U.S., there are 2,342 of us, give or take. There have been more, at times a lot more, but that's where the number has been for a while now. The number doesn't fluctuate a lot on any given day, but it does move."

"2,342 people under surveillance in the United States for data collection for what purpose?" Callie summarized in a way that she hoped wasn't too pointedly impatient, as the door to the sleeping compartment opened, and a thin, handsome man with distinctive Indian features and coloring, who looked to be in his late fifties, entered the room. Without waiting for introductions, he answered as he sat down next to Michael, "Atmospheric anomalies. 2,342 people are under surveillance so the Department of Defense, and a lot of other people, can understand what is only understood at this point to be atmospheric anomalies. Hi, I'm Trevor, Trevor Singh. And no, my name is not really Trevor, it's Tribhuvan, but the only person who ever called me that is my mother, and she's dead, so please don't start. Just Trevor. It's nice to meet you, but let's be done with this so we can move on." His accent was Midwestern American, but with just enough of a clipped Indian undertone for both Callie and Josh to assume, correctly, that his parents immigrated to the U.S.

The appearance of this new person, from who knew where, was disturbing to both Callie and Josh, but more so to Callie, who responded immediately, "Nice to meet you as well, but exactly how many more people are on this thing?" She didn't know whether it was a bus or a truck or a mobile home, so she just settled on *thing*.

"Except for the driver, just us here," Trevor answered. "But back to your question, since Michael is taking such a roundabout way of answering it," he said with something bordering on a smile in Michael's direction. "There are these packets of electromagnetic radiation, or energy, that have relationships to both of you. They exist just on the other side of the visible light spectrum, just past purple. So, they aren't visible to the human eye, at least to the majority of people the majority of the time. They were first discovered in the 1940s, when radar was invented, though no one knew then what they were looking at—people assumed they were atmospheric gasses of some sort. But as technology improved over the years, including improvements in lidar, which is like radar, but doesn't require a solid object, other theories have developed. You both understand how radar works, yes?"

Callie and Josh looked at each other with uncertainty, but Trevor continued before they could speak, "Briefly, when using radar, or radio detection and ranging, we send out electromagnetic waves, and they bounce off a solid object, and when the waves return back, we know where the object is, and can determine certain things about it, such as its speed, if is moving. That's how air traffic controllers use radar. With lidar, or light detection and ranging, no object is required, per se. At least, no airplane. It its infancy, lidar was used extensively in the exploration of the atmosphere, specifically the chemical composition, the gases, cloud formations, etc. Before the 20th century, we knew relatively little about these things. We still know very little, actually, but a lot compared to what we knew in the 19th century. The same is true for most of science, for most of what we know about earth, our lives on it. Take the case of the Friendly Floatees. You've heard of them?"

Callie and Josh shook their heads no, Michael nodded in assent—he felt like he was back in school.

"In 1992, a cargo container full of rubber ducks and frogs and things, children's bath toys, was washed overboard in a storm in the middle of the Pacific, on its way to America. This sort of thing happens all the time—the ocean is littered with hundreds of thousands of these intermodal cargo containers. But in this case, the container broke open, and 29,000 floating toys began drifting around the Pacific Ocean, and started showing up in all kinds of obvious places—Alaska, Japan, Washington state, and later in less obvious places, like Maine and Massachusetts—they had travelled through the Bering Strait, through the northern ice pack across the pole, and down into the north Atlantic. That whole time, up to now, oceanographers have been collecting data using the ducks to understand ocean currents more fully than we've ever been able to before. But the ducks are not the subjects of the investigation. Do you see what I'm saying?"

Callie saw. "We're the ducks. We're not the subject of the investigation."

"Right. You're the ducks. Michael misspoke before. These pockets of energy in the atmosphere, they are the subjects of the investigation. You're just ducks."

In Callie's mind, this realization brought forward what Sam had told them earlier about Lucy. *Ducks are disposable*, she thought. Josh's thoughts were elsewhere. "What kind of relationship? You said the pockets of energy have relationships to us. What kind of relationships?"

"Well, that is the question. That's the whole point. No one knows. We know more about them now—well, at least, we have observed them more, and collected more data, but it's probably not appropriate to say we know anything. But they exist, and each of you seems to have a special, though not entirely unique association with them, or to them. Whichever. I will share with you what we think. And by we, I mean not just the community, as Michael described it to you, but also generations of military leaders. At least their recorded thoughts. Speaking of which, Sam was a little dramatic with you earlier—every word you have ever uttered has not been recorded. Your surveillance has been going on through so many Washington administrations, with different goals and objectives, that your surveillance, while continuous on some level, has not always been consistently, say, intrusive. During the Carter administration, for instance, research was at the most minimum levels possible. The Reagan administration also didn't apparently see the point, while Bush Sr., as a former CIA—well, you get the point. The only data that has been consistently collected has been satellite imagery, which has become more detailed over the years, as that technology has improved."

Both Callie and Josh had become more comfortable and relaxed as Trevor spoke. The information itself was not comforting to them, but Trevor was. His emotional detachment from the situation—they each felt instinctively that he was not one of the 2,342 people under observation—was somehow calming. At the same time, each was waiting for some other shoe to drop—none of this felt real. They had each seen or heard evidence that it was real, but the singularity of the situation, though each shared it with 2,341 other people, seemed to have placed them in the inverted opposite of probability: *You have been selected to be hit by lightning not once, not twice, but three times, on the same day of the same month of three consecutive years.*

And yet, they were becoming less anxious, and the easing of tension was displayed in their physical ease. Callie was sitting back in her seat, one leg tucked under her. Josh, though in his rigorous, upright, almost aggressively masculine stance, with feet flat on the floor before him, still showed less tension in his face and hands than he had before Trevor's arrival.

Trevor continued, "The satellite tracking was not, at least until the 1990s, adequately advanced to be able to locate and track the anomalies on its own. We're talking about anomalies roughly the size of a kitten. And keep in mind, there's nothing there, except a distortion of light at a wavelength below the human threshold of seeing. Up until that time, the discovery of new carriers—that's how you're referred to in the literature, is carriers, or suspected carriers—seems to have been almost random. There were fewer than 200 known, tracked carriers going into 1996. From there, each year, the number grew, along with refined computer-aided detection and surveillance methods, until around 2004, when the known carrier count reached a population of 4,815."

Callie's expression changed at once from something like contentment into alarm. "What happened to the other 2,473 people?" Only Josh looked surprised at her appently effortless computational skills.

"Life, for the most part. Many of them were Vietnam Veterans. From that high number, something like 1,600 were holdouts from the war. But life for them, after the war, was never easy. You remember that Charlie Daniels song, *Still in Saigon*? Many of them never left Vietnam, not entirely. And as they stumbled through middle age, having suffered through years of depression, drinking, smoking, addiction, isolation, poor diets, poor healthcare, homelessness, you know, the whole gamut, they started dying off younger than their Baby Boomer peers. In fact," he began, but was cut off by Josh, who asked "Why so many vets?"

Trevor looked at him thoughtfully for a moment before he responded. "There are two basic schools of thought, or three, if you combine the two. One maintains that the anomaly association begins, or latent human potential for the association is actualized, at a moment of critical divergence—that is, when someone experiences something outside the acceptable realm of human experience—the loss of one's own limbs, or the forced killing of another person. The other school of thought maintains a chemical change in the brain, brought on by the introduction of a foreign substance with significant abilities to alter someone's mental and or physiological state. In a situation like Vietnam, where episodes of critical divergence are experienced while the body is in a state of heightened awareness brought on by the use of powerful methamphetamines, the opportunities for anomaly association increase significantly."

Josh replied with some skepticism, "Where would active soldiers get supplies of powerful methamphetamines?"

"From their commanding officers. They were originally intended, at least we believe, for fighter pilots who needed to remain in the air and focused for hours at a time. But, they trickled down—soldiers on the front line fought harder, longer, fiercer with the drugs. Many of the atrocities we associate with the Vietnam War are direct or indirect results of the liberal distribution of amphetamines among the fighting forces there."

"Can this be real? Do people know this? I've never heard this." Callie was skeptical. She was in fact skeptical of everything being suggested, but she was willing to take it apart bit by bit. This seemed like a good bit to discredit.

"Yes," Trevor answered. "It's common knowledge. You can go get on Google right now. It's part of the public record. There are military medical advisors even today advocating for the limited use of amphetamines in highly-specialized, rigorously-tested pilots."

"You're serious?" Josh questioned.

"He's always serious," Michael interjected.

"Okay, but I still don't understand how that means anything. What do the atmospheric anomalies do, exactly? You say we're carriers. Are they here, now? Are they in us? Around us? Is Lucy a carrier?" Callie wanted the conversation back on track.

Josh, prompted by her series of questions, added on, "And why do they call us carriers? Is it contagious? Whatever it is?"

"We don't know what they do. Or where they come from, or where they go to when they go off radar, or if they are the same ones. What we are relatively sure of, is that they are not generated by you. That took some time and data review to discover. Specifically, data review of the two of you. You are the first two carriers that were in some way observed becoming carriers. That is, we know roughly the time and place the Mollies—that's what we call them for short—became associated with you."

"St. Patrick's Day 1974." Josh and Callie said it at the same time, looking at each other as they did so.

"Exactly." Michael and Trevor replied, also in unison.

"But we'll get to that. The rest of your questions first. No, the Mollies aren't here, now, for several reasons. One, we're moving. The Mollies don't travel in any way that we recognize travel. If you're walking through the park, they will follow you about, but anything faster than a bicycle, and they're gone. Second, we're in a refrigerated truck insulated with chlorodifluoromethane, which the Mollies can't move through. There are several refrigerant gasses, mostly hyrochlorofluorocarbons, that work as a barrier to them. Finally, at least for the two of you, special circumstances are required for the Mollies to be present. For you, Callie, you have to be high, really high, on some sort of chemical accelerant. As long as you aren't doing cocaine or the like, the Mollies basically ignore you. They have for years. Josh, you're well, not quite the opposite, but the Mollies are always with you, unless you take active measures to keep them away. Since you've been in recovery, the prayer and meditation thing seems to work for you, but, as you know, only as a temporary measure. For Michael, they only appear in his sleep."

"If you could call it sleep," Michael added with a wry sort of smile. But Callie and Josh weren't really listening. Neither spoke. Each was travelling back through the course of their lives, those times when the intense presence of something else, someone else, had been almost, but not quite tangible. And now, someone was telling them that everything they had learned to tell themselves was a lie.

"They're real? The voices? They're real?" Josh no longer cared about Callie knowing about the voices, and guessed from the direction of the conversation it wouldn't be long before she knew anyway. He wanted, and felt like for the first time in his life, he was near, the truth.

"They're real to you. Yes, there is a relationship between the presence of the Mollies around you and what you have always perceived as auditory hallucinations. Most of us think the presence of the Mollies stimulate brain activity, and your nervous system, not knowing what to do with the excess energy, generates sound."

"But there are enough people," interrupted Michael, "who think the Mollies are trying to communicate with you, and with others, including Lucy, who is a carrier, yes, that they want to understand what they might be trying to communicate."

Callie came back into the conversation from her own train of thought, asking "The shadow people are real?" The visual hallucinations known jokingly, but collectively and almost uniformly among heavy cocaine and methamphetamine users as *shadow people* were not something she had given any real or serious thought to in years.

Trevor answered, "Again, for you, yes. The visual and auditory hallucinations you experienced when you were high dovetailed with times that the Mollies were present. On those occasions when you were so high that you actually began trying to speak with them, there was a reaction. More Mollies appeared. No one knows why, or how—most speculate it was the heightened activity level of your nervous system, and not your communication efforts, that caused the increase. But the more agitated you became, the more Mollies appeared. The same was true for Josh on the two times he tried cocaine as an adult, and when he was prescribed Ritalin as a child. And the data exists to support the conclusion. Enough data that the Department of Defense wants to understand. The three of you, more clearly than any of the others, except Lucy, are able to somehow interact with, or communicate with, or attract, the Mollies. And you have to understand, regardless of whatever else they are, they are energy. They have, or are, power. That is the military's interest in this. Not who or what you may be able to communicate with, but what untapped source of power may be available to them. Or, someone else."

"But, but, I haven't seen the shadow people since the last time I was high. Eighteen years ago. Why do they have a picture of me from two weeks ago? Why do you?" The sense of unreality was melting away from the situation, and Callie felt as though she were waking up from a dream of sunshine into a prison cell. She felt trapped.

"We get real time updates from their updates. Their interest in you, in all of the carriers, is really, fundamentally one of security. Since September 11th, your line item on the budget has steadily increased. It's part of the black budget. No one really knows how much it is. Why you? Because they believe, and we agree, that if they injected you with cocaine or amphetamines right now, and set you on the street, the Mollies would appear within six minutes. Then they could monitor you. They could monitor them." Trevor's voice softened as he added, "That's what they're doing to Lucy."

Callie's face paled, but Josh flushed with anger. His voice, low and calm, but layered with resentment, he asked "That's what Sam meant, by torture? That's what they're doing? They're injecting her with drugs? But why? How? Where? Is that where we're going?"

Michael answered with a forced businesslike tone, a poor imitation of Trevor's, "Yes, that is where we're going. And yes, that is what they're doing—that's what Sam meant. We have a plan to get her out. And it will work. Some of the best minds in the world have helped put it together. All we have to do is stay on schedule."

Josh sat back in his anguish, trying to picture his daughter, whom he had never seen, or seen a picture of, being tortured, being injected with drugs against her will, and he wanted to ask to see her face, but somehow he couldn't, just yet.

"I still don't understand why we're called *carriers*. This can't be contagious, or transferrable, if there are so few of us, with the numbers you described earlier." Callie was back on track to understanding.

Michael and Trevor were both looking at Josh with some concern, and it was Trevor who came around first to answer her question, "Well, you're right, to some degree. At least we believe you are. One of the reasons you, Michael and Josh and Lucy are of so much interest is because you're the first carriers who've been, for lack of a better phrase, born in captivity. Almost from the moment you became carriers, you've been under observation. They know almost to the moment Michael became a carrier, and they know you weren't carriers before that St. Patrick's Day because of the satellite positions on the V.A. hospital and the surrounding environs tracking the carriers there. Do you remember anything from that day? Or the days before?"

"I have no idea what you're talking about, to be honest. I don't recall ever being in Dublin as a child. I've driven through, of course, dozens of times as an adult, but I have no recollection of any event there." Even as she said it, the words felt wrong. She knew she wasn't lying, but she somehow didn't feel like the words she was saying were true.

"Nor does Josh, from newspaper accounts at the time," Michael added.

Josh had been watching the view out of the truck, its headlights cutting a parabola into the countryside, but roused himself, saying, "No, I don't. Nothing. I was questioned I don't know how many times, for years."

"For the first year after the incident, you were in weekly therapy sessions. You may remember them as spending time with a nice lady and playing with toys—she had an office downtown next to the Martin Theater. Do you remember?" Josh nodded, and Trevor continued, "There was a two-way mirror in the room, and you were being recorded. But they got nothing. You can watch if you want. We have copies of the recordings. After that first year, you were questioned at least once every three months, by various people in a number of positions in the community. That was for about the next five years. After that, you were questioned annually." Trevor repeated the information drily, as though reciting statistics about a certain species of insect.

"Was that planned? Was that part of the Defense Department? Were they operating through local officials? Through my school counselors?" Josh was incredulous at the thought that the people he fondly recalled as caring, bumbling hometown hayseeds had been part of some master plot to—but his incredulity stopped there. He still wasn't sure exactly what they were ultimately being accused of. The business about power and energy made some sense, but only in an abstract way, and when it was disconnected from him.

Michael answered the question. "Well, yes and no. The Defense Department certainly wanted to know, and updated their files regularly with questions asked for them by locals, but it didn't take much prodding of the judge and the sheriff, or anyone—everybody in Dublin wanted to know what happened. Those who remember still do." He paused for a moment, looking at the countryside passing by them, before continuing. "Most people didn't believe my father killed that young boy. The two of you showing up in that refrigerator in the Piggly Wiggly, well, it didn't make sense at the time. Now, it makes more sense." He gestured around him. "But only to us. No one in Dublin knows anything about any of this. Not that I'm aware of, anyway."

"What young boy? Who got killed? When?" Callie didn't think the information would help her understand any more than anything else had, yet it seemed to be a piece of the puzzle only she didn't have.

"Jonathan Vinson," Michael and Josh answered together. Josh then explained briefly about the death of the boy, what he remembered of it. The boy's death had in many ways shaped his own childhood, had shaped the town, even more than the storm. Josh and most of the children his age eventually forgot about the storm's destruction—as children, it was just another new thing, like seeing mountains for the first time, or a real train. New things are not extraordinary in childhood— most things are new. And in time, the roads and schools and churches and even the bridges were rebuilt. But the story of the crippled boy haunted the town as much as an actual ghost might have. The threat of *Do you want to end up like Jonny Vinson?* was a threat that kept children off streets and doors locked tight. Before the storm, before the boy's death, the idea of Dublin being unsafe would have been laughable. Afterwards, no one laughed. No horror seemed too far-fetched, no fear too irrational. Nothing of the sort ever happened again, but fear drove itself into the heart of the town as deeply as the rain had soaked into its soil, and precaution became a new way of life. Josh tried to communicate this to Callie, but the idea of safety in childhood was as foreign to her as birthday parties or a bed of her own, but he knew nothing about that part of her life.

"So who did kill him?" she asked, expecting the answer to be some form of military operation. Josh looked up as she asked the question, realizing the answer to a lifelong mystery was unfolding before him. One look at Trevor told him the answer—Trevor was, for the first time, expressing emotion in his countenance, and it was sadness.

"Well, we, we don't know, not exactly, but most believe it probably was my father," Michael answered. He looked her directly in the eyes as he said it, and his eyes were empty, entirely devoid of the excitement that had been animating them all evening. Callie was instant appalled at her own indiscretion. She barely knew the person sitting before her, but she liked him. She had liked him almost instantly, despite the bizarre manner of their introduction. He had been only kind to her, and her apparent indifference to his feelings caught her off guard. "I'm sorry," she said quickly, "I didn't mean to, to" but here her words faltered. Yet he was gracious, and cut her off.

"There's no reason for you to apologize. You assumed my father was innocent—and that was kind of you. More kind than many. But really, it wasn't my father that killed him. The man my father became in Vietnam, the man that returned, was so altered he couldn't really be said to be my father in any meaningful way. Between the shellshock, and the Mollies, and the chemicals they were feeding him, I don't know what he was, or who he was. But he knew me, and he loved me. He was scared for me. And he was right. He knew. Somehow, he knew."

"What did he know?" Callie's voice was almost a whisper.

"He knew we weren't safe," Michael answered, now looking at a cluster of mobile homes surrounded by mounds of filth visible even in the momentary light of the truck. "He was a carrier. And he was part of a group of ex-military who banded together—all carriers—to try to understand. They were part of the community, but it was much less organized then than it is today. No computers. No talking on the telephone. It was rudimentary, but it was part of the basis for what would become the community today."

"Not safe?" Callie looked from Michael to Trevor, who looked uncomfortable, even embarrassed, and on to Josh, whose puzzled expression reflected her own confusion. She looked back to Trevor and asked "Not safe from what?"

"This is where Michael and I diverge in our thinking, in our understanding of the data, if you will. Michael believes there is a point, a message, a sign, a purpose, something, I will let him explain it. I can't. He sees meaning in the Mollies. I see math. He believes in God—something he shares with you, I think, Callie. I believe if there is a god, he is a great scientist, not a great moralist magician playwright. We assign our human thoughts and values to a mystical creature-slash-creator who created the universe in the same way we anthropomorphize cats and dogs. The Christian Bible is no more real than a thought bubble floating over a cat's head in a Sunday comic strip. We humanize the universe to put it on a human scale. But the universe is not human. It is, if anything, unhuman, inhuman, unsuitable for the presence of beings like us. But—"

"What does any of this have to do with my daughter?" Josh interjected. He was growing impatient with them all, including Callie. He had not agreed to get on the truck to hear theological debates. He was interested in understanding what the purpose of it all was, but that knowledge seemed far secondary to how his daughter was going to be saved.

"Everything," Michael answered at once, and at the same time as Trevor, who answered "Nothing." They looked at each other and laughed, a congenial, well-worn laugh of old friends agreeing to disagree with each other's absurdity. And it was their laughter that finally sent Josh into the rage that had been building since Sam began his story in the grocery store.

"FUCK you people," he yelled, his face instantly flushed, and his neck marked with throbbing veins. "What the fuck is wrong with you? Does anything either of you retards believe have anything to do with helping my daughter? I could give a fuck about your gods. Where. Is. My. Daughter?" He stood and punched the ceiling as he finished speaking, a gesture he immediately regretted, as the ceiling was rigid as stone. He immediately half-screamed, half-groaned, cupping his injured right hand in his left. "Fuck. Fuck. Fuck." He was bending over with pain, his eyes closed.

Michael began softly, "Josh, why don't you—"

"Shut the fuck up." Josh interrupted, through gritted teeth. "Either tell me where my daughter is, and what our plan is to get her, or just shut the fuck up. I don't care. I don't fucking care."

He realized as he said it that he did care, and that he was scared of what they were saying. He did not believe in God, or any god, and he suspected they all knew it. An overwhelming sense of helplessness had begun to weigh upon him since Sam first blurted out the news about his daughter, a feeling that had only grown with the strangeness of the evening. But the God talk was just too much for him. It made him uncomfortable in any setting, but here, now, it was intolerable.

After a moment, Callie spoke, softly but firmly, "Your hand is bleeding, Josh. Why don't you sit down," and then, addressing Michael and Trevor, "Is there a first aid kit on this thing? He needs an ice pack."

Trevor almost jumped out of his seat, saying as he stepped towards the sleeping compartment, "There's one in the office. I'll get it." And he was gone.

Michael looked at the closing door with a look of mild amusement before standing up and opening a panel on the entry wall of the cabin, and retrieved a first aid kit from it. He located an antiseptic pad, and a bandage, which he held out to Josh, who was sitting, looking at his outstretched fingers. An indelible expression of despair on his face, Josh looked up at Michael and attempted to take the supplies with his left hand. Before he could, Callie moved next to him, took the supplies and immediately began tending to the cut. As she did so, she glanced up at Michael, who had seated himself, and urged him, wordlessly, to tell them the plan.

Michael pulled one of the on monitors away from the wall behind the sofa, and was busy tapping on the nighttime sky, now beginning to show more streetlights and houses as they neared suburban Augusta, but traffic was still light. It was past midnight. "Do you all mind if I turn off the exterior view? For some reason it's disorienting to stand with the world moving past like this."

"Not at all," Callie answered, and Josh replied "I can't imagine why." Everything about the trolley was disorienting to him.

"Just as a point of interest," Josh asked, with a groan poorly disguised beneath his words, "Why do you call this thing the trolley? Some Star Trek-sounding name would seem more appropriate."

Michael smiled. "Mr. Roger's Neighborhood. I was always fascinated by that trolley when I was a kid. I still am, really. The special effects, if you can even call them that, were so clumsy. You could actually see the hands in the hand puppets. But that was the whole point, I suppose—the trolley went to the land of make-believe. Make-believe for children is like the willing suspension of disbelief for adults—we can say we choose to believe or not believe a thing. For me, that's how this truck works. I can't feel the sun, but I can believe I can, and then I do. Anyway," he said, with a swiping motion, and the exterior view of the star-scattered suburbia disappeared and was replaced with what looked like dull grey paneling, except for the one panel he was manipulating with typing and sweeping gestures, which looked like a giant television screen, "back to the plan."

CHAPTER 4. SOUTH OF THE BORDER

A map of North America appeared, and like a television weatherman, Michael used his fingers to zoom in on an area of the east coast that stretched from Savannah to Boston. "We're here," he said, pointing to a blinking green dot near Augusta. We will refit at South of the Border, as we discussed earlier. We will refit again outside Baltimore. When we get to Bridgeport, we will pull into a distribution center for Applied Logistics Distributors in New Haven. Callie will go with Trevor by ferry from Old Saybrook in a refrigerated truck delivering dairy and ready-to-eat vending machine products to the Plum Island Disease Center. She will get Lucy, the two of them will get in the truck and back on the ferry, which will bring them back to us here at the distribution center. The four of us will then head to New York. The community keeps an office there, and there will be a safe place for us to stay while we assess Lucy."

As he was talking, he had been zooming into the areas of the map he was discussing, showing visuals of the places and things he was describing—the mechanic's shop in South Carolina, the interior and exterior of a distribution warehouse, a ferry, an island, an aerial view of Manhattan. When he finished, he looked at them, and, sitting, added, "That's the plan."

Based on his rambling explanations of everything else that evening, the brevity of the plan took both Callie and Josh off guard.

"Um, that's it?" Callie asked, trying not to sound underwhelmed or overwhelmed, though she was a little of both. "That's the plan?" added Josh, with less judiciousness, his eyebrows arched in what could have been either disbelief, or expectation, or possibly both.

"Well, those are the basics. Countless hours from who knows how many people have gone into the planning. There are terabytes of details if you want to go through them. Contingencies for most every possible thing that could go wrong. We have files on everything—the names, ages, location and employment of every family member of every employee of the distribution center, for example. But if we are actually going to execute the plan, there isn't time for you to read all those files, or even for you to know what all files exist, for that matter. Either we move in and get her, tomorrow, or we don't, probably ever."

"Let's get back to that in a minute. Why am I here?" Josh asked. He wasn't newly angry. There was some residual anger, but mostly he was confused by why his presence was necessary. "If Callie's going to do all the rescuing, why do you need me to stay behind with you?"

"Mostly because they will be looking for you. You're next on their list. They will be looking for you—it's only a matter of time, really. They haven't stopped looking for me for four years. They may even come to realize there's something larger at work, once you don't come out of that Kroger. They may realize we might be together. One way or the other, they'll be looking for you. Soon, if they aren't already. Speaking of which, hold on. Trevor," he said, again projecting his voice up to the ceiling.

"Yes?" answered the disembodied voice. But before Michael could say anything, Callie, feeling extraordinarily foolish, spoke up to the ceiling, asking "Any progress on the ice pack front?"

There was a long pause, then "I knew I was forgetting something. Be right there."

"Wait," Michael called out, "Any word from Sam?"

"Yes, he's live," was the response.

"Thanks. Unpage."

"Unpage?" Callie asked. Michael explained, speaking rapidly in an attempt to keep Josh's temper at bay, "That's the command to tell the system to stop broadcasting between any two areas. It had to be a word that wasn't a word. All those police radio words are everyday words—*over*, *out*, you know. It started out as *over*, but the system kept cutting us off in conversation, then we tried to stop saying the word *over*, and suddenly we needed to say it in every sentence. So we changed it."

"Right," Josh began, "going back to this group of brightest minds who've been developing these plans and backup plans and all. Is the man who just forgot about my icepack one of those minds?" Callie was privately pleased that Josh voiced what she had been thinking.

"He wasn't really going to get your icepack. I think he just wanted to get out of here. Emotions aren't really his thing. He didn't get out much, even before he got on the trolley."

"Why is he here?" Callie asked.

"We need him. And he didn't have a lot else going on. I mean, personally. No family or anything."

"Imagine that," Josh interjected, with a sort of smile.

Callie grimaced, but was pleased that Josh was making something like an attempt at humor.

"Anyway," Michael continued, standing back up "We realized when they took Lucy to Plum Island that some sort of intervention would probably be necessary. So Trevor joined me here. He's only been on the trolley a few weeks." With a few keystrokes, an image of a laboratory appeared, replacing the aerial view of midtown Manhattan that had been static on the screen for the past few minutes. It looked like any other laboratory — a low, wide, white landscape of beakers and computers and coils of tubing. There were glass double doors at the far center of the screen, and to the right was a black man in a white lab coat and Atlanta Braves baseball cap.

Callie laughed. "Who convinced Sam to wear a baseball cap?"

"Um, me." Michael smiled. "We needed to find a way for him to communicate with us nonverbally, and without signs or email or anything. This pin camera was installed in his lab two weeks ago, and we tested it when it was installed, but we turned it off because the battery will only last about two weeks. We don't have audio. I'm not sure why. But as long as he's wearing the baseball cap forward, no one's made contact with him. If he turns the cap around, it means they've made contact in some way."

Josh frowned, and looked from Callie to Michael, then asked, "I thought you all had access to everything they have."

"Well, most everything," Michael acknowledged. "Not everything. No one has access to everything. The world's just too complex now. For instance, we don't have active audio surveillance of them, not the way they've been recording you. We have a line in on some of their cell phones, but their organization is decentralized. Like many covert programs, they have some analysts in the National Security Administration, a couple in the Secret Service, even more in the Office of Net Assessment, some in the regular military ranks, but most of them are privately contracted, and virtually none of them ever have any contact with one another. They get assignments, they submit their reports, without ever knowing or probably even suspecting the nature of the investigation they're working on. We don't really know how many of them there are, or where they are. We have access to the servers at the Pentagon, and their satellite operations—most of them, anyway. But we don't know what's said in every meeting. If it becomes part of a record of a meeting, or the meeting is recorded, we can get that easily enough. But you've both been in meetings. You know the difference between what gets said and what gets written. And most of what gets written is a record of what has already happened, not what will happen. Decisions aren't always recorded in real time—especially when they aren't legal. We know they have at least a handful of people in the CDC, but we don't know who they are. Sam is very smart. He will be aware of any change in his environment. And he will let us know. All we have to do is watch. And, well, we, here, us, we don't even have to do that. Someone in the community is watching for us. I just wanted you to see Sam is okay." Here he made a nodding gesture as he made eye contact with Callie. "This is going to work."

There was a pause of a few minutes as each looked absently at the image of Sam on the screen, in his laboratory typing, and taking small bites off of what Callie and Josh were both thinking must be a granola bar.

"Can I see her? Lucy?" Josh finally asked. The vastness of the plan, whose details he could apparently not know, was fatiguing him. His anger was finally dissipated. "I would like to see her."

"You have seen her," Michael answered, "on multiple occasions. But yes, I can show her to you. Do you mean a picture of her as she is right now, or before she was taken?"

"Taken?" Callie asked, surprised. She had been working under the assumption that Lucy was being monitored somewhere as she and Josh had been, not that she had been taken from somewhere. "Where was she taken from?"

Michael looked surprised. "From you, Callie. She didn't run away from you. She was taken." Michael had believed, wrongly, that Callie's intuition would have told her the girl did not run away. For her part, Callie had no reason to believe that a troubled teen, whom she knew to have run away from multiple foster families, and unsuccessfully battle a war with addiction, would be a likely kidnapping victim. Even if she had ever had the thought, she would have dismissed it—there was no rational basis, no evidence, to support any such suspicion or conclusion. At least, not until this moment.

"You know this?" Her question was asked in a way that did not question the veracity of Michael's belief, but rather its basis in fact, in actual evidence. She believed Michael to be telling the truth as he understood it, but was it true?

Michael understood, and was not offended. "Yes. We knew it almost as soon as it happened. But we didn't know about it beforehand—it caught us off guard. It reminded us of the limitations of our own surveillance. We're watching the watchers, but, well, in the end, we're all human. We lost her for two weeks. They know how to shield from the Mollies as well as we do, and while they were transporting her to her new home, it appears she was in total lockdown. She ended up on a farm in New Hampshire. Two retired, married, Secret Service agents were contracted to shelter her in place. She tried running away a couple of times, but there was nothing there, no one there. She had the run of a 700-acre farm, with cattle and trees and a creek and all the rest, but she may as well have been in a prison cell, and she knew it. She didn't believe any of the cover story they gave her—ever. They had to keep her heavily sedated. Reports from that time are very limited—there doesn't appear to have been any significant research on her going on at the time. They just wanted her away from you and Josh."

"But that doesn't make sense," Josh interjected. "Why wouldn't they want us all together? And where did I ever see her?"

An image of a file folder appeared on the screen with a picture of a young woman on it. She was painfully thin, her face was without emotion, but her eyes were red and watery, and ancient. Her hair was brown with streaks of auburn, hanging limply almost to her shoulders. She was clearly not a child, but whether she was 16 or 21 was impossible to tell from the picture. Above all, Callie thought, she looked thirsty. Michael began, "In your first few meetings at Galano, you saw her on seven occasions. Callie was taking her to meetings. And the reason—" Here, he was interrupted.

"Oh my God," Josh whispered, his face turning pale. "I remember. She sat next to me in one of the meetings. She kept staring at me. She made me so nervous I got up and left. But how could she have known? Did she know?" He looked around, lost.

At first, Michael did not respond. He looked thoughtfully at each of the others in turn, and apparently resolving some internal dialogue, he answered, saying "I think she did. I don't know whether or not she knew you were her father, or bio-logically related in any way, but yes, she knew something. Why don't we look at that video. I will let you decide for yourself if she knew, or felt, anything."

After just a few clicks on the monitor, four boxes appeared, three with images focused on Josh and Lucy from different angles, and the fourth on Callie.

"How many of these cameras are there," Callie asked as the images appeared.

"You mean at the Galano Club or in all?"

"Both, I guess."

"Oh, well, I suppose the answer to both is the same. No one really knows. I think there are four in each meeting room at Galano. In the world, who knows. Millions. Tens of millions. Maybe hundreds of millions—every laptop, every phone with a camera—they're all connected to a network."

"That doesn't sound very likely," Josh added in, surprising even himself. He had little interest in intrigue of any sort, rarely even bothered to read the news, and was generally unobservant of his surroundings. He enjoyed the leisurely life of an orthopedic surgeon, and with the exception of the occasional terror event or war or stock market crash, didn't bother with the world at large at all. "Can that really be true?" he added.

Michael answered without hesitation. "They're everywhere. Take that Mellow Mushroom pizza place you all eat at after meetings sometimes. The owners of the restaurant have over 64 security cameras installed, all on, all the time, all the data being uploaded to a cloud server as well as downloaded to three redundant servers—one in the U.S., one in Spain, and another in South Africa. It has nothing to do with you all—these are just standard security cameras restaurants use to reduce liability and provide, well, security. The manager of a restaurant, or even a waiter, is much less likely to do cocaine on the job or sexually harass someone if he knows all those cameras are around. Because they suspect—rightly—that there are many more cameras they know nothing about."

"Why would a restaurant need so many cameras?" Callie asked, with mild but genuine interest.

"Several on each register and the safe. One on each table, to settle any disputes about who may or may not have paid, or if waiters are giving away food or liquor or whatever. A couple on each entrance and exit. And places like banks and high-end jewelry stores operate at a whole other level. The cameras you see mounted on the walls are dummy cameras—criminals can spray paint the lenses like in the movies, but it affects nothing. The real pinhole cameras are installed during the construction process—embedded in the mortar between bricks or marble or wood panels. Every light fixture is typically also concealing at least one camera, because there is a ready power supply there. The employees and even the owners of those places don't know where all the cameras are, because the employees and owners are the people most likely to steal from them. If they want the businesses to be insured, they agree to third-party security measures. The whole point of this is, there are legions of people across the country with significant experience installing cameras that are effectively invisible but give high-resolution, panoramic views of any space a client might need surveillance."

"So they're everywhere?"

"No, not everywhere. Not everyone, not every place is that interesting. Most aren't. But enough are to justify the payroll of a hidden army. We just passed through Richmond County, home of the Fort Gordon Army base. There are over 4,000 known civilian and military personnel there intercepting and interpreting phone calls for the National Security Agency. And that base is just one of dozens like it. And those are just the ones we know about. From what we can tell, it's mostly tedious, boring work, listening to Iraqis call their moms to say they have a new job, or new girlfriend, and Americans trying to determine whether or not they're talking about a bomb. Which they never are—it's like listening to millions of American teenagers on their cell phones and listening for the Columbine killers. Anyway, are you ready to watch?" The videos were still frozen, two rows and two columns of images neatly stacked on the monitor, like in an editing room.

Josh had not taken his eyes away from them, away from his daughter, himself, and Vicky—he could not now stop thinking of Callie as Vicky. Thinking about the images, he couldn't pinpoint the date they were made, but he didn't need to—it was embedded in the bottom right corner of each of display, and they were synchronized. It was two weeks after he first met Mama Ben. Josh had promised to attend one 12-step meeting a day for 90 days at the Galano Club. Mama Ben had said it didn't matter which kind of 12-step meeting it was, though he advised against Al-Anon, because it had no real relevance, but had suggested that even Al-Anon would be better than sitting home alone. Josh was also required to introduce himself to at least one new person at every meeting, or speak to someone if there was no one new for him to meet. This was awkward for him not because he wasn't outgoing—he just didn't have honest answers for many of the questions he was asked, such as "Why don't you want to fuck me?" It was a question asked of him several times in his first week of attending meetings. After it became generally known that Mama Ben was his sponsor, and that he was not allowed to have sex during his first year of recovery, most of the men left him alone, but a few took it as a challenge, and approached it with vigor. But that day, a Thursday, he had purposefully shown up a half-hour early to avoid the throng that usually congregated by the front door and served as a sort of gauntlet—one that reminded him uncomfortably of his undergraduate fraternity initiation. He sat alone for twenty minutes or so, as others trickled in, and then pairs and groups began filling the room, until one of the few empty seats was one next to him. Right before the meeting started, this girl, Lucy, walked in, and from across the room looked him directly in the eye, and moved toward him without taking her eyes away. She then sat next to him, and continued looking at him as the meeting started, and for the first few minutes of the meeting, until he couldn't take it anymore, and got up to go to the restroom, and left. At least, that was his recollection as he said, "Yes, let's watch it."

Michael made a couple of swiping gestures on the monitor, and the images came to life. Michael was apparently comfortable observing multiple adjacent views of the same scene unfolding simultaneously from different persepctives, but Josh and Callie were not. Callie decided to try looking at just one display at a time, but as soon as she focused on it, her peripheral vision drew her away to another. Josh just looked at Lucy at first, who was in the top right of the four stacked boxes, but soon she appeared in all four, as did he and Callie, and he became overwhelmed.

"Okay, stop," Josh blurted out in frustration. "Can you just show us one at a time? And tell us what we're looking for?"

"Right, let's try something else" Michael responded. "Give me just a second." He fast-forwarded to a specific moment, pressed play, and then pause, while leaving all four images up. "Tell me what you see."

Josh and Callie both looked at each of the still images in turn, Josh moving more rapidly from each to the next and then back again, but it was Callie who spoke first. "It's Josh who's staring at her. Lucy's looking in his direction, but she's not looking at him, really. She's looking, what, around him?"

"Exactly," Michael answered, smiling. "That's the conclusion we've all come to. Them, us, everyone who's watched it. Now I want you to watch the thermal imaging from the satellite. This is from the time Josh sits down until the time he leaves. Its twenty-two minutes, but I'm going to show it to you at 4 times the speed. Josh, you're labeled SC8742, Callie, you're labeled SC8743. Lucy is SC8997. The SC is for suspected carrier, the number identifies you in their census of carriers."

"Can I just say how gross that sounds?" Callie suggested as Michael began typing and swiping at the monitor.

"And fucked up. Just very, very, fucked up," Josh added.

"It's their system, not ours. I'm just letting you know who you're looking at."

This time there were three video images, lined in a row, each labeled with the SC number, and the date and time, in the bottom left corner. In the bottom right of each image were two vertically-stacked strings of numbers. Josh's numbers were constant, while Callie and Lucy's were changing rapidly. "The numbers in the bottom right are your longitude and latitude positions," Michael provided without prompting.

"What's going on here?" Callie asked, trying unsuccessfully to make sense of the moving images, which were just radiant patches of shifting rainbow light on the screen.

"You and Lucy are speeding through midtown Atlanta, trying to make it to a 6:30 meeting. You were on a conference call with clients that ran late. Josh is just sitting waiting for the meeting to start. Just watch."

"Do we each have our own satellite? How does this work?" Callie asked, watching as the Lucy and Callie patches of red sped through a psychedelic landscape, and Josh just sat with other red patches slowly moving into the rectangle of black he was sitting in. Just barely visible, though plainly there, were faint white wisps that looked like smoke gathering around him.

"What are those things moving around me?" Josh asked, fearing he knew the answer.

"Those are the Mollies, Josh. And, no Callie, you don't each have your own satellite. It isn't necessary. All of these images are gathered from the same thermal imaging satellite. Think of how your local weather channel shows just the satellite imagery for your town—your town doesn't have its own satellite, or camera. Your weatherman focuses in on what he wants to see clearly, but that's done at the television station level, not at the satellite level—the satellite is constant. Right now you and Lucy have the same image onscreen because you're in the same place—that's what the technician chose for us to see."

"Why don't they have any Mollies?" Josh asked, with some annoyance, though he didn't understand what he was talking about, or know if he believed it.

"They're in a moving car. The Mollies, as I mentioned before, have certain limitations, which I suspect are human in nature. They can't move faster than a human can move on its own, they cannot go underwater deeper than a human can safely go, they cannot fly. I say they can't, what I should say is we have not observed them doing those things. Callie hasn't had interaction with Mollies in nearly 18 years, but they've never entirely left her. They will appear as soon as the car has stopped moving, usually within six minutes. They've been with Lucy her whole life. It's coming up now."

Sure enough, the Callie and Mollie patches of color came to a halt, and the latitude and longitude numbers abruptly stopped changing.

Both patches of color moved towards a building, which Michael confirmed for them was the Galano building, and the Callie patch of color stopped to interact with other patches outside the building. Lucy kept moving, and here their video images diverged from the same image for the first time. Within a minute of leaving the car, the same wispy images of white light visible near Josh began appearing around Callie as she stood outside, and Lucy, as she walked quickly to a bathroom.

"This is obsene," Callie voiced, her voice more disdainful than angry, as Lucy quite clearly sat down on the toilet. "Even in this thermal imaging whatever, this is just inappropriate."

"It's all inappropriate," Josh corrected her. "It's immoral. It's unethical. It's almost certainly illegal." No one immediately responded to him.

"But also," Callie added with some apprehension at her own words, "a little amazing, to see this, now. One of the reasons I was speeding was because Lucy desperately had to use the bathroom. I remember now. I ran a couple of red lights. She has an incredibly small bladder."

While the video showed Lucy on the toilet, Josh kept his attention on his own image, and the people walking in and sitting around him. Michael, realizing this, said as he reduced the playback speed to real time, "Okay, here's Lucy walking into the meeting room." Josh again looked at the other images.

When they first started watching the thermal imaging videos, it had been easy for Callie and Josh to identify themselves—not only were they numbered, they were at the center of the screen, and there were only three total people in the three monitors. Now though, the crowding in of others, whose thermal images were more or less identical to theirs, made it more difficult, even with the identifying SC numbers. They could also now see other identifiers, less bold, on other people in the clubhouse. "Who are the POIs?" Callie asked.

"Persons of Interest. Mama Ben, Sam, anyone you all have any sort of real relationship with," Michael answered with a tone that suggested the information was unimportant. "Keep watching."

It wasn't possible from the overhead position of the thermal camera to determine exactly when Lucy first saw Josh, but when she started walking his way, the scene changed. The wispy patches of white light became more luminous, and more numerous around both Josh and Lucy. The brightness of the white kept growing until the red glowing shapes of the people in the room were almost entirely obscured, and all of the black background of the images was gone. Then, when Josh got up and walked out of the meeting room, the intensity of the white immediately dimmed, and over the course of the next few minutes, the three images eventually returned to something close to what Michael then described to them as the "more-or-less natural, or at least typical, state of the Mollies. Josh, as soon as you got in your car and started moving, the Mollies were gone again. You drove around Atlanta for almost two hours that night. Later you told Mama Ben that you were driving to clear your head. Had you ever made a connection before between being in a moving car and being able to tune out the voices? We know you speed a lot, but we are curious to know about any conscious connection."

"Yes," Josh answered immediately, and then, "No. I don't know. It's something my father always used to do when he and my mother would have disagreements. I thought it was just something people did to calm down. My father didn't have these Mollie things did he?"

"You're right," Michael answered, "Driving is its own sort of self-soothing for many people, and no, your father has nothing to do with any of this. He is not a carrier. But we've been wondering for some time if you ever made the connection between driving and the voices going away?"

Josh considered before answering. "It wasn't driving that did it, it's like you said before, it was moving fast. If I was in a bad spot and got stuck in Atlanta traffic, the voices came back. I knew that, yes, I guess. But not until I was in my twenties."

The video onscreen followed him to the bathroom, where he paused to wash his face, and go outside. The Mollies lingered near him as his car slowly navigated the cars parked on both sides of the narrow Dutch Valley Road, but once he was speeding down Monroe Drive, they disappeared into the black nothingness of the thermal display, and the three of them watched for a minute as Josh turned onto Piedmont Avenue, Lucy sat turning her head around to see if he would return, and Callie just sitting still, oblivious to it all.

322

"So what just happened?" Callie asked.

"We don't know. No one knows. But it kept happening. Anytime Josh and Lucy were in a room together, the thermal imaging and the video surveillance recorded a rise and drop in the presence of this light that coincided directly with the time the two of them were together. It's important because all other known living carriers appear to be able to interact, even with Mollies present, without there being any change in the quantity of energy present. Adding chemical stimulants to either or both carriers appears to change that, but carriers experience such a bad high, that they avoid getting high with each other."

"What do you mean by living carriers?" Josh asked, taking his eyes away from the image of him moving along in his car on the Atlanta bypass.

"There was a set of twins who fought in Vietnam, both carriers, who had a similar effect on one another, but one of the two shot himself before any data could be gathered. We think the effect was only between the two of them. At least, the other brother never showed any signs of accelerated activity with other carriers before he died. That was in the early eighties."

"Did they kill him?" Callie asked.

"Wh-Who?" Michael stuttered, and then "What? You mean Defense? Did they kill the twin?"

"Yes. Based on everything else they've done, there must be a body count. Somewhere. We're all expendable, right?"

"No, not if they want to study and understand the Mollies and our relationship to them, we're not. And no, there is no direct association of any carrier deaths with any work done by Defense."

"No carrier deaths? Who did die?"

"No one died, not that we know of, not for sure," Michael responded hesitantly, not liking the turn of the conversation. "But there were two investigators who became problematic. One from Bethesda, Maryland quit his job and moved to Los Angeles in an attempt to meet Callie, in the eighties, and another took archived digital video of you," he said to Josh, "and uploaded it online. He had passed all the clearance tests, but he still somehow became addicted to child pornography after sifting through hours and hours of watching you as a teenager. They only found out when they found video of you online through facial recognition technology. They thought they were finding new video, but it was their own. Anyway, both of them disappeared. Literally. That's one of the gaps in the surveillance I was talking about—all we know for sure is that both of these men were being discussed as problems, and then, suddenly, they were never discussed again, and neither of them exist anymore."

"There's pornography of me on the web? As a child?" Josh asked, half indignant, half incredulous, entirely unconcerned about the men who had disappeared.

"Not anymore. They were able to find it quickly enough that they were able to remove it from the internet. Any home or office in the United States that was a download or upload site was raided, some covertly, some that made it into newspapers, and all remaining video was destroyed. For international downloads they just sent a computer virus out to destroy the host computer and network it was on, if any. You haven't resurfaced. But they keep monitoring—you were an, um, a very popular download."

Callie thought briefly about suggesting there were worse things in the world, but decided not to venture down that road unnecessarily. Michael looked at her for a moment, saying nothing, with an unspoken suggestion that she might want to say something comforting to Josh, but she didn't. She wanted to hear more about the plan.

"So this Plum Island. What is it? I've never heard of it," she said. The uncomfortable silence was made more awkward by the abrupt reversal of topic, but Michael went with it.

"It's a federal research facility. Part of the Department of Homeland Security Science and Technology division. It's been around since World War II under various names. Its primary, public purpose is to protect American livestock from disease. But it's been used for all kinds of things, including developing biochemical weapons, temporarily housing prisoners, stashing weapons, hiding people. Lucy is far from the first person to be held there."

"So this is a military base? We're breaking into a military base? I'm breaking onto a military base? And releasing a prisoner?"

"No. You're saving Lucy. The rest is all true enough. Technically, though, she's not a prisoner. Technically, she's not even there. There is not a single piece of paper, or email, or any piece of evidence anywhere, that could confirm she is a prisoner there. But she is."

"How many guards are there?" Josh asked instinctively, sounding too much, he realized immediately and with some embarrassment, like the gun-toting hero of a loud summer blockbuster movie.

The other two both turned to look at him. "You're not going, Josh." Michael's voice was firm, but kind.

"That's why I'm here. To rescue my daughter."

"And you will. We all will. It will take all of us. The island is just the beginning. Within six minutes of getting out of the delivery van, the defense satellite will pick up Callie. We have just enough time for her to get in, get Lucy, and get out. Lucy trusts, knows, and loves Callie. She cries out for her. I personally think she's somehow waiting for you, Callie. Josh, she does not know you. You're her father, yes, but she does not know that, and in the time it would take you to explain it, the Mollies and the small arsenal on the island would be surrounding you. And, you saw the effect your presence has on her. It happened every time you were in the same room together, including one time when neither of you ever became aware of the other's presence. She is incredibly high right now. We don't know what might happen if you go in there. So you can't. It has to be Callie. And she has to be alone. It's that simple."

Josh bared his teeth and made an angry, resentful noise, but sat back on the sofa nonetheless.

"It's going to be important for us to get some sleep tonight," Michael suggested after a moment's silence. "Tomorrow is likely to be a long day, even if everything goes perfectly."

"Wait," Callie blurted out, caught off guard by his abrupt suggestion and not the least bit likely to fall asleep any time soon. "Why now? We've all been under all this surveillance all this time. So, why her? Why us? Why now?"

Michael hesitated. They did need their sleep—it had been a long and emotional day for all of them, including his own breakfast meeting with Sam, which had taken over four hours. It had been a risk to involve Sam, but in the end it paid off. Michael knew that Callie and Josh would never see, that he himself had never seen, all the pieces to the puzzle, and his intention had been to show just enough of the pieces that they would have a sense of the overall shape of it, put just enough pieces into place to show them where they fit in it. He had received an incalculable number of suggestions, and comments on those suggestions, on the community's electronic bulletin board messaging system, but none of them accurately addressed the scenario before him, which really was unprecedented. Behavioral specialists, physicists, computer networking engineers, and all manner of other people eagerly participated in the discussion about how best to tell Josh and Callie about their lives—some members of the community had been involved in Project Anna, as it was officially known, since or near its beginning in the 1950s. It was important to get it right for the two of them, and the timing had caught the community off guard. They always knew they would have to act quickly when the time came, and it had finally arrived. Michael's introduction to the community, to the trolley, had been entirely different. He himself had suspected he was somehow unique, or different, for most of his life—when he received the piece of paper from Trevor at the conference, it had come as a surprise, but only in its form, and where it led to. He had more or less been waiting since eighth grade for the mystery of his life to be revealed to him at some point. Reason had led him to rationally deduce, and instinct to reinforce the belief, that there was more to his life than he was being shown. Callie and Josh, who had no Eleanor to guide and protect them, had experienced a fractured reality they worked hard to repair, and were not likely to be prepared to let their carefully reconstructed lives shatter before them. How to explain had been a nagging question for months and years, but intensified in the past few weeks. In the end, it was a retired NASA communications specialist who provided the advice Michael followed. *Trust yourself,* he had written. *Your instincts have always been right. Callie and Josh will trust you. They will believe. They will do the right thing.* Michael decided to answer Callie's questions in the most direct way possible—to show her the evidence, which he knew she would ask to see, anyway.

"I'll show you." Michael stood and started typing and swiping on the monitor again, and this time two maps, of the eastern and western hemispheres, filled the screen. Like the thermal images, the background was black, and the contour lines establishing the state boundaries were light grey. "This is a time-lapse model of the identified Mollies worldwide from 1958 until day before yesterday. It will take about 10 minutes. Just watch."

Almost instantly, hundreds of white lights the size of pin heads spread over the maps in irregular patterns, their locations appearing to Callie to be more or less a population density map—anywhere a population cluster occurred, such as New York or London or Hong Kong, an apparently corresponding cluster of white lights shown. There were other smaller isolated clusters, and individual white lights spread throughout the map. In the bottom right corner of the screen, a digital readout showing the date and a series of numbers appeared—April 17th, 1958, 13:20:18. "It's military time. One-twenty. East coast U.S. time."

The time display started moving rapidly, and with it lights began to appear and disappear with startling speed. The points of lights around the cities made them seem to throb. There would occasionally be a bright flash of lights in one corner or another of the globe, but by the time they looked at it, it was gone. The general effect was disorienting.

After just two minutes, Callie finally spoke up. "I don't get it. I have no idea what I'm looking at."

Michael wondered if he hadn't explained properly. "These are the Mollies."

"I understand that. I'm talking about the maps. I know nothing about geography. I barely know where most of the states are. I can pick out Italy's boot, and England, but I couldn't find Japan or Iraq or Ethiopia if my life depended on it. If I'm supposed to be making a connection between time and geography and the appearance of these Mollies, it's just not going to happen."

"Seriously, I had geography in sixth grade, but I didn't care even then." Josh added, grateful Callie had spoken up first. "Why don't you just explain to us what we're supposed to be looking for?"

Michael thought for a moment as time sped by on the screen, then stood and zoomed the map in on just the United States. He touched another couple of buttons and the outlines of the states appeared, very dimly, providing the context the others seemed to need.

"Let's try this. Just watch. I will explain."

Lights continued to flicker on an off, but this time the information was more meaningful. Florida, California, Texas—these were things that could be understood. Still, trying to look at the time, the lights, and the map was an effort. At around the nine minute mark, Callie's head tilted to the right—her customary physical response to uncertainty. Around the same time, Josh scrunched up his nose. Neither was aware of making a gesture, or why. As the time counter moved closer to the current day, flashes of lights intermittently lit up the screen, moving in what appeared to be a counter-clockwise circular motion, like a hurricane without a fixed center, covering the entire expanse of the United States. There was some movement just above the Canadian border, and just below the Mexican border, but those movements appeared to be aberrations. Then the movement and the timer ended, at 9:02:32am on the previous day. The lights that were left on appeared to be in no discernible pattern, but looked much like the lights at the beginning of the scene in 1958, where most of the lights were just clustered around major cities.

"So what did you see?"

"Why don't you just tell us what we are supposed to see?" Josh asked, with annoyance creeping back into his voice.

"Well, because I'm genuinely interested in what you think," Michael responded. "There is no right answer. No one knows. I mean, we can all agree on certain apparent patterns and movements, but beyond that, your guess is as good as the physicists, geologists and atmospheric chemists who've been studying this for years."

"Do you really think that's true, Michael?" Trevor's voice issued from the ceiling, causing Callie and Josh to jump, but Michael to smile when he answered that yes, he did think so. He added that if he did not value their opinions, he would not have asked them. Callie asked again about the ice pack, but Trevor said Josh's hand appeared to be fine, which Josh confirmed, before asking "Are you watching us? Are we being taped, even now?"

"Of course I'm watching you. Of course you're being taped. We're all being taped. This is important stuff. We need you to be safe, but we also need to understand what this is. You aren't being rescued from science, you're being rescued by science, for science."

Michael jumped in, "Well, that's one opinion. Trevor, do you mind if we go on?"

"Certainly not," came the answer from the ceiling. "As you were."

A sort of collective heave of the shoulders, a regrouping of the three back into three, happened before Callie asked, "Can we go back just a minute, a minute and a half maybe, and look more slowly?"

"How far back?"

"December 2000 maybe? I don't know why. It just felt like something happened."

Michael made the necessary motions to replay the film, this time slower, and they sat for a few minutes as they watched the patterns unfolding on the screen as December 2000 played, then January 2001 and on through the year. When they reached October, it was Josh who blurted out "Stop. Wait. Go back. What just happened?"

But he knew, and Callie knew. September 11, 2001 had just happened.

"Can you start in August and slow it down some more?" Callie asked.

"Sure," Michael replied, his voice expressive of nothing in particular, though there was a sheen of excitement layered onto his implied indifference.

This time, they both saw it, with certainty. It was Josh who spoke first. "The Mollies were gathering before September 11th. Did they know? Was it them?"

Remembering the swirling pattern of light from the months leading up to the day before yesterday, Callie added, "Are they back? Are they the same thing as the things that follow us, or whatever they do?"

"They appear to be back in mass, yes. I was first brought into the community when it became apparent that there was something big happening. As you saw, there appears to be something like a storm of them gathering, but with something like a geopolitical border, which, well, defies scientific explanation. As to whether or not they're the same thing, yes, they are the same energy—light is always light. But light is light in the same way that carbon dioxide is always carbon dioxide— there is the carbon dioxide we animals breathe out, and there is the carbon dioxide generated when fossil fuels burn, or volcanoes erupt. It all looks the same under the microscope, but it has different sources. It's the same product, if you will, but the result of a different process."

"And we don't know," Trevor added, "that the Mollies are the product, or if they are part of a process, or if they just are." Trevor's disembodied voice was no longer jarring to Callie and Josh, but neither especially liked it. "September 11th is the most dramatic and obvious example of the Mollies appearing in a way that suggests a relationship, but there are literally hundreds of other examples we could show you. Oklahoma City, Columbine, every major, most minor, and some seemingly tiny events where Mollies were present before and or after an episode, and then disappeared."

"They are all," Michael added, "events that were man-made, or at least initiated by humans. Natural events, for the most part, don't seem to draw Mollies. The 2004 tsunami in the Indian Ocean, the earthquakes in Haiti, blizzards, avalanches, flooding, these sorts of things have no apparent association with the Mollies."

"But what about the storm in Dublin? Are you saying that wasn't natural?" Josh asked.

"The storm was natural. Unusual, by all accounts, perhaps unique, and still unexplained, but apparently natural. The flooding wasn't, though, at least not entirely. That was manmade. The opening of the floodgates at Lake Sinclair, the construction of the floodgates in the first place, that was all manmade," Michael responded. Here, Trevor felt obligated to add a corollary to what he privately considered Michael's nonsense.

"This whole business of manmade versus natural may be completely irrelevant. Statistically, we do not know it is meaningful at all. Science is very bad at determining cause and effect relationships. Including that information in this discussion is like including the brand of footwear of children injured in bicycle accidents. If all of the children are wearing Nike tennis shoes, that doesn't make the shoes the cause of a head injury. We have to be very careful when we are looking at this data. Michael assigns meaning to things based on his personal beliefs, which I don't find very useful. You may do with it what you will, but keep in mind, as I've heard countless times listening to your recovery conversations, feelings aren't facts."

"And many times," Michael added, "Facts aren't facts, either. The world was once flat—it was a known, scientific fact. Rats caused disease. It was a known, scientific fact. As children we were taught the facts about plate tectonics as though the facts of the Earth's crust were well-established, but in reality what we understand about the basic mechanics of the planet we live on changes almost daily. The list of so-called scientific facts that have been disproved is far longer than the list of things that we know, absolutely, beyond any doubt to be to true, because the second list is just a waiting list for the first list. We know nothing—we have just disproven the last thing we believed to be true, and believe something else. In reality, we think things, we feel things, we believe things. Nothing more."

Callie had stopped listening to the men's conversation minutes before. She still heard them, but once she realized nothing they were saying was going to help her get Lucy off the island, or understand why she needed to, she tuned them out, choosing instead to stare off into the map still illuminated in front of her, and consider what lay ahead of her. It was at this point in their conversation that she finished gathering her thoughts, and joined back in with them, saying "I'm going to need something else to wear."

"What?" Josh asked. Michael looked at her, slightly taken aback. Trevor remained silent.

"Tomorrow. I can't wear this to the island. You all must have something else planned for me. What is it? Where is the map of this island? How do I access the place where Lucy is being kept? How do I find her in it? Will there be anyone in the room with her? Will I have to shoot and kill that person, or those people?" She was looking at Michael as she spoke. She felt he must know that she had purchased a handgun and taken two years of shooting lessons after a relapsed addict followed her after a meeting and tried to get into her home. She was an excellent shot, and she suspected everyone in the community knew it. "Well?"

The men realized at once that she had cut out, and cut through their abstractions with surgical authority and precision. The only one really surprised by her interruption was Josh, who understood her least well of the three men. He liked her—he had always liked her. Mama Ben had warned him against liking her too much, even though, as Mama Ben had always said, "What's not to love about Callie? She's a perfectly lovely creature. Middle age becomes her." And it was true. Perhaps because she had never had a proper childhood, or perhaps just because she seemed so content, there was a youthful presence to her middle age that made her glow, but it was anchored in the authority of understanding gained through experience. She smiled freely because she understood the value of a smile, and she thought critically because she had learned how costly not thinking can be. Throughout the course of the evening, Josh had increasingly looked to Callie for assurance and guidance—he did not know her well, but she became his anchor in this increasingly foreign place. He knew that she was as surprised by the revelations of the evening as he was, and yet she remained determinedly focused on the task at hand. And as he looked to her, he began to see her, really, for the first time. Before this, he had experienced her mostly from afar, and in settings where she might be expected to be comfortable and secure—surrounded by friends and admirers in places she had spent years. But he now saw her in a place where she should be as scared and discomfited as he was, and she was not. He had seen her falter, or thought he had, as she parted ways with Sam, but that only secured him in his belief that beneath her rational exterior there was a real, caring, compassionate woman—one who was now asking, not exactly with detachment, but with something like emotional rigor, whether or not she would need to kill another person, or people, the next day. He sat back in his seat, not knowing if it was admiration, or fear, or love he was beginning to feel for her.

Michael likewise was at an immediate loss for words, but Trevor was relieved by the pragmatic turn of the conversation and soon filled the pregnant pause that seemed to be filling the cabin. "Yes, Callie, we have clothes for you. It is a uniform for the delivery service. This is the woman you will be filling in for on the truck." The map of the United States disappeared and was replaced moments later with several images of a woman who looked not unlike Callie, but not very like, either. "We know you don't look very much alike, but no one will be looking very closely. The service has been making deliveries like clockwork for the past fifteen years. The truck will be waved through. Here's the island." An aerial photograph of the island appeared. "This is the truck you will be going in on. This is where it will be parked to unload goods into this building." As he spoke, crudely drawn circles appeared on the screen around what he was describing. "You will walk to the front door of this building. It is the old guard's cottage. It has pretty basic card-swipe hardware on the door. We will let you in remotely." A series of arrows appeared showing how Callie would get to the door, then the aerial view of the building disappeared and was replaced with a floor plan of the two-bedroom cottage, complete with furnishings, accessories, and even what appeared to be bars of soap in the bathroom soap holders. Trevor continued, "Once inside, you go through the old living room, down this short hall, and into the bedroom on the right. The other bedroom, on the left, is where the treatment team monitors her. There will be one doctor and one nurse there. You will use this tranquilizer gun to stun and sedate them. The grip and weight are almost identical to your own Walther PPK handgun, and you will aim for their upper thighs. All of the electronic alarms will be disabled—you just have to immobilize those two. You will also have a PPK identical to your own, including your scope. We don't think you will need it, but if it comes to you being taken into custody, or taking out a couple of their guards, your safety, and Lucy's, is our priority. We'll have four snipers in place on and around the island—you only have to be concerned with the interior. And really, not even that. The bullets are for just-in-case. You will have a minute, maybe two, to get Lucy out of there. She is experiencing constant and intense auditory and visual hallucinations, in addition to the Mollies. She may not even accept that you're real, or that you're you, or she may change her mind. You will need to remove her IV, and she will almost certainly be very sore. She will be in pain, but you will need to get her moving quickly without agitating her. You will walk back out the same door with her to the delivery truck, get in, secure yourselves in the freezer, and I will drive the truck out."

Everyone was quiet for a moment. "Six minutes? Really? You think I can do this in six minutes?" She wasn't questioning whether or not she could, or would do it—only the timing.

"Five would be better," Trevor replied, but she ignored him.

"With that much detail in the drawings, you must have video of the interior. Can I see it?" Callie asked.

This time, Michael answered, attempting to sound casual. "We don't think it would be that useful."

Callie was not fooled, nor Josh. "Is her condition that bad?" Callie asked.

"Yes," Michael answered simply. "It is."

Trevor added "Everyone who has seen that tape, including myself, agrees that she must be retrieved. And she will be. That's what we're doing. "

"If you think it's worse than what I'm imagining, you're wrong," Josh said softly.

"This situation is emotional enough for both of you. For all of us. Let's just let it be for now. You will see her tomorrow. You will help nurse her back to strength. You will help her detox. You will be her father. Tonight, you need to rest to be prepared for her. She will take all of your strength. I promise." Michael's voice had the desired calming effect. Josh shrugged his shoulders in resignation, but his face expressed his displeasure.

They sat in silence for several minutes before Callie asked "Can we turn the exterior cameras back on? I'm getting carsick, or something." Within moments the panels surrounding the cabin were filled with the cars passing by on I-95. Michael repositioned the one panel he had lowered earlier, and the sky snapped into place around the cabin. They soon saw an illuminated billboard with a giant sculpture of a sausage attached to it, and a cartoon man in a sombrero saying *You never sausage a place! South of the Border – 10 Miles.*

"Why? Why do all of you people, the community, care? Do you care? What can my daughter mean to you? What can I mean to you? Or Callie? Or any of us?" Josh's voice was level, but it was clear that he did not believe the community cared.

"We are responsible for the military having the abilities they do. This isn't a guns-don't-kill-people-people-kill-people conversation, though some even in the community attempt to frame it that way. We, science, technology, have given the military abilities humans aren't supposed to have. And it should come as no surprise to us, though it usually does, or we say it does, when they use those abilities inhumanly. Did you know there is enough radioactive material in the Y-12 storage facility at Oak Ridge to create over 10,000 nuclear bombs? We have the power to decimate life on this planet over and over and over again, from one storage facility. That's not science. That's not defense. That's just stupid. It's un-science. It's indefensible. And *we* did it. Science. And we gave them the tools to destroy that young girl. Or any young girl, or boy, or man or woman, anyone. With no accountability. None. And, now they're trying to use Lucy to gain even more power that we quite frankly don't understand, and we decided, well, enough. We can't save everyone, we can't save everything, but we can save Lucy. And, she may be the answer. The patterns you saw on the monitor earlier are making the military desperate. Movements of light they cannot see or understand have led them to torture with impunity. The government has made us many of us very rich, and now we can use our wealth in a way that is actually useful."

It seemed to Callie and Josh that Trevor might go on talking, but Michael knew his speech patterns better—Trevor never modulated the tone or inflection of his voice to provide conversational clues—he just kept talking until he was done, and then he stopped. He did not pause to think, he just spoke until he was through. But Michael picked up where Trevor left off, adding, "And before it's over, some of us will probably lose our lives as well—not the two of you, but us, the community. We will have ten minutes, tops, once we get Lucy out, before the powder keg will blow. It's likely that despite our best efforts, they will uncover the community. Those of us who are more deeply connected, especially those on site, and have risk of being captured, have kill pills— cyanide capsules at the ready to prevent us from having your whereabouts tortured from us. They will never find us all—*we* couldn't find us all. "

Callie looked away from the billboard facing them, the same cartoon man from before now saying, *The Sky's The Limit, South of the Border, 2 Miles.* Her face was alive with rage. "You gave one to Sam, didn't you, one of these kill pills?" she asked, but it wasn't really a question. Michael opened his mouth to answer, but before he could speak, Callie spoke again, saying "Don't say another word. I don't want to hear any more about your plans right now. I don't want to know anything else about the community. I want to read my file. And Lucy's." She waited for half a heartbeat, and when there was no immediate response, she added with hostility, and finality, "NOW. There must be a way to stop this thing and get off. I swear to God I will find it. I may not be able to drive this thing, but I can stop it. I know I can."

It was Trevor who responded as Michael sat gulping air. "Callie, the wall in your bunk is a monitor. So is the ceiling. You can sit, or lay down, and read. Or you can have the files read to you. The woman's voice who reads is bad, but not as bad as Siri. Just lower the tambour door to the sleeping compartment, and the voice activation will come on. If you would rather sleep, your music and books are downloaded into the system. You can just say 'Play Alanis Morissette,' for instance, and it will play that record for you."

"Thanks. I think I might just do that." She didn't bother asking how they knew one of her few secret guilty pleasures was singing *Jagged Little Pill* all the way through at the top of her lungs, alone, in her car, with the volume set to maximum, on the rare occasion she felt anger or resentment—it was a release for her. She had never discussed it with anyone, even Mama Ben—it was juvenile, and absurd, but it worked for her much more quickly than prayer and meditation. As she was standing up she became vaguely aware of the truck beginning to slow. She looked at the exterior view and saw the landscape on the right being illuminated in bright bursts of yellow—the turn signal. She paused, standing, looking out at the giant water tower shaped like a sombrero, and the haphazardly arranged assortment of brightly-colored buildings muddied by the cheap lighting in the desolate expanse of asphalt parking lots. "You're no different than them. You may think you are, but you're not. You're deciding who lives and who dies, for your own purposes, using your knowledge and your machinery to achieve your goals."

"You're wrong, Callie. Sam has a choice. You have a choice. Lucy has no choice." Michael's voice was firm but with just a touch of pleading.

"Sam always chooses to do the right thing. You filled his head with this rubbish, and then gave him a pill so he could sit alone in a laboratory and wait to die? Alone? For me? For me. Without giving me any voice, any choice, any say so at all? That's no choice at all. That's just bullshit."

"It was the right thing to do," Michael began as the truck pulled off the service road and moved slowly towards the automotive repair warehouse.

"I don't know what the right thing to do was, or is," Callie said, with her teeth clenched, as she walked towards the door to the sleeping compartment and put her hand on the wall, "but I know I'm not going to let you decide for me. Not them, and not you. Not anymore."

The door slid shut behind her. Trevor's voice came over the intercom system again, saying with complete detachment, "Overall, I think everything has gone better than anticipated. But there's some movement in Dublin you might want to look in on, Michael."

The exterior view of the truck had changed to the interior view of the massive mechanic's shop, filled with dozens of repair bays, and several cars on lifts hovering near the dark ceiling. In the distance, three men could be seen through a window in a small office set into the space. They were passing what appeared to be a glass pipe and butane lighter between them.

"Is that our driver? Is he smoking crack?" Josh asked, incredulous.

Michael stood and moved his hands across the screen to zoom in on the image of the three men, one of whom was exhaling a dense cloud of opaque smoke so white it was almost blue. With his hands shaking, the driver handed the implements to another of the men, and sat back on a desktop covered with invoices and magazines, and closed his eyes, his limbs twitching.

"Meth," Michael replied, resignedly, looking down at his watch. "But he's not our driver anymore. Our next driver will be showing up in one hour and 54 minutes." He saw the expression on Josh's face change from shock to fear, and added, "Everyone has their demons. We're all imperfect. The plan, it may be imperfect, too. But, it will work. Why don't we see what's happening in Dublin?"

With that, he turned off the view of the mechanic shop, and began typing again on the black screen.

CHAPTER 5. RUMMY

"Evening Ms. Ida Mae, Ms. Eleanor, ma'am," the Laurens County sheriff said in what he hoped was a confident tone, but it was not. Tired, annoyed, and confused, yes, but certainly not confident.

He had received a call two hours earlier that a Georgia Bureau of Investigation officer would be arriving by helicopter with a federal agent to interview Ida Mae Edmonds about the location of Michael Isaacs. He did not ask what kind of federal agent—he had been through the files of the events surrounding the Great Storm of 1974 just like every sheriff between then and him had done, and he knew the whole business was shadier than a pecan grove in springtime. When the woman known in Dublin as Eleanor Allen had shown up three years earlier, with no apparent knowledge of where the man was that she had taken away as a boy just after the storm, he suspected that sooner or later some shit would hit the fan. And this appeared to be the moment—Ms. Eleanor was not supposed to be at the Irish Acres Retirement Center. She was supposed to be at home, in bed, like all old people. But somehow, here she was, playing cards with Ms. Ida Mae, and some other woman he did not know. And Ms. Ida Mae was supposed to be in her room, alone, asleep, and not sitting in the common room where another group of patients and nurses were half-dozing, half-watching the second half of the *Tonight Show* from a sprawling sectional sofa and Queen Anne style wing-back chairs pulled over from a seating area on the other side of the room. Three of the old people were in wheelchairs. The room was relatively dark, but there was a brass chandelier illuminating the antique oak table where the three women sat playing cards, seated on contemporary, upholstered side chairs. An upright piano sat in a dark corner, but its bench was missing. Overall the place gave the appearance of a well-tended country club, except for the smell, which was consistent with that unique combination of ammonia, medication, mush, and powder smells that is characteristic of all nursing homes, regardless of how many brass chandeliers there may be.

He had seen the three women from the outside window of the main entrance as they walked up the sidewalk to the front door, which opened onto the common room, and suggested they return in the morning, but the G.B.I. man said no, it had to be now. The federal agent had yet to say a word since he got off the helicopter, which was more than a little unnerving. So they just walked through the double doors, into the common room, and started talking to the women as though every-thing happening was just nothing at all. But the tension the men carried with them suggested that no, it was something. The women, by their own lack of reaction to being approached by the men, suggested that they knew it was something, too.

"It's mighty late to be playing cards, ain't it, ladies?" the sheriff asked. It was past midnight, and not that long past his bedtime, but each minute of the night since he got the first call suggested it would be hours before he was back home in bed.

"Not for us. We play right reg'lar. Time don't mean so much when you get to be as old as us here," Ida Mae answered.

"Speak for yourself, Ms. Ida Mae," laughed the unknown woman sitting at the table with the two older women. She was a sleek, carefully sculpted and manicured black woman in her mid-sixties with close-cropped, graying hair, perfect teeth, and jewelry and clothing of a superior quality that suggested to the sheriff she must not be from Dublin. Her appearance had at first confused him, but now he was outright alarmed. She was laughing—a deep, throaty, confident, somehow masculine, laugh. Even though he considered himself a good, kind, and fair sheriff, generations of discrimination had taught the black people of Laurens County to show deference, humility, even submission, in the presence of a uniformed officer. This woman was having none of it. He could sense, somehow, that she was laughing not at what Ms. Ida Mae had said, but at him.

"I don't believe we've met," he said, taking off his western-style felt sheriff's hat, its wide brim always comforting to turn slowly around when he was nervous. "I'm Sheriff Jack Saunders."

"Nice to meet you, sheriff. What can we do for you? As you can see, we're in the middle of a game here. And I'm about to win." She had just drawn from the deck on the table, and discarded the card she drew—the three of diamonds.

His confidence would have been shaken more had he not been backed up by the two agents behind him. "Sorry to interrupt you all, but we need to have a few words with Ms. Ida Mae. Police business, you understand. If you could just come with us, Ms. Ida Mae? We'll have you back in just a few minutes."

Ida Mae didn't move, or even look his way. She drew from the deck, and kept the card she drew, discarding the seven of diamonds from her hand. Eleanor drew a card, and held it, considering. She looked up at the three men over the fan of her cards, but said nothing.

The youngest of the three women was the one to respond to the sheriff, saying "As a matter of fact, I do understand police business, as you say. Just what kind of police business could bring you out here to disturb a feeble old woman in the middle of the night?"

Eleanor smirked as Ida Mae looked askance at the younger woman.

"Well, now," the sheriff answered, "That's between us and Ms. Ida Mae." His voice suggested this ruse may not get him far, but that he was obliged to follow it through.

"Who is this *us* you're talking about?" She gave the two men standing behind the sheriff a frank appraisal before turning to look back at her cards. "Ms. Ida Mae isn't in the habit of going off with groups of strange men in the middle of the night. What kind of woman do you take her for?" She looked over her cards at the men, her eyebrows arched in a mocking gesture.

Eleanor felt an incredible urge to laugh, but the laughter only made it to her eyes. Still, the sheriff and the other men saw—they were being played. And they weren't the only ones who saw—the group watching the television had, at some point during the exchange, turned down the television volume and were now watching the scene with undisguised curiosity. One man, clad in his pajamas and wrapped in blankets, so old and hunched he appeared to have no neck at all, had turned around, and rolled his wheelchair a little closer to the unfolding scene.

"Ma'am, my name is Garret Stokes, I'm a commander with the Georgia Bureau of Investigation. We need to speak to Ms. Edmonds on a federal matter." Stokes was a rare presence in the G.B.I.—he was one of a handful of black men to rise in the ranks. He realized as soon as they approached the building and the sheriff pointed out the women at the table inside why he had been sent to Dublin—all white people seemed to think all black people have some mysterious way of getting each other to cooperate in situations where white people would have no success. He never understood it, but he had been dragged out on occasions like this for so many years, that it no longer came as any surprise.

"Nice to meet you, Commander Stokes. Two down, one to go. Who is your companion here?"

Eleanor finally discarded her ace of spades, and Ida Mae drew from the deck.

"I'm not at liberty to say, ma'am. This investigation has nothing to do with you, I'm sure. I understand you may be concerned, the circumstances are a little unusual, but Ms. Edmonds is in no danger, not in any trouble at all." Stokes spoke calmly, but like the sheriff, he was also a little nervous with the situation, and it showed. "We just need to ask her a few questions is all."

Ida Mae and Eleanor watched as their companion cocked her head first to the right, then back, and said with something close to a sneer, "You don't know, do you? You don't know who that man behind you is, do you? You haven't even asked to see his identification, have you? You didn't call Atlanta or D.C. to verify that he even exists, did you?" She laid down her cards as she spoke, and the other two women followed her lead, as she looked at the three men with frank contempt.

She cocked her head to the left. "You just brought some stranger, with a loaded weapon, probably more than one, into a nursing home, in the middle of the night, with no explanation. Are you crazy, negro?" It had been years since she called anyone other than her husband negro, and she wondered distantly if it was because she was back in Dublin, or because of the situation, that she said it now.

Her husband had been dead for six years, and had always feared for her travelling the back roads. *Baby love, I need your love, you come on back home safe*, he would always sing when she was leaving for the judicial circuit. She wished he was home waiting for her now.

"Ma'am, let's just dial this back a bit. Could you please identify yourself?" Stokes was going to try taking over as bad cop.

"Certainly, commander. I am the Honorable Charlene Eugenia Smith, Circuit Court Judge for the United States Court of Appeals for the 11th Circuit, and I have been since 1997. And I want to know why the hell the woman who raised me from a baby is having her civil rights violated left and right and up and down by you three, and on whose authority. But first, I want to know, and my security detail who is listening in on this conversation and have this building surrounded want to know, who the hell is that man right there?"

As she raised her hand and pointed her finger at the federal agent, who still had not spoken, several things happened, seemingly at once. The unnamed federal agent began backing towards the door the three men had just entered through, and reached for a gun in his shoulder holster. The four members of the security detail traveling with Judge Smith entered the room from each of the four available exit routes, including the door the agent was backing towards. As the nearest detail officer shoved his service revolver into the narrow of the federal agent's back, he turned to fire, but the hunched old man in the wheelchair raised his head slightly, pulled a Sig Sauer semiautomatic pistol from under his blanket, shot and killed the agent and the detail officer with two shots, both of which went through both men and shattered the glass door behind them, before turning the pistol to his own temple, blowing off the entire front of his head with results as horrific as they were unexpected.

The mayhem that followed was quite unlike anything the Irish Acres Retirement Center had ever seen or prepared for. It was a rural, relatively upscale retirement home, that frequently left the front door propped open, negating the desired effects of the security cameras and buzzer entry system installed there. The only crime they were accustomed to dealing with was the occasional pilfering of small amounts of cash and somewhat larger amounts of oxycodone and similar drugs from the patients. People died there all the time—death being the natural result of checking into a place like Irish Acres, which was designed with one wing for assisted living patients, and another wing for patients requiring medical supervision—it had double doors at the end of the hallway to let the morticians' gurneys pass through easily. But murder was another story.

The sheriff, like everyone else, was left temporarily deafened by the shots from the old man's pistol, which had no silencer. The gunshots and screaming woke up everyone in the home, and those who were able to leave their beds without assistance did so; those who were not able to leave their beds began frantically pressing the call button for a nurse to come explain what happened. All of the nurses, though, had been in the common room, and none were able to hear. They were, in any event, running and ducking for cover, unaware that the danger had passed with the deaths of the two men—the sheriff and GBI agent were as confused and scared as everyone else.

Judge Smith had anticipated that something might happen, but not this. She had sat face-to-face with more murderers than she could count, and had watched murders played out on video many times, but she had never witnessed one personally. She was, however, as prepared for it as anyone is ever likely to be. As a federal judge, she regularly received threats in the form of letters and anonymous emails, and the occasional posturing in her courtroom, but the reality of being a black federal judge in the deep South was never lost on her. Unlike some other judges, she never travelled without her security detail. After she was first confirmed as a judge, she spent a week with the Secret Service, receiving training in how to react to various situations that might arise, from bomb threats to actual bombs. At the first sight of a drawn weapon, she had reacted with more training than instinct, reached her arms out around the backs of the two older women, forcing them face down onto the table with her. They huddled there, trying to look at the scene behind them, until two of the remaining security detail pulled the judge up by the arms to lead her out of the scene. At the same time, she grabbed the arms of Ida Mae and Eleanor, showing every intention of bringing them along. When the sheriff and Commander Stokes made motions to intervene, they found themselves with weapons drawn on them by all three of the remaining security detail, one of whom spoke to the men in a loud, carrying voice, knowing their ears were likely still ringing. He mouthed his words slowly and carefully in case their hearing was gone altogether.

"Gentlemen, you brought an armed assassin into the presence of a federal judge. Until you're cleared, you're considered suspects. Drop your weapons, now."

The two men did not know what to do. Without lowering his revolver, the sheriff yelled back, "This is a crime scene. These women have to stay here." He pointed down to the floor for emphasis. In the background, nurses and patients were scurrying around in what appeared to be circles—everyone seemed to feel an urge to move, though suddenly no place seemed safe enough.

"This is the scene of your crime, sheriff. The F.B.I. is already on its way, as is half the county. The safety of Judge Smith is our priority. If she says these ladies go, they go. We're going. Agent Larkin will stay here to secure the scene." He nodded to the agent now checking perfunctorily for signs of life of the two men on the ground, though there had been little doubt about the results. There was blood and bits of bone and tissue on the walls, curtains, door, ceiling and floor.

The three women were now standing, and the man who was apparently the head of the security detail, his weapon still drawn, started walking, his hand wrapped firmly around the upper arm of the judge. "Move, move," he said, and they began walking out, the three women holding onto each other as they followed him, and the other security officer trailing behind them, walking sideways and looking backwards, his weapon drawn, his eyes quickly scanning the population of the retirement home and its attendants for signs of another assassin. He nodded a farewell to the remaining security officer, who was beginning to bark orders at the nurses and patients, as well as the sheriff and Commander Stokes, all of whom seemed relieved to have someone telling them what to do.

The sheriff looked with dismay as the women and security detail walked through his crime scene, leaving bloody footprints behind. Commander Stokes looked at the sheriff with a face that expressed the uncertainty the sheriff was feeling: *Did we follow protocol? Did we do the right things? Was the judge right? Is she a judge? What just happened here? And who are these dead men?*

CHAPTER 6. FRIEND OR FOE

"What just happened there? Did it just happen? Where is that?" Josh was the first to speak, with questions as rapid-fire as the seemingly-decrepit old man's bullets.

Michael looked at him with a mixture of surprise and something like sympathy as he answered "Yes, it just happened. You can see the timestamp on the screen. It's Irish Acres Retirement Center."

It was the place where Josh's own father had moved two years earlier, but which he had visited only twice. He knew from the look on Michael's face that he had been expected to remember the place, but he had not.

"Is my father alright?" Josh asked, swallowing his shame, as his face twisted up in sudden confusion, anger and fear.

"We'll find out soon enough," Michael answered, adding, "Right now you know as much as I do."

"Who were those women?" Josh asked, more looking for something to say than out of any real curiosity, and this time it was Trevor who answered, his disembodied voice now welcome to Josh, and providing the information that Eleanor was the woman who had adopted Michael, and that Ida Mae was a neighbor and family friend of Michael's family. "The other woman, we know nothing about. I don't, anyway. Do you, Michael?"

"Never even heard of her," he answered, as he began typing on the nearest display screen, still showing a Jeep elevated on a hydraulic lift in the garage. "At least, I don't remember her. I don't know." He was distracted by the carnage of the scene.

"Could she be part of the community?" Josh asked.

"Possible, but unlikely. There are some former Justice Department higher-ups in the community, but no sitting federal judges that I've ever known of. Or heard of."

A plain black screen replaced the scene in Dublin, then words, names and numbers began appearing, filling the center of the screen in an irregular shape that at first seemed almost organic to Josh, until he realized the words were not only moving, but also changing in size, color, and intensity. Before he could ask, Michael explained, "This is the visualization of the community's electronic bulletin board system. These are the topics being discussed for the past hour. The most recent entries are at the top. The most active entries at the moment are in red, the least active are violet, and everything else is in-between. The largest are the ones with the most entries in the past hour, the smallest have the least. But as you can see, at a busy time like now, pretty much everything is in a constant state of change."

It was true. Even as Michael spoke, new subjects were appearing at the top of the heap of words. "What do you call this thing?" Josh asked, trying not to interfere with what he assumed was important work. "A cloud, just like you'd see on any blog" was Trevor's response. He continued, "Josh, why don't you let me get you signed into the system, and you can see for yourself."

Trevor talked Josh through the same steps Callie had followed, and he soon found himself looking at an image of a file folder with his name on it. His picture, though, was from a few hours earlier, taken at the Starbucks. "Someone's been busy," he suggested wryly, but his tone was lost on the other two men, whose focus was suddenly not him, but the scene they had just witnessed.

"We have to stay busy, otherwise, what's the point? They have literal armies of people working 24/7. There are just a couple thousand active members of the community, and most of them have full-time jobs, families." Trevor's tone was, if anything, more matter-of-fact than it had been before, which Josh would have thought impossible.

Michael and Josh were now sitting facing away from one another, looking at and manipulating the monitors on opposite sides of the cabin. Michael continued his instructions, describing for Josh how he could change the date at the bottom of the screen to change the cloud's parameters to any given period of time since the bulletin board began. "When you're on the discussion board, if you see blue text in a file, it's a link to the Annopedia page. It's like Wikipedia, but it's just about this project. It's mostly basic information that saves newcomers, or newcomers to a topic, time. So you don't have to read back through years of discussion board threads to get a general idea of something."

When Josh saw Sam's name growing larger and brighter red, he clicked on it, and was startled to see that literally thousands of posts about Sam had been made within the past 24 hours, hundreds in the past five minutes. As he was going down the page reading the subject lines, a new one appeared at the top, labeled *Audio file Rogers_to_Smith* with the date and a time earlier that afternoon. He clicked on it, and found what looked like the Windows icon for a sound file there in the body of the message. "Can I play this?" he asked out loud, not knowing who he was asking for permission, adding quickly, "this audio file of Sam'?"

"Sure," Michael answered, adding "Somehow I don't think it's going to be about cats."

Josh pressed the icon on the screen, and the recording began, with the judge answering her phone. "Sam! Girl! It's been a mess o' hot minutes since I've heard from you. How the hell are you? What's going on?" They both relaxed into their childhood Dublin accents when they spoke on the phone—at least, when they thought no one else was listening.

"Not enough o' the good stuff, too much of the other, girl."

The love the two friends shared, which extended back into Sam's infancy, was evident in both their voices, which expressed not only affection, but also regret that their lives had become so distant when they had once been inseparable—the loss was audible. It was the judge who had first let Sam wear a dress and heels, at the age of five, when she had been watching after him at Ida Mae's house. She had been Sam's role model, showing him how to navigate public school to end up in a fine university with a promising career. She had stuck with him through the insanity of his addiction, though she had never quite understood it, and didn't really know how insane it had been for him until it was all over and he told her about it.

"Alright, tell me. What kind of mischief you in? I thought you were done with all that. You're not back on the pipe are you?"

"Don't start with me. No, I'm not back on the pipe. Girl, I'm gonna read you. But first I need to ask, how far are you from Dublin right now?"

"About an hour. I'm just leaving Macon, but I was headed home. What you need in Dublin?" There was more than a little shock in her voice—they both avoided Dublin whenever they could. They felt guilty not visiting their relatives still living in poverty, but they felt worse if they did.

"You. I need you to go check on Ms. Ida Mae. I can't go. I'm sort of stuck in the lab here."

"She alright? I haven't heard from anybody."

"She's fine, as far as I know. But I think there may be something going on... something she may be in the middle of... I don't really know how to explain it. But she called me last night, and asked me to go meet her special little boy this morning. And I did. And well, I can't explain it, really. But you know she's been spending every day watching TV with Ms. Eleanor?"

"I'd heard something about it. You mean *that* special little boy?" She understood now that they were speaking in code, and she understood why. Ever since Michael had left with Eleanor more than thirty years ago, Ida Mae had ended every prayer, every blessing at meal time, every conversation with God she had, public or private, with the request to "watch after our special little boy, Michael." When Eleanor had moved back to Dublin, Ida Mae's prayer had changed. The words hadn't changed, but she ended them with a smile—a knowing, satisfied smile, quite unlike the fretful expression of the previous decades. It gave the impression more of gratitude than supplication. The judge and Sam had discussed privately that there must have been some secret exchange of information between the two old women, and this conversation appeared to be confirmation of their suspicions.

"Yes," Sam answered, "That special little boy."

"What do you think she might be in the middle of?"

"I think Ms. Eleanor might be the best person to answer that question."

"You think I should go now? Tonight?"

"If it's possible. You know I wouldn't ask you to—"

He was cut off by the judge, who said, "You never have. Anyway, I could go for some peanut brittle. If you're at the lab I'm assuming you'll be up late. Want me to give you a call later?"

"I've got nothing but time right now. But just a text saying everything is ok will be fine, if you have your hands full."

"Alright, sweetie, I'll see what's going on and let you know."

The recording ended.

"That didn't tell us very much, did it?" Josh asked.

"Well, it confirmed what we suspected. Sam didn't think we should have involved Ida Mae. And he took steps to protect her. And it appears he was right," Michael answered. He sounded genuinely concerned, but whether it was because the carefully constructed plan was falling apart, or possibly that he had put those women in danger, or both, was indiscernible.

"We don't know that, Michael. There's no evidence that Ida Mae, or anyone was in any danger. The judge may have forced a hand no one intended to play," was Trevor's quick response. "What's more concerning to me is No-Face Man." The way he said *No-Face Man* suggested that was at least the dead man's temporary identifier. "He's been in that nursing home with Ida Mae for six months, and he never came up on anyone's radar. There's no reference to him anywhere. We've already gone through all known video from Irish Acres, and not once has this man's face been caught on camera. And it was entirely intentional—there are times, when his back is to the cameras, when he raises his head and rubs his neck. He was avoiding being filmed. He was working for someone, doing something, but what? And who? If he was working for Defense or Intelligence, he was so deep undercover no one there, up the ranks so far, knows anything about him."

"Then that means he was part of the community, right?" asked Josh.

Michael looked at Josh in frank astonishment, and demanded "Why on earth would anyone from the community do such a thing?"

Josh answered with something bordering on scorn. "Why on earth would anyone be in the community in the first place? I mean, I remember all your noble talk from before, and all the high-and-mighty whatever, but you know this is fucked up, right? You all are normalized to this, but it's like you're playing some fucked up game of chess with real people as your pawns. Who would want to be a part of this? I mean, literally, what is the psychological profile of the adult human who sits around on a computer to hack into things to win... well, I'm not sure what they think they will win, or earn, or whatever. Put aside the moral atonement business, and just ask yourself, who does this? Grownups tired of Dungeons and Dragons? You admit yourself you don't even know who's in the community. Maybe an aging programmer in Rhode Island needed to retire somewhere warm and just inserted himself into the action in Dublin. People from the other side have gone rogue, you said. Why wouldn't one of you? And don't try to answer that, because you don't even know who you all are. It's a question you can't answer."

Michael just sat looking at Josh, until Trevor spoke up, saying "He's right, you know. I'm sure someone in the community has already thought of it, but Josh is the only one with enough external clarity to readily assess and present it. And he's been here, what, four hours? Very good. I'm getting on the bulletin board now to get someone to make sure no electronic signatures are connecting No-Face to us. He may have left some files behind, or who knows what else."

"I think we can be pretty sure his hard drive is clean," Josh predicted aloud. "Anyone who is willing to shoot off his own face isn't going to be likely to leave lots of loose threads lying around."

Michael resurfaced into the conversation. "True, but we don't have a lot of time, and we need to be certain. That computer, if he has one, will be going offline and into an evidence box in hours, maybe minutes. We need to get moving on it. Trevor, can you put a call out?"

The cloud was still on Josh's screen, and he just sat looking at it, lost in thought as his eyes watched the slowly shifting words change position, size and color. He thought about all of the people sitting around at their computers, watching the action unfold, typing in the words that caused the screen to change, that caused the lives of the people on their monitors to change. He understood the lure—he realized, with sudden clarity, how much like internet porn this was. But it was life porn, where the participants had an opportunity to direct the action. *Turn this way. Turn that way.* He wondered how much of his own life had been guided, directly or indirectly, by these people that he would never, could never know. "They have it all on film," Sam had said in the grocery store. He saw his own name, in a dull forest green color, swimming lazily near the bottom of the screen. He was safe. Or at least the community thought so. Inspired, he changed the date of the visualization from the past hour to the past 24 hours, and as he anticipated, his name, and Callie's, and Sam's, shown bright red at the top of the screen. He thought briefly about clicking on his name, or Callie's, or both, but then a wave of exhaustion fell over him. He could almost literally feel it weighing down on his shoulders, and move down through his body. Suddenly, even his feet ached. It was as though his body was telling him, *You don't want to know.* He muttered to himself, aloud, "I don't want to know."

"What was that, Josh?" Michael asked, distracted.

"Bed. I think I'm going to bed."

"Good idea. We all should. The community can handle this. Trevor, you should follow us."

"Yes, I will. You should sleep through 7:00am. The community seems to be getting distracted by this thing with Irish Acres and the judge right now. I need to get everyone refocused on tomorrow. Lucy should be our primary focus right now."

Yes, Josh thought. *Lucy.*

CHAPTER 7. CLOUDBUSTING

Callie walked into the sleeping compartment shaking with rage. It had been years since this much anger had rushed through her, and it was disturbing. Part of her was watching, as though from a distance, allowing the anger to run its course. She could not think about the arrogance, the disinterestedness, the heartlessness of the decisions of those people. *Those people. All of them.* She would not, could not think about them. She had to sleep. She had to do whatever she was going to do tomorrow to get Lucy from that place, and then she was going to see Sam. If she had to walk a thousand miles, she would be there, with him, thanking him for his foolish, senseless selflessness.

She sat on the nearest bunk, her back held straight, her feet on the floor, her knees aligned with her shoulders, and her hands resting on them palm down. She bowed her head slightly and closed her eyes. Slowly, she breathed, first in and then out. Long, soothing, deep breaths, carried the oxygen from her nostrils down to her toes. *With this breath, I breathe the world in. With this breath, I breathe the world out.* As the air flowed in, she could feel the anger dissipate, as she blocked the idea of anger from her mind by focusing on her breath. *With this breath, I breathe the world in. With this breath, I breathe the world out.* The tension in her back and neck and shoulders eased. Soon, she was herself again, or close enough as made no difference—she would be able to think, and possibly to sleep.

She opened her eyes and looked around the room. It was the same as before, but on two of the closet doors there were now Post-It notes, one with her name and one with Josh's, both written in black marker. She opened hers and discovered that it was less a closet than a 21st century armoire, like something from Ikea, but attached to the walls and floor. There were clothes on hangers at eye level with a shelf above for shoes and another below for sweaters and a sweat suit. There were four drawers at the bottom. It took her just a moment to realize that the clothes she was looking at were near duplicates of clothes she actually owned. She opened the drawers and found an oversized men's Fruit of the Loom v-neck undershirt, and a pair of Danskin black tights—her pajamas. She took them and the cosmetics kit into the bathroom in the next compartment to change for bed.

As she slipped on the undershirt, she realized that it was, like her own at home, worn with age. She wondered as she pulled on the leggings, also soft with apparent age, if the garments had been purchased second-hand, or intentionally distressed. *If God is in the details, these people are saints*, she thought. And then, *These people are not saints*. She found, with some mild relief, that the toothbrush they provided her was not broken in for her—but it was her brand, and her color, and the bristles were soft. She had been considering changing brands of toothpaste, but was comforted to discover that they could not read her mind—the toothpaste was her old brand. She considered flossing, but decided against it. She washed her face with her usual brand of fig-scented glycerin soap, and dug around in the bag to see if they had her eye cream. They did, of course. She typically applied the absurdly expensive cream in miniscule, vanishingly small amounts, but she opened the large jar—larger than any she had ever seen, but still relatively small—and dug her index finger in deep, applying liberal amounts to both her eyes. *You look like death*, she thought, looking at the signs of middle age in the too-close mirror. And then, *Well it has been a long day*. And then, from some deep reserve, she realized, *But you've had much longer days*.

When she returned to the sleeping compartment she couldn't easily discover anywhere to put the clothes she'd had on all day, so she just stood holding them as she tried to determine which bunk was hers. There were no Post-It notes on the beds, and she thought at first they must be first-come first-serve, but then she noticed in the shadows of one of the lower bunks that it had three pillows. She felt them and discovered one feather and two memory foam pillows, and knew that was hers. It was not the bunk she sat on before, but she did not care. She threw her dirty clothes into a far corner at the foot of the bed, pulled back the sheet and blanket and crawled in.

She tried pulling the tambour door to her bunk down by its handle, but it would not budge. She could see the wheels sitting in the track, but no matter how hard she pulled, it just wouldn't move. Remembering what Trevor had said about using voice commands, she tried that instead, saying "Close the door," but nothing happened. Looking up at the glossy grey panel that was the bottom of the top bunk, she tentatively put her hand on it, and a computer monitor appeared directly above her. At first glance, it had the same dimensions of her MacBook Pro at home, and the same default Apple background. When she looked closer, she saw those were her icons. They didn't just have her music, they had her entire computer replicated on the bottom of the overhead bunk. *Nifty*, she thought with not a little sarcasm, *but that still doesn't tell me how to close the door.*

In the bottom right corner of the monitor display she saw a new icon, an image of a cable car with the word *trolley* beneath it. She tentatively touched it, and another monitor image appeared beside her MacBook display, which moved to the left, so the two monitors were side by side and the same size. On the new monitor, the word *start* appeared in flashing blue text. She touched it, and a woman's voice, soft, polite, and British, seemed to whisper in her ear, "Welcome, Callie. How can I help you?" Callie was startled out of the quiet reverie she had fallen into, as she was passively not-thinking about Sam. She looked around quickly, realized there was no woman, and asked, "Are you a computer or a person?"

"I'm the voice of the operating system. If you would prefer another voice, there are several genders, ages and nationalities programmed into the system."

"No," Callie responded quickly, almost apologetically, "you're fine. Can you close the door please?"

"Certainly," the voice replied, and the door quickly, quietly slid down, as vents opened at each end of the bunk and fresh air began to pass through, and the two side-by-side monitor displays dimmed to adjust to the darkness of the enclosed bunk. It took Callie a moment to realize the lady's voice sounded almost identical to the voice of the British Airways automated phone system.

On the trolley monitor, the word start had been replaced with the question

What would you like to do? Callie decided to think about it before she answered that question.

She went to her MacBook screen, opened iTunes, and selected her bedtime playlist. One of her bedtime favorites, *Floating*, by Julee Cruise began to play, but just a little too loudly. She couldn't see the source of the sound, so she adjusted the volume on the monitor, and then, using the same weatherman gesture she saw Michael use earlier, she resized the MacBook monitor to the size of a playing card and moved it just out of her field of vision. She centered the trolley monitor where she could view it comfortably, made it larger, and asked with just a touch of hesitancy, "May I see my file please?"

The British Airways lady answered back immediately, "Yes, but it is not recommended that you read your own file." Callie paused, looking at the blinking blue words, *What would you like to do?* before asking "But I can, right?"

"Certainly," was the immediate reply.

She could not say how, exactly, but a part of Callie felt that the information in her file would somehow prepare her for the next day. Whether it was a feeling, or a belief, or curiosity, or some combination, she did not know. Not opening the file felt wrong. It was beyond her capacity to not open it, given the opportunity. So much of her life had been so strange, and she had made her peace with the events of her childhood and youth, but she had never received anything in the way of an explanation for them. And this seemed like it might be her chance, and her only chance, at that—her aim was excellent, but a part of her felt that this, her first night on the trolley might well be her last, regardless of the day's outcome.

"Well, that's what I would like to do, please," she said. "I would like to see my file."

Instantly, the image of the manila folder she saw earlier reappeared, with her picture and name. She paused again, still just a little unnerved by the warning from British Airways. But as always in her sober adult life, when she felt in the right, her resolve persevered. She wondered if they knew that about her—if that was why they had chosen her. She thought she might find out soon. She opened the folder, having no idea at all what to expect.

What she found was one document, 220 kilobytes, named summary.txt, and an index of subfolders in chronological order beginning from the year of her birth. She thought about skipping the summary file altogether, and just moving through each year of her life. She was almost desperate to see what they could have discovered from when she was two, or six, or even ten—years she had almost no recollection of herself. Then she became aware of how small a file 220 kilobytes was for a summary of her life, and thought with some smugness that it was unlikely a life as long and complex as hers could be summarized that succinctly, even by the brightest minds in the world. She opened it with a touch of her finger. What looked to be a piece of plain white paper appeared on the screen. In the upper left corner of the page was the label *SC8743*, and beneath it, *Vicky Ann Pennington*, and beneath that *aka Callie Pennington*, and then the date of the last revision to the file, from the day before.

In the first paragraph, her world changed, word by word, and as she lay looking up, the unbearable weight of knowing pressed her down into the bed. Her mother was alive, and serving a life sentence in a women's prison in Alabama for setting an abusive boyfriend on fire a decade before. *My mother is alive.* Her father—her real father—died in Vietnam before she was born. Her parents met a month before he was sent to boot camp. Her father died in combat as an undecorated private, and never knew he had, or would have, a daughter. Her mother had married the first man she could find as soon as she discovered she was pregnant. He never knew Vicky wasn't his daughter. He was murdered three days after Vicky disappeared, by the men he sold her to that night. *My father is not my father. My father is dead.*

She did not cry, but she did not continue reading, either. Her eyes remained looking in the direction of the luminous rectangle, but she could no longer see words, just black and grey shapes swimming in a pool of white. She lay motionless for several minutes.

"Close my file please," she whispered into the small enclosure, and the bunk became almost instantly dark, the only illumination coming from the animated screen saver of her small MacBook screen, still out of her field of vision, casting a dim, shifting light like an aquarium.

British Airways was right, she thought. *British Airways is always right. How can this help?*

She turned on her side, putting the feather pillow beneath her outstretched arm and one of the memory foam pillows beneath her raised knee. The other memory foam pillow she kept beneath her head, as she always did. The weight of knowing pressed down on her, crushing her into the bed, and exhaustion came like a wave that filled her bunk, so tired she could barely breathe, yet her heart was racing, in time with the music thumping softly in her pillow.

On the periphery of consciousness she was aware of Kate Bush singing, but she could make out neither the words nor the song. She reached back into memory, from just a few minutes before and from years before in early recovery, to remember how to breathe—she had to go to sleep.

With this breath, I breathe the world in, With this breath, I breathe the world out. With this breath I breathe the world in, With this breath, I cannot believe this. With this breath, I always wondered, With this breath, I always knew. With this breath, I'm glad he's dead, With this breath, I forgive them all. With this breath, I hope I can do this, With this breath, It's what I was born to do. With this breath, I'm going to sleep, With this breath, I'm breathing. I'm breathing. I'm breathing.

***

The Ferris Wheel was rising into a picture-perfect sky. The sun was enormous and glowing, partially hidden behind a patch of lazy cumulus clouds, iridescent white and radiant. Callie held her father's hand as they moved up into the atmosphere, higher than she had ever been, but his large, warm, dry hands held hers clasped in his, and she was safe. And she was clean, in freshly laundered clothing, and new white sneakers. Her glistening hair was combed back in elegant plats. Her teeth felt clean—she had flossed that morning, she knew.

She looked at her father, who smiled down at her with big white, square teeth, the wide open smile of a father who loved being with his daughter. His hair was a sleek, black military cube, and his skin was the color of vanilla ice cream, with two warm patches of pink coloring his high square cheekbones. His lips were full and red, the color of apples. His eyes, like hers, were bright Kelly green. His dress military uniform was immaculate, and the bars of multicolored ribbons covered his heart like a piece of enameled armor. Medallions of honor, of valor, of glory, of things she didn't know, seemed to almost cover him. Everything about him shone—his shoes, his buttons, his eyes, his teeth, his hair, all sparkled in the wash of white sunlight. "You know what you have to do, don't you," he asked as they neared the top of the wheel. His voice was deep, and kind, and caring, and had no accent that she knew.

Below them the white Portland cement of the parking lot glittered and looked soft enough to dive into. Families dressed in their Sunday best walked, holding hands, down the midway. Clusters of multicolored, translucent balloons festooned each of the sideshow attractions, where young boys and girls were winning stuffed animals and model cars and hula hoops. Strings of multicolored metallic pennants crisscrossed the midway. At its far end the carousel spun slowly, as *I'm looking over a four leaf clover that I overlooked before* played out from its calliope.

She wanted to know the answer, desperately, but she didn't. "No, I don't. I don't think so. Can you tell me?" Her voice, though young, had the crisp diction of a New England finishing school.

His smile didn't falter. "You have to use their weapons against them."

They were well into their descent, and the smile was fading from her face as they neared the angled steel girders that supported the massive wheel.

"But I don't know how to use any weapons. I don't know what the weapons are." The expression on her face was pleading, but not desperate. She wanted to please him. She was looking directly into his eyes as he said, "You, my sweet Vicky, you are the weapon."

They passed through the shadow of the girders, and in that instant of shadow, she could no longer see his eyes. The scene changed around them.

They were still on the Ferris Wheel, ascending now, but the sky was dark with clouds, as though it were night, but it was not night, she knew. From horizon to horizon, every type of cloud crowded the sky, heavy and dark with rain, but it did not rain. The air was swirling, and filled with smoke, tarry and dry, and she looked down and saw the white cement and everything and everyone on it was gone. There was nothing now but fire, belching up from black asphalt, stretching into the infinite distance.

She looked into her father's eyes and saw only the reflection of the fire beneath them. She looked away from his eyes, and saw his hair now hung to his shoulders, greasy and matted with filth. His cheeks and eyes were hollowed, his lips cracked and dry and the color and texture of uncooked fish. She looked down at his uniform and saw that it had changed, too. There were no ribbons, no insignia, no shiny buttons, only drab olive green canvas smeared with dirt, and blood, and worse. She became aware that he was not holding her hand anymore only when she saw the jagged stump of his arm drooping from the blackened hole in his jacket. She looked down to look away, and saw that he had no legs. She had no shoes, and even in the fire-filtered darkness she could see that she, too, was filthy, and she was ashamed, and closed her eyes.

"Look et me, gurrrrl," her father said, his voice a growl, a threat, a curse. His accent rang with the memory of cheap beer, beaten up trucks, beaten up wives, and black boys left dead by the road. She looked at him. "Do you understand whut it is you have to do er not?"

They were rising incredibly fast, but the wheel seemed to be expanding as they moved upwards, and they were getting no closer to the top.

"No," she said, and something about her voice seemed wrong. That scared her more than her father did.

"You gots to fly, gurl."

"I kaint," she said, in a defiant, whining tone made even more appalling to her by the deeply southern twang. *Who am I?* she thought. *Who is he?*

The Ferris Wheel was moving faster again, impossibly fast, but now she could see they were moving, nearing the apex. "Oh yes you can, little gurl," the man laughed, loud and hard and cruel, as the wheel jerked to a stop, and she soared aloft from the seat beside him. There was nothing below her but burning asphalt, nothing in front of her but clouds. She wanted to scream, but the smoke had filled her lungs.

When she reached the first low-lying cloud, black and dense, she burst into it, and burst apart into an infinity of drops of rain, water from the beginning of the beginning. She scattered into the atmosphere, bursting every cloud, and soon the earth was drenched, and cold, and wet. She could see the sun was shining. But she had no shadow. She was nothing—she was gone.

***

Callie woke with a start, up out of the sheets, and hit her head on the overhead bunk. "Fuck," she screamed, and then moaned, and then mumbled "fuck" again as she rubbed her head.

"I'm sorry, Callie, I don't understand," the British Airways lady said in the darkness.

"I don't, either," Callie mumbled, wiping the sleep from her eyes. And then, "What time is it?"

"4:07am" was the reply.

"What time am I supposed to be up?" Callie asked, guessing, correctly, that her entire life—past, present, and future—was within reach of the nice British Airways lady.

"You are scheduled to have breakfast at 7:30am. Your morning alarm is scheduled to ring at 7:00am."

Callie thought for a minute, trying to look around in the darkness, but the darkness was absolute—her MacBook had gone into sleep mode. She raised her hand and placed her palm on the ceiling, and the MacBook and trolley monitors appeared on the ceiling in the same positions she had last seen them. Her bedtime playlist resumed playing, picking up with something from Imogene Heap. She repositioned the pillows, putting all three under her head, and asked aloud, "Can I see Sam? The Sam video stream?"

"Which Sam would you like to see?"

The question took Callie off guard. How many men named *Sam* could possibly be under observation at any given time? She decided she didn't want to know.

"Sam Rogers at the Centers for Disease Control in Atlanta."

"Certainly," was the immediate response, and almost instantly she saw Sam sitting at the same desk, wearing the same ridiculous hat in the same position as he had been hours before. Now though, he was talking on the telephone. Not his cell phone, but apparently a desk phone, with a cord. Who could he be talking to at this hour if he isn't talking to me? she wondered absently.

"Can I send Sam an email?" she asked aloud.

"Certainly. Which email account would you like to use?"

Callie thought for a moment. She had several Gmail accounts she used for different purposes, but she and Sam emailed each other back and forth through all of their various accounts using their phones, and frequently she had no idea which one she was actually using. With her few accounting clients, and her sponsees, she was much more aware of what she was sending and from where. As she was considering, it suddenly occurred to her that emailing Sam might put him, or her, or Lucy, or someone, in danger, or more danger.

"Is emailing Sam a bad idea?" she asked, looking up at the monitor.

"I cannot make decisions of ethics, morals or emotions. I can suggest statistical probabilities of outcomes if I am provided sufficient data, but I cannot tell you if a proposal is good or bad or right or wrong."

Callie heard an almost apologetic tone in the computer's voice, and wondered if it existed or if she was hearing something that really wasn't there.

"Is anyone else awake? On the trolley, I mean?"

On the monitor, Sam was returning the phone to its base. He looked troubled.

"Yes, Trevor is awake in the office."

"Can I go see him?

"Certainly."

"Can you open the door for me?"

"Certainly."

Callie rolled out of the bed and stretched before padding in her bare feet and pajamas in the direction of the office, which Michael had told her was on the other side of the bathroom. She knew her pajamas might be considered immodest, but the reality that everyone in the community, including Michael and Trevor, had already seen her naked as many times and in as any positions as anyone could ever want to, made any notion of modesty seem ridiculous.

She paused before she opened the door going into the bathrooms and asked, "Computer, do you have a name?"

She noticed that the doors to the two bunks on the opposite side from where she slept were closed. The one above her was open, and the bed was still made. Apparently someone had not slept.

The voice answered "I will respond to any name you assign me."

"B.A. I'm going to call you B.A."

"Certainly."

"And can you close that door for me?" She didn't want anyone to see her bed wasn't made, but she also didn't want to waste time making it.

"Certainly."

Callie placed her hand on the wall, and the door to the bathroom opened. Behind her, she thought she could hear the faintest suggestion of movement as the door to her bunk lowered, and she moved on into her day, all memory of the Ferris Wheel and her father sealed in the compartment behind her.

CHAPTER 8. DRIVE

The judge's black, four-door Mercedes S550 sedan was a safe distance behind the black Ford Explorer on Highway I-16, but 90 miles per hour still did not seem like a safe speed. It felt fine—in fact, travelling in the luxurious cocoon of leather and chrome, it felt no different than doing 50—but the idea of driving at this speed was not something she had considered when she insisted on driving herself. The two security officers in the Explorer had been trained to drive at these speeds, she knew, but she had not. Still, she had told them to *Get us as far away from here as possible, as quickly as possible*, and that is just what they were doing. "Your honor, are these two women in custody?" the lead officer had asked. "What answer will get me what I want?" the judge had answered back. "Yes," he responded. "Then yes, they're in custody. Now let's move."

Twenty minutes later, they were already approaching Macon, headed towards Atlanta, and would have to slow down while going through Macon's congested urban bottleneck. They had barely spoken since getting in the car—the only sound, when they could all hear, was Ida Mae humming. It was a song Eleanor did not know, and one the judge could not remember.

"Can you hear yet, Ms. Ida Mae?" the judge called to the backseat, her voice raised.

From the darkness Ida Mae responded "I can. I guess. But I don't know whether or not to believe anything I'm hearing or seeing. Where are we going?"

The judge opened the storage compartment between the driver's and passenger's seats and retrieved a small metal canister. She carefully unscrewed the lid and rested the two pieces in her lap. She then reached to the collar of her jacket and removed a small enameled brass lapel pin showing the insignia of the Department of Justice—an eagle with its wings spread above an American flag—and dropped it in the container. She resealed the lid, and placed the container in a cup holder.

"Well, that depends on you all. Alright ladies, talk."

Eleanor turned round in her seat to look at Ida Mae, but Ida Mae just looked back at her blankly, without any suggestion of what they should do next. Eleanor had refused to speak until Ida Mae could hear, but even now that she could hear, neither woman knew exactly what to say, so neither said anything.

"We may need somewhere more private to speak," Eleanor suggested cautiously. She would have liked to have written it down, but did not want the judge trying to read a note at night while driving at that speed.

The judge looked at her in astonishment, and looked up in the rearview mirror to see Ida Mae slowly shaking her head with just the corners of her lips turned down.

"This car is secure, ladies. No one can monitor our conversation, internally or externally—I'm a federal judge. This car is regularly swept for listening devices, and emits an electronic signal that prevents eavesdropping. That lapel pin I just removed is a microphone so my security can follow what's going on with me, but they can hear nothing now. As long as you two don't have cell phones on you, there's no way for anyone to listen. Now, tell me what's going on. Where is Michael? And why is Sam involved in all this? Why are you all involved in this? And who is that crazy cracker that just killed my Andy and shot his own face off?" Andy was the name of the security officer who had just been shot down. He had been on the judge's security detail for five years. He had a wife and two children, all lovely people, from what the judge knew. She wasn't angry, but someone needed to account for this madness, and somehow, these two little old ladies seemed to be holding all the answers.

"Hmph," said Eleanor aloud. "How much time do we have?"

"As much as it takes. We can drive to Alaska if we need to."

"Well, alright then," Eleanor answered, and swiveled around again to Ida Mae, who nodded once in a deep, slow, resigned gesture of consent.

Eleanor exhaled deeply before she began. "We don't know exactly what's going on, or exactly where Michael is. But he is safe, in a secure location, somewhere.

He's been communicating with me regularly since he disappeared. When I moved back to Dublin, he began communicating with me and Ms. Ida Mae together. It's safer at Irish Acres—Ms. Ida Mae has audio surveillance on her, but not video."

The judge looked over at Eleanor, then in the rearview mirror as she asked "You two are both under surveillance? Why? And for how long?"

"My special little boy," came the voice from the backseat, "is more special than we knew, it seems."

"Michael," answered Eleanor, "has been under surveillance since his mother died when he was three. But his father was under surveillance before that, so you could say basically his whole life, until he disappeared four years ago."

"He was under surveillance when he lived with you?" The judge asked.

"Oh, yes. There were cameras and microphones everywhere. Things weren't as sophisticated in the seventies as they are now, of course. Clumsy things, they were. I just worked around them."

The expression on the judge's face was consternation with a whiff of impatience. "Why don't we go back a bit. I'm not understanding something. How did you know about all this? And why? Why Michael?"

"I can't explain the *why*. I won't attempt to. Michael is extraordinarily gifted, with language, among other things. But I knew about it because I was a part of it." As they passed through Macon, and slowed to 75 miles per hour, Eleanor explained briefly the circumstances of how she came to adopt Michael, and the course of the next fifteen years—the payments, the doctor's visits, the special camps Michael attended each summer, his enrollment at M.I.T. When she came to the part about Michael's disappearance into the community, the judge balked, and interrupted Eleanor as she might a witness on the witness stand, saying "You don't honestly believe this, do you?"

There was no contempt in her voice, and she hoped it was not unkind—she was more concerned about what the truth was behind the lie the old women had been led to believe. She wondered if someone had been taking advantage of their old age and naivety. But to what purpose, she couldn't imagine.

Eleanor's reply was steely, cool, and unforgiving. "You said you wanted to hear. This is the truth as I know it. I know what it sounds like. I'm no fool. Either you want to hear it or you don't. I imagine those two dead men back there would want you to listen. You did see them, did you not? Do you believe your own eyes? Or wasn't that real enough for you?"

"Charlene Eugenia Smith," came a sharp rebuke from the backseat, "who taught you to interrupt your elders that way when they're speaking? I know it wasn't me."

"Yes, ma'am," was the judge's patient reply. She knew she would never listen to just any elder with the deference Ida Mae was suggesting, but these weren't just any elders. These were the proper, wise elders one hoped for, that one needed, even if they had somehow been confused, manipulated, or threatened. She would listen. "But how has Michael been communicating with you? How did this, today, this night, those deaths, come about?"

When the judge had arrived at Irish Acres two hours earlier, the two women had been seated at the same table where she joined them. Neither of the two older women left the card table except to go to the bathroom, and the judge had noticed that each woman carried her purse with her when she did. When the judge had tried, several times, to bring up the subject of Sam, she was summarily silenced by one or both of the women, but with the laser-quick and ephemeral sounds and motions of someone ending a forbidden topic at the Sunday dinner table. The message had been crystal clear: *We can't talk about what we can't talk about, so be quiet.* This, though, was the time for disclosure.

Eleanor gathered herself up with a dignified shrug before she continued to speak. "I don't understand the technology of it, of course—I don't even understand how my toaster works—but once a week or so, sometimes more, sometimes less, but usually once a week, Michael takes over the video part of *The Young and the Restless*. The sound of the show keeps coming through, so to the people eavesdropping

370

on me and Ida Mae, it sounds like we're just watching the TV show, but what we are actually watching is Michael. He is sitting somewhere, usually in an office, but sometimes in a little sitting room, and as he talks, his words show up at the bottom of the screen, like that closed captioning."

The judge just accepted it for what it was at the moment, and continued with her line of questioning, asking without a hint of disbelief, "But how do you communicate with him? Is it completely one-way?"

"Well, since he disappeared I've been under more surveillance than before. All of my audio is recorded, probably the N.S.A., but well, who knows. Anyway, this community of Michael's has access to all my files, and since I've been in contact with her, Ida Mae's, and we just talk out loud to ourselves, like doddering, senile old ladies. And we pass along messages to him. Let him know how we're doing. Encourage him."

"It's important work he's doing, but I think it's rough on him," broke in Ida Mae from the back seat, her voice sad but loud. "He told us way back when that it was dangerous, what he was involved in. I think he knew it might come to something like this, one day."

The judge could not believe she was having this conversation. "How on earth could the two of you get mixed up in something like this? When you knew you could be putting yourselves in danger?"

"Why do you travel with a security detail?" Eleanor asked, looking at judge's silhouette in the glow from the dashboard.

"That's entirely different. I'm a judge. I'm helping people."

Eleanor arched an eyebrow, which the judge could not see, but Ida Mae responded by saying "You don't hold the patent on helping people, Charlene."

"But who is he helping?"

"Us, he says. All of us. He's trying to help all of us," was Ida Mae's matter-of-fact reply.

What the hell has Michael gotten mixed up in? was the judge's first thought, but somewhere, in the back of her mind, she realized that whatever else might be happening, there were, as Eleanor had pointed out, three dead men back in Irish Acres, one of whom had come with what seemed professional or military training, with what she believed to be real government officials, into a nursing home in the middle of the night for some less-than-genteel purpose—if not to hurt someone, then to take something, if only information, by intimidation, or force, if necessary. That much was clear. But what could these two women possibly know? That line of questioning, though, seemed like the least direct line of questioning to get to an understanding the situation they were in.

"But I don't understand how you became involved in any of this, Ms. Ida Mae. Or why," the judge asked, with sincere interest. The judge had been a child when Michael was taken away from Dublin, and while the memory of both he and his father haunted the Quarters for years, even decades to come, she had no personal remembrance of him, though they had certainly known each other as children.

"I would think you'd never have heard me pray for that boy in the past thirty years," was the old woman's answer.

"Of course I have," came the judge's prompt reply, "but there's a difference between praying for someone and dying for someone, or going to jail for someone."

"I'm not so sure of that," was Ida Mae's calm, but emphatic, deliberate reply.

The judge was startled by the words as well as the tone they were delivered with, and she looked in her rearview mirror to see if maybe Ida Mae had the playful, Cheshire cat grin she sometimes wore when she was stirring for a fight. She did not. She looked as thoughtful and content as she almost always had. The judge looked away from the mirror to see if Eleanor was reacting to Ida Mae's radical pronouncement—to the judge, it seemed like a radical thing for Ida Mae to say—but Eleanor was just looking out at the roadside signs as they passed them, increasing in density as they neared Atlanta.

The judge realized she would soon need to make a determination as to where to take the women. She wouldn't take them to her home. She wouldn't take them to her office, or the local F.B.I. or Secret Service field offices, but she needed somewhere safe. She realized when she did not know what to do that she needed to call the person she called when she did not know what to do.

"I'm going to make a quick phone call. I need to figure out where to take you ladies."

She pulled her phone out of the center console, put the battery she had removed back in it, and searched for a number not in her recent call log, ignoring the 12 missed calls and many texts she had received. Eleanor smiled when she saw the name that appeared in the Bluetooth display on the dashboard, indicating the recipient of the call.

The call was on speakerphone, and it rang twice before it was answered. "Good evening, Chari. I've been hoping to hear from you."

Before the judge could speak, Eleanor spoke up, with a note of levity in her voice that surprised the judge. "Hello, Stick. It's not just Charlene. I bet you don't remember me, do you?"

"I certainly do. And I don't want you to say another word. I want to hear all your news in person, Ms. Eleanor. Chari, have you passed the Perimeter yet?" The Perimeter was the eight-lane stretch of asphalt circling Atlanta, allowing motorists to circumnavigate the city center.

The judge was shocked beyond measure that Stick knew her rough location, but chose not to comment on it—she knew that they were now on an essentially open line. Her phone was a military-grade encrypted Blackberry, but that meant nothing if it was the military doing the surveillance.

"Not yet, no," the judge said, looking at Eleanor, whose expression was a nearly perfect balance of grim satisfaction and resignation. She added, "We're about two miles away."

"Good, just stay on the line with me. There's just one other person in your car besides Eleanor, yes? That you picked up at the same time?"

"Yes."

"Is your security detail still in front of you?"

"Yes."

"Can you see the turnoff for the Perimeter coming up just ahead of you on the left?"

"Yes."

"Slow down a little. Turn west. Don't use your turn signal. Just turn. Do it now."

In the days to come, when she reflected back on that moment, the judge was never able to satisfactorily explain to herself why she did what her old friend and mentor Stick Strickland told her to do. Leaving behind the safety of her security detail, heading away from every safe location she knew of, into the wilds of west Georgia, in the middle of the night, with two old ladies who almost certainly needed their rest and medications as much as she did, was beyond reason, beyond logic, almost beyond comprehension. But at the last possible moment, she cut off two lanes of light nighttime traffic to take the steep, sharp curve into the unknown.

"Did you do it? Did you turn?" Stick's voice was eager.

"God help me, yes, I turned. Now will you tell me what's going on here, Walter?"

"I will, but not now. Take the battery out of your phone. Stay on 285 west. I'll be in touch."

And with that, the line went dead.

The judge slowed to a more reasonable speed and merged into the moderate traffic heading west on the Perimeter. She looked over at Eleanor, whose smile was wide, her eyes alive with mischief, even in the dim light of the dashboard. "What?" she asked the lady, with a little impatience.

"Well, now you know why," Eleanor said with more than just a hint of satisfaction.

"Why what?" the judge asked, fumbling to take the battery out of her phone, looking at Eleanor out of the corner of her eye. But it was Ida Mae who answered.

"Why we took a leap of faith without having all the answers. Whatever you think it is that made you take that turn back there, whether you call it instinct, or trust, or intuition, you're wrong, girl. It was God. Nothing more, nothing less."

No one said anything for several minutes, though the judge turned to look at Eleanor, and in the rearview mirror at Ida Mae every few seconds, as though to assure herself that what was happening was real. They soon began passing stretches of woodland that hid the middle class suburbs and strip malls of West Atlanta.

"I hope you're right, Ms. Ida Mae. And whatever is going on here better resolve itself soon. My security detail is gonna be hot. Me taking off, not answering the phone, with armed men running round opening fire. It won't be long before they're on us. And God only knows who else. They'll probably call out the National Guard. I'm a judge. Good Lord. And I don't know how Stick thinks he's going to contact us."

"Have faith, Charlene," answered Ida Mae, and she began humming the same tune from before.

Without warning, a chill of recognition stabbed down the judge's spine, sharp and steely cold—the song was a hymn she remembered from childhood. She sang the long-forgotten lyrics in her head as she looked back in the mirror to Ida Mae, who sat smiling, looking out at the landscape speeding by. *I have decided to follow Jesus, no turning back, no turning back.*

She turned her eyes back to the road. The fear of the faithless filled her, and she could not speak.

CHAPTER 9. STICK

Stick Strickland retired to New Orleans in 2003 after a long and seemingly undistinguished career as a clerk for various judges in the federal court system in Atlanta. That same year, he also officially retired from his role as a special agent for the Central Intelligence Agency, in an intelligence-gathering role he held for almost as long as he was a court clerk.

The circumstances of Stick Strickland becoming a spy were as quotidian as they were coincidental. One spring Wednesday in 1970 he was having lunch with one of the young women from the federal courthouse secretarial pool. They were on a sunlit bench in a park in front of the courthouse, and they were both talking animatedly about an episode of *The Carol Burnett Show* they watched the night before. Across the park from them two men, both intelligence officers, sat having a cigarette and discussing how to gain the trust of a German banking executive and known homosexual on long-term assignment in Atlanta. "What we need," said the C.I.A. field director to the Justice Department mole he was sharing the bench with, "is a patriotic homosexual we can trust. And we need him here, now."

Officially, at the time, no such person existed. Homosexuality was still a diagnosable mental illness, and illegal throughout the vast majority of the United States. And yet, there were homosexuals all over the world with access to information the United States wanted or needed, so the discrete employment of certain "confirmed bachelors," as they were known, while not commonplace, was not entirely unusual, either.

The Justice Department official just shrugged and asked "What about him," gesturing with his head in the direction of the young woman and Stick, who at that moment happened to be waving his arms in the air in movements more feminine and aquiline than most women are capable of.

"You know him?" the field director asked, more than a little surprised.

"He's in Justice. Just some clerk. Family connections. Educated, well-spoken.

U.G.A. law school, I think. Good southern mama's boy. Everyone assumes he's a fairy. He doesn't especially try to hide it."

"You don't say," laughed the field director as the young man kicked one of his brightly polished wing tips above his head, apparently demonstrating some dance move he'd seen.

The director spent a few minutes observing the young man. He wasn't sexually attracted to men himself, but reasoned that if he was, this one would likely do. Very tall, thin, with curly blond hair, and angular, Aryan features—he guessed this was the sort of thing a German banker might go for. The young man's suit was almost comically conservative when contrasted with his flamboyant demeanor—the deep cuffs and high waist of the trousers, and narrow lapel on the three-button coat, worn with a plain white cotton dress shirt and striped silk bow tie, altogether looked like a throwback to another era. Around him, even conservative judges and lawyers could be seen wearing the exaggerated lapels, bold prints, and polyester blends that typified the dawning of the Age of Aquarius, even in Atlanta.

"Does he always dress like that?" the director asked.

"As far as I know. He loves old movies. He can tell you anything you wanna know, or don't wanna know, about any old movie you never wanna watch."

"Put a tail on him, see where he goes, what he does. I'll see what a security clearance would look like, run his bona fides. What's his name?"

"Stick."

"His name is Stick?"

"That's what everyone calls him. I never bothered to ask his real name. I'll get back to you."

"You know you work in intelligence, right?"

"Right."

***

The two men met the following Monday on the same bench, at the same time, and again watched Stick and his friend have lunch. The mole handed the director an envelope filled with surveillance photographs from the past five nights.

"Well, what do you think? Could he work?" the director asked, taking the envelope.

"If I didn't know better, I would say he's already working for someone else. He's a regular chameleon, this one, and always on the go, one thing to the next. Knows people everywhere, fits in everywhere, everybody's happy to see him. The homosexual leather bar Friday night, a fish fry in Dublin Saturday, back for the symphony here Saturday night, then out to a piano bar, gets up Sunday and sings in the choir at First Presbyterian downtown, then to Piedmont Park to play tennis. He doesn't just change clothes, he changes his whole personality—his walk, his accent, his hair, even way he holds his head. We almost didn't recognize him when he came out of his apartment in this leather getup." He handed over an 8" x 10" glossy photograph of Stick exiting his apartment building wearing a leather harness, torn faded jeans, and black cowboy boots. He looked like an entirely different person.

"What's a leather bar?"

"Like something out of Amsterdam. All the fairies dressed up in leather costumes, blue jeans, cowboy hats. It's like Halloween, but every day. And no women. Not one."

The director flipped through the photographs. "Did you find out if he's the man or the woman?"

"What do you mean?"

"When he's having sex with other men. Is he the man or the woman?"

"Both, I believe. He's what they call versatile, apparently."

The director nodded in approval. "He's versatile all over the place, it seems. Smart, as well, according to his transcripts. He could have used his connections to really make something of himself. But he's carved out this little place for himself where he can have this homosexual lifestyle, but still participate in society. He can't rise too high—he seems to understand that. But he has some family money, so he doesn't really need to rise. He can just enjoy the ride. He's not entirely without ambition, or at least, motivation—he's not lazy, that is, by any means, but doesn't seem to be in pursuit of anything in particular."

"Maybe he has everything he wants?"

"How could he have? He's 25 years old."

"Still. When I was his age, my apartment wasn't even fully furnished. He has monogrammed towels, and a wet bar, with vermouth, and cognac. *Cognac.*" He repeated the word with emphasis, as the director hadn't reacted when he said it the first time.

But the director continued not to react, appearing for all the world as though he was staring off into space, but he was looking intently at Stick.

Finally he responded, but apparently continuing his private train of thought, saying "Patriotic, too. Some of his papers from law school—very well-written. I never really thought a homosexual could be patriotic. No socialist leanings at all. Very free-market, pro-democracy. Very surprising, for a homosexual. You know?"

"I've really never given it a thought, chief."

The two men sat silently for several minutes as they watched the young man, dressed in what both men now separately regarded as his work costume—all of his clothes now seemed liked costumes. "Which symphony did he go to Saturday night?" the director asked.

"There's just the one, I think. The Atlanta Symphony. They were playing something by Ralph Van Williams, something like that. It's in the report. Thought it would never end." He crushed a cigarette on the park pavement with vigor, the memory of the interminable evening bringing fresh resentment.

The director's smile widened. "This is going to be easier than I thought. Our German banker was there, as well. Do all the fairies go to the symphony?"

"Mostly blue haired old ladies. But of the men there under 50, yeah, I would say most of them had a little more swish than swagger. Not exactly a place to meet a girl, anyways."

"Right." The director stood to leave. "We're going to make contact this afternoon. If all goes well, and I think it will, he will receive field assignments from you, and report back to you, and you only."

"Right."

***

The meeting went well, and Stick's first assignment, which lasted for the next two years, went even better. For the next three decades, he would continue to work for the C.I.A., long after his summer-blond good looks aged into maturity. The need for newer, fresher faces was endless, and he became something of an expert at picking out patriotic young men who could be relied on not to venture off into alcohol and drugs, who loved their country, and could keep their mouths shut and their legs open.

It was one of those young men who first introduced Stick to the community. The call came shortly into Stick's retirement, from a young man employed by a software developer for the National Security Agency who also worked for the C.I.A. on occasional short-term assignments overseas. Stick by then had relocated to New Orleans—his parents in Dublin were long dead, and the little family he had left were scattered through the southeast. Like so many good old southern families, they kept in contact mostly through email and Facebook.

The young man, named Alex Atkinson, was in his late twenties, and was not only a recruit but also a protégé of Stick's, one that he took a personal, almost paternal interest in. When Alex telephoned in mid-August 2005 and asked, *Can we meet? I need to talk to you*, Stick agreed immediately. It wasn't unusual for new agents to become uncomfortable with different aspects of their assignments—responsiveness to moral ambiguity was something the agency actually looked for, as an unwavering obligation to complete any assignment without question could lead to mistakes, should someone in the chain of command become compromised. For complex human assignments, they needed complex humans. This young man was one of them.

They met in a small private room Alex rented for the afternoon in a gay bathhouse in the French Quarter, with the weary pulse of decades-old disco music providing sufficient cover for their quiet discourse. Both men were wearing only towels, with their room keys on lanyards around their necks.

The scenario he presented to Stick took nearly two hours to explain. Alex had been the lead programmer on a proprietary software program code-named *Omnivore*. It worked somewhat like the web-based software that determines trending topics, but more like a data aggregator that calculates the most popular search terms across on a number of search engines. But the Omnivore was different in a number of ways—it included the data in private email accounts, along with text and images from websites the email user had accessed, and data and voice delivered through cell phones and even land lines. A simple sound, such as *um* or *er*, would be included as vital information, possibly providing a clue, a sign, or a code. Even the length of time between sounds, between texts, calls, and emails was measured and compared. And all of this was not only directed at perceived or potential enemies of the state, but everyone. Part of the rationale was that society at large provided the baseline against which aberrations could be determined—if the average American waited two seconds between any two given words and someone else—anyone else—spent four seconds, or eight seconds—that person became suspect. It was simple enough, from a technological perspective, but deeply troubling to Alex from a moral perspective. *This is not America*, he thought to himself at the time. "This is not America," he said to Stick.

"So what did you do," Stick asked, aware that the tone of the young man's story so far was not that of someone seeking permission, but forgiveness.

"I put in a kill pill," answered the young man simply, and then stopped, looking away from Stick.

"Well that's not so unusual, is it? I thought all developers left some backdoor into the software they developed so they could change it later without getting permission. Isn't that sort of common?"

"Yes, it is," Alex blurted out quickly, now, apparently getting to the point of the visit, "which is why they always look for it. But I went a bit further. I gave myself several back doors. One of them was found—and closed—by N.S.A. But the others weren't found until later. And they weren't found, still haven't been found, by the N.S.A. They were found by a group called *the community*. I think you'd be interested in what they're doing."

Alex explained what he had been doing for the community—simply providing technical expertise on potential situations the community might encounter while protecting certain vital assets of the United States. He had been recruited slowly and very carefully, he said. He knew he did not have full access to what the community did, but that was part of what gave him some mild comfort in what he was doing—not everyone in the community would even know there was someone providing the expertise he was giving.

"Why are you coming to me now?" Stick asked.

"Am I wrong? I don't know. I believe these people share the same values, and beliefs, and love for our country that I have—that we have—but sometimes when I think about the scope of some of the things that come up, just exactly what we're talking about—sometimes I wonder if it's actually another secret branch of the government. I know it's not though," he added quickly, at a sharp look from Stick. "None of the agencies involved would ever agree to this level of oversight, or disclosure, or whatever it is."

"Which agencies are compromised?"

"All of them."

Stick breathed in the stale bathhouse air, a warm mix of cologne, disinfectant, and sweat, and asked, "How deeply compromised are they?"

"I know what you were wearing on the day you were recruited. You looked great in that harness of yours, by the way," he added with a nervous smile. "I never knew you were into leather."

Stick ignored this, his face expressionless. "How do you communicate with them, this community?"

Alex had no idea if he was about to be turned in to his superiors for insubordination, or espionage, or treason, but he had taken it too far not to cooperate with whatever Stick suggested.

"This," Alex said, retrieving from a backpack what appeared to be an aluminum legal pad holder, but was actually a fully functioning laptop computer, the thickness of a typical weekly magazine.

"Impressive," Stick commented. He knew there were similar computers, or at least prototypes of them, all over the world, but he had not seen one personally—in 2005, few people had. "So how does it work?"

"Just open it. The current password is on the back of this bracelet." Alex took off a chunky stainless steel link bracelet that gave every appearance of being a medical alert bracelet, and turned it over. On the back of the smooth center metal panel where his name might have been engraved was a small LCD screen with a series of 12 numbers, letters, and symbols. "The password is regenerated every 60 seconds," he added, as Stick looked at the bracelet.

Stick entered the password on the laptop, and a scrolling list of topics appeared—the community's bulletin board system. But as Alex rightly guessed and explained to Stick, his access was limited—"I'm only invited to participate in subjects where I might have some knowledge, something substantial to add. I have a feeling that what I'm looking at is just the tip of the iceberg—literally the tiniest tip of it. The people on this list are smart. Really smart. Most of them much smarter than me, I think."

Stick didn't doubt that. He had seen Alex's testing, and while the young man was clever, and well above average, and a computer programming wizard, he did not have big-picture capacity. He lacked imagination—one of his few failings as an agent. He could follow directions perfectly, but deviations from a planned scenario often resulted in something just short of chaos. He wondered why they had chosen Alex as he scrolled down through the topics.

"Why do you think they chose me?"

"I don't know," Stick answered. "What network is this connected to?"

"I don't know for sure. I'm almost certain it's a satellite. And a good one—the connection is constant. Anywhere on the planet, this thing works."

"I see. Talk to me a little more about how you were contacted."

"Someone I went to school with was responsible for investigating the Omnivore software for the community. When they saw the number of back doors and kill pills I included, they did an assessment, and decided I might make a good recruit. After a series of secure meetings, I was given this laptop and this bracelet, and was told I would never have personal contact with the community again."

"The community? You mentioned that before. Is that the group's name?"

"No. I don't think so. I don't think there is a name. That's just how a few people have referred to it in postings. It sort of stuck in my head."

The topics of the subject lines Stick was reading were at once arcane, specific, and diverse: *Northeast Power Coordinating Council Redundancy Nodes, Intermodal Transport Load Variances, Submarine Transport and Docking, Turbidity Currents and Submarine Slumps; NTSB Bridge Data.* It went on and on for screen after screen as Stick scrolled down. As he randomly clicked on a topic, *Van Allen Radiation Belt*, he saw dozens of entries, and clicking on one entry, he saw hundreds of lines of discussion.

"Do you know about these things? I've never heard of a Van Allen Radiation Belt." Stick did not necessarily think of himself as smarter than the Alex, but the breadth of what he was looking at he felt was beyond both their abilities.

"Well, no, but I don't know that that's exactly the point. I don't believe topics are posted for idle speculation—there's usually some actionable outcome, or at least a potential for action, or a decided inaction, for every posting. This one, the Van Allen Radiation Belt, is there because, or at least I think because, the community uses an older satellite to house its servers and communications. The Van Allen Radiation Belt consists of these layers of atmospheric radiation that cause deterioration to satellites that pass through them. So this discussion board is about the necessity of transferring data and communication abilities from one satellite to another at a specific point in time. I think because the community's current satellite will fail, at some point. The discussion is about establishing a redundant satellite but not activating it until close to the time the current satellite fails. It never actually says it's the community's satellite."

"So your part in the discussion is really about how long it would take to transfer the data and communication abilities, and nothing to do with the radiation belt itself?"

"Right. There are other people, atmospheric guys, discussing those things."

"But that information you're providing could also be used to take control of another satellite, steal its data, shut it down?"

"Possibly." Alex tried to inject some uncertainty into his voice, but it didn't work—they both knew it could be done.

Stick clicked on one of the more technical looking postings and saw strings of scientific jargon and equations that meant nothing at all to him. He closed it, and looked for entries by Alex, then realized he didn't know Alex's username on the discussion board.

"What name do you post under?"

"They assign them. I'm Lisa Simpson."

Stick smiled, despite himself.

"Don't laugh. Adonis was already taken. Literally. They started with the names of mythological figures, at least I think they did, then they went to great artists, then musicians, that sort of thing. When I got recruited, they were using cartoon names."

It took a couple of minutes of clicking around to find a posting of Alex's.

"What do these highlighted words mean?"

"They're links to Annopedia, it's the wiki of the community."

"What does that mean, Annopedia?"

"I don't know. It's actually not referenced on any of the pages I have access to."

"How did you come across my name? My clothes? From 1970?"

"For a while in the 1970s you were what is called a Person of Interest, or POI, to the community. There was a storm in your hometown, and a lady who would become important to the community called you for assistance. For a while after that, they were monitoring you to see what connection you might have to whatever it is that was going on there. After a while, they stopped monitoring you, but whenever they get more data, it gets added in, updates to inactive files, you know."

"Yes, but," Stick began, then paused, trying to measure out how far the laptop he was holding extended back in time, and out in scope. "They've been around this long, this community?"

"I don't know if there were a hundred of them, or a hundred thousand of them, then or now. Somewhere in between, I would guess. But yes, I think they've been around for decades."

"But still, how did you come across my name? Did you search for it?"

"Oh, no, not at all. I was working on something related to the agency, and when I went to the C.I.A. Annopedia page, there was a list of every known C.I.A. operative. Every single one, probably, I think organized by date of first employment. Most of them it's just a link back to their agency files, but a few others are marked with one asterisk, some others marked with two. Yours is marked with one. The ones that are marked with two have links to files I don't have access to. I think they're part of another agency. Something higher-up. Something black budget."

"I need to sleep on this. I need to think about this." He paused before lifting up the laptop and asking "Can I borrow this? Can I take it with me?"

Alex had been expecting the question, and he knew that he could not refuse. He dug in his backpack and found the laptop's case and power supply, and handed them to Stick. "Of course. I will feel a little naked without it, to be honest."

Stick laughed. "You are a little naked."

"Right."

For a moment there was only the sound of violin-heavy disco thrumming through the space, and the smiles faded from the men's faces as they both came to the same inevitable conclusion of their conversation.

"I can't promise I'm going to return it. I may have to hand it in. You understand that, don't you?"

"I do. I want to do the right thing." In that moment, the needful expression of a child took over the young man's face, alight with regret, and fear, and the overwhelming need for absolution.

"I know you do." Stick stood to leave. He wished there were words of comfort he could offer the young man sitting before him—somehow more naked in his towel than he would have been without it—but any words of reassurance would have been a lie, and they both knew it. He wanted to be kind, but more than that he wanted to be honest. Not knowing what else to say, he said only "I'll be in touch," and closed the door behind him.

***

Two weeks later on a Saturday afternoon, as Stick was getting organized for the rapidly approaching Hurricane Katrina, which would be his first hurricane encounter, he retrieved the community laptop from the downstairs closet where he had left it untouched since getting home with it, and prepared to take it with him in the event he decided to evacuate. He had a freestanding home on Esplanade Avenue in the French Quarter, built in 1892, which had survived a couple dozen hurricanes, according to the realtor, but he still didn't think he wanted to be around for all the rain, even if the hurricane didn't hit. He had six tenants in four apartments just behind the main house, all hurricane veterans, and they weren't leaving, so he was waiting until the last minute to decide—he would just need to throw his things in the car. But, he had everything together in case he decided to stay—lots of bottled water, canned fruits and vegetables, crackers, batteries, lanterns and a camp stove.

The laptop had been sitting on the outer edges of his consciousness since he first received it, but he had not opened it. He had been considering, in the way he always considered things, what it meant, what it could mean, what it had meant for Alex. He had been waiting for a call from Alex to prompt him into action, into a decision, but the call hadn't come yet.

One of the things he had discovered over his long career, both in the Justice Department and in his work for the C.I.A., is that all intelligence has a cost. Whatever form it takes, whatever the method of delivery, there is always a cost. For the average person, and for the companies and organizations they collectively animate with their weak and limited humanity, sometimes the cost is just the loss of other intelligence—the name of a sixth grade history teacher disappears from memory as it is replaced unknowingly, irrevocably, with the name of a thesis advisor in college, or maybe later with the name of a coworker's child, or even later with the name of a grandchild. It is not only a problem of capacity, it is a problem of priority—who and what matters most.

He also believed strongly that people are task-oriented, and that successful multi-tasking is a myth. Not only that, he believed other people inherently believed it as well—in conversation on the topic, he would ask "Do you want your heart surgeon texting while he's operating on you?" to bring what he considered clarity and finality to any discussion of human ability to successfully perform multiple tasks simultaneously. With new agents, especially the younger ones, it was becoming increasingly difficult to emphasize the need for singular focus. But he understood it—it was one of several abilities that had enabled him to serve his country proudly, and well, for decades. And it was for that reason he wanted his mind absolutely clear when he sat down with the laptop—he knew it was important. It deserved his undivided attention, whether he decided to open it or not.

Whatever else it was, the laptop and the information it contained were incredibly valuable, and incalculably dangerous. The street value for the information on the C.I.A. alone was easily worth tens of millions, possibly hundreds of millions of dollars—if it was real. He felt that he could reasonably easily determine whether the information was genuine or not—at least the information about himself and a handful of others—but even that held certain risks. There was likely classified information relating to his file that he was not authorized to know. The fate of an Italian man he had lunch with in 1986, the whereabouts of a car he had once driven from Antwerp to Le Havre and left in a marina parking lot, the real identity of a man who had been introduced to him as *Nathan Nobody*—these were all loose threads that had crossed his mind over the years, and while likely not actually matters of any import, they were technically classified matters of national security. It was against the law for him to know, or knowingly seek out, that information. But as he walked up the stairs that Sunday evening, with dusk beginning to fall, barely discernible behind the darkening clouds, he knew that the time had come for him to decide: Stay, or go?

He had made it a practice throughout his life, drilled into him at an early age by his father, to do nothing when he did not know what to do, because tomorrow, he might know. There were very few decisions in life that required immediate action—most decisions, most actions, most conversations, most everything could wait another day. So he had waited until the moment of knowing, and in that moment, the certainty of action became as real as the laptop itself. He would stay in New Orleans, but he would leave the comfort of his restful, elegant, southern gentleman retirement. He planned to assess the laptop and the community it was connected to with the efficient, methodological approach he had used for decades. He would take his findings wherever it was necessary, but he would not end up like Alex—overwhelmed, indecisive, morally and ethically confused. He was older, wiser, and stronger.

***

He began cautiously enough, just as he had planned. In the end, it was the emotional detachment that lured him into the deep end from which he could not escape, even if he had tried.

The story of his life—almost the whole story, certainly more than he remembered himself—was told with the dispassion of a court recorder reciting the details of a violent murder, an insipid indifference he could not bear. He kept reading to see what someone, anyone, might actually find interesting. He kept on reading and clicking and reading and clicking, through the thunder and lightning and the sounds of things—who knew what, just things, tree limbs maybe, or flower boxes—slamming his home's clapboard siding with a dull thud, or against the storm shutters with a hollow vibrato—but the interest in his life that he was looking for never came. There were no exclamation points, not a single notation of amazement, or wonder, or even interest. He read through the night, but none of the external noises penetrated his internal engrossment. It was not until the power went off the next morning at 8:36am that he became really aware that there was a storm. Unable to peer out of his storm-shuttered windows, he opened his front door, and the Plexiglas storm door began rattling in its frame, speckled with rain despite being eight feet in from the roof line. The street before him appeared to have been washed away during the night, and a shallow black stream had taken its place. A forlorn, wet calico cat he had never seen looked up at him from his porch with suspicion. He shut the door and went back inside.

His intention when he turned on the laptop and put in the password had been only to confirm his personal information on the Annopedia page as Alex had described it, and not to look into his C.I.A. file, or any government file, at all. But the intoxicating effect of seeing page after page of text about him, his life, the people in his life, the people around, about, over, under, and through his life, was more than he had anticipated, or could ever have prepared for. It was only when the electricity went out, and his first impulse was to worry about how long the laptop's battery would last, that he realized how far in he had gone.

"Am I wrong," Alex had asked. Now, Stick felt he knew the answer. "No, you are only human." It was information Stick sometimes forgot to remember, but it sounded weak and insufficient, even to him. It was an excuse for anything, and everything, which meant nothing at all. He didn't feel wise, or strong—just old.

***

During the days after the storm, Stick was sometimes required to be away from the discussion board and Annopedia, but he disliked being physically away from the laptop, and usually carried it in its case in a backpack. He wore the bracelet that came with it at all times. When he was grilling out with the neighbors, or standing in line for more fuel for the generator that kept the air conditioning going and the laptop powered up, he would absently rub the bracelet as though it were an amulet. He would take furtive glances at the bottom of it to confirm it was still generating passwords. He considered taking the bracelet apart to see how it was powered, but decided it was not worth the risk—he would replace the battery or whatever it was when the time came.

It was two weeks and two days after he had first opened the laptop when it finally happened. Stick woke on that Tuesday and began his new morning ritual. He poured his small glass of orange juice, set the four-minute timer for his French press coffee, and put one of his favorite morning concerts on the stereo—the pianist William Kapell playing in a 1951 performance of Rachmaninov's *Rhapsody on a Theme of Paganini in A minor*. It was upbeat, but not overwhelming.

The coffee ready, dry wheat toast on a porcelain plate, cloth napkin over his silk robe, he sat at the kitchen table, opened the laptop, and put in the password. For the first time, it did not work. He re-entered it on the off chance he had entered it wrong—though he knew he hadn't. He waited for the next password to appear on the bracelet, and when it did, he entered it, and got nothing.

He could see his reflection in the monitor glass. His eyebrows were furrowed, too dramatically for 7:30am, and the corners of his mouth were turned down in a way that reminded him of his mother. *That face isn't going to help anything*, he told himself, relaxed his features into something more like how he liked to see himself, and raised a piece of toast to take a bite and think about his options—he knew even before thinking there wouldn't be many, or any, really, as he had been through this scenario in his head dozens of times since he had first logged in. But before he could get the toast to his mouth, a voice came from the laptop—a surprise, since he didn't know it had a speaker.

"Good morning Stick," it said. It was a man's voice, baritone bordering on bass, without any accent at all—just American. Stick held the piece of toast before his open mouth, afraid to move, afraid to breathe. He looked at his reflection in the monitor, the word *Password* blinking on his forehead.

A woman's voice came out of the laptop. "You may as well eat your toast. This is going to take a while, Stick."

"Don't even think of closing the laptop," the man added.

It sounded to Stick as though the man and woman were in different rooms, maybe different places, but he couldn't tell for sure. "No, of course not," he said aloud. He took a bite of the toast. He was no longer hungry at all—fear was stretching his skin at the seams—but he did not want that to show. He put the remaining toast back on the plate.

"Before we start," the woman asked, "I would like to ask, we would like to ask, what is it you think you've been doing? I mean to say, we know what you have been doing. We've gone back and reviewed every minute you've spent on the laptop. We know what you know that we know. But to what purpose? To what end?"

The man continued, "The idea that you were doing anything noble or self-less disappeared within ten minutes of you being in our system. So what is your objective?"

Stick sat looking at his reflection, and he had no answer—he did not know.

The woman's voice began again. "We can disconnect the laptop, disconnect you, from us, permanently, and immediately. The box you're looking at doesn't have a hard drive, per se. It stores no data—none. It has no way to connect to us—we connect to it. There's no identifying mark on it or in it. Either you give us a satisfactory answer right now, or you're going to become the owner of a very expensive paperweight."

There is a right answer was Stick's first thought. He didn't know what it was, exactly, but he knew it had to be the truth. He was smart, but not smart enough to lie to these people convincingly.

"I don't know," he began, watching his face as he knew they were watching his face, hearing his voice as they would hear it, "I don't think I had an objective.

I got…" he watched his face crumple in confusion as he searched for the word, "lost." He saw the expression of surprise register on his face, unplanned, as the word fell, like a crumb, from his lips.

The silence from the laptop seemed to come at him in waves that were somehow synchronized with his breathing. He felt suddenly, and surely, that the man and woman were in a room together. They were talking about him. They were looking at him. He wondered for the first time where the camera was. In the computer? Yes, he felt certain, there was a camera behind the monitor screen.

"I want to help," he blurted out. "I want to help you."

"What is it you think we do?" the man asked, his voice somehow amused.

"Why do you think we need, or would want, your help?" the woman added before he could respond.

"You collect and analyze information. I've spent my entire adult life doing that. If you can use Alex, you can use me. I can do this. I'm not as sophisticated with the technology—I know that, obviously. But I can think help. You know that from my files. And I've thought more in the past two weeks than I have in years. I feel… alive again." And he looked alive again. He could see it in his reflection—his eyes were animated in a way he had not seen them in decades. Most importantly, he saw truth in them, and he was almost certain that was what the people watching him would see, as well.

"What about Alex?" the man asked.

Stick answered almost immediately, "Is there some reason we couldn't both, independently, continue to work on—" he stopped, not knowing how to finish the question. It felt suddenly like a trap, and it was, but not the one he thought.

The woman answered his question, her voice sarcastic and weary, yet forceful. "The reason you cannot continue working with Alex is because we believe him to be dead. As does the city of New Orleans and the Federal Emergency Management Agency. And the C.I.A., and the N.S.A., and the community itself. His name is on dozens of websites of missing people, but you haven't looked for, or even tried to call him. You've been so *lost*," she spat out the word with undisguised contempt, "that you haven't lifted a finger to find your friend. Your protégé." She took in a breath, then continued. "We are many things, Mis-ter Strick-land," she said, in four overly-long syllables, "but we are not unkind. And we do not abandon our friends, or colleagues. Even those we have never met. We've been searching for Alex. The community has been looking for him, and two other of its members, for the past two weeks. What have you been searching for?"

The community, he thought. "Answers," he said aloud. And then he watched on the monitor as a smile slid onto his face, and he added, "But you're wrong about Alex. He may have gone underground. Off the radar. Out of the country. The pressure of all this may have been too much for him. I may have scared him. But he is not dead. I know him. I trained him. He isn't dead. I never considered it before, and I won't consider it now."

Silence. A wall clock in his kitchen measured out the void in staccato clicks.

And then, a change in tone. A shift. The man's voice returned, softened, and with a shadow of what sounded like relief, he spoke again through the laptop, but as a friend. "Well, Mr. Strickland, welcome to the community."

"On a temporary basis," added the woman, whose distrust of him was plain in her tone—she had not agreed. "You may continue to dig around as much as you like. We will have you under continued surveillance."

"To answer your question from before about you and Alex, you do lack his technical expertise, but you are not being actively surveilled by anyone, which he has been, 24/7, since you began recruiting him."

"They don't trust him," the woman's voice said matter-of-factly, the aggression all but gone. She apparently hoped she had made her point.

"But they trust you. They have for years now. We could never have had this conversation with him. They have ears everywhere."

"But not so many eyes?" Stick questioned.

"Right. In any event," the man's voice said, with a tone that suggested the conversation was coming to a satisfactory close, "you will find the discussion boards and topics available to you on Annopedia more suitable to your experience and knowledge than what Alex has been seeing and working with. Except for your own file, of course. That file, at least for now, will be locked for you. I'm sure you understand." He sounded genuinely sorry to be sharing the news.

"And," the woman added, almost cheerfully, "If you could spend some time in Annopedia reading and updating Dublin, especially going back to the big storm, 1974, the community has a special interest in that, for some reason" the woman added, in an offhand tone meant to suggest it was a throwaway request. Stick immediately realized the reason the laptop was not already just a paperweight—he could give them firsthand information and perspective they could get from nowhere else. It all went back to Dublin.

"We'll be in touch," the man's voice said. "Goodbye."

"Goodbye," added the woman's voice.

"Goodbye," Stick said aloud, not knowing whether or not anyone heard, but knowing at least that his words were being recorded, somewhere, and that someone, now or later, would review them, would watch him.

He looked at the bracelet again, and entered the password shown there into the blinking box on the screen. With a blessed sense of relief, he saw the box disappear, and the scrolling list of the discussion board appear. At the top of the list was Dublin.

***

In the beginning, it did all go back to Dublin. For the first six months, he dutifully created entry after entry after entry, all from memory, all about Dublin, all radiating out from the year 1974. Much of the heavy lifting had already been done—the names and locations of businesses, schools, families, churches, and parks—most everything—had already been meticulously laid out onto a digital map of the town, and then, somewhat incredibly, the entire town, every building in it, was built as a three-dimensional model. When, and by whom, and for what purpose, there was no mention of—just a link from the Annopedia page to *Dublin, city model*, that he happened to click on. Some of the individual building models were just three-dimensional boxes, while others were incredibly detailed, with fully-articulated architectural elements such as windows and doors. Some even had furnishings. The home he grew up in was just a box, but he was able to open every door and window of Moore Street Elementary School. And the city model as a whole could be made to change over time. There was a software feature that allowed Stick to establish a camera location and view, and dates and times, to create a time-lapse video of pretty much anywhere in the incorporated town. He could see the Oconee River Bridge being built, and destroyed, and rebuilt, three times, from any streetcorner or building window, or random X,Y,Z coordinate where he placed himself in the model. He liked playing with it for the first few hours after he discovered it, and thought it was great fun, but could not imagine the purpose of it. He began to wonder if someone, somewhere, was watching him playing with the map in the same way a parent might watch an infant playing with a television's remote control, grasping the basic mechanics of the thing, but nothing more, not the context, not the meaning of the sounds or pictures. He felt the answer was *Yes*, and stopped, and went back to work.

His enlargement of the Dublin files quickly began to take on a life of its own, becoming a wiki within a wiki, the embedded links growing and crisscrossing with dizzying speed and complexity. He tracked down friends he hadn't spoken to in years, on the premise he was using his retirement years to write a memoir. He made his notations of the sources of the new material, and the map, which had been a stagnant digital ghost town, seemingly abandoned just after 1974, came alive with the collective memory of Stick's friends and relations, and their friends and relations.

He waited some time before he called the young woman he helped get into the University of Georgia, and Emory University's School of Law. She was, after all, a sitting federal judge. He knew basically nothing about the black community in Dublin, from 1974 or any other time. It was a gaping hole in the community's

396

understanding of the town—if anyone in the community was actually observing his work. He sometimes wondered. But she owed him a favor—a lifetime of favors, really. But they were friends, and friends don't count favors. At least, not out loud. He had helped her navigate the political system when she first graduated law school. She learned quickly and well, and advanced further than he had ever imagined, but still, she owed him. So he called her.

He didn't like lying to her, and wasn't very good at it, either. His decades of spy work had not taught him how to lie to a shrewd, intelligent, perceptive friend. After he tried introducing the topic of Dublin in 1974, and explained he was writing a book, she stopped him without even a hint of apology and asked abruptly, "What is this bullshit? What are you really up to?"

"I better not say. You're right. Never mind," he answered meekly, humbled. She owed him a lot, it was true, but he owed her the truth. He could not, would not lie to her. They only spoke a few times a year, and he would not spend that time lying to her.

Stick's suspicion that his work was being monitored by the community was confirmed one day about eight months after he first signed in as himself. He was told, quite simply, to stop work. He was being moved on to other assignments.

From there, he moved quickly up the ranks, or at least felt he was advancing. He first became involved in the logistics and execution of complex assignments, then part of creative development teams that drew specifically on his experience as an intelligence officer, and finally as part of a select group—at least, he felt it was a select group—of former intelligence agents who spoke regularly to discuss strategy. None of them ever knew the others' names, or locations, or any other identifying information. He did not know, with any certainty, that the men and women he spoke with were ever actually agents like he had been. But based on the way they spoke, and how they communicated, more so than the information itself they shared, he felt it to be so.

He never knew fully, really, how interested the community was in Dublin until he received a call letting him know that in four days Carrier 1623 would be taken into shrouding, and that he, Stick, would be responsible for debriefing him.

"On what? Debriefing him on what?"

Michael had been introduced to the community years earlier, but he, like everyone else, was only aware of what he needed to know when he needed to know it. Now, he needed to know more, and Stick was the person who told him. Stick had helped on the design of the vehicle he knew as the *Shroud* but which Michael would soon begin calling the *trolley*.

Over the next 24 hours, the life of Carrier 1623, a person known to the wide world as *Michael Isaacs*, was explained to Stick in more detail than he could have imagined before he joined the community. Michael was a person who existed in Stick's mind only as the vaguest of memories, an aside in one of the many stories that came out of Dublin after the storm. There had been talk—whispers—of a lynching, of Eleanor taking a child away, of a government conspiracy. But Stick was already living in Atlanta, living his own life apart from the smallness of Dublin. His capacity for caring about a child he had never seen or heard of before, in a place he didn't live anymore, was about the same as anyone else's might be—very little, even in passing. But he learned, and learned to care, quickly.

What he learned frightened him. He had never believed in any sort of anything *out there*. He wasn't even sure what out there meant to him. He hadn't not believed—he wasn't an atheist, or an agnostic, but he wasn't a believer, either. He was a Christian, sure, but in the same way he was white, that he was male, that he was a homosexual, that he was Southern, that he was American—he never really chose to be a Christian, it was a part of who he was, how he was raised. It was more of a habit, a lifestyle, than a choice.

The Mollies, the atmospheric anomalies, changed all that. Before he spoke to Michael, he looked at the evidence that would be shown to Sam, and Callie, and Josh later, and he saw... something. The something *out there* turned out to be something *right here*, something that some—but not him, not Stick—could see. And they were something that one person, and possibly only one, could talk to, or communicate with. He had the gift, or the curse, or the talent, of language. That one person was Michael. And Stick could talk to him, and he did talk to him, and he believed.

He wasn't sure what he believed before he joined the community, but now he believed what the community believed, and he believed what Michael had eventually told him.

After spending a day with Michael showing him the features of the rolling shroud, already moving down the interstate, well on its way to its first scheduled refit with Michael aboard, Stick had asked him the question that no one and nothing in the community had been able or willing to ask him. "What is it you know?"

Michael looked at him and said simply, "It's coming." His smile was benevolent and trusting, warm and encouraging.

"What's coming?" Stick's mind hit a wall. All of the possible answers a court clerk or government agent might have to this question seemed laughably wrong, feeble, and small.

"You know," Michael's smile widened. "Everyone knows. The answer is inside us. It's all around us. It's almost time. We have to get ready. That's all."

That answer, entirely unsatisfactory to Stick, was still all that he received. And it made him thankful that he never brought his young friend Chari into the community. She would not have understood. She would not have believed.

CHAPTER 10. LUCY

The interior of Applied Logistics Distributors looked like the interior of any state-of-the-art automated distribution warehouse—fully mechanized with a robotic retrieval and packing system that allowed the products coming into and leaving the building never to be touched by human hands. This particular distribution center was different from most regional distribution centers in that it was entirely refrigerated—Applied Logistics had a separate dry goods facility just a few blocks away.

As she sat looking through the pseudo-windows of the cargo container's interior out at the apparently surgically-clean warehouse, Callie wondered indistinctly if the exhaust from the trolley would contaminate the food in it. Her yogurt, which she had been eating much too quickly, suddenly seemed less appetizing. She put it down and returned to sipping on her espresso, which Trevor had prepared for her when he was notified that she was awake. She had already changed into the Applied Logistics Distributors uniform he provided her, and she did not like it—a knit polo shirt with the company logo, and khaki trousers, and both were synthetic blends, which she despised. The black sneakers were horrible, and used, and she was looking down at them trying not to imagine their previous owner as she waited for Trevor to return.

He found her in the study, where they had been talking the night before, and he was also dressed in an Applied Logistics Distributors uniform. "Aren't you a little conspicuous," she asked. "Are there many Indians in Connecticut?"

"I don't know, honestly. But Applied Logistics is a wholly owned subsidiary of Eko Global Industries, one of the larger military suppliers. Everything from butter to bullets. We'll have a barcode on the side of the delivery truck. We won't need identification. We aren't really us—we're Eko Global employees, which in most cases means ex-military."

"It's a little scary, isn't it? Being on the island with no way off except the ferry?" Callie asked after a moment, distracted, apparently not very interested in the population of Connecticut or of Eko Global.

"The ferry is our best way off, not the only. Contingencies for contingencies, remember. You don't have to remember the whole plan, or even part of it. You'll have this earpiece in the whole time. There will be someone telling you what to do every step of the way." He held a small piece of transparent silicone out to her. She could see tiny wires and a small circle of mesh embedded in it. She took it, and turned it over in her hands, rolling it like a small pebble.

"Then let's not go over it," she said with a shrug of her shoulders, and turned her head back out to the view of the warehouse, where she saw a metal arm in the distance move a pallet of what looked like a million crated eggs.

"What?" Trevor was surprised. "Why not?"

"If I'm supposed to be following what people are telling me to do, it doesn't make any sense to be trying to remember a plan I'm not following. I should just be using my eyes and ears, yes?"

"Well, just in case," he suggested encouragingly, though halfheartedly.

"Just in case what? If everything goes to hell, we're just fucked, right? I don't want to remember contingencies of contingencies. If the earpiece goes out, my plan is to swim like hell. It's an island, right?"

"I see your point. I'll go get your weapons."

He returned not just with weapons, but also with Josh and Michael. She barely noticed them, her attention focused on the guns instead. But even from her brief glimpse of them, she could see neither man looked like he had slept much, which neither had. Trevor laid down the guns and holsters on the bench beside her before going into the truck's refrigerated cooler to get breakfast for the other two.

The next twenty minutes were uncomfortably tense. At one point Josh asked her if she was ready, in an overly-pointed kind of way, and she looked back at him in amazement and disbelief, and asked back, "Ready for what? To kill someone? To die? To get my hair done?" And then she looked away. After that, no one asked any questions or talked about what was about to happen, until it was time to happen.

Michael, who had been fiddling around with a laptop, stood up and activated a monitor where one of the views to warehouse had been. "Okay, our shots are in place."

"Shots?"

"Shooters. Snipers. Lookouts. Whatever. I'm not entirely sure what all they're supposed to do, or be, but they're in place. And our cameras are live. Here's the island," he swept to a block of twelve video images at the top of the screen. "Here's the ferry." He pointed to two monitors just below. There were 20 or so other video images playing at the bottom of the screen, which Michael didn't reference. All of the exterior shots appeared to have static.

"What are those?" Josh asked, pointing to the video images at the bottom of the monitor. They showed a variety of cars, trucks, doors, gates, driveways and windows.

"Locations of backup plans. Callie, I need to get your earpiece in. Trevor, can you do your own?" Michael was all business. "You leave in six minutes."

"Why six minutes? What about traffic?" Josh asked.

"Traffic is being monitored remotely. The ferry is waiting on us. We will be arriving on the island just in time to board the 1:00pm ferry."

"Why is there so much static?" Callie asked.

"It's not static, it's rain," Trevor answered with a shrug. "Lots of it. There's a major storm going on out there right now. Thunder, lightning, etc. We're in an insulated truck in an insulated warehouse—when we get on the ferry, we're going to feel it."

"Is this good or bad?" Josh asked, his brows furrowed.

"Good," Trevor and Michael both answered at once.

"Test Callie," Michael called out to the ceiling, and at once Callie heard a woman's voice—not the British Airways lady, but another—say gently in her ear, "Callie, please repeat the following sequence of numbers for confirmation. Ten, nine, sixteen, forty-two, seventy-six, twelve."

Callie said the numbers out loud, feeling more than a little foolish, since no one else in the room had heard the woman's voice giving her the command. Josh looked puzzled, but when Trevor recited a similar string of numbers immediately after, he seemed to get the idea.

"Ok, let's go," Trevor said, standing and walking towards the door to the refrigerated cooler, and the warehouse beyond.

"Do we have different people talking to us?" Callie asked as she slipped the shoulder holster with the tranquilizer gun around her arm, and clipped her own pistol, in its holster, to her belt, nestled along the base of her spine.

"Different teams," answered Michael, as held out the Applied Logistics Distributors rain jacket out for her to slip her arms in. When she was in, she turned to face him as she buttoned it up, hiding her weapons. She looked into his face, this man she barely knew, and saw a calmness she wished she could take from him, or at least share in.

"What am I doing? Have I lost my mind?" she asked aloud, and in her head she added *And who are you?*

"You're doing the right thing. And you have to go do it." Michael picked up a baseball cap with an ADL logo on it, but before handing it to her, he embraced her. It was sudden, and strange, and unexpected, but not unwanted. She felt she could stay there with him all day—it was the embrace of a big brother she never had. But he pulled away from her, and handed her the cap. Trevor was already out the door, and in the warehouse.

The voice in her ear began to speak, "Callie, we need you to get moving, if you're ready to go."

"Back soon," Callie said, and she raised her hand in what might have been the unfinished thought of a goodbye wave as she walked distractedly into the trolley's refrigeration compartment. She walked towards a rectangle of light that was a door in the side of the truck, and down a set of portable metal steps.

The voice in her ear said "Turn to your left and go around the back of the truck. Trevor is already in the white delivery truck. Get in the passenger door. Go into the refrigeration compartment immediately and close the door behind you."

She followed the directions, making momentary eye contact with Trevor, but saying nothing as she passed through the truck's cabin.

And then, all she could see were prepackaged, prepared, refrigerated foods, apparently for vending machines, nestled in trays stacked in racks along the walls. There were sandwiches of all sorts packed into triangular plastic wedges, some dismal looking oranges, pints of milk, juice boxes, fruit cups, yogurt, and Jello-O pudding and gelatin in a variety of flavors. She looked for and found a place to sit, a tire well cover that provided something like a bench, and she sat, just in time, as the truck lurched forward.

"Does he know how to drive this thing?" she mumbled aloud, grasping onto one of the racks for support. She hadn't expected an answer, but she received one. "He hasn't driven this truck, but he is proficient at driving standard transmission, yes."

Callie looked up and around for the cameras, but saw none. "Ok, thanks," she said quietly. The truck was moving and she could hear the rain begin to patter on the roof. She heard a crack of thunder, but she couldn't tell if it was far away, or if it was very close and the sound was muffled by the refrigeration and insulation.

"The cameras are in each of the four upper corners, Callie," the voice said. "You're doing just fine. We have a few minutes before we get to our destination. Are you sure you wouldn't like to review the plan?"

The woman's voice was comforting, encouraging. Alone in the cramped, strange space, so very far from home and everyone and everything she knew, she agreed to listen to the plan, just to hear the woman's voice.

It wasn't much more than an elaboration of what she had already heard—she suspected they were trying to keep her mind occupied, and give her confidence. She was grateful for their efforts. Each bump in the road, each turn, made her body react. She could feel spasms race down her arms, and though she tried to control them, the muscles in her face twitched involuntarily. She was a nervous wreck, and they could see it, and she didn't like it. She forced herself to talk.

"What's your name?" she asked, not knowing whether or not the woman could, or would answer, or do so honestly if she did.

"Call me Maggie," the woman answered.

"Nice to meet you, Maggie," Callie answered back, very much wanting the conversation to keep going. "Tell me, what's happening with Lucy right now? I'm not really concerned with getting in the house or stunning the doctors, but her mental state, Lucy. What's she like?"

"Your guess is as good as ours, Callie. Maybe better. How many drug addicts experiencing a euphoric high can or will say everything that's going through their minds? And how quickly can that change? We know she is very, very high, and almost certainly experiencing auditory and visual hallucinations. We know the Mollie population around her right now is extraordinary. There is a possibility you may experience it yourself, on some level, without really registering what it is."

"So the shadow people are there. Like, a lot of them?"

"You could say they're having a convention on that little island. And that's the goal, remember. That's why she's there."

"Right. How much longer 'till we get to the ferry." She forgot to add the inflection to make it a question, but received an answer anyway.

"Almost there."

"So this traffic control thing you guys do. How does that work? Is every traffic light hooked up to a computer now?"

"Traffic surveillance and automation systems are used in all of the larger cities, and in at least parts of smaller-to-medium size cities, and they allow us, or anyone interested, really, to change traffic flow. Even with older systems, if there is electricity being used to operate them, there are ways to control them remotely."

"Oh, cool," Callie said. She didn't think this was especially interesting—in fact, she was fairly certain she already knew it. But the idea that someone was actually using that technology in real time to get her from point A to point B was interesting, even under the circumstances.

"Tell me about yourself," Callie said, not knowing what else to say, but wanting to keep Maggie talking.

Maggie took the hint, and began describing herself. Callie learned that Maggie was a psychologist and former law enforcement agent with a specialty in crisis negotiation.

"So you're not really directing any of the action, you're just the voice in my ear reciting, but not deciding, what I need to hear to get from point A to point B?" Callie interjected at one point.

"Well, not really, no. I'm not reading a script. I'm looking at the information being put in front of me electronically by a team, and telling you what I feel you need to know. I just saw a red Honda Civic pass by you, heading south, but that wasn't important information, at least in my opinion, so I didn't share it. A colleague sent me a message a few minutes ago suggesting I tell you that if you want something to eat, you can just grab something from a tray, but it seemed irrelevant to me, so I didn't tell you."

Right, Callie agreed silently. *I would have just taken a sandwich if I wanted one.*

Maggie continued, "You are, however, about to be loading onto the ferry. Strictly speaking, the ferry driver can inspect the truck. He's an employee of the island. Having an unknown driver would generally make him more likely to inspect the truck, but not in the pouring rain. Personal comfort trumps national security, every time—especially when you think no one's looking. The water is a little rough, but nothing extraordinary. It might feel like the truck is floating in a bath."

That was exactly what it felt like just moments later, as after a few fits and starts, the ferry began moving. Maggie explained that Trevor would be making the usual three delivery stops at different locations on the island. Since it was raining, he would enter the refrigerator through the cab, and exit through the back with the necessary trays. At his third stop, she would be 40 yards from the entrance to the cottage where Lucy was being held. That is when she would exit the truck with him. Then she would have her six minutes.

With her back pressed against the side of the truck, she could feel the pistol pressing through the clothing, into her back. She had never shot at a moving target, much less a person, and she wasn't certain she could, if it came to that. She would, she knew, but she didn't know if her willingness and ability were aligned.

"Is there any risk of the tranquilizer causing any permanent damage?" she asked, as she felt the ferry coming to a stop. She felt the answer would be *No*, regardless of what the truth was. And, she was right—the answer was *No*. But her thoughts were on her real gun, the real bullets resting just along the curve of her spine.

It seemed like no time before the truck stopped and Trevor was passing through, taking an armful of trays and disappearing into the rain without a word. The rain swirled in in gusts—it was a real storm out there.

As the truck was slowing for the second stop, Maggie announced a change of plans. "Callie, we've decided to take the power on the island down, and the backup generators with them. The storm gives us enough cover to make it plausible. We're going to wait until you have the cottage door open, then all of the power on the island will go down. You'll still only have about five-and-a-half minutes to get Lucy in the truck, but that's enough."

"Why take the power down?"

"It's the best way to make certain they don't have video of your face. The longer it takes them to connect the dots, the better."

"Right. You're still going to be walking me through? You'll be able to see? With no lights?"

"We will be able to see."

"Will I be able to see?"

"There are emergency lights, one in each room, and floodlights by the front door. The sudden lighting change will disorient the doctors and give you another advantage."

"Another? What advantages do I have?" The truck was moving to the third stop.

"You have a long list of them Callie, and most of them you had before you ever stepped onto that truck. I've read your file. There are some people in the community who think you were made for this moment. I happen to believe you were made for much, much more. You're strong. You're smart. You have a capacity for caring in a way that helps others grow. You're special. This is strange, this new beginning, this yet-another new beginning, but I think this will be your best one yet."

"You don't think I'm going back to my life in Atlanta, do you?"

"I think you can have any life you want, Callie Pennington. But it's time. For Lucy. When Trevor opens the doors, get out. Turn left. The cottage will be 40 yards directly in front of you. Walk to the front door. Don't touch the handle until I tell you."

Trevor opened the door and walked past her, with barely a look in her direction. He was soaked. She followed him, and when he opened the doors, she got out, carefully navigating the slick metal. She walked purposefully towards the cottage, which she could barely see. Almost as soon as she thought *What happened to Maggie?* she heard her say "Perfect, keep going just as you are."

"Can you see a red light to the left of the door?" Maggie asked. Callie was 10 feet from the door.

"Yes."

"Do not touch the doorknob until it turns green or an alarm will sound."

"Ok." She kept walking.

"When you open the door, close your eyes."

The light turned green. "It's green."

"Open the door."

She closed her eyes, and opened the door. At once she heard the many sounds of mechanical and electronic systems stopping.

"Hello, is someone there?" She heard a man's voice call from down the hall of the cottage. It was interested, but not alarmed. She also thought she heard, just barely, the sound of a girl whimpering. *Lucy.*

Maggie urged her, "Open your eyes. Pull out the tranquilizer gun. Say out loud, *Maintenance.*"

"Maintenance," she called down the hall, her eyes adjusting rapidly to the contrast of the dim emergency lighting and the emergency floodlights.

"Walk down the hall, quickly. They are both in the room on your left at the end of the hall, as we planned."

"You might want to come back when we have some power," the man's voice called, and he was moving into the hallway, into the glare of the floodlights, which blinded him to Callie's weapon. And then she was on him, and she pulled the trigger, and the dart was in him, and he was down.

"Carl, is everything okay?" asked a woman's voice, startled, from the room the man had just left.

Maggie spoke with urgency, "Step over him, now, get her, now."

Callie hesitated because she was so surprised that a woman would be here, would be part of this. *What kind of woman?*, she thought to herself as she pulled the trigger, and the woman's expression of shock melted into unconsciousness, and she slumped to the floor.

"Perfect. Turn around, Lucy is in the room behind you."

She turned, and it was true. Lucy was in an oversized hard-plastic hospital bed from the early 1980s, more the size of a compact car than a bed. And she was strapped at her ankles and her wrists to the sides of the thing. And she was looking at Callie with a wild mixture of emotion that denied immediate identification, but which also belied a lack of likely helpfulness—Lucy appeared to be in no state of mind to be of any assistance in her own rescue. She was skeletal, swimming beneath a hospital gown, and looked barely alive, except for her eyes, which were darting around and behind Callie in terror. Her breathing was short and frantic, her chest moving in shallow waves as though she had just run a race.

"Say *Hello*, Callie, walk into the room, say *Hello*. Tell her you're there to take her away. You've got to get moving."

Before Callie could speak, Lucy did. "Is that you? Callie? Are you here? Are you real?"

"Yes, it's me. I'm here. I'm real. I'm going to take you away. I'm going to unbuckle these straps." She had walked to the bed, and was unsnapping the hard plastic buckles securing the straps.

"I'm cold. Can we go? Can we go?" Lucy's staccato speech was irritated, disturbed.

"Yes, of course. There's a truck outside. We're going. But you need to be very still so I can take out this IV."

Maggie spoke again, her voice soothing but insistent, "Callie you have to bandage that IV. It cannot be left open. The bandages are in the tall metal cabinet behind you."

No one had mentioned that the IV was a central IV going directly into Lucy's right atrium—Callie had been expecting to pull a tube out of Lucy's hand, not out of her heart.

"Lucy, I'm going to get some bandages, ok?"

Lucy nodded silently and pointed to the cabinet. Callie took off her jacket, turned and shook the residual rain off it, and handed it to Lucy. "Hang onto that," she said, and turned back and started digging through the many drawers. She quickly found what she needed and turned back to face Lucy. She tore four pieces of medical tape and attached them to a thick square of gauze.

"Ok, girl, you ready? This is going to hurt a little, ok?"

Lucy bared all of her teeth in a manic sort of smile that passed for affirmation, and Callie, terrified, bent in to begin.

"Just slide it out carefully. One quick pull. Keep your eyes locked on hers." The voice was steady and reassuring in Callie's ear.

Callie leaned in, and held Lucy's chin up to look into her eyes. "We're going to get through this, ok?"

Lucy could only mouth back, *Ok*, but she appeared more frightened than assured. And she pulled her elbows tight to her sides, and balled her hands into fists. Every part of her was trembling, and cold.

Their eyes locked together, and Callie slid out the tube with her right hand, and began applying the bandage with her left, and then, suddenly, Lucy's eyes left hers, and then Lucy was reaching behind her, and Callie felt her gun dislodging from the small of her back, and then she heard a shot, as loud as the end of the world, and she spun around just in time to see Trevor fall to the floor, his body jerking in spasms as blood sprayed from the hole in his chest. She was vaguely aware of more movement as Lucy threw the gun across the room, and it disappeared into the shadows, and suddenly Maggie's voice, urgent in her ear, "Go, Callie, go now. They'll have heard the shot. Get Lucy and go. Leave Trevor. He's dead."

And Callie could see it was true, or soon would be. And Lucy could see it was true. And the terror rising in Lucy's face told Callie she had to get control of her immediately, or she never would.

"Lucy, look at me, look at me," she forced the girl's eyes up from the man still dying on the floor, "Look at me, it's ok, but we have to leave, we have to go now, ok?"

Lucy struggled to form the word "Ok," and failed, but Callie took it for what it was—her best effort—and smiled at her. Lucy looked back down at the floor, though Callie was still holding her face, and suddenly, in the midst of his struggles against pain, shock, and even gravity, Trevor waved an arm dripping with blood in front of his face and said in a garbled whisper, "I can see. I can see them."

Lucy tried again to form the word *Ok*, like she had before, but she got stuck on the O, and began gasping, and her mouth formed a tiny O shape over and over again, a fish desperate for water, finding only air, and her eyes went somehow even wider than they had been, a width that seemed impossible on her small, fragile face.

"Good, here, put on this jacket. We're going to go." Callie ignored all of the obvious signs that she should not take the girl anywhere, and led her around the man, who was unmoving now, and moved back toward the front door of the cottage.

"Lucy, we're going to get in a delivery truck, ok. Can you sit in the back of truck? Can you be very still and quiet for me?"

Lucy nodded, and Callie could not see, but she felt the nodding movement.

"Good," she said as they went through the door, "let's go." And with that, they were in the rain, and walking toward the truck. There was some movement in the far distance, but she had no idea what the buildings were or who the people might be moving around them. She opened the passenger door and helped Lucy into the passenger seat. She walked around and got in the driver's seat, and found to her amazement and delight that the truck was still idling. She would not have to go back and check Trevor's pants for the keys.

"Put Lucy in the back, quickly." Maggie's voice was insistent.

Callie opened the door to the refrigerated unit, and urged Lucy in, holding her index finger to her pursed lips as she did so. Wide-eyed, and with some awkwardness, her limbs unused to moving, Lucy made it into the cooler and sat down. Callie smiled at her and shut the door. The smile fell from her face like an anchor.

"Now what?" Her teeth were gritted and she was just barely whispering.

"Drive. Slowly. Just follow the road for now, I will tell you when to turn. It won't be long. This road will take you straight back to the ferry. Ignore the people running around. They have no idea what's wrong yet. We still have time. That's good. Just keep going. Remember to breathe, Callie."

Callie was grateful for the reminder. She breathed, fully, deeply, repeatedly, before she heard Maggie say "Turn right at the next road. Here. A hundred yards and you'll see the ferry. Don't wait for the driver, drive onto the ferry."

Callie was pulling onto the ferry when the ferry boat driver came running over from the boat's cabin waving his arms.

412

"You see him?" Callie whispered into the cabin of the truck.

"Yes. Stun him. In the heart. Draw your weapon now. He's almost to the truck. Let down the window. Do it now."

Callie drew the tranquilizer gun from the shoulder holster, held it in her lap until he was at the window yelling at her, "Hey, lady, I don't know what you think you're doing—" and then she aimed directly at his heart, pulled the trigger before he saw what was happening, and he dropped like a stone to the ferry's concrete surface.

"Get out of the truck. There are two ropes securing the ferry. On your right. Untie them."

Callie did so, and the boat almost immediately began to be pulled out into the current, strong even in the small marina.

"On each side of the ferry, there are wheel chocks attached to chains that will keep the truck from rolling. Stick them under each wheel. The water's a little rough. We don't want you going overboard."

Callie managed to find the chocks, which were really just large triangular chunks of grooved rubber, and put one under each wheel. She jumped back in the truck, shut the door, and repeated the same question from before, "Now what?"

"The cabin is ahead of you. Go in now, close the door."

Callie groaned, opened the truck door and worked her way over the slick, moving deck to the ferry's cabin, regretting that she had not listened more carefully and asked for more details of the plan and the contingencies before—she was doubling back on herself when she should be frantically escaping. Once in the cabin, she barely had time to look at the controls around her, and determine that they were not unlike boats she had been on in the past, when instructions started to flow into her ear.

"There is a red button at the top left corner of the control panel. Push it in. The key should be in the ignition, turn it to the right."

Callie could feel the boat shudder and begin to tremble in the water. She looked up from the control panel to look out the window and could see only nothing.

The rain was washing in sheets over the ferry and the water, which she could not distinguish from one another. She knew the Long Island Sound and the Atlantic Ocean were surrounding her, but she didn't know which direction either was, or even where she was on the island—she had not, after all, watched the arrival of the ferry, she had been in the back where Lucy was now.

"Push the black throttle back just a little. All you have to do is make one sharp right to get out of the marina, and then you're making a beeline for Orient Point, the tip of Long Island. It's just a few minutes away. A car is waiting for you."

"What about the trolley?"

"It's pulling out now. The distribution center will be crawling with law enforcement in fifteen, twenty minutes, max."

Callie followed the instructions, and after turning the ferry what felt like 90 degrees, she asked "Is that enough?"

"Just a little more, and you're set. You're going to be shooting straight out between two jetties that serve as breakers for the surf coming into the marina. It's going to get a little rougher as you go through. Ok, stop, you're good. Pull the throttle and just keep moving straight."

How the hell can I tell if I'm moving straight? she thought, but answered her own question—either Maggie would tell her, or she would run into a jetty.

The change Maggie had described became palpable very quickly, and the boat began to roll and lurch.

"Is this safe?"

"Safe enough. You're holding it steady, that's the important thing."

It did not feel like she was holding it steady at all—it felt like she was trying to drive a bumper car.

"Should I go check on Lucy?"

"No, she's fine. She's putting on clothes now."

I don't remember seeing any clothes, Callie thought. Then aloud, "I don't remember seeing any clothes."

414

"They were in one of the trays," Eleanor responded, "But we need you to focus on getting the ferry to Orient Point.

"I can talk and drive at the same time. How does she know to look in the trays for clothes? Or to put them on?"

"She's talking to Josh. There is a communicator—it's like a phone, she can see him talking to her. It rang, so she answered it, and now he's talking to her. She recognized his face. She's comforted. The tip of Long Island is right in front of you. Can you see it?"

"No, I can't see anything."

"Well, it doesn't matter, there's been a change of plan. Make a sharp left. Ninety degrees, just like before."

After a brief pause in which she turned the boat's wheel, she replied, "Ok. Is that good enough?" She had never considered before just how much more mechanical boats were than cars—it took actual strength to turn the ferry's wheel.

"Yes, go straight ahead for just a few minutes here. We're going to East Hampton instead."

"Why? And why didn't I get a communicator phone thing?"

"You didn't get a communicator because you need your eyes open to what's in front of you. She needs one because she has just gone from one traumatic, alien environment into another one. We're going to East Hampton because the drones are on you."

"What drones?"

"A surveillance drone. There are hundreds of them, thousands really, up and down the eastern seaboard. The same ones we use for fighting in the Middle East. They're everywhere, watching everything. And right now, they're focusing in on you and that ferry you're on. You're not in any immediate danger—they want you both alive—but we have to get you off of that ferry and under the radar."

"What do I do?"

"Go ahead and open up full throttle. It'll be a little rough, but they're ready for you."

"Who's ready for me? Us? Who's ready for us?"

"You're going to be landing on the beach on Gardiner's Bay. It's on the north side of the island. There's a party that's been going on all night on Kings Point Road. There's a red Jaguar convertible on the road in front of the house. You're going to be driven to another house on the other side of the island. There's a safe room for you there. But first, we have to get you to Kings Point. You're almost there."

"I'm just crashing on the beach? Is that what you're telling me? That's the plan?" Callie was trying to keep the rising anxiety from her voice. The smallness of the ferry cabin, and her inability to see beyond it, was creating a sense of claustrophobia she had not experienced in almost 20 years. The increasing complexity of the unfolding plan added to what was beginning to feel like hysteria. She would not allow herself to think of the man they had just left, dead, behind them.

"Yes, you'll be totally fine. There will be a lurch, and you will have to be careful jumping onto the shore, but we've tested it. This will work."

How they could have tested crashing a federally-owned ferry onto a private beach was beyond her comprehension, but she felt the futility of arguing. "How much longer?"

"You're almost there. Bring in the throttle, slowly."

Callie did as she was told, and in a few moments, she could feel the scrape of the ferry as it touched the shore, then was pulled back out with the current, and the ferry started to turn.

"One sharp thrust, and you're there," came Maggie's voice, with some urgency. "Now."

Callie opened the throttle, a little too much, she realized quickly, as the ferry slammed onto the shore, and she was thrown into the wheel and her forehead smashed into cabin window. It took her a moment to get her bearings.

"Callie, are you alright? Callie, can you hear me? Callie, are you there?"

"Yes, yes, I'm ok," she said, realizing it was true as she said it. "How's Lucy?"

"She's fine. She's on deck now waiting for you. You have to move."

With one hand Callie reached for the door handle, and the other reached to her forehead, where she could feel a lump rising. The rain had diminished, but it was still coming down. She found Lucy standing at the front of the ferry, motioning her forward. She made her way towards her, and they both made their way down carefully from the slick deck onto the wet sand, as the ferry fishtailed in the surf behind them.

"Can you see the red umbrellas?" Maggie was back in her ear. Callie looked around and saw patches of red light in the distance.

"Yes, I think so."

"Walk towards them, quickly. Don't run. Lucy shouldn't be running. She has an earpiece in now. She will know what to do. Just walk. Now. Go."

Callie doubted either of them could effectively run in the wet sand, in any event. She looked down and saw Lucy's hand outstretched, fingers spread open, waiting for her. She looked through the rain into the girl's terrified eyes, entwined their fingers, and began walking. Lucy was shaking, but whether it was from the drugs, or the rain, or the excitement, or some combination, Callie couldn't begin to guess.

"Are you ok?" Lucy asked her, her voice tight and thin and dry.

"Yes, of course I am. And so are you. I'm so happy you're safe. We're almost done, I think," she answered. She didn't believe it was true, but it seemed useful to be hopeful.

The house was much closer than it had first appeared. She was just getting ready to ask for more direction when Maggie said "Keep walking towards the umbrellas, but not to them. Walk around the house. You're going to hear a loud bang and see a flash of light from the beach. Don't turn around, just keep walking. There will be a rush of people from the house to their cars. You will fall in with them. You'll disappear into the crowd."

As they neared the steps leading up to the house with the umbrellas, a familiar rhythm could be heard distantly, through the rain. As they approached the steps, Maggie instructed "You go first, Lucy will follow." She let go of Lucy's hand with a squeeze, and began.

The short flight of wooden steps opened onto an immaculately manicured lawn, where a few smokers were gathered beneath one of the red umbrellas. "Keep walking, they won't notice you," Maggie urged her on, Lucy now back by her side.

Massive windows designed to overlook the bay provided a perfect picture of the scene inside, not unlike hundreds of parties Callie had been to, or been taken to, or from, in her life. There were people there—hundreds of them, upstairs and down, skirts impossibly short, heels improbably tall, bodies pressed comfortably together—and their forced laughter spilled out through the open kitchen door. As Callie and Lucy passed the corner of the house, close to a thick hedge row of privet, she could make out the lyrics of the song—Debbie Harry, singing *Now you see what you wanna be, Just have your party on TV*.

"Cover your ears, quickly." Maggie's voice was insistent. In her peripheral vision, Callie could see that Lucy had received the same command. Both covered their ears, and at once the ground beneath them shook, and their jittery silhouettes were traced in a bright flash of red-orange light on the side of the home they were passing. They could hear screams from inside, and felt through their feet the herd of people as they began to jostle one another on their way away from the home that was soon to be a crime scene.

"Keep walking. The red Jaguar is just in front of you. Walk around the car, get in the rear door."

Callie made eye contact with Lucy before she walked around the car. People were buzzing all around them now, and in the distance they could hear sirens. Both of them got in the car and sat, waiting, silent, holding hands, watching as the orange flickers of flame were beaten down into flickers by the rain and surf.

"It was just the ferry. No one in the house is hurt," Maggie said in her ear. "You should both remain silent. Your escort is approaching. Say nothing."

Callie wondered about the fate of the ferry captain she had tranquilized, then realized she wasn't even sure if he was still on the ferry when they landed on the beach.

A young man opened the driver's side door, a young woman the front passenger door, and without any acknowledgement of the two women in the back of the car, the Jaguar took off down the road, joining a stream of cars that dispersed quickly along the many quickly intersecting roads and streets connecting the far end of the island. They found themselves moving down Accabonac Road towards East Hampton. Two fire trucks passed them, moving at substantial speed, their sirens swallowed up in the rain that seemed to pound the car down into the road. The car turned onto Abraham's Path, and Maggie's voice came alive in her ear again.

"In about two minutes the car will stop and you'll get out under a covered carport. Just stand there until the car drives off and is out of sight."

Two more turns and the car was on Further Lane. The car stopped at a gate nestled in a massive hedge stretching as far into the rain as they could see. The gate opened, and they were down a drive, then under the carport.

"Get out, now. Not a word."

Callie and Lucy looked at each other, opened their doors, and stepped out into the carport, deep in shadow, but dry.

The Jaguar made its way back down the driveway, and through the gate.

"Turn around, there is a pool in the yard behind you. There is a pool house to its left. There are double doors on the front, go in. Go, now."

As she turned, Lucy turned, and the two walked together towards the edge of the carport. The rain was finally not pounding anymore, and the beginnings of sunlight were beginning to peak through.

"Hurry. Go. Now."

They went, carefully navigating the walkway of slick slate pavers, made their way to the pool house, and Callie opened the doors.

"Down the hall, quickly, there's a bathroom on the right, second door on the right."

Making their way around overstuffed floral furnishings, the two made their way down the hall and into the bathroom. The light came on automatically as they entered. As Lucy closed the door behind them, a mirror that took up the opposite wall began to slide back into the wall, revealing a narrow, well-lit passage.

"In, quickly, now, and down the stairs. Carefully. Let Lucy go first."

Once they were in the passage, the wall of glass slid closed behind them.

"You're safe now." Maggie's voice sounded surprised at hearing itself say the words.

Certain her voice would be masked by their steps as they descended the concrete stairs, Callie ventured to ask in a whisper, "How close were we?"

"Very. They found the gun. They already ran the prints. They know it was you. They're hot. But you're safe. Lucy's safe. Thank God for the rain. There's a doctor waiting for you both at the foot of the stairs. We're waiting on word from him before we decide to transport Lucy. I'm signing off."

"Thanks," Callie whispered. She wasn't sure if anyone had actually tried to kill her, but it felt as though someone had. That someone still was. *It's been years since anyone's tried to kill me*, she thought, and smiled at how strange it was to be someone that people had tried to kill over and over again. And even though her streak of non-violence had ended, she somehow felt comfort knowing that there was, at least some purpose.

At least, she hoped so.

***

Within minutes, both women were in warm, soft clothing, their hair towel-dried, and each had a Coca-Cola. The room they were in was small, and looked like nothing more than an at-home office, though it had more computers and monitors than usual. The man who greeted them introduced himself as Steve, and he looked like a Steve—unexceptional in every way. He explained that he was there to make certain they were both alright, and asked each woman a series of questions, and

420

took a series of measurements. He took out two syringes and explained to both women that the syringes contained lorazepam and haloperidol, and would help ease Lucy's transition from her high, but that she would still be awake, and he asked permission to administer the drugs. Lucy looked to Callie, who nodded. Lucy sat in one of two upholstered club chairs, and grimaced as the needles entered her nearly-translucent skin. Callie pulled her chair over closer to Lucy's, and held her hand, which was clammy and wet. A small electrocardiogram machine sat on a table between them, and the numbers were disturbingly high.

Callie began telling Lucy about Mama Ben, and how much he missed and wanted to see her, just to have something to say, and Lucy began to cry, very quietly, and very slowly, and so Callie stopped talking, but Lucy encouraged her to go on, so she did. She talked about the preparations for the New Year's Eve party at the Galano Club, and how excited everyone was going to be that she was ok.

"You didn't believe I ran away, did you? They said you did."

"No, I never believed it." Callie lied, wanting it to be the truth. She clasped Lucy's hand again, more tightly, and felt the chill racing through the girl's veins.

"Are you cold?" and then before Lucy could answer, "Can we get a blanket?"

Within just a few minutes Lucy's demeanor began to change. She stopped shaking. She asked for water, which she received. Steve then gave her a pill to slow her heart down a little. After she took the pill, she looked around, as though looking for something or someone.

Callie started to ask if anything was wrong, but caught herself. "Can I get you something, sweetie?"

"No," she began, looking more than a little confused. "It's just. They're gone." She seemed embarrassed.

"Who's gone, sweetie?"

Steve sat straight up at the monitor where he was typing with his back to them at the same time Callie heard a man's voice sharp and firm in her earpiece where Maggie had been, "Callie, stop. Do not discuss the Mollies with Lucy. In her current psychological—"

Callie reached up and took the earpiece out of her ear, saying as she did so, "Sorry, sweetie, that thing's been irritating my ear all night."

"Mine, too," Lucy said at once, taking her earpiece out and placing it in the palm of her upturned hand.

"Who's gone, sweetie?"

"What?' Lucy looked genuinely confused.

"Who's gone?

"Nobody. Nothing. Just these things I think I see sometimes. Most of the time. Most always. But not here." She looked up at the ceiling as though she expected something to appear through the ceiling. "That's what they wanted back there, at that place. They wanted to see them, but I don't think they're real. What was that place?" Through all of this she looked to Callie with the tone and expression of a much younger child with her mother.

Callie looked deeply into the girl's face, and then at once more superficially, and saw that the girl's lips were extraordinarily chapped, as through dehydration. "Steve, do you have some lip balm?"

"What?" he asked, turning around.

"Lip balm? Something for her lips. They look painful. Do they hurt, sweetie?"

Lucy nodded.

"Some Vaseline if you don't have anything else," Callie insisted.

"I d-do," he stammered, "I do have something else. It's for lips after plastic surg-g-gery. It's amazing. I'll be right b-b-back." He stopped and turned back, asking "Is the inside of your m-m-mouth dry, too?"

Lucy nodded.

"I have something for that, t-t-too." He disappeared through a door, and the women watched him go.

Callie looked back at Lucy. "I'm not really sure what that place was, to be honest with you, or this place. But this place is a better place. I hope. Steve, is this your place?" This last she directed in a raised voice towards the man in the other room.

Steve appeared back in the doorway. "What, sorry?" he asked, his hands filled with tubes and jars of creams and ointments.

"Is this your place?" Callie asked.

"Um, yes, it, it is." He answered, though clearly uncomfortable at being drawn into the conversation.

"Are you going to chain us up?" Callie asked, her face entirely serious, but Lucy knew Callie's deadpan as well as she knew her own freckles, and she began to grin. She did not remember it, but it was the first time she had smiled in months. She did not know what day, or week, or month, or even year it was. She did not know what city or state she was in. But she did remember how to smile. And even though it was painful, it felt good to her.

"N-n-no, of c-course not. I'm here to help you." He looked genuinely puzzled, until Lucy began to laugh, and Callie smiled.

"There ya go, kid. That part of your life is over."

Sensing that he was dismissed, Steve turned round to go back into wherever he'd been.

"What about the other part? Those things. Do you think they're real?" A visible chill ran through her scrawny limbs as she asked it. Callie could remember seeing very few people look so scared and vulnerable in her life—and one of them was herself.

"I've been thinking about that a lot, sweetie. This past day has been unlike any day in my life, ever. And you know my story." Here she grinned a crooked jack-o-lantern smile, and arched an eyebrow, but Lucy only nodded her head in solemn acknowledgement. "It's been a big day for you too, I know. A big life, I think."

She paused, stroking the still-damp hair before she continued, "I think they are real, but I don't understand exactly how they're real. So far, they seem to me sort of like television. Like, when I see people on my television, they aren't real. I can't touch them. Not like Willy Wonka. At the same time, they were real at some point, maybe still are real somewhere. And there are these things—forces—electricity, anodes, diodes, whatever, that makes it possible for me to see them, or what was them, or is an electronic or static or whatever memory of them. And, you just have a better television than most people, I guess? It's all confusing. I don't think anyone understands it, really. At least, no one I've talked to. But yes, I think they're real."

"You don't think I'm crazy?" The question was sincere, a question she had been fearing to ask for years, maybe her whole life. Her eyes retreated back into their dark, hollow sockets, and she trembled.

"I think you're crazy beautiful. But crazy? No. Never crazy." Before the words were out of her mouth, Lucy leapt from her chair and into Callie's lap, curled up in an impossibly small ball of limbs, and felt almost as weightless as she appeared. She sobbed so hard Callie thought she must wretch, but she didn't. Steve came and stood in the door, a tube in each hand, a look of terror on his face, but Callie shook her head, almost imperceptibly. She could feel the girl's strength waning, overwhelmed by the effort of being awake, of being alive, of being not crazy, of being held, of being loved, of being.

"Are they gone? Forever?" Lucy's whisper was almost inaudible.

"No, sweetie, they're not gone. But you're here with me now. And everything will be ok, sweetie. I promise." Another lie that she wanted to be true.

Steve moved the electrocardiograph machine back onto end table from the edge where it was teetering after Lucy's movement, and he opened one of the tubes, handing it to Callie as he moved his index finger across his lips in a put-it-on-this-way gesture. She did so, and handed the tube back to him. He tried to hand Callie the earpiece to put back in, but she would not take it.

Not yet, she thought, as she held the girl, the young woman, the incredibly small human whose body still trembled, and jerked, and shrugged, working out the complex changes in chemistry. *I came her for her.*

CHAPTER 11. PBR

It was the wet metallic sound of the can opening that startled the judge. The three women had been sitting in the storage room of the massive Flying Z Super Stop Station for more than twenty minutes, and they were all more than a little jumpy even before they hid, if they were hiding. They couldn't come to an agreement on that between the three of them, as to whether they were *just hiding*, with an emphasis on the *just*, which was Eleanor's opinion, or if they were *in* hiding, which was Ida Mae's opinion, or if they were just waiting for this to get cleared up, and they *weren't really hiding at all*, which is what the judge said, but none of them really believed she actually thought. She was a judge, and a grown woman, and no fool. And only a fool could believe that she was not in hiding as she sat on a cardboard box full of Castrol 10W30 motor oil, getting her St. John Collection ivory knit skirt dirty. She had paid half-price for it at Saks Fifth Avenue, but it was still the nicest suit she owned. She liked to wear it when she was traveling around to the backwoods of rural Georgia. It gave her a little oomph. She felt she could use a little oomph in that storeroom—it made her uneasy.

And despite Stick's assurance from earlier that the storeroom was safe, and where they should wait for their ride, the relentless sweeping of the security cameras over the ladies made the judge feel vulnerable. The camera's mechanical motion was silenced by the whirring, spinning, swelling tick-tocking of the countless motors keeping the beer, milk and soda cool, but that made it somehow more sinister to her. She wondered how many more there might be. Who might be watching. If the police had already been called. The teenagers honking their car horns in the parking lot weren't helping matters, but those sounds, and the sounds of competing car stereos, could only be heard intermittently over the noise of the machines.

Lost in thought, and nearly overwhelmed with nerves, she was unaware of Ida Mae opening one of the many big metal refrigerator doors and retrieving a six pack of Pabst Blue Ribbon from the massive cooler, at least until she heard the pop-rip-hiss of the can being opened.

"Woman, what do you think you're doing?" She turned and looked at Ida Mae with frank disbelief.

"I'm having a beer. What does it look like?"

"Is this the time?"

"None better. From where I sit." She was sitting back down on her own recent perch—a pallet of energy drinks—that she was sharing with Eleanor. She spoke with the authority of a grandmother sage, but her lips let slip a smile that reached up to her eyes.

"You don't even drink. You don't believe in it." Despite what they had been through earlier in the evening, the judge was still surprised to see the octogenarian sipping the can of beer.

"Hmph. You so sure you know what I do? What I believe?"

"I've known you all my life. I hope I know something."

"That's true enough, you have known me all your life, but you haven't known me all my life. I was past thirty when you were born. Tell me, did most of your life happen before you turned thirty, or after? I don't mean the awards and the promotions, all that money and foolishness. I mean the parts of life that make you blush when you sittin' in church? That make you smile when you wake up from dreaming the dreams of the good times? Of the best times? The times that matter?"

She took a long sip from the Pabst Blue Ribbon can, as the judge looked on in wonder and Eleanor looked on in amusement. The beer's acrid, metallic taste reminded Ida Mae of youth, of freedom, of her husband, before the worries of children and church elders.

"Why don't you have one? Maybe you'll stop jumping around like some crazy old housecat," she suggested to the judge.

"I think I'll pass, Ms. Ida Mae. I'm not saying I don't want one—I could use one. I can't remember when I could use one like I could use one right now. But I'm so tired I might just pass out."

"No, nobody's passing out," Eleanor interjected, "and nobody's driving, either. Stick said someone was coming to take us away. Why don't you take the gavel out your ass and have a beer? Ain't nobody here but us chickens." Her smile was half mischievous, half bored—she had been dealing with judges since before this woman was born. There might be some differences here and there, maybe, but the past few decades had apparently done little to diminish the self-importance of judges, no matter the sex, or the age, or the color.

The judge bristled, seeming to sense more than a little of this…*indifference* was what it most felt like. She didn't know who this woman was, not really, but she wouldn't have liked the casual familiarity she was using, even had she known her well. She met Eleanor personally for the first time just a few hours earlier, sitting at the table with Ida Mae. And despite the circumstances, she was, still, a judge. At least, she thought she was—she couldn't not be a judge. She didn't know how. The only other person she knew how to be was this uncultured little black girl from Dublin who made good grades but couldn't sing, couldn't dance, didn't know how to use cutlery, and lived in a shack in the Quarters. She *had* to be a judge, and a judge could have a beer if she wanted one. So she got up, and took one. As she took it, she gave Eleanor a shady sort of look she usually reserved for women who wore sundresses to church, but she did take it.

She found a paper towel over a mop sink to wipe the can off with, and then opened it, and smelled its contents, but wasn't convinced she was making the right decision until the sour golden bubbles fell in the valley of her tongue, and ran down the back of her throat. It washed down the insanity of the past few hours, of the present moment in the storeroom, of waiting on a stranger to take them to some strange place for reasons she still didn't, and might never, understand. And, it was the best beer she ever had in her life. It was the best drink she'd ever had. No crème de menthe, no Corvoisier, no Grey Goose with pineapple, even on a beach, even with her husband, ever tasted so good. It washed the judge in her, of her, away. She took another sip, and felt like Chari again, maybe for the first time.

Not that honorable, not even that well-behaved, but also not a young girl living in the Quarters. Just Chari.

She looked down at her feet, scrunched up in her favorite black Salvatore Ferragamo pumps, with the remains of what she thought must be blood crusted on the soles, turned down the corners of her mouth, and asked "Now why didn't I get my sneakers out of the trunk?"

"Cause you'd look like a fool wearing that Sunday suit with sneakers," shot back Ida Mae.

"Who you think is gonna see us?" Chari asked, with genuine curiosity, turning to look at Ida Mae. She had stopped actively trying to imagine the outcome of the evening before they were even out of Dublin. Imagination had never been her strongest skill, and years of reading law journals and opinions, and writing for law journals and writing opinions, had stripped whatever imaginative faculty she ever had down to a minimum so bare it was rarely worth engaging.

"We might be on the front page of the *New York Times* before it's all over with," Eleanor suggested.

"You think so?"

"Well, I think something big is going to happen. And I want to be here when—" and then the thing happened that they were waiting for.

***

All told, it had been less than an hour since Stick first told Chari to turn. But it felt like an age of ages to her. She had turned into the unknown, and it felt strange to someone so used to knowing, and not just knowing truth, but creating it. Her thoughts, written into opinions, shaped, and sometimes—if only by default— became law. She did not like ambivalence, but Stick did not make her wait long.

It was less than two minutes after her Mercedes flew onto I-285 westbound that her car's navigation system appeared to turn itself on. She and her passengers had been sitting, driving, waiting, twitching, making little uncomfortable noises. Neither of her passengers knew that Chari had not turned on the navigation system, and she felt no need to explain. Within moments of the illumination appearing, text began to crawl across the top of it that was not part of the navigation system itself, but certainly appeared to be. Chari did not yet know it, but the community had remotely taken over her car's operating system. She was still driving, but they were in control.

Chari, it's the man from U.N.C.L.E. When you finish reading this and each line, sniffle.

The Man from U.N.C.L.E. is how the two of them had obliquely referred to Stick in his capacity as a specialist for the C.I.A., though Chari never knew what agency U.N.C.L.E stood in for. It had become apparent to her relatively early in their relationship that there was something more than a little unusual about Stick's travels, and before she even finished her undergraduate studies at the University of Georgia, she knew he was more than a clerk. At that point, being a clerk had seemed a much more realistic personal goal for her than being a judge, or even a litigator. But he encouraged her, and nurtured her, and she, being bright and curious, asked questions—and it came to a point where he either had to lie to her explicitly, or let her know the truth, without knowing. "I can't really tell you," he said in response to her questioning one day. "Are you the man from U.N.C.L.E?" she asked jokingly. "Let's just say yes, that's exactly who I am." It gave him the freedom to discuss some of the more romantic aspects of his job without jeopardizing national security—the same way she would later discuss judicial happenings without jeopardizing the judicial process. But in telling her even that, he told her more than his family, or his sometimes-boyfriends over the decades.

She read the sentence on the display, then sniffed, loudly.

That sentence disappeared and was followed by another. *You are under drone surveillance. You are being followed. They can hear and see you.*

She sniffed again.

We can hear and see what they can. We're going to get you out of this. We need a minute.

Another sniff. She looked over and saw that Eleanor was following along with what she was reading. From the backseat, Ida Mae asked, "You got a runny nose Charlene? Blow it. You know I can't stand all that sniffling. Here." And she attempted to pass to Charlene a tissue retrieved from the depths of her purse—she could not read or even see the dashboard monitor.

"I think I'm fine. Thank you Ms. Ida Mae."

Take the Washington Road exit going south. Do not call me. I am compromised.

Another sniff.

"Here, Charlene. Blow your nose."

Charlene took the tissue being waved wildly in her peripheral vision, and said "Thank you, Ms. Ida Mae."

And, for good measure, she blew her nose.

Just follow the directions on the GPS. You'll end at a Flying Z Super Stop Station.

She sniffed again.

Go inside. Use the bathroom. Go into the Employees Only storeroom beside it. Wait.

Another sniff.

"Here, Charlene, take another tissue," demanded Ida Mae from the back seat, waving another one at the judge.

"No, ma'am, I don't think I will, but thank you. I spend too much on my moisturizer to scratch up my face with that—you call that tissue? I think I'm going to have to find something to blow my nose that doesn't feel like sandpaper. You ladies need anything? There must be a store around here somewhere."

A harrumph loud and clear echoed from the back seat. "If it's good enough for your seniors, it should be good enough for you."

"I am a senior now, Ms. Ida Mae."

"You're not as old as me yet."

They're trying to decide what action to take. It will take time. Unprecedented.

Charlene understood—she could not recall anything as bizarre as what she was in the middle of ever coming before her as a judge, or possibly even in a law journal, or the tabloid magazines. It was because she was a judge that it was unprecedented, she knew. There were layers and layers of strangeness giving her discomfort.

Sniff.

Leave the keys on the driver's floorboard. Lock the doors. Take your things.
Sniff.

They were nearing the intersection of Flat Shoal and Feldwood Roads, where the GPS showed the Flying Z Super Stop Station. As the judge knew from her travels, it was a trucker's paradise, with dozens of bays of gas pumps, a grocery store of sorts, a mechanic's shop, a truck wash, probably even a McDonald's or Popeye's Fried Chicken. On a night like tonight, it would be swarming with people—there weren't that many places open this late, even in Atlanta. But the Flying Z was open 24/7.

She did not like the thought of leaving her Mercedes behind, not one little bit. But since it seemed she needed to be preparing to leave much more than that behind—everything she thought she knew about everyone in her life—the car began to seem like the most easily replaceable thing.

When the power goes out, leave through the storeroom emergency exit. Linus will take you.
Sniff.

And then, suddenly, they were at the store, and after exchanging looks both dark and uncertain, Charlene and Eleanor began to get out of the car. Ida Mae, however, wasn't moving.

"Come on, Ms. Ida Mae. We can't leave you out here," Charlene encouraged her.

"No, I'm fine. I don't need anything. Ya'll go on."

"Ida Mae, get out of that car right now, and bring your purse. I need you in the ladies room." Eleanor was getting frustrated.

"In the ladies room? For what?" Ida Mae was genuinely confused, and absolutely comfortable where she was sitting.

Charlene opened the back door of the sedan and whispered through clenched teeth, "Get out the goddam car, woman." She had never cursed before Ida Mae in her life, and she hoped cursing at her would get her moving. It did.

More than a little startled, Ida Mae gathered her things, some of which she had spread on the seat when digging for tissue, and found her way out of the car, looking at Chari with both contempt and bewilderment.

"Have you always been this difficult?" Charlene asked through pursed lips as they walked into sea of fluorescent light spilling out from the high glass curtain walls of the store.

"I'm the same as I ever was. What's all this foolishness? And who do you think you are, cursing at me? I'll tell you one thing," she began, before Eleanor cut her off as she opened the door to the store, "Get inside, Ida Mae."

"I don't understand," Ida Mae began, but Charlene cut her off, saying, "You will," as she herded her along past massive pyramids of Coca-Cola and motor oil to the back of the store.

They had to wait for the ladies room. There were several young women in line. And as Charlene looked around, she could see an extraordinary number of young people in their weekend finery, especially for a gas station, and so far from downtown. As she looked out through the station's massive plate glass windows, she saw cars streaming into the parking lot, where already there were few parking spaces left.

She hazarded a question to the young woman standing closest to them in line, asking about all the commotion.

"There's about to be a party here, ma'am. It's what they call a flash mob. I never been to one, but it's all over the Twitter." The young woman was as white trash as she was apologetic, but when she came out of the bathroom, she had a newly-painted face on, ready for the party, and she disappeared into the store after saying "Ya'll ladies drive safe, now."

That should be distraction enough, thought the judge, who knew just enough about flash mobs, Twitter, and bored Atlanta teens to see the making of a major headache for someone. The line behind them reached back now to the pyramid of soda, and there was barely room to move in the store, which was getting rowdier with

432

each passing moment.

Once they were in the restroom, Charlene whispered to Ida Mae what had just transpired in the car, and what they were doing—more than a little scared that Ida Mae would balk at going into the storeroom if she wasn't in on the plan.

Her only response was, "Well, alright then," and followed the other two women into the storeroom without complaint. The girls in line didn't bat an eye.

None of them knew that at that moment, there were over forty local, state, and federal vehicles circling the neighborhood at a distance, brought in not by local police to control the flash mob, but by the drones, which were now having a very hard time identifying exactly where the three women were. Their heat signatures had been lost for some time. There would be three helicopters, from different agencies, maintaining a safe distance from the store, and from the women by the time the power went out at the Flying Z.

***

But the lights did not simply go out. They did not dim, or suggest with a flicker that it might be time to leave. A surge of electricity from who knew where or how slammed into the Flying Z with the speed and ferocity of lightning travelling through wet cotton string. Every light bulb in and around the store was shot out, with glass and flames and electric currents shooting out everywhere. The three women screamed at once, and they weren't the only ones. They could suddenly hear quite clearly the competing rap and country music from the cars outside, and screams of terror from all directions, including the door they were to walk through. The three of them, at least, had warning that *something* would happen—the rest of the Flying Z's patrons were, quite properly, terrified.

"Merciful heavens. What are they doing?" asked Eleanor, who remained startled, which surprised her in itself.

"They're getting us out of here. Come on, let's go," commanded Charlene, trying to be heard over the sudden alarms and sirens wailing. Sparks flew in the room all around them, and the women from the bathroom line poured into the storeroom, running, screaming, looking for a way out.

The three old women joined the throng, holding onto one another, and as soon as they were out of the emergency exit, a man appeared and, gesturing with one arm towards an idling parts truck, said "Good evening, ladies, I'm Linus. This is our truck. In, please. Quickly."

The women did not even stop to look at him. They just got into the Southeast On-Time Parts Delivery truck—the judge having more trouble than the other two ladies, who had worn sensible shoes—and worked their way around the passenger seat and into a door going into the back. Linus followed them into the back compartment, slid the door closed behind them, and the truck pulled out of the lot behind a series of other cars fleeing the mayhem.

At the same time, unknown to the three women, 45 seconds of radio silence ended. The problem was, none of the officials—state, local, or federal—could or would say how it happened. But for 45 seconds, every communication device, every radar, sonar, lidar, every sonic and thermal observation device, every walkie-talkie, every cell phone, satellite link and internet-based device in a 1,000 yard range of the Flying Z became inoperable, including the three stealth drones being operated by the Army Forces Central Command at Shaw Air Force Base in South Carolina, which were much further out of range. When all three drones went offline at the same time, the first thought at Shaw was that the drones had—somehow—been shot down on American soil. But the lack of any radar of the area prevented them from knowing for certain, so fighter jets were immediately scrambled. At the same time a decision was made somewhere, though no one could say where, to move in and take the three women into protective custody. But as soon as the command was given, the power outage at the Flying Z began to spread, like a virus, radiating out in a pulsing circle from the station. It took just two minutes for the outage to reach the Hartsfield Atlanta International Airport, and another three for all of downtown Atlanta to be black as pitch. At the same time, the electronic control systems of the government-issued cars began to crash, along with the ability of the cars to move, or even crank. The sounds of breaking glass and exploding transformers littered the quiet night sky for the next two hours, by which time Linus and the three women were in the parking lot of a 24-hour Target Supercenter outside of Montgomery, Alabama.

Their conversation with Stick, once in the back of the truck, while brief, gave them assurance they needed, and some they didn't know they needed. "I have to stay in Atlanta," he said, as the women sped down I-85 south towards the Alabama border. "But I'll be following you back to New Orleans soon. I was in Atlanta on other business, but when Sam contacted you this afternoon, Chari, it put a whole other set of wheels into motion. As soon as they realize they can't have you three, they're going to walk it back—they're going to want Sam. We're getting him out now, even as we speak. I have to go, but we should just be a few hours behind you, ok?"

The women all assented, with only Charlene asking back, "Yes, but Stick, who are *they*?"

His answer was frustrated, distracted, uncharacteristically inarticulate, and very nearly meaningless. "I don't know, exactly. They don't exist, but they're everywhere, and they have ears, and eyes, and money, and guns. I will explain it to you when I see you. Linus will get you whatever you need, and get you where you need to go. You're in good hands. Love you, Chari. I have to go." And he was gone.

***

Secure in the truck in the parking lot of the Target, the three women put together a list for Linus that included everything from a pair of walking shoes for the judge to Sanka for Ida Mae. "It has just enough caffeine in it to keep me awake 'til New Orleans, I think, but get the big jar, it's cheaper that way," she added. When Linus tried to explain to the women that they only needed enough supplies for the next couple of hours, and their list wasn't really necessary, the women would have none of it—the night had already taken too many turns for them. And, Linus couldn't be much more than 20 years old, so regardless of what Stick might think about the young man, the women were not having it.

A sharp look from any one of the three women would have been enough to quell his resistance, but such looks as he received from the three of them at once removed whatever of independence or sass the young man had in him. He returned to the truck with a shopping cart spilling over with food, candy, gum, over-the-counter medications, powders, lotions, shoes, pajamas, a garment bag for the judge's suit, and on and on. And to top it off, a trunk and a cooler to hold all of the new purchases, so they wouldn't be rolling around the otherwise-bare floor of the truck.

Linus had already apologized for the starkness of the transportation, but the women, who had no idea what other transportation the community had it its fleet, were initially surprised and amused by the appearance of comfortable, upholstered club chairs secured to the floor and walls of the truck. From their cursory glance at the truck's exterior, they had naturally been expecting to find auto parts there. Instead, it was stripped bare, with hastily-installed panels to shield the interior of the truck from surveillance. It wouldn't stand a much closer inspection, but Linus had very little time, and even less choice, in how to get the women from point A to New Orleans. And he hadn't known until shortly before he picked them up what point A would be—in what state, much less when he would be picking them up. That it all happened in Atlanta was good, and the timing seemed more like prescience on Stick's part than luck on the part of the community, at least to Linus.

Once they were on I-85, they did—as Linus and the community had rightly predicted—create an area too vast, with a high volume of fast-moving traffic, for the type of net necessary to snare them. Short of shutting down every road and interstate passing through and around Atlanta, there was no way to locate the three women. The Georgia State Patrol had become very excited at one point, just after the electricity failed, when the judge's car, with three passengers, was seen speeding out of the Flying Z parking lot. The patrolmen followed the car, anticipating a high-speed chase, but when they turned on their flashing blue lights, they pulled the car over to find only three teenagers, who had been given 500 dollars cash to drive the car to the judge's home, by a man they could not identify. They were taken in for questioning—which everyone agreed would be pointless—and the Mercedes was towed to a county impound lot. But the judge and her passengers were gone. And the city of Atlanta, and the skies above it, had very quickly turned into a dark, dangerous twin of itself. Every alarm system was inoperable, every cell phone, land line, data cable and computer was dead, and every criminal—it became clear very quickly—was wide awake. Almost as though someone had given them notice. Almost as though the whole thing was planned.

***

Linus answered whatever immediate questions he could for the women after the brief call with Stick, but then he returned to his laptop, where he was helping coordinate the massive effort to get Sam out of the C.D.C. It had already become apparent to everyone in the community who was watching that whatever happened with Lucy, Callie's next move would be to get to Sam, and it was not something Callie would have time for. But Linus knew nothing of that. He had never heard the names *Callie, Michael, Sam, Josh*, or *Lucy*. He knew nothing about the Mollies. His access to Annopedia, and to the discussion boards, was limited to postings discussing transportation—routes, methods, theories, and application. Though he was only 19, and one of the youngest members of the community, he had been a transportation specialist for the Los Olvidados drug cartel in Mexico since he was 13 years old. A natural born hacker, and the son a chop shop owner, he began working for his father hacking the onboard computer systems of the new generation of luxury cars that required thumbprints or voices for ignition, not keys. He created electronic back doors into not only the manufacturing facilities of the largest luxury auto manufacturers in the world, but also into the subsidiaries that supplied the hardware and software components that made the cars run. It did not take long for his digital signature to be recognized by automotive security experts, and for him to become a potential recruit for the community.

The opportunity for his recruitment came when he was arrested in a DeKalb

County Sheriff's Office sweep of a large, predominately Hispanic apartment complex on North Druid Hills Road where he was sleeping in a guest bedroom of people he did not know, having just finished a delivery run of crystal meth from Matamoros, just on the other side of the Mexican border from Brownsville, Texas. His profile had been promising, so the community took a calculated risk, and bailed him out. He showed no particular signs of interest in the drug or mafia trades—he was just a very talented young hacker making the most of a situation that kept him out of poverty in his hometown 200 miles south of Matamoros. They knew from their surveillance of him that everything he loved, everything he wanted, was part of the American dream. He never acknowledged this love in front of his family, who were fiercely patriotic Mexicans, but when he went online, his digital footprint showed his allegiance to another land, another dream. His identity in the online gaming community was of a young man named Linus who lived in the suburbs of La Jolla, California. His character in the online game *City of Heroes* was a chiseled, inflated version of himself, in red-white-and-blue-and-stars-and-stripes from head to cape to toes. He developed strategies to lead packs of his online friends—all identified as Americans—to win countless battles. He became an American hero, at least on the internet. His life online showed the outline of a young man who wanted better, who wanted more, who wanted out, who wanted north.

Within six weeks of being bailed out of Dekalb County, his arrest record disappeared, and his identity as a Mexican citizen disappeared along with his actual identity—some minor plastic surgery on Long Island allowed him to travel freely without fear of being identified by the hundreds of gang members he had met and known in the chop shop, in his parents' kitchen, at school, and at church, who regularly crossed the border to complete tasks for Los Olvidados.

His first assignments for the community, which he greeted with the anticipation of a full-scholarship freshman at an Ivy League school, were a series of increasingly complex logistics operations having nothing to do with automobiles per se. The objective was to see if the intellect and ingenuity he displayed in stealing cars and winning online battles could be readily adapted to other pursuits. It could. He displayed a plasticity of mind that enabled him to move swiftly and nimbly from Spanish to English, from Mexico to America, from Linux to DOS to Windows to any other dozens of programming languages. He could also diagnose and change a spark plug or carburetor with pinpoint precision and startling speed. And from the very beginning of his relationship to the community, when he first met the man who had hired the local bondsman, he displayed an unerring loyalty and devotion to *Mi Familia*, as he preferred to refer to the collection of people that he never met, but who plucked him from obscurity and ill-fortune to become—he did not know quite what. But the prospect, the reality, of this other, was more than he had dreamed of before.

He was first introduced to Stick a year after his rescue from the DeKalb County lockup. It had been decided in the aftermath of Hurricane Katrina that the time was right to finally do what the community had debated the wisdom of doing for years—to create a physical headquarters. It was to be built not from the ground up, but down, underground, just far outside of the city of New Orleans to be discrete, but near enough to be serviceable. It was to be massive, larger than they thought they would ever need, because this was a singular opportunity—tens of thousands of welders, carpenters, plumbers and drywall hangers crammed every inhabitable space of southern Louisiana, and were willing to work on most any project without question for the right price. The rebuilding of New Orleans was the great construction Gold Rush of the 21st century, and the men were there to make money, as much as possible, as quickly as possible. They questioned nothing. Some guessed they were working on a secret government facility, some guessed that a criminal enterprise, the Mafia, the Masons, a modern-day paranoid Howard Hughes, or even a terrorist enclave might be their employer. Their utterances were monitored as best as could be under the din of construction in an underground manmade cave, but with little worry. The envelopes full of cash each man was provided with at the end of each day, according to his talent, did much to dispel any inquiry. And the inevitable gossip that came from the men in the bars and makeshift brothels was assimilated into the myth and legends of the rebuilding of New Orleans. Theirs was not, after all, the only building being built without zoning approval, without permits, without even the vaguest awareness of the city, state and federal authorities overseeing the reconstruction of what Katrina had destroyed. If an eyebrow was raised here or there by the wild tales of a few drunken laborers from the far corners of the continent, there was neither time nor funding to go after them. Bridges, highways and entire towns lay in ruins—the scofflaws would be dealt with when the heavy lifting was done. But by then, of course, the far-flung men and the cash-flow that kept them in Louisiana would be long-gone.

It was Linus' job to secure these men and take them to a facility where they went single file through a series of rooms, first disrobing, then taking a urine screen for drugs and alcohol, then putting on uniforms provided to them, and then into a windowless van that took a circuitous and disorienting route to a job site that was both unremarkable by any physical landmark and undetectable by any method of electronic surveillance. Few of the laborers spent more than a few days at the site, and none of them ever saw all the plans. And they never met anyone from the community other than Linus. At times acting as a general contractor, at others as a labor supervisor, and sometimes just as translator, communicating construction details from an earpiece to the workers standing in front of him, Linus' role was as critical as it was diverse.

The laborers never knew it, but they were working in an abandoned sugar cane processing facility that was turned into a cement production plant, supplying cement to building sites throughout northern New Orleans, and to itself, underground. The van that dropped the men off came in through a back entrance where any suggestion of the building's purpose or exterior was stripped away. They could have been in a shopping mall or hospital for all they ever knew.

The name of the facility was provided by Linus himself. When he began to understand the sheer volume of semi-precious and precious metals going into the structure, he thought first of Fort Knox, which he knew from watching the History Channel, but later thought of Alexander Dumas' fabled cavern, and began calling it *Monte Cristo*. Stick thought that too obvious, and they settled on *Oglasa*, the original name of the Tyrrhenian island of legend. Once the two of them agreed on it, the rest of the community followed suit. Stick and Linus had become a seemingly unlikely and inseparable pair. Linus was completely heterosexual, but in that nearly universal and completely idiosyncratic way of his generation, he thought no more of Stick's sexuality than he did of his teeth or brand of luggage. It was a thing, yes, but not a thing that mattered in their relationship. And, it was certainly not something that prevented Linus from becoming Stick's more or less adopted son. There was mentoring, yes, but their capacities in the community were so disparate as to make communication on any topic other than Oglsaa almost pointless. They talked about books. They talked about life, and family, and God, and America, and Mexico. They laughed and shared bottles of wine, and occasionally Stick would go out on the town with Linus as his wing man—because for all of his intellect, Linus had little or no skill at meeting women. Stick, however, could turn his southern charm on most any woman, complement the things that were begging for attention, ask the flattering questions, and introduce her to his nephew, Linus. And he would usually see him the next morning or evening, and would never ask intimate questions, only a hopeful *Buenos dias?*, which would usually be answered with a blush if the answer was *Sí*, or a shrug if the answer was *No*.

Neither man had any say-so in the design or furnishing of the space, which was specified by engineers, architects and designers from across the globe—many of whom never knew if the project they were consulting on was even real. From afar, Stick oversaw the complexities of keeping the construction secret, while Linus did the same at the job site. When construction was done, they visited regularly with cleaning and maintenance crews to keep the space ready, but neither ever knew exactly what it was they were waiting for. All 216,154 square feet of the underground space was ready to be inhabited by up to 150 people for as long as a year. The space was entirely self-contained, able to provide its own energy, clean water, even its own clean air. Who all of that energy and water and air would be for was not in any part of Annopedia that either of the two men had access to. They would sometimes sit having dinner together in the courtyard between Stick's house and the adjacent apartments, where Linus had moved in, and conjecture in the most obtuse way, throwing out increasingly obscure potential populations—a game of their creation in which no group of people could be repeated. It went on for years, beginning vaguely, with groups like *The President's Cabinet*, or *Football Coaches of the SEC*, but went on to increasingly more arcane, specific, and in their own way less-easy-to remember groups, such as *Ex-Wives of the Rolling Stones*, or *People from the City of Des Moines with Five Names*.

And then, that afternoon, Sam called Chari—and everything changed. The countless other groups, real and not-real, that Stick and Linus had considered as potential inhabitants of their secret fortress disappeared into memory. As they saw notifications pop up for them to sign into their separate discussion boards on their laptops, something about the urgency of the message—a priority one message, something they hadn't known existed—told them the time had arrived. *They're finally coming*, both men thought. And, *Who are they?*

***

"Here we are," Linus said, as they pulled into the Bayou Concrete and Cement Company, watching on his laptop as their icon moved toward the building. The plant was closed for the day—the manager had received a call earlier that an unscheduled corporate safety inspection would be taking place and to notify all workers they would have the day off, with pay.

The women exited the truck, not commenting on the absence of the driver, who was gone before Linus opened the door. The cavernous, industrial interior of the space was filled with heavy machinery and lifts and buckets, and most every surface was coated in a fine white powder of sand and limestone and granite dust.

"This is it?" The judge asked, incredulous. "This is headquarters?" That she still wasn't exactly clear on what she would be entering the headquarters of made the appearance of so much machinery and dirt that much more discomforting.

"Come with me, quickly," he beckoned as he made his way towards a small building set within the building, with a cheap adhesive metallic plaque that read *Office* on the door.

They followed, and once inside, he asked, "Can you ladies come stand with me around the desk? Put your hands flat on the desktop." The women looked at each other with some uncertainty, and just as much resignation, as if to say *We've come this far.*

But none of them moved, looking instead at the nondescript but sturdy metal desk in the center of the room, its surface strewn with workplace flotsam and jetsam.

"What about the trunk and the cooler with all our stuff in it?" Ida Mae asked, interestedly—she was less interested in going without than she was readily willing to admit.

Chari cocked an eyebrow up and "Are we going to the Batcave?" Linus shot a sharp look in her direction that said without question, *Yes, we are going to the Batcave,* and *Shut up. Now.*

All three women saw the look, and were taken aback—the young man had been nothing but kind and amenable all through the long, strange drive, but he had become commanding and abrupt instantly. He relaxed his features, and said, with obvious restraint, after a quick glance at his watch, "I will come back for anything you need. Please, put your hands on the desk."

They did. And with one of the four of them on each side of the desk, Linus nodded his head, and the floor began to descend. The descent began almost imperceptibly, with each of the women looking around in wonder. There was no mechanical noise, not even the shushing of a hydraulic lift. When their heads were below the level of the floor above them, a three-inch thick horizontal plane of reinforced concrete began to slide smoothly into the place where the floor they were standing on had been. The sides of the lift shaft were smooth concrete, with vertical insets of fluorescent light on each of the four walls, illuminating the startled faces of the women.

When the concrete sheet was in place, forming a ceiling above them, Linus began, "I'm sorry, ladies, but it is turning into sort of a crazy day. This facility should be as electronically secure as any military command in the free world, but we didn't want to take any chances until we were in." He took his hands off the table, being long-familiar with the slow downward movement of the office. The women hesitantly followed suit.

Soon, when they were 20 feet below the surface of the earth above them, a sliver of horizontal light shot across the floor, illuminating their feet, the legs of the desk and chair, the trashcan, and the fine coat of silt that dusted the floor. As they continued descending, the sliver grew into a wedge, finally filling the shaft with light, and opening onto something that looked like a cross between an artist's studio, a high-tech startup's lounge, and, strangely, someone's living room. What appeared to be sunlight was pouring in through a wall of windows, and an enclosed exterior space with small shrubs, beds of ivy, and a small lawn of centipede grass. The furniture was mostly mid-century modern, but all of it serviceable, and most of it vintage, with visible wear. There were massive shelves of books, with plants, and knick-knacks. There were long, low sofas spread out in seating groups with club chairs and coffee tables, and white paper lanterns suspended from the ceiling, which was 16 feet high. To left of the living area, there was a kitchen with two large Sub-Zero refrigerators, visible from a distance, and a Kitchen-Aid stand mixer, and plenty of knives and spices and cutting boards, lots of counter space—it seemed like a great place to cook in, except for the lack of a stove.

"What is this place?" Charlene asked, since no one else appeared willing to.

"A bomb shelter," answered Eleanor, somewhat unexpectedly. Ida Mae, like Eleanor, had lived through World War II and the Cold War, had seen countless bomb shelters in the movies and on television, even advertised in the Atlanta and

Dublin papers. She nodded in agreement, taking another glance around as she did so.

"Well, yes, I guess, yes," Linus began, stammering. It was a bomb shelter, surely, but only in the same way that the trolley was a cargo container. And, though he did not have time to explain, he felt some pride and more than a little ownership of the place. He began to explain, "This is the great room. It was based on the living room of some dead designers. Brothers, I think? Ray and Charles Eames but I don't really—"

"Husband and wife. Her name was *Ray*," Eleanor interrupted, her correction gentle but firm.

"Right," Linus said, changing course at once, "Okay, listen, I need to get back to work. Velma is going to explain what this place is and what's going on. At least, as much as she can. A lot of it is still happening."

"Who's Velma?" asked Ida Mae, looking around in expectation.

"I have no idea, I've never heard of her before," Linus answered. "She's a member of the community. Just have a seat over here," he gestured towards a farm-style wooden table, with two long benches on the sides and mismatched armchairs at each end, that separated the living room area from the kitchen. A plain pewter platter piled with apples, pears and oranges was at the center of the table.

"Is there a bathroom in this place?" Eleanor asked.

"Of course. Just down that hall. Actually, any of those three halls. You ladies can show yourselves around. When you're ready to talk to Velma, just sit at the table," he replied, and then, somewhat sheepishly, "She's waiting on you."

"Well by all means, let's get moving," Eleanor said, with some asperity.

"No need to get all snippy, Eleanor," Ida Mae said. "We're all tired."

They continued in that way for some time, but Linus had already left them, retreating to a far corner of the living room where he took out his laptop and began typing away before the women even agreed on which hallway to go down first.

It didn't take them long to finish looking around. It wasn't that they weren't impressed—they were. But they were asking one another questions that they couldn't answer, and the circular nature of their questioning led them back to the table in short order. They knew what beds looked like, but they did not understand why the beds—or they themselves—were there.

Once they were seated at the table—Ida Mae had located a plate to peel an orange on, and fixed some instant coffee she found in a pantry—a transparent piece of clear, synthetic material descended from the ceiling to eye level and swiveled around so that the image of a woman's face was looking at them. She appeared to be in her mid-to-late sixties, with radiant silver hair cut close to her head, porcelain skin, and a warm, friendly expression.

"Good morning, ladies. I'm Velma."

"Is that your real name?" the judge asked, without hesitation or embarrassment.

"No, of course not, but I'm stuck with it," the woman laughed, with genuine, hearty laughter. She explained briefly about how names were assigned within the community, and how the community maintained anonymity in general, explaining that even while she could answer any questions about the interior functions of Oglasa, she had no idea where it was, and that if the laptop and bracelet she had stopped working, she would have no way of contacting the community. "What would you like me to explain first? Where you are, or why you're here, or who I am, or about the community?"

"The community," Eleanor and Chari answered at once, and in unison. Then they and Velma turned to look at Ida Mae, whose face held an expression of surprise, and a shade of disappointment as she looked at the women at the table beside her and answered, "Michael. I want to know my Michael is safe. And Sam, too. Where are they? How are they? Why aren't they here?"

Eleanor turned down the corners of her mouth, feeling the mild rebuke, and Chari spoke up, more tentatively than was comfortable for her, and asked "And Stick. How is he connected to this? Is he ok?"

446

"They're fine. Michael, and Sam, and Stick—they're all fine. They're not out of the woods, I'm not going to lie to you. And when we're done talking, you'll be able to follow along with others in the community who are watching everything unfold. Well, directing everything as it unfolds. That Sam of yours, he really threw a wrench into the plans yesterday. I tried to tell them—you see, I'm not a scientist, not even a programmer, or engineer, or anything practical to the community in a technical sense. I taught philology at Kenilworth University—I'm retired now. But, I was considered something of a language expert in my time. Published important papers, that sort of thing. But unlike most people in the community I've worked with, I'm also a mother, and a sister, and I have friends. For all their high-flying good intentions—and they are good, I believe that—most of the people in the community, the men, especially, have no sense of what a real person might do in any situation, how anyone will react. They can determine probabilities based on past events, but they have no real sense of what life is. They've lived in computer laboratories and gone to conventions where they exchanged ideas and developed professional networks, but for the most part, they've never been a part of an actual community, not in any real sense. They've never volunteered at a homeless shelter, or led a Boy Scout troop, or given a toast at a wedding, or even had people over for dinner. They're as useless at understanding people as I am at understanding how this laptop works. My friends call me when a husband gets sick, or a child dies. Their friends call them when they want free technical advice. There's a difference."

"That's why you're giving us the introduction, then? You understand people?" Chari asked.

"I think so, yes. And, well, quite frankly, everyone else is pretty busy. A lot is going on. Have you ever spent months, or years, planning something, an event, like a wedding, that was planned down to the second, and then at the last minute, just as it was starting, a storm came out of nowhere?"

All three women murmured their assent and nodded.

"Well, the clouds are shifting. Quickly. And no one in the community understands why, or at least, no one can agree on what it is they don't understand. Some think the storm is coming because of the wedding, some think the two things are just linked, some think there's no relationship at all."

"What do you think?" asked Eleanor, knowing that an explanation of the storm would be coming soon enough.

"I have a son who is a meteorologist. Works for a local channel in Boston. He's always trying to explain weather—an occupational hazard, I guess. So I understand that part of it, enough, probably more than I want to. But I can tell you that if I was a bride, standing in my wedding gown in front of hundreds of guests, or even if I was a guest, and a perfect summer sky opened up during the ceremony, pouring rain, I wouldn't feel like it was a coincidence, some random meteorological event. I would feel it was fate. Now whether I laughed, and considered it God's blessing, or trembled, and felt God's wrath, well, that's entirely another story. The thing is, I believe my son, and any of these people in the community would feel the same thing in the same situation, but they wouldn't believe it." Her face was expressionless as she finished speaking.

"You're saying the community doesn't believe in God," Eleanor said.

"They believe in… something. Not themselves—they don't believe in themselves. They believe in the systems they create. They consider themselves great thinkers, great architects, masters of the universe—until they stand on a beach, or have to visit someone in hospice. They see the software and hardware they've developed in the homes and offices, even the hands, of billions of people. And they feel that power, that sense of self. But put them in a storm they could not predict, and well, they feel, how should I say…" Her face dimmed with uncertainty as she searched for the words.

"Human?" Eleanor suggested.

Velma's face came alive with gratitude. "Human, exactly right. Human." She paused for a moment, and the smile slipped from her face, and she continued, "Keep in mind, all of this is circumspection. I've never met most of these people.

At least, not that I know of. In the early days, there was more of that—we would get together every now and then. But now it's all done through computers, discussion boards, email, messages. What we're doing now is the least common way of communicating. I've only ever seen the faces of a few of them. But times are changing, and quickly."

"Now, about this storm. How about we hear some more about that." It was Eleanor talking. She had slid Ida Mae's plate closer to herself, and was peeling an orange of her own.

"Okay. Everybody comfortable? This is going to take a minute." And so she began. At least, she began at the beginning she knew, where she was asked by a testing company she had never heard of to evaluate a young man—Michael—for his language capabilities. She described meeting Eleanor in 1975 in a doctor's office in Amherst, Massachusettss—at which point Eleanor's face paled with recognition. She described the following decades, how the technology kept expanding, how the community kept growing, and the data sets began to demonstrate more convincingly that something was happening. She described how her position in the community changed over time, how she went from being a language specialist to a general advisor on projects involving humans. She described the Mollies, just as Michael and Trevor had done a few hours before, and patiently answered their questions, accepting their disbelief as part of the natural pattern of understanding. And then, some two hours later, she showed them, how in the past 12 hours, the Mollies had moved. There were clusters, as always, around New York, and Chicago, Dallas and Los Angeles.

"But why did you take them out of that circle there?" Charlene asked, pointing to a place on the map Velma was showing them on the screen. There were no Mollies in or around Atlanta, or Charlotte, or Nashville, or Cincinnati. It was as though someone had drawn a circle on the map, and erased them.

"We didn't do anything. They're just gone." Velma's face had no expression, no suggestion of her thoughts or reactions to what, if anything, had happened.

"But what's in the middle of the circle?" Ida Mae asked.

It was Eleanor who answered. "Oak Ridge." And she looked at each of the three women in turn, startled, but only Velma understood her alarm.

"Yes, Oak Ridge. And we have no idea why. It may be connected to what's happening in New York, or Atlanta, but we don't know anything. We can't make the connection. Eleanor, what do you think?"

"I think I'm going to need a cup of coffee. No Sanka." She stood up and stretched, and moved in the direction of the coffee maker on the far counter, but stopped, and turned around, facing the monitor. "And, I cannot keep calling you Velma. It's ridiculous. What is your name?"

"Anne."

"Well, Anne, this is why I'm here, isn't it? Oak Ridge?" It was a question, but there was no uncertainty in her voice.

Anne's response was less certain. "I believe so. I don't know. I believe you were supposed to be here, yes. I believe you were always meant to be exactly where you are, right at this moment. An oversight of the community—a flaw in the system, they would say—had you in that retirement center. But Sam's actions remedied the oversight. The community sees Sam's call to Chari as a flaw in their plan. I say it was their plan that was flawed. And the plan corrected itself. Or, someone, something, corrected it. In any event, you're here now. And, I think, we think, we need you."

Eleanor nodded, and went to make the coffee.

"What about us?" Charlene asked. "What are we doing here?"

"Do you believe in coincidence, Charlene?"

She deliberated before answering. "I do."

"And you, Ida Mae?"

The old woman's face was full of pity as she looked at Chari and said, "I believe in God."

"Whether either one of you is right, or you're both right, I don't know. But you're here for some reason. I'm sure of it."

CHAPTER 12. DIM SUM

When Lucy woke 18 hours later, Callie was still with her, but they were in a different place. At least, Lucy thought they were in a different place. She opened her eyes, and looked around, and smiled even before she saw Callie sitting at the foot of her bunk.

"They're still gone," was the first thing she said, wiping the sleep from her eyes, then adding quickly, as she saw Callie's face turn to smile at her, "and you're still here."

"I don't know that they're gone, but they're not here. And I am. What can I get for you?" Callie laid her laptop down on the blanket, and took the earbuds out of her ears.

"A bathroom. I have to pee so bad. I'm pretty sure I've been dreaming about peeing for about an hour."

"Come this way. Watch your head."

As Callie used her handprint to open the door to the bathroom from the sleeping compartment, Lucy looked at her in horror and confusion. "Are we on a spaceship?"

She wasn't joking, and it was hard for Callie to contain her laughter. So hard to do, that she didn't, immediately apologizing, "I'm sorry, sweetie, I don't mean to laugh. We're not on a spaceship. Here, pee. I'll explain. Just tap on the door when you're done."

Two hours later they were still lying in Callie's bunk, looking up at the monitor on the bottom of the bunk above them, and Callie had just finished describing the community, the Mollies, everything that Trevor and Michael had explained to her. She had left out Trevor's name, for the moment, dreading the inevitable time that the topic of his death would surface. She thought this must be what Lucy was thinking of, when she said instead, "So he really is my dad."

"You knew?"

"Not... exactly. You know how you said Michael communicates with the things, the Mollies? It sounds like he does it with language. That's not how, how it's worked for me."

"What do you mean?"

"They talk to me in pictures."

"How do you mean?"

"Maybe not pictures," Lucy said, thinking. "More like, memories, maybe, but it's all, like, visual. There aren't words. Just these images pop into my head. And I live them. And it's.... it's horrible, even when the memories are good, because then they're gone, and even when I try to hold onto them, I can't."

"So you saw pictures, memories, of Josh's when you were around him?"

Lucy's forehead crumpled with the effort of remembering. "I don't know that they were Josh's. They were maybe just *of* him, or contained him, or something. Some of them were scary. Some were really sad. Some were just memories of dreams, I think, dreams of the future, maybe. But I don't know that they were his dreams. They were so... in focus. I just had the sense that he meant something to me. And I never knew my dad, or knew who he was... I try not to think about it. I've tried so hard to forget. Not just him, all of them. Always. Usually they don't make any sense at all. These past few months...living in that place, it was like someone had a television remote pointed at my head, going through thousands of channels of flashes of things that were totally unrelated. The doctors tried to make me tell them what I was seeing, but it was too much. I couldn't remember. And a part of me thought if I ever told them anything, they would never let me leave. Really, I just wanted to forget."

"Sometimes trying makes forgetting harder. Like picking at a scab instead of letting it just heal. Sometimes *not* trying is what we need to do."

"Right." Lucy sat up and retrieved a juice box from a tray on the bed. She was too old for juice boxes, she knew, but she loved them—she had always loved them. So far, while talking to Callie, she had been through eight, and been back to

452

the bathroom twice. After a moment, she asked, "Where are we going? You told me what this trolley thing is, but you never said where we're headed. Or what we're going to do when we get there."

"Apparently, we're headed to New York. City. Someone in the community has a secure place for us there, I guess. I think we're just waiting for everything to settle down. Some people you've never heard of—that I've never really heard of, except in passing—got wrapped up in all this. Sam, and some of his family, I guess. They're ok," she added quickly, as Lucy's eyes widened in fear. "They just need to get somewhere safe. I'm not exactly sure where they are. We can check, if you want to. And when you're ready, your dad is here."

"Here? You mean on the trolley here?" Her face showed excitement as well as trepidation. "Why didn't you tell me before? Is he ok?"

She still doesn't trust me. Not entirely. "Yes, he's fine. The powers that be wanted me to take some time with you this morning. You've been through a lot. You've learned a lot already this morning. And, I agreed. We didn't want to overwhelm you. But. Would you like to see him?"

Lucy nodded slowly, and smiled a very tender, raw smile—the smile of a child. "I wanted to see him when he was just Josh." After a moment she added, "Who are the powers that be?"

"I dunno," answered Callie, "but they got you out of that place, and they got us back together. So, they can't be all bad, right?"

"Right," Lucy replied, without enthusiasm.

***

Their reunion was as emotional, and awkward, and charming, as any such reunion might ever be—even in a modified cargo container travelling at speed up the New Jersey Turnpike. Before Lucy entered the study, she brushed her hair with Callie's brush, and put on an oversized grey sweatshirt and skinny jeans that were still baggy on her. Josh had been watching her without ceasing, even watching her sleep, until Michael promised he would wake him whenever she woke. But Josh had not been able to sleep long. He woke in the early morning, and sat in the study watching her sleep on one monitor as the other monitors around him showed the sun rise over the sprawling urban landscape of Grand Central Parkway in Queens. He listened to her breathing, and heard his own breath in hers, and felt a connection to humanity he had never felt before. He wanted to hold her, to protect her, to love her—but most of all, he wanted her well. So, he waited.

It took longer for them to get back on the road than anyone had planned. The explosion of the ferry caused quite a commotion on the eastern tip of Long Island, quite apart from ending a party that had already been going on too long and too loud, as far as the neighbors were concerned. While publicly attributed to an engine malfunction, the N.S.A. and state investigators knew that remotely detonated C-4 explosives were the real cause of the ferry blast, though that was kept quiet during the ensuing and discrete terrorism investigation. The explosion was not publicly linked with the young woman who was abducted from the island that same morning. The New York State Police issued an Amber Alert for Lucy within minutes of her disappearance from the party, though they made no mention of her likely travelling companion, because they themselves did not know there had been or a murder, or that there was a gun with fingerprints on it back on Plum Island—they were only told a mentally unstable girl who was in protective custody was missing from the eastern tip of Long Island. Road blocks were erected on every road back onto the mainland as soon as police could be summoned there, and they were sure the girl was somewhere on Long Island, but they had no idea where. The rain had washed away any scent of the women the search dogs might have hoped to find. A door-to-door survey conducted by the village and county and state police yielded nothing, but the N.S.A. had not expected it would. The surveillance drones were brought in too late to be of any real service. The one real hope had been the oceanfront home of a plastic surgeon named Steve Boyett, a site where one of the drones showed two women being let off under a carport, then going into a pool house. A search of the house and grounds found only two young women in their late teens who swore they had not been to a party the night before, without convincing the police, or apparently their father. It was sometime after the investigators left that a Pottery Barn delivery truck arrived at the Boyett residence with new furniture for the pool house. It took longer than usual for a furniture delivery, but when it was done, the old furniture, and Lucy and Callie, were safe inside, tucked away behind what appeared to be a fully loaded truck.

The reunion tears were ended by the time the truck entered into Manhattan, and despite knowing she was with her father for the first time in her life, and knowing it was him, and the indescribable comfort of his touch, the excitement of seeing the skyline—even knowing she wasn't really seeing it, but just pictures of it, knowing it was there—threatened to take her attention away from him. Sensing this, he said, "We'll have plenty of time to catch up. Let me tell you what you're seeing."

Michael and Callie were both on laptops by this time, and other than occasionally correcting Josh on the names of buildings, or their architects, they left the new parent and child in peace, sitting, holding hands, watching the skyline emerge before them, as lane upon lane of traffic converged in bewildering knots of asphalt, and signs appeared for off-ramps to places Lucy had never heard of before, but immediately wanted to see and know about.

For the carriers—Lucy, Michael, Callie, and Josh—Manhattan represented one of the best places in the world to disappear, but also one of the easiest places to be identified, and ultimately caught. The Mollies were everywhere in the city, and the group of the four carriers, unshielded, would present an irresistible magnet—at least as far as precedent could be understood. Moreover, they were four of the most carefully recorded humans in the history of electronic surveillance. Their voices or faces would set off alarms in most any public place in the city, where hundreds of thousands of public and private cameras scanned the city streets and public places without ceasing.

Once they were in place in the community's apartment, they would be more or less safe, most everyone in the community agreed, but getting the four of them out of the truck and into the loft-style apartment where they would be living, at least in the interim, was less of a ballet than a salsa—they were to be loaded off the truck individually in a custom-made lead-lined box disguised as a new refrigerator. Were it just one of them, the task might be easy enough, but repeating the process four times, double-parked on a congested cross street, in the middle of a busy work day, might lead to trouble. They were attempting to be inconspicuous, after an unexpectedly conspicuous day on Long Island.

They need not have worried—there was, almost miraculously, parking in front of the building, despite the apartment's location on 23rd Street between 5th and 6th Avenues. The handsome ironwork on the front of the building was all that remained of the former early-20th-century toy factory. The building had been purchased and converted into luxury condominiums in the early 1980s by a group of five wealthy, single men, each of whom had originally occupied one of the building's five floors, and had carved out sprawling caves of early postmodern chic for themselves. The only shared spaces were the small entryway, the elevator, and a basement with storage spaces assigned to each unit in the building and delineated with chain-link fencing. The top floor had originally been owned by the photographer Robert Mapplethorpe, and the building saw a brief moment of fame when erotic photographs from his *The Perfect Moment* series became the subject of a national debate over arts funding. The series included highly-stylized erotic photographs of—among other things—a bullwhip inserted into the photographer's own anus, which may have been shocking to the politicians in D.C. who publicly denounced them, but they were not offensive, or even surprising, to the photographer's neighbors. They did, however, find the newshounds on their doorstep distasteful, and were delighted when the controversy passed. All seasoned veterans of the sexual revolution on its New York City battlefront, those original tenants of the newly-renovated building had long been scattered by time, AIDS, and gentrification to the far corners of forever by the time Pottery Barn truck arrived.

Michael was the first to make the strange, dark, slow, trip in the box from the back of the truck, down its lift, over the curb, through the small lobby, into the elevator and the small, private third floor elevator lobby. Next went Josh, then Lucy, and finally Callie, who said goodbye to the truck driver/delivery man after he opened the box door for her, but she received not so much as a blink in reply—as though she weren't even there.

"Well that was weird," Callie said, as she crossed the elevator lobby and through the gloss-black metal doorway to the others, who were cautiously looking around the sprawling apartment while waiting for her. "Did that guy say anything to any of you?"

The other three shook their heads in reply, as a man Callie hadn't seen before appeared from around a corner. "He wasn't supposed to say anything to you. He never saw you, you don't exist. To him. But hi, I'm Ted," he said, extending his hand out to her with a smile. She shook it, reflexively, as she looked around the apartment. It seemed smaller than the 2,800 square feet she had been told to expect. "I'm Callie," she replied, distracted and still somewhat disoriented from being carried like a piece of freight on a dolly to yet another completely foreign space.

"Is this it?" she asked with bravado, looking around, and seeing only what looked like a black slate runway two steps up that ran the length of the apartment, and divided it, running from four windows on the north side to a sunken living area with six adjacent windows on the south side, facing 23rd Street, each window nine feet tall and three feet wide, and providing actual views to the Chelsea skyline. Perfectly square black-lacquered columns, two feet wide on each side, marched in a double, triple, or quadruple rows from north to south, every ten feet—depending on where one was standing in the loft space. Many of the columns had low benches running between them and connected to them. Even without any furniture, the apartment could easily seat dozens of people. The smooth plaster walls were painted a soft dove grey, and soared 14 feet from the landing below the central runway to a smooth, crisp white plaster ceiling that covered the entire space. White track lighting ran in continuous lines from north to south, visually reinforcing the length of the apartment. A single canister light shone down on an octagonal glass dining table, elevated on an extension of the runway that connected to the kitchen, where black laminate cabinets and gleaming stainless steel hardware were visible because the pocket door usually used to conceal the small space was tucked back in its pocket. Somewhat incongruously, to the right of the kitchen, and on the same elevated level, was what appeared to be a closed old-style mechanic's garage door, on metal tracks, with mirrored panes where transparent glass would typically have been. The carpet that appeared wherever there wasn't black slate on the floor was tightly-woven black and grey wool, almost certainly designed for commercial use.

There were only two decorative elements visible in the space. On the dining table was a massive, ornately-carved, antique silver candelabra with eight arms, each holding a beeswax taper. The base of the candelabra was a hunting scene of a pack of pointers flushing a brace of pheasants from a thicket of young oaks, whose slender trunks formed the stems of each of the eight arms. The birds were shown mid-flight, among leaves swirling up from the densely-packed forest floor. The intricate articulation of the silver, of each leaf, each snarling dog, of the spray of feathers, seemed impossible. One look at it told Callie that it was worth more than the homes of most of her friends back in Atlanta. Josh and Michael paid no attention to it. Lucy recoiled from it in horror, and looked away.

On the other side of the dining table from the kitchen there was a small sunken sitting area with a fireplace, with no ornamentation at all—just a massive rectangular column of grey plaster with an unfinished rectangular opening for gas logs. Above it hung the other decoration—a framed canvas showing grey and black lines with occasional blocks of red, blue and yellow. As Michael moved towards it, Ted said, "It's a study for *Broadway Boogie Woogie*, the painting by Mondrian. It's considered important by people who know about these things. But to answer your question, Callie, the rooms are all sort of disguised. There are three full bedrooms, three full baths. Three of those sofas over there pull out into beds." He pointed to the sitting area on the south bank of windows. "The original owner was very wealthy, but very discrete. Most of his houseguests, even some of his close friends, never knew how large the place really was. Since we're all here, let me give you a tour. You all can decide how you're going to sleep."

"How long are we going to be here?" Lucy asked, not knowing that everyone except her knew the answer.

"We're not sure," Ted answered, smiling. "We were hoping to slip you out of the country, somewhere safe, without a lot of commotion, but that doesn't seem like it's going to happen just now. But, we're working on it."

"Me? Just me?" Lucy was terrified at the prospect of travelling alone, perhaps in a lead-lined refrigerator box, to some other country, alone.

"No, of course not," Josh said, with a stern look at Ted, who he'd already taken a dislike to, for reasons he couldn't quite identify. "You're not going anywhere without me," he added reassuringly.

"Or me," Callie added, her eyebrows arched with undisguised wonder at Ted's seeming indifference to Lucy's still somewhat-fragile state, and to the likely somewhat-fragile state of them all.

"No, no, of course not," Ted added quickly. "You aren't going anywhere you don't want to go. Your safety is what's important. Here, let me give you the full tour."

It took only a few minutes to get a full tour of the space. The doors to the bedrooms were hidden in plain sight—the same color and texture of the walls, they were discernible only by the light peeking out from under the doors where there was baseboard on the walls around them, and almost imperceptible outlines of the doors where they met the walls. All of the door hardware was in the rooms' interiors. Callie guessed—rightly—that at night, those seams would disappear in shadow. The only real surprise came when they learned that the garage door was the entry to the master bedroom—when the lights were on in the master bedroom, and off in the rest of the apartment, they could see into bedroom, in a sort of at-home peep show. Whole groups of people could, presumably, stand around on the slate runway, or even sit on one of the benches, and watch what was happening in the bedroom. Josh was amused, Callie appalled, Michael confused, and Lucy outraged.

"Who the fuck would do that?" she demanded, still somewhat shaken by the recent knowledge that almost her entire life had been recorded—even from conception—and that she had been on display the whole time, for countless others to see.

"It's a relic of another time, another age," Ted responded. "It was all consenting adults, I think. In any event, you can just leave the door up." He located a remote control on one of the bed's two nightstands, and the garage door's tambour panels clanked up, the door disappearing above the ceiling.

"That's just fucking creepy," Lucy said, unimpressed.

"I've seen worse," Callie added, noncommittally, but with something like a shudder.

"So this was just a big orgy party house?" Josh laughed, unable to contain himself.

Ted blushed, "Well, no, not at all. There were mostly proper parties here. But it's been years since anything like even that happened here. The community bought it in the early 90s, and after some really minor adjustments, it's been a sort of meeting place, hostel, whatever, ever since. Very discrete, conveniently located, all that. It's perfect."

Josh and Michael appeared to agree, or at least not to disagree, but the looks on Callie and Lucy's faces expressed mild disgust. Callie started to speak, but Lucy interrupted her, demanding "Does the community even know what a house looks like? Are you just naturally all creepy, or is it something you have to like, work at? This place is like something out of a horror movie. There aren't even any blankets or pillows." Blankets and pillows were the physical things Lucy had missed most while strapped to the bed back on Plum Island, but she didn't want to say that.

And while not exactly Callie's sentiments, they were close enough, so she waited for Ted to answer.

"Um, no, I mean, yes, there are pillows, they're on the beds. And blankets, here in these towers." Two of the rows of columns were not concealing structural columns—they were storage cabinets with hidden pressure-release hardware. Ted pressed on one of them, and the door swung open, revealing shelves holding an assortment of household supplies—candles, tissues, a bike helmet.

"That! That's what I mean," Lucy almost shouted. "Why can't anything just be what it is? This isn't perfect. This is nuts." The architectural slight-of-hand seemed to be alarming the young woman—even Callie wondered how many places there were for someone to hide in the bizarre man-cave. She wrapped her arms around Lucy from behind, and Lucy accepted the soothing gesture—she did not want to be upset, and she wasn't entirely sure why she was angry.

"Ted, we're all exhausted. But I think what Lucy meant was, there aren't any pillows on the sofas," here Callie pointed to the geometrically rigid, grey wool sofas that looked as warm and welcoming as a stone bench in a freezing rain. "Couldn't we get, you know, just some throw pillows? Maybe an afghan? Some flowers? Even if we're only going to be here for a night, this place is like a tomb. Seriously, I'll pay for whatever it is, but we can't just stay in this morbid place like this." She looked at the sunlight glinting off the grey walls, and realized that with some pictures and flowers, she actually could live there.

Ted looked at the two women as if they were exotic creatures from a zoo that had suddenly learned to speak, but were using words inappropriately. "I'm sure we can do something. I need to go out now to get some things for you. Most anything in the world you can have delivered to you from where you are, but I need to order it, and be here when it gets delivered. I live just a few minutes away, so it's no bother. If you have any other special requests, just send me a message through one of the laptops."

"Where are they?" Michael asked, speaking for the first time.

"In the lobby. All of the things you had in the truck are in that refrigerator box. We're going to keep it here, the box, for when we relocate you. But not the food," he added thoughtfully, "It's not in the box. I'm getting fresh food and milk and all that. A doctor will be stopping by in about 20 minutes to check on you,

Lucy. Her name is Lou Kincaid. Michael, I think you've met her?" Michael nodded, and Ted continued, "Buzz her in here. You'll be able to see her on this screen." He gestured to a standard-looking video entry system by the door.

"You do know I'm a surgeon, right?" Josh interrupted, both confused and curious.

"Yes, but—" Ted became flustered.

"You can't examine your own daughter, Josh," Callie said, stepping in with a quizzical look on her face.

"Oh, right," Josh replied, making a mock-mortified expression—until two days ago, he hadn't been a father. It would take some adjusting.

"Right then," Ted added, "Anything else you all need?"

The three newest passengers of the trolley looked at him in astonishment. They needed everything, and the idea that he could not see that made them more uncertain about where they were, and who he was, than they had been before he asked. It was Michael who answered, "No, we can work things out. Maybe there's a pack of cards here somewhere?"

"I'll pick one up, just in case," Ted answered, heading quickly for the door, not wanting to miss an opportunity to leave an environment he felt was becoming more anxious because of his presence in it.

"Pick up two," Callie suggested as the door closed behind him.

"So what now?" Josh asked, looking at the other three.

"I, for one, am taking a bath. There were Jacuzzi nozzles in that big tub in back, and I call first dibs. Unless you want it, Lucy?" Callie was long overdue for a long, hot soapy bath.

"No, I guess I have to wait for this doctor lady."

"You could just hang out with me?" Callie added, but she really wanted time alone, and she suspected after she spoke that she had given her game away.

"I can wait with dad." Lucy's voice was calm and even as she spoke, belying nothing. It was the first time she had called him that, and they all knew it, though they all pretended nothing had changed, or happened.

"Right-O. Michael, Josh, does one of you want to explore all the hidden cabinets in this place just so we can know what all is here?"

The two men looked at each other, shrugged, and started moving about, looking for places where things might be hidden. Michael had stayed there before, but only briefly, and his curiosity at those times had been about the city outside.

Callie turned to look at Lucy, and, with intuition taking over, saw some feeling beneath the expressionless face. "What is it, sweetie?"

Lucy burst out with unanticipated emotion, "Is anything ever going to be normal again? Will we ever get to go back to our house in Atlanta? I loved that place. I loved being there with you. It was my only real home." She looked like she might cry, but she didn't.

Callie hesitated before answering, "Sweetie, I don't know. I miss it, too. And I miss Mama Ben. And I miss Sam."

"Where are they?" Lucy asked, interested, and recovering from her outburst.

"Let's find out. And let's get those laptops going—I want to find our throw pillows and some throws. Ted seems nice enough, but I don't trust his judgment when it comes to housekeeping. Can you believe he said this place was perfect?"

"Perfect for a strip club," quipped Lucy, and the two laughed together as they walked towards the elevator lobby and began bringing in armloads of clothing, laptops, toiletries, and other things they couldn't identify, all of which had been piled in the refrigerator box. They put them on the runway and benches in something like piles.

As Lucy joined Callie at the dining table with a glass of water, Callie thought to call out, "Hey, did you guys hear that? Lucy and I are going to pick out the throw pillows. Tell Ted to wait 'til he hears from us." Callie's face was pointed at the track lighting in the ceiling.

"Who are you talking to?" Lucy asked.

"The community. I have a feeling there's about one chance in a trillion we're not being monitored right now."

A track light near them blinked on and off twice, in apparent confirmation that the message had been received.

"There ya go," Callie quipped, with exaggerated resignation.

"Doesn't it creep you out a little?" Lucy questioned, uncertainly.

"Actually, no. It explains a lot in my life. And yours. Do I trust the community entirely? God no. But based on what I've seen, I'd rather it be them watching me than the others—the ones who had you."

"I guess so, yeah." Lucy didn't sound entirely convinced, but Callie wondered, since Lucy knew they were being listened to, if she was actually convinced at all. She tried to read her face, but it was as expressionless as the blank grey wall behind her.

***

By 6:00pm, the third floor of 23rd Street was beginning to resemble something like a makeshift home. A delivery of 36 throw pillows in jewel-colored velvets and chenille, and a similar assortment of blankets, had been scattered on the sofas, benches, and floor, and in a makeshift grouping in front of the fireplace, which had been lit. Bunches of flowers from the corner bodega were in drinking glasses throughout the space, and the Mondrian had been replaced with a digital display screen the community sent over along with an assortment of other computer gear that Michael was working through. The silver candelabra had been banished to a back closet, out of sight, and apparently out of mind. Everyone except Callie had taken a nap, who had opted for her bath, and, except for Michael, everyone looked rested and well.

Ted asked, when he returned from picking up the pillows and throws at ABC Carpet and Home, "How is it possible to spend $6,428 on pillows and blankets?"

"It was possible to spend ten times that," Callie said without blinking an eye. "We're being prudent." She looked over to see Lucy smirking as she pretended to be asleep, or listening to her iPod. It was almost like the Lucy she had known before, and it made her happy, and though it felt tentative—everything felt temporary, suddenly—she welcomed it.

"The flowers look really nice," Ted said encouragingly. Callie frowned as she imagined what Mama Ben would say if he could see the shabby little things with their baby's breath and dyed carnations, and smiled as she said "Thanks, Ted."

Grocery bags with pantry staples and soda from Fairway Supermarket, and more bags with prepared foods, meats, and cheeses from the upscale Balducci's market, were piled on the small granite countertops of the galley kitchen, and on the floor, and on the dining room table. Ted had ordered pizza, salad, lasagna and garlic knots from a neighborhood pizzeria, and everyone seemed mildly, though somewhat inexplicably, happy. Their distant plans were uncertain, but their immediate plans seemed blessedly, pleasantly normal.

Everyone except Lucy had spent time that afternoon communicating with the community, both directly through video and through the discussion boards, and it appeared some agreement had finally been reached. It was only when Sam—alive, and well, and healthy—appeared on her screen that Callie actually began to care about where they were going. She wanted to be where he was, as did Lucy. Josh wanted to get back to his life, with Lucy; but that, he learned, was impossible.

There was a standing order to take any of the four of them into protective custody immediately upon detection, and all of the surveillance mechanisms available to the combined forces of the overlapping, interacting United States and state and local agencies were actively seeking them out. The terrorist alert had been raised to red earlier that day, based on the kidnapping of a U.S. Circuit Court Judge in Dublin, Georgia the night before. From what the community could gather from the limited intelligence it was intercepting, the N.S.A., the C.I.A., and the Justice Department believed their intelligence gathering systems were compromised. They believed the disappearances of all seven of the missing people were linked, and were coordinated by a single organization, and they were mobilizing to find it. Students, colleagues and business associates of the community, and many members of the community itself, were being called in to identify the gaps in security without being given any indication of why. But the community knew, and the community was prepared—it had always been prepared. And despite her apparent disinterest in anything other than the people she knew, Lucy was being provided detailed information about what was happening as she sat with the others around the glass dining room table, eating their Italian dinner.

"Oh my God," Lucy exclaimed after taking her first bite of the pepperoni slice that dripped grease down her t-shirt and onto the table, "I never knew why people liked pizza so much. This is *so* good. I want to stay here forever. Is there pizza like this where we're going?"

Everyone laughed, except Ted, who replied with the enthusiasm and compassion of a rental car agent explaining the terms of a rental agreement, "It's unlikely there will be this same type of pizza, but yes, you will likely be able to have pizza, or some other regional specialty."

When Josh turned to look at him, he realized why he had taken a dislike to the man, and that it wasn't a dislike at all, it was discomfort: This man, Ted, reminded him of Trevor, a man he actually *had* disliked, but who had died to save his daughter, had in fact been killed by her. Dead, and left behind, uncared for, unattended, discarded. Left to be searched, probed for evidence of how to find them—him and his daughter—and their friends. Josh realized, looking at this man Ted, looking at and seeing his features for really the first time, that Ted, too, was placing his life at risk by being with them—if Ted hadn't known it before Trevor died, he certainly knew it now. And he was running around midtown Manhattan buying pillows and milk and pizzas as though his life might not end with it.

Josh looked closely at and saw the man for the first time—his brown hair, cheaply cut, probably by a stop-in barber, and his neck in need of a shave. His white button-down shirt, dingy and wrinkled from a day of running around. His green eyes, a scar beneath one of them. He had an athletic build, which surprised Josh, who thought of the community as a vast network of computer nerds living in their basements. He realized then that the man wasn't pasty at all, but surprisingly robust and healthy looking—he must lift weights, or play some sport. Again, a surprise. But why? Why should he be surprised that every member of the community wasn't the same? He had no idea how many people were even in it. He was vaguely aware of the sounds of the monitor above the fireplace playing the television show *Full House*—Lucy's favorite, he had learned on Annopedia—in the background. The audience was laughing.

"Something wrong?" Ted asked, aware that Josh was looking at him minutely, scrutinizing each part of his appearance.

"No, no, nothing at all," Josh answered too quickly, recovering himself poorly. "I was just wondering what it is you do when you aren't helping lost souls like us get pizza and pillows."

"Oh, u-u-um," Ted stuttered, and everyone else at the table, including Ted, suddenly realized that no interest at all had been expressed in him throughout the day. He had been treated, if anything, like some sort of servant or errand boy, but he merely blushed, and continued, "Special effects. I develop special effects. Freelance. Usually on a team. But I work freelance. Not from my home," here he picked up a garlic knot and began untangling it, getting olive oil and bits of garlic all over his fingers, "I don't work well at home. I keep an office, sort of thing, a shared space, really. A collective, they call it. We share an assistant. She answers calls, keeps books, looks up checks."

It seemed he would keep going that way indefinitely, sputtering along with information about himself, until Lucy interrupted him, interested by the idea of special effects, wondering if he had worked on her favorite Pixar films. But no, "Nothing like that," he assured her, with a lingering disappointment in his voice. "All military. Or at least, violent. I help develop games that train soldiers. I'm a ballistics specialist. If you're playing a game with a machine gun, I show them what will happen if you hit a bottle or a wooden door or a metal door or whatever from this distance or that distance, with wind or without, that sort of thing."

Josh expressed his admiration, and engaged Ted for as long as seemed reasonable after a day of total disinterest, and learned that Ted played racquetball twice a week in the winter, and tennis in the summer. As that bit of conversation waned, and the pasta began having its soporific effect, and the bursts of audience laughter from the nearby monitor became more pronounced, Lucy asked, seemingly out of nowhere, "Why isn't Mama Ben going to the place where we're going? Won't the police arrest him? Won't they hurt him?"

Callie looked thoughtfully over her half-raised glass of chilled Perrier and answered "His place is with his chickens, sweetie. He would never leave. And, the police already know everything he knows, and they're watching him. They've been watching him. We think he's safe. But I know he would never leave his chickens. It's better not to ask—that might actually put him in danger."

"You don't think he'd want to be with us?" Lucy asked, a little hurt escaping her pretend selflessness.

"I think he'd want us to be with him. There. You know how many people rely on him. Who need him, every day. He would never just disappear." And as she said it, she thought, *I need him. I rely on him. I would never just disappear.*

Lucy seemed to read her thoughts, but did not argue. "Okay," was her only intended reply, but "I miss him" snuck out without permission.

"So do I," said Callie and Josh together, and looked at each other, for the first time really realizing how deep the connection was that they shared through Mama Ben. Callie turned her eyes from his and toward Lucy and said, "But we have each other now, and he would want that more than anything." She had spoken without thinking, and she wished her words hadn't implied anything to Josh that wasn't there, and hoped even more that there wasn't anything she was feeling that she didn't know. And that hope told her the wish was a lie. Confused, and more than a little alarmed, she looked for a change of conversation, distinct and irreversible, and landed quickly on a question that had lingered at the back of her mind all afternoon.

"Ted, how is it that we're shielded from the things here, the Mollies, and from all the people looking for us, without the refrigerant gasses and everything on the trolley? Can't they just look through the windows?"

Ted was wiping the oil from his fingers with one of the many paper napkins the young Korean man had delivered with the food, and looking up, answered with mild hesitation, "We're not shielded. We're disguised. The young man on the floor above us is the beneficiary of an irrevocable trust, and has had a meth binge going on for more or less the past 18 months or so. He sleeps occasionally, but he hasn't been truly sober, what you would call sober, in years, since his early teens. The Mollies come and go in waves with his using, and with the company he keeps, and he usually has company. He's providing you cover."

"That's really, really awful," Callie said, sorry for the turn of conversation she had chosen. They all looked up at the ceiling, even Ted, and wondered at the suffering going on upstairs.

"Isn't there something we can do?" asked Lucy. Her concern was as genuine as it was likely to be ineffectual, and her father, who was seated next to her, reached under the table and held her hand, and she did not withdraw from him.

"That's not our battle, sweetie," Callie answered, not unkindly. "We have enough on our plates. It's sad that he's an addict, yes, but you know how it works."

Lucy shrugged in agreement of sorts, but Josh was more interested in the latter part. "But what about the others, the people who are looking for us?"

"This place is virtually soundproof. Trust me, there's a 24-hour-a-day party going on upstairs—but you can't hear a whisper. The slabs between the floors are six-inch-thick concrete. The walls are 18" of brick and steel and concrete. And the windows are basically what you might find on a space shuttle. If they knew you were here, they would probably be able to spot you, yes, but they don't. And general surveillance won't do it. They could systematically search the interior of every space in New York, but they don't even know that you're here. They suspect it, but New York is one of dozens of places they're looking at, and not all of them in the U.S. You're safe right where you are."

"What do you think, Michael?" Josh asked, in his awakened sense of appreciation and gratitude.

Michael had not spoken throughout dinner, and had been quiet most of the day. He had lost his friend, Trevor, his sole human companion for what felt like an age, and he was lost. He looked up from his leafy green salad, drenched in ranch dressing, and answered, "I want a drink. I want Dim Sum."

Everyone looked at him in surprise. Even Lucy, who knew virtually nothing about the man, was surprised that he would suggest drinking in front of people that he must know were recovering addicts and alcoholics.

"Beg pardon?" Callie asked, wondering if he meant what they all thought the meant, or something else entirely.

"I want a drink," Michael repeated. "I want to go to the Odeon—a restaurant. Downtown. It's my favorite. I took Trevor there. He liked it. A lot. It's everything the trolley wasn't—full of light, and life, and people, and French fries hot out of the fryer, and cheeseburgers. Bacon cheeseburgers, made to order, with fresh ground beef, hand-patted. An amazing goat cheese salad with Granny Smith apples. French onion soup. And the Croque Monsiuer, just perfect. We would eat at the bar. With vodka gimlets. Stoli—Stolichnaya gimlets. We called it Dim Sum because we only had time to safely eat a few bites of each thing because of the surveillance around the place. But it became sort of our place. The lunchtime bartender knows us. Knew us. And I want to go." Throughout this, Michael's voice had been rising and falling, in tone, and in speed, his warm recollections tinged with the sadness of passing, of letting go. But his ending, his *I want to go*, was clear and decisive, not a wistful longing, but an actual desire—his decision had been made.

The others at the table, except Lucy, looked around at one another in alarm, waiting for someone to respond. All eyes settled on Ted, but it was Josh who spoke first, haltingly, asking "Doesn't that seem a little risky? I mean, a lot risky? Just going out to a restaurant? In front of God and everybody? For a drink and a burger? We're safe here. We can get you a cheeseburger and a bottle of Stoli, right, Ted?"

Ted looked terrified, but nodded in agreement.

"No. The Odeon," Michael said, before Ted could say anything, looking at Josh with an awareness dawning on his face that showed he knew the others at the table thought he might be going a bit mad. "I know what you're thinking. It will be complicated, yes, but it can be done as easily now as it has been in the past. We aren't prisoners, you know. We can leave—we can all leave. The community is here to protect us, not to keep us prisoners in this gilded sort of grey cage." He waved indistinctly with his fork at the apartment around them. "I want to go, and I will go, and the community will help me or not. They're free to make their own decisions as well."

Ted finally spoke, resolving to be firm but kind, "I really don't think now's the time to—"

But he was cut off by Michael, who was more firm and less kind, and whose eyes were alive with a passion the others had not seen in him, though they had no idea of knowing how truly rare—in fact, how unprecedented—the look was, and the feelings it grew from: Michael had changed. He had somehow come alive not with curiosity, as he had been, as he had always been, but with anger, and with certainty of some new knowledge. "Now is exactly the time," he said, his voice clipped with authority, any question of his right-mindedness dispensed with. "There's something happening. Something the community doesn't know about. Something the authorities don't know about. But I know. And she knows."

And he looked Lucy directly in the eye, with the tiniest flicker of uncertainty in his gaze as he watched her face for confirmation.

She looked back at him, unmoving, unflinching, her face giving nothing away. The audience laughed on the soundtrack in the background, filling the silence.

"Stop it, Michael, you're scaring her," Josh demanded, his voice thick and parental. Callie looked confused and concerned, but not scared—and she sensed, rightly, that Lucy wasn't scared, either.

"He's not. I'm not scared," Lucy said, again, not giving anything away.

And suddenly, Callie *was* scared. Without thinking, Josh let go of Lucy's hand, to focus his attention on looking at her. "What is it, Lucy?" he asked.

"Michael, tell us what you're talking about," Callie demanded. "And no more of this hamburger crap."

He looked at her, surprised, but did not answer.

Then together, as if in one voice, Michael and Lucy said, "They want us to leave."

Callie dropped her glass to the table, and while nothing broke, the clattering thud of glass on glass shot through the suddenly-alive nerves of the others at the table. Ted looked as though he might bolt for the door at any moment.

"Who?" Josh asked, fearing the answer—knowing the answer.

"We're in danger. It isn't immediate, but it's real. Just leaving here won't help us," Michael said, almost as if in a trance, and with sadness in his voice.

Lucy continued, "We have to go far, far away. We have to go underground—there's a place for us, it's underground. And we have to get there. It's a storm—but not a storm, not a real storm. The sky is going to burn," and her voice, too, was sad, but certain. "Can I go to bed? I'm tired again."

"Of course," Callie answered, still more surprised, her nerves frayed. The two women would be sharing the back bedroom with two of the windows on the north wall. She stood to walk Lucy back to the bedroom.

"No, I'm ok," Lucy said as she stood, her forced smile not quite a lie, but nowhere near the truth.

Ted spoke up, nervously, but with conviction, asking "Would you like to take the medication Dr. Lou left for you? It might help you sleep. It might help with," he began, but she interrupted him, saying "I don't want any more sedatives. I have Callie. And dad."

They all watched as she wandered off into the crisscrossing shadows the track lights made with the columns.

Ted was the first to speak. "Michael, I think the community is going to be more than a little interested in what you're talking about. Perhaps we should consult with—"

"No, we shouldn't consult with anyone," Michael cut in. "Tomorrow's the day. It all happens tomorrow."

"What?" Josh demanded, his voice rising, "What happens tomorrow?"

"I am going to have Dim Sum. And the world is going to end. Or at least, begin to end. We didn't cause it, but we also can't stop it. And Lucy is right, we have to get out of here. But somehow, I'm right too—Dim Sum. It has to happen. I have to be there. I think Trevor was supposed to be there, too. And maybe, somehow, he will be. But then we have to go."

"Says who?" demanded Callie. "Please just explain what the fuck you're talking about." She wasn't hysterical, but everything they had been trying to achieve since she first walked into the Kroger loading dock seemed to be spinning out of control, beyond reason. It was reason, after all, that had convinced her to come along—evidence of her past, from her past. She had not come along out of some emotional longing or because of some spiritual insight. She had come to save and protect Lucy, and she suddenly felt that ability, if it had ever been more than an illusion, was slipping away from her.

Michael replied, looking calmly between Callie and Josh, his hand still holding the fork, upright now, on the table. "When I took my nap this afternoon, they came to me, and we talked. It has been a long, long time since I was unshielded. These were new voices, but somehow still familiar. And they told me about the pictures Lucy is seeing, has been seeing all her life. She has been seeing you, Callie, since she was born. You, on a Ferris wheel with your father, and your not-father. And the landscape burning. And the sky, burning. And we are here together now, and the sky is going to burn. And we have to go. Tomorrow, we have to go."

Ted spoke again, "We have got to get the community in on this," he began.

"They're already in, Ted," Michael cut in. "They're the reason we're here. And their job now is to get me safely to Dim Sum tomorrow, and to plan us a way out of the city."

"This is nuts," Josh began, "Even after everything else, this is just fucking nuts. Michael, you're in shock, your friend is dead, I get it, but there's no way that you having a dream can—"

"It's my dream," Callie cut in.

The three men looked at her, each confused in his own way. "It's not her dream, it's my dream—it's me, on the Ferris Wheel. But I never had it before the night before last. Before I met her."

"What. The. Fuck. Did everyone take a hit of acid when I wasn't looking? Please someone tell me what the fuck is going on here." Josh was growing impatient, his temper beginning to flare for what felt like the first time in a long time, but really wasn't—it was just a departure from the mild, productive-seeming day. But he kept his voice low, aware that his daughter might hear his voice echo through the sprawling apartment.

Michael hesitated, then began, looking at Josh earnestly, with desire for him to understand written all over his face—with compassion in his voice, saying "Imagine driving down a road, like a country road, for miles and miles, seeing nothing and no one, and you're just driving, for hours, and there's no one else, and then you see a plume of dust rise in your peripheral vision, and you look and see a car coming along the horizon, and then another, from the other direction, and you keep moving, and you all come from nowhere, from nothing, and the three of you meet together at a four-way stop at the same instant. Who goes first? And how did you get there? And what about the fourth stop sign?" He paused. "That's what this is. It's the beginning of a, a convergence. We are together because we are supposed to be together."

Callie had had enough, but wanted to sound reasonable in her reply. "Ok, fine, we're supposed to be together. Just leaving aside the fact that the community brought us together, very purposefully—we weren't out on some road somewhere, we were at Starbucks, minding our business, and they swooped down and shoved us into this insanity. That isn't luck, or chance, or providence, or whatever. It just isn't," she paused, taking a breath, but continued before anyone else could start, saying "But ignore that—what about the rest of it? My dream? Or Lucy's dream? Or whatever it is? Suddenly dreams are supposed to mean something, too?" Callie began in that moment to feel weary of it all—not angry, not resentful, or even surprised—just really, incredibly tired. Yet she had strength enough to lean over the table and whisper, with purpose, but without malice, "And what about Trevor? Was he supposed to die? Is he in the car that never arrived?"

"Well," Michael began, slowly and somewhat purposefully, treading lightly with each word, aware not only of the emotionally charged people around him, but also his own uncertainty. "I don't think it is a dream. At least, not your dream, or Lucy's dream, if it is a dream. I think it's—something else. As far as destiny—I don't know. But you did have a choice. You weren't shoved into this. And you can leave right now, walk out that door. That sad young man upstairs—he had a choice, still has a choice. Was he destined to be upstairs injecting amphetamines so that you could be here safely today? I don't know—but he had a choice. So do I. So did Trevor. And as far as the fourth car goes, I never said it didn't arrive. I think it did arrive. But only Lucy can see it."

***

The cleaning up was left to Josh and Ted. Lucy and Michael had somewhat abruptly, though politely, stopped talking and become intractably introspective after their exchange about the imagined crossroads. Whether it was because neither had anything else to say, or didn't really want to hear want anyone else had to say, was an open question that hovered over the table until they left it.

When they were gone, Ted asked gently, but with some exaggerated meaning, "How are you doing, Josh?"

Josh looked at him with a stern but focused look, a pizza box half-crumpled in his hands, and said, "I don't want to talk about it."

"They're back?" Ted insisted, polite but firm. "We need to know." His tone was encouraging, sympathetic.

"Not, not entirely," Josh replied, his voice uncertain. "They're not really there, or here, but they are. I think, somehow, having Lucy—maybe she's acting as a sort of shield? I don't know. But I don't feel attacked, or chased, or scared. Not really." He looked up at his own unexpected acknowledgement of fear, regretting it—then realizing this man, Ted, probably knew as much about his life as he did himself—knew how much fear Josh had lived in.

"Maybe. It could also be that learning that the Mollies are real has taken that aspect of fear—the unknown—away from them. At least, partially. It could be a combination. It could just be that you're stronger," Ted said, using a paper towel to remove the drops of excess olive oil from the glass top table before he sprayed it with window cleaner.

"But is that what we want, right now?" Josh asked curiously. He felt more than a little left out of the shared dreams or whatever it was that seemed to connect the other three. "Shouldn't I be trying to communicate with the things?"

"No, not necessarily. What is supposed to happen is what will happen. I think—we think—you need to be here for them. To be strong."

"They're already strong. They're all strong. Stronger than me." Josh's tone was without self-pity. It expressed a detached awareness of self that surprised him.

"You think so?" Whether Ted was asking out of interest, or because it was what the community would want him to ask was impossible to know from his tone, but the inability to determine the other man's interest triggered a change of topic.

"Do you think the community is going to let Michael go to this Odeon place? Doesn't it just seem nuts?" Josh asked.

"Of course. To both. It seems highly risky, but they're probably working out the logistics of it right now. Michael's right—you're all free agents. And, Michael doesn't usually change his mind. When he's uncertain of something, he says so. When he wants input, he asks. He's done this before, multiple times. The risk is probably about the same, really, despite the heightened awareness. And, he seems to have made his mind up."

"But couldn't his emotions be impacting his judgment?"

"They could." Ted hesitated, putting the used paper towels into a black plastic garbage bag with the rest of the refuse from dinner. "But I don't think so. He isn't like us."

"Are you a carrier, too?" Josh asked, startled, looking at Ted with renewed interest, as though there might be some glow about him, some mark of distinction that connected them which he had somehow overlooked before.

"No. I'm just... human," Ted said, opening the door to leave, the trash bag in his hand. "Get some rest," he added, smiling encouragingly. "Meditate." The elevator door opened, and Ted looked back at Josh, standing with the metal door to the apartment held in his hands. "You need to clear your mind, Josh. This is not your moment."

And with that, the elevator door closed, and Ted was gone.

Josh looked around the empty apartment, motes of dust dancing in the shafts of dimmed track lighting. He could sense, just outside the range of perception, the shadow people. The community might call them *Mollies*, but he knew what they were, what they had always been. And they were there, in that apartment—he knew it as certainly as he knew his name. They had been there all day. He suddenly realized he had known that since he had stepped off the elevator, but he had shelved it, shoved it somewhere out of sight like a piece of unwanted mail from an old lover.

A part of him wanted to give in, to let himself go to the unknowing of the other, the blissful oblivion of not having, the security of not feeling. He wanted to grab a pair of scissors, and run, and not care who he hurt. But more than that, he wanted to be a father. Her father.

He thought of her as he sat on one of the large velvet pillows, his face turned north towards the Empire State Building, but without knowing it.

He sat quietly, patiently removing each thought of the day, his eyes seeing but not seeing the lights of the city beyond the windows, seeing but not seeing the tiny particles of dust scatter and drift in the beams of light shooting softly between him and the window, hearing but not hearing the exhaust fan in the bathroom, the whirr of the air conditioning, the almost-snoring-but-not-quite from behind Lucy and Callie's door. Some hours from when he sat down, though he would never know when, when his mind was completely clear of all thought, all fear, all emotion, and he began to see into the life of each speck of dust—each had a history, some millennia old. Each one told a story, he knew, and it wasn't just a story of what it had been, but what it would be. He needed only to find the right one, to find the right bit of dust, to pluck it from infinity, and read it. Then he would know. But these were not thoughts that occurred to him in words he could have articulated—his body simply knew it to be true.

He remained unmoving, his eyes focused on the middle distance between 23rd Street and forever, as he sorted through them, each speck a strand connected to and through where he sat: A young laughing boy with yellow hair opening a package wrapped in Raggedy Ann and Andy wrapping paper, orange and aqua, with a thick rope of orange yarn tied round the top; a woman in her thirties speaking Polish to her young daughter in their small apartment block in Poland right after the revolution—and he could not speak Polish, but he understood; Patty Smith, bundled in scarves, throwing a tennis ball to a black Labrador, whose name was Winter, sunlight streaming through skyscrapers and oaks into the little park just down 23rd Street; a group of men in black leather boots and little more, grinding and hairy and sinewy and sweaty, music too loud for speech, lights blinding out thought and memory, but the feeling of their touch warmed his skin, and he wasn't scared, but he pushed on, looking for the right particle. He pushed through them, forced himself away from stories he felt he wanted to hear, visions he wanted to share, until just before daylight, when a score of thousands of lifetimes had sifted through him, and he found the right one.

He recognized it at once—a Ferris Wheel, turning in time with the wisps of clouds washing past in the picture perfect sky. And he realized at once that something was different. There was not just a single line connecting this speck of dust to others, a single dot in a sinuous, endless strand. In his mind he turned it, and the perspective changed, and the sky was aflame, and then he turned it again, and it was not. And he turned it, and turned it, and turned it again, looking for the right strand to follow, until the wheel was not a wheel, but a spinning mass of light, an infinitesimal gyroscope with strands not extending from it, but being drawn into it. He saw what was about to happen before it happened—he found the right strand, and followed it out, as daybreak broke around him. A warm hazy glow began to spread across the rooftops of midtown and strike the sides of the towers uptown. The Empire State Building sat in the middle distance, squat and square compared to the elegant skyward strokes of cement and steel further uptown, but somehow more solid, more real, resolutely grounded to the place where it stood looking out at the morning.

He had needed to piss for a long time, but had been unaware of it. He did so now, before drinking a long drink of freshly squeezed orange juice from a plastic bottle in the refrigerator, and taking a bottle of Fiji water to the living room, where he put in Callie's earpiece from Plum Island, sat in front of the community monitor and whispered into the morning light, "Alright, we need to get Michael to Dim Sum."

The monitor was still coming on when a voice he didn't know said in his year "What happened? What did you experience?"

"I know what Michael knows. I've seen what Lucy has seen. And we have to get ready, now. And we're going to need running shoes."

"Why running shoes?" The unknown voice was curious, but without any hint of disagreement.

"I've just seen how this day ends. There are an infinite number of ways it could end. Might end. Will end. I've seen them all, I think. But in every one of them, we're running. And the sky is on fire."

***

The others slept well into mid-morning, giving the community plenty of time to make the Dim Sum arrangements, and for Ted to go to Paragon Sports off of Union Square. He bought five pairs of running shoes for each of the occupants of 23rd Street, but was wearing his own broken-in ones—just in case.

Josh was continually making coffee in a French press, which seemed overly-laborious and messy, but gave him something to do to keep him from looking at the others. He had seen into their pasts, and their futures, or at least glimpses of what might have been their pasts and futures, and he couldn't stop looking at them. And it was creeping out Lucy and Callie, he was sure, though Michael seemed to be in his own world. The kitchen was really only large enough for one person, so he stationed himself there. When the fruit was cut and croissants warmed, he called the others to the table, but had not set out a plate for Michael.

"Why isn't Michael eating?" Lucy asked. It was the first time she had asked about him. Their connection seemed to have grown overnight, and Josh knew why, though Callie did not.

"He's having Dim Sum at Odeon at 11:30. It's all been arranged," Josh answered, matter-of-factly.

"I thought you didn't want him to go?" Callie asked, sensing deception of some sort.

"Apparently we can't stop him," Josh said with feigned resignation, "so he might as well enjoy the food, right?"

"Um, right," Callie responded, not believing, but much more interested in a poppy seed bagel, cream cheese and smoked salmon from Balducci's than she was in interrogating Josh—she had always wanted Michael to go, so she wasn't going to question it.

"Why can't we get juice like this back in Georgia?" Lucy demanded, finishing her second glass. "Is everything just better in New York?"

"I can answer that," called a voice from the doorway—it was Ted, with 20 pairs of running shoes. "Yes, everything is better here. Bigger, better, louder, prettier. It's a city of superlatives."

"I wouldn't say that nature is better here," Callie quipped, gesturing out at the concrete landscape.

"Our nature may not be as big as the Grand Canyon, or the Rocky Mountains, but it's certainly better." He laid the bags of boxes of shoes down on one of the built-in benches, poured himself a glass of water, and sat with them. "Inch for inch, Central Park can put any of your natural beauties to shame."

"What's with all the shoes?" Lucy's energy and interest seemed to reflect more than just the elimination of sedatives from her system—she appeared really alive, and happy to be so. Her frame was still gaunt, but her face was flush with light. While too thin to be considered healthy by any conscientious parent, she wouldn't stand out among the model-thin weight-conscious young women roaming the streets just past the windows.

"Everybody needs shoes. When you're done with breakfast, everyone try some on. Keep whatever fit, but keep a pair by the door in case you need to go out."

"You think we'll be running?" Callie asked curiously.

"I think New York streets are hard on feet," Ted replied noncommittally.

***

As Michael was showering and dressing for Dim Sum—khaki pants, a black v-neck cashmere sweater, and a brand new pair of Adidas running shoes in lurid neon green, pink and yellow—Lucy asked the others, "What is it we're supposed to be doing? Are we just sitting here?"

"Yes, we're just sitting here," Josh said, standing to help Callie with the dishes as Ted reorganized the reject shoes into the right boxes to return to the store.

"I've been thinking," Lucy began, and already Josh felt the dread of any parent whose child has been thinking, as she continued, "Couldn't we just write to Mama Ben? Email? Or something? And let him know we're ok?"

"He knows. It's taken care of," Callie replied, "I took care of it yesterday."

"How?" Lucy asked, looking up from the game of Enchanted Fortress she was playing on the phone she'd found ringing in the delivery truck two days earlier.

"My phone doesn't actually connect to anything. Except, well, those people I guess. But I can't even call them, I don't think."

"I think if you need to talk to them, you can probably just start talking into the phone, and they'll answer," Callie suggested.

"They definitely will," Ted confirmed.

"So how does Mama Ben know we're ok?" Lucy persisted.

"I'm not sure about all the mechanics, exactly, but a vase full of eucalyptus was delivered to him during the meeting at Galano night before last. The card said, We're all ok. We love you. And it had our initials."

"Do you think that's enough? Will he believe it?" Lucy sounded doubtful.

"He knows us," Josh said, "and he knows we love him. That's the most important thing to believe, and he does."

Both women looked at him, and regarded his uncommon stoicism with expressions of wariness.

"What's into you?" Callie asked. "You've been strange all morning. Breakfast was great, by the way." He had really only opened packages and put things on plates, but still, it was nice to sit at a table.

"Adjusting to our new life, I suppose," Josh stammered out, without much conviction, as he returned to the kitchen with the leftover plate of fruit.

***

In less than two hours, Josh, Callie and Lucy were watching as Michael stepped into the lead-lined refrigerator box, pressed his back flat against the back of the box, and Ted gently leaned the box back on the appliance dolly. They disappeared into the elevator, with Ted waving a meager sort of goodbye, and Callie wondering aloud, "Is it strange that this seems normal now? I mean, this would have been completely bizarre three days ago, right? Watching a grown man climb into a box to be driven to have a meal where he's almost certain to be apprehended?"

Josh looked at her, surprised. "What makes you think that? Why would he be apprehended? The community is on top of this." He sounded remarkably sure of himself, for someone Callie believed to have as little understanding of the community as she did.

She looked back at him, troubled by his apparent sangfroid. "The community makes mistakes. We know that." She did not want to mention Trevor, but his name seemed to hang in the air around them. Lucy walked away, pulling her phone out and apparently continuing her game.

Callie went on, "He's going to a restaurant conveniently located halfway between the World Trade Center and the Holland Tunnel, two of the most obsessed-over terrorist targets in the city. There must be a million cameras down there. And the N.S.A. has footage of Michael from every angle that exists, and every age until he got on the trolley. They probably only need a glimpse of his nose to catch him."

"But they won't get it. Not a single glimpse. There is not a camera, or monitoring software that the community can't remotely control. Anywhere. Even now. They've had all night to plan for it, not like at Kroger, which was sort of unexected. They've done this before. They're ready."

"Are they going to take down all of lower Manhattan? Like they did Atlanta? That won't help matters downtown—he'll never be able to leave."

"No. They're just going to make him a ghost in the machine. The New York State Office of Counter-Terrorism has the most closed-circuit televisions, tens of thousands of them in the city altogether, all with a direct feed to the federal database of known faces—and most are known. If you've been in a yearbook, you're in it. If you've been in the newspaper, you're in it. If you've been arrested, have a driver's license or passport, you're in it. The databases are searched in order of priority, right now Michael is a top priority, so he would be an almost-instant hit, if seen. But he won't be seen. The system is incredibly buggy, and it will go offline downtown for two minutes when he's going in, and down again for two minutes when he's coming out. It's that simple."

Callie didn't believe him, but she pretended that she did. "What about inside?

Don't they have cameras there? In the restaurant?"

"They do, and a lot of them, but the recordings go to a hard drive in Jersey City where they're stored in case they're needed for investigations. Insurance companies require most of these places to keep them on file for a year—it's like we heard about before. The N.S.A. will intercept and review the feed, but there is always a delay. The community will digitally blur Michael before the file ever makes it across the Hudson. The same way faces are blurred on Google maps. This is easy stuff for them"

Callie frowned. "Shouldn't they be looking for real terrorists? I mean, I understand scientific inquiry and all, but aren't there bigger threats than us?"

Josh looked at her, and fought back an impulse to reach out and touch her as he said, "Callie, we are real terrorists. We broke into a federal facility and stole one of the military's most valuable assets in a war they've been fighting for decades. And they still don't know for sure what or who they're fighting. There's nothing more terrifying than not knowing. We're at war now."

Callie staggered backwards, and looked over to make sure Lucy wasn't listening. She wasn't responding, and her earbuds were in, but Callie knew that meant very little. Lucy was smart. Callie motioned Josh to the kitchen.

"Have you lost your fucking mind?" she began in a whisper when they safely were out of Lucy's range. "What kind of thing is that to say? Do you want her to think we're all going to be shot and killed?" Callie was seething, and the words punched through gritted teeth.

Josh wanted to smile, but didn't. He tried very hard not to sound condescending, to not seem like he knew things she didn't know. But he did know things, or he thought he did—at least, he believed he knew more than Callie. He said, "I think she knows that no one is going to be shot and killed. As much as anyone knows, she knows."

He saw in her face he had said too much.

"What do you know? How? Tell me." It was a demand he felt incapable of denying under her brutal gaze, so close to his, and so full of love for his daughter. But before he could respond, Lucy called out from where she was nestled by the fireplace, "If you guys want to watch, he's about to get out of the truck."

They turned their faces in her direction, but before Callie could make a move in that direction, or question him further, he suggested as mildly as he could, "I'll finish washing up. Why don't you get dressed and I'll meet you in the living room?" Callie was still wearing the tights and t-shirt that passed for her pajamas.

"Are we going somewhere?" she asked first, then continued, still whispering, though she wasn't sure why "Is something going to happen?"

"I think so, yes," he said with only mild confidence, then, sensing the weakness of his statement in her lack of reaction, he added with more conviction, "And soon. It's going to happen quickly, I think."

"Fuck," was her singular response as she darted past him to go tell Lucy to get dressed, and found Lucy already putting on her shoes, almost ready to walk out the door.

"Is there some reason no one could tell me earlier that I needed to get dressed?" Callie shouted at no one in particular as she turned and walked with speed to the back bedroom where her things were. She quickly located some black Marc Jacobs cargo pants and a black Armani Jeans sweatshirt—if they were going to be running the streets of New York, she at least wanted to look like a New Yorker. She grabbed her watch and toiletries kit from the nightstand, some socks, and the white-and-red Nike running shoes from their box. She regretted having chosen this pair, without immediately understanding the regret. If visibility mattered, she reasoned, Ted wouldn't have brought such a conspicuous pair for her to choose. *If he knew*, she thought. *If he knew what they know.*

She threw herself down on the sofa between Lucy and Josh, looking up at the monitor over the fireplace, which was showing three of the CCTV feeds, and one of the interior feeds from the restaurant's security system. "Ok," she said, trying to sound more authoritative than she felt, "would someone care to tell me what's going on?"

"The fries are taking a minute. The grease wasn't hot enough. He's waiting until everything is on the bar before he goes in," Lucy answered, not looking away from the screen.

"I'm not talking about the food. Why am I putting on running shoes?" she asked with impatience, as she was putting on her socks. "And can we get some audio? Can I hear what's going on?"

"Here," Josh said, and handed her an earpiece. "Can you put it in yourself?"

"Well, yes, I suppose," she began, flustered, "Why am I putting in an earpiece? Why can't we all just listen together?"

"The fries are coming out," and unknown voice said in here ear. Then a different voice, "Michael is preparing to leave the van."

Callie resigned herself to not getting an immediate response, and watched the *We Move NYC* moving van idle on Thomas Street, beneath the Odeon's red neon *Cafeteria* sign. The main entrance was around the corner on West Broadway.

Suddenly, there was a rapid fire succession of clipped announcements in her ear: "New York State down," "American Apparel down," "Supreme Court down," "Gina's down," and the mysterious voices continued until one finally said, "Go, go, go," and the three CCTV images on the living room monitor switched to interior views of the Odeon, and Michael walking into it.

"Why does the Supreme Court need to go down?" Callie asked, in alarm.

"New York County Supreme court is across Thomas Street from Odeon," a detached voice said in her ear, giving her little reassurance. She wondered vaguely if Michael could have picked a more conspicuous place to eat if he had tried. Then she wondered if he had tried.

"It's like from a movie," Lucy whispered, looking at the interior of the restaurant, and it was true.

The terrazzo floor, crimson and red leatherette banquettes, upholstered bentwood chairs, rippled glass partitions, and white tablecloths set with stainless steel cutlery, all immaculate, and joined together by a high bright ceiling punctuated with milk glass globe pendants, altogether created a more theatrical, yet somehow timeless and permanent setting than Lucy could have imagined possible. *It's like a dream*, she thought, and the thought cut through her consciousness like a laser. *It's like a dream I've had.*

The entire space was ablaze with light, the morning sun sparkling off the Art Deco stainless steel and chrome architectural flourishes, and immense light-reflecting mirrors—larger than many bedrooms in the city—hung at angles around the restaurant, giving everyone in the space a gleaming view of everyone else, and especially of the bar. Immense and ancient, the soft curves of the Art Deco bar rippled down almost the entire north wall, reminiscent of an aging but fierce battleship. The veneer gave it a soft, warm radiance, but it was a hard-wearing, hard-drinking bar, its back mirrors reflecting the dozens of bottles that pinged the morning sun back into it, its bar top dented with the pushing and shoving of drinkers clamoring, friends carousing, lovers pushing back into its soft, rough, curved edges. Looking at the thousands, perhaps hundreds of thousands of reflections of Michael that a high-definition camera would most certainly see, Callie whispered softly, "Good God."

"Don't be alarmed, Callie, everything's under control," came a voice, warm, familiar, soothing. "Everything's going to be just fine."

Callie gasped. "Sam? Is that you?" Lucy turned to look at her, and smiled.

"Yes, it's me. Of course it's me. Who else would it be? Child, if I could tell you about the past few days. And I will, but not right now. We need you to settle down, missy."

"What do you mean settle down?" she said, perturbed that this man she had been so worried about was speaking down to her like a schoolchild. "Who the fuck—"

"Your anxiety level is apparently too high. It's registering in your voice. Can you meditate for a minute?" He sounded like he was reading from a script, and wanted her to know he was reading from a script.

Callie turned to look at Josh and Lucy to see if they were hearing what she was hearing, but they apparently were not. They were listening intently to something else, presumably the exchange Michael was having with the bartender as he sat down at the bar, his face a curious mixture of delight and sadness, his blackness glowing white in the countless crosscurrents of the morning light reflecting through the space.

Callie closed her eyes and exhaled. "Sam, I love you, but if I don't get some answers, or at least get to hear what is happening right now, I swear to God I will burn every wig, dress, and stiletto you have ever owned. You will be the worst-dressed drag queen this side of the Mississippi. I swear to God. Do you understand me? Am I making myself clear?"

"Alright, girl, just making a suggestion," he said with a sardonic uplift of his voice. Then he added quickly, and apparently off-script, "I'll see you soon."

She would be seeing him—she was going to the place where he was. That was one mystery settled for her. And then she thought to herself, *Why all the mystery, if everything is so secure? Why can't we just openly discuss it?* She asked the same questions aloud, and was surprised when Josh answered, explaining what might have been obvious—if members of the community could go rogue, and he had been right, one had, back at Irish Acres Retirement Center, one could go back to the other side, might actually still be working for the other side. "There's no reason for everyone to know where anyone will be," he finished. His explanation provided little comfort, but as explanations went, it was one of the more reasonable ones she had received recently.

As she watched Michael taking a bite out of the bacon cheeseburger, she was more than a little jealous—the high definition of the cameras and monitor, the brilliancy of the room, and the light in Michael's eye made the whole scene appear as nothing so much as a commercial for the restaurant. The audio in her earpiece came to life, and suddenly she could hear the sounds of the restaurant, Depeche

Mode playing in the background, the sounds of chairs scraping as the early lunch-time crowd began to wander in. Busboys and servers, fresh and clean, suited in black and white, began to appear from doors on either side of the kitchen. She could hear glasses and bottles clinking, the sounds of car horns and heavy trucks from the street, and somewhere out on the street, an argument. Michael ate some fries, dipped in a miniature white ramekin filled with ketchup. He savored them for just a moment, then moved the plate down the bar, and, took a sip of what Callie assumed to be his Stoli gimlet. He then began his next course, the French onion soup, which had time to chill, but when Michael pulled the thick layer of Gruyere cheese back from the white crock, steam rose from the slick surface of the soup, thin slivers of onion swimming in the broth. Callie could almost taste it.

"I'm starting to wish we had gone with him," Lucy said. "I can't believe he just ate two bites of that cheeseburger. And all those fries..." she drifted off with longing, "They look so—"

But here she was cut off with a scream, and everyone froze, and then a voice called out, full of wonder and delight, "Michael! Michael Isaacs! Oh my God!" And a blur of a black and white uniform topped with long yellow hair raced through the restaurant to stand beside Michael at the bar, her arms spread in anticipation of a hug. Michael turned and smiled, but his smile could not mask his confusion.

"It's Gillian! Gilly Connors! From Brattleboro! We went to school together. Oh my God, I can't believe it! I heard you were dead, or in some kind of trouble." The last part was said as he embraced her, remembering her fondly from another age—junior high and high school in Brattleboro, Vermont. She moved to New York after graduation to become a star of stage and screen. He was pleased to see her, and it showed on his face and in his clinging to her arms. "I can't believe you're here," she continued, "and that you're the Dim Sum man. I've been hearing about you since I started work here last year—I usually only work nights, so I've only ever heard about you. You're kind of a legend," she said, her face alive with pleasure. "I can't believe you're here. Michael Isaacs!"

In his earpiece, Michael was hearing a warning, "Michael, you've got to get out of there, now. Go, go, go. Now, Michael, go." But he did not go. He stood, placidly, looking at her beaming face, and could not tear himself away that quickly. It had been so long since anyone had been happy to see him—just him, being him, having lunch. "Gilly, it's so good to see you. You look amazing." The perfect gentleman, he pulled over a stool for her, and gestured for her to sit down next to him, and reached for the crème brulee, topped with fresh raspberries and a dollop of crème fraiche, and put it at the place he made for her.

"Oh my God, no, I can't. I need this job," she said, laughing. "How long are you in town for? Are you on Facebook?"

Throughout New York City and State, across the river in New Jersey, at the Pentagon, at Fort Meade, Maryland, and at Special Operations Command Central at Macdill Air Force Base, Florida, men and women were mobilizing, preparing to swarm and lock down the entire southern tip of Manhattan, casting a net so thick and wide and dense that Michael could not possibly escape it. The swarm of anomalous figures that had been swirling around the southeastern United States for the past three days in an increasingly complex and refined pattern appeared to coalesce almost at once in time with this movement, and the eye of the storm—if it was a storm—spread, though no meteorologist, no astronaut looking down from space could see, the hole forming in the center of the swirling mass of white light. Part of the community listened to the military mobilization with increasing alarm, while another part watched the changing pattern of light with amazement. Those with access to both discussion boards tried not to overreact. But they wanted Michael to act, and quickly.

"Just here for a couple of days. No, my work won't allow me on Facebook," he said with a grin, and a cautious glance up at one of the cameras that he knew must be watching him at that very moment.

Across the restaurant, two suited men stood and threw their napkins on the table where iced teas with sprigs of mint had just moments before been set down by a waiter who asked, "Is everything alright, gentlemen?" as they reached behind their backs, towards their waistbands, in slow deliberate gestures. Michael saw in the mirror behind him as the morning sunlight hit the barrels of their drawn weapons, and he ducked below the glass partition separating the bar from the dining room, pulling Gilly down with him. The rest happened so quickly he could not distinguish, but the front windows of the restaurant exploded in a shower of glass that sent both of the suited men to the floor, bloodied and unmoving. In his ear Michael heard a voice demanding "Through the kitchen, now, GO, Michael, for the love of God, GO." And he did.

Leaving behind a restaurant full of screaming, crying and bleeding people, his friend Gilly on the floor in hysterics, he raced doubled-over to and through the kitchen and out a side door onto Thompson Street. He was headed towards the truck when he received the command, "Not the truck, Michael. Turn right, and run, just keep running up West Broadway." As he ran, a man who looked just like him, and was dressed like him, ran past him towards the Odeon. And then two more men, who looked less like him but had his same build and features, crossed Worth Street ahead of him, one running east, one running west, then two more crossed Leonard Street, again running both east and west. Another ran past him in the direction he was running, and turned left. And then another, who turned right.

In the confusion of all the people running he wasn't sure anyone would notice all the tall, slender, elegantly and identically dressed men; but, there was a critical difference he noticed, even in his haste—all of the shoes were different. Only he had the Adidas.

"Varick Street is veering off to your left. Follow it. You'll see a covered entrance to the subway directly in front of you. Run down into it. Someone will meet you there. His name is Lucien. He'll guide you." Behind him he heard two explosions, and people began running and screaming in earnest, some passing him. Sirens sounded in every direction. "Your earpiece will not work underground. Just follow Lucien."

As soon as he heard the young woman scream in delight at seeing Michael, Josh knew what several of the next outcomes might be, and he stood. "Where is the key?" he asked, to no one in particular.

"What key?" asked Callie and a voice in his ear simultaneously.

"The key to the 72nd floor," Josh asked, with a little impatience, and some confusion. "Isn't there a key to the 72nd floor here?" Callie and Lucy looked at Josh with frank bewilderment, trying to listen to Michael's high school reunion and follow along with the rapidly-evolving, increasingly-disturbing developments on the security front.

"Michael has the key," was the reply, almost apologetic, that fell flatly in his ear. He groaned, stood, and looked around—uncertain for the first time of what he had seen last night. He had seen the key—he had known it was there. How could Michael have it? He hadn't seen that.

"What's happening?" Callie asked, then Lucy screamed as the sound of gunfire and shattering glass exploded in all their earpieces, causing them all to jump, and Callie to drop a mug of coffee on the slate floor.

"We're leaving, now," Josh said, "Come on, let's go," he demanded walking towards the door, "Lucy, now, come on, get up," but Lucy stayed on the sofa until Callie nodded. Callie looked back down at the coffee spreading on the slate tile beneath her.

"Leave it. They'll be here in minutes. They'll trace the truck back. It's out of our control now." Josh opened the coat closet by the front door and took out a shopping bag before he entered the elevator lobby and pressed the call button for the elevator.

Sam urged Callie gently through her earpiece, "You better go, girl. I gotcha back. Get Lucy. Go."

She heard the elevator's gentle ding of arrival and walked through the puddle of coffee to grab Lucy's hand as they stepped down the slate steps, through the little lobby and into the elevator. The apartment door shut itself behind them with a thud, but they did not lock it—there seemed to be silent consensus among them that there was no reason to. And, no one had a key.

The earpieces did not work in the elevator, and it was the first time any of them had their thoughts to themselves in some time, and it was uncomfortable.

"You ok, kid?" Josh asked Lucy, with an extraordinary amount of awkward paternal affection layered on.

Lucy looked back at him with a fake disgruntled-teenager face. "I'm fine," she said, "and don't call me kid. I'm not a child."

Callie realized she was right—Lucy was not a child. At least, not entirely. Less than most.

"Okay," he said, distracted, "we need to put these on. They won't help much, but they're better than nothing." He pulled two baseball caps, one platinum blond wig, and one black wig from the shopping bag. Callie and Lucy each snapped a ball cap from his hands, but as the elevator door opened, he said, "Seriously, come on, guys," and Callie reluctantly traded a New York Yankees cap for the blonde wig. It was synthetic and horrible, and she wouldn't have liked it even if she didn't despise wigs, which she did. "Sam, how do you wear these things?" she whispered aloud as she followed Lucy and Josh out onto 23rd Street, heading east.

"I would never wear that wig. That's just nasty," Sam answered voice in her ear, "and slow down. Walk a few steps behind them, and closer to the buildings. You're only going to the corner. You need to get underground. You're going to lose radio contact once you're on the train." Unmarked sedans and sports utility vehicles were careening down Broadway, most without sirens going, but enough sirens were wailing to draw attention from passersby, even in New York.

"Why?" She whispered, disquieted. The street was bustling with lunchtime pedestrians. She passed a street vendor selling hot dogs and some sort of spiced meat patty, the smell of which almost made her retch.

"How should I know? I'm a chemist. You're almost there. Just to the corner, that's all." Sam's voice, just the idea of Sam, reassured her. Soon, he had said. Soon. He continued, "They're going to go down the entrance to the N/R line. Follow them. And Callie, I love you."

"I love you, too, Sam." She paused as she passed the green globe that marked the entrance to the 23rd Street Uptown station entrance Josh and Lucy had just entered, and asked "No suicide pills, right?"

"Girl you should know me better than that. That was never an option. I'm all about a blaze of glory. But there won't be one for me, or for you. Not tonight. Us bitches got plans. Just follow Josh. Go."

"What bitches?" Callie asked as she jumped down the steps, herded along by an impatient throng of commuters anxious to get on the train they heard pulling into the station.

"Go girl. See you later."

Josh and Lucy stood by the turnstile, waving her forward, and Josh swiped a MetroCard for each of the three of them to pass through the turnstile as the train arrived at the platform. They jostled their way onto the uptown N train, and just as the doors began to close, they heard from the street—distant, yet clear and distinct—the sounds of explosions, and people screaming. The doors closed and the train pulled out of the station.

The explosions heard on 23rd Street, and throughout Manhattan, were the sounds of every critical piece of communication infrastructure in the city exploding—117 in all. The relatively small number of routing centers in the city allowed the N.S.A. to efficiently monitor millions of terabytes of data as it passed through the cables, wires, and airwaves of the city—but it also provided anyone who knew where those 117 critical junctions occurred to leave the city effectively mute. Most of the explosions were very controlled, but several sparked fires on rooftops and underground channels throughout the city. Within minutes, no cell phone, land line, internet connection, or radio dispatch call could be made. At 12:03pm, power to major rail lines failed—no Amtrak, Metro-North, Long Island Railroad or PATH trains could move, and they sat idling on tracks mid-route as railway administrators began to frantically adjust the afternoon train schedule to accommodate for what would quickly become an escalating delay, but to no avail—the power at Grand Central and Penn Station went out three minutes later. Within minutes, there was no power flowing anywhere into the city, as though it had simply been cut off from the power grid. Backup generators at hospitals and airports went into automatic duty, as word spread in Albany, the state capitol, that every power plant transmission substation supplying power to New York City was suddenly incapable of routing power there. Unable to immediately divert the excess electricity elsewhere, power plants across the state began going offline.

At 12:57pm, the Federal Energy Regulatory Commission issued a press release saying power could be expected to return to New York and New Jersey in waves throughout the afternoon, as fire crews were readied for potential hazards that might arise. The press release was issued on behalf of the Northeast Power Coordinating Council, whose own offices on the 10th floor of the 1040 Avenue of the Americas building were without power. The news was broadcast on CNN out of Atlanta and local stations across the country, as the major television networks in New York scrambled to get their networks back online.

CHAPTER 13—ÉTOUFFÉE

"Now when you say *us bitches*, who exactly do you mean?" Eleanor was looking at Sam over her cup of tea with feigned outrage—she wasn't actually offended at all by his comments, but if they were going to be living together in an underground fortress for an indefinite amount of time, she did not plan to be called a *bitch*, or a *ho*, or a *skank*, or any of those other outrageous words young people used to address each other—she watched cable television. She knew how young people were these days.

And more than that, he wasn't young. While he had apparently accomplished a lot professionally, his deportment, his demeanor, his very approach to living was almost sophomoric, if not entirely juvenile, particularly for a man of his age, old enough to have grown children. He was worse than those 70-year-old men who insisted on driving around in red convertibles, acting like teenagers, with the liver spots on their balding heads exposing the lie. They at least were what they were—ridiculous old men trying, like all men, to have more fun than they were entitled to. But Sam was something else, and she couldn't quite figure out what it was, and it made her uncomfortable. His behavior, his very being, she took as an affront.

She understood sodomy as well as any woman could—again, just men trying to have more fun than they should, in her opinion. But this business of dressing like a woman, acting like a woman, even singing—*singing*, for heaven's sake—like a woman, she could not understand. She remembered Phil Donohue appearing on his television talk show dressed up like a woman, and she didn't understand it then, and she still didn't. She had never particularly liked the extra effort it took to be a woman, particularly after her husband died. The heels, the make-up, the sitting in a chair for hours with noxious chemicals curling her hair, with her aching legs crossed demurely—it all seemed so completely pointless. She had no one to impress—no man, at least. But if she wanted to be taken seriously at the courthouse, at PTA meetings, if she wanted the bank teller to serve her promptly, and with proper deference, she knew she had to play the part—her part, her right part, her assigned part—and she had done it. And this man, this Sam, seemed somehow to be telling her she had been a fool, that she needn't have done the things she did. That she could have been anything she wanted, had she simply been sassy enough, rebellious enough, even woman enough; if she, like him, had simply refused to accept things for what they were, she could have been anything she wanted. His swagger—his *pride*, she supposed he would call it—suggested to her that he thought she was weak, or lazy, or morally inferior to her because she was a product of her age. But he was wrong. She would have been run out of town. And more to the point, he would have been lynched. It was another time. And this, she knew, was its own time, was *his* time, and she would let him have it. But she would not be disrespected. That, she would not let him have. *Us bitches, indeed.*

"Eleanor," he said looking across the large wooden table they were seated at, "I meant no disrespect. Callie needed to feel comforted, and that is how the two of us communicate. Had I spoken to her in a more genteel manner, she would have been made more suspicious and uncomfortable than if she hadn't heard from me at all. This isn't about you."

Eleanor was preparing her rebuttal when Stick sat down at the table and interrupted, "Sam, could you please help Linus with lunch? I need to speak with these ladies for a moment."

Stick's cover, such as it was, had been blown when he first guided Chari off the interstate. He had been preparing for his disappearance since he first entered the community—the apparent evaporation of his own protégé, combined with his own decades of duplicity and double-dealing, had suggested to him the need for prudent planning. He had turned over the deed to his home to a local hospice, and arranged all of his legal matters in such a way that his own eventual evaporation-into-thin-air would be as tidy as possible. He had also worked to make Olgasa as tidy as possible, sensing that when it came time for him to go underground, it would most likely be a literal move to the headquarters he helped build there.

And so it was. As soon as he was able to extract Sam from the lab at the C.D.C., and navigate the post-blackout Atlanta traffic snarl, they followed the same route, in the same truck, as the women had a day before them. Sam had barricaded himself in the lab with enough snacks, candy and gum to last for days, but the place still did not have a bathroom. He made those trips as infrequently as possible, however, and when he did so, he made a great show of putting a barcoded glass vial in each of his lab coat's four pockets—anyone watching would know that he was a walking biohazard. On one of these trips, he ran into a cleaning lady in the men's room and she passed him a note, unseen by any camera, before she left him. Following the instructions on the note, he climbed through the two-by-two drop ceiling in the bathroom, replaced the tile, and dropped into the adjacent stall in the women's restroom, quickly shaved, put on the wig and cleaning uniform left there for him, and was out of the building before anyone realized he was missing. The cleaning lady they later identified as him could be seen on camera getting into a Federated Cleaning Services van at the loading dock of the laboratory, and though it had certainly returned to the Federated central supply office on East Cleveland Avenue, no one there remembered seeing any such woman, or the man shown to them in pictures. "That is one fine lookin' woman," one of the men in the front office suggested, adding somewhat unhelpfully, "I sho' wouldn't of let a woman that good-a-lookin' get away from me."

The appearance of Stick and Sam at Olgasa had provided some immediate diversion for the three women, who, though only there for a day, had already grown somewhat weary of the place. When the men arrived, those who had known each other before were delighted to see the others, those who didn't know the others greeted one another with detached, even suspicious enthusiasm.

The first thing Eleanor had learned about Sam—at least, that struck her as meaningful—was that he did not follow the rules. Any rules, apparently. It was his call to Chari that had precipitated Eleanor's own decampment to the forlorn, if well-appointed underground cavern, and she resented it. There was a lack of order in the place that made her uneasy, and she somewhat unreasonably held him responsible, though she was, in her own way, more implicit in the dealings of the community, through her communication with Michael on the trolley, than Sam had ever been. Eleanor's participation had been entirely voluntary—Sam had been dragged into it. That it was her friend Ida Mae, and not the community itself, that had first brought Sam into contact with Michael was a fact that Eleanor simply chose to overlook.

So this sit-down with Stick, whom Eleanor regarded with a sort of grudging respect, was welcome to her. She hoped it would give her the opportunity to ask some questions, and make some pertinent observations that had been on her mind since the conversations the day before with Velma-Anne, as they had taken to calling the woman on the monitor. Before Eleanor could arrange her thoughts in the most politic way, however, Stick had begun.

"My apologies for not being able to spend more time with you this morning. As you've seen, we've been quite busy. Michael and the others are safe for now, and we're going to get them out of New York, and to somewhere safe. Ideally, we will have them all here before the day is through. Once they're here, though, your flexibility—your ability to leave here as you please—will be limited. Right now, we can safely get you to the federal authorities without any real risk. You would probably be held for several days for questioning, but in the end, they would let you go. Once the others are here, however, that will change. You might not be able to leave for weeks, possibly months. You didn't ask to be brought here, and we won't keep you here against your will. But you will need to decide—and quickly, I'm afraid—whether you want to be part of the community, and stay here with Michael and the others, or go back to your lives as they were.

"You don't really think I'm ever going to be a judge again, do you?" Chari asked, with a heave of her shoulders and a humph that was close to a laugh.

"I think you are a judge. A good judge. With the potential to be a great judge. The community needs more wisdom. We need you." His face, however, told another story: *I need you*, it said. *I need a friend here.*

"And what about us? You certainly don't need us, do you?" Eleanor joined in, unexpectedly. He turned to look at her.

"I think you're wrong, Ms. Eleanor," he began cautiously. "I think the whole world is about to change. I think there are few enough people like yourself, and Ms. Ida Mae, with a voice. You understand change, and the potential for change. The devastating effects that technology, that mindless indifference to tradition, to what was, to what has been, to what should be.... what effects that can have."

"You're saying I'm a conservative? That I'm old-fashioned? And that you need a living relic of the past sitting around telling you how we did everything wrong before?" She was directing her animosity towards Sam at Stick, which she regretted almost immediately, and softened her tone, adding, "I'm really not any of those things, you know. I'm just an old woman, and getting older each day."

Ida Mae laughed in agreement, "Yes, you are, Ms. Eleanor. You certainly are. But I've made my decision—where Michael wants me to be, that's where I want to be. And I believe he would want me here."

"Fine, then. Is Sam staying?" Chari asked, with interest.

"Yes, Sam is staying," Stick replied, and looked to Eleanor and whispered "He's not that bad, Ms. Eleanor, once you get to know him, I don't think." She turned down the corners of her mouth as a sign that she had heard, but would not be responding.

"What exactly is it that you all think is going to happen? And why do you think it's going to happen now? I mean, those graphs and swirling maps and Oak Ridge and all the rest—what does it all mean? Do you know?" Chari asked.

"I don't know. But I believe something is going to happen. And I plan to be right here for it." Stick's voice was uncharacteristically firm, and suddenly, disconcertingly sad.

"Well then, I'm staying," Chari said, searching his face for a sign that he knew more than he did, but finding none. "Whatever happens out there—up there, my life won't be the same whether I'm back in two days or two weeks or two months."

"Well, I'm not certainly going back there alone and trying to explain all this mess," Eleanor said with resignation and finality. "They'd think I've lost my mind."

"Who's to say we haven't?" Chari suggested with a weak smile as Sam moved towards the table with his arms full of plates piled with cutlery.

"Ladies, if I may," he asked with a little aloofness, and a sarcastic sort of curtsy, and began laying plates at the other end of the long table after receiving a sort of silent assent to proceed.

Eleanor stood up, and with the air of an experienced military commander ceding her place on the battlefield to someone younger, and less experienced, and from a different army, she smiled as genuinely as she could muster said, "Here, let me help you with that."

Disarmed, and outflanked, Sam lay the dishes down and said, "I'll bring the food over, then."

Eleanor rolled her eyes at the others, who moved down to see what they were having for lunch.

"Quesadillas Étouffée, everybody," Linus called, following Sam to the table with a platter of folded, stuffed tortillas.

The women looked at each other with eyes so expressive of disguised alarm that each suddenly laughed in turn at the other.

"Is something wrong?" Linus asked as he set the platter down on the table.

"Don't mind us bitches," Eleanor said somewhat wryly, and even more pointedly, adding, "We think everything's funny."

They all smiled—except Linus, who didn't quite understand what was going on—and they sat down together to enjoy an unexpectedly good meal together. Still, afterwards, Ida Mae and Chari did a thorough inspection of the pantry and cabinets and made a list of everything they needed from the market before Linus left on what was expected to be the last supply run for the foreseeable future.

CHAPTER 14. EMPIRE STATE

Michael was halfway down the steps into the subway station when he realized he had no way of identifying the man he was supposed to be meeting. As he stepped off the bottom step, a young blond man in his late twenties or early thirties who was standing by the ticket machine turned and faced him—he was wearing a black sweatshirt with the name *Lucien* spelled out in white felt letters across the front, and had a backpack slung over one shoulder. "Hey, my man," he said, walking towards Michael, his arms stretched out in the exaggerated way of men who are old friends that hug with closed fists. Michael smiled, and it wasn't entirely insincere, and returned the hug as the man whispered "Just follow me, don't say anything," and turned to walk through the turnstile, swiping his MetroCard to pay both his and Michael's fares. "It's so good to see you," he began, and continued with the sort of mindless banter not atypical of conversations where one person has a lot to say and the other person can respond with nods, shrugs, or a smile. None of the scattering of people on the platform was paying them any attention, anyway—the commotion from the street was drifting down the steps, across the turnstile, and down the echoing tunnel, drawing the attention of the few people not wearing headphones.

An uptown number 9 train approached, with few enough people on it, and the two men entered the nearest and least-crowded car, and seated themselves as a computerized voice announced "Stand clear of the closing doors. This is a Bronx-bound number 9 train. Next stop, Canal Street."

"Oh, here, your glasses are in your backpack," the young man said, and handed the worn black nylon backpack to Michael, who found a black hoodie as well as a pair of matte black plastic eyeglasses. With a nod from Lucien, he slipped both things on, to the typical indifference of their fellow passengers. He returned the backpack to the floor, and Lucien slid it between his feet.

They got off the train at 14th Street, and began a labyrinthine walk up and through twisting stairs and passageways. They made their way to the underground passageway connecting the Seventh Avenue station, where they had just departed the number 9 train, to the Sixth Avenue station. Lucien's pace slowed markedly, and he began to speak in exaggerated tones about his personal views on a number of penalties called by a referee in a football game the week before. About two thirds of the way down the tunnel, with no one else in sight, a service door with no handle opened from the other side, and they quickly stepped in. The low-ceilinged space was dimly lit by a few bare light bulbs housed in protective wire cages. How far back the space went was not immediately clear—it seemed to be filled not just with floor buffers and mop buckets and the unassembled parts of barricades stacked to the ceiling in every direction, but also an assemblage of the less-portable debris of the station outside: old magazine racks and newspaper boxes, innumerable waste bins, dingy traffic cones, and piles of abandoned clothing. The sound of the heavy, industrial door closing on its rusty hinges was surprisingly almost noiseless. The place smelled of dust, chemicals, beer, and stale, secret tobacco.

The person who had opened the door came into view—a short, balding, stocky man in black polyester pants, white shirt with breast pockets, a black braided leather belt, and black utility shoes in a style somewhere between a sneaker and a dress shoe—and he beckoned Lucien and Michael away from the door. On one hip he wore what looked like a policeman's UHF radio, and on the other what looked like his personal cell phone, and a massive ring of keys, all clipped to his belt. When all three were blocked from view of the door behind stacks of boxes of cleaning supplies, Michael saw the man's Metropolitan Transportation Authority identification card hung round his neck with a lanyard. "Tony Alvarez," he said by way of introduction, "I'm the station manager here. Good to meet you, Michael, but we only have a minute," he began, but Michael interrupted him before he could continue.

"She wasn't supposed to be there," he said, looking back and forth from Tony's face to Lucien's. "Gilly, she wasn't supposed to be there. Those men, they weren't supposed to be there. They're not supposed to be here." He kept looking between the two men, desperate for some information that would make sense of the words he was saying—he appeared to not be exactly in control of them. Having stopped forward movement, his thoughts seemed to be catching up with and overwhelming him. "They weren't supposed to die. They weren't supposed to be there. What if it's wrong? What if it's all wrong? What if I'm wrong?"

Lucien looked at Michael and spoke with more assurance than he felt, "Michael, everything is going to be ok. It was never likely that things were going to go exactly according to plan, but that's why we had backup plans. Have backup plans. We're going to get you out of here, and back somewhere safe."

"Listen," Tony began nervously, as his radio crackled uncertainly, "I have to get back upstairs. When these lights go out," he gestured to the ceiling, "that means it's safe for you to go. You'll only have a couple of minutes before officers come down for these barricades. You know where you're going?" He looked to Lucien as he asked the question, and Lucien nodded. Tony took from his pocket a somewhat smaller ring of keys than the one on his belt, but still containing more than two dozen keys of various shapes and sizes. "These will get you in any door on the 4/5/6 line. Be careful, get your flashlight ready." He looked at Michael and added, "You, too. Be careful."

"Were you supposed to be here?" Michael asked, with a hard note of desperation cutting his near-whisper. Lucien pulled a small flashlight from the bottom of the backpack.

"We're all where we're supposed to be," Tony said, adding, "And I have to be somewhere else now." He smiled a grave, determined smile, and walked around the stack of cleaning supplies. The two men left behind did not hear the door open or close, but they did see a patch of light appear and disappear on the ceiling.

"Michael, are you ok?" Lucien was looking at Michael with frank and unapologetic concern stamped upon his every feature.

"Josh knew," Michael began, faltering as though admitting some horrible, unspeakable truth, "Josh knew that the dream wasn't real. He knew it could all go wrong. Would go wrong." He looked down at his feet, the three jagged stripes a visual repudiation of everything he had believed. "We were supposed to be able to stop it. They won't let us," he said, his voice nearly in panic.

"Michael, you have to calm down. Breathe. Don't say anything else. Just breathe. The lights are going to go out any minute now, and we have to leave, we have to stay focused." Lucien grasped Michael by the shoulders, and looked him in the eyes, "Michael, we can do this," he said.

"Who are you? I know you. Who are you? You aren't Lucien. What's your name?" Michael's speech was insistent.

"Alex. My name is Alex. I came up from New Orleans. I've been learning the New York City subway system for over a year, getting ready for this day, for this moment. I'm ready. Are you ready?"

"You're going to die," Michael said, and sadness and anger ran down his face. "The voices keep changing now, but I can hear them. I'm sorry," he said, seeing the color that had drained from the face of the young man standing there wanting to help him, "I can't stop it. They're coming for us. For us both."

The light flickered and was gone, and the screaming out in the tunnel began, as Alex turned on the flashlight, grabbed Michael by the hand, and pulled him towards the door. He pulled it open as the emergency floodlights in the tunnel flickered on, illuminating people who were searching for their cellphones to light their way in the subterranean passage. He turned off the flashlight and let loose of Michael's hand, grabbed him by his forearm, and began pulling him towards the Sixth Avenue tunnel.

As they walked, apparently recovered from the dire warning he had just received, Alex began, "A few minutes back, you said *here*. You said they aren't sup-posed to be here. Who were you talking about?"

"Them. All of them. They weren't supposed to be here. It was supposed to have stopped."

"What was supposed to have stopped, Michael?"

"The storm. Being there, with Trevor, was supposed to make everything right. I thought it would make everything right. But Josh knew. And now they're here."

"This is all going to work out, Michael," Alex said as he began moving up a flight of steps that would take them to the platform for the L train. People were shouting and bumping into one another, waiting for an announcement that would tell them how long their trains would be delayed. The two men made their way to the platform for the east-bound L train, and stood waiting for the announcement. The meager light of the emergency floodlights, so bright in the small, tiled tunnel, was insufficient to light the gaping, endlessly black train tunnels or the cavernous platform where they stood, Alex in anticipation, Michael simply lost. People had out their cellphones, and their faces, flush with frustration, were illuminated by the screens that told them there was no service. A chill, wet wind whipped down through distant grates and across the platform. The blaring, piercing, honking horns of frustrated motorists, unmoving on the streets above, escalated into a discordant, but constant chorus. No one was moving up there.

But one man was moving below, his feet dragging along the concrete platform in accumulations of tape and twine and scraps of leather that might once have been shoes. His voice, ragged and derelict, sounded like the articulation of the rags he wore—soiled and matted with age and disease, layer upon layer of folds of fabric of indeterminate color and shape. He appeared to have been called to the dark platform from some near-distant place down the tracks. He smelled of rot, and rat, and retch, but his eyes were dancing as he moved from one indifferent person to the next, accepting their silent shrugs and lack of generosity with shuffling curses. "A little change? A little change?" he asked in shrill, torn supplication, and then "Motherfuckers, motherfuckers," under his breath in an agitated, hollow whisper that seemed to be carried along down the platform by the collective hope that he would go away.

His shuffling stopped when he came to Alex and Michael. He looked at the latter and barked, full in his face, "You're late!" and the sickness was stripped from his voice. He spoke with the command of a general on the battlefield, prime, and lean, and full of purpose, and rage. His eyes were fierce and unforgiving as they connected to Michael's. The commuters nearest them backed warily away, unable to avoid paying attention to the voice ringing in their ears and disappearing down the tunnels, while others further down the platform positioned themselves discretely so that they might see without looking like they were seeing, tucking their useless phones into their pockets, and preparing for a quick departure.

"And you!" he shouted, jabbing a crusted, swollen finger in Alex's face, "You're not supposed to be here at all, now are you?" And saying this, he withdrew the neck of a jagged beer bottle from one of the folds of his makeshift vestments, and shoved it through the black sweatshirt into the young man's lower abdomen. Supporting him with one arm while twisting the glass into him with another, he reached into the man's pants pocket and took out the ring of keys, which he held out to Michael. "You're gonna need these, boy. Go, now, you're late! RUN!" he shouted, and pointed down the tunnel as the last of the panicked commuters made their way up the stairs.

Michael's hand shook as he took the keys from the man, and quickly lowered himself onto the train bed.

"RUN!" The voice commanded again, and Michael took off running, navigating debris and crossties and pools of filth as best he could. It was not long before the shallow light of the station dimmed to nothing, and he stopped running for fear of falling over the tracks or running into a wall. From an overhead street grate in the distance, he could hear rain softly pattering the sidewalk, and dripping down onto the tracks. His shoes and socks and feet were already wet with oil and muck, and he wanted to take them off, but he dared not. His eyes began to adjust, and what seemed like the light of a single candle a mile away brought his surroundings into focus for him. He wanted to sit, to think, but there was no place.

He reached into his ear and took out the earpiece that was still somehow there, and threw it into a glossy puddle. The tiny splash echoed, but the sound was lost with the dripping of the rain. Abandoned, confused and alone, he wanted to lie down across the tracks, stretch himself out, and make the wet cave his tomb. *It was all for nothing*, he thought. *I am nothing.*

You're wrong, a voice spoke from the darkness, and Michael wasn't sure if the voice was in his ears or in his mind, but he knew it was real. It continued, *But you are nothing, have been nothing, without me. Come now, and I will lead you. And you will lead.*

***

Lucy had never been on a real subway before, and was excited, though the anxiety of being pursued and the excitement of being in New York and on a subway and with her dad and her Callie, were all sort of mixed up together. It was a lot, particularly for someone still physically reeling from the months in which she had been subjected to isolation and chemical torture. While no one spoke of it, she knew, and everyone else knew, that she was still in shock. She didn't mind—she suddenly had everything, and everyone she needed. Compared to her condition four days earlier, she felt as much like a warrior princess as anyone on an N train can feel.

When the train suddenly stopped, and the lights in their train car went out, she was one of the few passengers who did not scream. The stop was violent, and the darkness more black than what any of their fellow commuters were accustomed to. They stood on the somewhat-crowded train for 35 minutes, while waiting on word as to what they should do. With the emergency flood lights from the 42nd Street-Times Square stop clearly illuminating a path to steps that led up to the station platform, their fellow passengers gave up on waiting for directions, and forced open a door between cars. After the first few daring youths made the trip without any injury or arrest, an apparently-harried businessman in a chic Burberry suit followed them, and after that there was a jostling queue of people waiting to make the short but treacherous journey across the slick crossties, gravel, and debris.

Josh held Callie and Lucy back, and they walked through the car doors to the back of the train, where they disembarked, and as quickly and quietly as possible they made their way back through the curving tunnel in the direction they had just come from. Their plan was to make their way back to the 34th Street-Herald Square station, where an emergency exit was on the east side of Sixth Avenue, and would leave them just half a block from the Empire State Building, which Josh assured them was their rendezvous point. And it worked, to a point—by the time they reached Herald Square, the station had been locked down, and they couldn't get to the emergency door Josh had planned for them.

"There's an exit sort of in Macy's," Callie suggested weakly. "Maybe it's unlocked?"

It seemed like a better plan than walking back to Times Square—the trip had been laborious, and an affront to all their senses, and none of them wished to repeat it. They found the exit into Macy's properly secured, but they also discovered that their earpieces came to life in the narrow passageway from the subway stairs to the locked turnstile, though they dared not linger there very long for fear of drawing attention from the street. Rain pelted the pedestrians who were running and bumping into one another on the sidewalk and as they navigated the unmoving phalanx of taxicabs on 34th Street, and a small throng of people were huddled under the Macy's canopy just a few yards away from where the three stood looking out with trepidation.

"Where are you, exactly?" Sam asked her, and she described the spot with precision—the two of them had been there together shopping. "One second. They're working on it. You doing ok, girl?" He asked, again off-script.

"I've had better days," Callie said, "but also, much, much worse. Two days ago, for instance."

He cut her off. "Here's what you all need to do. Go back down the stairs," he began, and continued giving her detailed instructions for making their way east across 34th Street without going above ground. A ConEd power specialist was in the sub-basement of the Empire State Building cutting power to the building at the main switches located there. He would let them into the building, and into the emergency service stairs to climb to the 72nd floor. Callie looked down at her wet shoes, grateful she was wearing sneakers, but unable to imagine what kind of condition her feet would be in by the time they reached their destination.

Twice along the way of their subterranean passage from Sixth Avenue to Fifth Avenue they encountered men who opened doors for them. Wordlessly, without any acknowledgement other than motions pointing them forward, the men disappeared back into the shadows of the passageways they gave entrance to, which wasn't difficult at all—the corridors seemed to be made of shadows, and in many places weren't actually proper corridors with walls at all, but simply the space between spaces, between forests of wet glistening pipes, many of which turned at right angles, branching out across their path or to run beside them, narrowing or widening the path in alternating, irregular rhythms. Bundles of cables ran in every direction, some tagged with labels showing a corresponding street address, others with names of businesses, but most were anonymous, bare of any mark except the name of the manufacturer. The smell of urine was faint but distinct, masked somewhat by infrequent gusts of misty wind that somehow wound their way down from the street. Occasionally a door would appear out of the gloom, always metal, and usually with the street address of the building it opened onto scrawled in marker or chalk. *No Smoking* sings appeared at irregular intervals, invariably amended with graffiti to read *No Smoking Crack* or *No Smoking Cock*.

It was when they passed a door with *22 E 34* written on it twice—once rather ineffectually with pencil, and again below in what appeared to be Sharpie marker—that they first began to hear the voice of a man somewhere in the distance ahead of them arguing with a woman on the other end of what sounded like a radio. "And I'm telling you," he said, in a voice that suggested he would not be to blame for anyone else's mistakes, "We have to bring them up one by one. Bringing all these signals back on at once just ain't an option—we'll blow the top of the tower off. You get a list to me, which ones come back on, in which order, and when the time comes, I'll do it. But it don't matter right now, cause we ain't got no power." His thick Staten Island accent seemed to fill the room.

"The New York State Department of Homeland Security has a list, but we don't have it yet," the woman on the other end began, tiredly, "but in the meantime," the voice continued as the man in the ConEd uniform caught a glimpse of Josh, Lucy and Callie emerging from a doorway into the roomful of electric panels and meters where he stood.

"Alright, I gotcha, save ya battery. Let me know when you have the list," he interrupted her, and turned the power on his radio off, looking at his watch as he did so. He began to smile an almost-smile at them, reconsidered, and turned the corners of his mouth down. "Alright, once we go out that door," and he gestured to one of the room's two other doors besides the one they had just entered, "Don't say anything," he said, his Staten Island accent replaced with a nondescript but soft Midwest tone. "There are still a ton of people in the building. We don't want them asking questions. It probably doesn't matter, but still. There's a helicopter on its way here with a replacement microwave antenna—You'll be getting on that helicopter when it takes off. Everybody clear?"

Josh nodded, Lucy shrugged, and Callie's eyes bulged out. "Isn't there a less conspicuous way to get us out of town?"

"You need to get out now. Michael is upstairs—he needs to get out, now. I let him up just a little while ago. Something's not quite right. But here, we need to hurry. Your earpieces will work once you're in the stairs. But remember, no talking." He pushed open the door, and after three quick turns, illuminated by his flashlight, they were in the stairwell, level SB2. The stairs were more-or-less regularly illuminated with emergency floodlights, but it was more glare-and-shadows than an even distribution of light. As they began their ascent, they were alternately blinded or seeing flashes of light with each step they took, each turn at each landing was another dull shock to the senses. By the tenth floor, all their legs were aching, and they could begin to feel blisters cutting into the soft, wet skin of their feet. Lucy, who had been immobile for most of the past few months, felt the ache of her muscles sooner than her older companions. By the 40th floor, she felt a burning cramp grab hold of her upper thighs, both at once, and a gentle moan escaped her despite her best attempts to contain it. Josh and Lucy sat with her on the landing of the 41st floor for a few minutes, until a voice in Callie's ear urged them on. "Your way out is up, Callie, you have to keep moving," Sam said cautiously, not knowing the cause of their hesitation.

"Lucy's in pain," Callie whispered angrily, and the small sound ricocheted off and up and down the concrete steps and walls and doors.

At the same time, she heard Lucy describing the pain to some other person, but Lucy's whispers did not carry. In a few moments, Lucy stood, and when Callie stood, she could feel her own legs protest—one look at Josh told her he was not fit for this climb, either. But they began, and continued somewhat more slowly, until they reached the 60th floor, where Lucy crumbled onto the landing, and tears began to stream softly down her cheek. "I can't," she whispered, and they all sat for a few minutes, before Callie heard Josh whisper *Okay* aloud, and in a jerky movement, he lifted his daughter and began to carry her up the stairs. It was fitful, and awkward, and Callie was scared at times that he might topple backwards with her, but he didn't. When they made it to the 67th floor, he leaned down, and Lucy stepped lightly from his arms. "I can make it now," she whispered, and they continued up, their eyes now dull with the pain of adjusting and readjusting from shadow to light.

***

Once down a service corridor they found unlocked, they discovered the door to the 72nd floor terrace was propped open with what were clearly Michael's running shoes, though filthy, like their own. Callie reached out hesitantly to open the door as a voice—not Sam's—came to life in her ear, asking "Can you see Michael? The helicopter is almost there. We need all four of you on the terrace. Can you see him?"

"Jesus Christ," Josh mumbled, pushing past Callie into the cold, blustery dark sky. "Michael. Michael, Michael," he called out, but his voice was blown away with a curl of chilled air. Callie and Lucy followed after him. A row of round, white microwave antennae stood sentinel in a row against the exterior wall of the building at the back of the terrace. The distance from the door to the edge of the deck was short, as was the three-foot ledge preventing them from going over the edge of it. Josh stepped forward slowly and carefully, and looked out over the edge of the building. At the sight of the street below, he stretched out his arms to hold back the other two, but only Callie was there, looking with awe and trepidation at the unexpected view of the darkened, wet city. Josh called out for Lucy, but she did not answer.

"Shit." He turned away from the dull, wet, sprawling spectacle before him, adding "She couldn't have gone far, anyway. Unless she went back."

"She didn't go back." Callie was pointing to a far corner of the terrace, a figure standing in the distance, just out of sight in the swirling mist, down a narrow walkway filled with translucent boxes with cables snaking out from them. "The lights. These must be the lights that light up the spire." Callie had been to the city many times as an adolescent, and a few times as an adult, and the illumination of the Empire State Building had always been marvelous to her.

"We've got to get Michael and get out of here," Josh said with determination as he started towards the figure, then paused as his eyes adjusted to the darkness, and he pointed to a mound on the brick terrace and asked "Are those Michael's pants?"

"Just go," Callie answered as she picked up the pants, and the two began slowly working their way down the wet narrow walkway, which seemed to grow longer, and narrower, and further from the street below, as their feet became tangled in the cords and metal housings anchoring the lights to the deck. They realized quickly that grabbing onto one another in the gusting mist wasn't at all useful—they were each on their own, 72 stories above the pavement below, without a net, without even a rail.

As they approached, it was Lucy who emerged first from the mist, standing, looking down at Michael, who was sitting naked on the cold wet brick, his arms draped casually over his knees, as though he might be basking at a summer picnic, being painted by Manet.

"Why are you so, like, naked?" Lucy was asking, as Callie and Josh entered into hearing.

He looked at her, with an almost childlike sweetness, warm and glowing, despite the chill. "I, I don't think I'm human anymore. I think it has left me. I think I'm an angel now. Or maybe I always was. I don't know. But I do know. You know?"

"Sort of. But you know, not really. But that doesn't really explain why you're naked." Lucy was more concerned for Michael than she was discomfited by his nakedness.

"Since I've been off the trolley, clothing has become more and more like those rubber Halloween masks, when you can no longer breathe, and all you can smell is synthetic, awful. Your face is sticky with sweat, and the mask sticks to your face in awkward places. And no matter how hard you try, the mask won't stay on right, so your vision is obscured, and keeps changing. You know, like that. A second skin that you can't keep on because it would be so easy to take it off."

"I guess that makes sense. Sort of. But, if you're an angel, why don't you have wings?" Lucy asked, and there was less doubt in her question than there was curiosity, it was an innocent question—a child asking for clarification about grown-up things.

"I do have wings," Michael answered, and his face spread out in a radiant smile, as though he was pleased she was beginning to understand.

Callie had had enough. "Michael, you don't have wings. We are looking at you right now. You don't have wings." Her voice was stern. Confused, exhausted, and freezing, she wanted this day to finally be over. She heard a helicopter in the distance, but when she turned and looked out at the sky with focus, she could see there were dozens, perhaps several dozen helicopters darting around the dark wet sky. "Michael, you have to put on some clothes. They're coming to get us. We have to leave."

514

"Hello, Callie." He turned to look at her, still sitting on the terrace. "Are you suggesting that because you can't see them, I don't have thoughts? Or lungs?" He wanted her to understand.

Josh spoke for the first time. "Michael, it's cold. You really need to put on some clothes. We have to go." Josh actually was uncomfortable with Michael's nakedness, and like Callie, was ready to go home—wherever home was now. He held out the wet pants.

Michael's voice was patient as he replied, "No, I don't. And no, I'm not. I'm where I need to be, and how I need to be." He paused for just a moment and continued, "Did you know an airplane hit this building? Right up there." He pointed in a general direction to the space just a few floors above them. "Right up there. A B-52 bomber just flew right into it. Death. Destruction. Fire. The summer of 1945. The war in Europe was over, but we were still fighting Japan. Everyone was just so… confused. The world was on this threshold, everyone could feel it. Things were changing. There was this energy, like the final minutes before a close game you know your team will win, and we did, we beat Hitler. We won! And then, this American pilot flies his bomber plane into this great symbol of American pride. An American does something Hitler never managed to do, but wanted to do desperately. Kill Americans on American soil, spectacularly, generating the kind of sensational terror we see over and over again now." Michael got up on his knees, and turned his back to them, and spread his arms out over the city. "Look at all the witnesses to mankind's inability to understand. But I understand now. Science cannot save us. Science never could."

"So, is that why… Are you like, a nudist now?" Lucy was still trying to understand.

"No, I'm an angel. Not at all the same thing. I don't think. I don't know, I don't think I know any nudists." Michael's smile faded for just a moment, burdened with the apparently mundane thought that had just filtered through him.

"You don't know any angels, either. Michael, you are not an angel." Callie's impatience was creeping into her voice. "We have to go Michael. Now. Please put on some clothes." She had just heard in her ear that the helicopter was making its approach. She took the pants from Josh and held them out to him with urgent little thrusts.

Then a blue-white floodlight rose from the side of the building, blinding them all. The whisper of aircraft blades cutting into the night could be heard from behind the light. Michael turned his head and said to his friends, "I will see you again, soon," then smiled, and turned back, standing on the ledge to face the city and the world beyond it.

"This is not my body. It belongs to my father," he called out to the night.

An almost-deafening electronic hum filled their ears in the moment before every light in the Empire State Building lit at once, a beacon again in the dark city sky. The floodlights where they stood on the 72nd floor now washed them and the tower in white light. It took them a minute to realize there were only three of them—Michael was gone. They looked down into the street, and then up into the sky, but they could no more see him in the mortar of the streets below than in the ether of the wet heavens.

A metal walkway, six feet wide and 15 feet long, slid out on two hydraulic arms from the rear of the helicopter, and rested, jittering, on the short parapet wall. Three men in fatigues, wearing harnesses attached to cables snaking out from the aircraft, slid a large wooden box down the slight incline of the ramp to where Callie, Josh and Lucy stood in shock, as they were each clipped to one of the three men.

"You have to go, go with them," each of the three heard as the men gently urged them to step up onto the ramp.

Without a rope, without a net, so far, so far, Callie thought, looking at the wet metal ramp. But her thoughts could not help her, so she tried to stop, but those thoughts were replaced with the name, *Michael. Michael. Michael.*

"Please Callie, go." It was Sam's voice again, "Please, for me. Walk."

And she did, but not before grabbing hold of Lucy's hand—Lucy, who seemed to be as lost in that moment as she had ever been. Josh went before them, bent over and charging with speed into the aircraft, pulling his escort beside him, then turning back and beckoning the others towards him. Lucy and Callie moved slowly forward, clinging together, and holding onto the cable, in front of the two remaining men in camouflage, until they were all in the craft. Then the walkway retracted, and the cargo doors closed, and their flight west began.

Callie tried not to sob, but she could not stop herself, and Josh tried not to embrace her, but he could not stop himself, and suddenly the three were together standing, clinging, unsure of anything but each other.

"Please, we need you to sit down," a voice said, and a hand rested on Josh's shoulder. He looked and saw yet another face he did not recognize—not from his own past—and he relinquished his hold on Callie and Lucy, and guided them towards a bench that extended almost the length of the other side of the helicopter. Lucy sat between Callie and Josh, and the three tried not to look at the anxious faces of the people strapped to the bench across from them, as they were being strapped in. They just held onto one another, Lucy clutching at Josh and Callie, as in terror they too might vanish.

With one hand, Callie held onto Lucy. With the other, she carefully untied each shoe, and removed it, and the socks, and pulled her blistered feet up into her lap gingerly. Unwilling to let go of either of the hands holding her, Lucy just kicked her shoes off, and she looked at them, and finally asked the question no one else would.

"Where did he go?"

Josh answered, haltingly. "I, I, I don't know, sweetie. I don't know."

"Neither do they, do they? The people in my ear?" Lucy was somehow certain of it.

The people in her ear did not answer, but in Josh's ear he heard, "No, we don't know."

Callie heard Sam, "Soon girl, soon. You'll be here soon. You alright?"

She nodded, and then, not knowing if Sam could see her, forced herself to say

"Yes, I'm fine," and in saying it, realized it was true, and was able to stop her tears.

"Things here are a little crazy right now. You just holler if you need me." He answered.

She wondered where *here* was, but said simply "I will."

Josh and Lucy looked at her curiously. "Sam," she said, her voice cracking. "He's watching out for us."

The helicopter navigated its way out of the city and began flying west towards Morgantown, West Virginia, where yet another method of transportation would take them to yet another place, but none of the three asked what would be taking them, or where they were going. They were tired of plans, of going. No one tried to look out a window. No one spoke as the city behind them disappeared—the place they had entered so recently, and so full of hope, but which had betrayed them.

CHAPTER 15. TOUCHDOWN

The three young men who hired the helicopter to take them from Knoxville, Tennessee to the Nashville International Airport were the very picture of affluent American youth trying to appear both older and poorer than they actually were. Shaggy-haired, unshaven, unkempt, all in dirty jeans and flannel shirts, but with good teeth, better posture, and excellent guitar cases, they gave the impression of what they said they were—three college friends trying to start a musical career. They said they had an audition in Nashville, but their car had broken down. In the time it took them to get to the airport to rent a car, they would never make it on time. "Is it possible to get us to like the Nashville Airport in like, 45 minutes?"

The owner of the Ed's Transport Service, who was not named Ed, but Larry, eyed them carefully before he answered. He decided they looked more like trust fund brats playing make-believe than down-on-their-luck musicians, so he answered matter-of-factly, "If you have six hundred dollars it is." He had learned, over time, that people who could not afford to charter a helicopter would not wander into his office asking for helicopter rides—most people knew their limits.

"Thank God," replied the one who was doing all the talking. He opened his wallet and pulled out a gold American Express card. "Do you take American Express?"

"We sure do. Let me call Ed." Larry smiled at his own sagacity as he turned to find his cell phone amongst the clutter of an office that looked more like a mechanic's shop than an airline terminal. "And I'm going to need picture ID for the three of you." There was already a helicopter preparing to leave in five minutes to make an organ transplant delivery to Nashville—except for a little extra fuel, taking the boys along would be pure profit.

From their licenses, Larry learned that two of the boys were from the same town of Cleveland, Tennessee, and the other was from Columbia, South Carolina. They were each 20 years old. "Ya'll looking to make it big?" he asked as he handed the licenses back to them.

They all smiled nervously in response. Only the apparent leader of the trio spoke, answering, "If we don't make it big today, we might not ever make it. This is a pretty big opportunity. We've been planning for it a long time." His friends shifted nervously.

Ed walked in and introduced himself. An affable, casually dressed, retired Air Force captain, 42 years old and 42 inches around, he looked too large, at 6'4", to fit in the helicopter he guided them towards out back behind the office. As they walked, he explained by way of apology that he would normally be wearing a uniform with a tie if they had been expecting passengers today. "So I'm real glad ya'll didn't call ahead. The uniform was Larry's idea."

The relatively small hangar was home to just two helicopters, with an adjacent landing pad enclosed with razor wire. The Augusta 109E was a small, tidy, efficient workhorse of a helicopter, painted navy blue with sky blue and white racing stripes running down its body. A small American flag was painted on the tail fin. It held five passengers, the pilot, and two crewmen, but there was no crew on the quick flight. The boy who had introduced himself as Eric asked if he could sit up front in the copilot's seat.

"Best seat in the house. Sure, come on up."

The other two young men arranged themselves in the back passenger area, with the guitar cases and their light luggage and knapsacks. Eric kept his knapsack up front with him. When the doors were all secure, the mighty sound of the helicopter blades was almost indistinguishable. "Wow," Eric commented conversationally, "it really is quiet in here."

"Yeah, it ain't like the movies. It's loud outside, for sure. Here, let me get this thing up in the air," Ed replied with an almost apologetic tone that suggested he needed to focus for a moment, but would be back to chatting shortly. He pulled on a headset with a covered earpiece and microphone, and began communicating in official-sounding chatter. Eric pulled a tablet computer from his backpack and began looking at maps, eventually identifying their location on a topographical map, and zooming in on their location. Once they were in the air and moving, Ed reopened their conversation by letting Eric know they would be on the ground in twenty minutes.

"Awesome," Eric replied, with what sounded like excitement at new information, though Larry had already told them the anticipated duration of the short flight. "I just saw on my map we're going to be flying over Oak Ridge. Is that the same Oak Ridge they built for World War II?"

"Sure is. But we won't be flying over it. Still a federal base, used for all kinds of stuff. No-fly zone. We'll be flying around it. But you can almost see it already. Right over there. See them white buildings off over there?" Ed pointed to a distant mass of buildings on the edge of the horizon.

"Wow. Cool, I've always wanted to see that place." Eric's face was alive with anticipation.

"They do tours there during the summer. For Americans—American citizens. There's a waiting list, but it's worth it. It's amazing to see it all firsthand. What this country can do when we put our minds to it." Out of the corner of his eye, Ed saw Eric digging around in his knapsack for something, but had no time to react at all to the gun before he looked into the young man's eyes, the same ice blue as the sky behind them, and the bullet went through the pilot's head and lodged in the cockpit door. Eric put the gun on the floor of the craft, and immediately began taking over the flight controls as he had done hundreds of times in simulations in preparation for this flight. He gave a thumbs-up to the two young men in back, but they did not see it—as soon as the pilot had slumped over, they had begun opening the guitar cases and luggage in final preparation for their descent into Oak Ridge.

The craft had been moving northwest to skirt the no-fly zone around what had been a nuclear research facility in World War II, but had grown over time to become one of the largest known sites in the world for nuclear material processing and storage. Eric shifted the course of the craft due west, heading directly for Y-12, the site of the Highly Enriched Uranium Materials Facility, where more than 400 tons of highly enriched uranium sat stacked in highly insulated cans in a single, cavernous room spreading over more than 100,000 square feet, where every aspect of humidity, temperature, and seismic activity was intensely monitored. Seismic activity was of particular concern because Oak Ridge was situated less than 300 miles from New Madrid, Missouri, the site of the most powerful earthquakes to hit the eastern United States in recorded history, and likely long before that. The scientists at Oak Ridge knew well that their site was connected by a vast array of underground fault lines, some crossing over like spiderwebs, to the epicenter of the New Madrid earthquakes of 1811-1812. Any significant activity anywhere in Missouri would likely be felt at the Oak Ridge facility—an understanding that the architects and engineers who designed the facility could never have imagined, as the science of plate tectonics was not developed until decades after the original facility was constructed. Any movement was unlikely to have any impact on the stored uranium, but what impact it might have on the nearby research facilities was another question entirely. The science of earthquake prediction remained more guesswork than actual science, and with the exception of insurance and liability companies, who are required, by necessity, to fabricate numbers suggesting the relative probabilities and possibilities of most every potential event, no reasonable scientist had yet to make a guess as to when the next great earthquake in the eastern United States would happen. But everyone—insurance companies, geologists, seismologists, and the nuclear researchers at Oak Ridge—agreed that one day, it would happen. There was no question of if.

The three young men in the helicopter had no knowledge of the seismic entanglement of the Oak Ridge facility. In fact, they had very little knowledge of the physics that underlay the weapons they were very rapidly assembling and preparing for detonation. They weren't entirely certain that the weapons even *were* actual weapons. They had purchased them on the black market, in a plan they had developed over two years at the University of Tennessee. Their original intent had been simply to blow something up—as American a dream as getting married and having children. But it had grown over time, fantastically and improbably, to this moment. They had thought throughout that they would be arrested. Surely, someone must be watching them. Someone must know. Despite their caution and subterfuge, as they approached detonation day, or D-Day, as they must call it, their paranoia escalated, and at times they seemed almost waiting, possibly wanting, to be arrested. Up until the moment the helicopter lifted from the concrete pad, they assumed that someone would stop them. Now, as the two young men gave thumbs-up from the passenger cabin, no one could stop them. The detonation was set for two minutes on each of the three improvised nuclear devices, so-called dirty bombs, waiting to be tossed onto the roof of the Y-12 facility.

The call Eric had been waiting for finally came through on the headset. A voice, old, male, and stern, not unlike his father's, boomed into the cabin, "Nashville Air Control to unidentified craft. Identify yourself. You are entering a no-fly zone. Alter your course to the northwest by 26 degrees immediately. You will be escorted to Nashville. Pilots are en route."

Eric smiled as he responded, with a voice shaking with a nervousness he did not feel, "Sir, um, sir, hello, my name is Eric Reese. Our pilot just had a heart attack or something and the helicopter is just going on its own. I don't know what to do. Me and my friends, we don't know how to fly a helicopter. They're in the back. We're students from UT. What are we supposed to do?" He made his voice rise several octaves as he spoke, increasingly slowly in hysteria, to a pitch in his final question, making him sound much more like a frightened ten-year-old than a young man planning to set the world on fire.

"Don't worry son, we've got everything under control. Position yourself where you can see all the dials on the dashboard. It's just like driving a car. We'll get through this fine. Give me just a second here." The man's voice was calm and assuring now, the threatening tone gone entirely.

There was a brief pause. In the control room, women and men scrambled both to verify the story they were hearing and to put multiple plans in place. No one believed for a minute that the defense department would shoot down a helicopter with three American college students in it, but Defense had been notified and the fighter pilots had already been scrambled and were on the way as part of standard protocol. By the time they arrived, however, the helicopter would have already passed through the no-fly zone. The immediate concern at Nashville ground control was who would walk the boys through landing the craft safely, and where. Eric and his friends had predicted the scenario almost perfectly, and he was waiting for a new voice to come on the line to walk him through the steps to safely land the craft in an out-of-harm's-way location. As they had anticipated, no one had even asked him to try to take the pilot's pulse to see if he was alive—that was not a concern.

Eric looked down at his computer tablet to confirm that the building just ahead of him, that he knew from practice was the Y-12 building, was actually the right one. The tablet confirmed it. He held up two fingers, and his two friends prepared to throw open the emergency door on the side of the helicopter.

A female voice came on over the headset, which surprised Eric—he had been expecting another authoritative male. But the woman's voice was deep, calm, and he supposed would have been reassuring, if he had needed reassuring. He did not—at that moment, he had all the assurance in the world.

"Eric, this is Sonya Martinez. I'm going to be guiding you through your landing. We've done this plenty of times before, you're going to be just fine. You're at the controls now?"

"I am," Eric answered. Now that they had reached Y-12, and were positioned 300 yards above the building's exact center, he began a direct aerial ascent, slowly moving the craft straight upward. The young men did not know whether or not dropping the bombs from any height would have any impact or not, but figured it couldn't hurt.

"Eric, according to our controls here, you've stopped moving. Can you tell us what's going on there?" The woman's voice was troubled, disturbed by what she was seeing.

In the distance, Eric could see two faint shapes, which he assumed to be F-15 fighter jets, approaching from the southwest.

"We just started going up. I think I might have hit something." He was almost laughing with delight. They were doing it. It was really going to happen. It was happening.

In the Nashville Air Control Tower, things became very tense and very quiet very quickly. Everyone in the room knew that the helicopter would not just stop forward movement and begin a vertical ascent because of an inadvertent movement in the cockpit. There was some quick discussion with the command center at Arnold Air Force Base, where the F-15 jets had flown in from, and the commander there assumed authority from Nashville.

"Okay, Eric, this is Commander Lewis with the U.S. Air Force. We have made visual contact, and we can see that you are in control of the craft. I don't know what is going on in that cockpit, but we need you to land that craft, now, in the parking lot ahead of you and to the right. Immediately. Start your descent now."

Eric looked around and could see the F-15s now circling in the distance less than a mile away, and knew that if they could see him operating the helicopter, they could see the bullet and blood on the pilot's window. He stopped smiling, held up one finger for his friends to see, keeping it raised, and continuing to move the helicopter skyward.

Up and down the Atlantic seaboard, phones had been ringing, and alarms sounding, for several minutes as the video from the stealth surveillance drone a quarter mile away was broadcast on hundreds of defense department monitors. Almost as soon as the helicopter went off course, a call was put into Ed's Transport Service for the passenger manifest of the helicopter. Within minutes, hundreds of analysts were pouring over every detail of the lives of the three boys. Every college course they had taken, every baseball coach, every cell phone call, every Facebook post, every YouTube video they had ever watched. And they were coming up with nothing. Beastie Boys, Nirvana, Phish. They didn't look like terrorists. They didn't read like terrorists. But the blood on the window made it clear—they were terrorists. But what were they planning to do? And what did they have in those guitar cases? The background radiation from the site, and the jumble of gear on the helicopter, made it impossible to tell from thermal imaging if the boys had nuclear weapons. But the drone said they did.

"Son, we need you to bring that helicopter down, now. No one needs to get hurt here. We can work this all out."

Eric broke his radio silence with the commander. "Dude, did you seriously just call me *son*? Who are you, like John fucking Wayne? Seriously dude, what the fuck? You got no game here." The smile was back on his face. He was radiant. He looked down at the countdown clock on his tablet computer, which was synchronized to the detonator timers in the back of the helicopter. It was at five seconds. "This is game, motherfucker." He lowered his index finger, then punched his fist in the air, yelling "This is motherfucking touchdown. Touchdown!"

The two young men in back had been watching for his signal. They threw open the exit door, and without so much as a word or glance at each other, each tossed a metal cylinder out of the opening, as casually as though they were on a country bridge dropping pebbles into a stream below. Eric had turned to watch, and when he saw the mission was complete, he gave them a thumbs-up, and as one of the F-15 jets flew in close enough that the three men could see the pilots, Eric gave John Wayne, and all of the John Waynes before and after him, spontaneous, responsive, gleeful salute with both his middle fingers. And he laughed.

CHAPTER 16. THE FORETOLD

The helicopter was preparing to land at Morgantown, West Virginia, when it happened. The whole sky ignited in a blue-white sheet of light, and the aircraft began spinning, alarms ringing in the cockpit that echoed into the cargo hold, and the breath was ever-so-briefly and gently pulled from their lungs.

After several spins, the pilot was able to regain control of the helicopter, but all radio contact was gone. Everyone was jostled and thrown where they sat, but the safety restraints did their jobs, and other than some bruises and bumped heads, no one was hurt. Medical supplies and bottled water bumped and rolled down the floor of the hold. And the air somehow tasted different. The quality of the light itself coming into the craft seemed altered. No one seemed to have been injured by the aircraft's unanticipated, jarring movements, but no one seemed especially well, either.

Josh's eyes were closed, and he was weeping, and slowly, everyone became aware of it, and looked at him, to him, but he did not speak, and he did not open his eyes.

"Is that why we were running?" Callie asked. "Damn it, Josh."

He did not answer.

"Answer me," she demanded, almost yelling, "Is that why we were running?"

"We almost made it," he said, without opening his eyes.

"We still can make it," Lucy whispered.

The helicopter landed not at the airfield, but in a nearby pasture adjacent to an enclosure where a herd of fawn and white Guernsey cattle shuffled and stomped and cried out in fear, but none ran, seeming to sense there was nowhere to go. They registered the change in the light, and the air, and while spooked, they were not panicked. But the birds began to fly away, in the thousands and tens and hundreds of thousands, countless birds took flight away from the light, away from the sickness and death now spilling out of Tennessee with every gentle breeze, which the

Earth quickly supplied, once the sky was no longer on fire.

In the helicopter they quickly discovered their radios were useless. They had no radar, and no satellite to guide them, to tell them where to go, to tell them what had happened—though somehow, everyone knew. They had not seen the mushroom cloud, but the magnitude of death somehow filled the air. And, so, too, did something electric. A charge in the atmosphere.

"Can we get out?" Lucy asked suddenly, unbuckling herself from the straps crossing her. And just as suddenly, everyone wanted to get out of the helicopter with her, to put their feet back on the earth outside. When she began to move, everyone moved with her.

"Let us check first, it may not be safe," one of the camouflaged men suggested without much conviction, hoisting a rifle as he spoke.

Josh had opened his eyes when Lucy let go of his hand, and he spoke for the first time. "I don't think this helicopter can protect us. But bring those guns, by all means." And after a pause he added, "Are there more? Guns?" The people in camouflage shook their heads in unison. A woman with close-cropped salt-and-pepper hair said, "Here, you can have mine. I don't even know how to use it. I'm not even sure if it's a real gun, or if there are bullets in it." Josh took the assault rifle from her, but slung it over his shoulder without checking the clip.

The cargo hatch was opened manually, and everyone walked out into the afternoon light, the verdant landscape untouched by the destruction that had just illuminated the sky. The sky itself seemed changed, though. The sun was a shimmering ball of white, threatening in its purity. Along the horizon purples and blues shifted uneasily beneath a line of orange that glowed and glistened like the edge of a tangerine hanging on the vine on the dewy morning—but it was not morning. And the air was palpably dry—the air of an arid desert displaced into a northeastern meadow.

The pilot and copilot of the craft soon joined their passengers—the copilot looked as though he might vomit, while the pilot, though shaken, seemed ready and able to guide the aircraft back up in the air when and if electronic communications were established again. The pilot verified that everyone was unhurt, and then they all stood around, just looking, before Callie asked "Couldn't you just use the sun to navigate us? I don't feel safe here. It feels so….open." It was open. The sky stretched from horizon to horizon, conspicuously, menacingly vast.

"I could, yes. The problem is who else might be trying to do the same thing. We have no way of knowing. If we knew the sky was empty, it wouldn't be a problem. As it is, it's just too dangerous. I think we're safe here, for now." But he didn't sound sure—wasn't trying to sound sure, as he looked around at the scattering of farm buildings and the distant woodlands providing the jagged edge to the horizon. But there were no vehicles or people present, and somehow they all knew that if people had been in the buildings before, they would be outside now.

They stood around a few minutes more, watching the sky sparkle—in places, it looked like there were children in the distant woods, using mirrors to flash the light of the sky back into it. At other times it looked as though there were lasers pointing to and through the fabric of the sky, making tiny rips and tears that sealed themselves up immediately.

"Are you all military?" Callie asked, somewhat incongruously. The others all appeared to be thinking of other things—personal, impossible, infinite things.

"I'm a physics professor," answered the woman who had given Josh her weapon, and continued, "We're all community, but I don't know what any of these people do, or who any of them are. I never met them before today—haven't met them, really. My name's Annie."

"Hi, Annie. I'm Callie, but I guess you know that?" she asked. The woman smiled and nodded in confirmation.

The others in camouflage did not introduce themselves. The oppressive weight of the sky seemed to make introductions meaningless. Their utter isolation from the electronic world, the inability to get or receive a text message or phone call, or even to know exactly where they were, overwhelmed the members of the community, who likewise seemed unaccustomed to seeing the sky so full and wide at any time. They continued their gazing, distant and filled with stupefaction. Callie seemed impatient with their inaction, while Lucy appeared to be waiting for something to happen from without the group, and Josh stood alone, somehow more alone than the others, more lost. Whatever he had seen that morning, it wasn't this, not just this way. Something had changed, or he had read something wrong, or maybe it was all a hallucination—he was no longer sure.

Callie soon realized that colors were beginning to drift in from the horizon, and were settling in the air around them, luminous and shifting like butterflies, and massing above the cattle. The cattle sensed it too, and began to move, and their shuffling half-measures became full steps, and then they were running, and at first they were the clumsy, awkward shifting of mass typical of cows, but as the spots of color began to accumulate above them, the cows and calves formed two great circles, running in opposite directions, the outer circle running clockwise, the inner running counter to it. Their speed increased as the people watching nudged each other somewhat unnecessarily to look towards the herd's enclosure, as the impact of their hooves, mighty with determination, slammed into the loose earth. Their centrifugal stampede became a blur of color and movement.

Great clouds of dust began to rise up, and mix with the colored light borrowed from the sky, and it too began to spin in circles of opposite rotation, and seemed to draw in the light from the sky around it, building in speed and rising up from the enclosure, until all at once, as on a single unheard note, the cows stopped dead still, not blinking an eyelid or twitching a tail, and the dust fell to the earth like lead.

In the center of the two circles of motionless cows and calves stood the single bull in the herd, his head bowed down so that his horns touched the ground. On his back, surrounded by the blue and purple and orange light, sat Michael. His face radiated with sadness and joy, an equanimity of emotion both sublime and frightening. His right hand was raised, pointing up to the merciless sky, and his left pointed down with equal force and measure. His robe was roughspun wool, unbleached and undyed. His feet were bare, and his head was shaved. And after their eyes adjusted to the flickering light around him, the small crowd of people saw that his eyes were gone—in their places were two rough clumps of granite. An odor of sanctity filled the air—lavender and cedar, with lemon and myrrh—and replaced the acrid, metallic smell of modernity that filled the distant landscape.

Lucy tried to run out to him, to climb over the fence, but as she approached, the two circles of cows began to move again, and the docile animals suddenly appeared mighty, deadly, impenetrable. Callie ran forward and pulled Lucy back, and the cows stopped moving again, as suddenly as before.

"Michael," Callie called out, unnecessarily loud, for even though she could plainly see him, it felt as though there were an impassable gulf between them, ages and miles and years—Where had he been? When had he been? "What's happening? What is this? What's going on?" she continued, still yelling.

"I've come to take them home," he spoke, and it wasn't a whisper, he was just talking, but his voice filled their ears, and the sound was warm and rich. Each heard his voice in a different way, in the way that would best say to each of them, *I am here now. Be Still.*

"Who? Where?" Callie asked. She was not scared, and she was not angry, but she did not want to be still—she wanted to understand. Josh and Lucy were not scared, but they knew it was not their time to speak. Something in his voice in their ears, but not Callie's, had told them.

"I have been to see my mother. I have been to see my father. And your father. And they are all waiting on the other side. But this side is not done yet."

Callie closed her eyes and breathed. More than anything, she wanted it to be done. Whatever it—this—was, she wanted it to be over. She dug her toes into the dirt and felt a pebble between her toes, and in that moment, she loved that pebble—it felt so real, so completely and perfectly solid and manageable. It needed no understanding, it had no questions, no answers.

Michael raised his voice when he spoke, "Open your eyes." His voice filled the meadow and the clearing and the sky beyond the forest. It reached through their flesh and grabbed and rattled their flimsy human forms. "You have been chosen to lead, and I will lead you. I, I, I, see, I, I, I, speak, and I, I, I will be heard." It seemed impossible that anyone, anywhere, any corner of creation, had not heard him. It was not menacing, but majestic, and demanding in its majesty. The basso profondo reverberated in the soil, in the sky, in their skin—but not Callie's. She was unmoved by his presence, by his voice, by his eyes-not-eyes looking into her.

Slowly, she looked up and raised her eyelids, and looked into the place where his eyes had been and said, without so much as a quiver, but with anger beginning to rise at the back of her throat, threatening with each syllable to spill out from her lips, "You told me I had a choice. You told me. You said we all had a choice. And I, I, I do not choose this. I, I, I will go back. I, I, I have no father." The word father fell from her lips as an unfinished whisper, a sadness unmarked by regret.

Michael's expression did not change, but his voice now was for her alone, and not the world. "You have many fathers, the one and the many, going back through time, and all here, all now. You have many mothers, the one and the many, going back through time, and all here, all now. Always, all here, and all now. With you, always. But I, I, I have come to take them home. I, I, I am the one that was foretold, come again and for forever. You were foretold, and Josh, and Jonathon. He was taken, but he is here too. And I, I, I will take him home."

"You, you, you, will shut the fuck up." Her anger could no longer be quelled— she was no longer willing to try. Lucy reached out to grasp Callie by the arm, but Callie rejected her touch. Gently, but with purpose, she lifted the girl's hand from her arm and pushed it away, without ever looking away from Michael. She did not know if he was an angel, or a demon, or an alien, or a monster, or a figment of her imagination, or even a dream, but his talk of taking children had awakened something within her that despised him, despised everyone who took, and took, and took—never giving. "Take whatever you want. You always do, all of you. But I will not help you. Whatever this is—whatever that was," and she gestured here towards the southern sky, "That's your problem. It's nothing to do with me." His smile remained complacent as she spoke, and she wanted to run at him. She knew she could not hurt him—knew somehow that the cows would not let her, or something more frightening than the cows would take their place if she somehow did make it past them.

He did not speak—he just sat, waiting. After what seemed like an eternity in which no one and nothing moved—only the disc of white fire was lower in the sky—she asked, "Why can't it just stop?"

"It will stop. This is the beginning of the end. I have been to the beginning, and to the end. I have seen it all—every way it might end. I have seen what Josh tried to see, I have seen what they have been trying to show Lucy. I have seen, and I know, and it is you. You are the one who can set them free so I can take them home."

Take. Take. Take. The word made her teeth harden in her mouth, made her not hear all that he was saying. "If you can take them, take them now."

"I can't take them now. They are outside the kingdom. They were spirit made flesh, but their flesh was taken out of the realm of man, out of the realm of nature, by the weapons put here by the Other, the One. These weapons and shields and transmissions and emissions are not of God."

"Well then let God deal with it."

"He has. He sent a storm to save you."

"Me? Just me?"

"Us. The four of us. But this is your time."

"Three out of four isn't really a good average is it? I mean, for God? We are talking about big-G God, right? Especially when, how many did you say died in that storm?"

"They're still here. Waiting."

"Of course they are. Here, but dead."

"In the human sense, yes, they are dead. They are, as you say, shadows of themselves. They are shadow people, but they are real. They are not human, but they are powerful. They weren't before, but they are now. And you can lead them. You will lead them."

"Callie, Queen of the Shadow People? Is that my new name? Do I get to wear a cape? This is nuts. I haven't seen the shadow people in 18 years, and I don't want to see them now, Michael. You know that. Or is your name still Michael?" She looked into the place where his eyes had been with some anger, but with even more trepidation.

He smiled at her anger, and welcomed her contempt—but the time for questions had passed. "My name is always Michael. And you will see. And everyone who sees you will see, and everyone who sees you will believe, and will follow." And with that, he lowered his right hand, which had been pointing skyward throughout their discussion, and raised his left hand, which had remained pointing downward, and he covered his eyes. And light began to pour from the sockets, as tears, and where it slipped around his fingers it slid down and branded the bull, which did not move, and scorched the earth where it fell. Michael removed his hands from his eyes, and with his left hand he cupped a puddle of the shimmering light, and with his right he dipped two fingers into his cupped palm, and withdrew them. He raised the two fingers in front of his face, and touched his thumb to his forehead. And then without warning, with a single flick of his wrist, the light flew across the enclosure, and landed in Callie's eyes.

She cried out, and for the first time since Michael arrived, the others around her moved, as if awaking from a dream, but in a burning house. They began to scream and shout and moved to cling to her, but she would not remove her hands from her face.

"Leave her," Michael commanded from his seat upon the bull. "Let her see." There was no thought of disobedience—the cries and murmurs stopped at once. And the hands began to fall away from her, though some lingered—the touch of her seemed different. They wanted to touch her, to be more in her presence.

The sun was even lower now, just beginning to touch the tip of the horizon, preparing to sink them into darkness. The blue and purple and orange surrounding Michael had begun to slip down to the earth around him, spread between the hooves of the animals.

Finally, Josh and Lucy's hands fell away from her, and her hands fell away from her face, and she saw the shadows, all of them, tens and hundreds of thousands of them, shadows so dense they blocked the sunlight stretching out across the distance. They radiated out from where she stood, and she knew they stretched back beyond the trees, beyond the mountains. They were crossing rivers to come to her. They were legion times legion times legion, of all nations, and kindred, and tongues, and they were hers.

"They are my army?" she asked, and her voice began to shape itself like Michael's had done, in the ears of the living. Her eyes were not harmed, but they were changed—all her senses were sharpened with fire to a state at once primitive and wise.

"They are your army," he answered. "They are the beginning."

"Then I will lead them. Come on," she added as she turned and looked back to find Josh and Lucy, who were just behind her, and she beckoned them forward, holding her hands out to them as they came. Out of the corner of her eye she saw Annie standing with the others in camouflage, and added, "You better come along, too, Annie."

"Where are we going?" Annie asked as she nearly leapt forward, prepared—or so it seemed—to go anywhere.

"We're going to the table of my elders. You should probably hang on." Annie reached out and clasped her shoulder. The shadows began to move in and spin around them, quickly gathering speed, and Callie turned her head to yell to the helicopter pilot, "Thanks for the ride. You better get out of here." And at the end of the last word, the whirling blackness of the shadows swallowed up the four of them, and they were gone.

And then the cows and calves began to move in their great circles again, and the bull lifted his head as Michael called out to the pilot, "She's right, you know." And as the sun dropped below the horizon, the last twinkling bits of purple and blue light sank through the earth, and the dust began to rise, he called out "We're at war. You better get moving."

And then, Michael was gone, and the cows slowed their pace, and the circles disbanded, but the herd stayed awake through the day and night, nudging each other with their muzzles, and taking turns to rub against the bull, to where Michael sat. His return had been foretold, they knew—in their blood, they knew—and they had been part of the crossing over. They sat there at the threshold, their eyes big and black and wide with knowing. Sleep would come, in time, but on this night, they were awake with joy, and fear, and sadness. *Hallelujah!* they called out in their secret language, as the stars filled the sky. *Hallelujah!*

EPILOGUE

Josh was waiting for Jonny on Friday morning, standing in the rain at the end of his parents' driveway as he watched his friend make his slow, wet progress down and across the street. Jonny had more trouble crossing the street than the other kids. He had more trouble doing most everything than the other kids, except homework. He was good at homework, because he didn't have to use his legs. But Thursday, he didn't do his homework. Like all of the other kids in the neighborhood, he had been out playing in the rain all afternoon. He was strictly forbidden to get his leg braces wet, but they were already wet, so he decided to enjoy the rain with everyone else.

There was a group of eight of them out playing on Thursday after school, all between six and 12 years old. They had wandered on their bicycles over to the K-Mart shopping center to see if the travelling fair was all set up yet, and if it was, if the rides would work in the rain. It was only a mile or so from where they had been playing on a zip line, without permission, in the backyard of a home where the children were grown and had gone off to college. But the parents would be home soon—might be home early, because of the rain—so they had set out. Jonny rode on Josh's handlebars, as he always did, and the rain just added another element of danger for the pair as they traversed the low, rolling hills in the neighborhood. To get up a hill with his passenger, Josh had to speed down the previous hill, which was always perilous, and in the rain was even worse. No one wore helmets, because no one had helmets—there was no fun in that.

When they got to the parking lot, they could see all the rides were assembled, but none appeared to be running yet. There was a red Ford pickup truck parked in the center of the midway, and a scrawny, red-headed girl holding a beaten-up old umbrella over the head of an older man who was down on his haunches trying unsuccessfully not to get wet as he made adjustments to a junction box that had wires going into or out of all four sides of it. Everything was wet, and his flat-head screwdriver fought him with every turn. The girl was looking at the pack of children through the rain, her face more curious about than jealous of these children out playing in the rain on their bicycles, and her face twisted up in confusion as she observed the boy on the handlebars whose metal leg braces made him look as though he was part of the bicycle.

She did not see her father drop the screwdriver, or see it roll out of his reach under the truck holding the ring toss game, until he reached around and slapped her with the back of his wet, oily, calloused hand. "Git it, you stupid gurl. Whut's wrong witchu?"

He took the umbrella from her hand and shoved her towards the battened-down truck, which gave no hint of the hundreds of cheap stuffed animals crammed inside, that moved from town to town, un-won and unloved.

She blushed with shame as she saw the confused looks on the children's faces, and she knew that no one ever shoved them. No one ever called them *stupid*. She got down on her knees to reach under the truck for the screwdriver, and heard her father yell out, "Ya'll best git on out from here. Fair ain't open."

Her daisy-print dress did not cover her knees, and the rough tarmac of the parking lot dug and scraped into the soft, wet flesh of her kneecaps. She was scrambling, trying to find the screwdriver, because she knew a blow would be coming her way if her daddy had to stand up to come help her. To her relief, her fingers found and clasped onto the ridged plastic handle, and she withdrew from the ground to hand it to him, taking the umbrella back as she did. She was even more relieved to see the other children were no longer there—they had given her an unbearable sense of shame that she felt no storm, no amount of time, could ever wash away. She knew they didn't mean it—they hadn't done anything—but she was still glad they were gone.

When they got back to the Candlelight Motel that night, her daddy's new girlfriend—her new momma, he told her—wasn't in his room. "She got company," he told her, so instead of sleeping in room 36, alone, Vicky slept in the room with her father. At least, she did get some sleep after he finally had his way with her and passed out drunk.

***

"They'll never find out," Josh told Jonny as they trudged together towards Moore Street Elementary, rain pelting their yellow slickers. "I heard mom on the phone—the busses ain't even running."

Jonny looked over at Josh, and had to turn his whole head to see him—the hood of his rain slicker blocked everything from sight except for what was immediately in front of him, which was just a narrow wedge of rain and street. He responded with the voice of an older boy, explaining something down to someone much younger, though they were the same age. "We don't ride the bus, Josh. Everybody knows that."

Josh was unmoved. "Lots of kids won't be at school today. We weren't going to do anything today except watch movies, anyway." That part last wasn't entirely true—they were going to be turning in their homework, which Jonny was all-but-too aware he had not done.

"I bet Mrs. Sturgess would call mom."

"No she won't. Dad said he bet more than half the kids don't show up. They won't have time to call everybody's parents."

Jonny had heard his own parents have a similar conversation, before they had their mild, familiar argument over whether or not he could walk to school. He always insisted on walking—even in the rain. Everyone who lived within walking distance walked, and he didn't want to be any more different than he already was. And one of the other kids—usually Josh—would always wait for him, and slow down to walk with him, anyway.

But skipping school was brand new territory for the two boys. They had talked about it—everyone talked about it—but hardly anyone ever did it until junior high. And then, it was usually kids who smoked, and stole things, and got suspended from school all the time. Jonny and Josh did not smoke, or steal things, and they had never been suspended.

Jonny realized that Josh was right—the school wouldn't have time to call all the parents, even if they tried. "Okay," he said, but without smiling, and not entirely convinced. He added, "So where should we go? The Treehouse?"

Josh scrunched up his face, unseen by Jonny, before replying, cautiously, that "It's too early. Too many cars on the road. Probably Caruthers, too. Even in this rain. Asshole." He paused, thinking. "We have to wait 'til after school starts. Let's just wait in the damned woods." The boys had just recently begun swearing, and it was still sounded forced, the words uncomfortable on their tongues when they did.

They were halfway down Roberson Street, just down the block and around the corner from the school, when together and without discussion they cut through one of the few back yards on the block that did not have a fence, or a dog, or both. When Josh was alone, he could and would climb any fence, and most dogs would have left them alone, but with Jonny, they needed to use one of the shortcuts without obstructions.

***

They did not see the young girl who had ducked behind the fishing boat permanently parked in a driveway midway down the street. She had woken up before her father, and taken a dollar from his pants to buy some breakfast. After that she took the beaten up umbrella from the back of his truck and wandered down the street to the Jiffy Mart, where she bought a Honey Bun and a bottle of Sunny Delight, which she consumed under the overhang of the store. People on their way to work and school stopping into the store took no notice of her. She asked a crumpled-up looking old woman for directions to the fair, and the woman didn't know what she was talking about, so she waited to ask again until she saw someone who looked like they might actually go to the a fair—a woman in her twenties who left two children in her idling car, as she went inside to get some cigarettes before she went to work—and the woman replied, "You should be in

540

school, not at the fair," and the girl replied, without hesitation, "I do book learning at home. My daddy works at the fair."

Wanting the conversation to be over with, the woman pointed the girl down Moore Street, told her to follow it until she got to Moore Street Elementary, then walk around to Roberson Street and follow it until it ended, then make a right, and the big red K-Mart sign would be down the road. It wasn't the most direct path, but the woman was thinking of her own route as she gave directions, and she would be dropping her own children off at the elementary school as soon as she could get her cigarettes and get back in the car. She never thought of offering the girl a ride, and the girl never expected she would. "Thank you, ma'am," is all the girl said as she started off walking with the umbrella providing just enough protection to make it worth the bother of holding it.

It was a long walk, but for most of it, there was sidewalk. She first encountered a mass of cars and people at Dublin Junior High School, just two long blocks from where she started at the Jiffy Mart. Teenagers darted out of cars and up the steps of the imposing brick building, which had a very narrow portico where clusters of teenagers stood smoking. No one else lingered, though—there was nowhere to linger in the pouring rain. She kept walking, passing some youngsters, but not many, on their way to the junior high. As she made her way several more blocks down, she encountered other children walking in the same direction she was—younger children, on their way to the elementary school.

When she arrived there, the scene was quite different. Cars were backed up and down the streets in all directions, as mothers and fathers waited their turn to drop off their first-through-sixth graders to teachers waiting with umbrellas to herd their charges under the boomerang-shaped portico and into the school. Most of the fourth-through-sixth graders got out and walked from the street, but with third graders, one never knows—so the parents waited.

As she turned the corner going past the school, a crossing guard that she couldn't readily identify from the side as a man or a woman asked, "Shouldn't you be going to school, missy?"

She looked up in the guard's face and saw that it was a woman, who looked both kind and interested, but the girl replied as she kept moving, "That ain't my school, ma'am." The girl had no way of knowing there were no more schools in the direction she was walking; but, the guard didn't recognize the face as a Moore Street student, and let the girl move on.

When she turned the corner onto Roberson Street, the scene changed again— there were almost no cars, and no people that she could see in the misty downpour, but there was also no sidewalk. Since the rain was already running in swift little rivulets down the sides of the street, and in sheets cascading down its middle, she chose to navigate the higher terrain of the front yards of the houses on the north side of the street. She wended her way around boxwood hedges, birdbaths, and azaleas; dodged the few parked cars, fishing boats on blocks, and abandoned bicycles; and, she had to watch each step for footballs, Frisbees and baseball bats abandoned mid-play, apparently without fear of them being stolen. As she made her slow and meandering path, she considered how different this world was from her own. In her world, she feared everything, everyone. She had been taught, and trained, and beaten, to fear. In her world, everyone knew you can't trust anyone, ever. People will take, and steal, and lie, and cheat, and hurt for any reason, or no good reason at all.

These were her thoughts as she saw the two boys in the distance ahead of her. She was older and taller than both boys, and they were turned walking away from the houses she was walking in front of—they were cutting through to the woods. On an impulse she could not satisfactorily explain even to herself, she followed them. She recognized one of the boys—or at least she thought she did—from the day before. He had the same rain slicker and leg braces, and she reckoned there couldn't be too many of those. And, if she needed to outrun them, or even beat the boys up, she knew she could.

They had a head start on her, but they were moving slowly, and her lithe, quick

542

steps caught her up to them almost immediately, though she held back. She lost sight of them twice after they made their way through a backyard littered with playthings, and through the metal gate that stood in the center of a pierced brick fence opening onto a thick planting of teenaged pines.

She heard their laughter before she found where they had stopped. It was a lean-to constructed of an old metal Colonial Bread store sign, pieces of rusting corrugated tin, and odd scraps of plywood and pressboard. There were only three sides to the small structure, which looked more like an oversized doghouse than anything else, and it had a dirt floor packed firm, and bare of grass or weeds, but crisscrossed with small isolated puddles from drops of rain that worked their around and down the layers of roofing. The boys sat on old metal milk crates, and the floor was littered with candy and gum wrappers, soda bottles, some cigarette butts, and red circles of plastic—the remains of cap gun ring caps. A formation of ants marched across the floor and up one side the back wall of the fort, but disappeared from there.

She couldn't hear what they were saying, but standing in the rain, and feeling more than a little foolish, she felt she only had two real choices: Turn back and go the way she came, or make herself known to the boys. Again, for reasons she didn't fully understand, or couldn't have articulated if she did, she chose the latter. In a move both fearsome and brave, she snuck round the side of the fort before she planted herself in its entrance with one hand holding up the umbrella and the other anchored firmly on her hip, and demanded "What'chall boys doin' out here?"

Both boys yelped more than just a little. They had been discussing the likelihood of being found out when she jumped out at them, and while her timing was inopportune for them, she felt it was good for her—their fear gave her a slight advantage, somehow.

"We ain't doin' nothin'," Josh replied, too loudly, as soon as he saw it wasn't a teacher or a parent or anyone likely to make a public record of their truancy. He was angry at being scared. "What are you followin' us for, anyways?"

"It's that girl from the fair," Jonny said, recognition setting in, and speaking to Josh, but looking at her.

"So what if it is? Ya'll ain't s'posed to be out here. Ya'll s'posed to be in school." She spoke with the authority of someone older, which she was, and someone wiser, which she wasn't sure was true—she was jealous of book learning.

"It's a rain day," Josh answered, with some bravado—but not enough.

"It didn't look like that to me back there. All them other young'uns at school." She didn't live in the world, but she knew enough about it to know that boys their age—and girls her age—were supposed to be in school, even if it rained.

"What's your name?" Josh demanded.

"Who wants to know?" she answered, this being the most common response whenever anyone from the fair was asked his or her name.

"I'm Jonny. This is Josh," the smaller boy answered without even considering that he should lie, which is what Josh had been thinking, and which is why Josh then scowled, without considering that he should make his face lie.

The girl could see in their faces it was the truth, so she answered back, "My name's Vicky. What'chall gonna do out here all day? It ain't nothin' but rain."

"We were gonna walk to the fair and see if it was open yet," Josh answered, feeling somewhat stupid.

"It ain't s'posed to open 'til tonight. We got to test all the rides to make shore the 'lectricity is runnin' right."

"Can we come watch?" Jonny asked, without thinking. There were few places in Dublin more public than the K-Mart parking lot. The idea that they might get to ride the rides for free, in the rain, and before anyone else in town had immediately taken hold of him, though he didn't speak it aloud.

"Shore," the girl said. "How far is it from here?"

Neither boy had any idea how far it actually was, though they had a rough estimate of how long it would take them, either way they went. Roberson Street would be the most direct route, from where they were, but they would likely be identified by some parent or another, walking down the street in the wrong direction at that time of day. The other way—down Cedar Creek to where it passed the backs of the houses on Pine Forest Circle, and then onto the back of the K-Mart, was the safest route for not being caught, but the longest, and the most treacherous—especially for Jonny. He seemed to sense this calculation forming in Josh's head, and before Josh could complete it, he blurted out, "We have to take the creek. It's the only way we can go without getting caught."

They spent the next few minutes discussing the pros and cons of each plan, before all agreeing to follow Jonny's suggested creek route. They would all be covered in mud from head to toe, they agreed, including Vicky, who had never seen the creek; but, she was so surprised at being included and accepted by the boys, she readily agreed with them. Whenever clean boys like this—*nice boys*, she thought—tried to talk to her at the fair, their parents would shoo them away from her like her poverty was contagious. These boys didn't seem to judge her at all. She wondered if their parents would judge her if they could see her, then decided she didn't really want to know.

Their journey was longer and more treacherous than they could have imagined. Cedar Creek was normally more of a sunken path than an actual creek, a deep trench worn out and down over time, but it felt like a mighty river as they tried to navigate the rushing water, slick red clay, and the projecting limbs and roots of the surrounding trees. Vicky gave up on her umbrella before she even made it down into the creek bed, though she held on to it, and the boys' rain slickers were ineffectual against the swirling rain.

She was as eager for information about life in a house, and a school, as they were for information about life in a travelling fair, with no school, and no homework, and getting to stay in a motel most every night. Their conversation was punctuated with lots of *Huhs?* and *Wows!* and *Whats?* Their imaginations roamed as their knowledge grew of the world outside their own very different, distinctly sheltered lives. They all watched television, and saw lots of other people when

545

they went places, but most of the people they actually got to talk to were just like them, or who they were supposed to be when they got older. This was something different. This, somehow, felt real. They weren't learning what their teachers, or parents, or television told them—they were learning some fundamental truths about what the world really was like. The small-town boys were jealous and amazed by nomadic life of the girl who could ride carnival rides every day, not knowing that to the world at large, she was just carny trash, as ephemeral and disposable as the paper cones that held the cotton candy she sometimes sold. To the girl who felt she had nothing, the two boys had everything any child could ever want, and she was confused by their apparent ingratitude for their lives of privilege. She had not yet learned envy, and they had not yet learned pity, and this freedom enabled them to ask questions freely, without fear of learning—or giving—resentment.

They were not slowed down by the rain itself, but they were slowed down by Jonny. Somehow though, no one seemed to mind. Once they were all good and thoroughly drenched, they couldn't get any wetter, and it became a day like any other day, but with the added excitement of being out of bounds—the boys were supposed to be at school, and she was supposed to be with her daddy, wherever he was.

***

It was close to 11:00am when they first sensed something was wrong. They were nearing the shopping center, the boys knew, and had shared that information with Vicky, but they felt something change in the air. It wasn't just anticipation, though there was a certain anxiety consistent with nearing the end of a long and dangerous journey. And, it was still raining—it seemed like that would never change—but something in the air felt charged. It seemed tangibly alive, but the smell was almost electric. It was not something they could pinpoint, but it was something not right.

Without discussing it, they all slowed, and then stopped walking altogether. They stood there, ankle-deep in mud at the edge of the gushing stream, and looked at one another, breathless with expectation. They looked around, quiet, waiting to hear something. They each seemed to expect something soft—a deer, or a dog, maybe even a turkey vulture, all familiar to this little stretch of wilderness cutting through suburbia like a theme park. They thought it must be something they would just barely be able to hear, just above, or below, or just out of time with the pattering rain.

What they got instead was the manic, wailing, unnatural force of Willie Isaacs, charging down the bank of the creek at them, his eyes as wide as heaven, his arms cartwheeling wildly, as he jumped and slipped and hopped down the wet clay walls of the creek, then running towards them, through the water, splashing, yelling, "GO, go, go, now, you're not supposed to be here, GO, hurry, GO, go on." His stream of commands, urges, requests and entreaties began as soon as he set eyes on them, and did not stop.

The children were all good and properly terrified, but none of them moved. They were too scared—even Vicky, who was used to all manner of sudden rages and terrors from the drunks and addicts who populated her narrow existence. "GO!" the man yelled as he got right up on them, but they could not move. He was wearing a camouflage jacket with the name *Isaacs* embroidered on a patch above his heart. They could see through the rain that he was crying. "Josh, Jonny, Callie, you've got to go, go now, go back. You're supposed to be at the Treehouse. Not here. Not here. You've got to go. It's coming. It's right behind me."

And with that, he took off running through the creek, right down the center of it, the water above his knees. He turned to look at the children, who still weren't moving, but were watching his progress in the rain. "You've got to follow me," he called back to them, pausing to look back. The earnestness of his sobs scared them, but they still did not want to follow the man. He balled his fists and thrust them down as he bent over and yelled "NOW, you've got to come NOW."

"How do you know our names?" Josh demanded, not moving.

"I know. I can see. And I can see them. They're coming. It's coming. You've got to come with me." His voice was desperate with pleading, and his fatigued breathing punctuated his words.

"My name ain't Callie. That ain't no kinda name. Why you call me that?" Vicky was trying to regain her composure—her carny composure: tough, fierce, and unafraid.

"Vicky, Vicky, I'm sorry, your name is Vicky. Please, come with me. I need you to come with me." He was temporarily thrown off by the girl's name, but it was of no matter—he had to get them away. He was gesturing them forward as he looked in the woods behind them, his eyes wide with the fear.

"You been following us? That how you know our names?" Jonny was trying to be as brave as the others, and was, in his way. He knew he could not outrun the man. He knew no one could hear him scream in the woods. Bravery was the path before him, so he took it. He began to walk towards the stranger.

"No, that's not how I know your names. I know your lives. I know what you've lived, what you will live. Vicky, I know what your father does to you, and I know you're scared right now, you're always a little scared, but you won't be, not always. Jonny, I know last night you dreamed of waking up fully grown, with legs that run. Josh, I know you're going to live your whole life running, running, running. And that is what I need you to do, right now, is run."

Jonny was still walking towards the strange colored man, who had his arms outstretched, beckoning him forward like the boy was a spooked pony. And that's when they heard it—they all heard it. A great whir of mechanical clicking noises, like a million tiny, shrill, insistent metal crickets crashing through the trees and the rain, and it was coming for them. No one doubted anymore. The three took off running through the creek bed towards William.

And as they ran, with Jonny quickly falling behind, the sound changed, and the earth began to tremble as though hell-born beasts had crashed up from beneath the churning wet clay, and Vicky screamed, "WHAT IS THAT" and William yelled back at her, "DEATH."

They just barely heard the splash as Jonny fell. They felt it, sensed the lack of forward momentum, more than they actually heard it. Josh turned back to look and see, and he saw Death, knew it at once, knew that the man with *Isaacs* on his jacket had been right, but what he saw wasn't a beast at all. It was a shimmering, wet, rectilinear plane of black that looked at once like glass, then tar, then water, then a bottomless square pit in the sky that sucked the rain into it, and it changed size as it moved through the treetops with deliberation. It appeared to be alive, but its movements were skewed and distorted, like a geometric abstraction of animal, but an abomination, electric and cold, all-knowing, but knowing only death.

Josh knew at once it was a lie that Hell was a lake of fire—Hell was this thing, this eternal, unnatural fleshless plane of flexing symmetry, its hunger made more terrible by its lack of teeth, by its lack of anything created or touched by the hand of God. And it was going to take Jonny, and he would be gone, forever.

Josh began to run towards the boy as the black void began to descend from its place among the trees. Jonny was trying to right himself in the water, and Vicky began screaming, and William started running back towards them, his voice booming inarticulate rage and despair; and then, it was 11:09am, and they heard the sky as it began to fall, a sudden exhalation of displaced air somewhere in the distant heavens. And as they heard the branches above them begin to groan and creak and crash down, they covered their heads, and they were crushed down into the creek, with the weight of the universe pushing them into and under the water, cleansing them of time and remembering, of seeing and hearing and touching, of doing and of being. It held them there, safe and secure in the resurrection—of their resurrection.

William was the first to pull free. He looked up without noticing the changed world around him, except for the trees and limbs now scattered across the creek bed, immense tangled knots of splintered wood between him and the children. Vicky was closest, and he pulled her out of the water, and she gasped for air and tried to cling to him, but he shook her free—she was breathing—and he climbed a tangle of branches to pull up Josh, who spat out water and words in equal measure, but they were incoherent and William wasn't listening, he was already looking for Jonny, and then he found him, and pulled him up, but Jonny did not sputter, or spurt, or gasp or cry. He did not whimper, or shiver, or cling, or shake. The rain fell into his open eyes, and the creek spilled from his mouth and nose and ears, and William held him as his own child, and mourned for him as he would his own—in his heart, as he did mourn his own, that he now knew he would not see again.

The other two children approached William with caution, and as best they could, traversing the swelling mass of water and sticks and leaves, searching their bodies gently for breaks and scars and lumps.

They were walking through the rain, not knowing what to say, or do, or even feel—should they be scared or sad or angry or dead?—when they heard a voice boom from the top of the ravine, "He ain't gone yet Willie. Look at him. Look at him close."

The children knew what to feel now—scared witless. The old man looking down at them through the rain was terrifying to Vicky because it was yet another strange man to be scared of, and terrifying to Josh because it was a man he knew, and knew to be scared of—Dyson Caruthers.

"We didn't do nothin', Mr. Caruthers. We didn't do nothin'," Josh began babbling at once, somehow as scared of Caruthers as he was of Death itself, but Caruthers cut him off short. "I know you didn't do nothing, boy. Willie, put him down on the ground. Over yonder," he pointed to a small rise of earth on the side of the creek. William obeyed, and lay the boy face up on the mound of wet earth and forest debris.

"Look at him, Willie, look at him." Caruthers' voice was loud, but there was no anger in it—there was a sense of urgency, and perhaps excitement—the expectant thrill of revelation unfolding.

William did look at the boy, and so did Josh and Vicky. They did not want to, but they could not stop themselves. As the reality of what they were seeing became real, Vicky grabbed Josh, and Josh grabbed Vicky, and they stood in the water and felt unsure of anything in the world except each other. They could see light seeping from Jonny's mouth, and where it met the air, it turned into shadow.

Caruthers' voice was soft now, but still loud. And like a stage whisper done right for the first time ever, it cut through the rain as he urged him, "Breathe it back into him, Willie. You can do it. You've seen it. I know you have. I've seen it, too. Do it now. We have to go. It might come back. We've seen that, too. Do it now."

Josh did not believe it would come back, but he wanted the Isaacs man to do whatever it was Caruthers wanted him to do. "Please, Mr. Isaacs, Mr. Willie, is that your name? Please?" he asked.

"Willie. Willie is my name, son," he said, looking deep in Josh's eyes, and then he lowered his face down to Jonny's, and put his mouth to the boy's mouth, and he exhaled a deep, long, tearful breath deep into Jonny's lungs, and when he withdrew his head, no more light spilled out.

"Looks like that done it," Caruthers barked from his lookout, all business now. "Come on, now, let's get him back to the fort. We got to figure this out. Things have changed. Willie, keep that boy's mouth closed tight now. I thought Jimmy and Edwin would'a been here by now. Guess they'll meet us at the fort. Come on, now."

William began moving at Caruther's first suggestion, but it took several minutes to find a place where he could safely navigate the steep, wet embankment while holding the boy in one arm and keeping his mouth closed with the other.

When William was safely at the top of the ravine, Caruthers shouted down impatiently to the two children, "Well, come on, we ain't leavin' you two out here. We've got to get you somewhere safe. Good Lord." The children, though yet strangers, still clung to each other, and looked to each other for guidance, their feet still sunk in the muddy water. "It ain't a suggestion. Get your asses up here or I'm coming down there for ya." His expression turned from taciturn to fierce in a heartbeat, and their hold on another strengthened briefly before they released each other with a glance and began scrambling up the muddy wall. Josh had always thought of Caruthers as old, and frail, and withered, but the man seemed to loom over him, impossibly tall and broad and strong, as the children emerged from the ravine and stood, and the old man said, somewhat more kindly, "Come on now, we got to get moving."

As they started walking, Vicky spoke up for the first time. "I ain't got no shoes."

"What hap—never mind," Caruthers stopped, cutting himself off, and turned back, and picked up the girl with the grace and ease of a ballet dancer a quarter his age. He carried her to his car, which was a few hundred yards down the road. William was almost there, and Josh was struggling to keep up with Caruthers, who could more easily navigate the thicket of wet fallen pines, even with the girl in his arms.

"What fort are you talking about? Why aren't we going to the hospital?" Josh was a few steps behind Caruthers, and calling out ahead of him in the rain.

"We're going to the Treehouse, son. And we ain't goin' to the hospital, cause there ain't nothin' they can do for this boy there."

"But he's alive, ain't he?" Josh asked, catching up to Caruthers as he spoke and looking up into the man's face, and into Vicky's at the same time, her face taut with terror, looking down at him. The man didn't answer.

Josh knew, he could feel, if Jonny was dead, it was his fault—all his fault. The weight of the burden compelled him to keep talking. "If he's dead, we have to tell somebody. We can't just take him to the Treehouse." In his fear, it had not yet occurred to Josh to ask how Caruthers knew about the Treehouse.

"We don't have to do any such thing." They were at the car, which had a broken windshield but looked otherwise unharmed by the storm. Caruthers added, as an afterthought, "Not yet, anyway," as he stood Vicky on the wet ground. Josh climbed into the front seat beside Caruthers, and Vicky got into the back with William and Jonny. William was holding the boy in his lap so tenderly, and pressing his index finger against the boy's lips with such compassion, that the girl, for the first time since she saw the man, was not scared of him.

"Is he gone? Willie, is he gone? Look at him and tell me." Caruthers' voice was firm, and filled with authority, but not unkind. He was eyeing the man in his rearview mirror. His voice filled the car, but the rain kept it from escaping out into the morning. Josh turned around to look in the backseat, getting muddy footprints on Caruthers' front seat as he did.

William did not immediately speak. He kept looking at Jonny's mouth beneath his finger.

"Of course, he's gone, he's dead," Josh said, his voice rising as he did it. He had not yet begun to cry, but everyone could hear the threat of it.

Caruthers did not look away from William's face as he responded, almost gently, "Dead and gone aren't the same thing, son. Not by a longshot." As he was speaking, Willie's head begin to move from side to side, and Caruthers asked, speaking to the mirror, "We need to stitch him up, Willie?" William nodded in the back seat.

The old man started the car and began driving, very slowly, to their destination, which was just a few blocks away. The roads were relatively clear, despite the devastation in every direction, but the great spider's web of cracks in the fogged-over windshield, and the rain, and the lack of a visible road made the drive difficult. He parked the car beside the road, and they began their walk across the remains of the pine trees. They approached the Treehouse from the opposite side of the creek from where the neighborhood children entered it, and as they neared it, and Josh realized it really was his Treehouse, their Treehouse, Caruthers was leading them to, and he asked, somewhat sheepishly, "So you know about the Treehouse?"

"Know about it?" And the old man laughed, though his laughter was impeded by the weight of the girl he was holding again, and was maneuvering around and over the remains of pine limbs and scattered across the nearly open expanse. "I helped build it. I helped keep it safe for you all. All these years later...this was where you were supposed to be today. That is where you were supposed to take this girl here."

"I don't understand," Josh said, very simply, and his legs stumbled in time with his thoughts.

"Well, no, you wouldn't. And you won't, not for a very long time. I don't understand all of it, myself, but that isn't my job. My job was to keep this place for you. For today. And, well, it has worked out, sort of, in its own way. You were on the path… But the darkness, it drew you away. Ah, well. Best laid plans, and all that."

He looked at the steep, slick path down to Cedar Creek and asked the girl in his arms, with an almost apologetic and sincere supplication, "Do you think you can make it down on your own, little lady?" She said "Yessir," still shaken by the events of the past few hours, including the kindness of the man who had carried her so far—her own father would never have done that. Why had this man?

They waded through the creek, which was now up to the grown men's waists, and Josh and Vicky held onto one another as they crossed, Josh clinging to Vicky, who was taller, and Vicky clinging to Josh—she did not know how to swim. Willie's crossing was the most difficult. He was burdened with an unmoving, unbreathing boy, and he was unable to see from the rain and his own tears, and his arms, though strong, were weak from the effort of holding the boy with one arm, and keeping his lips closed with the other. But he was a soldier, and he had done the same thing before dozens—countless dozens—of times. Even in the rain. Even being chased, and shot at. His intimacy with death was as real was the shirt he was wearing.

Midway through the stream, it was Vicky who first saw the shadows moving in the rain. At first she thought it was a trick of the lighting and the rain, but then she heard them.

"What is that?" she whispered to Josh, stopping in her tracks, the creek rushing around her, the daisies on her dress floating up in the muddy water. He stopped with her, and looked, and listened. And he heard them. And he saw them. "Mr. Caruthers, I think it's back. I think there are more of them."

Caruthers, who was on the landing in front of the hidden door before them, said, "No, son. That's something else. That's nothing to fear. Come on across, though. We need to get in." They could all hear sirens in the distance.

Vicky did not need telling twice—she lurched through the water, dragging

Josh behind. They scrambled up and into the Treehouse, and the door closed behind them.

Willie laid Jonny down on one of the beds as Caruthers began looking on a set of shelves, asking as he did, "Josh, where's the first aid kit?"

"The what?" Josh had been listening for the voices he had heard outside.

"The first aid kit. We left a first aid kit here. Where is it?" He was looking under the unmade bed where William sat still, his finger still pressed on Jonny's lips.

"Um, I think we might have, um." Josh faltered, then added "It's gone."

"Damn it. Is there any string here? We need some string. For stitches. Now."

William spoke for the first time since before they got in the car, saying to the man, "Dyson, you hold the boy. I'll get it."

Dyson traded places with William, who sat on the floor where two Barbie dolls lay with a G.I. Joe. He picked up one of the Barbie dolls as Josh and Vicky, who hadn't moved from just inside the door, edged closer in.

"Whut er you doin'?," she asked, as he began to pluck strands of the synthetic hair from the doll's head, barely distinguishable in the weak fluorescent lights.

"I'm preparing him to rest," William replied, and his voice was distant, marked with a melancholia that seemed familiar to it.

He lay the strands end-to-end on the floor in front of him, and began passing his right hand over them, in a back-and-forth gesture, saying words that might have been a prayer or incantation—the children could not make them out—and when he was done, in his palm he held a single gossamer strand, clear and brilliant, even in the fluorescent light.

"H-h-how did you do that?" Josh asked, audibly and unabashedly afraid.

"You a magician?" Vicky asked, less frightened—she had known many magicians, and knew some of their tricks.

"No, he's not a magician," Caruthers answered for him, as William walked back over to the bed.

"Hold him," William said, without looking at the other man, his eyes intent on Jonny. Caruthers held the boy's head up, and William held his lips closed, and slid the thread into and out of the boy's skin, stitching them closed, making sounds that might have been words, and the thread went in and out without blood, or even any pressure, as though the strand knew its purpose. His hands moved with the skill of a surgeon, and the tenderness of a newborn's mother.

The children were both terrified and amazed by what they were seeing, and stood dumbstruck and silent.

When William was done, the soft pink flesh of the boy's mouth was tucked inside a single straight line that did not smile, and did not frown, but simply disappeared. Jonny's eyes stayed open, unmoving. Mud still dripped from the folds of the metal braces, which held his legs firm, though the rest of his body was as limp and lifeless and dull as the boy's yellow rain slicker, splattered and streaked with mud.

William looked to Caruthers and asked, "What are we supposed to do now?" His voice was soft, unsure.

"You're the prophet. I'm just a fixer." Caruthers spoke with a jocularity that disarmed the children from their silent revelry. "We got to wait on Jimmy and Edwin, though. They'll have to carry the board."

"Whut's a prophet?" Vicky asked, and added, "Whut's a fixer?" Before either man could respond, Josh asked, "Who's Jimmy and Edwin?"

Once the children looked away from the boy, they did not look back, keeping their eyes moving from William to Caruthers with fixed determination—they did not want to see.

"I'm not a prophet," William answered, and his voice was sad as well as a little vexed—it seemed that he and Caruthers might have had this discussion before, with no agreement on what he was, or possibly what they were. A tension hung in the air that seemed to have nothing, or maybe very little, to do with the boy whose mouth had just been sewn shut.

"So how did you just do that thing?" Josh asked, and then, when he received no response, turned to Caruthers, asked "And how did he know our names?"

"I'm not going to spend a lot of time explaining this, because Willie will need to take this memory from you—all of this, everything that's happened so far today, everything up until the time he leaves you. You won't remember any of this for years. Decades. But, the short answer is, war changes everybody, and it changes most people in different ways. You, the two of you, have been changed today. Not the way the Other wanted you changed—you ain't dead—but you're changed. Those voices you heard, those shadows you saw? They've always been there. They're always around. Sometimes more, sometimes less. That's what would've become of Jonny, if William hadn't been able to help him. But he did, and it may be that he—Jonny—might come back to us one day. No time soon, though." He looked at the children thoughtfully for a minute before he spoke again.

"Willie, why don't you find something to take down one of these panels?" He gestured to the upright, unfinished plywood panels that lined the Treehouse walls. "And I guess we'll need something to tie him down with, too. We'll have to leave him somewhere they can find him. We don't want them coming here again. Of course, this place will have to come down. And, soon, too." He said it with sadness, a combination of nostalgia and regret that seemed uncomfortable in his voice, on his face.

The children were more confused than ever, but William apparently understood, or at least could comprehend what Caruthers wanted from him, as he immediately stood and began scrounging around in boxes and crates. Josh saw immediately from the way the man was searching that he, too, had been to the Treehouse before—he was looking in all the right places. Josh started to speak, but Caruthers stopped him, and gestured to one of the beaten-up sofas—the one facing away from Jonny. The children sat, still wet and dripping, and he sat facing them, moving an old shoebox filled with random parts of games out of his way as he did so. He appeared to be having a difficult time keeping his focus on just the two of them—the dead boy was not far behind them, and William was having a time removing screws from the drywall with the Phillips screwdriver he found from who knew where.

Caruthers let out a sigh and began, "I'm making a shit-show of this, I can see that. I was hoping we wouldn't have to have this conversation at all. I was hoping it would turn out another way, a different way. But, we take what we get. We have to. That's the thing, you see—I told you before, war changes everybody. In different ways. It's an inhuman thing, an unnatural thing, to take the life of another man. It's hard. Very hard. Even when it is for the right reasons—and hardly anyone can ever even agree what those are—the right reasons to kill a man. Some say there are none. Some will just as soon take a life as cross the road. But when it comes time to look a man in the eye and kill him, well, it's just hard. And these machines we use now, they make it easier, to kill more, faster, easier." He stopped to collect his thoughts.

"Whut does that have to do with that boy back thar?" Vicky thumbed behind her head behind her, keeping her eyes straight ahead at Caruthers. She understood little of what Caruthers was saying, and she imagined—rightly—that Josh understood even less.

"Sometimes in war, you fight a battle that seems like—it becomes—a whole new war. There are wars within wars within wars. It's always been complicated, but it'll soon get difficult, much more difficult, to untangle right from wrong. There will come a time when men will sit in a room half a world away and drop bombs and kill people whose faces they never see. There will be great machines—computers, we call them—that make decisions for the men. And the women. There'll be women there, too, killing with the push of a button, never even getting their fingers dirty, same as the men. Never working up a sweat, never feeling the heat of battle. That heat, that fire, that comes from inside. It's the body working itself up to do a thing it knows it ought not do. They'll play these war games on their computers, hooked up to a television, and it makes it look like war, and it doesn't take long for them to get confused, for the real war and the make-believe war to get all mashed up. Sometimes one side thinks they've won, another time the other side thinks it won, but every time, it's really the computer that wins. It's the Other."

None of this made much sense to the children. The distant future seemed impossibly far away, and the thing that had chased them seemed very close. Though it had only been a few minutes, really, it already seemed almost not real to them. It couldn't be Death. It was just—something else.

"Is the other that thang we saw in them other woods, or them thangs out yonder?" Vicky asked, pointing to the metal door that separated them from the outside world. His earlier reassurance had done little to ease her mind about the voices she had heard.

"Those voices are nothing to fear. You won't believe me. I didn't believe it myself, not at first. None of us did. I was in Korea, fighting, dying—at least I thought—when it happened to me. The battle of the Chosin Reservoir. So much death. And so cold. We were hungry, and thirsty, and tired. So very tired. We thought we were hallucinating. Even though we were all hallucinating the same thing, most of us—that's not so unusual. I ask you if you hear something, you listen, and maybe you start hearing something even if there's nothing to hear. But we did hear. Not all of us. Just some. Most. We stuck together. Even after the war. Long after war. Even now."

He looked at the blank faces of the children, and sighed before he continued. "After a while, we discovered that some of us could, well, not exactly see the future, but if we came into contact with a piece of the flesh of another person—no matter how small… microscopic, even, just a fleck of skin, even dandruff—we could follow that person's path, or paths, into the future. We could see the past, too—but there, there's only one path. Whatever has happened, is done. No changing the past, regardless of what the scientists say. The future, though, there are many paths, for most of us. Things change. Circumstances. Events. Storms, for instance." Here, he laughed, not entirely without humor. The children's expressions did not change.

"What I'm saying, children, is we've seen your path. Your *paths*. We know what led up to this day, and now, we know at least in part, what the path forward is. We have to get you somewhere safe, and we have to get Jonny somewhere he won't be found until some people can get here who know what he is. Who he is. We can't have that sonofabitch Doc Parry cutting the boy up." Josh winced at this, and looked as though he might cry, while Vicky looked straight ahead at Caruthers, uncomfortable but unflinching.

"Why somewheres safe? Is that thang coming back?" she asked, with more courage than she felt.

"It's coming back, yes, but not for a very long time, we don't think. Not in... human time. To the infinite, our lifetimes are barely noticeable, but our lives—every life—is important. Your lives, especially. When it returns, the earth will be on fire. The very rivers will burn. Man will turn on man. Brother on brother. And you will be there to fight it."

He smiled as the children turned to look at one another, their smallness compressed by the eternal strangeness of the man's suggestions, and by their wet hair clinging to their heads, and their bodies swallowed up on the sofa made for people larger than they were, or felt they might ever be. Before either could question anything, or speak, Caruthers stood abruptly, and called to William, who had been sitting quietly with Jonny.

"The parking lot, then?" he asked, over the heads of the children, who turned their heads in William's direction, but did not actually look back, stealing glances at each other instead.

"Yes," William answered, softly.

"And you're going to stay with them, watch over them?"

"Yes," he answered again, and sadness snuck out with his breath.

"You're sure? You've got to be sure, Willie. You know how the shadows can get. How they will get." He looked at the younger man with uncertainty.

"I," William looked up, his face streaked with tears. He had been weeping, silently, the whole time Caruthers had been talking to the children. "I'll do it."

"Well, then, I guess we just have to wait for Jimmy and Edwin. Ya'll can follow the creek back to the lot, take the kids back with you. You should be ok. You still got the key to the Piggly Wiggly I gave you?" William nodded in confirmation.

Vicky's nose scrunched up as she peered at Caruthers with suspicion and asked, "Where you gone be at?".

He smiled at her as he answered, "You know, I've been looking at this day for years. We have. Trying to get a fix on it. In some threads, you all died on the Ferris Wheel, just like the Other planned. In some, the fair never made it to town. In others, something close to this happened, but not this exact thing. Not that I remember, anyway. The future is so fragile, so flimsy, so hard to read. You'll learn that, Josh. I've seen you, the future you, sifting through time, trying to make sense of it all. You'll see," he said, turning to the boy, who looked back at him with the blank expression of a child listening to a foreign language for the first time.

Caruthers sighed, and continued, "But, back to your question, Vicky, every way we've seen today, I die. Always. At the end of this day, I will be dead. There were some paths that ended with William living through next week, and getting well, and raising his son. But I'm afraid this isn't one of them." William did not speak or change expression when the children looked to him for a reaction. Caruthers raised his voice to regain their attention, saying, "But the two of you—you will live. Your path is long, and strange, and painful. Most paths are. But you will live through today, and that's what matters."

A sudden rat-a-tat-tat knock came from the door, which flew open, and in walked two men as wet and muddy and bedraggled as the others. The expression on their faces, when they saw the occupants of the space, bore the indelible mark of finding what they had expected, but had not truly believed they would find. *It really is true*, their faces said, though the men remained speechless as they stood in the open door.

"Let's get moving then," Caruthers said, and, directing his voice at the two men, ordered, "Jimmy, Edwin, take that board there. Vicky and Josh are gonna follow you all down through the creek."

Josh looked at the man as he stood, and asked, "Where are you going?"

"I'm planning to die in the comfort of my own home, and it's gonna be hell to get there."

It took a few minutes of introductions and adjustments, including finding a pair of shoes for Vicky—an old pair of Converse Chuck Taylor trainers that were much too large for her—and then they were ready to go. As Caruthers' path diverged from the group headed back towards the parking lot, he called out through the rain, "Remember, the future isn't real until you make it real. And what seems real isn't always real, anyway." And then, he disappeared into the rain.

Their path back through the creek was tedious. They all were already weary of rain, and in dread of the thing returning—if it had even been real. The voices had returned as soon as they stepped out of the Treehouse, and seemed to be growing in number, and volume, though the words—if they were words—remained undistinguishable.

At one point, a little more than halfway, Josh spoke aloud what Vicky had been thinking. "I want to go back. To the Treehouse. It's safer there."

The three men were ahead of them, but it was William who stopped and turned round, as Jimmy and Edwin maneuvered around him with the piece of plywood. "No, it's not safer there. That place will be gone soon. Maybe in hours, maybe a few days. I'm not sure. But the Piggly Wiggly will be safe. There's a locker there. You won't hear the voices. And your parents will find you." He tried to smile, but couldn't, so he just added, "Come on, we don't want to fall behind."

The three caught up with Jimmy, standing by the piece of plywood, behind the Sears store. "Edwin went to get some rope from the fair out there," he said, as the three approached him.

"Alright," William said, "I'll take the kids on over." He held his arms out for Jimmy to take Jonny from his arms, which the man did, with stuttering reverence. The other three then continued walking behind the stretch of shops, behind the K-Mart, and then back round behind the Tog Shop Outlet, stopping at the Piggly

Wiggly. William extracted a key from one of his jacket pockets, and led the children through the back of the darkened store to the door of the meat freezer, all of them bumping into crates and corners and walls as they moved.

"Wait here," he said, and went to find distilled water, but none was left, and he brought them bottles of ginger ale instead. He opened the door, went in, and gestured for them to follow, though they could barely make him out, a shadow in the shadow of a shadow. "Come on in."

He found places for them to sit as they entered, and handed them the bottles. "Why do we have to wait here? I want to go home," Josh questioned, thinking of his warm bed.

William smiled, a real smile for the first time since the children first saw him. "Well, when I take this memory away from you, the voices, they'll go away. For a time. But that other thing you saw… Death. It might come back. The storm might not be over. It can't get you here. But at home, well, it can." He said the last part apologetically, not knowing for certain how deep the memory of the morning might be hidden, or if it would just be veiled. His own understanding of his powers was little more developed than the children's.

Josh didn't need to hear anything more. He was ready for the memory to be taken from him, because that would mean, somehow, that Jonny was still alive. Vicky, who had lost the too-big shoes in the muddy creek bed less than halfway down the creek, was just happy to be sitting, and not hearing the voices, which had stopped the moment she walked into the freezer.

"I have to get going," William began, and the smile dropped from his face. He chose his words carefully before he began again, "Vicky, Josh, there will come a time when your eyes will be opened. You will see. You will remember this. All of it. My son, my Michael, my Peanut, he will open your eyes for you. You tell him I love him. And go with him. Follow him. He is the one. This was all for him. Remember."

"Yes sir," Vicky said, because she was in the habit of saying it.

"Okay," Josh agreed, because he didn't know what else to say.

William began to whisper words they could not understand, and with his right hand, he swept down Vicky's face, and her eyes closed, and she fell back against the stack of boxes behind her. He continued, making a swiping motion down Josh's face, and the boy's eyes closed as he fell back into the girl. William paused for just a moment to look at the two before he walked out of the freezer and closed the door behind him.

The voices swarmed into his head at once, filling it, crowding out all thought, and all feeling—except fear. He sobbed as he ran through the rear of the store and back to where he left Jonny with Jimmy, but the men and the boy were not there, so he kept running, and when he turned the corner of the Sears he could see the boy and the plywood board were in place over the stormwater drain, and the rain was steadily rising up over them. The men were gone.

He dashed back into the corridor of shops beside the Sears, and fell down in front of the Wonderland of Crafts store, crumpling his body up into a ball from which he could watch over the boy, make certain he stayed safe. He felt into his jacket and pulled from his shirt pocket the wet remains of a report card, with his son's name streaked but still legible, above a grid that showed the child to be *Exceptional, Exceptional, Exceptional,* all the way down.

He held onto the card, and tried to follow his son's paths into the future, trying to remember what he had seen before, and what was new, or different, all while trying to block out the voices that had followed him down the corridor. He could see the Ferris Wheel from where he sat, saw the water rising up above the electrical boxes, and knew that at least for the time being, he and his son would not ride it. Not together.

"Please, Dear God," he cried softly, as he rocked back and forth, seeing the future spin out before him, "Please let this be right."